David,
My David

A 20th Century Saga

2018 Edition

Eduard Qualls

DANAAN PRESS™

As explained on www.DavidMyDavid.com/music,
David, My David **is perhaps the first multimedia novel.**

The embedded QR Codes (and embedded URL hyperlinks in some eBook versions of the text) are links set up by the author, connected to pages within the book's website:
www.DavidMyDavid.com/music/chapters

These will allow readers to proceed to sites that provide further links to streaming versions, of the musical works cited within the text. Note that these are not a background soundtrack: for greatest effect, pause reading and listen intently to the music at that point.

Note that the QR codes provide the alphabetic text of quick URL-links to the pages on the book's website that detail those playlists; they transmit no additional data.

Three selections among the MP3's were written and/or played by the author himself. These are located only on the website itself. They can be downloaded for free from the pages for DMD-26b, DMD-28a2 and DMD-28b.

• All translations into English, except for that on page 295 (which is from the King James Version, *SRE*), or into other languages, were done by the author, himself. • Quotations from the German Scriptures are from the Luther-Bible, 1912 edition. • Temperatures and other such measurements appear in metric units while the story is situated within Europe, but in customary, human units whenever the scene changes to the USA. In noting pre-war, German currency, "*ℛℳ*" stands for *Reichsmark*(s). • Please note that France and Spain were on Greenwich Time until World War II, during which they switched to German (Central European) time (by military force in France; by Franco's dictatorial decree in Spain), and that they have remained so thereafter, the geographic, longitudinal nonsensicality of that situation notwithstanding. • The book contains embedded phrases or abbreviated personal titles in Catalan. Of these, the most common is "Sr", which is *senyor* in Catalan (*cf. señor* in Spanish). • Please note that the Catalan personal name *Joaquin* is pronounced approximately as it would be in French (but without nasalizing the final vowel): within this context, it is not Spanish. • Anglicized Hebrew within the text may appear in Ashkenazic form, thereby reflecting the Eastern-European origins of the book's Jewish characters. • Yiddish appears, as closely as possible, in the romanization standard established by YIVO [yivo.org]. • The Aramaic *Kaddish* appears in standard, English-based romanization. • The few lines of Russian appear in the more complicated, pre-1918 orthography preserved by Russian émigrés who escaped from Lenin's fatal seizure of their democracy.

• The German nickname "Edi" is pronounced like the English nickname, *Eddy*.

• All German quotations appear in the original, classically literary orthography.

"Steinway" is a registered trademark of Steinway & Sons: *www.Steinway.com.*

The resemblance of any character within this text to any person, living or dead, other than those public individuals cited, is purely accidental.

𓀭𓀮 𓊽𓎛𓂝 𓂻𓃾

Library of Congress Control Number: 2018904733

ISBN: 978-1-890-000-16-5

DP: 300-0321-092770-3

To the Memory of All Those
Murdered
in the Name of Hatred
Masquerading
as Social Norm
Political Necessity
or Religious Prerogative

It is far better to love, braving any chance of being wronged, than to hate, and with it, to be eternally wrong.

p. 260

Author's Preface

In the early 1990's I watched a television program, the plot of which had been extended from a true story of how, during World War II, a Jewish teenager had avoided being arrested and sent to a death camp by blending into the everyday life of Berlin. This facility of "hiding in plain sight" from Nazi terror became the central idea behind the outline that I produced in 1994 for a screenplay.

However, not satisfied with it at that point, I put it aside, and it fell out of memory for the next two decades, while other, more vital events overtook it.

One sunny Saturday, a November afternoon in 1997, in a bar in Dallas I saw the most beautiful man I had ever seen. Although contending with an orthopedic boot on his right foot, he followed me around that bar, up and down the stairs, till he cornered me and made sure I had his name and phone number. After I had gone to the club next-door, there on the dance floor I turned around, and he appeared again, with that glistening, raven hair and those piercing blue eyes. We stared, touched and pretended to dance. From there, soon afterwards that evening, we went our separate ways.

The very next day, he phoned me three times: we talked for over four hours. I was not sure of our chances together until, while he was telling me of the car wreck that previous June that had crushed his right foot and done such serious damage to him, my heart drowned out my doubting mind with its inner yell of: "I almost lost you!"

I knew to listen to that inner voice, the one that had guided me for as long as I could remember. The following February, Jeffrey beat gay-marriage legalization in the U.S. by more than a decade when he went to court and had his name changed to mine.

We were that central, male couple within Thomas Mann's works. I, a broad-shouldered, 6-foot blond with blue-green eyes, and Jeffrey a slighter and only slightly shorter, raven haired, blue-eyed beauty: we were the American version of *Hans Hansen* and *Tonio Kröger*, but without the angst of Herr Mann's own, perpetually unfulfilled, unrequited love.

The next twelve years were a dream, but heavily accented with travail.

Jeffrey had suffered a severe concussion in that wreck in 1997: it had been ignored by physicians then, and was not diagnosed by a neurologist until 2007. Those nine previous years of psychiatric misfeasance and malpractice had taken their grievous toll on us. But with that successful diagnosis by a gifted neurologist-psychiatrist, our life was coming together again. Jeffrey was so relieved and happy: he had found his calling in creative writing, and (after seventeen publications as an undergraduate) was heading to a guaranteed position in graduate school. I was also busy writing: computer programs and music.

Then, on Saturday, July 11, 2009, I lost the love of my life.

But "lost" is far too weak a word.

When Jeffrey didn't answer any of the phone-lines at the house on that afternoon, I rushed away from my weekend visit with my mother and, as fast as I could, drove with anguish and roiling apprehension those almost 300 miles back to the Dallas area.

There, in the evening-darkness of our living room I found Jeffrey: collapsed, cold, having suffered a fatal seizure sometime during the early hours, not long after we had last spoken, at around 3:30 that morning. *I stood there, in a suddenly, dreadfully empty, echoing, deserted room, in a distant land, living darkly: abandoned, dejected, rejected.*

The only solace has come from knowing that the last thing I said to him that early morning, before our good-nights was, "I love you, too, Baby!"

Yet there was so much left to say, to do together: he was so young, only 34…

After continuing years of labored coping with the loss and the trauma of its sudden inception, in 2013 I discovered that outline from 1994, read it through, and decided that it "had legs". But no longer could it be a screen play. Now with a far greater story to tell, it demanded a more capable medium. Thence comes this novel. For me, its time had obviously come: in the first three days I had written 14,000 words.

The story I tell here is an expansion on historical events.

Yet, in the telling those events became so personal that I gave the main character, and his uncle, my own (and already German-spelled) first name. Thus, too, was I required to tell the story in the first person.

In form, inner strength and intelligence, though not in personal history or religion, Jeffrey appears both as *Reinhold* (and Reinhold's dealing with his own concussion), as well as the first *David*.

The portrayal within the text of events that appear arbitrarily coincidental reflect the too common facts of life of those who are mobile, and are members of specific, often constrained, professional, religious or other communities. It can be surprising, but it is not unusual for entire series of such real-life events to be linked "as if from afar."

Two years of early research, and of plot and manuscript polishing, are present in the fact that all the public places referenced, and their individual histories, are historically correct. (And images of all those are easily retrievable by searching the Internet.) For scenes within Germany, even the weather is exact for place and referenced date.

The settings and conditions in this novel are real-life, historical events.

Amalgamated from several life-stories, this text is fiction only in that the main characters are inventions who live within, and must contend with those historical events. Some actions of real-life characters have been invented and inserted for effect and fullness of presentation, but abide respectfully true to their temperaments.

As one of the few Westerners to have witnessed Communism in one of its most brutal heartlands—Ceausescu's Romania—I am singularly prepared to speak of the problems of tyrannical government, and how its worst effects arise from the conservative drive for self-preservation. Tyrannies will present themselves as the answer to ill-defined decline, the insanity of a single answer to a complex of problems, or simply as the satisfaction of a yearning for the false memories of a nostalgic past. My university studies of Western History and of European History, in particular, provide me with insights into the reasons behind the 20th Century rise of that era's conservative trinity of tyranny—Communism, Fascism and Nazism—that the main character witnesses, and must survive. From that come the insights into the resurrection of those problems in the early 21st Century expressed throughout this book.

When, concerning the seizure of power by Hitler's minority party and its subsequent, easy outlawing of all other parties, Reinhold states, "The Germans did not become suddenly evil in 1933," his explanation not only describes Germany then, but stands as a potent warning to the United States, Western Europe and the World now.

This 2018 edition, a revision of the first version, came about for several reasons.

First of these was that readers found the text of the original, printed edition to be too small. The second was that, in doing the German translation, and being forced to re-read every word, I found places that required improved formatting or divisions: for example, the original 20th chapter was split into two in this edition. The third was that the deteriorating political situation in the United States since 2015 (and its reflection of events from the 1930's) required a few lines of edits or expansion. The fourth reason was that I simply wanted to, perhaps, had to.

Between the two editions, I had had my genes analyzed by a reputable firm and, beyond confirmation that my great-great-great grandmother had been Black (the poet, Langston Hughes, was also a distant cousin), discovered through it that one of my grandparents in the generation just previous to that had been an Eastern European, Ashkenazi Jew.

The knowledge of this, and its establishment of my own vital connection to the great human losses of the Holocaust, imbued my effort with just that much greater purpose, and sorrow.

———————————————

And now, after my experiences—the joys, the shock, the yearning, the abiding sorrow—I warn all couples, young and old, never to take their time together for granted: everything can be lost in an instant.

Live, love and make memories while you can, or you will find yourself suddenly consumed by silence, able only to repeat my own words, as spoken here by Reinhold:

"Don't be like me: living, just waiting to die,
wrapped in the shroud of my own regrets."

Eduard Qualls
11 July 2018

CHAPTERS

David, My David

Abreise: Das Paket
— Chapter 1 —
Departure: The Packet

I turned and walked slowly into the security checkpoint.

Simple, solitary steps through a metal-detector arch followed by the cursory search, screening now, in 1995, merely shadowed the terror of the 1970's and '80's, of recently fallen radical groups, striving to unsettle the strength and determination of the West.

It hadn't worked, had it?

Within my 74 years, I had stood intimate witness, too much, too often.

And indelible memories—unwelcome, wild, harness-rending specters—can bolt flagrant, to flow pyroclastic, all-scorching, unreined! I longed for the cooling presence of sister, niece, friend: I had always been blessed by the company of strong women.

Welcoming the machine's muteness, I moved forward.

"Destination!" the officer ordered, bluntly, detached.

Politeness mobilized: "Dallas … the USA, sir."

A curt, blank-faced sweep compelled me forward into an immediate pat-down.

My only companion there, a time-worn satchel stuffed with literal and literary music—Beethoven, *Beowulf* and *Buddenbrooks*—had set off on its own slow, disjoint holiday, reclining warm-beach lazy beneath intense, intrusive beams.

Jerking back, spasming head-tilt toward the surface at his side, the officer snapped, "Empty your coat and pants pockets onto the table!" His tight-eyed, *are-you-watching-this?* glance shot toward the other officer manning the station.

My wallet, spare pfennigs and ancient rosary fell first.

Chasing my every movement, he passed over those apace, to motion roughly toward one coat pocket that I must have been too slow in clearing.

I held the jacket open as I extracted tickets, notes, random tissues, an errant piece of hard candy (upholstered in my Max's fawn-boxer fur) and, finally, that packet, the one my elder sisters had fussed and worried over, back in the evening's earlier *bon voyage* party on my Frankfurt am Main, *Altstadt* sidewalk. I slipped the emptied jacket off as well, in hopeful assurance that I harbored no other, secluded stash.

He recited my full name from the passport his spine-cracking grip still forced open, "Eduard Gottlieb Meyer," then cast it onto the table. His stabbing the air toward the small bundle emphasized an irritated, "Open the packet!"

"With pleasure, officer," I said, hoping to allay our disparate concerns.

As I started so carefully pulling age-tender twine, then yellowed, dark-creased paper apart, he shifted closer to my left side, increasing curiosity seeming to conquer his ready causticness.

In unexpected interest, that other officer, as yet only standing by, observing, stepped up and moved in on my right, completing a privacy cordon to each of my sides. Did they understand the intense, personal nature of the contents inherently? Perhaps something inspired or someone conspired their shielding this packet from the prying notice of others.

Deliberate fingers at last delivered it fully, without adding rip, wrench or wrinkle to the aged paper.

The guards stood close, quiet, their reactions hidden, like the packet, from the rushing airport around them, staring down at those few, secreted pieces.

"For my nephew … in America," I explained with mollifying caution.

Each stared at the slight scraps, in self-consuming silence.

That grace evaporated a-flash.

The irascible officer to my left lurched into a solid backwards step. Calling the other away after him, he strode off.

That first guard used his hands to force pointed statements toward the other.

Ever more heated, he worked down a list enumerated with the index finger of his right hand, ever angrier as it pointed to, almost dug into, those of the left. At each point, his affective agitation grew.

Within the day's mounting exhaustion, from this trip's so heightened emotion, my misgivings, my nervousness burgeoned, then doubled with the frightful recall: forced into strictest line, the ominous-hanging stench, the threats, black-jacked officers striding pompously, their impersonal, arrogant inspection, pursuing the slightest imperfection, the merest provocation to single out, to call forward, to condemn. Deep-anguishing memories that I had so assiduously suppressed those many years resurged.

Sweat prickled a reborn anxiety.

"Dammit!" I scolded myself, "I should have shipped the package ahead of time, or just posted it!"

I swallowed my breath, tightened my chest, struggling against rising, jagged heartbeats: each one, a pounding, jarring flashback into that line, forced amongst countless cattle-car loads, of facing paired, black-uniformed, death's head officers, one volcanic, the other, a distanced, icy observer.

"Remember, Edi! Remember! This is no longer the Germany that dragged you, helpless, to the death-fed, fiery pit, to the very dragon's coal-fired, flaming maw!"

Fighting fiercely to subdue the rising throes, I studied the second officer's response intensely, yet caught only a final, "You may certainly continue your questions!"

They marched back toward me.

The instigating officer stepped forward stiffly to say, "Herr ..."

"Meyer," I inserted, too nervously.

"Yes ... Herr Meyer," he restated in even curter acknowledgment.

"To whom do these items belong?" pointing to the packet's contents.

"They belong to *me*, sir."

"And you have a permit for them?"

"Only this."

I exposed, held forth the evidence I had.

The color collapsed from his face.

Though fading, those fifty-year-old stains could still startle, still chill.

Making no conscious sound, immobile, staring: his breath fell to a slit-mouthed breeze; his nation's, his own inescapable inheritance there manifest.

His eyes scoured slowly back and forth, peering into the triune visage: the packet, its contents, its receipt.

Waking a-jolt, he nodded a tacit "OK" to the other agent, secondarily to me.

A pause, a glance over his shoulder, back toward the growing queue extending from the entry to the metal detector, and he stepped away with a second nod of deflated acquiescence—but no other word—to attend to the increasing crowd, grown restive at the guards' inattention.

At once bureaucratically separate from my situation, he set to work, scurrying to pull the fidgeting travelers through their physicals, to rush them on toward their self-important flights.

The officer still standing to my side was again gazing at those contents.

He looked up: "You are *the* Eduard Meyer, right?"

Assuming he meant the once-prominent musician, I nodded and sighed deeply.

"Yes, sir."

As I watched him, the now-growing ease in his bearing, I began to sense the degree to which he had recognized me. Was it, perhaps, from those cultural remnants still clinging to my life's long journey, as extensive concert pianist, organist, even as the occasional conductor? I could only wait.

"I beg your forgiveness, Herr Meyer!"

"Born and raised within the old DDR, the other officer has only recently been graduated from the academy: he remembers too many confusing, or faulty, details, those oppressive attitudes and operations from his youth," he revealed with a confident, *I've been here longer and know better* smile.

Whew. I could breathe again.

Within this other, still very official security-bureaucrat I began to sense a deeper, Western—perhaps Rhinelander—humanity, and a fan, to all appearances, with all the solicitous and patient attitude notables receive from this extended tribe of admirers. It is the familial balm, assuaging our self-doubt and insecurity: what we ever crave to help fill in and pave over that precarious, attention-craving, stage-life quicksand.

"Wrap up the packet, please, Herr Meyer."

He watched patiently as I arranged the intimate pieces once again, nestled securely within their ancient caddy. Suddenly, he stood straighter and, with a hand-to-shoulder touch of excited informality said, "Please wait here a second … OK?"

I reassured him with knowing nod and "Certainly!" After all, I was still within *his* security-check area!

He hurried to the officers' desk, dodging passengers the others had cleared and set to path, and returned quickly, pulling a couple of obviously only recently purchased music CD's from a more populated sack.

Handing them to me he explained, "My son, Klaus, is completely enraptured with music and the piano! I've been shopping for presents for his seventh birthday next week…" In his unmistakable proud-papa glow he added, "Would you autograph these? For him?"

With a confirming, furtive glance at his nametag, I assured him in renewed confidence, "With the greatest pleasure, Herr Frey!"

I looked at the CD's. One held Schumann's *Three Sonatas for Violin and Piano*, a disc that I had recorded only a decade ago with my Viennese conductor-friend, Maestro Seidler, here soloing on violin.

The other disc was one from among my slightly earlier, multi-volume set of the complete Beethoven piano sonatas.

I choked a sudden surge of memory; besides the *Waldstein*, and the *Appassionata*, this particular disc held his Op. 78, *"à Thérèse."*

The title startled me with the sudden sound of the lyrical progression of its opening nine chords and their sweep of emotion: my own David, those longing, blue eyes, Leipzig, December 16, 1940…

Colors, colors!

Eyes, hair!

Names, noses!

Parents, Grandparents and the Nuremberg Laws!

The bone-breaking ache! Death and undying yearning!

I blinked away the rash race of moisture, fussed minutely with the CD, struggling to staunch up-surging memories. Perhaps it was simply tonight's tension, the physical strain, that had rushed it all to mind. Stress stoked the depression, refueled the repetitive, ever-ambushing recall.

Nevertheless: *seize it, control it, throttle it!* I simply had to power through!

Noticing my inept fluster with the discs, Herr Frey produced a key and used its jagged edge to pop open those annoyingly unwieldy, plastic-film shrink-wraps to expose each jewel-case before handing it back to me. Carefully, I extracted the too friable liner notes; he handed me his pen.

Watching as I searched for an open-space in which to write, he volunteered, "Die Waldsteiner—*that rocks*!" [*The Waldstein (Sonata)*—…]

That one had been one of my father's and grandmother's favorites, too. I looked up from starting the dedication to his son, *Unserem Kläuschen* [*For our Little Klaus*], and chuckled in relief.

Where else in the world besides Germany might you find an ordinary person, a security guard at his everyday duties, who not only knew of Beethoven, but his sonatas by name, as well?

Achtung, Edi! [*Pay attention...*]

I slipped the autographed liners back into the jewel-cases and, while handing those over to him, noticed that there was at least one other CD poking at the straining bag.

Herr Frey caught my glance and explained, "Actually, I bought him some other CD's, too. It was so difficult to choose!" Pulling a third CD from the cloth bag, he stopped, stared at the picture on its front then looked at the autographed discs.

Then he did it again.

"You rather resemble each other, Maestro," he remarked before turning the CD-front toward me. It held the photo of my nephew, David Eduard Ziegler, on his recording of the Schumann and Grieg piano concertos with the Berlin Philharmonic. I knew it well: his playing of the Grieg had influenced my own interpretation, it was that damned good!

"Very true, Herr Frey. My nephew. Taken a few years ago," I explained, unable to disguise a strain of sadness.

A puzzled, then sudden flash of recognition, of painful recollection, passed over his face. He turned the front of the CD again toward himself, looked at it and replied softly, "Indeed."

Carefully, deliberately, he returned all the CD's to the bag, carried it to his desk to put it away, and returned promptly to me with an interrogation-closing, almost regretful, "Your jacket, Herr Meyer!"

Regathering his bureaucratic composure, and in a smiling, rather theatrically overdone, *Prussian* maneuver, he snapped to attention, "Everything is in order, Herr Meyer! I thank you ... most heartily."

I nodded a "Danke" as he called an aide over and told him to bring an electric cart, followed by a sterner, "Be certain to get Herr Meyer to his departure-gate well in time!"

Just as I had stepped up and taken my seat in the buggy, Herr Frey called out and ran after us, hefting my neglected satchel. Gratefully, I stashed it beneath my left arm. He then grabbed my right hand in both of his.

In a slightly breathless, but almost familial tone, he added warmly, "I bid you a most pleasant journey, Maestro!"

"Thank you very much, Herr Frey. And my best wishes to your entire family!"

With a sudden, "aaah! leg cramp!" jolt, the cart spasmed itself awake, to collapse just as suddenly into a rolling, "ugh, damn! that hurt!" stall and shudder. But another angry jounce of forced recovery regained its wits, and we rushed off through the antiseptic, nauseatingly high-pitched sting of the airport corridor's blanching fluorescent lights.

Wheeling among the few solo-walkers, skirting the distracted pedestrian-clots and with expected, Teutonic efficiency, my driver had me at the gate within plenty of time.

Stepping down, I thanked him.

He replied with a business-like, unmoving, "Bitte schön!" [*You're welcome!*], then sped off, without nod or notice, back toward a distant posting.

6

My mind, still aswirl in the airport's madding prelude, now paused to regain its earth.

Taking seat before the floor-to-ceiling, cathedral-of-flight windows to the side of the gate, I could watch from there the distracting dash-about beneath the spotlights on the field, particularly of those ministering to the looming 747, prepping it meticulously for its heavy flight from Frankfurt's Rhein-Main into DFW.

A tarmac flash blanked my vision: the rush of attendants servicing the plane yanked me back unbidden to that gravel-bed siding, of train-cars spilling their milling masses, frantic in raw thirst and gnawing hunger, the long journeys' captive, unwashed stench, redolent waves of fear, desperation...

"Stop, Edi! Stop!" I gorged the urgent agony.

"Not now! Not here!"

Looking around, scanning the crowd-filling area's disinterested faces, I compelled myself forwards: it was not the same Germany! I respired myself slowly, slowly, back toward a saner present, to the flight.

The distant echo of *Herr Offizier* Frey's adulation recalled those emotional rewards of public performance, of rising, welcomed applause resurging in fond temptation. I felt my fingers moving once more across glistening key-tops, playing that *Waldstein* he had praised, on the keyboard of my mental grand piano. Yes, I had played it back then, for the inmates, the starving, the diseased, the dying ...

Stop!

Aghast, I realized that I had been repeating the physical movements of recital! Such "spastic hands" and pedal-pushing feet could be taken for insanity!

"Musicians fall into such near-loony idiosyncrasies," I reasoned.

Music affects and infects everything we do; everything we do comes back to manipulate it, too. Our hands move, our voices hum along, and sometimes, we dance!

Absentmindedly, I repeated a different, long-practiced motion, rubbing the inside of my left forearm lightly with my innumerable practice-hours' sensitized fingertips. Within those numbers, *my* numbers, though concealed beneath soft, camouflaging layers of fabric, I could yet feel the stabbing pain of hammered, tattoo-needles, even now, when that indigo ink had surrendered to a blurring-edged, muted black.

Fear-wracked panic: my right hand's spasm hit my chest!

The packet was there, returned, secure.

From the gate, a sharp, too tinny announcement banished my momentary release. I gathered my goods, eased myself forward, up and into motion.

This wasn't my first trip to the USA, nor to any other such far-distant destination. But at least this one time I had the solace of knowing that I would receive the amenities of first class!

Maestro Seidler and Unterbürgermeister [*vice-mayor*] Jost's gift of an upgraded ticket was a rare treat for me, since I could never convince myself that I was that big of a "star" even after LP's, CD's, radio and television appearances, printed reviews, plus the odd mention in this or that tell-all tome.

Unless we've reached the highly acclaimed status of a Caruso, a Callas, or of a present Pavarotti, classical-music performers are never so well paid as those in other, often less studied, but oftentimes more medicated, types of music. So, I had made a habit of frugality, and coach class.

Just let no one call me miserly! I'm prudently sparing, not insanely cheap.

"Hesse, not Swabia!" I chuckled.

Within minutes, a young lady stepped from the counter, popped open the door to the jetway and took the microphone to give us our boarding orders: first-class, and otherwise impaired passengers, first. So, rescued satchel securely under arm, I threaded my way, pushing sideways through the anxious throng, toward the gate.

At last I pushed free of the crowd, to the front of the line. The young man standing there took my boarding pass, and as he was tearing off the stub, did a double-take of the name on the ticket.

Looking up, he smiled, "Welcome, Maestro!"

I nodded slightly, as if acknowledging polite applause, and said, "Thank you very much," extending courtesy with his nametag's "Andreas!"

He commenced his airline-presentation.

I tried to listen, forced myself to listen. Even now, at my age, such handsome men just made it so difficult to hear past their effect: the rising, *con fuoco* heart-beat pounding in my ears!

As a companion gate agent came to serve the other first-load passengers, to dispel this second traffic-jam I was causing, Andreas took the time to detail how I should make my way past this gate and jetway, which seat was now my assignment, and to warn about the stairs up to first class.

His extensive presentation complete, I set out, alone.

The long jetway's walk at last fading behind me, I maneuvered my still slender, but not entirely cooperative, carcass up those steps. Once I had reached the upper-room, Sonja, another solicitous attendant, ensured my numeric seating, and invited me to spread out, for no elbow-jabbing armrest-wrestler was to lurk in the corner beside me!

I stared through the window, into the darkness, pacing instinctively my inventory-list of invasive, pre-flight concerns: the apartment; my boxer, Max; my elder sisters and their worries; the packet.

A slight jarring of the plane: jetways popped, then swung away.

The address system crackled to life, and the captain went through his welcome-aboard shpiel, first in German, then again in English. Within the themes of this flight-prelude, I was pleasantly surprised to see Andreas performing the seatbelt-hula, the *dance of the seven exits*, on my side of the cabin.

Past the traditional bump-and-sway of taxiing, we paused at the end of the runway. In a sudden, surging rush, the plane coursed down the concrete, faster and faster. The wings and engines at last compelled the possessive tires to release their jealous, lover's grip on the ground, and we sailed suddenly, soaring upwards rapidly into the starry sea of the European night sky.

A piercing pang of doubt: my right hand sprang again, compulsive, to that coat pocket, frisking for reassurance the packet's slight, extrusive bulge with those keyboard-intense tips of my fingers.

But relief fled.

The parcel's rationale cast me down, like a meteor burning itself to cinder-black, falling fitfully to the too-common sorrows of Earth.

I was doing my duty.

If Great-aunt Franziska were still alive, I might seek her out, ask her to weigh my life, my actions, against that high standard she had held of our family. Was I a man amongst her "good ones—so many in our own family"?

It was I who had created, and promised, this packet, this gift.

I had just never conceived that I should be its courier, too.

With leveling flight, musical scores spread into out-flowing layers.

I played my way through each one mentally, marking here with the red pencil, there with a blue one, and occasionally the green, my own, idiosyncratic set of melody-, tempo- and attack-mapping, brightly colored, antique hieroglyphs.

"A glass of wine, water, perhaps a beer?

"A little more champagne, Maestro?"

Andreas, sometimes Sonja, would slip a stemmed vessel very carefully between the music-sheets. Or one of them would materialize suddenly with menu, a small plate of hors d'oeuvres.

Andreas had stepped over, to observe my scribbling for a while, going so far as to rub my neck and shoulders lightly while watching. Comforting, the moves were just too reminiscent of another, recalling those hands long gone: of Leipzig, the music, the ghosting of points east.

Several minutes of serious work completed, I pushed it all aside, stretched and yawned. Of course, Andreas was there in a snap to see if I were in want of anything. I had underestimated the effect of the drinks and, with this ready and eager audience, was basking in the attention.

"No, thank you, Andreas. I'm fine."

He smiled, certainly having witnessed such flight-finally-underway induced (and alcohol-advanced) mellowing before.

"Shortly, we will be showing a movie, Maestro," he proffered.

I considered the suggestion, but it took a notably special film to get me interested, to maintain that attention. After all, I had lived through and survived far more than most screenwriters, novelists, or other such feeble scribblers, could ever fantasize!

A quick pause, and he reminded me, "Or … we have classical music channels in the on-board audio system. You may listen to these with earphones if you'd like."

"Thank you, Andreas. The earphones. That would be very nice!"

Before I had finished the sentence and managed a steadying breath, he had returned with instructions, schedules and equipment. He reassured me as he handed me the headphones, "I've already tested these. *Ces écouteurs, ils marchent!*" His lapse into French, *'these headphones work!'* tickled my Rhinelander ear. He seemed to know instinctively how to entertain, to raise my spirits. I took the headset; he explained the plug-in, then where and how to select the channel and set the volume using the handrest's exposed roller-buttons.

As I looked through the schedule—various piano, orchestral and choral works, Beethoven, Schumann, Bach, Brahms, Granados, Wagner (the entire *Ring Cycle*? *Tristan und Isolde*, too? Was the flight going to be that long?)—and was scanning some of the channels, I even found two of my own performances!

The knob was subtle, the division between stations easily knocked, switching unbidden from one station and its musical playlist to the next: light classics, full symphonic, chamber, mixed instrumental, opera, and beyond, into big-band, country-western, pop or rock.

An easy, errant forearm swipe and the audio (and I) jumped: "Oh, damn!" and I set it back quickly.

This style-station swerve, this musical aberration was so easy, so jarringly distracting, I hoped I wouldn't endure such accidents throughout the flight. My mind was simply too susceptible to the imagery, the memories each style would evoke, or could inflict!

———————

Peeking from behind curves and points of another brace of pillows, Andreas reappeared, armed with more blankets.

I leaned forward; he helped me out of my jacket and offered to hang it up.

Meticulously, obsessively, I made the packet secure, nestled tightly within the depths of that inner pocket, then surrendered it.

Leaning back, before my head could settle against the seat, one of those pillows lay readily inserted for my neck. Earphones on and schedule near, everything else was safely away.

The lights lowered comfortably. Blankets crawled over and around me, and I found that I had been securely, although disappointingly maternally, tucked in.

"What beautiful hands!" drifted to mind, lyrics melting into the now-flowing melodies.

Suddenly alone, I stood basking in the acoustic breeze grazing a distant, orchestral meadow. Resurgent memories no longer repressed, music surged. My mind surrendered, regressed.

"Let the anguish fade, Edi! The melody! Always the melody!"

"Oh, sweet, devoted, bereft Clara!" I sighed.

The rolling Taunus, the ancient Hessian villages, farms and forests of my life, arose, sweeping through note-lofting waves, coaxing ever more tightly closed these lolling eyelids, to shield the visions, the dancing projections of a long-lost, tightly-held world.

I heard my mother humming as she scurried, almost danced about the kitchen. Was it already time for supper?

Der Anfang – Chapter 2 – The Beginning

"I can't bear this Czerny-jerk!" I shouted.

From Mama's wiping the kitchen table, she looked up with a gentle rebuke.

"Edi! You mustn't say such a thing! Remember what Herr Fuhrmann told you! The Czerny fingering and velocity studies first, then comes Beethoven, later!"

She obviously had more respect for my piano teacher, and ole Czerny, than I possessed at the moment!

"But the Czerny études are so-o-o-o-o booooooooooring! I've already memorized aaa-aa-a-all of them!" I puled before falling forward onto the keyboard for the loud, unmusical, but dramatic (I hoped!) effect.

Mama waited for the heavy din to die away before continuing, undismayed.

"The last time I spoke with him, Herr Fuhrmann was very serious that you practice the exercises thoroughly! He said that you should remember that Czerny was Beethoven's student, and so had learned directly from the master himself!"

"Aber der Herr Fuhrmann hat gesagt, daß ich Hände wie *Raketemannen* aufnehme!" [*But Herr Fuhrmann said I'm {getting} hands like rocket-men!*]

She paused, looking puzzled, silenced by what I had just said. It was what I thought I'd heard him say: I didn't believe my words were *that* strange!

After a quiet few minutes, though, she broke into a laugh, shook her head softly then, still smiling, corrected me.

"No, dear! He told me that you are simply grasping the music so rapidly, developing hands like those of the famous Russian pianist, Rachmaninoff!"

"So. I'm getting some sort of hands!" I thought.

Wondering, I flipped them over and over in front of me, searching for some distinction.

"Desiß gúod?" [*Izzat good?*]

"Very good, dear! Herr Fuhrmann met and heard him in concert only two years ago, just before Rachmaninoff returned to his new home in America!"

She smiled before continuing more sternly, "Und sprich einmal echtes Deutsch!" [*And do speak proper German!*]

I paused for a second, not quite understanding it all, except, of course, Mama's perpetual insistence on "proper German."

She told us often about her early years at school in Hannover, where she had learned "schönstes, echtes Hochdeutsch" [*most beautiful, proper Standard German*] and had become so devoted "to the enchanting language of Goethe, Schiller and Heine." She would stop us kids—and sometimes even Papa!—in mid-sentence, with "Oh! Do be quiet! You sound like Swiss cows!" Then she would correct us.

If she were really annoyed, she'd call us "baa, baa, Österbauern" [... *Austrian farmers*], and make us stop whatever we were doing and go study, "until you can express yourselves in proper German!" But between Mama's German practice and Herr Fuhrmann's piano-fingering exercises, I really thought I was being corrected enough!

I reached over to scratch my boxer, Eva, behind the ear. She raised her head and licked that one of my "Rachmaninoff" hands, whatever Mama and Herr Fuhrmann had meant by that!

Going back to the keyboard, I ignored Czerny and his exasperating, pianist's *School for Velocity*.

Closing my eyes, listening intently to the lady's voice that came now so often into my mind, teaching, encouraging the music, I scooted forward on the old stool to reach the pedals better, and started recreating what I had heard on one of Papa's gramophone records.

I got all the way through the first movement of that piece, although I knew that it wasn't absolutely right. I couldn't reach a few of the keys quite fast enough: they were still just a tiny bit too far apart, even for growing "rocket-man" hands! Yet all the colors, aromas and flavors were there, flowing freely, vibrantly through my mind while I played.

I could see and savor the notes! Different musical keys made me sense lots of differing things: the wind on my arms, or even taste bright-yellow potato salad: the good kind that Mama and Gramma made, not that watery, dull stuff you'd get in those factory-made cardboard tubs down in the village!

"Edi, when did Herr Fuhrmann give you the score to that sonata?"

Papa startled me: I hadn't heard him come into the house!

"Never. Or not yet, *I should say!*" I answered snippily.

"Stupid Czerny!" escaped in an angry whisper.

I looked up from the keyboard, over to the two of them. Mama was wiping an eye with the corner of her apron; Papa watched her, rubbed the small of her back consolingly.

"Mama? ... Is something wrong?" I asked. The Czerny-rage had fled on first sight of her tears.

She didn't say a word until she had circled the dinner table, come over to the piano, bent down and hugged me.

"Nothing is wrong, dear. It's just that you have made me so proud!" she explained, pushing a lock of hair back from my forehead before kissing it.

"Among all the sonatas that Beethoven wrote, the 'Les Adieux' sonata is my very favorite!"

With that, the old farm-house stood soothingly quiet.

But then, with an untuned wail, my baby sister, Margaret—I called her *Gretchen!*—announced to the world that she had awoken. Mama rose and went quickly to check on her. I didn't understand how Gretchen could sleep through those loud note-runs in the Czerny studies unless, of course, she was already as bored with them as I was!

Arguing about stuff that I couldn't, and generally didn't want to understand, my two older sisters, Marianne and Anneliese, burst through the door into the farmhouse. They were the best of friends, but what they were actually best at was … arguing!

While Mama was calming Gretchen's fret, Papa got out the haddekuche and apple juice, and the older girls' sipping and chewing finally calmed their noise. Then he called Mama and me over to the kitchen table, too. He had an announcement!

"You all know that I took eggs and vegetables this morning to Herr Fuhrmann."

He looked over at me. A properly brought-up German, I shrank a little from shame at having been disrespectful towards my teacher and his authority!

Shmuel Fuhrmann was a patient, talented teacher, a kind man, and his and our families were generations-long, close friends. I knew he was immensely dedicated to helping me play better and better. But that Czerny! He was starting to test my patience!

I sighed; Mama and Papa were right.

"Well, after I had visited him, I walked over to the post office. We had received another letter from Berlin by special delivery."

He held up the envelope, showing us all the postage and other official stamps it had earned on its long journey from the capital.

"Edi, because of the amazing progress you've made in your music lessons," he continued, bringing it even more pointedly in my direction, "Your uncles Edo and Reinhold have sent enough money to all of us, to buy tickets for the next performance of the symphony orchestra at the Opera House in Frankfurt!"

My older sisters were already getting excited.

"There, from the post office, I called the Opera House, and have already reserved the seats."

"Bravo, Uncle Edo!" the girls shrieked, and jumped and fidgeted with joy: they always wanted to go to Frankfurt, to the stores, whatever might be the real reason!

"Should we call your brother, to thank him?" Mama suggested.

"No, my dear! All the way to Berlin? That would be too expensive! And on his own receiver, too!" he replied. "No, we're not having an emergency. It's not necessary."

As for me, I would have been much happier if we could have telephoned Edo and Reinhold right then!

I was overjoyed, but uncertain how to show it: my disrespectfulness toward my teacher made me contrite; but then this great gift had suddenly appeared! I started to think about the gift, the tickets and my uncles. Saturday was only two days away! How could I send a thank-you note in time?

My dear Uncle Edo!

Papa's older brother's name was really "Eduard" like mine.

But he was "Eduard Friedrich" and I was "Eduard Gottlieb." *And*, he was "Edo" and I was "Edi", so people could be sure who was who! He was just the best uncle you could possibly have!

Uncle Edo and his friend Reinhold were both so smart, handsome, funny and so great to be around! They had come to visit at least twice a year while they still lived in America, but they had visited us much more often after they moved back to Germany, to Berlin from New York City in the early summer of 1925, just before my fourth birthday, the eighth of June! Whenever they were here on the farm, they ran around with us like big kids, playing ball, leading around the big Norikers with us on their broad backs (the horses', not my uncles'!), or chasing the chickens and geese with us, laughing as they squawked, honked, flashed and fluttered away.

"Lazy hens lay weak eggs!" Edo always laughed to his playfully disapproving mother when we would scatter them, running and cackling with their wings all flapping.

Because Edo and Reinhold came here to the farm so often, they had paid to have the telephone company run a line to the farm! They had the installers put the receiver in the parlor but, because Papa had said it was too expensive to be left out, the crew had hidden it behind one of the doors of the small cabinet built atop the sideboard, one that could be locked. After it had been installed, Uncle Edo let me place the first call, to talk to his secretary, Matthias, at their business in Berlin!

Every time they were coming to visit, Papa would unlock that door, grab the receiver and pull its long, cloth-wrapped, stringy cord out of the treasure box and have it ready, in case they needed to use it. A couple of times, Herr Fuhrmann had come over and borrowed it to make emergency calls to his sister in Vienna. That's even farther away than Berlin! Herr Fuhrmann asked my uncles how much he owed them for using their telephone, but they just chuckled, "Don't worry, Herr Fuhrmann! You are too near family for any such concern!" My uncles were so great!

Whenever Edo and Reinhold arrived after that, the first thing they did in the morning and afternoon was to call Berlin, and I always got to talk, too! Sometimes, they even called across the ocean! To New York, Chicago, Galveston, New Orleans, Baton Rouge and San Antonio! The places all sounded so exotic!

Earlier this year they had driven—driven!—the whole 650 km from Berlin!

Uncle had this big, black sedan that he had named "Marlene Beatrix" (because those were its initials!). This last time they were here, Uncle Reinhold called it "Naughty Lola" and chuckled, but I had to ask him why he'd said it. I didn't know that such a nice car could be naughty: it was so big, shiny and powerful, and the leather seats smelled so good!

They both laughed and said, "Aber nein, Edchen!

„Nicht *freche*! *Fesche*!" [*But no, dear/little Edi! Not naughty {or saucy} girl! Elegant!*]

"It's from a project we're helping our friend, Zuckmayer, with, back in Berlin!"

Oh! Now I understood! *Das war famos*! [*That was great!*] But I still wondered what was so funny about the pianola!

14

When they drove up in the beautiful *Marlene* one following, early June afternoon, I ran out to greet them, jumping immediately up onto the running board on the driver's side. Reinhold had just rolled down his window as the car itself rolled to a stop.

He held his hand out to me. It held a furry brown and white, leggy lump with big brown eyes and floppy little ears. He exclaimed in English, "Edi! Look what *we* found!"

A Deutscher Boxer puppy!

Uncle Edo flung open the door on the rider's side, stood tall on its running board to see me over the top of the car and proclaimed, "Happy birthday, Cowboy!"

I jumped back down onto the grass quickly as Uncle Reinhold pulled his puppy-filled hand back inside, to open the car door and step out. He knelt down with me and handed her gently into my excitedly trembling arms.

"Happy birthday, Edi!" he said.

After he had passed her over to me, making sure that I was holding her to my chest very, very carefully, he watched as I stared, still open-mouthed in delirious surprise, at my wondrous gift! She wiggled to get settled, moved her pointy little head around, sniffing, then stretched up to lick my chin!

A puppy! A puppy! Reinhold said something about how she had slept, held securely against his collar, snoring into his neck, all the way from Wiesbaden, but I didn't hear everything! I was enraptured by this leggy, tennis-ball body with ping-pong ball head and such floppy ears! My own baby boxer!

Eva adored Reinhold! Every chance she got when they visited after this, she would sit as close to him as she could, stretch to put her head on his chest, staring up at him, and lean as hard as she could against him. As she grew, she would even try to push him over while he talked and cooed and petted her!

Mama, Papa and my older sisters spilled out of the house, followed just as determinedly by Gramma Meyer, wielding the cane she had been forced to use since one of the cows had kicked her a few months before, in a milking accident. They went through all the familiar family hugs and happiness.

Barely able to contain my excitement, I brought the puppy over to Papa to show her off.

"You guys! You shouldn't have done it! So expensive a gift!" he said, in a feeble rebuke of our visitors.

Edo just laughed.

"But, Hänsel! Little brother! You know for a fact that our entire purpose in life is to spoil these beautiful children!" he pronounced with a lordly sweep of arm over the three of us standing in front of him, before stopping to rub Gretchen's cheek as she looked on from Mama's arms. The baby laughed, spun away and hid her face from him. The adults all laughed, too, but my older sisters froze when they realized exactly what he'd said, stopped pestering me, trying to pet *my* puppy, and stepped expectantly over to Uncle Edo, with that "did you say you were going to spoil us, too?" sheepish-greedy look in their eyes.

"Ah! Yes, my dears!"

Der Anfang — Chapter 2 — The Beginning

He cupped each of their faces in turn between his hands and kissed their hair.

"How could I ever forget such beautiful princesses? Come with me!"

They ran over to *Marlene* with him. He opened the door, reached into the backseat and pulled out two—almost as tall as they were!—bundles wrapped in fancy, city-store paper, and handed one to each of them. Their eyes had gotten huge when they saw how big their gifts were! Immobile, they held them tightly, as if they might vanish, then looked up at Uncle Edo.

"Open them, sweethearts!" he urged.

The two of them walked so carefully, like Mama does with Papa's hot coffee, over to the front doorstep, sat down and started unwrapping their treasures.

Marianne, the elder, told Anneliese, "Be careful! The paper is really exquisite!" But when they had pulled the wrappings apart just enough to get a peek inside, the tissue flew!

China dolls like movie stars! with hats and shoes and purses and eyes that winked and clothes with snaps and… I almost got jealous, but then the puppy in my arms wiggled and did little boxer snuffles against my hand. Nope, mine was definitely **the best**!

Edo and Reinhold stood close together, watching us enjoy our gifts; Reinhold rested his forearm on Edo's shoulder. Gramma moved over to them, slipping her left arm between them, sending it around Edo's waist. Pushing in, she slid them apart. Then she put her right arm around Uncle Reinhold's waist, and pulled them both tightly to her.

"You! You, my dear sons!" she looked up at each in turn, "You are definitely spoiling these children!"

They smiled. Edo put his right arm around Gramma, then Reinhold extended his left arm, protectively over Gramma and onto Edo's shoulder. I noticed that Reinhold was squeezing it, sharing Edo's subtle glances.

"Both of them are so handsome," I thought.

"They should have been in the movies!"

A Taunus forest-breeze arose, vagrant. Watching all, with nose installed within new-gifted puppy fur, my mind feasted on the spreading polyphony of pleasing aromas, sweeping, circling, settling peacefully around my family.

My earliest memories of Mama and Papa were of their singing.

Soft, comforting little songs surrounded, insulating, elevating, so many of their daily chores. That's how I had learned to talk, by listening to their songs. Music extended my language and, together, forged bold my emotions: "Das Deutsch ist mir das erste Lied gewesen." [*German was my first song.*]

By 1927, after all the troubles from that big war, Mama and Papa had succeeded in re-establishing a stable, but not overly ostentatious prosperity on the family farm, perched on the northwest ring of hills rising from the village of Singhofen. At least the Taunus was far enough away from the big cities that the sporadic, bloody street-fights between red-neckerchiefed Communists and Nazi brownshirts were only distant side-notes in Papa's Frankfurt newspaper!

I was six years old, "and never an infant," Papa would say.

Never spoken to in "baby talk" I had already been reading from Gramma's big encyclopedia set for a year, and could even recite sections of Goethe's works by heart. On top of that, my music teacher, Herr Fuhrmann, had started me in the real (not the beginner, simple-edited versions!) of the works of Bach and Mozart.

Tall, almost lanky, for my age—just six, most people thought I was eight!—I still ran around in lederhosen (like every other boy, and lots of farm-working men in the Taunus), chasing the chickens and geese out of the grain fields closest to the house, standing on boxes to brush the flowing manes of our huge, black Noriker plow-horses, playing with the barn cats and with my baby boxer, Eva!

A big, fawn puppy with a band of white flashing from her chest up around her neck, Eva wasn't supposed to sleep on my bed. But every night after Mama fluffed up the feather bed and comforter, and she and Papa kissed me good night, I would get Eva up on it, in amongst the covers!

I'd fall asleep with an arm over her back, my head pressed into hers, where I would launch into dreams after confiding to her everything that had happened that day, especially the secrets! Eva was my boxer-confessor, and never made me do penance! But I had long before memorized the *Ave Maria* and I always said— sometimes sang—it there, to and for Eva, in those golden moments before I fell deeply asleep, with soft fur cushioning my forehead and that velvet aroma of warm, boxer puppy caressing my nose.

Eva usually sat, but sometimes lay, beside the piano stool while I practiced on the old (1884!), massive-oak, upright piano.

In 1901, my Grampa, a singing farmer (as Gramma often reminisced) from whom we seemed to have received our individual musical gifts, had traded three precious young milk-cows for it, hoping each of his (then eight- and five-year-old) boys would learn to play. He had held a particular fondness for the music of Brahms, having sung in his youth the baritone solo in the first performance in Bad Nassau of the *Deutsches Requiem*: "Herr, lehre doch mich, daß ... mein Leben ein Ziel hat, und ich davon muß." [*Lord, teach me indeed ... that my life has an end, and I must {live} by that.*] And he had made sure to purchase this upright piano, after having seen a photograph of the composer working at his own!

However, although both of Grandpa's boys loved music, neither could abide spending that much time belabored, cramped and bored indoors, and so did everything they could to hide from their lessons. Papa still used a phrase about big letdowns that Grampa had exclaimed about this piano: "Das ist wohl eine dreikühige Enttäuschung!" [*That's really a three-cow disappointment!*]

And now, when Gramma heard me play, she would often say, "*Der* ist aber keine Dreikühige!" [*But he's no three-cow {disappointment}!*]

It took me a little while, but I came to understand that not being a "three-cow" whatever was definitely a good thing!

About six months before that sixth, "boxer" birthday, back on the first Friday of December, 1926, Mama had loaded us kids onto the earliest train to Berlin, to go visit Edo and Reinhold in their huge apartment near the *Tiergarten*.

It was so elegant, clean and bright in the frosty, early-winter light: and not so close to the Zoo that you had to smell the animals! Mama was terrified we'd break something. They had to order her to relax!

That evening after we arrived, though, I got very sick. I was burning hot, then cold, didn't want anything to eat, didn't want to do anything, didn't even want to talk! Uncle Edo found a doctor who came to the apartment that Friday night. He was kind of chubby and balding and stank of tobacco smoke.

The smelly old doctor made me strip down to my knickers. Then he pushed his cold heart-and-cough listening-thing all over me, poked me with his crooked fingers, and pulled open and prodded everywhere. After all that, I lay down on the sofa; he called Mama and my uncles over, to the far end of the room to talk.

I was too shivery and tired to get up and walk.

"What are they saying over there? I can't hear anything! I really have to go, to hear everything they ..."

Suddenly, I was gone: lights out in mid-thought!

The next thing I knew, I was dreaming of music, that a lady, her long, graying hair pulled back along her head into a bun just like Gramma's, was teaching me, encouraging me. I was playing the music on her piano, too!

I could see colors, glowing then fading ones that changed with different pitches and tones. They floated with shifting aromas, some tasted familiar, others strange. After what seemed hours and hours, I started to open my eyes. The sensations, the music and its long dream of the teaching-lady, were fading.

Slowly, I awoke.

The trees outside the tall windows of the big parlor were immense shadows against a deeply dark, weakly city-lit, freezing night sky. The room lay in the gloom made by a tea-towel draped partly over the shade of the lamp on the small, round table nearby. That table held a thermometer; someone's silver wristwatch; a small, open tin of aspirins; a crystal water-pitcher and its glass not half-full. I seemed to remember having been urged by Mama's voice to take sips, small sips of water, a pill, to swallow.

Being rocked ever so gently, I was held on someone's lap, against someone's chest by arms around me, thick ones that kept me wrapped tightly in a wonderfully soft blanket.

Raising my eyes, I saw Uncle Reinhold's cleft chin, its valley of black, whiskery stubble. His head was leaning back against the top cushion of the tall rocking chair, his chest expanding rhythmically as he breathed slowly. He smelled so good: being held tightly and smelling him felt so good.

I watched; I breathed; but I finally had to move a little. My legs were starting to tingle!

At that, Reinhold stirred, opened his eyes a slit, looked down, noticed I was finally awake and whispered, "Good morning, sleepy head!"

With some effort, I managed a croaky, "Mornin'."

He yawned deeply then leaned forward, sitting up further to adjust our position. I could see Mama, lying on her back, asleep on the couch opposite us, still wearing her dress from Friday night; a handkerchief rested over her eyes.

"Maria," he called softly. She moved slightly.

"Maria," he called again, louder.

She slipped the kerchief off her eyes and looked over. She seemed puzzled, but then jumped up and almost fell the meter or so over to us: she seemed to have realized suddenly that I was watching, fully awake.

With both hands, she reached out, anxiously caressing my head, my neck, feeling my chest and arms.

"Now, no fever … no fever … My little son, my baby! Thank God! No fever!" her voice got gradually louder and more emotional with audible excitement and growing relief.

I lay there, letting her investigate, enjoying the attention. But I had to stop her!

"Mama," I said.

She continued her inspection unaffected.

"*Mama*" I repeated with growing frustration.

"*Mamá*!" finally broke beyond her own emotions to get her attention back to *me*.

She turned from the physical search and centered her gaze on my face, still interrogating my eyes for something: I didn't know what.

"What is it, dear?"

"Mama, I have … **to pee** … … and … *I want some strawberries*!"

She looked quite shocked.

Softly, she giggled then laughed, then she cried, then she laughed some more. I glanced up; Reinhold was laughing, too.

"But strawberries aren't *that* funny!" I said with a petulant frown.

From inside the blanket, I started flailing my arms and kicking at the covers.

"Ugh! I'm too too too **too hot**!"

I had to get some cool air onto those sweaty, clingy pajamas!

Reinhold put me down, leaving me draped loosely in the blanket, standing in front of my kneeling Mama. He was still chuckling as he told her, "I'll get the strawberries, Maria! But *you* can handle the rest!"

He stood, pulled at the wrinkles in his clothes, grabbed his watch from the table, walked a bit stiff-legged to his bedroom door, opened it narrowly and called out, "Edo! Get up! We have a strawberry-emergency! Quickly, cowboy!"

I heard a deeply groggy, "Whaaaat?" from that dark interior. Opening the door wider, Reinhold made one quick step into the room, flipped a light on, turned and closed the door behind him.

Mama walked me to the bathroom, a slow, regal procession, as I saw myself, with the blanket-of-state trailing me across the mirroring wood-floor. When I was finally done in there, after having watched the flow go from almost-brown to yellow to clear as I relaxed more and more, I moved rather unsteadily back out into a hall growing slowly brighter with the day. Mama had knelt with the blanket, waiting for me.

I was getting drowsy again; I leaned into her soft, welcoming shoulder, rubbed my eyes against the glare, waited for a chest-deep, leg-shaking yawn to pass, then asked softly, "Mama, what happened to me?"

She straightened out the twists and untangled the knots that I had managed to tie in my pajamas. Only after that did she answer.

"Honey, you became terribly, terribly sick, very suddenly.

"You had a very dangerous, high fever. Because of it, you slept all of a day and a half! Edo, Reinhold and I took turns holding you to keep you warm so that you could fight the fever! Whatever you were sick from, the doctor didn't know precisely, so we were forced just to wait and pray, that your fever might break."

I tried to take it all in; but now that I had discharged my most pressing issue, I was definitely hungry.

We returned to the parlor.

Mama held me close, re-blanketed on the sofa, and kept watching me, feeling my head and arms. But eventually she seemed to have assured herself that I was better, to have become certain that I was going to stay that way, and so let me sit, both of us relaxed, beside her. Edo and Reinhold had stepped out; in the quiet, Mama dozed. And whenever my eyes settled softly into a nap, the lady would return. She would teach and encourage, and I would play her piano!

I snapped awake when a heavily wrapped Edo and Reinhold clacked and clattered back into the apartment, carrying cloth bags and small boxes completely filled—I discovered!—with sausages and crepes, oranges, bananas, pastries, a bundled gift. And strawberries!

Soon, everyone else was up, even my sleepy-bear sisters (including my five-month old sister, Gretchen) who all appeared to have hibernated through everything! Uncle Edo made coffee for the three adults, and the apartment warmed with the marvelous aroma of the most wonderful feast-day breakfast you could imagine!

Mama was amazed.

"Where did you two manage to find all this? Oh, bananas and oranges! At this time of year? And so early on so frigid a morning! What day is today? Sunday? The fifth? Edo! Strawberries in December? And this lovely, thick sweater, how did you get it?"

Uncle Edo just winked and said, "We have many good friends among the most skillful neighborhood merchants!" then set quickly to getting the banquet laid out in style.

"And we ran into some of them, just setting out with their two, adorable little four-year-old twins. Herr Schraeder led us back into their store, fetched the sweater for you, to present it with their welcome-wishes and most deeply-shared concerns!

"Reinhold keeps trying to talk them into opening another store, in Frankfurt, so that we can stop by there whenever we travel to the farm!" Edo added as he placed the bowl of dressed strawberries before the china-and-silver setting he laughingly pointed to as *mine*!

The feast at last fully spread, we sat and ate, and ate! With my crisis over, the adults seemed ready to relax, to indulge, to release the tension of the previous few days. But *I* had something to tell them!

"Mama, in my dreams I was listening to music!"

I paused to see if she heard.

"And I played it, too!"

"Really, dear?" she replied languidly, sleepily yet patiently, as if she expected me, now recovered, just to keep talking. She sat before the still very tempting remnants of the layout covering one end of the long dining table, and was gratefully relishing the steam swirling up toward her face from a cup of coffee. Now that I was obviously recovered and awake, talking was the one thing she seemed to expect of me.

"Yes, music ..."

I looked over the crowd around the table. Were they paying attention to *me*?

My uncles were busy, restocking their plates as my sisters sparred over melon-cubes. Mama was leaning forward, visibly exhausted, her arms a triangle with the cup in apex beneath her nose, the brew held expectantly at her lips. No one seemed to pay notice as I walked from where I had been sitting across from her at the dining table over to *der Steiner*, as Edo and Reinhold called the beautiful, ebony Steinway concert-grand piano they had ordered all the way from Hamburg.

I mounted the bench and sat down. They would pay attention to me now!

I reached over, touched keys that now tingled their place so exactly beneath my hands, and started to play, to recreate melodies that I had heard during my fever: at least to play as well as my going-on six-year-old fingers would let me! The lady, who had first talked to me while I slept, returned, urging, "Rhythm and melody, Edi! Let it sing!" This whispering-lady had taught me those two pieces.

When I had finished them, I looked over at the table. I thought my efforts sounded pretty good. But *they* were quiet.

Staring at me, no one said even a word!

Like Gramma looks sometimes after a farmhouse-shaking thunderclap, they were all rather pale, even in the morning light that had started helping the crystal chandelier illumine that side of the long, high-ceilinged room that was their parlor and dining room. I had had only beginning, but promising, music lessons so far. However, to me, I appeared to have advanced considerably, with audible skill, within those past, lost days.

It seemed like hours before anyone moved, or even made a sound!

When they had finally recovered, Uncle Edo said, "Very good, Edi!" then spoke softly to Reinhold, "*Knecht Ruprecht*, and *Erinnerung* [*Memory*] from Robert Schumann's *Album for the Young*: on the radio yesterday afternoon, while he was 'out of it'...".

Then he turned and asked Mama more loudly, "So, he has already been on the old *Dreikühige*?"

"Your mother has given him permission to touch the keyboard with supervision," Mama replied.

She added, sounding unsure of what had just happened, "He has been playing extremely well in his first lessons with Herr Fuhrmann, but Mother-in-law has insisted that he have more, serious piano studies before he be given completely free access to it."

Edo looked down at his plate, pointlessly using his fork to push around some pastry crumbs, eggy bits and butter-blobs. After a very quiet few minutes he looked up, over to me, winked and smiled his huge "I gotcha now!" smile. Then he turned to Mama, using that fork to emphasize his words as he said, in almost formal, businessman-like phrasing, "Dearest Sister-in-law, from this moment you must allow me to pay for music lessons for the boy!"

Mama had put her coffee cup down and watched me, her hands raised, held pensively beneath her chin, seemingly trying to think through everything that was happening so suddenly. When she took her hands away, she was beaming at me, as I sat there at the keyboard watching her and absentmindedly moving my fingers, feeling and taste-hearing the musical tones in my mind, without pressing the actual keys.

"If your brother will allow it, I have no objections."

I cried, "Hurray! Thank you, thank you, Uncle Edo!" jumped down from the piano bench and ran over to hug him.

But instead, I slipped on the polished floor and ran my shoulder into his chair just as he was raising his coffee cup.

Before he could absorb the bump, the coffee had spilled onto his hand!

He dropped the cup when the heat hit his fingers, knocked his plate onto the floor while trying to catch the cup, and the crash and clatter of bouncing and breaking dishes echoed across the room! Edo looked up from the racket rather confused, and exclaimed, "Well! That was another bolt from the blue!"

Reinhold laughed out loud as they all rose from the table to help clean up the mess, "After the lightning, there's always the thunder!"

"And the Zoo!" I yelled.

Even Uncle Edo had to laugh at that!

————————————

Late that next week, after we had returned to Singhofen, the morning post brought a large, special-delivery envelope from Berlin.

Addressed to me, it was cardboard-stiff, with "Nicht verbiegen!" [*Do not bend!*] across it in tall, red, thick-Fraktur letters.

I opened it, very carefully, to find a photograph from our trip: one of me, standing on a zoo-bench in front of Uncle Edo and Uncle Reinhold. There's that elephant trying to touch Reinhold's hair with its trunk! Mama found a frame for it, and I made sure to put it beside my bed, so I could always see it.

When Eva was older, and could jump up onto the bed with me, I would pick it up and show it to her, tell her all about the zoo, and the big piano, and the train rides between Frankfurt and Berlin, but she always just wagged her stubby butt and tried to lick the picture!

————————————

Uncle Edo was different from the rest of us.

He was something called an "American."

And he was a cowboy!

He had gone over across the ocean a few years before the big war—the one that the adults *just kept on talking about!*—had even started. After becoming one of those Americans, Edo had met Reinhold and stayed there with him during and after that war, and made lots of money selling things to Europe.

During their visits here in Singhofen with us, they both had started teaching me *American*, helping me read the books, maps and magazines they brought me! I learned really fast, and Uncle Edo would talk about cowboys and longhorns and Indians and Texas and some towns called San Antonio and Austin and Fredericksburg, how the hills around there made him a little homesick, except that they only had lots of scrawny trees that he called "mosquitoes" or something.

One time he even brought his old cowboy boots, chaps and hat for me to see! (He always wore cowboy boots, and those dark-blue cotton pants with the shiny brass rivets! because that's what he was: a real, free, rough, tough cowboy!)

His hat was so big that it flopped down over my head, and the brim came almost all the way down to my shoulders! Everyone laughed, but I didn't see how it was so funny. I wanted to wear it like Tom Mix had in the movies we had seen at the cinema over in Bad Nassau!

He pulled it off me, laughing when it tugged at my ears, then held it in front of me while he explained, "The brim of the hat is broad against the strength of the sun, and curved to channel the rain away!"

The big, black boots with all the fancy stitching were so tall that they went all the way up my legs; and the heels were so tall that they almost made me fall over!

Uncle Edo bent down and held one of them between us, pointing with his finger to different parts as he went into detail, explaining things to me—listening as hard as I could!—from when he had worked "punching cows" (that was so funny!) out west, in places around Fredericksburg called Harper, Comfort, Kerrville and Cherry Spring!

"Cowboy boots are tall, up to the knee, to work with the chaps to protect you from cactus and brush, and mean cattle. They're sharp-pointed so you can slip them right into the stirrup, fast! The narrowing heels are tall, often 7 cm or more, to hold the boot snug in the stirrup: it mustn't slip off it or through it, especially when the horse runs fast or wheels quickly! Any other kinds of western boots, well," he laughed, "they're just for goat-ropers, not cowboys!"

I laughed so hard at that! Who would want to rope a stinky ole goat?

He showed me the hole punched into the right boot and leg of the chaps, where he had protected his horse from being gored by a longhorn bull! He even had the scar on his leg where the horn had ripped through, from where the blood had dripped into his boot! That was better than books or even the movies!

But he said he had had to leave his six-shooters and all his ponies in Texas!

He explained that there were lots of Germans around there, especially out west and north of San Antonio in dusty little cow-towns ("Tell me about the stampedes and the saloons and the shoot-outs!") in the hills west of there, near where the Indians had once been—the "Comanches" he called them!—and that San Antonio had been like a little Frankfurt, with its beer, sauerkraut and sausages, local German newspapers, and because of all the people who had moved there from Germany: good people run out of the Taunus and the Rhine Valley in the 1850's.

"Just as those blasted kaisers started pushing everyone around!" Gramma added, and Edo just laughed and shook his head, 'yes'!

Uncle Edo taught me one sentence that he was very proud of, about how things had happened over there, in what he would smile and call "the *German Hill Country*" emphatically: "Texas ist die einzige erfolgreiche Bauernkolonie des deutschen Volkes." [*Texas is the only successful farmer-colony of the German people.*] He explained that the other German colonies, the ones in Africa and Asia, had just been more of that ole Kaiser's military adventures. And, boy! did Gramma jump in on that!

He promised, too, that one day we would all go over there so I could hear them speak their own "mittelrhein'sches Texanerdeutsch" [*middle-Rhine Texas-German*] myself! "*Gut'n Tag, y'all!*" And he said they had real *haddekuche* [*ginger cookies*] and *Frankfurter Kranz* [*almond-crème cake*] there, too! in a bakery not far from the big house they still owned in San Antonio, on *König Wilhelm* Street.

There in San Antonio, "on a fine Fall Saturday" in the café of that bakery, was where and when Edo had met our Reinhold in 1915!

Orphaned in 1910, Reinhold had moved to San Antonio from Germany to stay with some of his relatives, and talked Edo into staying in Texas longer! Then, with Edo's cowboy and ranching contacts, and help from Reinhold's family— they owned a big brewery there!—the two of them had set up a business that shipped sides of beef, bales of cotton, and barrels of oil to other countries, especially over here to Europe.

Just after that big war was over, they had decided to move their business to New York, right there in the skyscrapers! He said that New York was mostly a lot cooler than Texas. Reinhold added, "Absolutely right, cowboy! But so crowded! A million more just in that city than in the whole state, and *it's* bigger than France!"

They described, sort of dreamily, how they had taken the train back to Texas lots of times, to the quiet, the winter warmth, and all the nighttime stars they loved, out around a huge rock that they said was magic. I tried and tried, but just couldn't remember it all! Several times, Uncle Edo brought us loads of pictures and postcards and books—even some big flags, posters and gramophone records! —all the way from America! He explained about them, "Flags like that are very important to Americans, as representative of their democracy, just like ours is to your Gramma: they are *their* flags." I loved our flag, too, because it displayed— just like Gramma had told me—in its *black-red-gold* the colors of a glorious sunrise, but I wondered why ours seemed so unimportant to so many other Germans.

Then, a few years after that big war, Edo and Reinhold had decided to move back to Germany, to Berlin, and set up their business there, too. I heard Papa tell Edo once that he didn't know how to thank him for all the help. And I had also overheard Papa tell Herr Fuhrmann, when they were talking by themselves, that we had made it through the bad-money time because Uncle had sent us these things called "dollars." Somehow, they made things better: we had gotten electricity, and even our farm had grown bigger back then! Papa and Mama always spoke gratefully about my uncles' help!

But there was still that problem of the thank-you for my music-gift-concert that coming weekend!

I had written them a special note earlier this year, thanking them after they had sent me a big box of sheet music from New York. It contained a complete set of ten preludes in an Opus 23, autographed by someone whose name I couldn't read: it started with a capital "P", but lots of it wasn't even real letters! Gramma explained they were called "Cyrillic".

But most of the music was by an American called Gershwin, including one thing called a "rhapsody" and it was "in blue" (I wasn't sure what those meant, either); and he had even signed his music with notes written to my uncles! I hadn't thought about there being any composers actually *alive*, that I might be able to meet, talk to, play for!

Although Herr Fuhrmann told me to wait about the "opus" music, I had started learning by heart all of the Gershwin pieces that I could! They were happy, and had neat harmonies! Gramma, and Mama in particular, really enjoyed them!

After all these minutes of memory-distracted pondering, I happened upon what I hoped would be a good solution to my dilemma.

"I'll wait until after the concert to write the thank-you letter to my uncles! In it, I can describe *everything* that happens there! A great plan!"

Now, satisfied with my scheme, I turned back to watch Mama and Papa and my silly-acting older sisters. They had started bugging Mama about going to look at dresses and doing other yucky girl stuff. Mama tried to calm them down, but she seemed weary already.

"The tickets are for the Saturday afternoon matinee, Dear," Papa confided.

She looked so relieved. I guessed that, even within this short time, she had already started to dread, and to feel exhausted from the prospect of having to chase, clean and dress all four of us, especially my fussy sisters!

After Papa had read more from the paper that Uncle had sent, he started to explain the music of the concert itself to us.

"In this performance, thirteen years after the battle, the orchestra is celebrating the 1914 victory of the present Reichspräsident, Field Marshal von Hindenburg, at the Battle of Tannenberg."

He paused while reading the rest of the sheet before detailing it further.

"And the only thing on the program is the Eighth Symphony of Gustav Mahler."

"Apparently it was chosen," he continued, scanning the text and talking at the same time, "because it includes a setting of the Final Scene of Goethe's drama, *Faust*. And you know that both the play and its author are tightly associated with the city of Frankfurt!"

He paused and took a deep breath. Then he looked up, somewhere into the distance before continuing, seeming to measure his words.

"However, I do find it unusual that they would insert a full intermission between the two parts.

"Admittedly, this symphony *is* rather large, the second part in particular..."

I already adored Goethe.

His poetry had shown up quickly on Gramma's reading list for me, "the greatest and the best" she called him, always with that direct, "This is really important, Edi! Remember it!" tone in her voice.

But I didn't recall ever hearing that piece by Mahler, or even seeing it among Papa's gramophone records. And I had never been to a real, living orchestra performance!

We had only ever heard orchestras over the static-crackles of the radio, or listened to them on the gramophone.

"Tooth-grinding reconstructions! Dull, miserable, feeble imitations!" Papa would proclaim in growing exasperation at the rhythmic *scritch–scritch–scritch* of the needle eating away so rapidly at his fragile, dizzy-spinning, black-wax discs.

Now I was going to see and hear real, live musicians creating real, live music!

I wasn't sure what kind of human lived solely by making music.

Were they like Herr Fuhrmann, very serious, kind of lonely, and way too strict about fingering studies and velocity exercises? I only knew that they had to be somehow different from the farmers, teachers, merchants, tinkers and coopers we had around here. I just hoped they weren't too different!

But suddenly it was bedtime.

With a waggy-butt and a bounce Eva was up on the featherbed, making circles, tromping out her snakes before lying down; I grabbed and hugged my big, always happy puppy. Only Eva would hear tonight's confession of my deepest secrets: of my uncles' gift, and just how tremendously excited I was!

Unvollständiges Konzert
— Chapter 3 —
An Incomplete Concert

"Hurry up! Just because it's early in the morning doesn't mean it's going to stay cool in the car! After all, it's almost still August!"

Like me, the fabric of the car's backseat was getting bristlier the longer I sat, grumbling and waiting for my silly sisters to get ready so that everyone else could get out of the farmhouse to leave for Frankfurt!

The early morning of Saturday, the third of September had dawned clear and, though cool, the sun was succeeding rapidly at pushing us toward the 24° high that Papa had warned us to dress for. It was already quite warm in the car.

I sat there in my best-dress short pants and knee-socks and fumed.

"The concert starts at three this afternoon, and we have to go the whole 85 km from Singhofen to Frankfurt! Papa said that's over two hours away, but only if we don't have any problems with the car! And I wanted to be there early!"

Papa had pulled the sedan to the front of the house, close to the front door.

From its interior, I could spy into the deep shadow of the kitchen. The morning was so still that I heard almost everything they said, including every sound Mama made as she bustled about, trying to keep things organized. I saw it all with my ears, even if, like those quarter-hour peels of the tall, ancient clock, the reports came from the further, shadier part of the big, front room. Like all families, we had patterns and rituals, comfortable, predictable, noisy ways we had just grown, or simply fallen, into.

"Hänsel!" Mama called out.

Then again, "Hans!" still to no avail.

"Johann Gottlieb Meyer!" she yelled. Papa should have been able to hear *that*! (Although, with *Meyer* so common a name in Germany, she was lucky half of Hesse was not running to the door!)

We had all grown accustomed to Mama's three-part Papa-calling. He seemed to like it, a lot. Whenever he finally appeared, he would start whispering to her to make sure she wasn't really angry. Then they'd get all soft-talk-y and gooey-eyed. That's when we knew they weren't paying much attention to us kids!

"Yes, ma'am, dearest Frau Meyer!" he joked, in a most obedient tone (for my

Papa!) as I heard him walk in the mismatched rhythm of uneven steps, obviously still trying to dress himself, across the heavy wooden floor to where Mama stood at work in the kitchen.

She started her usual, "Uh-huh … turn around … again," words that told me she was directing him in her "Inspektionswirbel" [*inspection twirl*], as my oldest sister had started calling it. "Again. Slower … well …"

Papa laughed.

Suddenly though, Mama stopped sternly: "Johann Meyer! Where is your son?"

Without my persistent interruption of the otherwise continual summons, pleas and petulance from everyone else (except Gramma!) in the house, she had apparently lost track of me.

"O-ho! *My* son! *He* is outside in the car," Papa replied.

"He got himself up near sunrise, around 5:30, is completely dressed and ready, and has been sitting in the car for almost the past hour."

In a snap, I heard Mama rinse her hands, wheel, and with quick, almost military steps march outside to find me in the car, waiting. When she looked inside its still-open door, the tempest in her voice ebbed.

"Honey, why are you sitting out here? And in such heat?" she asked me.

Her palm worried over my forehead, making sure I wasn't too warm, or feverish again. The big windows in the sedan were trying to turn it into a hot-house, and I was too irritated to be anything but a prickly rose!

"Let's open all the windows, OK?"

She went around to each door and rolled its glass down.

"It's already time, Mama! We've got to leave!"

I swiveled to be sure to appeal directly to her as she walked around the car. "It's already half-past six! Die Zeit drängt!" [*Time is fleeting!*]

She came back around to me, patted me on the head.

"Understood, my captain!" she said in jest: not wanted and not funny, as far as I was concerned!

"Why can't the others just hurry up?" I asked her, with a goodly tinge of whining thrown in. I couldn't help it; I wanted her at least to cringe with my personal anguish!

"We're all coming in a moment! Just relax!" She turned to leave but stopped herself to add, "And if you get too hot, come right back into the house, OK?"

I sighed. Did she really understand how important this was?

"Yes, Mama," I replied, dejected.

I wished Eva were here: *she* always understood! But she was staying with Herr Fuhrmann's bouncy, barky little dachshund, the one he called *Attila*. I closed my eyes, remembering how they would run around chasing each other—Attila's wiry tail spinning like a fan to keep his balance whenever he skidded around a corner—then play tug-of-war, pulling each other with that sausage-looking, old brown sock that Herr Fuhrmann had stuffed with cotton-wool.

With Mama back in the house, suddenly feeling abandoned, I decided I was thirsty, so I jumped down from the car seat and followed.

Papa was already dressed and had started working with the older girls. The baby, running unsteadily between Papa and her sisters, was next on Mama's

28

work-list.

But first, Mama grabbed the couple of dishes she had laden with Gramma's breakfast. I ran up the stairs, to catch up and walk with her as she ascended to Gramma's room.

She gave a gentle knock, and a pleasant, "Mother-in-law? Are you awake?"

Even after fourteen years of marriage, Mama still treated Papa's mother with great, almost formal, respect. She had told me once that she was so grateful to Gramma, that it was her upbringing that had made Papa the man she adored. She told me, too, that I should appreciate all Gramma's attention: that it had been Gramma who had helped me so much by starting to teach me to read when I was only three. "𝔉rü𝔥e𝔰 𝔏e𝔰en–lebenslange 𝔈rfenntni𝔰𝔰e!" [*Early reading—a life of discoveries!*] Gramma taught.

A light throat-clearing, then a soft, "Certainly, Maria! Please, come in!" sounded from beyond the door.

Mama handed me the small plate holding two toasted, flaky rolls beside some jam and fresh-churned butter, then turned the doorknob with her right hand. I leaned against the heavy oaken door to help her push it open wider, slowly, before she led us into the room behind a still-steaming cup of tea.

Placing the cup on the small table next to where Gramma was sitting up in bed, Mama took the other plate from me and arranged both cup and plate there, within Gramma's easy reach.

Up on the bed, atop the homemade quilt was lying the ever-present picture of my grandfather, "my late Opa [*Grampa*]," taken of him in his army uniform not long after he had been drafted at the start of 1917. Gramma explained to me often, "He was murdered by the Kaiser!" outside Ypres, that very same year, at the battle of Passchendaele. Only ten years ago the previous month, in a still too vivid past, all of that was something she was certain to have me memorize in greatest detail. "Any nation that has to draft its forty-year-olds," she would preach, "is already at the very edge of the abyss!"

I could see this morning's moistness in Gramma's slightly red eyes.

Still holding her rosary, Gertrude Magdalena Meyer's hands grasped Mama's.

"Thank you, dear daughter! And our handsome Edi! But you are too good to me!"

Gramma patted the bed; Mama sat carefully at its edge.

I stepped closer, stood with Mama's leg at my back, and tilted my head and shoulder over onto the covers, toward my Gramma; she leaned forward, pulled me up toward her and kissed me on the forehead.

It was so comfortable, standing there, leaning into the quilt atop the puffy featherbed, that I drifted dreamily, almost falling asleep. Before I did, I reached over and flipped open the cover of the book Gramma had taken out: Lessing's play, *Nathan der Weise* [*Nathan the Wise*]. She had started us reading it together just that past week: I got to be both *Saladin* and the *Templar*!

Only fifty-three, Gramma was still suffering from leg problems after one of the cows had kicked her, just last year. She was getting around better and better, but still used her cane. I had said that I hated that ole cow for hurting my Gramma! But she admonished me not to talk like that, not to speak of hate. The cow hadn't meant to hurt her; Gramma had just been in the wrong place when it had been frightened.

"You may disapprove, dislike, admonish, find fault, or reprove, Edi, but do not hate. Hatred is for the weak, the shallow, the ignorant: for the fool!"

I leaned my head onto the bed, looked up from the soft folds of the comforter and watched my grandmother's eyes intently; she noticed, smiled and winked at me.

"Mother, you remember that Hans and I are travelling with the children into Frankfurt today, right?" Mama asked, then added, "And that Herr and Frau Brandt are coming to spend the day with you, and to do the farm chores? We will be back late this evening."

Gramma looked up from taking a sip of her tea, and nodded, "I remember it all, thank you, my dear! Having the Brandts visit will certainly be very pleasant."

"We're leaving shortly."

Mama smiled, stood, smoothed where she had sat on the featherbed, before sighing, "Well, back to work!" Then she called me to go with her, leading me by the hand into the hall. She closed the door quietly and followed me back down the stairs to finish getting her brood ready and on the road.

But, as for me, I was going back to the car: the others could just hurry up!

The sun was warm, and the air very fresh, streaming through Mama's recent-ly-opened windows. I leaned back and closed my eyes, trying to remember those pictures of Frankfurt that I had seen in the encyclopedia: the *Dom*, the *Römer*, the Opera House…

Papa jolted me awake when he popped the trunk open to start stowing the packs that Mama had worked so diligently to get together. Suddenly, I remembered her instruction, "Do everything before we leave!" so I got up and ran into the house, toward the bathroom.

"Well, now! What next?"

Papa looked up as I rushed around him, into the house, oomphed as he bent quickly back down to face that cavern, to stow all the cargo the sedan had to schlep to Frankfurt and back simply because there would be four children aboard.

I heard Herr and Frau Brandt drive up. Now dressed, Gramma had made her way downstairs. When I returned to the kitchen, she had already gone outside to greet them and usher them into the house, while Papa and Mama were outside, finishing Mama's list of chores. They both returned to the house to bid their quick goodbyes; we kids had already said goodbye to our Gramma.

Mama came to the car and checked that they had gotten everything done, and all the bundles and children stuffed into the vehicle. Papa walked around the car, again, inspecting the tires, and the spare before getting in behind the wheel.

Mama placed my littlest sister, Gretchen, in front, right between her and Papa, because she was the one Mama had to spend the most time feeding and cleaning. My older two sisters and I had the big back seat to ourselves.

"Finally!" I muttered as Papa started the car.

He looked over the gauges, checked his watch and whispered toward Mama, "A quarter after seven. Good. Maybe Edi's whining got things moving, after all!"

With a jolt and a grind, we headed down the hill and out, to cross mountains, fields, forests and farms of the Taunus, and on, toward Frankfurt. I watched from my window seat as the progression of familiar trees and houses melted into the nervous excitement of the unfamiliar, the new and unknown.

Before we had even gone the nine kilometers from Singhofen into Holzhausen an der Haide, Papa mentioned to Mama how little the road toward Wiesbaden had been improved since before the war. I moved to the middle of the back seat to listen. I leaned closer to them, onto the back of the front seat to ask, "Papa, why was there a war?"

"Because the Kaiser was completely crazy!"

I could hear the anger he still held for the specific man that he and his mother blamed for his father's death.

He slowed the car so that he could talk to me and drive at the same time.

"At that time, he held the government powers himself, and no one would or could contradict him." he said, growing more emotive.

"That was the reason the war happened: he had to have his own way, no matter what the people wanted! His generals, the newspapers and the industrialists are the reason it continued."

"All you children!" he paused to see that my sisters were listening, too, and waited until he was sure they were.

"Kids, always remember that a dictator, Kaiser or tyrant, each one can do how, what and when he wants to do *anything*, even when he's nothing but nuts!

"Democracy—a well-functioning democracy—is the only thing that protects us from such insanity!"

Mama reached over and touched his arm, "And that would be the political broadcast for today, right?" she pleaded gently.

She always calmed Papa when he started talking about the war.

Although he was 18 the year it started, he had not been sent to it. He had survived something called *polio* when he was a baby. It had taken the sight from his left eye and had bent that side's little finger permanently. Otherwise, he was fine, but that had meant the army wouldn't take him away. He had had to work very hard to keep the farm running after Grampa was called up.

Papa sighed, grinned, uhm'ed a bit, then turned to her, winked and said in a low voice, "Jawohl, meine Liebeskaiserin!" [*Yes, ma'am, my Love-Empress!*] Then he sped back up; I sat down. I had seen the hint of gooey-eyes. It was time to leave them alone; they didn't seem ever to make much sense after that started, anyway.

Soon, we three children in the backseat fell asleep amid the cool forest breezes and the smell of late-summer haystacks blowing in through the open windows from the trim farm-fields of the Taunus. The temperature had started climbing, even though it was still well before noon. At around 22°, it was so comfortable— and I had been so nervous that whole morning—that the nodding whisper of naptime could not be ignored.

We woke each other just as we were coming into Wiesbaden. Everything was so interesting, so exciting that we made a thick Kinderklumpen [*clump of children*], pressed up before whichever window presented the most siren view.

So many buildings, built so tightly together! Ones of exposed timbers completed with brick, a few of stone, all with varying tints of tiles on the roofs, and people wearing so many different types of hats, clothes and costumes!

The downtown smelled of ancient, worthy things: old and strong like our barn, but without the hay, and all the cats and cows!

Because it was a Saturday morning, the townspeople were running about, getting things done before the shops closed at noon for the rest of that day and all of the next. We had several near-misses, when people stepped into the street without looking, or horses would paw the pavement, or rear too close to the car. I guessed they didn't expect automobiles to be passing through some of those streets; they were so narrow! But Papa still got us through all the noise and bustle of Wiesbaden, where we turned east, heading finally—at last!—toward Frankfurt!

———————————

After a quick lunch-stop, full of sauerkraut and sausages, refreshed and suddenly rather sleepy again, we came into the heart of Frankfurt am Main, and much sooner than I had expected!

Across busy Mainzer Landstraße, past the train station, at the corner of Kronprinzen-Straße, Papa stopped, looked at his watch, checked and rechecked his maps, admitted to Mama that he'd missed the turn at the Landstraße, then headed us off toward the sentinel cathedral tower, into the Old City. So many medieval buildings, streets so crowded with cars and people, it all looked just like the pictures of it that Gramma had shown me in the encyclopedia, but real, and in color!

We passed the Römerberg slowly, with Papa and Mama pointing out things we kids were supposed to remember, but (in the excitement) wouldn't. Papa said that we would have to make time later to come back to tour the *Römer*, the *Dom*, the Paulskirche and the other sights there in the *Altstadt*.

Later was OK with me: right now, I just wanted to get to the Opera House!

Over by the cathedral he turned up a little street I thought he called Trierische- or Hasengasse as he pointed and talked more and more. He followed that and others until we reached High Street—*Hochstraße*—at this really tall old building. Papa said it was the Eschenheimer Tower. It looked really medieval and pointy; I definitely wanted to go see it, to climb up into it, but still, not as much as I wanted to get to the concert!

Papa said, "And now, we're only half a kilometer from the Opera House!"

We could have been on the moon, it seemed to me so far away!

But finally, the columned, stone façade of the Opera House came into view.

I couldn't say anything! I was awestruck! With its classical architecture, it looked like some of the buildings in the pictures of ancient Rome that Gramma had shown me, but more majestic, and definitely better because it was here, now! right in front of me!

Gramma had also shown me closer photos of the chariot on the front roof, and more pictures of the winged horse, Pegasus, that pranced, up there on the highest point. "The gift of the Goddess of Wisdom," she had said, "Pegasus represents humanity's potential to rise above the base, the mean and evil, to great heights of sagacious goodness!"

Papa discovered where we were supposed to park the car. We got out, stretching and trying to brush the journey from our clothes. After extracting what we needed from the car—but making sure to leave everything we didn't!—we shut its doors and walked toward the grand building.

It was already 14:30 and the cloudless sky was warming the plaza in front of the Opera House. I was ready to head for shade when we finally approached the front arches, below where the big letters proclaimed,

DEM WAHREN SCHOENEN GUTEN

[For the True, the Beautiful, the Good].

The stunningly handsome, classical building made me want to be all three!

We walked into the tall foyer. It was suddenly so nice and cool!

After Papa made his way through the crowd and retrieved our reserved tickets, we were allowed to walk further in, across the foyer, then up one side of the grandiose double staircase. We stepped into the concert hall.

My head almost swiveled off my neck, I was looking around at so much, so quickly! I wanted to take it all in, remember every detail for my thank-you letter!

Our seats were about halfway back from the front, in the center section.

"Wow!" said Papa, "right in the middle of the middle!"

I sat between Mama and my oldest sister, Marianne, on my left; Anneliese sat beyond Papa, who was just beside Mama, holding Gretchen. As usual, Gretchen was happy and quiet, but Mama was ready to shield her if she thought things were getting too loud for baby-ears.

I stood on my seat to get a better view; Mama touched my leg and told me to get down. I should have pouted, but I was too excited to remember to!

Some would have said we looked out of place. Mama and Papa weren't dressed quite so showily as most of those there. But I didn't care! I loved Mama and Papa because they had done this for me: without them I wouldn't have received my present! There also weren't very many children present, even for a Saturday afternoon. To me it seemed a pity that other parents hadn't brought their own children to the concert. I thought they might have enjoyed it, too!

Suddenly, so many people started walking out onto the stage! Men, women— and even boys not much older than me!—stepped onto the risers behind a flat area of chairs and music stands. Some were slow and friendly, like they were meeting friends on the sidewalk in town; others walked in a rush, like Haydn trying to escape his tone-deaf wife!—had Gramma told me about that?—right to where they wanted to be, then stuck fast.

As those were coming on stage toward the back, musicians, carrying their instruments, came onto the part closer to us. Some of the instruments I had already seen: just who in our modern, 1927 Germany hadn't ever seen a violin, a flute, a cello?—but I was enthralled to see other, less common kinds. Contrabassoons, tubas, the mix of wood and brass was so compelling, then the horns! Is there anything more beautiful than a horn, with its shining, golden bell, and ring on ring on ring of sparkling tubing?

"Play yours for me, Siegfried!"

The audience grew quiet as the instrumentalists sat and arranged their scores, and the people on stage behind them all got into their places.

Then, the nearest violinist stood up and used his bow to threaten the closest of the oboe players.

The oboist played one note.

"That's an *A*," I said to myself.

I didn't remember why or how I knew that, but I knew it, and not from being told that this was the note that orchestras used to get themselves in tune. The sound of that note moved through my mind distinct from all others, flashed in streaks of bright yellow, and filled my mouth and nose with that rich taste of freshly churned butter on steaming, just-baked bread.

All at once, the orchestra responded with a cacophonous cobweb of dissonance, playing jumps, runs and scales. That made a big mess in my ears, my mind, and in my nose and mouth: it tasted horrible! I almost stuck my fingers in my ears to shield them from the noise, but because I didn't see anyone else doing it, I didn't dare either. So, I squeezed my jaw muscles tightly and made my ears roar and roar, loud enough to block the painful racket!

After the din of that first blast of noise had subsided, the violinist pointed into the woodwinds again. The oboist played another lovely A. This time, however, everything got better very quickly: no need for fingers in ears or roaring jaws!

The house lights dimmed. Everything and everybody got suddenly very quiet.

Four ladies in long, fancy dresses and three men in long-tailed, black coats stepped out onto the stage, moving across, in front of the orchestra. Right behind them came a man with longer tails on his coat. Gramma had explained how wolves (and dogs!) used their tails to show who was the boss; I guessed this was the same sort of thing!

When this pack had all reached the stage, the audience began applauding.

Papa had explained that a lot of people would be in this performance, but I hadn't thought there would be such a crowd! I hoped they shouldn't, but it looked like some of them were very close to falling off the edge of the stage!

After the applause died down, that last guy out stepped up onto his little platform and waited for the soloists to take their positions. He got the chorus standing up, paying attention, raised his hands and baton, and waited. He lifted himself up on his toes, swung the baton back and forth, one, two, three, four, then on the next 'one' he snapped it at the organist!

A deep E-flat boomed from the loudest, lowest voices of the organ and the orchestra—*one, two*—a *forte*, both-hands, E-flat Major chord from middle and high voices of the organ—*three, four*—and the chorus joined loudly: *Ve—ni, Ve—ni creator spiritus…* [*Come, Come, Creator Spirit…*]

The brass burst forth and I was gone: elated, elevated, shot heavenwards, lost in a world of sounds, of colors, tastes and experiences, of visions that my six-year-old mind had never imagined could exist!

Planted at the very front edge of my seat, I could feel warmth hit my body, my hands gripping the armrests hard. I was transfixed, bewitched—by music and spectacle!

And so I sat, teetering but immobile, painfully aware of everything before and around me while absolutely transfixed, through that shifting, mountainous, Alpen landscape of the entire first movement of Gustav Mahler's Eighth Symphony, *The Symphony of a Thousand*.

By the time the entire crowded stage—organ, orchestra, choirs and soloists—had traversed the vast panorama, an eternity in those lofting measures, to hold, hold, then release those final, fortissimo E-flat major measures of that section's terminal "Gloria Patri," I had transcended several levels of musical paradise. My mouth still hanging open, a sudden gasp-gasp-gasp shudder cast me precipitously back to Earth. Just twenty-five minutes of music had transformed my life, perhaps even fulfilled that rewiring of the circuits in my brain that that Berlin-fever had so eloquently incited.

The applause rose; I looked about. It was honey-filled magic!

The accolade continued as soloists bowed, the conductor, then orchestra, too.

They exited the stage; the house lights rose.

I released my cramping grip on the armrests, took a deep, re-inflating breath. I rubbed my hands to drive the pin-prick tingling from my fingers, squeezed my eyelids together, pulled them apart, back together, then again apart to urge the moisture back onto them. I felt something else odd, and looked down.

A darker spot on the front of my short pants: it had already started drying, but still showed.

I had wet myself—just a little—in the initial, inarticulate ecstasy of that surreal moment, overpowered by my discovery of the true heart of Music and my new-fulfilling, emotional, physical, and spiritual, existence within it.

We arose from our seats and wandered out into the foyer with the rest of an audience that was obviously unaccustomed to sitting still for very long. I made sure to keep a hand in front of the spot until it was dry and no longer so noticeable!

Papa had explained that the intermission was a very good idea: the second part of this symphony was twice as long as the first part! When we reached the foyer, he had started talking to someone who also turned out to have lived in the Taunus. He joked with him, dropping into Hessian dialect (beyond Mama's hearing), "At least there's no Bruckner!"

"I agree completely!" replied the man, "Else we should have had to bring pillows and night-caps with us!"

While they were still laughing at that Austrian composer's expense ("Ugh! So repetitive and long-winded!" Papa always added whenever Bruckner or his works were mentioned), we heard someone in an usher's uniform call from across the room, "Herr Meyer! Paging Herr Johann Meyer!"

Papa looked up. Two men stopped the usher in sequence as he walked by.

He paused, asked the gentlemen something, then moved on, again calling out, "A message for Herr Johann Meyer!"

Papa walked over to intercept him. They exchanged information, making certain Papa was the one he sought, then the usher handed over the message.

Papa opened the note; he turned white as aspirin.

Looking up, he bit his lip. Then he came over to Mama and started to pull her to the side, pausing only to tell Marianne to keep her sister and me with her there.

After they got across the room, he held out the note, and they both read from it silently. Mama moved Gretchen into her left arm, and hugged Papa, rubbing his back, standing in a way that hid his face from us. Then they started talking intently, mouth to ear.

After a few minutes, just as the lobby lights flickered to hurry people back to their seats, Mama took the paper from Papa, folded it with one hand and pressed it down into the little purse she had been carrying. Then they came back over to us.

They called us over to where they could sit down, to be at our level as we stood before them.

Papa said haltingly, "We've received a message from the Brandts … at home with your grandmother."

He curled his lower lip in and bit down as we watched him try to impede the too obvious flow of emotions. He stopped; he simply couldn't go on.

Gracefully, Mama took over, continuing his explanation, "The message says that your Uncles Edo and Reinhold were in a very bad car-accident yesterday."

Marianne started whimpering; Anneliese joined her.

Papa was silent. He stood up, staring into the mirroring, polished stone floor.

"Shouldn't we go home, Papa?" I asked quietly.

He raised his misting eyes to mine, looking rather surprised, I guessed, that I would surrender the rest of my musical present without the hint of a fuss.

He knelt, hugged me tightly, pulled away to look me in the eye, and with a struggling voice agreed.

"You're absolutely right, son. Let's go home."

———————————

That next day, the sudden, chill autumn rains were washing the sky a frigid, anemic gray. Information came in from Berlin; so Papa and Mama called us together in the parlor to let us know what had happened. Mama talked; Papa couldn't.

Uncle Edo had died? Reinhold was in a coma?

My older sisters cried.

I was stunned, confused, shocked. I couldn't get it to fit, to work in my mind. My uncle Edo? It was just too much to understand!

So I didn't react; I didn't know how.

When Mama had finished giving us the news, I turned, vacantly, and walked slowly up the stairs to my room. I jumped up on the bed with Eva and hugged her, held her as tightly as I could, then just lay there staring out through the window panes into the whispering rain. Eva started her little boxer snores; I fell asleep.

There were voices downstairs; some of the neighbors had stopped by. I pushed myself off the bed and stepped quietly to the top of the stairs.

Papa was talking about what had happened, about the wreck, the information he had obtained from the Berlin police. I could hear much of it.

Some Nazi and communist gangs were fighting, running through the streets and slugging it out on the sidewalks. Sudden gunshots, and a man driving a big delivery truck too close to those blasts panicked. He stepped on the gas pedal and the truck sped up, too fast; he lost control. The truck crossed over and crashed right into the front of Uncle Edo and Reinhold's car; Edo was driving.

Papa's ability to talk about it drained away.

The neighbors stepped in, started saying how sorry they were, "… what a shame, and so young, just 34! …"

I turned and tiptoed back to Eva. She was asleep again. I held onto my baby boxer, and soon I had fallen asleep, too.

───────────────

Gramma never left her room. She wept.

Even after her sister, Franziska, had arrived by express from Zurich, she kept to her bed.

I could hear her sobbing, with Great-aunt talking softly, then weeping, too.

The priest came and met with her. I could hear them praying the rosary. Whenever they got to an *Ave Maria* part, I would say it with them. I wasn't sure why, but right then it just made me feel a little bit better.

Papa had had to get Uncle Edo's telephone out of its lock-up, to place some calls to Berlin. He told them where and when to deliver it. I didn't know what this 'it' was, and I wasn't going to bother him to ask.

I had never seen my Papa struggle so. Sometimes all this seemed to overcome him, to push him down, almost drown him. I didn't like that: my Papa was always strong and happy and fun. But now, only when Mama came over and hugged him, spoke softly to him, and rubbed his back or caressed his arm did he seem to get any of his strength back.

Then came the day that Mama said we all had to go to church, all the way over to Bad Ems. Frau Brandt arrived, somber, to stay there and take care of Gretchen. I had never known Frau Brandt not to have a big smile on her broad, always near-chuckling, Hessian country-woman face.

My older sisters and I dressed quietly, putting on the dark clothes that Mama had picked out, then we slipped into the car. No fussing, no arguing, we watched the adults and stayed quiet.

Papa was completely silent as he drove. Mama sat on the back seat with us, and once in a while would check on us quietly, just that way mamas do.

Gramma and Aunt Franziska rode in front with Papa.

Standing behind Papa, against the seat, I watched. Gramma dabbed her eyes with her handkerchief several times; Aunt Franzi patted and rubbed Gramma's hand.

When we got closer to Bad Ems and could see its buildings in the distance, Gramma turned and asked her sister, sadly, "You do remember, Franzi, that the Requiem for my Erich was sung here at St Martin's, don't you?"

"Certainly, Gertri! *He* was a good man, among all the good ones—so many in our own family!"

Gramma bit her lip, nodded slightly and produced the uneasy hint of a smile. Mama rubbed my arm; I looked up at her.

"Shall I be among those 'so many', too?" I wondered.

Again, the car fell to silence.

───────────────

Visible from the Kaiserbrücke across the Lahn, St Martin's nestled in a glade near the river; its narrow façade moved into view as we reached the Ems side of the bridge. A pinnacled, woodland-gothic fairytale, the marzipan-cake church stood pale, at the western end of a long, grass lawn, framed between two rows of trees, waiting beneath a frail, September-morning sun.

We were the first ones there.

Papa had so much to attend to. Gramma and Aunt Franzi stayed outside with him, waiting there to greet the priest. Mama led the rest of us into the building.

The light shining through the high windows played weakly down the length of the tall, slender, reddish-stone columns, across the light-gray pavement and onto the rich tones of the oaken pews. The nave smelled rather *A minor*: comfortably old with hints of incense, candle wax and long-used, thumb-smudged prayer books.

Up the center aisle to the second pew on the right, we four progressed as a single, hand-holding mass. As we came to it, we each crossed ourselves and genuflected, turned and made our way down the pew single-file, sitting down quietly, to wait.

I looked about, feasting on all the images, icons and furnishings, all the rich impressions they conveyed, all the sonorities they sounded on the keyboard in my mind: beautiful harmonies like those singing out from an ancient, voice-rich *Kyrie*.

I found all the images and figures of the Madonna, her countenance so serene, as she stood arrayed in gold, white and deepest blue. To each one I whispered, "Ave!" as if they were the loose jewels, the cardinal beads of a disjoint, figured rosary.

I sat back, pulling my jacket together against the chill, and looked up, toward the embracing, widespread wings of the golden altar piece, the towering, thin-column images within the stained-glass lancets above it. Then I pulled my gaze down, closer to the Earth.

At the altar end of the aisle there was a long wooden box with a large bouquet of freshly cut flowers laid out upon it.

I stared. It was as long as a bed. But it was also slim, long like a slender person. My eyes bore into it. Could that be Papa's 'it'?

Suddenly, I understood.

I shuddered; the tears burst.

The torrent flowing down my cheeks, flooding my vision, hurt simply because of what my heart could now see too clearly: I understood.

Uncle Edo was *dead*.

I sobbed.

And that box held what remained, what remained of my tall, beautiful, golden blond-haired, blue-eyed, *Wild West* cow-herding, *New York subway* riding, *Coney Island hot-dog* eating, *American* teaching, *his very own out on the range adventures* storytelling, "You're just the best nephew in the whole world!" cowboy!

I wanted to run up, rip off the lid and fling that box open, just like we had done with all those so many gifts they had brought us, and pull him out, make him stand up, smile and laugh, toss us up onto the horses' backs! chase chickens with me! and count kittens!

"And where is our Reinhold? Why isn't he here with us?"

I had to run to get him, "Where is he? *Where is he*?

"Hilf' mir! Hilf' mir! **Helft mir**!" [*Help me! Help me! (Both of you) Help me!*]

Marianne leaned down, asked quietly why I was crying: did I want some gum, some candy? Mama leaned over, too, to see what was wrong, but how could I tell them, anyone?

The loneliness. The vacuum.

The anguish of utter, desperate helplessness.

We sat. We waited.

I was painfully drained. Empty, empty.

More people entered the church for the service; I could hear them whispering into the other pews, behind us, across from us. Then I heard Papa's voice. I looked back toward the door.

He and Franziska walked in, bracing my Gramma between them.

She glanced up and spotted the box.

The shriek of a mother forced to bury her own child shattered the air.

It smashed your chest, grabbed your guts and ripped them out in one furious jerk, one arm's ever-tightening muscles strangle-holding your neck, the other wrenching out your heart, lungs, throat—yanking them farther and farther as you fought, wrestled, flailed—battling just to draw one more breath!

Gramma collapsed.

Her cry's resounding echo scraped the bloody, bony inside of my ribs raw with its rough-whet, rusty knife-edge, leaving an empty, blanching shell.

I was barely six years old.

And I had already met Death.

[1927]

Die Erbschaft – Chapter 4 – The Legacy

My world had collapsed. Colorless. Joyless.

The black and white of the old, upright piano's keyboard, the words and pictures in the aging encyclopedia set, of music and schoolbooks, all made a monotone world. I withdrew, stayed irretrievably busy, because I didn't want— couldn't allow myself—a moment to stop, to think, to ache.

Even Czerny and his pianist-exercises didn't faze me now. I wouldn't give him the pleasure of controlling how I felt, of forcing me to feel anything, even if good ole Beethoven had been his teacher!

But I longed for Gramma to come back from Aunt Franziska's in Zurich! I was so very close to needing a new reading list from her, one with more, heavy requirements to burden my time, to provide the ache-shielding silk for my self-secreting cocoon.

"He is so sad. He never laughs," I had heard Mama say quietly to Papa.

He tried to reassure her, "He will get better. It just takes time."

But the improvement was so very, very slow in coming, impeded by starkest emotional isolation.

―――――――――

We heard nothing from Reinhold.

The week after the funeral, when Papa had recovered somewhat from its work, its ordeal, he called the hospital that Reinhold had been taken to. But the staff there reported that, after Reinhold had awoken from the coma its third afternoon, he had been taken by his doctor to his own *Kurort*, a sanitarium near Potsdam.

Later in the week, Papa had located and was finally able to reach that sanitarium, but they said Reinhold had already left. Papa called Edo and Reinhold's *Tiergarten* apartment, but there was no answer. He contacted the police office for that area of Berlin, but they could only confirm that they had no change of residency information on file.

Then, early one evening, some nine weeks after the funeral, there was an unexpected knock at the front door. Papa opened it carefully, to find a courier bearing a large envelope. Papa stepped outside the open door, to handle the delivery-details.

With the package in hand, he closed the door gently and walked back toward us slowly, all the while studying the envelope, carrying it over to the big table.

He sat down, opened the packet carefully and started reading slowly through its slight pile of paper. He leafed through all its sections, shuffled it back together, popping the edge of the papers down onto the tabletop to get them all neatly re-aligned. He turned to Mama, who had come to stand behind him, sipping her coffee, stroking his hair.

"A letter and papers from Edo and Reinhold's solicitor," he explained.

"It seems that, as surviving business partner and sole heir, Reinhold has or-dered him to sell off the apartment, almost all its contents and to liquidate all business ventures that Edo or they both owned or had a shared interest in. He says that he doesn't yet have the revenue estimate from that, but asserts that it definitely won't be small. He states that Reinhold has directed him to make pro-visions for us from the proceeds.

"He also writes in assurance that everything Reinhold has ordered him to do should be accomplished within eight to twelve months. 'As a small, promissory indication of my good intentions,' he continues, 'I have sent along a check for *RM* 1000 from the legacy.'"

Papa held the check up to show us, then replaced it and went back to leafing through the papers, even though his rapid flipping of pages made him seem un-able to stop and concentrate on any of them, or even pause long enough for any-thing beyond a very cursory scan. One thing had obviously caught his eye, though, and after leafing past it, and whispering something (that he didn't want us to hear), he flipped back through the sheets searching for the point in the text at which the words had struck him.

He paused his nervous frittering, looked over at me, then to Mama with a slight smile. He returned his glance and said to me directly, "He also writes that we should be on the lookout for a concert grand piano, since the big Steinway now belongs to Edi, and will be delivered very soon, as it has already been shipped."

I stared at him blankly, then my voice broke as I tried to say, "I don't want it."

Sudden tears strangled my voice.

Mama stepped over to where I was sitting at the table, knelt down and placed her hand lightly on my arm. I looked into her eyes. "I don't want it!" I pleaded.

I jumped up and spun around toward them.

Half-begging, half-scolding, I repeated the painful phrase, *"I don't want it!"* then ran in a panic up the stairs to my room. I flung the door and fell onto the bed sobbing, burying my face, desperate to block out the pain.

The bed shook.

Eva had jumped up, and was walking across the covers toward me. She sniffed my face and gave my tear-wet nose a quick lick. I pulled on her and final-ly got her to lie down beside me. Then I happened to look up. The photo from the *Tiergarten* was still standing there on my bedside table. Edo and Reinhold were there, smiling back with me, at me.

I buried my face in Eva's back; I could still smell that warm boxer puppy aro-ma she had radiated, when Reinhold had first handed her to me.

"Slowly, it will get easier and easier for us all," Mama said softly, entering the room to sit next to us on the bed.

Eva's stub-tailed rear-end started waggling; she squirmed and pushed me back to give herself room as she rolled over into her "rub my tummy!" pose. I shifted myself nearer her, my forehead against her neck, and ran my hand slowly over her deep chest and soft, smooth belly.

After several minutes, Mama spoke again.

"Honey, from all the most beautiful times of your life, you must hold in your mind everything that you can, and in your heart, cherish everything it will allow!"

I couldn't say anything; I didn't *want* to say anything.

I wanted my uncles!

Just lying there, the *D major* aroma of boxer floated in my mind: swirling waves of golden brown, sunshine on bouncing puppy's back, music.

Although there was no hand doing it, I felt my ear being tugged, the same way Uncle Edo would pull it playfully to get my attention, and somewhere in my mind I heard the *D, D-F♯-D, A* notes of the articulated D major chord starting the presto-finale of Mozart's *Prague* Symphony. I needed it; it was happy, fast, and had been Uncle Edo's favorite. He had been a fan of Mozart in the same way I had been drawn to Beethoven and Schumann.

I had sat in rapturous attention during his visits, as he told me stories of Mozart's journeys from court to royal court, through those then-dazzling musical capitals of Europe: of Vienna and Linz, of Paris and Prague.

But now, all of that was gone.

Achingly, I realized: I had to watch; I had to feel; I had to remember everyone and everything. Who else would I lose now, too?

We stayed there on the bed for what seemed ages, with me, lying next to Eva, stroking her belly, and Mama watching silently.

Within the music, I began to relax, and felt my heart open, just a crack.

"Thank you, Mommy," I said softly.

I moved my hand to touch hers, where she had before reached to stroke Eva, too.

"I love you, Mama."

She gave me that smile-from-the-heart that only mothers can reveal, when one of their children says that phrase, unbidden.

"I love you, too, Edi!" She said before raising my hand to kiss it; then, still clasping my hand, she leaned over to kiss the side of my face. She sat back up and stroked my hair. I lay unmoving against Eva; she was snoring again, little slupfpf-pfuff's as her upside-down boxer-lips blocked, then fluttered in her breath.

After prolonged, blessèd quiet, the tall clock in the parlor sounded the hour; Mama asked softly, "Do you want to go back downstairs now?"

I replied with a slight, unsure shrug.

"You have to think of one thing, Edi. There's no avoiding it. We still have to rearrange the furniture to make room for the new, grand piano: for *your* new piano!"

———————————

It was good that we lived on a farm!

Papa measured; Mama considered, then told him how to measure again. This was repeated several times until they (Mama!) had decided how to fit all the pieces of furniture into the big room, at least all the ones that could stay there!

"Der Mann denkt; die Frau lenkt," [*The husband proposes; his wife disposes,*] I thought, remembering what I could of one of Gramma's many sayings. It was only later that she corrected me: "Mann denkt; Gott lenkt." [*Man proposes; God disposes.*] Well, maybe that's the old *tradition!*

The big room was just that: a large, country-kitchen area, a long dining table with its mixed-generations of chairs protruding from the kitchen, the old upright piano farther in, against one wall, and little tables and comfortable chairs spread toward the western side of the room, centering loosely on the big fireplace.

They had decided to leave the old upright exactly where it was. Papa said it weighed only a little more than a locomotive. They couldn't get the horses into the house to shift it, and he really didn't fancy ruining his back just to edge the old *Dreikühige,* one way or another!

On the morning after our day spent arranging the room, a big goods-truck showed up with four burly guys in it. They had muscled the piano off the train, loaded it into the truck and driven all the way, from Bad Ems through Bad Nassau to Singhofen and up to the farm!

There were three crates, one smaller, one bigger and one *huge!* It was over three meters long! It took all of them, pushing and puffing, heaving and huffing, sweating and almost swearing, to get the largest one safely off the truck, edged through the door and into the house.

Finally! They had it reassembled, almost in the broad middle of the big room. Its keyboard, on the same side as the old upright, was shifted to leave plenty of room between new bench and ancient piano-stool, for us to walk (or for me to chase Eva!) between them.

Mama and Papa stood and gazed at it. Very long, it looked so shiny-new and amazingly modern in the midst of all the farm-worn, but dearly inherited, furniture around it. Papa nodded at me and said, "Well? Play something!"

I moved to its side, raised the keyboard cover and lowered my gaze to look down the line of keys. One eyebrow rose as I spotted waves: slight but noticeable unevenness in the lie of the tops of some of the stunningly white keys.

"It wasn't like that in Berlin!" I thought to myself.

After sitting and pulling the bench in, to the best distance for my reach, I brought my hands down, playing a very simple, basic harmonic sequence of chords: *C major, G major, F major, A minor, F major-minor 7* and then had to stop, unresolved.

The pain hit me like a resounding thunder-clap.

"Aaa!" I spat, nearly yelling. Then I ordered sternly, "It has to be tuned!"

I stood up, and walked away.

Turning, I called out rather imperiously, "And somebody has to level and rebalance that keyboard!" still stepping from the room. With that, no matter whether anyone asked nicely, begged or cajoled impatiently, I would not touch the piano until it was tuned and repaired!

When I told Herr Fuhrmann at my next lesson all about that gorgeous piano, just delivered from Berlin, he had remarked excitedly, "Fantastic, Edi! With such a beautiful instrument, you will make great progress!"

In a far sterner tone he continued, warning, "But you must treat that new piano with great respect! It is a marvelous, precision, world-class instrument, one that you must always maintain, protect, love!"

And that's why, when it came to that lustrous Steinway, I would often demonstrate what Papa came to call, "jene Flügeleinstellung" [*that grand-piano attitude*]. But when it came to my piano—or Edo and Reinhold's piano, as I so often caught myself referring to it—I brooked no bings, bangs, bashes or other carelessness, or its ever being out of tune!

————————[1928]————————

Life on the farm meandered slowly, predictably in step with the seasons' cycle.

After paying for the piano adjustments, the Reichsmarks that we had received from the attorney in his inheritance-introduction letter had gone in three different directions. Some was used to help Herr Fuhrmann, who never had enough students and always undercharged for his lessons; some was spent on a brace of new horse collars; and the rest was stored away, "securely," Papa said.

In mid-1928, some nine months after that first, specially delivered, attorney's letter, Papa received another.

It appeared late one August afternoon, while Papa, Mama and I were sitting at the big table, finishing lunch. My sisters had rushed through their meal and run off to play. Gretchen had been doing her two-year-old best to get into everything within reach, until Mama at last persuaded her to lie down for a nap.

Instead of the usual, German stamps with eagles, castles, frilly numbers, or those new images of the late President Ebert, or of the current Reichspräsident, von Hindenburg, this large, tan envelope was decorated with a splash of multi-pastel foreign stamps, many showing an airplane over a map or a landscape, and a coat of arms in the upper-left corner that looked like it had a dead worm dangling from the necklace that surrounded it. Papa explained that it was the *golden fleece* from the Argonaut myth. Whatever it was, it still looked dead to me!

The letter had come from a manager at the Barcelona branch of a Swiss bank, a man whom a short-leaf enclosure from the Berlin attorney introduced as Bartomeu Ferrer.

Within his own letter, Herr Ferrer explained that he had met Uncle Edo and Reinhold while they, and Herr Ferrer, resided in New York City. Their resulting friendship had led my uncles to seat their financial concerns with him at his bank. This explained why he had started his letter in expressing his shock, sorrow and deepest condolences "upon this almost inconsolable loss suffered by us, each and all."

In the following part of the letter, he detailed that my uncles' Berlin lawyer had informed him that Reinhold had designated him, Herr Ferrer, the executor of the monetary estate. He would be responsible for setting up the accounts and transfers that were to be established for the family as part of the legacy.

Papa's face showed confusion—mixed with amazement—that seemed to grow with every line I saw his eyes move across.

He had been scanning the text silently, but then he started reading it aloud, to Mama more than to me, apparently just to make sure he was understanding exactly what he thought it said.

"Herr Meyer, the size of the monetary amounts involved requires that you travel here to Barcelona, to sign all contracts and currency forms in person. Your personal visit will also make everything that we might be able to help you with, such as transferring money between accounts or banks, *etc.*, easiest and simplest.

"Please inform me at your earliest convenience when you might be available to travel here, to Spain. If you could also apprise me of how many will be coming along and the length of your visit (one or two weeks will afford all the time requisite for our tasks), I will make all necessary arrangements, including visas, travel permits and rail tickets. The bank will be very happy to book your lodgings and pay on our own account.

"Best wishes to your wife and family, *Bartomeu Ferrer.*"

Papa sat speechless. A look of sorrow-tainted wonder came over his face.

A couple of times, Mama had started to say something, but had then stopped herself.

I knew that my uncles had always loved us. I knew it because of the way they were so warm and patient, taking as much time as we needed to help us learn about and enjoy new things. And they taught me that teaching, itself, is a form of love, love for the growth and success of others. My school had already moved me out of the first-year class and into the second year because I paid such close attention to the teachers and their lessons, and could already read so well, thanks to Gramma and my uncles. And I heard one of the teachers sigh, "Forwards to the third-year class!" after one of our second-year history texts had had English sentences in it, and I had just read through them, without stopping, like my uncles had taught me.

When Mama and Papa had each awakened from their pensive silence, Mama voiced her bewilderment aloud, "the size of the monetary amounts?"

Papa looked into her eyes, sighed, and shook his head in denial, "Of the meaning of that, I have absolutely no idea!"

"Should I go along with you?" Mama asked pensively, then added with more spirit, "And if I go, shall the children come along, too?"

Papa tapped his finger on the table, made little "I'm thinking" noises and then broke into a boyish smile.

"Why not? We can certainly take a week or two of vacation from this glamorous peasant life!

"Mother can stay with Aunt Franzi in Zurich. The Brandts can take care of the farm and, this time, we can pay them for their work!"

Papa stopped talking, and fell deeply silent.

He was pushing the remnants of his meal around with his fork, building this or that little castle, lining up a hedgerow or plowing a cabbage field with the tines. Mama started worrying, talking over the trouble kids can cause on a trip, especially if they're bored.

"Our older girls are good travelling companions. But Edi? It would be better if he were to have someone along on the trip, too," she said.

"Well," Papa started, obviously trying to pull things together as he spoke.

"We don't know what arrangements might be made, but even if we don't leave *from* Frankfurt, every train from the Taunus region going toward Spain still has to go *through* Frankfurt," he stopped, pondering.

Then he continued, "It would be only a small inconvenience to pick up Edi's cousin Albert there."

Mother was hesitant: "I really wonder if that would be such a good idea.

"He's almost three years older than Edi," she added, gazing at me, sounding rather protective of her own, still little, boy.

"Hans, at our age, the three years between us is no big deal, but the younger children are, the longer the years between them and others stretch. And, if memory serves, these two are growing to be rather different from each other!"

Papa laughed. He knew that each of us had been spoiled: me by my uncles and grandmother, and Albert by his paternal grandmother, Waltraut. They talked it over some more, but eventually Mama agreed that it would be better to see if he could go. Papa added it to his mental schedule saying, almost as if rather dreading it, "I'll get in touch with Konrad, or Waltraut, next week."

I knew, or thought I knew, my cousin fairly well.

Albert Neumann had been raised by his father, Konrad's extremely religious mother, Waltraut, who would drag him to mass almost every morning, unless he could escape to school, or just hide from her. He had told me last summer that she had agreed to start rewarding him for going to mass with her so often by stopping at a local bakery on their way home. "Pastetenerpressung," [*pastry-extortion*] he had called it, with a smirk.

Albert had fallen to the care of his grandmother because his own mother, my father's first cousin (and Grampa's niece) Sieglinde, had died in the big influenza epidemic when she was 23 and Albert not quite three years old. Because he was so young, and because Konrad couldn't be bothered with what he labeled "women's work," he had handed Albert off to his mother.

When Albert and I were together (he came to visit for at least a couple of weeks regularly, every July) most people thought we were brothers. We had the same basic shape; and Papa, whom Albert always called 'uncle', said we both looked like his own grandfather did when he was young. The main difference between us was that I was already a little taller than Albert, and he was a little chubbier, probably from all the communion wafers and pastries! His blond hair was also a little whiter than mine. But otherwise, I guess we did actually look rather alike.

Eight weeks later, on an already chilly Monday morning in the middle of October, we were trundling along, the six of us and all our impediments, from the farm to the closest train station, the one in Bad Nassau. Mama had said that riding the train from there instead of taking the car into Frankfurt would be much easier.

Easier I was glad of! Just packing for the trip had been an ordeal for all of us, thanks to my sisters. My oldest sister was turning into a real teenager rapidly, dragging the younger one along with her. They kept trying to pack almost every

46

dress and pair of shoes they had: "just in case!"

Papa made sure all our documents were together and tickets ready, and that we arrived early. Two days before, he had put the passports and visas into a satchel, together with all the letters, forms and cash he had gotten from the attorney and the bank-manager. Every couple of hours or so after that, he would return to it, leaf through its contents, checking and rechecking that all was there, that he hadn't forgotten or mislaid anything.

He had told Mama that we needed to get to the station early, so he could talk to the station officials, to make sure of the details in handling our baggage. Since we were required to change over to a long-distance express in Frankfurt, he wanted to make sure he knew exactly what he had to do to ensure that the luggage was transferred correctly, too.

The son of our friend, Herr Brandt would drive his father into Nassau later that day. Herr Brandt would then drive our car back to the farm, where he and Frau Brandt would stay to take care of all the farm chores those days that we were gone. It was nice to have neighbors we could always depend on!

Our local train from Bad Nassau left early, but then stopped at every little town along the route, threading its way northeast, up the mountain-looping valley of the River Lahn. I prayed we wouldn't have to go the whole way to Barcelona sitting on tough bench-seats like the ones on that local train! Even part of our baggage had stood there, shoved in between us! We kids got restless very quickly, despite the views and our persistent search for people, animals, buildings, anything odd or unusual within those deep, folded rills of the Taunus. And we were already seat-sore!

At last, the train chugged beyond Eppstein, passed through the final few hills, and descended into the Main River Valley. After those 96 km of seemingly endless stops and starts, it pulled into Frankfurt's main station on time.

From there, Barcelona lay around 1200 kilometers farther.

Before we could reach Spain, we would have to cross a large part of central, then southern France. I had pored over the maps in that part of the atlas very carefully, making a list of the towns I thought we would be going through, at least as far as I could tell from all the tiny, red, railroad lines limned onto those charts! I was hoping to get real route-maps at the train station in Frankfurt, because I wanted to take them to school with me after we got back, so I could show my teachers. Maybe then, too, the kids who had started teasing me by calling me *Flügelhorn*, just because I talked about my *Flügel* [grand piano], would be impressed enough to stop their mean jibes.

Once we arrived in Frankfurt, we had to exit that train and wait in the station, surrounded by all our baggage, extracted and stacked on the platform. Mama and the girls had their warm coats on, and decided to stand with the pile, to keep our bags in sight, despite the cool wind blowing in from beneath the great, open, wrought-iron arch under which the smoke-belching trains entered and left.

The train to Strassburg wasn't due to arrive for more than half an hour, and wouldn't leave for at least thirty minutes beyond that, so Papa had gone to talk to the station master. I was searching for charts in the little shops and on the shelves near the ticket windows.

While I was lost in thought, poring over brochures and maps, Cousin Albert jumped suddenly around the corner of the kiosk.

"Hey, dumbass! Whatcha doin'?"

"Albert, you jerk! Why did you try to startle me like that?"

"Shut up, kid! Don't be a wuss! It was just a bit of fun!" he laughed and gave me one of his "ha, ha! I'm older than you" punches to the shoulder. I hated them. And now that I had started growing taller faster than he was, he had just better watch out!

Albert started yammering about the trip; I continued not finding anything else that I was looking for.

So, we left the kiosks and walked back out, under the filigree-steel arches holding up the thousands of filthy-gray panes of glass that roofed the wide vault of the central hall. We ducked adroitly between winter-bundled walkers and their ill-guided carts overloaded with trunks and suitcases, to reach our platform.

Waltraut had already scoured the terminus, found the girls, and was now talking rather animatedly with Mama.

"Betcha she's raving about our new parish priest, Father Arno. I almost believe she's got the hots for him!" Albert offered with a sneer.

He was right, at least about her topic. As we got closer, I could hear her extolling the virtues of Father Arno Hagen, newly arrived from his studies, in Rome no less, replete with all the latest Vatican rumors, and full of praise for Mussolini. But when she finally noticed us, her voice trailed off, then regained its volume to announce, "But here come our treasures!"

Mama greeted Albert; he returned her welcome with a thank-you and compliments. In those few seconds, he had turned into the sweetest angel his grandmother could ever have dreamed of!

After the pleasantries, and his becoming no longer the center of their attention, Albert moved away from this flock of family-females. I stepped over to him and watched him as he inspected the crowds, waiting, walking or running, on the other platforms. His glance was quick, thorough, almost furtive.

He stopped his scan, and with a sudden, back-handed punch against my gut said in a loud whisper, "Damn! Look at the tits on her! And such long legs! I've got exactly what she wants!" He grabbed, then just as suddenly released, his crotch. As if he remembered in that split second exactly where he was, he cast a worried look over his shoulder toward his grandmother, then turned back around with a relieved sigh when he knew for certain that she hadn't been looking in our direction.

"Don't be so disrespectful!" I scolded him.

"And you—don't be such a faggot, you pussy!" he shot back at me, with an angry, narrow-eyed glare.

I wasn't sure what those words meant, but I knew I didn't like them because of the way he had used them. And I didn't like his attitude!

But suddenly his mood lightened, "No worry! When you grow up, you'll become acquainted with the great carnal pleasures of the female sex!"

I looked at him askance. He was barely ten years old! Where did he learn such big, and adult-sounding, words? And where did such an attitude come from, from someone who went (well, was *taken*) to mass almost every day?

"Crap!" he sputtered, "I'm so edgy! I really need one!"

"A what?"

"A cigarette, of course! I started smoking this year. Haven't you?"

"No, of course not! No one at our house smokes!"

I looked easily over the top of his head—yep, I was definitely growing faster than he was!—to check the time on the big wall clock above the ticket counter. Maybe Mama was right about smoking's stunting your growth! Although two and a half years younger, I was already almost three centimeters taller than Albert.

"I think smoking is so adult. At home, my dad smokes. Granny begs him almost daily to stop, but he won't. He smokes like a chimney! That's why Granny can't smell them on me."

I could imagine how awful their house must stink! Even a whiff of smoke coming backwards down our chimney into the fireplace and out into my face could make me sick. I was glad that I had never accepted any invitations to stay with him in Frankfurt!

I had to tell him, "But I certainly can! And my parents will detect the odor. You had better not smoke while we're on the trip."

"So says mommy's wimp! I'll be careful to hide it from them."

He had really changed from the Albert of last year, and this new, rough attitude didn't really make so great an impression.

"What a jerk!" I thought to myself.

The only benefit from having him along, that I could think of at that moment, was that at least I wouldn't have to spend the trip embedded within my sisters' competitive arguing!

A great, smut-black engine chugged its long line of drab, obedient train cars alongside the platform, their windows reflecting the rays of meager sunshine struggling through those coal-smoke dingy glass panes of the roof. It was our train to Strassburg.

Papa got the luggage stowed. Mama and Albert said good-bye to Waltraut, and we all got on and settled in. Only a few minutes later we heard the whistles and calls of "Alle an Bord!" [All on board!] Great clouds of steam and smoke burst onto the platform, then a rattling jolt shook us as the cars pulled, bumped, kissed away from each other, at last settling into a smooth acceleration as we chuffed out of the Frankfurt Hauptbahnhof into the Rhine Valley morning's autumn sunshine.

———————

We had been assigned two first-class couchette compartments, adjoining each other about halfway along the car. Mama was going to stay with the girls in one, and Papa with us boys in the other—at least that was our "Locarno Plan", as Papa called it—to avoid sibling conflict.

Albert and I settled into our own compartment, spreading out our kit where we chose, while Papa was still sitting with Mama and the girls.

As quickly as I could, I had taken my window-position as observer. Albert sat, lay around, stood up to check each knob and fiddle with every gadget he could find in the compartment, then repeated. He just generally fidgeted, obviously

bored almost before we had crossed the Main into the southern suburbs of Frankfurt!

But I was entranced by the vision of this, the Imperial City, so near our village
in distance, yet so distant from it in character.

My face left light smudges on the window. I would step back and wipe them
away to clear my view, then return to position, pressing my face again tightly
against the glass, just to spread yet more, unconscious smears.

I could not believe how fast the train, at last, was going, south along the Rhine
valley! The sweet smell of early autumn, newly-mown hay-fields awaiting the
barn, of the forests and quaint, ancient towns, all arose to douse my brain in their
historic magic. We were riding just to the east of that ancient squiggle that
Gramma had detailed as separating the Roman West from the Germanic East—
the Rhine—and I wanted to see it all!

"Somebody's gonna hire you as a housemaid if you keep scrubbing that window!" Albert said, poking fun at my struggling to keep the glass clean, to see
clearly everything that rushed by so rapidly.

After a while I simply had to sit down; my legs were almost cramping, and I
wanted to review my projected train-station list well before we got to our first big
stop, in Karlsruhe. As it turned out, the few printed tables I'd found in the railway office showed that we would be going around cities I thought for sure we'd
go through or stop in, while stopping in other places I hadn't considered. The
bank manager had put us on a series of those express trains available between
Frankfurt and Barcelona, so I wouldn't see as much of the Rhine Valley, and of
France, as I had so fervently hoped!

———————————

The slowing rhythm of the wheels and the change in lighting combined to
rouse me. Rubbing my eyes and yawning, I stirred slowly from my long, unin-
tended nap. We were coming to a stop at the station in Kehl, on the eastern bank
of the Rhine, just across from Strassburg. Albert had lain down with a pillow and
was still asleep!

The French border agents who boarded the train started their passport and vi-
sa reviews with the first-class carriages, so it wasn't long until they had stamped
our papers—the bank had made certain that everything was in order, particularly with what was left of the French Rhineland-Occupation forces—and we small
band of Germans were stamped as legal for temporary transport across the Rhine
and into France.

The tensions between the two nations after restoration of the German Imperial
province of *Elsaß-Lothringen* to France as *Alsace* and *Lorraine* were still very raw,
most likely because of the way that last, big war had gone, and then ended in
1918. Papa said this was probably the main reason the French customs officials
were being so nitpicky and fussy at the border, just making sure the people on
this German train got the message in no uncertain terms that those provinces had
been returned to France after almost 50 years of being held by the Kaisers. The
customs officers were going to hold the train at the station in Kehl for almost two
hours just to make sure they had time to interview all the passengers and inter-
rogate all the freight.

To fill the time, we walked, with Papa leading and Mama herding us along, from the station to a small neighborhood café, recommended by one of the railway stewards. Still within Kehl, it was comfortable, but unexotically still German!

Having eaten languidly, then fending a persistent drowse, we wove our way through the Rhine-misty afternoon, back to the station and onto our train. We had just shuffled out the cards for our family's own, particular, simplified version of *Doppelkopf* when the now familiar whistles, hand-cupped-to-mouth calls of "Alle an Bord," and the jolt and shimmy of reluctant carriages meant we were underway again; I shivered from the restarted possibilities.

My world was spreading its wings. Gramma's expansive training was inciting me excitedly into new, extended vistas. I pledged to myself, and her, that I would let my mind, my senses, lead: to further my learning, to deepen my understanding of people and places, of these, our national, close-cultural neighbors.

The late afternoon's fading sun witnessed aslant our crossing the Rhine, into France. I was terribly disappointed when the speed and shadow of the train meant my glimpses of the river as we crossed it were limited. That, plus the day's fast-diminishing light (it was 17:30 when we slipped into Strassburg) compounded by the situation of the tracks so far from the city's ancient center, kept me from being able to see anything but the fewest steeples within Strassburg's roofs as we made a wide, southern arc around the city, on a route leading directly into the main station, out on the town's western edge.

Halted again within *la Gare de Strasbourg*, we had to clear out of that carriage, haul ourselves and all our baggage from the German train over to a car of the French railway system.

Luckily, our next train was already waiting, despite any scheduling trouble the hour's difference between Germany and France might have caused. Mama and Papa made sure to take the opportunity to reset their watches to Greenwich—French and Spanish!—time.

Except for colors and lettering, the French railway cars looked almost exactly the same on the outside as those of the train we had just left, and when we got aboard, we found similarly that we again had two separate, adjoining, couchette-compartments.

Inside, though, the train looked a little more "artsy" (things had more curves than really necessary), something Mama called *art deco*. It was a little more *A minor*—musty and older smelling—than our original, German carriage.

I lofted to a renewed level of excitement from finally being in France. None of *them*, my ridiculing schoolmates, had ever been so far from home, so take **that** all you *Flügelhorn* callers! I wanted to stay in the window and watch everything that came into view, to see every building, person and animal that went by, just to have things to tell everyone about!

"But it's already too dark!" I lamented to myself.

The train pulled out of the station, and soon we had left Strassburg behind.

Within our separate compartment, Albert and I each had our own bunk, and so didn't have to worry about hiding from the girls! Papa had pulled the shades down over our windows, then he had gone back over to sit with Mama and the girls.

Albert and I took turns running down the passage to the toilet and back. Soon we were in our pajamas, bunked down and dozing off: the border crossing had

51

taken so long! We were sacked out well before Papa had finally come noisily over from the girls' compartment to go to bed. The excitement and stress of the day, rocked by the rhythm of the wheels and the swaying of the carriage, meant we were again deeply asleep before we could yawn twice.

This local train took us into Nancy where, late that evening, our carriage was shifted, inserted into a southbound express. Then, having passed through Dijon around 02:00, and Lyon by 05:30, it was nearly 07:00, between Vienne and Valence that Papa woke us, explained all that had happened in the night, then took us to breakfast—in a restaurant on a moving train! It was exotic, like something from Jules Verne!

Our French waiter—he introduced himself to us as Etienne Schultheiss—was from Alsace, and spoke Mama-pleasing *echtes Deutsch* [*standard German*], despite (he explained) having grown up speaking a kind of German he called *Alemannic*. Papa also spoke to him in a different language; he later explained that it was called *le beau français*, standard (Parisian) French. Etienne was the first French person I had actually met! With his German last name, and elegant, almost musical, way of speaking and moving, he evoked a convincing linguistic, cultural bridge!

Into Avignon mid-morning, it wasn't long before we had set out again, toward Cerbère, the last train-stop before entering Spain.

Just south of Frontignan the tracks went all the way down to the Mediterranean!

While we were right on the coast, even Albert got up from his bored flipping through his ever-present magazines, and his repetitive moans and "Just look!" outbursts about those picture ads and movie-star photos he flipped between: "Just look at her ... that pair ... what a butt ... what legs ... such big tits!"—to watch the scenery go by. I was very much relieved by his distraction; he was driving me crazy!

Something about the sea and the beach, the dunes, the distant waves, the bright sun and the smell of salt in the air made each of them irresistible, entrancing, even to those of us born and raised happily within the land-locked, dewy-morning mountains of foggy and snowy Central Europe.

It was not long though, before the train was forced to abandon the coast and climb westward, higher, up into the foothills of the Pyrenees, before it went south again, down closer to the sea and the easier slopes of its coastal hills. During the approach to the border, we had often traversed high above the arc of a siren beach lying deserted in an inlet cut deeply into the coastal hills.

At Cerbère the border-crossing banalities were repeated, but this time much faster, apparently because the Spanish border agents, unlike the French ones, had not been ordered to be so painfully strict with Germans.

In this third, Spanish train, the railway carriage was even older than the French one, although it smelled better: quite *F major*, all lemony and vanilla like those special cookies we got in the summertime, and with some old-oak aroma, like the heavy, old *Dreikühige* piano, mixed in with the lemon. The German carriage had been sparse but comfortable and efficient, the French one, more plush and a bit artsy-overdone. The Spanish carriage was older and wear-worn, the fabric of the seats had seen better days, but the woodwork was even more wonderful, with its deep-grained swirls, its lustrous feel: its smell evoked the shady coolness of those ancient, Teutonic forests surrounding the farm.

And we still had two compartments! Thank you very much, Herr Ferrer!

Sudden chuffs of steam shot out, then turned quickly into white clouds rising to mix with billowing, gray-black coal-smoke as the old engine strained slowly out of the station. It was struggling to get us up to speed quickly, drawing its charges through the long tunnel beneath the grassy-bare mountain that marked the eastern divide between France and Spain.

When we emerged from the tunnel, at last under the bright early-afternoon sun of Iberia, we were greeted by even more panoramic vistas of cliffs and sheltered inlets, of dry-grass hillsides punctuated with small, dark green copses, of pink-tile roofed, whitewashed seaside villages, of bleached sand beaches and blue, foam-lipped Mediterranean waves. We could have seen the coast the whole way through this length of the trip, except for the several tunnels on this part of the coast, detailing where the mountains had stretched out, all the way down from the high border, to soak their feet in the sea!

The tracks carried us back inland among the dry hills of Catalonia, with their patches of small, thin-limbed trees, spare farmhouses and occasional, white-and-black-wooled flocks and small herds of swarthy cattle.

No question about it, it made me thirsty! It was so different! The landscape, the sere sights, the dry smells, the different creaks and cracks of the carriage: all combined to rewrite my mind's association with where on Earth I had suddenly found myself.

A headache split my head; it was all too much, too fast!

Albert looked up from his perpetual magazines—it seemed he'd gotten one or two more, including a couple of risqué French ones, at every stop we'd made!—to see me rubbing my head in a rough, whimpering groan. He rustled the magazine away before going next door to fetch Mama.

She hurried over in a minor frenzy, reached down to put her palm firmly on my forehead (still checking for fever, after all this time) then sat next to me and drew me close. She rubbed lightly, my head, down my back, and kissed my hair before asking me, "What's wrong, honey?"

I could murmur only, "My head. Raging headache."

I kept my head down, shielding my eyes in the dark shade of my hands.

"I've been wounded by this countryside!"

She responded only with rocking, tender warmth and the humming hint of one of those Taunus folksongs she had sung when I was so young. The melody of her voice, and the harmonies of her aroma began to overpower, to push away that overload of sense-stimulation I had absorbed so suddenly from these new experiences, invading my mind from the afternoon's arid Catalonian landscape. I started to relax.

"This countryside *is* quite different, isn't it? But you needn't worry about that! You'll become accustomed to it very quickly," she said reassuringly, then asked, "And your stomach, is it upset? Does it hurt?"

I shook my head slightly: it wasn't my stomach that was out of tune, it was my head!

"Well, good ... Albert, please ask your uncle to come over here!"

He went next door and returned promptly with Papa.

"Hans, bring me the small aspirin-tin from my handbag, and have the steward bring us some cool water and sweets."

"Yes ma'am, my dear," he replied, sounding only a hint of his usual military-play at being ordered around, and turned to leave. But he stopped himself in mid-stride and asked quite seriously, "He isn't terribly ill, is he?"

"No, it's only a headache. Everything will be better quickly," she replied, trying to comfort me, and reassure us all. Then, to Papa, she added a softer, "The sweets are to prevent stomach upset from the aspirin."

To that I muttered, "My head is already upset!"

Papa delivered the medication quickly, then rushed off to find a steward. The minutes ticked along; Mama hummed more. The quietude that had come from hiding my eyes and tucking my head against Mama's side was already helping me recover from the pain when Papa came back to the door with a steward.

I peeked out of barely opened eyes to see that he was with a very thin—skinny like his own tiny mustache—slick black-haired, dark-eyed waiter in an overly starched, blindingly white shirt and very tight, shiny black pants.

Swinging the large silver tray around like a plate-spinning circus performer, he slipped it through the narrow door into the compartment.

Set upon a collapsible tripod, it was soon laden with a pitcher of water and several glasses, and alongside them, a plate stacked with pale, sugar-glinting cookies and varying brown pieces of chocolate. The waiter backed out; Papa gave him some coins; the steward slipped away, leaving only wisps of his wood-hinting, low-F-diapason cologne.

The spreading, sultry aroma of those milk- and dark-chocolate pieces swept away the strident, out-of-tune noise plaguing my brain and imbued a tightly-held, contented feeling, summoning a sumptuous, *warm, toasty and half-asleep after too much breakfast, wrapped tightly in a blanket, sitting in front of the fireplace on Christmas morning, hot cocoa caressing your nose* paradise.

Mama poured a half-glass of water and, following an aspirin, handed it to me. The tablet washed down under her watchful gaze, she then let me have first pick of the goodies. I grabbed two pieces of milk chocolate and shoved them into my mouth. I held them imprisoned between tongue and teeth, letting them melt into sumptuous, gooey goodness. The chocolate empowered my resurrection.

Albert stepped over, sat beside Mama on her opposite side and waited, looking up, plaintively. Mama reached out, hugged him close and said, "You, too, dear!"

He smiled at her, and reached over to grab a cookie and a piece of chocolate.

Papa poured water into more glasses, then brought my sisters over from the other compartment, to ooh and ah at the spread of treats. He stood, leaning against the door frame to steady himself against the sway from the occasional hiccup of the tracks, and held Gretchen, letting her try her best, two-year-old baby-teeth gumming at one of the cocoanut cookies. They were all quiet: even the girls held down their competitive sister-racket while they waited to see if my headache would clear.

Satisfied with sweets and assured that everything seemed to be settling down, first the girls, then Papa, and finally Mama, made their way back to the other compartment. I lay down, resting with my eyes closed.

A little nap and some more big, splashing glasses of water later, and I was back on my feet, standing at the window again, watching how the northern suburbs opened to let the train snake them into view. But then the actual city, the long-awaited city of Barcelona, started to appear!

I was still struggling to reconcile all the differences that were flooding my senses with so many variant strains of music, the product of so many, often such startling, contrasts between our little, haimish and hilly corner of Germany and the vistas of this ancient, Mediterranean city.

Albert sat up suddenly and peered out the window, shading his eyes against the still-bright, but West-hanging sun.

"We're approaching the station!" he announced with muted excitement. He had felt it first: the train was slowing down.

"You're right," I replied, my voice flooded with nervous apprehension.

What's it going to be like? Will I be able to understand them? Will they be friendly? What if I get lost? Would I be able to find Mama and Papa? Can we find the hotel? It's a big, foreign city, and I'd never been in one before!

I swallowed hard as the train pulled into the station and slowed to a belching, discordant stop. That, on top of my nerves (and too many chocolates), and I was almost ready to vomit.

Swallowing again, more strongly this time, I searched for reason and method to encourage my nerves to keep everything in place. I considered, "Herr Ferrer has gotten everything in order, and all has gone really well." So, I decided, "If Uncle Edo and Reinhold trusted him, so will I." And this calmed me.

Albert had started making those gawd-awful groans again, standing at the window, ogling women as they walked by on the neighboring platforms.

"Knock it off and get busy," I told him. Shutting all his distractions from my mind, I stood and gathered things to go back into my luggage.

Retrieving the satchel with those piano pieces, ones that I had completely forgotten about having promised myself I would study during the trip, and the colored pencils I had started using to mark the fingerings, highlight the melody lines and emphasize the musical dynamics, I headed toward the passage, to join the others who had already left the train.

I stopped before I stepped out of the door, turned and barked sternly at Albert, "Come on, slow poke! Let's go!"

He followed, struggling with his own load, and that satchel, stuffed with his hoard of magazines.

We stepped down from the train and walked over toward Mama and the girls, already waiting at the head of the platform. I was anxious to leave the train, to experience this new world, with its sights, smells and music calling to me through the still-distant, but wide open, Barcelona-beckoning portal of the *Estació de França*.

Das Hotel – Chapter 5 – The Hotel

The *Estació* was noisy, crowded and, for North-Europeans in mid-October, hot!

Yet, even awash in lingering, choking strands of steam and coal smoke, it was laced with the bright aromas I had first become aware of back before my late headache had started. This time, though, these landscape-smells didn't bother me but, rather, lured me toward the city, urging an exit of this painfully raucous, fume-filled terminus.

But then the acrid stench of steam-coal smoke, puffed from newly arriving engines overwhelmed, shoving me towards the exit. I started pulling my mother by the hand, "Come on, Mama! I'm drowning!"

Fighting the noise of a fresh train, holding her free hand over Gretchen's ear on the side facing the blasts of steam and rumbling iron, she knelt to ask, "What? How are you drowning?"

"In the dirty smoke!"

"Oh. You're right," she said. "It's bothering me, too!"

She stood up, draped a blanket-corner protectively over Gretchen's face, then cupped her free hand around the side of her mouth and called to Papa, "Johann!"

He had been helping pile our luggage onto an ancient, flat cart that one of the porters had brought over, but turned around to face her immediately on hearing her voice. He motioned something that looked like "just a minute!" then hurried the porter and cart down the platform towards where the rest of us had gathered, already having scooted small-steps away from the platforms, seeking the sunlight and air at the front portal.

"What's wrong, dear?" he asked when he had finally approached close enough to hear Mama.

"Forgive me, dear," she explained, "I didn't know that you were trying to get things together so quickly. We must move the children away from this smoke!" Even my sisters had started coughing.

"Right!" he said, and motioned a hurry-along to the porter, pointing toward the exit.

He let the porter lead the way toward the sunshine of the street with his complaining, iron-rimmed, oaken push-cart. Its spastic wheels turned him into a chattering mama-duck leading her brood, parting successive waves of other passengers milling across our way.

Just as we were about to move out into the early evening sunlight, a very well-dressed young man came toward us, at faster than a walk, but too stately, too self-composed for a run.

"Herr Meyer?" he asked Papa assertively, leaning to extend his hand as he approached.

Papa looked unsure, but returned his hand in greeting while responding with a tentative, "Ja?"

"Oh, wonderful! Herr Meyer! I am Bartomeu Ferrer!" he exclaimed in enthusiastic German as he grasped Papa's hand fully and shook it.

"Most pleased, Herr Meyer, to make your acquaintance!"

Papa looked almost giddy with relief, smiling as he replied, "Likewise, Herr Ferrer! *Very* pleased to make your acquaintance, Herr Ferrer! I am extremely grateful that you have come to meet us!

"May I introduce you to my wife and children?"

"With pleasure!"

I watched carefully as Papa introduced *Senyor* Ferrer to Mama (and Gretchen), then to each of my older sisters. I was looking at our new friend so intently that I almost forgot to shake his hand when Papa introduced me. I caught the hint of his cologne; I knew immediately that it was that very expensive kind that Edo and Reinhold had worn, too. Then Papa introduced him to Albert as "my dear nephew." This adapted, adoptive description made Albert smile.

With all the formal courtesies out of the way, we could relax.

We were no longer desperately alone in a city completely unknown, and of speech indecipherable to us. We now had a friend who, I thought—except for his more Southern complexion, darker eyes, and his being a bit thinner—looked so much like he could easily have been our Reinhold's cousin, or possibly, more exotic brother!

Senyor Ferrer had soon turned and was walking ahead with Papa, leading us fully out to the street, calling instructions back to the porter, now at the rear, struggling to keep up with us as he leaned forward to shoulder that squawking cart safely through the rush of a newly arriving throng. Sr Ferrer led with the sure grace of the stallion that one of our farmer-neighbors, the Baumgärtner's, had bought earlier this past summer; his mane was a glistening black, too.

Albert grabbed my arm to hurry me along; I had let myself slip away.

Outside, pulled parallel to the station's wide exit, a large black car (longer than Edo and Reinhold's *Marlene*!) was waiting for us among other cars, horse carts and carriages. Sr Ferrer had the porter and driver stow our baggage quickly.

A short ride later, we spilled out onto the walk, in front of a big, light-gray-colored stone building; it had several storeys of tall, arched windows above, repeating its majestic, street-level arcade. Another luggage-cart appeared from inside the hotel. I stood, engrossed in the sights, noises and smells that flooded the sidewalk, as the whole porter-procedure we'd witnessed coming from the train was repeated, in reverse.

It was I who had to pull Albert away this time from his absent-minded gawking at the sable-haired women on the street!

The arch-and-domed hotel lobby—so tall it had trees growing in pots inside!—the uniformed bell-hops, the creaking elevator ride, were all so exotic and 'big city' even compared to Frankfurt! Our suite was immense: it looked as big as Edo and Reinhold's Berlin apartment! Mama cautioned us so sternly, "Don't break anything; don't *touch* anything!"

But Herr Ferrer just laughed and said, "Frau Meyer, please don't worry! There is nothing here that cannot be mended or replaced!"

He then produced a printed schedule. Papa and Mama—and I!—had to be at the bank at a specific hour the very next morning.

"It's getting rather late," he said, "and you must all be tired and hungry. If you'd like, I can return in half an hour and accompany you to dinner here in the hotel's restaurant. You must remember that the bank will pay for everything. Because of that, you should let nothing out of your hand, except for any small purchases you may wish to make for yourselves!"

To that he smiled, "So long as you are in Barcelona, I am your guide, aide and companion, as well as banker!

"Also, about that," he said, pulling a packet from an inside coat-pocket, "I have here enough Spanish currency and coins for each of you to have sufficient pocket money with you." He handed the envelope to Papa.

Senyor Ferrer walked to the door, turned, and with a blinding smile and, "Until later!" he was gone.

Papa opened the envelope, and that shocked look invaded his face again.

Mama had given Gretchen to Anneliese to watch, so she went over and hugged him. "Everything is fine, Honey! Relax!"

I saw his shoulders drop as he sighed. He kissed Mama, and I could see his nervousness wane. When they stopped (please! no gooey eyes now!) Mama turned to us kids and said, "Come on! We have to hurry!"

And with that, she organized us: luggage put aright and stowed, and kids washed up and clothes straightened. She readied Gretchen, then had us each do the "inspection twirl" for her perusal, before she turned to her own concerns.

Papa was the quickest to freshen up, affording him time to take the contents of the cash envelope and divide it into six piles, two big ones and four smaller ones. He called us over to him and handed one of the little ones to each of my older sisters and one to me. Then he held out an identical one toward Albert, but bent down with it, to look Albert in the eye.

"And Albert," Papa said as he offered him the cash, "No cigarettes!"

Albert's eyes flashed angrily at me. Papa saw that.

"No, Albert. No one ratted on you: except yourself."

Albert looked very puzzled. "What?"

"At the start of the trip your breath stank like a cold ashtray, and your teeth, and fingernails, were already dirty, discolored. But in just these past two days those conditions have improved."

Papa was leaning, holding the cash out towards Albert: "Well now. Do you understand?"

Albert thought about it for half a second, reached cautiously for the money with a dejected, "Yes, sir. Understood."

Papa stood erect and said, "Well, good," then looked around at everyone.

During that exchange Mama had come back into the central sitting-room where the rest of us were already waiting. He whispered, "So beautiful!" to her, then asked, louder, "Everyone ready?"

We chorused the word, "Yes!"

Mama smiled. "Yes, dear! Everyone's scrubbed, polished, and ready to eat!"

Announced by three swift knocks, Sr Ferrer reappeared exactly on time to escort us to dinner.

With us gathered around a large, round, restaurant table, Sr Ferrer sat on Papa's left; Mama took her position opposite Papa, among the kids, while I sat just to Papa's right. From there, the adults helped control the childish clatter as we laughed and chattered through Sr Ferrer's patient translations of menu items, before placing our raucous, banquet-sized order.

Ever since the trip from the train station to the hotel, I had been observing, listening, my mind busy recalling the things that Gramma and I had read about Barcelona, its culture, its languages. So, once Sr Ferrer and Papa's discussion came to a pause, I just had to break into the conversation and ask, "Herr Ferrer, the language that I heard at the station and in the hotel—it's called *Catalan*, isn't it?"

He smiled and answered, "Absolutely, Edi! Just as it is with the majority of the population of Barcelona, and in this entire region, Catalan is my mother-tongue and I'm very proud of it. And, in the same way I am of my Catalan, so too can you be justifiably proud of your German mother-tongue."

"I am!" I said confidently. Then I added in English, "And I can speak American, too!"

He laughed at this, responding in kind, "Ah! Do I espy your uncles in this?"

"Yes," I said and tried to smile.

But I wanted to cry.

I stopped talking and made myself think of *Frankfurter Kranz*, so that almonds, angel food and butter cream might flood my mind with the music of happier memories.

However, once I had broached this still rather touchy subject, Papa appeared to summon the courage to ask Sr Ferrer how he had made the acquaintance of Uncle Edo and Reinhold.

Sr Ferrer began by explaining how they had met in New York.

"We ran into each other a couple of times at one Spring's Easter-week services and started talking. After I revealed that I was working for a Swiss bank in its New York office, they had started coming to me with business matters, and eventually transferred all their accounts, choosing me as their banker. Because of the troubles caused by the war, and their being ethnic Germans (even though Edo had been a U.S. citizen for several years), the staffs at the American-owned banks were often not helpful, and sometimes even hateful. So, finding a bank run by Europeans had made them feel that they were more accepted, and better taken care of.

"The huge problems caused for German banks in the U.S. during the war meant that my neutral-Swiss bank was able to help a lot of businesses with their transactions between North America and Europe. After the armistice, I was able to put Edo and Reinhold in touch quickly with businesses in Germany and Austria, ones who needed help with imports and exports after the Kaiser, and Emperor Franz Joseph, had so thoroughly ruined things for them, and for everyone else in their homelands." (I could hear Gramma's confirming exclamation!)

At that point, our table became very quiet, as if we were all swept by a sudden wave of exhaustion. Sitting back quietly in my chair at that moment, though, I became aware of the other diners, their loud conversations, gesticulations, and a consuming scrape and din of dish and silverware. Such painful disharmony made me turn off my ears, wishing I were back at home, listening to my Eva snore!

But just before I dozed off, our waiter and some helpers appeared across the room, balancing several large trays above their shoulders; and they seemed to be coming toward our table! They walked up and spaced themselves around the table, then each waiter popped open a portable stand, placed his tray on it and lifted its ornate silver cover so that the aromas steamed and floated all around us.

Ummmmh. Sleepiness had made me forget that I was so very hungry!

I was thrilled, on edge and anxious finally to see what we'd ordered! Like most of us, I had ordered *trinxat*, a Catalan specialty of potatoes, cabbage and pork. It was so good that I ate too fast, and almost fell asleep again, even before I had started feeling full!

My oldest sister, Marianne was sitting between me and Albert, making sure that we stayed in line, which we had to because she would thump us on the head if we ever caused her any grief! She hadn't had to do it tonight, though. I was just too tired and hungry to act up, and Albert looked that way, too!

When we had eaten our fill, and I was drifting very drowsy, Marianne leaned over and whispered into my ear, "D'ya suppose we could get some ice cream?"

I woke up! I cupped my hand beside my mouth and asked her in turn, "We can ask about it, can't we?"

She whispered back, "But *you* ask, since you've already talked to Herr Ferrer!"

So, I sat up straight in my chair, waited till the adults had paused their renewed round of polite chit-chat, then asked, "Herr Ferrer, was there any ice cream on the menu?"

He smiled.

"Certainly, Edi! Would you like me to order some for you? For you others? And for you, Herr and Frau Meyer?"

A four-voiced chorus of "Yes! Yes, please!" came from us children, and even Papa nodded his agreement with a grin, before adding his own vocal assent to the dessert chorus.

Only Mama said, "Thank you, Herr Ferrer, but none for me! I am already full. Any more to eat would definitely do me in!"

He chuckled as he said, "Very well, Frau Meyer. I understand completely!"

"He's really so polite, just like my uncles were," I thought. Except for slight physical differences, and the Catalan accent that broke into his German on occasion, he reminded me even more of Reinhold!

Sr Ferrer called our waiter back to the table and told him what we wanted.

The waiter repeated the order (so it sounded to me!), turned and walked briskly across the room. Within a few minutes he and his helpers had returned with plates, each one laden with big, individual scoops of vanilla and strawberry ice cream, next to sliced peaches, all with a voluptuous topping of what Sr Ferrer explained was called *crème catalan*. And alongside the ice cream were three baked pieces called *carquinyolis*, with pieces of almonds visible right in the slices!

An initial, prioritizing taste of each part of the dessert, then our spoons were a blur. *Mmmmh* ... almond bread with vanilla, strawberry ice-cream, and *crème* gravy!

At last, those eagerly scraped-clean dishes were removed, and we arose to make our way, staggeringly full of those fabulously rich, frigid sweets, back up to our hotel room and a night of bliss: one at last unbroken by the shriek of railroad whistles, unaccompanied by the never-ending clickety-clack of iron wheel against steel rail.

I tried to stay awake, to read again through the music that Herr Fuhrmann had given me, the pieces that we had worked on before the trip. But I fell asleep almost immediately, forehead pressed into one of the scores, with the grace notes of its opening bass line running *andantino, quasi allegretto* through my dreams.

Die Bankiers — Chapter 6 — The Bankers

We almost overslept!

Finally awake, I could hear Mama running around in a controlled tizzy, trying to get us all up and presentable before Sr Ferrer dropped by to take us to breakfast. The last of us was tottering, mostly kempt—OK! I couldn't get that one last sprig of hair to behave!—into the huge parlor just as we heard the *andante* of Sr Ferrer's rap-rap-rap on the door echo into our room.

Ugh! There was no escaping it: we had to go to breakfast. And I was still so blearily full from last night's late dinner! I trudged along with the rest, dutifully trailing Sr Ferrer and Papa, back into the big dining room of the hotel restaurant.

But it did smell amazingly, upliftingly good—fresh bread and bacon, chocolate, coffee and ancient, grand hotel—all the aromas wafting powerfully, harmonically distinct yet sonorously intertwined.

Despite the wondrous aromas, being still stuffed we ate only sparingly and were ready to set out quickly. After Sr Ferrer had stationed us in the lobby, he went to order the car brought around front for us.

Papa joked with Mama, "If we keep eating like this, I'm going to ask the bank for some bigger clothes!"

Sr Ferrer led us out onto the still rather chilly sidewalk in front of the hotel. The car was not long in driving up, and we set off to the bank. I was excited, nervous: uncertain what was going to happen!

But at least, finally, we would find out what this trip, all this fuss was about!

The bank looked rather like the hotel: columns with an arch over the front door, and a large lobby. But this one wasn't nearly so bustling, or welcoming!

We walked through the lobby, past desks and iron-gated counters populated by serious, dark-suit-wearing, mustachioed elder, and clean-shaven younger, men, to approach the elevator. We rode it to the third floor, the top storey according to the numbers on the elevator-cabin's dial.

A long, gray-walled hallway of muted tiles led past large paintings hung in heavy gilt frames. The man portrayed in the first wore a really old costume, but looked fairly pleasant. The next one appeared sullenly severe, painfully dour. Albert poked me and whispered, "What a sour puss! He really looks constipated!" I laughed: Albert was right!

Spaced evenly between tall, wood-framed doors, the pictures' effect was one of formal, imposing emotional frigidity. It reminded me, with some twinges of dread, of parts of the sick-houses in the spa-cities, Bad Nassau and Bad Ems.

Sr Ferrer conducted us into his office. His secretary, a svelte young man sat at a large desk near the door through which we had just entered. At the far side of this room was another door, open and leading to yet another office. It looked nicer in there: its windows faced the city outside.

Sr Ferrer said something that sounded like a Church-Latin "good morning" to his secretary, who had stood when we walked in. In German, Sr Ferrer introduced his secretary to us as an almost French-sounding *Joaquin*. Joaquin nodded when he heard his name, replied to Sr Ferrer's questions, then sat down and continued his paperwork. Sr Ferrer interrupted Joaquin's activities, speaking all the while in Catalan—I knew what it was called!—sounding like he was giving him instructions.

Sr Ferrer motioned for us to take a seat in the chairs and on the long wooden bench along one wall, directly facing Joaquin's desk. Papa sat down near the center of the bench, and I pushed in quickly to sit next to him. Its crimson, velvet cushion was thick and comfortable. I was full, and found myself being drawn inexorably toward sleep as I leaned into the warmth of Papa's side. Mama sat with Gretchen in one of the chairs, Liesel in another; the rest of us filled that long bench.

Once he had received all his instructions, Joaquin picked up the telephone receiver—it didn't have a dial like Edo's!—and presently started talking into it. At the same time, Sr Ferrer turned back to us and said, "The bank director should be here shortly. Please, relax and we'll get everything going, just as soon as possible."

With my head leaning comfortably against Papa, I watched Joaquin. I wanted to keep looking at him. He had such beautiful skin and lips (ones that looked like the bows the cherubs sometimes carry in the old statues), and an errant strand of black hair that he kept sweeping back from the long lashes of his olive-green eyes. He looked up and smiled at us, beautiful white teeth with just the slightest separation in front, like whole-notes tied over a bar-line between measures.

My heart beat faster. It was impolite to stare, so I closed my eyes. Sleep seemed like a good idea at the moment.

When Papa woke me, I was so groggy! I felt I'd been asleep for hours, but the clock on the wall beside Joaquin's desk disagreed; it had been only ten minutes! Ugh, I had to try to clear my head. I glanced back at Joaquin, but thought I'd better look somewhere else, just to be gracious. That's when I awoke enough to notice another person standing in the office.

The bank director had walked in. A distinguished-looking elder gentleman in a very fine, old-fashioned dark suit, Sr Millet was introduced to us by Sr Ferrer. Sr Millet spoke some German, but not nearly so well as *our Bartomeu*, as I found myself calling him in my thoughts.

Sr Ferrer explained that Sr Millet was the legal officer, designated to act as witness to the proceedings by the bank's directors. Motioning toward that other room, Sr Ferrer spoke a few words to Sr Millet in Catalan. Sr Millet nodded an acknowledging, slight bow, and stepped off in that direction.

With the same motion, Sr Ferrer then asked Papa and Mama—and me!—to accompany him into his personal office, too.

Mama told everyone else to move over, all onto the long bench. Once they were gathered there, she told them that Marianne, since she was the oldest, had authority and that they had to obey her. Poor Albert! I knew he would be so bored!

Marianne took to her task with pleasure, reaching to take Gretchen onto her lap even before Mama had thought to leave her with the others.

"Thank you, sweetheart!" Mama said to her.

With Gretchen transferred successfully, Mama followed us into Sr Ferrer's office.

I noticed immediately that it was furnished more expensively than the outer office, and was also a bit warmer.

Sr Ferrer closed the door after us. Sr Millet had taken the seat to the left of Bartomeu's, behind the big desk. There were three armchairs on our side, facing the desk.

"Please be seated," Sr Ferrer said, sweeping his hand across them. Mama took the closest chair; Papa sat in the middle. I got the one nearest the windows, with a clear view onto Sr Ferrer's desktop, its wide, immaculately emerald-green blotter and exacting array of pens, inkwell, papers and fresh stationery. Its neatness contrasted with my own usual, spread-out, disheveled tousling of scores.

Sr Ferrer opened the top drawer of his desk and pulled out a thick folder, its front labeled with "Meyer Family, Singhofen" in large, block Roman letters. He opened it to the first, perfectly placed page, one that held a short column of long numbers with a larger number in bold black numerals at the bottom of the list.

"Herr and Frau Meyer," he started, "I could not help noticing that you have not asked me why our bank would expend so much effort and expense to bring you here to Barcelona. Do you know the amount of the inheritance?"

Papa answered, "No, Herr Ferrer. We have no inkling, no experience in these matters. I knew that my brother and his partner had been quite successful in business, but he and I never talked about his private concerns, certainly not about monetary amounts and such." He held his breath, seeming to wait for Sr Ferrer to intercede with a continued exposition.

"Indeed. I thought as much. Along with required explanation of contracts and necessary signatures, this is precisely why you're here, in person.

"The original wills, written, and signed by both Eduard Friedrich Meyer and Reinhold Kristof Keller seven years ago, as amended from their original, partnership contract of 1916," he held it up for us to see, "stipulated one condition. That is: if one of them were to die before the other, all assets would transfer wholly to the survivor. According to this, with Edo's death, the entire inheritance was originally entailed to Reinhold."

He paused, as if to verify that Papa understood.

Papa nodded.

"But what happened after Edo's death was that Reinhold Keller caused their solicitor to draw up a new contract. In concert with this contract, which I also have here with me, Reinhold's attorney duly swears and affirms that everything promised herein has been carried out in the strictest manner.

"I have reviewed all matters, and stand witness to that fact."

Sr Ferrer stopped to clear his throat, take a sip of water, before continuing.

"You have already been informed that Reinhold has caused the sale of almost everything owned originally by Eduard Meyer or that the pair held in common at Edo's death. That was in keeping with the original testament. However, by this new contract and within its conditions and provisions, he directed his attorney to have the proceeds of that sale converted into gold and silver coins, or certificates, and deposited here in our bank."

He paused again, to get the papers back in order and (it seemed to me) for us to have a moment in which to rest our brains. It was so much! I thought I understood most of what he had said. I hoped I would remember everything!

"Herr and Frau Meyer," he then looked over at me, "and Edi," before pausing to look again at the value written on the paper in front of him.

"What Reinhold has done is this. Half of those proceeds, everything of theirs that belonged to Edo, he has given to you.

"In accordance with the stipulations of this new contract, Edo's half of the total proceeds, belonging to you now, comes to US $6.4 million in gold and silver. At the current exchange rate, that's nearly 27 million Reichsmark."

I looked over at Papa. I could see his head, unsteady in tiny circles; I thought he was going to faint. But he took a deep breath, leaned forward, buried his face in his hands and sobbed.

It was too painful to witness; I couldn't help but cry, too.

Mama reached over, rubbed Papa's back and shoulder, whispered into his ear.

We waited, wordless.

Sr Ferrer wiped his eyes. Edo had also been his friend.

He produced a box of white linen handkerchiefs from a desk drawer, gave one to me, took one for himself, then handed the rest to Mama to have ready for Papa.

When Papa was at last able to pull his hands away from his face and sit up, his eyes were red. After Edo's funeral, he had told me that he and I were now the only sons, and duty to the family had fallen to us. It seemed to me, with the way he had been bending over just then that, as the younger brother, he was already feeling a ponderous weight from that responsibility. Now, though, perhaps some of that task could be lighter.

Papa cleared his throat and said, "Forgive me, gentlemen. But it's an overwhelming, heart-breaking shock to me." He paused, looked over at me with deeply sad eyes, then back at Sr Ferrer.

In a lonely, wintery tone he added, "How perfect must be those scales, on which one can truly measure the worth of a brother!"

He worked diligently to regain his composure, wiping his face and eyes with the handkerchief Mama had handed him. He coughed, then folded it to wipe his eyes again. At last, he sighed deeply and sat aright, seeming to have recovered his emotional strength.

He swallowed hard, preparing his voice, then asked, "Herr Ferrer, just a moment ago you mentioned conditions and stipulations?"

"Yes, indeed, Herr Meyer. In order to inherit, you must agree to the conditions and abide by the covenants of the contract governing the legacy.

"The entire amount of the legacy is required to be retained at the bank as a permanent fund; payouts are defined by strict schedule. The contract's conditions are stated in thick legal language. Because of that, they are complicated and rather boring. Herr Millet"—Sr Ferrer indicated the bank director, who nodded in recognition—"has prepared a synopsis for you."

Sr Ferrer paused again, scanned the paper quickly to review the information, and clear his throat in preparation for what turned out to be an intricate read.

"The contract-conditions set these limits…," he started, listing the conditions, number by section-number. I listened as closely as I could.

For the first two years after returning home, I would sit and read and re-read the notes, to the point that I had memorized every letter. If Papa didn't have time to retrieve the synopsis, he would just ask me, and I would rattle it off.

The account had to stay at this particular bank for at least twenty years; Papa got $15,000 right then, at signing; we, as a family, would receive $30,000 on the first of every other year, starting in 1929; there would also be $50 a year for tuning and maintaining the Steinway, as well as $500 a year for my music lessons and schooling, with like amounts for each of my sisters. The other articles were accounting and legal talk, and talk, about who got what when or if a family member died; that any funds not distributed within a certain time would go back into the main fund; and specifying that Papa had final control over distribution of the payouts.

The very last section was just some instructions and restrictions Reinhold had directed at the bank, in particular: don't gamble on the stock market with the funds in these accounts! This sounded like so many familiar sayings of Gramma, and Uncle Edo: "Das Glückspiel wirft die besten Talente weg." [Gambling throws away the best of skill.], and "Der Fleiß verwandelt das Glück in die Tat." [Diligence turns Luck into Deed.], or "Gumption makes do into done," as Uncle Edo had taught me in English.

Sr Ferrer stopped and looked at us with an air of relief. This appeared to be all the legal-talk we were going to be subjected to from him: and I was very glad!

I had been watching the morning sky through the crystal panes of the tall window behind Sr Millet. It grew lighter and brighter as the sun moved ever higher, changing the way it illuminated the light stones of a tall, central, ornately gothic tower, and its accompanying shorter, delicate-tracery towers, paired and forward of the large one, all on what had to be a large church, one not very far distant.

The steam-pinging, ancient radiators under the windows had succeeded at dispelling any chill lingering in the high-ceilinged office. The saturating warmth was making me very, very sleepy again: I had been struggling to stifle a variation-set of huge yawns.

Sr Ferrer asked, "Alles verstanden? [Is everything understood?] Do you have any questions about any of this?

"Rest assured that we have copies of the original contract and of the synopsis, already prepared for you!" he said, holding up a separate, large envelope.

Mama and Papa shifted in their seats as if they were relieved that the ordeal seemed to be nearing completion. I was getting butt-tired!

But then, to get our attention, Sr Millet coughed into his fist, brought himself fully upright, edged closer to the edge of his chair. He turned to face us full-on, and placed his index finger on one of the sets of paper on Sr Ferrer's desk as he stood.

"Herr Meyer, dear Frau Meyer, dear little Son! I also have a few things about the bank and your accounts to explain to you," he said.

His address was straightforward, in stiff, rather formal German that he seemed set on making sound as monumentally bureaucratic as he could. He explained the bank's fee, as well as a guarantee (because of the size of the accounts) of the rate of return the bank would pay, after costs. He also revealed that Reinhold's directions had stipulated that, because of continuing fears about post-war economic, particularly monetary, conditions in Europe, all transactions be held and computed in U.S. dollars. After asking, and waiting, for any questions from the three of us—we had none—he nodded to Sr Ferrer and sat down.

The only remaining issue was a proposal from the bank that they relocate the account and its management from the Barcelona branch to the bank's home office in Zurich.

It appeared that Papa had progressed very well into the facts and rhythm of the presentation, since it took him no time at all to weigh the pros and cons of this suggestion.

"Why, certainly, Herr Ferrer! One of my aunts lives in Zurich.

"In fact, my mother is visiting her right now!" Papa said with some enthusiasm.

"Excellent!" said Sr Ferrer. "We also recommend that you allow us to amend your travel plans, so that you go home through Zurich, in order to have a short meeting with our bank director there."

"Certainly, Herr Ferrer!" Papa assured him.

"Very good. The Swiss managers will have all documents ready for your signature. For your local accounts, we also suggest that you allow us to contact a specific bank in Frankfurt, one with which we have worked quite often. The bankers in Zurich will provide you with all necessary information."

With this, he produced a series of forms, all in Fraktur-official German, an inkwell and a gold-nibbed, gilt and ebony pen. Sr Ferrer and Sr Millet both stood as Sr Ferrer announced, "And now, the time for signatures has finally arrived!"

Sr Ferrer explained each form. Papa signed, followed by Sr Ferrer as agent for the legacy, and Sr Millet as bank director. Another form, that Sr Ferrer said Reinhold had specified in order to protect Mama's interest was signed by her and the three men. Then they came to the two documents that I had to sign!

So, I got to write my name twice, in sharp-pointed *Kurrent*! Although Gramma had guided my penmanship in both styles, I preferred Kurrent over Roman-style handwriting, mainly because it made me feel a bit more *German* and much more *family*: it matched Grandpa's in his letters to Gramma from the Western Front!

Papa signed his name right under mine. The bankers countersigned again. And we were done!

It was great timing, too, because at that moment a wail from the outer office pierced the door.

A restrained knock, and Joaquin pushed the door ajar to look in and speak to

Sr Ferrer. Sr Ferrer then asked Mama politely if she might go out to help with the children: they were growing quite restless.

But as soon as Joaquin had stepped slightly to the side, in flowed three very unhappy sisters. Marianne had that "I'm so frustrated with Gretchen, if somebody doesn't take her from me I'm going to cry and make you all just as miserable as I've become" look on her face.

And, in her arms, Gretchen was now very fussy and squirmy!

As far as my other sister, Anneliese, was concerned, she was obviously very tired and irritable, too, seemingly now beyond arguing.

Sr Millet moved quickly to shake hands with Mama and Papa, and even more speedily to excuse himself; he looked rather anxious to extricate himself from the company of unhappy children, to return to the torpid banality of banking! He spoke to Sr Ferrer, who responded immediately with what I knew was a "thank you, thank you very much!" Some things in Catalan sounded so clearly like their more familiar, Italian counterparts, they were easy to understand!

I looked out into the anteroom to see what mischief Albert might have gotten up to. But he was sacked out on the long bench, lying on his back with an arm across his eyes, apparently sound asleep. It seemed he was as good at sleeping through my sisters' noise as Gretchen had become at sleeping through my piano practice!

Our mixed states of body and mind posed a big problem. Not one of us children was at the same state of tiredness or crankiness as any other: not unusual with five youngsters! The hour also wasn't near enough noon, so we couldn't all just head out for lunch.

Mama and Papa conferred privately, then sought Sr Ferrer's advice, having him join their impromptu conference.

Once they had reached agreement, Papa motioned for me, and the still-waking Albert, to come over to where they were standing.

Papa started to explain, "The girls are tired and cranky, so they and Mama will return to the hotel. Herr Ferrer and I will walk with the two of you within the old city, to see if we can discover some interesting and wonderful things."

"Does either of you have any idea of what you would want to do or see?" Herr Ferrer asked.

Albert shook his head, yawned and answered, "No. Not me."

I thought about it, then said, "I want to visit the big church, whose towers you can see through your office window."

Albert rolled his eyes and slumped his shoulders at me.

"Not for mass, Albert! Just to tour the building!"

Sr Ferrer broke into our exchange to explain, "That would be the Cathedral, Edi! Construction on it started in 1298, so this year it's celebrating its 630th birthday!

"High up on one of its walls is a very famous organ, one that was installed during the 16th century."

"I'd really like to see it, and if we might be able to hear it, too…" I replied with barely subdued excitement.

"My piano teacher has already promised me that I will soon be able to study

68

the organ, too!"

But Albert already looked bored, so I added, "Albert plays the cello, and pretty well, too. Is there anything nearby of interest to stringed-instrument players?"

Albert seemed pleased. Whether this was from the compliment or for my attempt at seeking something to allay his obvious church-boredom, I couldn't tell. He didn't talk about it much: it just wasn't as important to him, but he appeared to have inherited from his maternal grandmother, Rosamunde, almost the same gift of music that I had inherited from her brother, my grandfather, that singing farmer.

"Well!" said Sr Ferrer. "There is a good friend of mine in the area who has collected a large selection of antique and historic musical instruments. He has gathered them in order to furnish the city a museum on the history of Music. I had already been thinking that we might visit him, and now, after we've toured the cathedral, could be optimal!" Then he added, "Later, we can find us a good restaurant for lunch!

"Would that be OK with you two?"

Albert and I agreed that it would be fine, although Albert was still acting a little reluctant: we might have to find a pastry shop on the way, just to bribe him!

Sr Ferrer went over to Joaquin's desk: it looked like he was giving him instructions. Then he turned from Joaquin (who picked up the phone almost immediately), stepped toward the door, and opened it with, "Shall we go?"

Mama gathered up the girls, and we two boys tagged along with Papa and Sr Ferrer, as we all traced our entrance-journey backwards, heading down "constipation hall," descending in the elevator to the ground floor, traversing the ornate, but even more depressingly sterile (now that I had gotten a second look at it), stone-faced main hall, and out the front door toward the car, basking in the languid brilliance of the cool morning's sea breeze.

Mama and the girls got themselves in and seated while Sr Ferrer gave directions to the driver. Sr Ferrer opened the passenger car-door, leaned in to remind Mama of our room-number, telling her, too, that the people at the front desk had the room-key, that several of them spoke German and would help her gladly with anything she might need.

Marianne looked out the back window and waved at us as they sped away.

We stood a few moments in the warming autumn sunshine of the sidewalk, scanning the city-views that we had neglected during our earlier, sleepily preoccupied, arrival.

"Well! To the cathedral!" Sr Ferrer proclaimed as he turned to lead the way.

Musikalisches Geschehnis
— Chapter 7 —
A Musical Incident

Overwhelming!

My senses struggled to draw in every saporous trace of the fantastic airs flooding me during our promenade through this distinctively southern, exotically Mediterranean city. *Allegro,* then *adagio cantabile,* my mind darted to and fro, then stopped: listening, watching, breathing in the luscious, exotic melody of Catalonia.

Sometimes leading Albert and me, at other times following just behind us, Papa and Sr Ferrer had started talking about the banker's early life, where he was from, and when and why he had come to Barcelona.

"I first moved to Barcelona from a little village called Avinyó, up in the hills of west-central Catalonia, about 85 km away, to the northwest. It was there that I was born, and grew up, paying too much attention to sports," he laughed, "and far too little to my Latin, at least as far as my schoolmaster was concerned!

"We would rush away from school for wild, untimed, unbounded games of *futbol* in my street. So many times we had to run like crazy after the ball as my cousin, Aleix, the goal-keeper, let it roll past him, faster and faster down the *Carrer Major* toward any traffic along the *Carretera de Prats!*"

Albert and I joined in then, too, telling him all about chasing our own soccer ball down the hill, on the road that curled around those chicken-patrolled fields in front of the farmhouse!

After moving from the village into the city, Sr Ferrer had been hired by the bank, and worked his way up from being a teller. Here in Barcelona, he had studied English and German and, after proving his abilities, had worked with visiting, English-speaking, winter-season gentry-customers of the bank. He had then been transferred to its New York branch to work on extending his international-banking experience, and his fluency. As he had said last night at dinner, it was there and then that he had met Edo and Reinhold. Not long after those two had moved back to Germany, Sr Ferrer had been transferred back here, to the Barcelona branch of his firm, to receive his promotion to assistant director.

"Because I had learned English and German," he continued, speaking particularly to Papa, "and had practiced both so often in America with your brothers and other customers, the firm requested that I return to Europe. Since 1919, the larger American banks have gotten themselves so deeply involved in Germany's war-reparation payments and, because of the participation of both English and German speakers in this trade, the bank directors have come to value my expertise in those languages.

"The directors chose me as the best-qualified employee to handle such international matters. Evidently, they also thought that I, as a citizen of a neutral country, Spain, as well as the employee of a bank from another neutral country, Switzerland, would not be regarded with suspicion by the Americans, the other Allies, or by Germans, Austrians, Hungarians, or other remnants of the Central Powers."

Papa listened intently, even while we had rushed to cross streets, dodging the sporadic morning traffic of chuffing cars, and horse-drawn carriages and wagons, to reach the plaza in front of the cathedral. At that point, Sr Ferrer ceased relating his personal story, and started pointing out items more historical.

The ancient pavement of the plaza itself was all of a blond stone, only slightly darker than that of the cathedral façade, whose tall tracery and finials blessed the plaza with a very light, almost floating, heaven-pointing appeal.

The two smaller towers that I had seen from Sr Ferrer's office stood atop the corners at either side of the façade itself, where the bell towers usually are, on our own cathedrals. The much taller and wider, high-windowed tower centered between them, with its high-pointed, glass-filled arches and pinnacles rising into the air, shone with darker shadows as its summit of delicate, open-elongate triangles of tracery ascended, much loftier than the filigree of the front towers, rose serenely high into the embrace of the emblazoning morning sun.

Above the pointed arch of the cathedral's doorway was a triangular sea of trefoil and quatrefoil stonework, surrounding a six-pointed, curvy-edged, flame-tracery-filled star-window.

The double doorway itself was nestled in the center of an outward-spreading, nestled set of gothic arches, surrounding the portal itself. Centered in the arches, dividing the doors a-twin, was a post on which stood a statue of an unusually handsome Christ ("Who would not want to be *the disciple he loved*?" I thought) blessing on-lookers with his right hand, while the world-orb was cradled carefully against his chest by his left hand.

As we passed through, then closed one of those ponderous wooden doors, the din of city life faded apace, and we found ourselves amongst the glints and beams of sunlight shimmering from the great, high lantern: the tall windows of the soaring, octagonal cupola. This exalted, airy space—opened within the stone tracery of that grandest tower—perched perilously at the very top of the square of four pointed arches lofting it at this extreme, northwest end of the building.

Stepping into the nave was very much like entering a grove of very tall, beige-barked trees standing within the pale, but warming golden aura of sunrise: dark and soothing, with the glowing promise of enlightenment.

 We had arrived during choir practice. As we stood at the edge of the nave, we were greeted by that chorus intoning the soaring, soothing polyphony of Josquin des Prez's *Alma Redemptoris Mater*—*Ave Regina Caelo-*

rum [*Gentle Mother of the Redeemer—Hail, Queen of Heaven*].

Albert's face softened from his too typical frown into a serene, almost angelically peaceful countenance. He stepped up to the font, wet his fingers, made the sign of the cross while genuflecting toward the high altar, barely visible through the distant door into the choir.

He walked beyond the nave to a nearby statue of the Virgin, knelt, crossed himself and pulled a rosary—a rosary?—out of his left pocket! After he had apparently made his prayer, he crossed himself again, kissed the rosary and put it back in his pocket. Standing, he reached into his right pocket, and pulled out some of those coins we'd been given by Sr Ferrer. He held them over the slot of the coin box, but stopped to look back over at us, expectantly. Papa smiled at him, and nodded "Yes."

With that permission, he dropped the coins in the poor-box. When they had rattled their way to its depths, he turned back toward the image, lit a votive candle and, after it had taken secure light, placed it among its flickering brethren. Almost hidden from us, he crossed himself again, before turning to walk back slowly to where we had been waiting.

I didn't know what to think! What had happened to that loud-mouthed, vulgar punk who had called me "faggot" in passing anger, just those few days ago?

When Albert approached, Papa pulled him into a sideways, hip to shoulder hug then kept his hand on Albert's farther shoulder as we all stepped forward, across the shafts of light descending from the tower-windows above us, beams that spread across the polished slabs at this entrance into the deep forest of the nave.

We walked quietly to the door through the great, statue-studded stone screen into the choir. The music wasn't coming from there, but from the clerestory, aloft above the side aisle to the left, nearer the high altar.

The church was soothingly dark, almost cave-like in its cool, melody-wrapping shadows. The brightest lights shone only on the altar and on the great crucifix hanging above it.

We entered the choir, stepping quietly past banked rows of seats, within heavily carved, darkly wooden stalls. Above each one was a gold and red image of medieval heraldic arms. They were those of the knights of the Order of the Golden Fleece, Sr Ferrer explained: that "dead thing" on the stamps, I remembered!

Opening toward the high altar, beyond the three-walled choir was a set of stairs leading downwards, a wide-yawning opening that split those staircase-pathways, ascending to the high altar.

Sr Ferrer led us down the stairs to the protective metal grate: this was the grotto-chapel of St Eulalia. Beyond the tall ironwork I could see the casket-reliquary, a long box with every inch covered in carvings depicting the saint's life. Carried on two sets of delicately ornate columns, its one set of four supported the front, the other in back. The reliquary's lid, shaped like the roof of a house with its crest running lengthwise along the case, was also carved deeply with slender human figures. At each corner, an angel stood vigilant.

Atop the very center an exquisite, elongate statue of Mary—whom I greeted with an 'Ave!'—crowned with a halo of stars, held the Christ-child. The stonework was so intricate and sculpted so delicately into the pale stone that it all looked like a near-diaphanous array of ivory statuettes.

The wonder of the place was doubled by the change that had come over Albert. His face maintained its bliss: his manner had, well, *melted*. Following us up from the grotto, he walked so softly that I had to look back, twice, to make sure he was still behind us!

But when we did reach the top of the staircase, I looked up to my right—and almost fell back down the stairs a-shudder! It was the organ!

It must have been almost three stories tall! Against the high wall of the aisle, it filled the space above an archway and between two of the nave's columns as I stared at it from the center of the nave! Its four levels of keyboard pipes, and forward-pointing semicircle of trumpets, framed by the two pedal towers created an all-conquering, ancient-oak, gilded-scrollwork and diapason splendor!

A phrase that Gramma and I had found on a scrap of paper in one of her books flashed to mind, the single clause someone had scribbled in French and German: *et les orgues éclataient—und die Orgel donnerte*! [*and the organ thundered!*]

I wanted so much for it to thunder—like that one had, with that rumbling first note opening the Mahler concert in Frankfurt. But more so, I wanted it to be *me* who made it spit lightning and resound a rumbling, tonal cannonade!

"And it will be!" whispered Clara.

The sight held me captive. I could not look away: I stood immobile, entranced.

The air swirled with echoes of the choir's motet. I surrendered myself to the antique, soulful harmonies of Josquin des Prez's bell-like melody, his *Ave Maria*. It was a self-reconfirming, serenely rewarding reverie.

I hadn't noticed that Papa and the others had walked on.

Albert came back, put his hand on my shoulder, pulled me forward, surprisingly gently. He whispered, "Come on, dreamer!"

His soft summons ripped me back to the present. With longing, reluctant, Orpheus-glances toward the receding organ, I followed his steps away, toward the western, transept-like arch. When I had reached it, he turned to urge, to entice me onwards: "We're going to go see the cloister, its palm trees and pool—and the thirteen geese at its well!"

We exited the cathedral onto the narrow streets of the creamy-stone-built, medieval quarter of Barcelona.

Its narrow byways had none of the half-timbered, black and white, sky-squeezing balconies of Frankfurt's medieval *Altstadt*, but instead betrayed heady suggestions of greater cosmopolitan sophistication brought by intense, medieval Mediterranean trade, then the immense, new-world purloined wealth of the Spanish Hapsburg emperors.

At that same time, Frankfurt had been forced to make-do with the sporadic, dismissive attention of the Vienna-centric Austrian Hapsburgs!

The sounds and smells of close, city life assaulted my senses and forced a quick sequence of musical patterns, colors and images through my mind. Thankfully, though, they were all harmonious, especially those riding the wafting aromas of fresh bread, dark coffee and imminent chocolates! I fingered my pocketful of *peseta* coins anxiously, ready to fling them at the first bonbon that came within range!

We had stepped from the goose-echoing cloister, then rounded the corner onto Carrer de la Pietat, behind the cathedral, into the shadow of the semicircle of great, arched buttresses that supported the high walls and tracery windows above the Mary chapels arrayed behind the high altar.

Threading our way from there along the Baixada de la Llibreteria, we attained the Plaça de l'Àngel. Oh, the cream-filled, chocolate-drenched pastries! We had to walk quickly to keep my desperate feet from pulling us back, planting my lusting face at the windows of those lucious shops around the plaza! And who knew what twisted *pastry-extortion* schemes Albert was dreaming up!

Avoiding bakery- or chocolatier-inspired insurrection, we were across the Via Laietana quickly. Continuing southeastwards along the Carrer de la Princesa, Sr Ferrer stopped us on the sunlit walk before the door of a small pharmacy.

The owner looked up, greeted Sr Ferrer warmly as he entered. He shook his head 'yes' to Sr Ferrer's question before making welcoming arcs with his arms, sweeping our Bartomeu along the counter to the telephone receiver waiting near its end.

Sr Ferrer placed his call. He spoke quickly, taking only a few minutes to talk over whatever he might have needed to arrange. He hung up, then placed another call. After a very few, but obviously pleasant minutes of chatting, I heard him say, "Fins ara!" [*See you soon*] before returning the receiver very carefully to its cradle.

He slid a banknote across the counter, waved his passing farewell to the shop owner who, although now busy with another customer, smiled and waved back before grabbing the cash. Sr Ferrer stepped briskly out to where we stood, waiting.

"Please, excuse the interruption! But everything is good! I thought that I should call my friend, before we knock on his door! However, his assistant told me that he was not at the main site, but is working on the collection, quite nearby. I called him there, and he invited us to visit."

He led us down to the next block but one, where he stopped before the entryway of one of the many distinguished, five-story, stone-faced buildings—former homes of ancient nobles, notables and merchant princes—along the avenue and rang the bell next to one of the posted names.

A man answered, and Sr Ferrer spoke to him, with a bit of a "we're already here!" sounding chuckle. The voice replied; the door buzzed; Sr Ferrer opened it and motioned us in. Across the entryway to the staircase, at its marble summit he knocked on the very first door we had come to.

A distinguished man of around fifty answered the door, shook hands very warmly with Sr Ferrer, and invited us in. Sr Ferrer then introduced this, Sr Bertran, to each of us—which we handled as best we could, since it was done in Catalan!

Sr Ferrer then explained in German that Sr Bertran was a musicologist and conservator of a new museum, one specializing in historical musical instruments, that was being developed by and for the City of Barcelona, and was now open in two rooms within the Palau de les Belles Arts, a grand building just a farther, short walk away. But here we met Sr Bertran in a spacious room with ornate, old-fashioned stucco decorating its tall-windowed, ivory-hue walls. Electrified, antique brass chandeliers hung from rococo, plaster sunbursts embellishing the high ceiling.

Several keyboard instruments were arranged within this room, surrounding a very nice, but older-looking grand piano, which stood with its keyboard directly beneath one of those chandeliers. Stringed-instrument cases stacked in rows leaned against a couple of the walls. I noticed Albert's eyes searching them, as if running an inventory of their variant types.

Sr Ferrer explained that they had beautiful, historical or rare musical instruments stored in different places within the city, along with those in this largest one, Sr Bertran's workshop. They were switched in and out of the museum's displays from those storage locations. In the meantime, Sr Bertran endeavored to care for them: to repair, tune and maintain them. I could tell he had been at work; the rooms smelled amazing, a combination of the book-heavy shelves of an old library and that wonderful sap- and heart-wood-aroma of a carpenter's shop.

We then heard piano music—Mozart, as I discerned—echoing lightly against the heavily plastered walls, coming through the door leading into another room. Sr Bertran called out toward the sounds, apparently asking the other person to come to him.

The music continued, so Sr Bertran called out again. At that, the music stopped and a man answered, "Si? Un moment!" We heard his footsteps grow louder as they creaked toward us, across the unevenly aging, hardwood floor.

Another well-dressed man, slightly heavier than Sr Bertran, but of about the same height, with dark hair receding from the temples, accentuating his piercing eyes, entered from that Mozart-echoing doorway.

He greeted Sr Ferrer by name, then joined Sr Bertran, who promptly introduced him to us. Sr Ferrer translated, saying, in German, that this man's name was Frank Marshall King. He added quickly, "And Edi, you will definitely want to make his acquaintance. Herr Marshall is a great pianist, teacher, and he is the director of the Acàdemia Granados!"

With this additional information, I just couldn't repress the suspense his name had sparked in my mind. I blurted out in English, "Are you American?"

A look of sudden, ingenuous surprise crossed his face, but then, as quickly, he laughed and replied in kind, "No. My parents were English, and I'm Catalan, and Spanish. But you are so young! How did you learn to speak English?"

"My uncle went to live in America, and after he came back to Germany, he and Uncle Reinhold taught me."

"You must be quite a linguist to have learned so quickly!"

"Well, they made it fun, and easy."

"Yes, I understand! A good teacher can make all the difference, isn't that right?"

Sr Ferrer stepped in to add, "And Edi is quite a pianist."

"So you've informed us!" Sr Marshall replied.

He stepped over to the piano in the middle of the room, lifted the keyboard cover, hefted the lid to its full-angle, concert position, then pulled the bench out.

He turned back to me and, as he continued to speak only in English to me, asked, "Do you have something you'd like to play for us, Edi?"

I was startled, but immensely pleased, too! I had wondered how this piano sounded. Would it be better than my exquisite, ebony *Steiner*, back at the farm?

Plus, I loved to show off!

I walked over to the right-hand edge of the piano, ran my left hand over the white keys there, as if dusting them, but just to feel the finish on the key tops. Herr Fuhrmann's heavily used piano had keytops that felt different from those on my own keyboard; I had learned to change my attack based on how slick their surface was and how stiff the keys' action could be, following Clara's guidance, matching their tones to those in my mind. I pulled the bench into range and sat quickly, moving my hands back onto the keyboard.

"First," I told them, "a warmup," and rocketed into a dexterity exercise.

"Czerny! You monster! You're useful after all!" I thought to myself with a barely suppressed smirk.

When I had finished, Sr Marshall laughed and clapped his hand on his thigh, "I hadn't thought of that! Very wise, Edi!"

While the audience was enjoying itself at my supposed joke, I reviewed what I had just learned about the touch and temperament of this piano. Its keys were heavier to the touch than my *Steiner*'s, its tone slightly muffled, the keytops less polished and slick. So, it was a case of weighting my attack while also increasing attention to finger-positioning. Got it. Let's go!

"I usually start the day with Schumann, if I may," I said.

Sr Marshall nodded his approval.

I turned back to the piano and played my current, early-in-the-day fa-
vorites: the first three of Schumann's short pieces he had grouped as *Bun-te Blätter* [*Colorful Leaves* (or *Sheets*) {*of Music*}], his Opus 99. I followed this
with his *Blumenstück* [*Flower Painting*], Opus 19.

"Extraordinary attack, understanding and exposition of melody!" Sr Marshall exclaimed when I had finished. I turned and said, "Thank you" for the appraisal and applause.

"If Mama were here, I'd play the *Les Adieux* Sonata for her," I said pensively before turning to Sr Marshall.

"How about Number 18 in E-flat?"

"Whatever you wish," Sr Marshall replied. "*The Hunt* will do nicely!"

I placed those "*rocket-man* hands" onto the keyboard; my fingers flew through the Beethoven almost without direction. They followed the music I saw flowing through my mind, and the colors and textures, tastes and smells that caressed, in, around and through the harmonies. It had become my habit, whenever I performed, to play mostly with my eyes closed. It was while they were shut that I would hear the woman's voice, gentle and coaxing, with phrases of direction and encouragement. I just had to remember Herr Fuhrmann's warning not to bounce on the bench, while playing the paired *fortissimo* chords during this sonata's second movement!

When I had finished the flourish at the end of the final movement, I relaxed my hands, placing them on my thighs. The audience responded to my performance with generous applause, given how thin their number was. I turned toward them, or at least tried to … oh, no! The heat from my butt had my pants stuck into the bench's lacquer! So, I torqued my torso, angling myself toward them.

"Excellent! Excellent!" Sr Marshall said firmly.

"Outstanding technique, and a wonderful melodic and rhythmic sense, particularly for one so young!"

I replied, "Thank you very much, Sr Marshall."

The room fell quiet; the breeze was running past the windows, with the occasional push-rattle of a pane.

Then, remembering how I'd fallen asleep the night before, I said, "I have another piece that my teacher assigned me recently. May I try it?"

"How long have you worked on it?" he asked.

"A couple of weeks."

"And you have it memorized?"

I nodded, "Yes."

"Very good. Let's see how much life you can inspire in this music after so short a time! What is its title?"

"I can't remember at the moment," I had to admit apologetically, "I forgot to write it down! The score has only the number '5', and that's what I've been calling it. Everything has been happening so fast these past few days!"

He nodded reassuringly, "That's quite understandable! But, please, if you want, let's hear this *Number Five*!"

I turned back to the keyboard, closed my eyes and pulled the sheets of music into view—the *andantino, quasi allegretto* that my forehead had fallen asleep onto last night—and ran my mind's eye through the notes quickly. I let out a concentrating sigh, placed my hands in starting position and let the music come through me.

When I had finished, I extricated my pants diplomatically from the bench's adhesive finish before standing fully. I turned to find that everyone except Sr Marshall was clapping. I had no idea what I might have done wrong!

The room grew quiet; we were all looking at Sr Marshall. He seemed to be lost in thought, gathering his reaction.

After a few, very nervous moments for me, he came to himself, turned to Sr Bertran and, with some flourishes of his hand, said what my growing ear for the language (and with Sr Ferrer's enthusiastic repetitions later) heard as, "Té aquestes característiques innocents i naturals de la frase, úniques i subtils, les que no he escoltat en molt de temps." [*He has these innocent, natural characteristics of phrase, unique and subtle, ones that I haven't heard in a long time.*]

Then he sat straight up, looked directly at me and said, "I can only say 'Thank you', Edi. I have not heard that piece played with such lyrical clarity, and feeling, since 1916." He stopped, then cleared his throat before continuing. I was still very much on edge; I had not prepared myself for any particularly emotional response!

"Of course, at that time, there was a much larger mustache involved!" he chuckled, looking at Sr Ferrer who, with Sr Bertran, laughed along at the joke. Unfortunately, it was completely lost on me!

Taking note of my confusion, he explained, "Edi, the piece you played is called 'Spanish Dance No. 5' and it was written by my own teacher and mentor, Enric Granados. He drowned in the English Channel in 1916 while trying to save his wife during a shipwreck." He looked rather morose for a second, but then snapped back with a grin, "and he had a big, full mustache."

Whew! I could breathe again! So, I smiled, and managed a slight chuckle.

But I also knew the pain he had displayed; I had been having what must be similar flashbacks to that chill morning in St Martin's, in Bad Ems. I knew now that others must also carry such sorrows, inextinguishable ones; I wondered if I would bear them the rest of my life.

Sr Marshall turned to speak to Papa, relying on Sr Ferrer, standing at hand, for translation into German.

"Herr Meyer," he started, "if at all possible, I ask that you allow Edi to study with us here at the Acadèmia Granados. We can bring his prodigious talents to their full measure!" He then waited for Sr Ferrer's translation.

After some thought, Papa replied, "Thank you very much, Herr Marshall. But that would not be possible. His mother and I want him to remain with us in Germany. I thank you most heartily for your sentiment, but it's impossible!"

"I must request, Herr Meyer, that you at least consider it! We have another prodigy studying at the Academy, Alicia, a young lady of only five years of age now, who is destined for greatness. Edi has the same potential, which will, without doubt, come to full flower with our guidance and encouragement!"

"In the future we may consider that, Herr Marshall, but he must remain with us now, and return with us to Hesse."

"Please, do think about it!" Sr Marshall replied, not quite so dejected as I might have thought. He paused, then turned to me.

"Tell me, Edi, why do you close your eyes when you play?"

"To let me see the notes, the colors, everything about the music," I answered.

"And to hear the lady more clearly."

He looked puzzled.

"The lady?"

"Yes. She gives me hints, suggestions and encouragement."

I paused. Could he understand?

"She has very bright, kind eyes, and dark and gray hair smoothed and parted in the middle, pulled back into a bun. She told me that her name is Clara."

"Clara?"

"Yes. She often urges, 'Melody, Edi! Let the melody sing!' She has been whispering that to me this morning."

Sr Marshall looked quite puzzled, but allowed, "Well, she, and you, were certainly correct!"

Then he asked, "Edi, how old are you?"

"Seven—and a half. The eighth of June."

"June 8?"

I nodded.

He pursed his lips, lowered his brow in thought. Then he chuckled rather heartily, and said, "*Santa Maria!*"

"Edi!" he said enthusiastically, "This lady who talks to you also tells us now exactly where it is that you must study."

Then he motioned to Sr Ferrer to make sure he translated for Papa what he was next about to say to me.

"Edi! You must go to the Hoch'sche Conservatorium in Frankfurt. It is a school highly esteemed, being led now by a very gifted instructor, Bernhard Sekles. He will know the best courses, the finest teachers for you! I shall write a letter of introduction, and send it off to the Conservatory. You must certainly continue to study with your excellent local teacher until your parents allow you to attend the *Hoch'sche* for fuller instruction.

"But your attendance there must not be too long delayed!" he almost scolded before pausing to allow Sr Ferrer to finish the translation. He then looked at me and asked, "Do you understand?"

I nodded, "Yes, sir."

He looked over at Papa.

Papa nodded and smiled, "Completely understood, Herr Marshall! Thank you very much! That is completely doable!"

Papa looked at Sr Ferrer as if to ask, "it *is* possible now, isn't it?"

Sr Ferrer smiled and nodded, "Yes."

And so, as if by a strong, but unseen, hand at the tiller, my journey tacked surely to another heading.

————————————

The remainder of our stay in Barcelona was a sensual blur.

Mama and I spent an entire day with Sr Marshall and the teachers there at the Acadèmia Granados; I even sight-read some duets with the Academy's marvelous, little Alicia, Señorita de Larrocha. I thought it might actually have been fun for me to stay there to study, but then, I had to get back to my *Steiner*, and to my Eva!

We did finally get over to the majestic Palau de les Belles Arts on the Salón de San Juan to see all the instruments on display there in the Museu de la Música—twice!

Walking among pianos and harpsichords, seeing the designs and styles of the various keyboards, the instruments' decorations, and leaning over to look into them to gauge their variant stringing and musical mechanisms, I felt so joined to them that I could hear the very notes played by their former owners. They must have cherished these, their beautiful instruments, as I did mine!

The second time we went by, Sr Bertran himself greeted us there.

When he approached, Albert was standing enraptured before a display: he couldn't decide which one of two of the cellos on view to stare at the most. Sr Bertran noticed and offered to let him play the newer of the two.

Albert became quite red-faced, insecure at having been offered such a chance. Again, he looked to Papa for permission, who smiled reassuringly.

They found a chair for Albert. He was visibly nervous when he sat, grasped the bow, then the cello by its neck. The fingers of his right hand plucked each string in sequence, then repeated with his left hand pressing new notes into the strings. A few tweaks to the tuning pegs—I hummed the A, for him to get the note for the highest-pitched string—and it was in tune!

Holding the bow aside, he looked the instrument over lovingly, then caressed it into position. A moment's concentration, a deep breath, and he began Bach's G Major Suite for Solo Cello.

With the very first note he was again transformed: his face radiated the very same serenity as when he had arisen from kneeling before the Madonna in the cathedral.

I wasn't expecting it, but he played the whole suite, with barely a breath between movements! From memory! When he finished, everyone who had come into the room applauded. He awoke from his musician's delirium, rather surprised to find that so many had wandered in, stood and gave an acknowledging bow like I had, on that first day, when I had played the piano in Sr Bertran's museum-storage studio.

I had also noticed that, among the newly arrived audience, was Sr Marshall.

After Albert had finished, he came over to Papa and Sr Ferrer. I heard him say to them, "Well, it looks like we have another prodigy ready to study here!"

Before the audience had dispersed, Sr Bertran had Sr Ferrer ask me to play the Schumann pieces again, on one of the pianos there. I complied eagerly—couldn't let my cousin show me up!

After I finished the Schumann, there was a round of applause, so I turned and bowed for that. I returned to the keyboard quickly, but played a different piece, one that Herr Fuhrmann and I had worked on, one I *hadn't* fallen asleep on the other night, one whose lyricism I felt so dearly, a work called *Capricho Espanyol*.

When I had finished and looked up, I was shocked at the applause—it seemed that I had hit a nerve with the audience. I bowed to the applause, then turned quickly and sat down again. This time I repeated that "Number 5".

The audience's reaction to it was even louder, as more people had wandered from the grand salon of the Palau de les Belles Arts into this larger of the two side-rooms of the Museu de la Música.

Sr Marshall came over, still clapping, and bent down to say privately, "Excellent, again, Edi! And now you will be able to tell your own students that you played those pieces on a piano owned and played by the composer himself!"

I looked up at him in open-mouthed wonder; he squeezed my shoulder and laughed.

To hear that from him made me very proud. It was something that I definitely would tell Mama and Papa, and Gramma. But at that moment, it was an accomplishment I also wanted desperately to be able to share with my uncles.

That pain, the anguish, shot through me again!

I had already memorized that line of Goethe's, but now felt its true anguish: Nur wer die Sehnsucht kennt, weiß was ich leide... [*Only one acquainted with longing knows what I suffer…*]

Herr Marshall and the others talked more, but ultimately, Papa and Sr Ferrer called Albert and me away from our repeated, intent scanning of the instruments, to leave. As we stepped out of the room, Albert punched me in the arm and whispered, "Way to show off—and suck up—you talented ham!"

I hit him back and said, "You were pretty amazing, too—for such a dumbass!"

Papa saw us. "Boys! Musicians don't fight with their hands!"

Sr Ferrer added, "Yes! They fight with volume!"

"That's what I was telling him!" I yelled right at Albert.

"No you weren't!" Albert answered, even louder.

Sr Ferrer burst out laughing.

"Shhhhhhhhh!" Papa tried to quiet us,

"Boys! At least wait till we're outside!"

———————————

A short, sidewalk-conversation between Papa and Sr Ferrer, and we set off toward the southwest. Walking quickly, we crossed the Via Laietana—Sr Ferrer said we were half-way!—and past the Cathedral. (Albert looked worried there, like he was afraid he'd been tricked into going to mass.) But we hurried on, through the oldest part of the city, the *Barri Gòtic* [*Gothic Neighborhood*], to where the tall, tightly packed, stone houses fell suddenly apart, the narrow street spilling out into the long, inviting space of *Les Rambles*.

Sr Ferrer took us to a quiet little restaurant, and after another exotic (for a German farmer's kid!) meal, we stepped out onto the shaded boulevard.

Spying a postcard vendor, I walked over and started examining the pinned-up images, searching for one I thought Gramma would like.

Then it hit me, like snow falling off the farmhouse roof: frigid loneliness, the shocking chill of abandonment. I so wanted to see, just to hear my uncles again!

Papa knelt beside me, hugged me, "It's OK, Edi."

Had he seen me biting my lips? But with that embrace, I knew he understood.

I looked past Papa's enclosing shoulder. Albert stood watching, his face a mirror of my distress.

Papa stood, stepped back to say something to Sr Ferrer.

Picking a postcard, I called Albert over. "Perhaps if I help him," I wondered, hoping it might make me feel better, too.

"Here, Cello-Boy," I joked, "help me pick out some of these to take back!"

He stepped over, and started picking slowly through a separate stack.

"Well, Oma might like one," he ventured haltingly before I jounced the mood.

"Yeah, yeah, but let's spend my pesetas! Help me pick some to show those *Flügelhorn*-jerks back at school: they've never even been outside of Hesse before!"

He remembered the bullying; that riled him and he tore into the piles with me.

He was going to help me, too!

———————————

Even with deep autumn pressing in, Barcelona was wonderful, beautiful, a sensual feast. The golden-stone, ancient buildings, dark-haired crowds of flashing eyes and enticing accent-rhythms, the Mediterranean sunlight, its whipping, salty sea-breezes mixing with the sidewalk-wisps of roasting meat, or of citrusy, tongue-flooding sweets—such music echoed, reverberating within a mind just opening to the appeal of exotic, even sultry delight!

The *La Rambla*-redolent memories of the city, of our Bartomeu—and of those still-unfathomed visions of Joaquin—were ones that I would definitely pack resolutely into my mind and carry with me, back to the farm: to those secret confessions whispered securely into the always-attentive ear of my boxer baby!

In die Schweiz — Chapter 8 — To Switzerland

Intense sadness gripped me again.

Having to say "Good-bye" to Sr Ferrer, to *our Bartomeu*, as his name had become so quickly etched permanently into my mind, almost paralyzed me with this now-grinding repetition of separation: the rite of loss unfading, unbounded.

Sr Ferrer had come to the hotel early on our last day, to make sure we were getting about in time, and to help us with anything that we might need to obtain or have done before departing for Zurich. He had even brought along a packet of French and Swiss Francs: more pocket money sent by the bank in case we might need it on the way home.

After the big car had returned us to the Estació de França, Sr Ferrer made certain that we had our new tickets, papers and amended visas—the bank had re-routed us successfully through Switzerland to its headquarters instead of directly back to Frankfurt—and that all the baggage had been brought and stowed on the correct train. We were standing on the platform, milling about before our departure time when he gave us his own big news.

"The bank directors have summoned me to the main office in Zurich," he announced, "I've been promoted to *director*! In two weeks, I'll travel there to find a place to live; after six weeks, I'll be there full-time. I'll continue to manage your accounts, if that meets with your consent."

"Of course! That would please us very much, Herr Ferrer! Congratulations and best wishes on your promotion!" said Papa. Mama seconded with a "Yes, indeed, Herr Ferrer!"

"Thank you very much, Herr and Frau Meyer! I will always do the best I can in your service."

"Without a doubt, Herr Ferrer, we know that to be true!" Papa said.

"Thank you! I value the trust in me that you show so kindly. I wish you all a pleasant trip! I must now bid you only *au revoir*: till we see each other again!"

The departure thanks, good-byes, handshakes and cheek-presses commenced and passed. When I called out "Fins ara!" [*Adieu!*] he laughed and answered, "Fins ara, meu amic!" [*Adieu, my friend!*]

I liked Bartomeu! He reminded me so much of my uncle Reinhold—and by extension, Edo—that I didn't want him to be left behind, or me to be left alone again with nothing but memories.

The now-familiar, warning conductor-yells echoed down the platform, spreading like the scattered, rolling clouds of steam blasting throughout the station from the engines. In emotion-subduing haste, I moved away, delayed only by occasional, reluctant glances, and climbed the steps to board our carriage. Once again, our Bartomeu and the bank had worked their magic and afforded us our now-traditional, adjoining, first class compartments.

The train chugged slowly from the Estació just after four, into the pale blue afternoon of Sunday, the 14th of October, 1928.

This trip would be different from the first one! Its route ran through Geneva to Zurich, and after only one full day there would we leave to complete the return journey. This was my first chance to see either city, to glimpse the high mountains of Switzerland. I was excited by the prospects, but still, I was ready to go home!

The border into France crossed and trains switched at Cerbère by 19:00 that evening, we were heading east again, across the semi-arid far-south of France. Once smoothly underway from the border, we had gathered quickly in the dining car, to enjoy another hefty meal at the bank's expense.

Again within our compartment, we dressed quickly for bed. Albert and I ran back and forth to the toilet, in the now-customary race to see who could be in bed first. The steward had pulled the facing bunks down into position and prepared them with clean sheets and pillows by the time the two of us were approaching the finish-line.

We had jumped into our beds, arranged and ready for sleep, when Papa came in to make sure we were all set, before returning to the girls' compartment.

Spreading like a new coverlet lay the piano scores I had promised myself I would go over during the trip into Spain, but had neglected. But after meeting Sr Marshall, and my spending the day at his academy, they had achieved a new peak of importance. Albert had returned to his magazines. But I also saw that he had retrieved his rosary, too, not lying out in plain view, though: it was tucked away.

I was deep into marking differing issues along the important sections in the melody line of that "Number 5" by Granados when Albert interrupted.

"Hey, you! Bud!"

"Yeah?" I mumbled, still scanning my music.

Unexpectedly pensive, he said, "You know, Edi, you're really lucky."

Taken aback, I put down my green-leaded pencil, turned my head and leaned it into the palm of my hand, looking at him across the compartment. He was still eying his magazine.

"Whatcha mean?"

"Well… You're just lucky, aren't you?" He turned toward me slowly. Seeing that I had stopped to listen, he stepped carefully into his explanation.

"You have the perfect, spotless family, don't you? Attentive, caring father, interested, if bossy, sisters, supportive grandmother, now some money, and especially … your gentle mother. She's almost a saint, you know?"

He looked directly at me, as if searching for some sort of signal. I understood what he meant, but wasn't sure what he expected me to say, so I just nodded and smiled. That seemed to satisfy him, and he went on.

"The reason I started smoking is because my father found it funny. A kid that smoked was so entertaining to him and his friends: so pretend-adult. It wasn't easy, but it was one way for me to get his attention.

"Sometimes when he's drunk and comes home with his buddies, he orders me to perform for them, like a street-monkey. I refused once, and he whipped me hard. Grannie heard my screams and only she was able to stop him. He was drunk again."

He paused, his air sad and so very lonely.

"That's dreadful. I'm sorry…" I repositioned myself so that I could pay attention more fully.

After a second, he seemed to have built up courage to continue talking.

"Grannie invited that new priest, Arno Hagen, to dinner just after he had been assigned to the parish. He and Dad had a good time, and after supper Father Arno started to go on about politics. He's a National Socialist, and talked on and on about the party and that big-nosed Hitler.

"First, the Father trashed the Versailles Treaty. Later he damned the weakness of the Republic, and still later, after even more wine, beer, plus a little schnapps, he started railing against the Jews.

"By that time, Dad was too drunk to talk without slurring his words so, of course, he started agreeing with everything Arno said. At the end of the tirade, he had talked Dad into joining the Nazi Party.

"Grannie was so upset when she heard—about the drinking and smoking, not about the Nazis! Even though Grannie has been preaching at Dad always to vote the German Center Party because of its Catholic bias, she didn't say anything that night about the direction the talk of politics had taken. I haven't heard her say anything else, either. I guess she thought that if a priest was OK with the Nazis, it must be fine as far as she's concerned, too.

"Now the priest has come back to dinner a bunch more times. Whenever he greets Dad, they do that stupid straight-arm salute. Grannie just ignores it. It looks silly for two adult men to be falling over themselves about such things!"

He paused, looked over at me, then glanced at the door, like he was making sure it was closed. He narrowed his eyes.

"If I tell you something, you have to promise not to tell *anyone*," he said in a lower, mysterious tone.

Intrigued, I answered with a matching, subdued, "Of course, Albert! I promise!"

He repeated his glance back at the door, staring at it while he paused, obviously listening for any footsteps that might be coming along the passageway.

"OK," he started cautiously. "About a month ago, one night when Grannie was gone, Dad brought home this big prostitute."

He stared, like he was trying to gauge my reaction.

"Yeah, and?" I asked, matching his low volume, wanting him to get on with the story.

He continued, pausing between sentences, watching my reaction, "I had got-

84

ten out of bed and was peeking around the corner into the living room. Dad was so drunk that he had passed out on the sofa. She was drunk, too, but not as bad as he was.

"She was trying hard to get him awake, and undressed, but he was gone, and she was cussing because of the trouble. I turned and tiptoed away, back to my room, into bed.

"I heard her stop what she was doing, cuss some more, then move on shaky legs down the hall to the bathroom. After a while there was a flush, and I could hear those staggering footsteps again.

"She started opening doors and looking into all the rooms she found on the hall leading back to the parlor. Then she opened mine."

Again, he did his security check of the door, while I waited with growing interest.

"She saw me, mumbled, 'Oh, here's another one!' and came over and sat on the bed."

"You swear you won't tell anybody?" he asked again, more forcefully.

I nodded my consent, "Yes, I swear!" and he started again, slowly.

"Her blouse was open and her tits were pushing against the folds on the sides, ready to fall out!

"She grabbed my hand, put it on one of her big breasts and moved it all around over her nipple."

My eyes must have gotten wider; he started talking faster and more intensely.

"She groaned, grabbed my other hand and put it on the other tit, then groaned more, louder. She took her hands away and I stopped moving my hands. She spat, 'Don't stop! If your old man can't get me off, you damned sure will!'

"So, I kept moving them. She said, 'Pinch them!' I did and she groaned louder. Suddenly she fell forward, pushing her huge tits on both sides of my face. 'Lick 'em, sonny!' She ordered. I felt her shudder every time my tongue moved!"

Albert had turned over on his side, facing me. He had moved a hand down to his pajama bottoms and was rubbing himself.

"She stayed in that position, groaning. Then she raised, up, said, 'Let's see what's been hiding behind the curtain, and she reached into my pajamas and grabbed my prick. It was so hard it hurt, and her hand felt really soft! I didn't know what was happening to it, or me! She said, 'Well! Looks like it runs in the family!'

"She tugged on my pajamas and pulled it out, then started leaning over toward it, licking her lips…"

Papa opened the door and stepped into the cabin humming. Albert flopped onto his stomach, very fast; I flipped back to my music.

"What are you boys doing? I thought you guys would be already asleep!"

"Nah … we were just talking about all those old instruments in the music museum," I said, working hard to hide any guilty intonation.

A look of thankful relief came over Albert's face.

"Yeah, we were arguing about whose favorite was better," Albert chimed in.

"Well, that's great, but it's past time for you two to be asleep!" He said, turning to gather his toiletries and bedclothes. I moved my again-neglected scores out of the way, and started gathering colored pencils, reaching quickly after one of them as it tried to jump off the mattress.

Before heading down the corridor to the toilet, Papa pulled the sheet and blanket up tight to tuck me in, gave me a kiss on the head and said, "Good night, Edi!"

He turned to the other side of the cabin, got Albert tucked in, too, then stopped to look him in the eye. He said, "Albert, I'm glad you came along with us. You're a good boy!

"And … you have your mother's eyes; they, and the way you speak, bring such pleasant memories of my dear cousin back to me."

Then he gave him a kiss on the head, a hair tousle and made sure his blankets were comfortably secure, before reaching down to grab the toiletry kit and stepping out the door. It was the first time I'd seen Papa do that to anyone, anyone but me. I knew what it meant. Papa turned the lights down as he stepped out.

I closed my eyes, drifting as I listened to the music of the tracks in the swaying rhythm of the carriage. But shortly, I thought I heard a sniffle; I urged my reluctant eyes open to try to see what it was.

Albert was lying on his back, a forearm draped over his eyes. I could see the glint of a streak of tears running out of the corner of his eye and onto the pillow. His chest moved with muted sobs.

I watched him for a while, hoping that they were, somehow, happy tears. I wondered if his own father had ever said or done anything like what my Papa had just done. I doubted it.

No child, no one, should ever have to cry out to be rescued!

————————————

The next thing I knew, Papa was up, shuffling about, and sudden, early-morning sunlight was polishing the carriage to a high, eye-shocking sheen.

Albert was still in a sideways curl, his knees pulled up toward his chest, where his arms were entangled, holding each other beneath his chin.

Papa clapped his hands and said loudly, "Up and at it, boys! Get cleaned up and dressed for breakfast! You need to be ready within twenty minutes!" He was already dressed, and now stood and watched, to see whether we would start waking up and pulling ourselves together.

Certain at last that we were on the move, he opened the door, stepped out into the corridor to the next cabin and knocked twice. Mama called out, "Yes?" Papa answered, "Just me! Everyone decent?" I heard him open, then close their door.

Albert and I climbed down and started getting our day-clothes and things together. I was busy, not really thinking about anything in particular when Albert said, "Edi." I turned from my intense score-sorting to see what he wanted.

"Thank you," he said.

"For what?"

"You know … … everything." And he gave me a quick, *boys-don't-hug* hug.

"Don't worry about it, Albert," I said, trying to be consoling, trying to do what Gramma had taught, what I thought one good person would do for another.

"Right," he said. I saw the glint of water gathering in his eyes before he turned away quickly, back to dressing.

We didn't say anything else until breakfast, when the chatter from the rest of the family, and the fun of ordering and eating our big breakfasts got everything back to its normal lightness.

So, we settled in for a day across France, and back into the routines we had established. But Mama checked on me every hour or so—she made me drink lots of water—and the headache never came back.

This trip went so much more quickly! It seemed we had barely left breakfast and Lyon before we started seeing once in a while what looked like a big cloud-bank in the East. The closer we got, the easier it became in certain places to distinguish the snow of the distant mountain tops from the layer of clouds that clung to the summits of the highest peaks.

Papa came in and told us to start packing things up: we were approaching Geneva and would have to change trains again. We groaned and whimpered, but gathered all our stuff, anyway. Packing, unpacking, packing, again, and again: it was becoming so tiresome!

Out the window, stretches of west-Swiss farms and countryside passed by in a rush. We were in Geneva at 10:00 that morning!

Customs there was quick and efficient, leaving only a short wait before we could board the local train to Zurich. Our accommodations on it were suitable, but not overdone: I thought it another example of national character, prosperity, and (diminished) attitude toward decoration! Mama and Papa made sure to change their watches back to "Central European Time" (they explained), because we were back in the German time zone.

Papa exchanged almost all of the French Francs that Sr Ferrer had provided for additional Swiss Francs. There was less paper money and more coins. I liked them. They were real pieces of art, heavily made, with the "Confoederatio Helvetica" label surrounding high-relief, sculptural images, wreaths and seals. I wanted to be sure to take some home, for inspection and memories after the trip. Papa said that would be OK: he had been saving some souvenir-examples for each of us of all the currencies we had used on the trip!

Switzerland was almost startling!

The contrast of Taunus hills to Swiss mountains, the differences between forests and farms, houses and villages, these were all vibrant images that I wanted to hold onto, to remember for a long time. They even had good, not-runny cheese on the train!

The view from the speeding windows was of a tiny, fairy-tale land, autumn-hastily shoring up its farms before winter. We even spotted a parade of cows, wearing huge bells around their necks, trudging down from the mountains.

Suddenly, we were in Zurich!

With its hills and river, the city reminded me a little of Frankfurt, certainly more than any other city we had seen so far! But its river, so much smaller, clear—and without dirty smoke-stack ship traffic—flowed through the city from its own lake. Its great, crystal-blue width seemed to make Zurich airy and light, almost on the sea like Barcelona.

And the swans! Huge and beautiful, snowy-white—swimming easily between river and lake—looked like they were as big as cars, or even streetcars! "Wann fährt der nächste Schwann?" [*When does the next swan leave?*] I laughed, remembering Gramma's tale about that famous, funny tenor, Leo Slezak.

A rather ordinary-appearing Herr Lagendorf from the bank had greeted us at the station and transported us to our lake-side hotel. We roomed there only two nights, but it was convenient to the bank, and very enjoyable, particularly after we found the sweets store on the same block! Chocolates, chocolates, and more chocolates! Mama and Papa had to pull all four of us older kids away from that store window whenever we walked past it because we would press up against it and smear a row of monkey-see, monkey-want face-and-hand prints across the glass!

Great-aunt Franziska brought Gramma down to the hotel that night after we arrived. It was so nice to see, talk to, and to hug and hold my Gramma again! She was so happy to see her own grandson, as well as Grampa's late, elder sister, Rosamunde's grandson again, to fuss over us both. Gramma didn't get to see her grand-nephew, Albert, very much. Although at home in Frankfurt, not so far from the farm, his own Oma [*Granny*] held him there, close, as much as she could.

Aunt Franzi wanted us all to go back to her house for dinner that night, but Papa convinced her to stay and eat with us there at the hotel. It would simply have been too much trouble for her to have to cook for all seven of us, plus herself and Gramma!

Papa promised her that we would visit again soon, just to see her. This made her so happy! She seemed to be rather lonely. Great-uncle Kaspar had died three years before, and Aunt Franzi said that, although her son and his family lived in the area, they're on the far south side of the lake, and very busy. So, having her sister, Gramma, come to visit brought her such comfort and joy!

Aunt Franzi and Gramma were back at the hotel early that next morning, to stay with us kids so that Papa and Mama could go right to the bank as soon as Herr Lagendorf fetched them. This time there was no big car: the bank was so close by that they didn't need one. They just walked!

Their business completed in less than an hour, they hurried back so that we could all get out and see more of Zurich that day. By the next morning I was so sleepy, and full of chocolate, that I could barely wake up to get out of bed.

Yet the day summoned me: this was the last dawn of the trip, and soon I'd be back at home with my big piano, and Eva!

Aunt Franzi came to the station, to see us all off. Gramma was riding the train home with us: I was so glad! I had so many things to tell her, so many adventures to relate and souvenirs to go through! I was so happy I would finally have my Gramma at home again, to sit patiently and listen to me talk and talk!

We were all squeezed into a single compartment from Zurich to Basel, but once we cleared customs and had returned to a German train, we were divided once more into two couchettes.

Gramma sat in the one with Albert and me, talking with us about what we'd seen, explaining some of the things we'd observed or heard. It was like finally having the encyclopedia on hand again!

Of course, it also meant that Albert didn't get out his magazines, and that was a relief! He looked a little distracted at times, but I kept talking to Gramma, and he would eventually either pay attention or doze off. He seemed so much more calm and likeable now than he had been when we had first picked him up in

Frankfurt, nine days earlier.

The villages of the Rhine valley rushed by, and every kilometer made me more light-hearted, wishing the tower of the Dom would appear with every click of the wheels, every puff of the engine! I could hear each of the horns of Schumann's 4-Horn *Konzertstück* singing us closer and closer, ever closer to Frankfurt, my Taunus and home!

Waltraut was anchored to the platform, standing sentinel, waiting for us when the train pulled into Frankfurt.

Albert had spotted her: "Ah. There's Oma."

His voice betrayed only a little excitement, some relief.

However, when we stepped down from the train onto the platform, he ran over to her and grabbed her in a fierce, long hug. She bent over and held him tightly, too.

He had turned so suddenly back into his grandmother's only little boy.

I thought back, on what he had said on the train, "Edi, you're really lucky." I knew now what he had meant, and could see here that he was right, except that he did not know what I had already lost: that I was no longer anyone's "best little cowboy in the whole world!"

He had learned how to be bad; I was still not sure how to be good.

Albert had pulled his single piece of luggage and fat satchel from among the rest, when he came over to me. Softly, so that no one else could hear, he said, "Remember your promise, OK?"

I told him, "Don't worry; it's our secret!"

He smiled, punched me on the arm as he returned to his original, self-protective, tough-guy demeanor, and said, "You're a good kid, kid!"

He walked over to Waltraut, where she was still talking to Mama. He grabbed Waltraut's hand and, declaring, "Come on, Oma, we have to catch the streetcar!" started pulling her toward the exit.

Waltraut exclaimed with a laugh, "Well! I guess it's time to go!" and the rest of us waved and called out our goodbyes and see-you-soon's as the two of them set out for the apartment.

Once they were out of sight, Papa turned to Mama and said, "See, it wasn't as bad as you had feared. Now he's got something to talk about for months, in school and to his friends, and it was no trouble at all!"

"Well, Hans, you were right," Mama admitted, before adding with a smirk, "for once!"

He laughed as they both started to spin about, looking to shepherd baggage and children. Papa found a porter and a cart, and got it all moved over to the platform for the local train, the smaller one back to Bad Nassau.

This time, that 96 km trip couldn't have taken a couple of hours! It passed in what seemed only minutes! We were suddenly back in Nassau, our baggage taken off the train and being stuffed into our car for the short ride home.

With only Gretchen's occasional fussing, those nine kilometers passed very quickly. The onrushing, familiar surroundings—sights, sounds and smells!—made me feel more and more relaxed, happy, and excited to get back to the farm.

The car made the long sweep of our drive: down the hillock, along the edge of the woods, and then up to the front of the house.

Frau Brandt stood at the front door, waiting with Eva!

When Herr Brandt got out, I jumped to the ground, not even touching the running board, and ran around the car. My baby girl jumped and jumped, until I knelt, and hugged and hugged and held her! She was whimpering and yelping, trying to lick, wagging her butt as hard as she could, crying in frustration that she couldn't show just how excited and happy she was that I was back! I put my head on hers, my nose touching the top of her head.

Boxer-puppy, warm, D-major aroma, and I was home!

It was already past 5 o'clock when we walked into the house that afternoon.

We hadn't paused for a real lunch, so we obliterated what Frau Brandt had prepared for our supper. I ate so much that I didn't even touch ole *Steiner*, but pushed away from the table and went right up to my bedroom, climbed under the featherbed, pulled Eva down beside me, and slept until sunrise the next morning.

I dreamed of Zurich and its shimmering swans, of Barcelona and *crème catalan*, of the cool, shadowy cathedral and its snow-white, cloister geese, of the *Acadèmia* and the *Museu*, of Bartomeu, and of Joaquin.

Sr Marshall had said that Clara was calling me to Frankfurt.

With tomorrow morning's breaking light, I would start listening, listening diligently to discover just what her calling, this new life, would bring!

Lehrstunden – Chapter 9 – Lessons

"Yes, yes! Do go on!"

Herr Fuhrmann sat enthralled as I detailed everything that had happened in Barcelona: I worked earnestly to bring all the musical details to life for us both!

Reassured that he would continue to have me as a pupil, he offered to send his recommendation along with Sr Marshall's to the Hoch Conservatory.

"You have friends at the Conservatory?" I asked. It was the first I'd heard of it; he had never mentioned the *Hoch'sche* before!

"Yes, certainly! I studied there and at the Hochschule [*college*] for a while, but moved back to Singhofen to care for my ailing mother after my father died. My only brother, Herschel—may he be at peace with the Eternal!—our dear Hershlekh, who was such good friends with your father, died of measles when he was just nine. Your father, your good father, he wept like he had lost his own brother!

"With my sisters married and gone, only I remained to take care of Mamesheh. Then, after she passed away, the rabbi asked me to stay here, to teach and provide music for the synagogue. So, I have stayed." His voice trailed off, as if into thoughts of family and opportunities lost ... before his exuberance exerted, "And, Edi, I have events of my own! Good news, wonderful news, *kayn aynhoreh*!"

"Yes?"

I sat to attention. It was my turn to be intrigued! "It has to be good news if he said it three times!" I thought, giving my best guess at the meaning of that last phrase.

"Well, I was contacted last year by a shadkhen, a matchmaker in Ems who introduced me to a young lady of a family in Nastätten. We met and talked—so many things we talked about! I played for her; she was so wonderful!—she listened to me play and didn't fall asleep! Even once! Her family has been so very kind to me. And she is so lovely!

"Edi, I am going to be married!" he beamed.

"Congratulations, Herr Fuhrmann!"

"I will invite your family to the wedding! You, all of you will be part of my family! Would that be OK?"

"Certainly!"

"Fantastic! We'll talk more, as the date approaches! There are so many things to plan!" He had a smile broader than I had ever seen on his usually serious face.

"Well!" he clapped his hands on his thighs exuberantly and leaned forward, "But now, it's time again for you to do your warm-ups, before we start in on your lesson!"

I grinned. It had become so predictable: more Czerny!

————[1929]————

Shmuel Fuhrmann's marriage to Golda Chaiken took place the very next Spring, in March of 1929.

In the synagogue of Singhofen, Papa and I wore yarmulkes and stood among the men; Mama wore her hat and the older girls, lace head-scarves, all staying with the women. Herr Fuhrmann taught us what to say, when, so we didn't act too out of place. We had even called out, "Mazel tov!" at the right time!

He was so very pleased we were there! The only ones from his family near enough to attend were his oldest sister and her husband, who brought their three teenage children with them from Limburg. So, the ten of us, added to his students and friends from the village synagogue, helped impress his new in-laws with a demonstration of his substantial, respected role within our community. ("Kayn aynhoreh!" I learned to add!)

Not long after the conclusion of the ceremony, Papa and Mama paid their compliments to the newlyweds and excused us. On the way home, he explained that we had left early out of respect, "We don't know all the customs Herr Fuhrmann's and his new in-law's families have for their own celebrations, and it would be rude for us to impose our preconceptions!"

Mama agreed, relieved; she was aching to take off her too-seldom-worn—and already almost a size too small, she lamented—dress-shoes!

————————————————

The letters had been received, acknowledged, but little could yet transpire.

My expectations drew out, worried, exasperated, beyond weeks into months, but the big day did finally come! Very early in the morning, the 27th of that May, my parents and I set off in the car. We were traveling, at last, into Frankfurt to confer with Professor Sekles at the Hoch Conservatory!

Seven weeks previously we had received a letter from him, one in which he referenced his own, earlier receipt of the glowing commendation, and recommendation, from Sr Marshall in Barcelona. He had waited, though, to propose the day and time of the appointment, allowing a delay for concluding the school term. At my urging, Papa had telephoned to agree to it expeditiously.

It was at my next lesson that I told Herr Fuhrmann. He thought it fantastic, promising to affirm his opinion and assent to his friends at the Conservatory as soon as he could. He called out to his new wife, asking her gently to remind him that evening to write those letters. Frau Fuhrmann stepped in from the kitchen to answer him, contentedly wiping a plate dry with a towel. She beamed at him; to me, it appeared that she had gained a little weight around the middle.

She smiled and said, "Of course, dear!" before turning back toward her humming chore.

I was glad to see then that they were so happy together! Herr Fuhrmann stood taller, and seemed to have more energy for our lessons, too, even if they often had to be in the later afternoon now, because his wife had started getting sick when she woke up.

This morning, though, I was just overjoyed that the day had at last arrived!

We were within Frankfurt a little after 9 a.m., at least thirty minutes early.

"Ah, there's the Eschenheimer Tower, so we're very close … hmm, there it is!" Papa said and pointed out, toward the north.

I saw it: a stately, three-storey stone building with five tall, ornately round-topped windows on the first floor (visual extensions of similar, four smaller ones plus entryway on the ground floor) separated by a heavy cornice from the twelve, small rectangular ones of the top level. The text on the flat area beneath that front-spanning, floor-splitting cornice said "Dr Hoch's Conservatory" over the three high windows in the center, with twinned, ponderously arcane MDCCCLXXVIII over each of the windows at the sides. This was definitely the place!

Around ten minutes before the appointment, we pushed through the heavy front-door, into the Conservatory, crossing the threshold into this, my new world! I could hear differing strains of music, some instrumental, some vocal, coming from different directions and distances. I suddenly got a little shaky: not nervous, just trembling with excited possibilities!

We were directed to Herr Sekles' office. His secretary, pleased to learn we had experienced no trouble on the drive, asked us to be seated: Herr Sekles would be right with us.

At exactly 10 a.m. Herr Sekles emerged from his office, saying "Goodbye" to a departing visitor. Then he turned to us. He stepped immediately over to Papa, who stood to shake hands.

"Herr Meyer, I presume! Very pleased to meet you!" He then took Mama's extended hand and shook it, "Frau Meyer! The greatest pleasure!

"And you must be Edi!"

He extended his hand, and I stood, like Papa had, to shake it.

Before I could say, "Pleased to meet you," he continued talking.

"Only seven years old? Yes, Herr Marshall had mentioned that you were more mature, taller than your age would suggest! I would have guessed nearly ten, perhaps eleven from your hands!"

"I'll be eight within a couple of weeks, Herr Sekles!" I replied.

"Indeed! That will certainly be something to celebrate! Well, we must hear you play now, mustn't we?"

He turned to his secretary and asked if the room he had requested had been reserved. Her finger traced its verification, down, then across the text on a piece of paper she had picked up.

"Yes, sir. The recital salon is reserved for your use for the next two periods."

"Good! Have the professors I invited made time for this interview?"

"Yes, sir, they each responded affirmatively to your request."

"Excellent! Please make sure they are on their way."

She stood and walked briskly out of the office, turning smartly to head down the corridor.

Returning to us, Herr Sekles bowed slightly and said, "Please, walk with me!"

We ascended stairs, went down a hall and into a large room. On the slightly raised stage beneath the tall windows stood a concert-grand Steinway that was almost the duplicate of mine.

When we were all inside, Herr Sekles turned to us and said, "Now! If you, Herr and Frau Meyer, will sit toward the back, anywhere you are comfortable, please leave the forward rows empty. Edi! Please go on up to the piano. We need only await the arrival of the two additional professors I have requested…"

He was interrupted by the footsteps of two men, one of whom he greeted as "Rottenberg"; the other's name I did not hear well enough to understand. The three took seats, two or three chairs apart, spread across the center of the second row.

"Edi, the stage is yours. Simply tell us what piece you will play before you commence, then feel free to begin it as you wish."

I pulled the bench into position, sat down and ran my hands back and forth over the satiny keytops of the beautifully sculpted keyboard.

"Just like ole *Steiner*!" I smiled to myself.

Turning toward the professors, I said, "If it's OK, I'd like to warm up first! I haven't touched a keyboard since yesterday."

"As you wish," Herr Sekles nodded pleasantly.

I started with one of the simpler Czerny exercises, then went strictly through another I thought more taxing. My assessment of the instrument done—it was the virtual twin of my *Steiner*: no problems with action, tone or keytops!—I turned again to Herr Sekles and said, "I would like to play the *Waldstein*, if that's OK."

He nodded again, waved his hand lightly toward the piano and said, "Please!"

I closed my eyes, brought the music to mind, scanning the pages, my color-pencil markings, and prepared my fingers to sing their parts. I heard Clara whisper, "You're home now, Edi! Let the harmonies ring through you!" and I relaxed even more, hearing the soft voice of this, my musical guardian-spirit.

♪ DMD-9a1

When the inner colors and tastes swirling among the ending notes of the final movement had at last faded, I sat erect, sighed, and descended again into the physical world. After those 25 minutes of work, particularly concentrating on the final allegro of that last movement, I turned to look at the professors. Leaning in, towards each other, they whispered short phrases, with nods of agreement.

Herr Sekles said, "Excellent, Edi! If you would like to rest a few moments, please do!"

"May I have some water?" I asked.

"But of course! How foolish of me to forget to provide some! Just a second!"

He hurried from the room.

Within minutes, the director trailed his secretary's entrance with a pitcher of water and a glass, which she left on a small table that Herr Sekles positioned beside the piano. I stood, filled and drained the glass, not having realized how thirsty I had gotten! But with renewed energy and presence, I returned to the piano bench.

Watching the professors who, with Herr Sekles' return to his seat, had started talking quietly to each other again, I waited for them to return their attention to me.

When they had, I said, "Mozart. Variations in D major, K. 573".

Herr Sekles nodded his agreement, and I swiveled to face the piano. I liked this piece; it gave me a chance to show off my finger dexterity and range of light, subtle tone control, things you simply have to possess for Mozart or Haydn!

Clara whispered only, "Gently, Edi!"

When I had finished, with all three professors expressing their agreement, Herr Rottenberg pointed and smiled at the other. "See! I told you his middle name was *Amadeus*!" he said in quietly joking retort.

"Well, it *is* Gottlieb," I mused.

A short pause. I turned to them and said, "Schumann. *Davidsbündlertänze*, Opus Six. No 17, *Wie aus der Ferne [As from afar]*."

Again, Herr Sekles nodded his approval.

This tender, so soulful piece flowed easily, almost innately from my fingers: as did all the Schumann works!

After the gentle, ending notes, Herr Sekles said, "Herr Marshall had noted in his letter your gift for the melodic line. He was, indeed, correct! You have a natural gift for letting the piano sing!"

"Thank you very much, Herr Sekles!"

"Edi, do you always play with your eyes closed?" he asked.

"I do quite often, Herr Sekles. It helps me see, and experience, the music. And I can hear Clara better."

"Ah! Is that so? Now who is this 'Clara'? Frank Marshall mentioned something in his letter, but didn't explain."

My excitement, my concentration on the music and on the instructors' reactions to it, meant that I hadn't paid much attention to my surroundings. I hadn't noticed three portraits hanging on the far wall. But, as he framed his question, the center one glinted at me at just that moment, drawing my attention to it.

A rather plain rendering, it showed a woman with dark, somewhat graying hair parted in the middle and pulled back behind her head; she had the most piercing, loving eyes. Her simple dress of tan and darker, mourning shades, with just the hint of white lace at the neck matched her palpable, yearning melancholy. My jaw dropped.

I raised my hand, pointing in wonderment, and whispered roughly, *"That's her!"*

All three turned to see who it was that I had indicated. The other two chuckled, but Herr Sekles turned back to me and said, "Extraordinary!

"Edi, that's Clara Schumann, the wife of the composer of the piece you just played. So! *This* is what Herr Marshall had meant when he said that Clara was bringing you to us!

"She was the first piano teacher here at the *Hoch'sche*. A dear, most wonderful woman, she was the greatest of teachers and the most skillful, enchanting pianist! You could not have asked for a better guardian angel! Now I know whose technique yours reminds me of! When I was young, I strove to attend every recital she gave here at the *Hoch'sche,* and anywhere else here in Frankfurt."

The room fell silent as I was at last able to close my mouth. Finally, I knew who she was! I heard her voice regularly, encouraging, so warmly inspiring: was I crazy?

Perhaps; perhaps not. After all, who could say?

Herr Sekles asked, "Is there anything else you'd like to play for us?"

I thought it over.

"Yes, sir.

"First, Granados, *Escenas Románticas*: Mazurka."

"Very good!" Again, he made an inviting sweep toward the piano.

I closed my eyes to let the memories return: the music, palm trees, emotions, Clara's whisper, orange-scented chocolates, bright, warming vistas of Barcelona, visions of Bartomeu, of Joaquin's lips…

After the fading chord at the end of the *Mazurka*, I paused only reluctantly before announcing, "Granados: *Escenas Románticas*: *Allegro appassionato*."

When I finished its final, *pianissimo* chords, and had raised my hands from the keys, I was startled. One of the professors stood and applauded, calling out "Bravo!"

So, I stood up and bowed: I was learning quickly to acknowledge an audience's acclamation! At that, the other two professors started applauding, while laughing, poking fun at the first, vocal one.

Herr Sekles said, "Edi, you must excuse Professor Lehmann!

"He is very interested in more recent musical developments from Iberia, the Mediterranean area and the New World. And he has been feeling a bit lonely because he can't entice many students to share those interests!"

"Yes! You have made my day, my month and, with luck, several years!" Herr Lehmann exclaimed, to his colleagues' chuckles.

Herr Sekles stood, turned to Papa: "Herr Meyer, I'd like for you, all, to return to my office so that we can talk about what we might offer your son. I'm sure I have the agreement of my colleagues on this." As he looked at them in turn, Herr Rottenberger said, "Certainly!" Herr Lehmann exclaimed, "Without a doubt!"

Soon we were sitting again in Herr Sekles' office. He outlined all they had to offer, and the tuition. Herr Sekles then introduced the options for my residing, fostered, in Frankfurt.

"If we can, Herr Professor," Papa ventured, "we would like to keep Edi at home as much as possible right now."

Herr Sekles looked quite shocked.

Papa continued, "Would it be possible for him to have instruction, say, two days every other week for now? When he gets a little older and can be here on his own, we can extend the periods he attends classes."

The director thought about it, seeming to run options through his mind as he tapped the desk with his pen. At last he said, "It is possible, Herr Meyer, but we could not offer any scholarship if it were broken up in that manner, its being part-time, you understand. We had been ready to propose a full scholarship, with full attendance!"

"Scholarships and tuition don't matter, Herr Sekles," Papa asserted. "It would please us greatly if you were to award any scholarship moneys to others worthy, who truly need it."

Herr Sekles was definitely taken aback.

"If that is the case then, Herr Meyer, any schedule is possible! Let's get his teachers and course of instruction down on paper. If I were not able to convince you to have Edi study with us, I believe those two professors who sat with us today would rise in mutiny!"

They spent the next several minutes talking over ways to handle the abbreviated schedule Papa had suggested, and the actual dates. Herr Sekles said he would provide a plan that Herr Fuhrmann could work with me on, while I was not in Frankfurt, with completion of my non-music schooling with teachers or tutors in Singhofen.

Papa signed the tuition contract easily. I thought he would have been extremely nervous about it if Sr Ferrer hadn't gone over these things expressly, before we had left Barcelona and again, more recently, from Zurich!

The plan was that, starting around the middle of August, Papa would bring me to the Conservatory. We would stay overnight for a second day of instruction, then return to Singhofen. After two weeks had passed, we would do it again!

Thus, in the late summer of 1929 began my studies at the Hoch Conservatory, and my musical life in Frankfurt am Main!

––––––––––––––––

Papa switched us in mid-autumn to taking the train rather than driving. He located a smaller car at a good price to drive into Nassau, and leave at the station. That way, Mama could keep the larger car, for use at home.

In Frankfurt, Papa found a very reasonably priced boarding house within streetcar and walking distance of the conservatory. We would spend two nights each trip there with Frau Drescher in her tall, half-timbered house at the edge of the Altstadt's ancient Jewish Quarter. From our window, I could see that pointy top of the Eschenheimer Tower, not very far away!

We relished staying there, pretending we were real residents of Frankfurt. Frau Drescher was a good cook, too. Only a little older than Mama and Papa, she had been forced to open her home to boarders after she had been widowed. Her husband, Emil, had died in 1925 of the lung problems resulting from his having been gassed during the big war.

As Frau Drescher's only income, the limited cash her lodgers brought in compelled her frugality: her husband's illness had taken its toll. She always made sure that her boarders had a good dinner, that one meal a day included in most of their rents. Often, though, she and her children would have only some potatoes and lentils, with *shmier* that she had rendered from the remnants of chickens she had roasted for the boarders.

Her son, Daniel, had been born about seven months after I was; her daughter, Hannah, was already ten. But Hannah was sickly and never left the floor on which the family still lived. She had something called *palsy*: she could barely walk at all, spoke only with difficulty, and had to be helped to eat at every meal. Daniel did his best to take on some of the work his mother had to put into taking care of her. He would spend what seemed hours reading to Hannah, and had learned to understand what she was trying to say, so that he could converse with her more easily, even than their mother could. She was delicately pretty, and seemed really smart. I felt so sorry to see her trapped in a body that wouldn't let her move like she wanted! It made me appreciate the gifts my own sisters had, even if they still kept arguing so much!

But Hannah wouldn't stop trying: she wouldn't give up!

Late that October something big happened over in New York City.

Papa became very nervous when he started hearing the news reports on the radio; he even drove into Singhofen to buy a Frankfurt newspaper every morning during those two weeks. Every day it seemed there was another announcement that would make him pace the floor and fret. Finally, Mama convinced him to use Uncle's telephone to reach Sr Ferrer at the bank in Zurich.

When he connected to his office, Papa was able only to leave a message.

"He'll be back within the hour," he told Mama anxiously. So, he sat to wait; then stood up, made pacing circles around the grand piano, through the kitchen, sat down, got up to look out the door, sat again and drummed his fingers on the arm of his chair ... At last, the phone rang. Papa grabbed it; it was Sr Ferrer.

I heard Papa get out a set of sentences containing "Wall Street", "Stock Market" and "crash" in very worried tones before he stopped to listen as Sr Ferrer spoke. After replying "Well, that's very good news. Thank you! Thank you so very much, Bartomeu!"

Papa relaxed. He then asked for Sr Ferrer's recommendations on what to do locally, listened carefully before replying, "Yes, yes, I see." He thanked Sr Ferrer again, hung up the receiver, leaned back into the cushions of the chair, let his eyes fall almost shut, and let out a long, chest-collapsing sigh.

Mama had been watching worriedly, and listening, too. During his extended exhale, she had walked over to sit on the wide arm of his chair.

"Well, Hans, that seems to have calmed you! What did he say?"

He perked up, rubbed her thigh and smiled.

"It's very interesting, dear. About seven months ago, he and others at the bank had become quite worried about instabilities they were seeing in the markets, especially how greed, and something he called 'on-margin gambling' were rampant throughout the New York exchange, especially with so many of the American banks speculating with their depositors' funds. This had convinced the directors of the Zurich bank to pull all its holdings out of that 'casino,' as he labeled it, to shore up the bank's position. Herr Ferrer has moved all our interests into what he calls 'harder assets' that he asserts are very safe, and assures me that the bank is now in a very strong position, aided by those accounts Reinhold had him set up, and that we have no reason to worry!"

"No reason to worry?" she repeated.

"None." he said calmly. Then he started biting his lip. He bent forward, placed his face in his hands and sobbed in relief.

Mama leaned over, holding him and resting her head on his.

No money, however secure, could replace his brother.

Quietly, I left the room; I didn't want them to see me cry, too.

————[1931]————

In the late spring of 1931, Gramma was back at the farm after another sisterly trip to Zurich, and could stay with the girls, so Papa and Mama both drove into Frankfurt with me. This trip in mid-May, just before my tenth birthday, was the first time they had been to Frankfurt together that whole year.

They came along with me on my early trek to the Conservatory and sat outside each room I happened to be in, listening—until harmony class! That one was too much talk, so they took the opportunity to go for a walk.

Each of my lessons in accompaniment was always paired with an ensemble session for another student, usually a string-player, but sometimes flautist, oboist or horn-player. Most were older than me and had been at the Conservatory longer; so I made sure to be on my best musical behavior!

Midmorning, Herr Professor Nagel was working with me and a violist, rehearsing a piece written not long before by one of the Conservatory's ex-students, his Op. 11, No. 4. We were intent on getting the phrasing and tempos correct, pushing ourselves to follow Herr Nagel's directions. We got all the way through the melodic subtleties of the first movement and stopped. I had dropped my arms, resting them on either side of me on the bench when I noticed a man leaning against the doorway, observing. He started clapping as he began to walk farther into the room.

"Bravo, both of you," he said firmly as he approached. "And you, too, professor!" he added with a nod to Herr Nagel.

"Thank you very much," he said to the violist, as he shook his hand, and the violist replied, "Robert Lang, sir."

"Indeed, Herr Lang," our guest replied.

"Thank you! You played it excellently!"

Then, turning to me he said, "And you must be our rising Singhofen star!"

"Star?" I asked myself, then realized that I, too, needed to speak.

"Eduard …," I said as I stood and extended my hand in introduction.

"Eduard Meyer," he interrupted me, saying my name as he shook my hand.

"Yes, Eduard, I've heard of you. And I've been wandering around today, listening to you!

"I'm afraid that I must disturb your lesson in order to ask a favor of you, specifically. I am giving a concert here tomorrow and need someone to play during rehearsal this evening and again during the concert. Unfortunately, my regular accompanist has been laid low by appendicitis, and can't make it! Will you be available?"

Mama and Papa had entered the room from the hallway. I looked up at them; Mama nodded, granting their permission.

I responded, "Certainly, Herr …"

"Hindemith," he replied, "Paul Hindemith. I am very pleased that I timed my trip back here to my *alma mater* from the Berlin Music-University just right to meet you, and to be able both to hear you play and have you accompany me! I've met your parents." He raised his hand toward where Mama and Papa were standing.

"And I have given them the schedule and program. I look forward to seeing you there! Herr Nagel, you have scores that Eduard can use, don't you?"

"Certainly, Herr Hindemith, I have the ones you provided right here!"

He patted the stack of paper on his stand.

"He had already brought the scores?" I wondered.

Herr Hindemith shook my hand again, then turned to the violist, "Robert, you have extended the most lovely vitality in your instrument since I was last here. Please, do keep playing my music!"

The violist radiated his pleasure from this highly-appraised request.

And with that, Herr Hindemith strode toward the door, shook hands with Mama and Papa, and was gone.

After a quick, practice-room run-through of that concert music—some I had done; the rest were familiar, for a voracious score-reader—I had no more lessons or classes scheduled that afternoon.

So, we purchased some snacks and Papa drove the three of us to a suburban park beside a slow, quiet stretch of the river, for a small celebration. They asserted repeatedly how impressive it was that someone from Berlin—and in a different music conservatory, too!—already knew about me! I thought it was great just to meet a living composer!

We spread the blanket out over the grass; the summer-threatening sun felt so warm against the freshness of the light, northwest breeze. That slightest chill had not dispersed the few groups, and some loners, all out enjoying a bright, Rhine-Main, late-spring afternoon.

The snacks tasted so good after the lesson and practice session that morning! Mama kept talking about how marvelous the whole experience had been. I was very glad that she had been there with us—my travelling to Frankfurt with only Papa all the time must have been very lonely for Mama!

I was about to bite into my slab of the *Frankfurter Kranz* I had begged for in a pastry shop near the Conservatory, when a lady ran screaming to the riverbank, pointing to the water. Waving her arms up and down, she flashed a white handkerchief in her fist, the frantic semaphore of her distress.

Papa glanced up from his own piece of *Kranz*.

In a flash, he threw his wallet and watch, tossed his shoes, and was running toward the river.

The lady turned and screamed that her little boy had fallen in! Papa stopped, raised hand over eyes, spotted something in the river, raced after what he'd seen and jumped from the small, temporary pier into the water, swimming toward whatever he'd seen.

Mama and I stood up to watch what was going on. Behind me, Mama grabbed my shoulders, with anguished, "Oh, my! Oh, Hans? Oh, my!"

After what seemed several minutes, Papa stood up from the dive, as he splashed out of the water, rising as he neared the shore. In his arms, he was holding the boy, who had started coughing the moment he was lifted clear of the surface.

Papa carried him onto the grass.

The boy, who looked almost my age, dropped, sputtered a final, clearing cough and ran over to his mother, who pulled him tightly into a consuming hug. Others, who might be his father and sister, were close, running toward them.

They were all in tears. Repeatedly, the boy's mother kissed and rubbed him, hugged him, then leaned back to fan herself with that kerchief, trying to calm her near-hysteria before returning, almost to smother, to drown the poor boy again.

By the time Papa had walked from the water's edge over to them, the lady was bending over the lad, trying feverishly to dry him off with handkerchief, even the folds of her dress.

Mama said, "Edi, here. Take this to them," as she handed me one of the large, Gretchen-cleaning towels she packed automatically for all our trips.

I sprinted over to them, towel over shoulder. When I got close enough, I held it out with both hands, offering it to the lady. She took it quickly, saying, "Oh! Thank you! Thank you, *Bubbele*!" and started using it to get the boy (now seeming rather unexcited by the ordeal) and his clothes dry.

He looked up at me.

My heart pounded.

Under luxuriant black lashes, he had the most beautiful blue eyes I'd ever seen! His still damp, black hair had silver streaks, reflections of the sun's rays in the clear, bright, afternoon sky. To me, his eyes flashed bluer than the far, dark horizon, reflecting across that terror-strewn river from which he had just been raised.

He grinned: I stared.

The danger had passed, but parental panic was taking its own good time to abate. Papa was trying to lighten the mood of the situation.

"It was hard to grab him at first! He was really trying to swim—like a trout!" Papa laughed.

The boy's father chuckled uneasily. Then with a sudden gasp and spasm, he thrust his hand backwards and pulled out his wallet, almost panicking, "But, sir, how can I repay you? You saved the life of my son!" He glanced down at the boy, but continued, choked, "My only son!"

He started pulling 100 Reichsmark bills, even some 1000's, from his wallet. He tried to give them to Papa, but Papa put both his hands around those holding wallet and proffered cash, grasped them tightly and said, "Herr …"

"Schraeder. Jakob Schraeder, Herr …"

"Meyer, Johann Meyer, Herr Schraeder. Herr Schraeder, there is no need for this!

"You see, I have one son, too!" He released his hands to reach my shoulder and pull me closer with his left arm.

"I understand your anxiety very well!"

Herr Schraeder offered more; Papa blocked the offer with his free hand, "Truly, Herr Schraeder, I need no reward!"

"No! Please! Herr Meyer! You must let me do something for you! I would have given all I possess to have him restored to us! Please!" Herr Schraeder begged.

Papa looked him in the eye; I wondered if he would take anything.

"OK, Herr Schraeder," he said with knowing reluctance. He took one of the lesser banknotes Herr Schraeder held, still offering.

"I will accept only this."

"No, Herr Meyer! You must…"

Herr Schraeder tried with almost heart-rending determination to offer more.

"Herr Schraeder!" Papa held up his hand as if directing traffic to stop. "You must believe me, Herr Schraeder! Nothing more!"

When he realized Papa could not be swayed, Herr Schraeder put his wallet away. He shook Papa's hand again, fervently. Papa told him, "Let the rest that you offered be used in honor of your children, your family, to celebrate their lives!" Papa squatted down to our level, tousling the boy's hair, "And the day your little *Trout* was returned to you." Herr Schraeder finally smiled.

As Papa stood up, Herr Schraeder started, remembering social convention.

"Oh! Ah! Forgive me, Herr Meyer! May I introduce my dear wife, Deborah Schraeder!"

She extended her hand in greeting.

"Tausendmal bentschen auf ihnen! Tausendmal bentschen, Herr Meyer!" [Germanized Yiddish: *May [they] bless you a thousand times!*]] she said.

"Thank you, Frau Schraeder. This is my son, Eduard."

"And blessings on you, too, Schatzi!" she said to me, leaning down, caressing my face in a double-hand head-hug, "Such a good boy! And his wonderful father!" Her voice caught; she sobbed a little, suddenly recalling the danger.

Herr Schraeder continued the introductions.

"This, our son—whose life you brought back to us!—our, as you say, 'Trout', is David."

Papa shook his hand; David said, "Pleased to meet you. Thank you, Herr Meyer!"

"You're very welcome, David!"

"You will be more careful around deep water, won't you?"

"Yes, sir."

"Good! You're a brave lad!"

David turned and stuck his hand toward me. I shuddered slightly as I took it. It was still cold, so I put my other hand around it, to wrap it as I held it. I didn't know why, but I didn't want to let go!

"Your hand is so cold, David!" I said, trying to make sense of my action.

He put his other hand on top of mine, holding them together.

"This one, too!" he said and smiled, almost laughing.

"And this is our daughter, Esther," Herr Schraeder announced, pulling the girl into the presentations.

Reluctantly, I released David's hands and shook hands with her. She looked very much like him; but her curling hair was not quite so dark. Her blue eyes had flecks of green and gold.

"David and Esther are twins!" their father announced proudly, "Esther is four minutes younger!"

He paused.

"But we must move away from the water, well away!"

With a flourish, he turned and motioned inshore, toward the park, "Do come with us! We have food and drink, you must join us! Is that your wife over there? She must come over and be with us!"

Continuing to invite us, almost hurry us along, leading Esther by the hand, and trailing his wife and son closely, he set off toward their picnic, one with the visible makings for a full meal, rather than our hastily arranged snacks. I walked with Papa over to Mama; he told her what was going on while grabbing an extra towel for himself and sitting to put his shoes on. He gathered the pocket-contents he had strewn just before racing to the water, and they carried our things over to join the Schraeders.

The blankets were pieced together, with the towel shielding Papa's persisting dampness from the breeze. The adults sat and talked while they nibbled at the food.

The Schraeders were from Berlin. They owned a clothing store there, had a partner in Cologne, and were visiting relatives who had moved to Frankfurt recently to run the store the Schraeders had set up here several years previously. The adults had a little wine and talked on.

David and I kicked a soccer ball around. Exercise in the sunny breeze completed drying him. Not talking too much, I watched the sun glint from his hair, his eyes. Then we ran back for a little more food.

With our approach, the Schraeders revealed that David and Esther were both music students.

At this, Mama and Papa couldn't help but tell the Schraeders all about what had happened with me, the trip to Barcelona, the Conservatory, Hindemith, and so on. The Schraeders gushed their admiration, and followed it with best-wishes.

"We hope and pray that our two blessings can get into one of the better music academies, too. There are just so few openings! So many come from all over Europe—all over the world!—to study at our famous, German conservatories!

"But once in conservatory, they will join a select few, a community that will help each other to greater things!"

This close-knit society of musicians was exactly what I had seen in Barcelona, and was experiencing that very day, with the helpful attention of Herr Hindemith!

But David and I got bored with all the polite, parental small-talk about the weather, and about us, so we stood, walked a safe-volley distance from our folks and food, and started kicking the ball around again. David's eyes twinkled with laughter whenever I called him "Trout." His joy sent the spritely harmonies of Schubert's Quintet, *Die Forelle* [*The Trout*] swimming from ear to ear!

Growing ever less reticent, he and I were now so taken with talking to each other that the ball's free, variation-movements didn't particularly matter, as long as they kept us together, chatting, laughing and kicking in tempo.

Although rather beautifully delicate, Esther ran over and joined in the game, too. After a few minutes, we stopped, just walked around and talked.

I told them about all the instruments we had seen in the Museu de la Música.

They both said excitedly that they'd love to see the museum: they were especially interested in the older instruments, the harpsichords and woodwinds, that I told them about. I wished that I had brought along one of the picture-books Sr Bertran had given me, catalogs showing all the things that they had on display!

Very quickly the sun tilted toward the west. Papa called out for us to come back over to them: we had to leave. I had to be at rehearsal!

He made his apologies to the Schraeders while Mama gathered up our blanket and towels.

Among David's parent's renewed, effusive thank-you's, we said our good-byes, then loaded the car and departed for the Conservatory. I knew there that, if I had ever needed proof, I had it then, that very day: my father was definitely "a good man, among all the good ones—so many in our own family."

My gaze drew me backwards as we drove away: I was roiling in a flood of new, unsure emotions. But I so wanted to see the blitzing, mischievous laughter in those blue eyes again!

————[1932]————

By the start of 1932, when I was half-way to 11, I had sprung tall enough—most people thought I was already a teenager!—and we had befriended all the conductors and porters along the rail line, as well as everyone in the city that I had to deal with. So, Papa started letting me travel on my own to Frankfurt. My schedule also grew, so that I was attending four days twice a month, instead of the two days that had been my classes up till then.

Daniel's company made staying at the boarding house fun. Being in Frankfurt without Papa was daunting at first, even a little scary, and Daniel was easy to get along with, certainly easier than Albert! Although Daniel was only six months younger, my greater height made me look at least a couple of years older. He seemed much like a new-discovered little brother!

I helped him with his *Kurrent* handwriting, and he taught me how to decipher, then to read Yiddish! I enjoyed the musical, rhythmic sound of the language. It was so close to German but, like Dutch (Gramma had explained), was an old form of Germanic that had kept some things, lost other things and changed still other things that German itself had standardized differently. All of that, along with the exotic Hebrew words brought over into it made it unique, so interesting in its own right.

"Give me a little time!" I'd exclaim against his urging, "I'm having to read backwards!" and Daniel would laugh!

Very early in my life I had become so comfortably accustomed to left-to-right text, and music notation, that I hadn't realized just how much changing your assumptions about reading-direction could make your eyes follow new lines, and force your mind to become more agile!

I even found that taking time to read music from right-to-left helped me understand melodic patterns, voicing and harmonic progressions more deeply! And it was this greater understanding that I was soon able to put to good practice at the Conservatory.

Sometimes I would meet Daniel at the big synagogue on Börnestrasse, after his Hebrew class and walk back to the boarding house together. Once he introduced me to the cantor and, because Daniel had told him I was at the Conservatory and played at the Dom, he invited me to come inside to try the organ there.

Installed around 1860 at a cost of 8,500 Gulden, it was still quite good: smaller than the one at the Dom, but with clearer voices and not as, well, fluffy as that later, Victorian-era one. The cantor also explained that the Rothschilds hadn't liked it back then, but I thought it was still really nice. Then Daniel showed me the other parts of the synagogue and explained them, while I tried to think of matching parts of the Dom.

Becoming so close to the Dreschers, feeling useful in how I worked and lived with them almost like family, made my staying in Frankfurt alone much easier, and transformed that large city into a second home in ways I hadn't expected.

———————————

I did see Albert and Waltraut every once in a great while, but Albert's father, Konrad's perpetual, drunken rant against everything—from the Republic to liberals to socialists to the Jews—made him far too unpleasant ever to be around.

Soon, however, that situation would change.

Der Fall — Chapter 10 — The Fall

The farther the years had progressed since early 1929, ever greater were the privations pummeling the people around me, as more and more were cast down, onto the unrepentant, soul-bloody crags of unemployment.

I felt pangs of guilt: food from the farm itself, and funds from the inheritance meant that we were protected from the worst money-effects of the Depression. But now, in 1932, after the collapse of the American banks who had been financing German recovery, even we could not avoid witnessing ever more fights among the workless, split between Nazis and Communists, erupting in the streets of Frankfurt. The brawls weren't often as extensive or quite so vicious as those reported from other German cities but everyone, everywhere, was more frightened. I could only wonder how things could possibly continue like this!

Frau Drescher worked through several months in which I knew that she had too few business-boarders to make ends meet; she worried constantly about affording Hannah's medicine.

I had been in the boarding-house kitchen once as she was cooking, looking through lentils to extract any errant stems, twigs or field-stones. A spare seed threw itself off the table and rolled away, secreting itself quickly in a dark, out of the way refuge. She stopped and searched for it, going onto her hands and knees until she found it, cleaned it and placed it back amongst its less incautious brethren.

Was such a scene one that had come to His mind when Jesus spoke of the woman who sought diligently for a lost, tiny piece of silver, or of another widow whose utmost care allowed her to give her last two mites? Had He watched his own Jewish mother, diligently respectful for all gifts of Heaven and Earth, search for that one errant lentil, so that nothing ever be lost and fall to perdition?

I told Papa. He shook his head in dismay at her plight.

"I'm very glad you witnessed that," he said.

"We have had great fortune, reaped in sorrow; while all around us, others have great need that they bear with strength and grace. I am very proud of you, that you recognized, and learned from this, this lesson.

"Just remember, Edi, it is not money or power, but dedication, wisdom and compassion that make us human, that maintain our humanity!"

Having heard this all, Gramma called me over to where she was sitting, hugged and kissed me. I looked up into her warm, Hessian grandmother smile as she repeated with pride one of her well-worn sayings, one from an ancient she called *Euripides*: "Far better is it for us mortals to find a poor and upright friend, than one in whom evil is married to wealth!"

From the start of that very next week, Papa gave me an occasional envelope containing extra Reichsmarks to take along on the trip to Frankfurt. When I found that Frau Drescher was busy on one of the other floors, I would sneak into the little office-area in her corner of the family's parlor and slip it into the pages of her ledger. Hannah was often sitting in that room in her roll-about chair. I would hold my index finger to my lips and go "ssh!" She would smile conspiratorially, her eyes twinkling, excited to be part of the game. Not long after that, Daniel mentioned that his mother had been finding envelopes with extra cash in them stuffed into her ledger-book. He asked if I had seen anyone doing it.

I said, "No, but I wish someone would put money in my books!"

He grinned slyly.

I thought Frau Drescher had guessed the source, too, because I noticed that she became even more attentive, more motherly and huggy. And now, once or twice a week, she and her children would have fresh beef or mutton delivered from the shop of Herr Mendel, the *shoykhet* [*kosher butcher*] just one street over, to go with the persistent lentils and split peas. And at times, even some fresh fruit found its way home, too. I noticed that Hannah's complexion was returning to a more healthy tone: a velvet glow had returned to her visage, and she was coughing much less, too.

[1933]

One early-morning in late January, back at home on the farm, as I was once again arranging my heavy, winter clothes for the train ride into Frankfurt, Mama came and stood, leaning against the door to my room.

"Edi, your father and I are going into Frankfurt, too," she said solemnly, "by the first train we can meet in Nassau."

Puzzled at the abruptness of the announcement, I stopped my packing and turned to sit on the bed, facing her.

"Why, Mama?"

She sighed. "Waltraut has suffered a serious fall, and has been rushed to a hospital. We must go take care of Albert.

"So, pack an extra change of clothes: we'll be staying there until we can sort it all out. You'll go ahead to Frau Drescher's and to the Conservatory. Your father and I will find a room closer to Waltraut's apartment."

Poor Albert! What was left for him, now?

His father, Konrad, had frozen to death the first week of last December. After a night of boozing it up with his Brownshirt buddies, he had passed out in front of a bar and lain ignored in his uniform, almost in the street, the whole night. Mama had said that Albert showed no grief at the funeral, but was just rather sullenly quiet.

Even Konrad's mother, Waltraut, had not been overcome with grief. It was as if they had expected something like that to happen, almost as if he had deserved it, so Mama said.

Papa had also told us about Waltraut's revelation to him that, since Konrad's funeral, Albert had become withdrawn and moody. He had begun refusing to go to mass with her, sometimes yelling at her when she suggested it.

He had never raised his voice to her before; she was worried, distraught, didn't know what to do. That's why she had approached Papa: after Konrad's death, other than her, Papa was Albert's closest surviving relative.

Later that morning, I took my habitual path from Frau Drescher's to the Conservatory. My lessons trudged along in their winter-belabored, routine way. But well before noon, Herr Sekles' secretary brought Mama in.

"Edi, you must come with me," she said in her 'I don't wish to disturb anyone' voice.

"Waltraut has died and we have family business to attend to."

I was shocked! I had been told only that she had taken a fall in the kitchen. No one had said anything to me about a death-threatening catastrophe! Nevertheless, dutifully, I re-loaded my satchel with everything I had brought that morning.

January 25, 1933, was a very cold, gray morning in Frankfurt am Main, growing more dismal. Despite the below-freezing cold, on foot and by streetcar, the two of us journeyed, but quite briskly. The buildings of the inner city were packed tightly, stuffed within and conforming to the outlines of the long-gone medieval walls; the hospital was not very far.

I held the entrance-door open for Mama to duck inside quickly, out of the cold. Two steps forward and we slammed into an invisible, almost stifling wall of heat. Moisture condensed in tiny drops on the exposed parts of my face. The steaming air was almost overpowering!

We walked past hackers and spitters, coughers and groaners, in this room and that. The overwhelming nasal-stab of dissonant disinfectant almost made me faint! At last we topped the stairs and approached the first-floor ward in which Mother knew that Waltraut had last lain.

Papa was standing at the side of the room, talking to two, white-smocked doctors.

Albert was sitting on a now empty, disheveled bed, his face in his hands.

Mama went over to him, sat beside him and put her arm over him; he fell against her, not extracting his head the slightest from the protecting depths of his palms. I moved toward Papa, to see if I could discover what had happened since I had left them that morning.

I heard one of the doctors' final assertion, "It was fatal: nothing we could do."

Papa thanked them. Quick handshakes, then he turned to me and sighed. "All arrangements have been made. There's nothing else to be done here. We need to go."

He helped Mama maneuver Albert back into his coat. He had finally pulled his face away from his hands; it was red, wet, puffy.

"We have to go to Waltraut's apartment to prepare things," Papa said as he put his arm over my shoulder and Mama coaxed Albert toward the stairs. "The priest has already been here. Her funeral mass will be sung tomorrow morning."

We took our time descending the staircase.

"I know you have lessons scheduled tomorrow, so you don't have to attend the funeral if you don't want to. You haven't gone to one since Edo's; I will understand if you think it will be too difficult for you."

I had thought about it, playing scenario-variations in my mind, having already realized exactly what he had just said. I might not be able to sit through it!

"No, Papa," I said at last, just as we reached the bottom step, "I have to try; I need to be there."

"Good," he said thankfully.

"I'll contact the Conservatory this afternoon."

We stood at the bottom of the staircase, separate from Mama and Albert. He turned and stooped slightly, to face me directly.

"The thing I haven't told you, Edi, is that Albert will now be coming to live with us."

"Yes?" I replied, with rather less confidence than I had hoped.

"He'll take the spare room next to yours," he explained. "He will need your company and our attention to help him through this."

He bent closer, looking me in my eyes, "That will be alright, won't it?"

"Of course, Papa," I assured him, regaining some of my resolution: I would try to do what was expected of the men in our family, the *so many* good men!

I thought the arrangement could work out well, but then, only time would truly tell. Albert had been essentially on his own while his dad had been drinking so heavily, when Konrad had gone Nazi-insane; we'd have to see how he took to being absorbed into our farmhouse crowd.

One of the nurse-sisters had summoned a taxi for us. We took it back to Waltraut's apartment building.

At the rear side of a minimally maintained, old, half-timbered building was the tiny apartment into which Waltraut had moved the two of them the week after Albert's father's death.

We entered, walking in single file: that was all the door to the small sitting-room would allow. Albert stumbled into the room, still struggling blindly against his grief. We looked over the unfamiliar, pitiful surroundings. Musty and dark, cold and unwelcoming, the umbrous gloom of that apartment had been lightened only by Waltraut's love for this, her sole grandson.

Albert stepped over to the door leading into the tiny kitchen. Near collapsing, he slumped against the doorframe, groaned, grabbed his face and loosed the teen-aged wail of the abandoned.

The blood from Waltraut's head-wound was still visible on the sharp corner of the cabinet. Albert started talking—to us? to himself? to his grandmother?—trying to make sense, through a sorrow-ravaged voice, of the events and his place within them.

"I heard a thump and the clang of a dropped pan; I ran in from my room; Oma was stretched on the floor next to the cabinet, the frying pan flung against the wall; I called out to her!

"I raised her head with one hand, held her hand with the other. She turned her eyes to me slowly, and whispered, 'Be a priest, Albie' then turned her eyes away. I called her name again, but she didn't answer!

"The blood was flowing from the gash into her hair, onto my fingers! I didn't know what to do! *What to do*!?! I ran to get the landlord; he called for help; I ran back to hold Oma. The next thing I knew, the priest was at her bedside in the hospital, closing her eyes!

"Oma!" he sobbed, "Oma!"

Papa went over to him and hugged him. Albert was fifteen and had had everything he'd ever known—good or bad—ripped out of his hands!

Albert sobbed, great, gut-wrenching sobs. He pulled away from the hug, stood alone an unsteady few moments before turning back to Papa.

"What will I do, Uncle Hans?" he pleaded, lost in desolation.

"You will do what your grandmother and I had already planned," Papa said quietly, but reassuringly firmly. "You will come back to Singhofen and live with us!"

"You had?" he asked quietly. He looked at Mama. "I will?"

Mama stood up, took his hand and said, "Yes, you will, Albert."

He looked at her, almost smiling; he always smiled at Mama, for Mama.

His battered voice asked at last, "But … you had talked about it?"

"Albert, your grandmother had not told you, but she was very ill, deathly ill," Papa explained. "She had cancer deep within her, and the doctors had told her that it was only a matter of time before it would take her. She had started preparing a way to make sure you would be cared for. That's why she had written me.

"At the hospital, the doctors explained that she had probably fainted from excessive blood loss, internally. The head wound had only allowed the cancer to finish what its evil had already begun. There was nothing anyone could have done, particularly you. They said that she had essentially died here, at home, just after the fall. She never regained consciousness at the hospital."

Papa had to stop, to steel his composure before he could continue.

"I know it meant the world to her that she departed with you holding her, calling her name. You didn't know it at the time, but your loving attention at that moment was probably the greatest gift you had ever given her."

Albert whimpered, brought his hand back up to his eyes, sobbed; Mama hugged him.

"Thank you, uncle!" he finally got out, in a still-cracking voice.

Through all of this, I had struggled, struggled fiercely to keep my own emotions under control. I knew that feeling of loss exactly, the gnawing abyss of bleakest loneliness. But I still had close family to lean on; Albert's isolation was beyond fathoming.

Papa broke the silence.

"We need to get everything in here organized," he said, "into what stays, what can be sold, and what comes with us to Singhofen."

We set to it, slowly. With his emotions growing more steady, Albert started helping us sort through the apartment's contents, setting things in order for the next few day's rush.

That next morning, Waltraut's Father Hagen sang her requiem mass. Mama got Albert through it. I was there in body, distanced in spirit. It was only the music, and the blessèd serenity of the Madonna, that lifted me, carried me beyond the pain.

Albert mourned heavily the next few months.

The fact that he and Gramma had started a day-break custom of praying the rosary together had given him solace, and that accepting, nurturing attention that I had always known from Gramma, stepping gladly into an additional grandmother-role for this, her grand-nephew, had begun to fill the personal chasm in his life that Waltraut's death had torn open.

Because Albert was only fifteen, Papa or Mama would drive him, once or twice a week, to Bad Ems to work with the priest at St Martin's. He also stood ready to help the priests that came to Singhofen on their biweekly visits. It seemed he was taking Waltraut's dying wish seriously. Gradually, he had started laughing and joking again, returning to that Albert who had come to the farm on summer holidays those several years before. Outwardly, he appeared to be regaining his emotional strength, a sense of peace.

But when we were alone, he still loved to talk about women and his active, teen-aged interest in them. He luxuriated in their attention, sometimes with what sounded like shades of desperation. I would let him talk and joke, and go along with him, but slowly I was realizing more and more that this wasn't my own field of interest.

As an only son, being around Daniel had incited my appreciation of fraternal camaraderie. It was quickly becoming something that I was not only accustomed to, but looked forward to, and for the easy, affirming comfort that our near-brotherly help and companionship brought.

But that ease was also not to last.

After the Nazi-dominated Reichstag had passed the *Enabling Act* on March 24, establishing Hitler's dictatorship, it set about ripping away all signs and memory of our dear Republic. Soon thereafter, the Conservatory handed out official booklets detailing reverted, or new flags.

Gramma declaimed, "That dwarf has stolen the gold, our golden democracy!"

The beautiful black-red-gold tricolor of the Republic was done away with, replaced by that dull black-white-red scheme, reinstalled from the old Kaiser-devastated Empire.

Beyond that, the Nazi Party's swastika was installed everywhere.

I knew from using the powerfully concise and evocative signs and notation of Music, that if there was anything that the Nazis *did* understand, it was the power of simple symbols, and of facile—even if wrong or absolutely insane!—starkly stated slogans. They were using the power of propaganda skillfully to denigrate, to override, to erase German memory of democratic government, of civility.

On the 10th of April that year, the Conservatory was gutted of all its teachers who were Jewish, who had Jewish wives, a Jewish parent or grandparent, or who were foreigners. Its long-time director and my friend, Professor Sekles, was dismissed immediately, only to die shortly thereafter.

Music classes became very crowded as they had to be combined under the remaining faculty; or they had to be cancelled outright. All of us left there struggled to keep things going. I even started helping by teaching less-advanced students. Just imagine me, at 12, teaching! I had already been graduated from the school in Singhofen—Thank you, Gramma, Edo and Reinhold, and the encyclopedia!—so at least I was somewhat prepared!

The new director, Herr Wetzelsberger, asked my parents if I could be there full time, to help cover the reduced number of instructors, "for the good of the Reich." Of course, they agreed; what else was one allowed to do now, once that phrase had been uttered? Soon, I was staying in Frankfurt the full class week and going home to Singhofen only on occasional weekends.

The problem I faced was that the new teachers they brought in were, in many cases, ill-prepared, and in the worst cases, incompetent. I found myself having to correct things (very diplomatically, naturally) that other teachers had done during lessons, including instructions as rudimentary as those for finger placement! It did not bode well for the quality of the Nazified Conservatory!

Frau Drescher removed the mezuzah from the thick, ancient frame inside the front door; I found myself continuing to touch the shadow where it had hung whenever I stepped out that door. For these, my friends, I could still say a prayer for "the days of your children," even as we all slipped, step by too-little-noticed step, into renewed bondage.

My anxiety mounted feverishly late that summer.

The Nazis had pushed through their "Law for the Prevention of Genetically Diseased Offspring"—what everyone called "the Sterilization Law"—in July. It was to come into full effect the following January, 1934. This statute placed Hannah in great danger. Both palsied and Jewish, she was doubly in jeopardy.

While struggling over the situation, I began to form an idea, to nurture a plan. But I had to see if I could extract supporting information from Albert, first.

That next weekend we sat alone in my room talking. After leading him through some innocent questions about what had gone on at his father's Frankfurt apartment, I started asking about Konrad's activities.

"You didn't like your grandmother's priest ... who was it, Arno Hagen? ... did you?"

"Nah. He was too, well, *unholy*, ya know?"

"What do you mean?"

"You know how most priests—at least the ones you pay attention to!—are thin? They look like they take care of the parish first and themselves last."

"Yeah, I've noticed that."

"So, he was fat, a real *Goering*, and his nose was always red, like he'd been at the wine all day. His hair was always oily, slicked down like Hitler's. He was just, well, so greasy!"

"Ugh! Not what you'd think the bishops strive for, is it?

"Did your father or Arno complain about any problems they were having with other priests, or any of the Protestant churchmen around Frankfurt?"

"Well, I do remember their bitching about three main ones who kept confronting them about this or that Nazi policy. Arno was mad, too, because the two Catholics were his superiors; and, of course, he couldn't challenge the Protestant hierarchy directly about the other one!"

"You mean two were senior priests, or such? Do you remember their names?"

"Yeah, the one that bothered him the most was his own father confessor, Father Baecker. I remember that because he was one of the ones who often said mass, back when Oma and I would stop afterwards for pastries.

"The other was Father Vogler, the acting-assistant to the bishop, attached to the staff at the Dom. He'd call him 'Vater Vögeler' [Father Fucker] and they'd all laugh like it was the funniest joke they'd ever heard," Albert said with a sneer of undisguised disgust.

"I don't remember exactly who the protestant minister was, something like *Wolf* or *Wulf*," he paused.

"No! It was *Wurfel*!"

"Were your dad and his friends angry enough to confront, or even strike out against them?"

"Nah. They talked big, but at the end of the evening they were too drunk to remember what they'd talked about earlier. Even Arno got wasted. In fact, he was usually the first to pass out!"

I made a mental note of the names. I *had* to remember!

After Albert had supplied this information, I let him lead the conversation off in any direction he wanted, even talking about girls. I didn't want him to have any idea that I had actually wanted those names, or to ask why I had posed those questions.

———————

The weekend passed agonizingly slowly.

The first chance that next week that any free time coincided with a mass at the Dom, I rushed from the conservatory. Jumping onto the streetcar directly toward the cathedral, I attended mass there, then waited to speak to one of the priests.

I had made mental notes of who officiated, and afterwards, found a priest—a thin one!—that I thought I could talk to. I excused myself and asked if he knew either a Father Baecker or a Father Vogler. He smiled.

"I know Father Baecker, but I'm the only priest by the name of *Vogler* in the diocese," he said.

"What can I do for you?"

"Father, I have heard that you are a righteous person, not afraid to confront a problem."

"I would not be so bold as to claim that distinction, although I *have* gotten myself into trouble for things I hold sacred! But what is your concern, …?"

"Eduard Meyer, Father."

"So, Eduard, what is troubling you?"

He motioned for us to walk farther away from the sacristy, through the choir and toward the nave. He turned to the right, toward the Lady Chapel and stopped, directly in front of the *Sleeping-Mary* Altar. I hoped it was a good omen; surely Mary would be watchful over a girl bearing the name of the Panagia's own Jewish mother, Hannah! St. Anne!

We stepped to a distance from any stragglers, ones who had yet to leave after mass.

"Father, I have a friend who needs help, and I need your assistance to be able to help her!"

My voice rang with more emotion than I had expected.

"I see, my son, and what is this about?"

"The sterilization law, Father."

His eyes opened wide; his face lost its easy look; he glanced around. In a softer, more intense voice he continued.

"Tell me more, my son."

I explained the situation, Frau Drescher, the boarding house, and Hannah's intelligence, despite her disability. I emphasized her palsy, her physical helplessness.

"She's a cripple, Father, and a Jew. And I'm afraid if they take her…"

I had to stop, to clamp my quivering lips together.

"I understand, Eduard. You're a very brave young man, and a credit to your family and the Church. However, I'm not sure what I can do…"

"Why would they think they would have to do that to her, Father? With her physical condition, I don't understand how she could even have a child!"

He looked me deeply in the face. I could see in his eyes a mind now running through options, possibilities, courses of action.

"Well … hmm … perhaps … yes, *he* would know … … Eduard, you've just given me an idea. What is the address? I know a doctor that I might call on. When will you be back at Frau Drescher's? Will Hannah be there at that time, too?"

After detailing the boarding house, I continued, "… around 6 this evening, Father. Yes, Father, since the start of the year, she stays hidden within the house or its back garden."

"I will see if I can bring the doctor by at that time. No one else can be there! Can you manage that?"

"Yes, I believe so, Father. If it's necessary, I'll see to it."

"It is life or death, Eduard, so please do see to it!"

"Yes, Father, I will. Thank you so much, Father, thank you!"

I turned to go. He called my name, so that I turned back around.

With the hint of hope, he gave me the blessing, concluding "Vade in pace, fili mi!" [*Go in peace, my son!*]

"Thank you, Father!"

I crossed myself and started to turn to leave, but stopped in my tracks. The organist for the next, larger, Lutheran service had started his traditional, early-morning summons, the traditional hymn-setting of "𝔚𝔞𝔠𝔥𝔢𝔱 𝔞𝔲𝔣 𝔯𝔲𝔣𝔱 𝔲𝔫𝔰 𝔡𝔦𝔢 𝔖𝔱𝔦𝔪𝔪𝔢." [*Awaken! The Voice Calls Us.*] I walked at a snail's pace toward the door at the end of the northern transept listening, reveling in the rich, echoing tones.

I could not help but hum along, to sing the hymn in my mind. I stood, waiting for the swirling, final chords, for the caressing silence. Then I pushed the great door open, exiting the cathedral through this, the *Emperor's Portal*, and ran to the nearest streetcar stop to rush back to the Conservatory before I was missed by that local klatch, in a nation now infested with *foolish virgins*.

At lunch, I made certain that the Dreschers had no plans of visitors that evening. After classes, I rushed from the Conservatory to the boarding house, to find that Father Vogler was already there.

With him in Frau Drescher's sitting room was a distinguished, well-dressed man with thinning, gray-brown hair. He was holding a stethoscope to Hannah's chest, listening. As I stepped into the room, Frau Drescher came over, hugged me, and said, "Thank you, Edi! I would never have thought of this!"

Together, we moved closer to the examination.

Sitting on the sofa, watching, Daniel reached out and touched my arm as I passed him. I looked over and he smiled.

After several minutes of examination, concentrating on his stethoscope, his fingers holding Hannah's eyelids open, his hands checking her, repeating the motions again, punctuated by serious, sigh-inflated pauses, the doctor asked Frau Drescher, "You were in distress during your labor with her?"

"Yes, doctor. The midwife was forced at last to fetch a physician to help."

"And she is how old, again?"

"Fourteen, almost fifteen, Doctor Gutekunst."

"And she's never had her period?" he asked.

Taken aback by so blunt, so public a question, Frau Drescher answered protectively, almost a-whisper, "No, Doctor, never."

"I see," he said, standing, looking at Hannah and rubbing his chin in thought.

"Frau Drescher," he said, "I believe that the rigors of birth that resulted in her palsy may have caused some damage to Hannah's glands. In her case, I believe they are creating insufficient hormones now, female ones in particular, a deficiency that is causing her ovaries not to mature with the rest of her body. This may well be treatable in future.

"However, for your daughter's sake, right now, I can sign—in all good faith!—a statement declaring medically, officially that she is already sterile, unable to bear children. This will distance her from the threat of this noxious new law. Again, I assure you that her condition may not be irreversible, but for the current purposes of this horrible statute, she is sterile."

Father Vogler interrupted, "You are certain of this, Doctor? There will be no questions asked, no further imposition on the family from this statute?"

"Yes! Completely certain, Father! I will write my explanation, and declaration that there is no reason to move her, and in such plain and final terms as even a Nazi will understand! I have stalwart friends still in government who will assist us. We shall use this to make certain she is removed from any list, never to appear on any new ones!"

Frau Drescher did not seem to know whether to be joyous or crestfallen. The doctor leaned over to Hannah, "Don't worry my dear, when you are an adult, we may help you with this problem. You, too, might one day be a mother!"

"Excuse, me, Doctor, but when can you have this ready?" Father Vogler interjected.

"I will have it done by tomorrow morning!" he answered with undisguised pleasure.

"Thank you, Doctor," Hannah was able to say. It was one of the clearest, most easily understandable things I had ever heard her pronounce.

He rubbed her permanently cupped hand gently and leaned over to her again, "You are very welcome, my dear!"

Frau Drescher hugged and kissed her daughter, fussing with her child's hair and clothes, straightening here, folding there, smoothing it all, making sure her little girl was comfortable.

The doctor gathered up his paraphernalia and prepared to leave. As he stepped toward the door, Daniel stood to hand him his hat.

"Thank you, Daniel!" he said as he took it.

"You're welcome, Doctor, and thank you!" Daniel held out his hand; the doctor switched hat-holding hand to shake it.

"And thank you, too, Father," Daniel said to the priest.

"You're very welcome, Daniel!" Father Vogler said. "And Edi!"

"Yes, Father?"

"You did a great thing, coming to me to ask if we might help your friends. You may very well have saved a life today! You're very brave!"

"If I am, it's only because I've had a good teacher."

"What do you mean?"

"Three years ago, my father saved a boy from drowning. He told me that the one thing that gives meaning to life is service to others, even if at times it means you may endanger your own!"

He stood there looking at me, rather surprised.

"That is some lesson you've just preached, my son!"

He looked at the doctor, who smiled and nodded in agreement.

"You know…"

He paused, weighing his thoughts, "I want you to have something to mark the day. Hold out your hand."

He reached into his pocket and pulled out a small, velvet sack, which he placed onto my upturned palm.

"Open it."

I pulled the woven strings that held the velvet-soft sack's mouth closed, spreading it carefully. Through it I extracted a delicately worked, rosewood and silver rosary.

"I brought it back with me from Rome several years ago. It was blessed by Benedict XV, the 'Peace Pope' who—you are far too young to remember!—strove to bring an early, and quick end to the devastation of the Great War. I want you to have it, Edi, to take with you out into the world. It shouldn't remain hidden within a priest's musty pocket!"

"Are you sure you want me to have it, Father?"

"I'm certain, Edi! I pray it may give you strength to persevere!"

"Thank you, Father!" I looked down at it again: it was so beautifully wrought!

He then blessed it and me. Turning to the Dreschers he stretched his arms wide, out towards them.

"The blessings of the God of Abraham, of Isaac and of Jacob be upon you, your house and family, Frau Drescher!"

"Thank you, Father Vogler," Frau Drescher said, stepping quickly over to him. She shook his hand eagerly, and thanked him and the doctor again. I was distracted by the gift, and the depth of meaning residing within it.

Frau Drescher swung the heavy front door open for them; the doctor tipped his hat. The two men stepped out of the light, and were gone.

The deed was done the very next day.

I saw Father Vogler regularly after that. We became good friends as we talked more, and he arranged for me to give little concerts to entertain the infirm and elderly at the care-houses of the parishes in and around Frankfurt. I also played the cathedral organ for many of Father Vogler's masses, particularly the earliest morning ones, when no sane musician was yet awake.

I had never been forced, nor even encouraged, to go to confession. Father Vogler told me not to worry.

"I hear your confession, your contrition and your compassion when you play. Your notes are your novena!"

————[1934]————

That next year, Berlin commanded that we give the stiff-armed, Fascist, Hitler-salute, even in school. Herr Wetzelsberger was more than happy to enforce its use at the Conservatory.

We did it so much that it became a habit: you did it and didn't think about it, so that it became meaningless, whatever it was supposed to signify. But, unfortunately it could grind the conceit of Hitler-superiority into your brain, even if you didn't want to let it happen.

Inching a foolish, too-compliant Germany farther down that slippery path to perdition, the problems made for the Jews came in slight waves rather than one sudden, alarming flood.

But those waves were mounting ever higher as the months passed.

Frau Drescher was not the only one who now lived in daily fear.

When I went home for the first weekend of June, 1935, I told Papa and Mama what she was having to face. Just that week, SA-men had walked the streets, searching for (no longer advertizable) businesses owned by Jews, so that they could draw crude pictures and scribble hate-slogans on the store-fronts. Some of them searched out people they just thought looked Jewish, so they could taunt, humiliate, beat and abuse them.

I also let my folks know that I was no longer allowed to play Spanish music, merely because of the anti-fascist attitude of that government.

Later that day, from my room I heard Papa talking on the phone, downstairs in the great room. At that distance, I heard only the final phrases: "Yes. Yes, indeed.

"Very good. See you there."

I asked Papa what was going on but all he would say was that I'd find out in good time, that it was vital to keep things unexplained for the time being.

So, I was left in suspense.

Back in Frankfurt, on Tuesday of that next week I returned to the boarding house at lunchtime to find Frau Drescher in the parlor talking to Mama, Papa,

Father Vogler … and Bartomeu! I was so happy to see him! He was still svelte, so handsome and distinguished, and the sight of him reminded me immediately of those vibrant, freer days in Barcelona!

What was happening, Papa finally detailed, was that we were buying the boarding house from Frau Drescher! She would continue to live there and run it as long as she wanted, but it would be owned by us "Aryans" officially, allowing its rental-advertisements to return to the newspapers, and removing any goon-regime pretext for causing Frau Drescher trouble.

Papa had called on Bartomeu to handle the financial side of the deal. He had also asked Father Vogler to attend so that he might find us a favorably inclined local attorney who would handle the procedure without causing difficulty.

Couched in this subversive, liberal conspiracy, the deal went through quickly.

The insidious drive to deprive Jews of their property was already infecting the bureaucracy: we took possession quickly, the first week of July, that very next month, with the sale recorded at a very low price. This would please the Nazis, who were trying so hard to gouge the Jews.

Bartomeu would take the balance of the worth he had calculated from the building, its location, its potential income, and create an account at his bank for Frau Drescher, to hold this surfeit. Because this part of the sale would be a transfer within the bank in Zurich, Nazi officials would have no idea it had occurred, and could not misappropriate the funds. This was the only way Papa would have it: he would not steal.

Toward the end of their discussions that afternoon, after the deal and arrangements had been decided, Frau Drescher said unexpectedly that she had a favor to ask of Bartomeu.

As we stood watching, she stepped to her bureau, removed papers and an inkwell, and tugged on a secluded latch. The door to a wide, but thin, secret drawer popped open.

I could see that it contained some small stacks of cash, neatly bound in twine, and a few other small items, coins, a pocket-watch and such. But lying beside those was a flat object, ensconced in dark velveteen. She extracted it, extremely carefully, brought it over and placed it on the table.

She drew from it a richly worked, leather-covered case, bearing that so-ornate German imperial seal in high relief: bright gold embossed into the black calf's skin of the cover.

"Herr Ferrer, please take this back to Switzerland with you, for safe keeping."

We stepped closer; she continued her unveiling without pausing for a response.

The case was richly wrought internally with velvet on its inside top, again with the Kaiser's imperial seal in gold leaf. She extracted a yellowing piece of paper, unfolded it with tenderness, and laid it flat for us to see.

"𝔉ür tapferes 𝔙erhalten," [*For Meritorious Conduct*] it announced.

Beneath the Kaiser's stern, engraved image and the title announcing the grant,

Im Namen S. M. des Kaisers und Königs

[*In the Name of His Majesty, Emperor and King*],

ornate *Kurrent*-inked handwriting explained that, on 18 August 1917, Lieutenant Emil Daniel Drescher had "by bravest, selfless action put himself into the way of continuous direct harm, rescuing his men and other officers of his company from gas attack while under direct, heavy enemy fire" near Passchendaele.

At the bottom, beneath the repeated, boiler-plate proclamation, "für tapferes Verhalten vor dem Feinde" [*for meritorious conduct in the face of the enemy*], the commendation had been signed by General von Ludendorff, himself.

She shifted the container's inner sheaf to reveal what lay beneath.

"Iron Cross, first class," Papa said in quiet wonder. After his eyes had traced its form—the heavy, metal cross, with embossed imperial crown, capital 'W' and '1917'—and that vision had made its own deep impression, he looked up to remark, "Frau Drescher, that may well have been the battle in which my own father was killed!"

"Yes, Herr Meyer, Edi has told us about that," she said sadly.

"Before today, I hadn't wanted to bring this out, to avoid reminding anyone of that terrible war, or you of your loss. But I am forced to do so now, because I would like this, and his other awards, to be kept safely out of the hands of the Nazis. I have heard that they are confiscating and destroying the medals that had been awarded to even the bravest, most patriotic Jews!

"We, all of us," she looked around at her friends and family-remnant, "lost so much trying to help win that horrible war, yet all to no avail. Then—or now!"

"Frau Drescher, I will be very happy to keep it safe for you!" Bartomeu reassured her. "I will place it securely within the bank's vaults!"

She smiled weakly; regret at the separation seeming to temper her display of gratitude.

"Thank you, Herr Ferrer! And please add Herr Meyer's and your name to your records for access to it, in case I am unable. Times are just so uncertain!"

She gazed upon, ran her fingers lightly over this, the old Empire's at-that-time grateful memorial to her late husband. She reconstructed the precious parcel, hugged it, holding it tightly to her breast, then surrendered it for safe-keeping.

I grew distressed with the obvious, gnawing question. How could a nation that had inspired such selfless courage, that was still capable of eliciting such devotion, turn so viciously on these same men it had once acclaimed heroes? How could it be so double-faced, flighty and dismissive, to encourage and decorate them once, then denigrate and deny them thereafter, simply because they were Jewish? The very thought hung like a gray shroud over the face of Germany.

No one succeeds by disdain, by disunion, by hatred. No one!

———————

The weekend after our meeting in Frau Drescher's parlor was my 14th birthday.

Bartomeu stayed in the city that week to get all details of our purchase of the house worked through, and then accompanied me to Singhofen on Friday for a visit. It was a treat to be able to show him, finally, the big, beautiful piano, my *Steiner*—I hadn't realized he had already seen it at Edo's in Berlin!—and all the rest of the farm. He wanted to meet Eva, too!

My baby was now eleven, and starting to slow down. Papa had built steps for the foot of my bed, to let her climb up onto it since she could no longer jump that high, unless I grabbed her rear and pushed her!

She loved *our Bartomeu*, and would edge closer and closer, pushing against him, a 34-kg puppy scooting furtively onto his lap, like she used to do, so long ago, with Reinhold. Maybe she remembered my uncles, too, and caught their scent in the cologne he wore. I wondered. I hoped.

The weekend passed too quickly, too wonderfully. Bartomeu rode the return-train into Frankfurt with me, to catch the train to Zurich. At the main station, I wanted to hug him tightly before he left, but I was getting too old for that.

Sorrow shook me as he had to turn away, to board the train.

The engine snorted, puffed and wheezed its way out of the station, depriving me of the closest living memory of my uncles, and the utter happiness they had bestowed on my childhood.

Sad for myself, unsure of the world, I walked quickly to catch the streetcar for the solitary trip back to the, now *our*, boarding house.

Kristall — Chapter 11 — Crystal

The worst Christmas gift I had ever received came from Berlin in December of 1936.

The command was final: I had to join the Hitler Youth. Not just me, though; it was mandatory for all "Aryan" boys 14 years and older!

Hitler's grasp was everywhere and tightening. You couldn't walk down a block anywhere without being blasted by propaganda: posters, signs and swastikas. He was continuing to weasel his way not just into our transient, public attention, but into our everyday, private lives.

Gramma was both livid with rage and racked by anguish. She spoke angrily of the coming war, that Hitler was just padding the ranks of the Army, getting our young men ready to die under orders.

"Worse than the Kaiser! Worse, I tell you!" was her new mantra.

Papa became ever more alarmed by her saying such things, and tried time and again to get her to restrain herself.

"You can't fix this horrible situation by yourself, Mama!" he pleaded with her, seated at the kitchen table, "and if anyone hears you say this, they will make our lives impossible!"

"Hänsel! I didn't raise you to be afraid! And certainly not to go along with these gangsters!"

"Mama! You will get us all SHOT! Even the girls!"

That got her attention, at last.

They talked, argued round and round, talked some more. He seemed finally to be edging her closer to reaching comprehension, but not acquiescence. She was not happy, *at all*!

He stopped, made sure she was looking directly at him before continuing in singular severity.

"Mama, the area-gauleiter accosted me in the village this morning. He spoke threateningly, wanting to know why, as a prominent member of the community, I hadn't joined the Party."

Gramma frowned at him askance, as if she knew already what was coming.

"I told him I had been so busy with the farm that I thought it best to leave the decisions to men like him."

She twisted her lips in disgust.

"I told him that if he thought I could help, I would join."

"Oh, Hans! How could you!" She shouted and hammered the table with the side of her fist.

"Mama! I told you! I can't work against the dictatorship by standing outside it! You have to remember that an ant can't bite a dragon on the tail to kill it. You must work inside if you are to gain any control—at the least to gain some idea of where the beast is headed!"

The argument dragged on.

"Well, I will not have any of that ignorant troll's crap in my room! Especially not any of those hideous pictures of that Austrian traitor, that criminal!"

"Certainly not, Mama! We'll keep the propaganda near the front door. That way it will be easily visible to any nosey visitors, while not polluting the rest of the house. We *will* have to fly the flag, though."

"Shit!"

My mouth fell open! I'd never heard Gramma swear! It was shocking!

"I know, Mama! But at least if it's hanging outside, we won't have to look at it in here!"

Gramma was not pleased. But she was very smart, and crafty. Her disgust for the Kaiser had been overtaken by loathing of the new regime from early on. And now, although yet fighting infirmity from the old cow-kick injury, she was still fully ready to help Papa in any way she could. My Gramma was strong: wily and strong.

———————————

With Papa subsequently a party member, we started getting more information about instances of insanity set to infect the Taunus and Frankfurt. We made sure to hang a swastika-flag out at the boarding house in Frankfurt, and (because of its location within the edge of the erstwhile Jewish quarter) to put a sign up stating flatly "Aryan Owned" near its front-door. We apologized to Frau Drescher, but assured her it was best for her and her family's protection. Slowly, the surrounding houses and businesses had been sold to, or stolen by, new, non-Jewish owners as the age-old, Jewish neighborhood disintegrated under growing, pernicious Party pressure.

Father Vogler helped us locate a pharmacist who would continue to fill the orders for Hannah's medication. The package said it was for Gramma, but we made sure Hannah got it, anyway.

As a Jew, Daniel was no longer permitted to go to school, so Frau Drescher and I mapped out his home-educational program, and I helped him keep working ahead.

From staying more weekends, I became accustomed rapidly to being the Dreschers' honorary *oyrekh auf Shabbes* [*guest for Sabbath*]. Without realizing it, I was learning to span two cultures. It didn't seem like I was doing much by being part of their rites, but Daniel explained that it was very important to them, to be able to extend the hospitality of the Sabbath, to anyone of reverence, especially to a friend.

I was just happy that I could help, surrounded as I was by the loving kindness and innate decency of these three gentle people, people who had become my second family.

I fucking hated the fucking Hitler fucking Youth!

Militaristic bullshit, lying, *Wehrmacht*, fighting, *Luftwaffe*, Jew-hating, *SS*, propaganda, still more lies: more Hitler crap this and Hitler dreck that!

I understood now everything that Gramma had said about the Nazis, and shared her loathing! The only thing that kept my anger and revulsion from lashing out was the voice of Clara, telling me to concentrate, to keep the melodies flowing, despite the cacophony of this caustic flood.

I survived the Hitler Youth ordeal both because I looked so much like the propaganda-prize, typecast Nazi *Aryan*, and because I was taller than the boys in our local chapter. Farm-work had made me stronger than the rest: I had actually punched out one of the guys when we had been forced to box. A brainless, city-punk of a kid, he had called me a "piano fag" and I was damned sure that I was going to "make that varmint eat his words!" —as Uncle Edo would have laughed.

"Play them for the fools they are! Drain their strength into your own!" Papa and Gramma urged. And that was exactly what I did! I made them think that I was the best damned Hitler Youth I could be, because I was determined to learn everything that could possibly be turned against them when the time was right. At least that was my hope; and this hope fed my determination: it kept me strong.

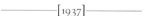

[1937]

In a summer's warm, clearing-afternoon breeze, I lay across my bed, leafing through Aunt Franzi's Zurich-discovered, regime-forbidden gift of a new, parallel German-Spanish printing of the complete poetry of Federico García Lorca.

Within the beauty of his language, his Iberian lyricism, he expressed an inner longing that I could hear, but was still uncertain of. He had been killed by Franco's fascists the year before because of those very sounds—shot by those terrified of a free voice.

Mama stepped softly past the propped half-open door, into the room, clasping a tightly folded newspaper. Sadness gripped her face. She placed the journal on top of my book, pointed to one notice, turned and, without a word, walked away.

The Nazi editor crowed: "the degenerate Jew-composer" George Gershwin had died suddenly two days before, on July 11, of medically-inflicted brain injury: only two months before his 39th birthday, in September.

I dropped my head and cried.

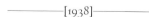

[1938]

The once so high standards of the Conservatory continued to fester, with ever more rot from the local Nazis who, of course, as "Aryans", acted as if they were the know-it-all godlings of earth. Even the regime-installed, Nazi Conservatory-director since 1936, Hermann Reutter, did nothing to avert the efforts of the city's party-controlled government to degrade the *Hoch'sche* into a musical elementary school.

Fear of saying, reading or merely referring to something prohibited, and of thereby being referred to the Gestapo, meant that no one deviated from Nazi-blessed *scripture*. Everyone was expected now to have, aside from the every-day, regime-blessed, ministerially controlled press, a copy of *Mein Kampf* somewhere close at hand. I had two. One sat on my desk at the *Hoch'sche*—I was teaching so much at Conservatory and Hochschule that the staff had repurposed an underused supply closet for me to use as a little office!—and one lay at the boarding house.

Not enshrined in worshipful display, that second copy was nevertheless ready to be grabbed for presentation in case of political emergency.

In late March of 1938, Paul Hindemith returned to give another concert. He was under constant surveillance by the Nazis, who held his compositions too close to the "degenerate" art they were set on destroying. I knew, too, that he had a Jewish wife; this set him firmly within their cross-hairs. Only his international stature had protected him so far from worse harassment, or arrest.

He complimented me again by requesting that I work with him in this performance, as soloist, while he conducted the local radio symphony orchestra.

Herr Hindemith surprised me by outlining a program quite demanding for any pianist! The first half would be Beethoven's Third Piano Concerto: enjoyable for me, but not the most strenuous of his concertos. However, the second half would top this with Brahms' Second Piano Concerto, a four-movement piece that was over fifty minutes of work! I hadn't had a chance to perform the Brahms before, so it was an innervating challenge!

The concert, given on the (for me, always emotion-laden) stage of the *Opera* went extremely well. Beethoven was always beloved; the so-lyrical Brahms was extremely well received. Standing ovations were followed by encores: one from the orchestra (Mozart's overture to *The Marriage of Figaro*) and, with Hindemith's push, two from me, first Schumann's Toccata in C, then his tenth Impromptu on a theme of Clara Wieck. (Yes, *my* Clara!)

The audience's reaction was so impassioned that Herr Hindemith motioned me back for an additional encore. I decided to pull out an emotional heavy-hitter on this one, so I played Schubert's soulfully ardent Impromptu No. 3 in G-flat major, again to great acclaim. But that was enough for one night!

A post-performance reception required our presence.

Among all its many well-wishers, Hindemith seemed most determined to introduce me to the visiting, imminent pianist, Angelike Gellert. I recalled that Papa had obtained some of her more recent gramophone-captured, prize-winning performances.

Frau Gellert, with delicate hands, not too tall and growing a bit wider in the foundation, was one of the few luminaries that the Nazis had persuaded to remain in Germany after the regime change. Goebbels had even talked her into leading the Classical-music program within the *KdF*, his ministry's *Kraft durch Freude*, the *Strength Through Joy* program.

She grabbed me excitedly by the arm before Herr Hindemith had even finished the introduction!

"Eduard! You were magnificent! Wasn't he Paul?" she exuded passionately.

"Certainly, Geli! Exactly as I told you, yes?" Herr Hindemith answered.

"No, no! Absolutely so much better! Your Beethoven was masterful! Your

124

Brahms, magnificent! Your Schumann, unrivaled! Your Schubert, astounding! You had me in great tears of tenderest ecstasy! So poignant! Such heartfelt, soul-caressing melodies!

"Dearest, you *must* come to work with me in the *KdF*! What are you doing now? Are you living here in Frankfurt? What are your plans? Have you ever toured? How large is your repertoire? It must be quite extensive! What concerts have you given? You must tell me everything!" she gushed without pause, latching herself to my arm and leading me, captive, to seize for herself an instantly refilled glass of champagne.

Her sips at last gave me the break in which to insert quickly what I was doing, where I was living, the situation at the Conservatory, everything that I dared, until she interrupted.

"But will you go to university, my dear?"

A startling question!

"I haven't thought that far ahead, Frau Gellert. Frankly, I am more concerned about the draft! I'm afraid I might be called up within the next couple of years!"

"Nonsense! Absolute nonsense! I will get you permanently exempted!

"You are a national prize, a budding treasure! We can't have you ever sent off to some ghastly Wehrmacht training, and possibly damage your masterful hands!" She grabbed them, "My God! They remind me so of dearest Serge!" clasping one to her cheek.

"Leave it to me! I will tell Goebbels to have the Führer give you an inviolable exemption!

"There is no doubt! No question! You simply *must* come to Leipzig! You will attend the University there! Just like Bach's sons, and Kuhnau, Wagner—even our dear Goethe!"

"Thank you, Frau Gellert! I hadn't even thought that much about it! I've just been so busy!"

"And you shall live in my house—I have a large, lonely house, with three grand pianos! I have long considered opening my rooms to protégés, and you shall be first!

"You will live there, and we shall play, practice and prepare, and then tour for the *KdF*! You will love Leipzig! Such a marvelous, musical city! The University and the Music Conservatory!—you remember, of course, that Mendelssohn himself founded it!—you simply cannot do better! Saxony will enchant you just as it has me! You know that I am originally from Hamburg, a lovely coastal town, but ah! The sea breeze can be so humid in summer and so cuttingly cold in winter! Have you ever gone there, dear? To Hamburg? Of course, you haven't! Why should anyone wander away from the Rhine Valley, the Lorelei and the marvelous Taunus? And so close to the most wonderful wines! When we tour, we shall travel all across Germany and you will see and fall in love with every part you have till now only read and dreamed about!

"So, dearest, you will come to Leipzig and play with my *KdF* program! We will make sure to keep you away from the army, and make you famous, acclaimed and beloved 'from the Maas to the Memel' as the anthem says! Wouldn't that be marvelous, dear? Most certainly, it would! Now, will you join me in the *KdF*?"

I stood, dumbfounded.

Waiting for the emphatic waves to subside, I had no idea what to say! Here, this national icon had swept in and planned my future for me! Not that I was convinced that I could object! If she could just get me excused from the draft, it would be worth any amount of trouble that anything else might attract!

I looked up at Hindemith, his nod a decided 'yes'.

"Thank you, Frau Gellert! That would be most kind! I would be honored!"

She smiled broadly, "Of course, you would be, dear! It's a fantastic opportunity! For both of us! You see, I have been searching for someone with whom I could play duets—particularly those of Mozart!—without having to worry about dragging an apprentice through fingering lessons. You are perfect! A teacher! A master! At what, only 16? You simply must come to Leipzig!

"I will speak to the officials at the University and make all the arrangements! And I will telephone Goebbels well before I travel to Berlin in two months.

"You shall make no other plans, you understand?" she declared, shaking her finger in a threateningly maternal way, pausing only to reach into a tiny handbag to extract a slip of paper.

"Here is my card: the address, everything! You will send me directions on how to contact you here, and I shall make *all* the dreadfully bureaucratic arrangements!"

She grabbed me by the shoulders—so strong for so diminutive a frame!—and pulled me down to her for adieu-kisses, then pushed me back aright.

"Now, away with you! You are far too young to be trapped at this horribly boring, old-fogey affair! Go home and rest, and start dreaming of how exciting life will be in beautiful, lyrical Leipzig!"

"Yes, ma'am, Frau Gellert!"

I bowed slightly, turned and stepped away. As I did, I heard her scold Hindemith, "Paul! How has this delicious treasure been hiding here all this time? You should have told me sooner!"

I was too far away to hear his reply. But it didn't matter. I was so excited! If this meant no army duty, it was absolutely fantastic!

Oh, happy Gramma! No Passchendaele for me!

———————————

The university-paperwork didn't exit the bureaucracy until September, and by then I was informed that I could start only after the new year. But the draft deferment had come through that spring, only three weeks after I had spoken with Frau Gellert! It was just in time, since I wanted to be sure to have it early, before I had turned 17 that June. The notice from the regime stated that a permanent deferment had been issued, signed by the Führer himself. Frau Gellert wasn't exaggerating when she said she'd procure it!

With the delay in enrollment, I was studying some, but more usually stayed in our Frankfurt boarding house, working at the sad remnants of my now-eviscerated Conservatory.

Toward the end of October, while at home in Singhofen, I explained to my family that I was getting extremely uneasy: the air of hatred infesting the city was growing ever heavier. When it was time for me to leave on the Sunday of that first weekend of November, Papa rode the train with me back into Frankfurt. He had business to tend to there, and also wanted to be at the boarding house, to review things with Frau Drescher, to make sure she stood in need of nothing, particularly in the face of this mounting trouble.

The next day, Monday morning, the papers announced that a Frankfurt-born, German diplomat, Ernst vom Rath, had been shot in Paris by a Jewish youth, Herschel Grynszpan. It took two full days for the Nazis to organize and stir up enough furor—they purposely delayed the outrage until the anniversary of the Beerhall Putsch!—but that Wednesday erupted in chaotic, targeted rage.

Although overcast, the warm-for-autumn, 11° weather of November 9th practically invited Nazi thugs onto the street. In a fury, they—the SA, the SS, party members, even common folk seduced into the mob—set violently upon anyone that they thought might be Jewish, anyone they just didn't like the looks of. The brutes even attacked older women and terrorized little kids!

They ransacked and burned the synagogues, and any yeshivas, academies or prayer-rooms they chanced upon. The surge was so powerful that those of us not infected by Nazi-disease could do nothing but stand by. Now oppressed, too disjoint, we could only resist tacitly, no longer fight openly against the regime's premeditated, murdering ways.

Papa and I stationed ourselves: standing watch in front of the boarding house.

He wore a fedora and a dark suit with a swastika armband and his Nazi-party pin displayed prominently on his lapel. I was in my brown, swastika- and award-bedecked Hitler Youth uniform. I had also worn my black, knee-high, cavalry-officer-style jack-boots—expensive ones I had won in the HY for horsemanship—specifically to make the uniform look more like that of the dreaded SS.

More than once, even with us standing there, crazed SA men had run up screaming, demanding to know who owned these houses, these businesses. Papa pulled his lapel forward to emphasize his party-membership pin and said with as much loud authority as he could muster, "I do!" The fact that he actually *did* own the boarding house bolstered our ethical strength and fortitude. Moving closer toward him, I helped face them down. They'd often look us over suspiciously—despite the fact that we were both so obviously, stereotypically "Aryan"—before running off to pleasure themselves in some other fetishist act of unthinking evil.

The late afternoon produced louder crashes of shattering glass, closer-rolling clouds of smoke, more desperate cries for help. The situation was eating very deeply at Papa's composure.

A beer-gutted SA thug ran up and shrieked, "Where's the other synagogue?"

Papa yelled, "How the hell should I know?"

At that, the sallow-faced brownshirt simply ran on. What did he mean by "the *other*"?

We stood there for hours; it seemed ages.

The smoke billowed, abated, then surged again.

 Through it all, one of us remained always on guard whenever the other had to step inside. We had no way of knowing the true extent of the pogrom, nor how bad it had become. "Es hat die Dunkelheit an vielen Orten überhand genommen..." [*In many places, darkness has taken over utterly...*]

sprang sorrowfully to mind. Who would not now mouth a needful prayer, "𝕭leib' bei uns, denn es will Abend werden!" [*Abide with us: for it becomes eventide!*]

We feared for all our friends, great and small, known and yet unknown.

A roiling gloom chilled me as I realized that, by all these acts of an utterly rancid inhumanity, what these goons were truly killing was *my* Frankfurt, and *my* Germany: Goethe's, Schiller's—Heine's soulful Denk' ich an Deutschland in der Nacht [{*Whenever*} *I think of Germany, in the night*]—Germany!

After this, neither city nor nation could ever be the same.

Ever!

But worse by far was that it was our very own people, our Germans doing this, obliterating their culture, their history, their nation just like, well, *vandals*. They had become the Kaiser's monster-*Huns*, now turned by Hitler against their own people.

Late that evening, the noise at last died down. The streets became still, largely vacant.

Papa sighed, "Let's go see."

Weak city lights glittered in the multi-colored sparkle of broken-glass diamonds coating the sidewalk. Not far from the boarding house, the sidewalk and half the street were fully carpeted in crystal shards, shattered windows fallen from storefronts and homes, all targeted for their assumed Jewish-association.

Hate-spewing graffiti was scrawled everywhere, some even still visible on the slivers of glass crunching beneath our feet. Scattered across the walk and street before Mendel the Shoykhet's shop were pools and strands of red, here and there mixed within the crystal.

Blood? Whose? I shuddered to think.

We picked our way through the debris, farther down Börnestrasse toward the main synagogue.

Stark against the night stood a still-smoldering, burned-out shell.

Its onion domes had burned into mere spindly metal frames, and the individual, tinted panes of the two-storey-tall, medieval-style window of its façade lay burst by outsiders' lofted projectiles, buckled by inner heat.

Papa approached the large front door, smashed and torn aside within its recessed, gothic-arched enclosure. We stepped through the gaping entry, walking warily into the building, trusting that the walls rose still firm enough not to crash in upon us.

I doffed my *Hitlerjugend* cap: an act of respect, however small, is still respect.

But then I replaced it: my *Drescher-Shabbes* yarmulke was not at hand.

Small fires continued to burn in distinct corners. Lead had flowed from above, where the wooden frame and windchests of the old organ had burned, its pipes melted into oblivion. The ancient pews had been pulled up and piled like kindling; the bimah had been bashed, broken and thrown onto the heap.

The ark ripped open, its scrolls lay shredded, burned, in scattering ashes.

By the light of the building's own angry rafter-candles—a menacing, mourning menorah—we stood, in unwilling witness to utter, mindless mayhem.

My wrath seethed; they had assaulted my teacher, and my second family! Yet the anger and frustration were numbing. Whether to run or to fight was now pointless: I could do neither.

Papa's anguish-graveled voice struggled against the mania of that noxious night: "You will never fully understand how much they mean to you, until you lose one that you love!"

He paused, scanning the painfully mute, deafening devastation, then turned, stepping slowly outwards, back toward a heavy oaken door: hanging forlornly askew in a rage-ruptured portal.

A charred scrap caught the fire-bred breeze and flew up, a parchment-leaf fleeing desperately from the shattered ark toward my chest. I grabbed and missed, then plucked it from that wisp of thieving, soot-stained air to rescue it, hold it securely, assuringly in my hand, not pausing, not daring to glance down at it, nestled close against my disguising, Hitler Youth shirt, lest I lose my way.

The smoke-shrouded journey urged us outwards.

Papa's guarded steps led in slow, deliberate exit, searching for progressive, reverent footholds between the glowing embers of the building's still-burning, rebuking remains.

The boarding house beckoned refuge.

We found the Dreschers huddled within a small, back room, where they had hidden while we were gone.

As we entered, Frau Drescher and Daniel rushed forward, full of anxiety and despairing questions. We told them what we could, but without adding to their anguish. Additional alarm would do them no good.

It was very late. Papa and Daniel helped Frau Drescher with Hannah.

I went to my room. Forlorn, I extricated myself from that feculent uniform, and at the wash basin, tried to scrub away the disappointment, the hurt, the shame, to no avail. I could not look into the mirror, to have to peer into this so "Aryan" face: helpless, feckless, humiliated.

That scrap of parchment!

I extracted it carefully from my pocket. It bore small, intricate lines of ornate Hebrew script: I could try to read it later, but would not let Daniel see it. I stuck it securely, deep against the binding, hidden within my 'safety' copy of *Mein Kampf*. Perhaps it could help cast out the stench of hatred that permeated that book.

I stepped over into Daniel's room. If I had thought that my own anguish was deep, it was as nothing compared to his. Lying in his bed, he shivered, quaking in juvenile fear until he finally tired.

I sat guard beside this, so near a little brother, attentive until, at last, he fell safely asleep.

I, too, dreaded the dawn.

We had to face the facts, the terrible, inescapable facts of the situation.

Yet one must also apprehend that fact-facing is the greatest fear of tyrants.

Still stinging from the terror of Kristallnacht, Papa, after returning to Singhofen, had decided in a moment of enlightened desperation that it was time to get Frau Drescher and her children to safety.

We talked it over and over. Both of us could see the insidious ways the regime was expanding its determined dehumanization of the Jews: it was only a matter of time before Hitler acted on his threats in *Mein Kampf.*

Even though winter had already shoved autumn out of its way and rushed in with its own raw, biting re-occupation, we ourselves had to move, and move immediately. There was no one else to do it; any delay could be too late!

Forced to be extremely secretive with the monies from the legacy, it was imperative for us to keep not only the arrangements, but all transactions out of the notice of the Nazis.

Our Frankfurt bank-accounts surveilled, Bartomeu had retained the payments in Zurich, to disguise the source and schedule of any disbursements. But despite this steep reduction in our condition, we simply had to spirit the Dreschers out of Germany.

Frau Drescher and her children had never had passports; this exposed a major obstacle. With the current state of the government—all Jewish passports had been revoked this year, on October 5—it was unlikely the Nazis would ever grant new ones to the Dreschers.

Shelter was considered, yet Hannah could not be hidden away! This meant that they could only escape overland, and it was we, alone, who would have to effect their transit.

Stealth, speed, and the connivance of not a few friends were of utmost importance. We, ourselves, would be at no little risk; but once it had been done, and done well, the affair should raise no reasons for Gestapo investigation.

With our purchase of the boarding house four years previously, the Dreschers were no longer on the property lists and asset-poverty had reduced their target-visibility to this rapacious regime to near zero.

Tyranny loves money; money adores tyranny.

Every society will learn this to their great cost, sooner or later or, as in our own, German case, too late.

Father Vogler put me in touch with one of his resistance-minded associates.

With the help of the Lutheran minister, Reverend Wurfel, we were able to hire a new boarding house mistress, Frau Guenther, a widowed parishioner of the reverend, one in whom he expressed the greatest ethical confidence. Large, older, with graying hair and soothing, but commanding, voice, she helped the Dreschers pack as lightly, yet as well, as they could. She doted on Hannah, and took leave of them all only after a cascade of grandmotherly pats, hugs, kisses and invocations of God's mercy for speed, safety, and good health. The reverend's confidence had certainly been well-placed.

Through carefully worded telephone calls and more-direct messages relayed by Aunt Franziska, we obtained the ready and active involvement of our Bartomeu.

The city of Barcelona was at that very moment one of the main, violent targets of Franco's Falangist forces. Franco had summoned the Fascist Italian air force to bomb Barcelona that previous March, inflicting the murder of over a thousand people and injuring twice that number. The Spanish Republic was falling quickly to Franco's Nazi-aided, Fascist-emboldened, conservative rebellion.

It appeared that Bartomeu would soon have no free Barcelona to return to.

This steeled his motivation to do everything possible to help us against our own, home-grown Fascists.

Gramma and Mama stayed at home with the girls; Papa and I set out for Frankfurt on December 23rd with tickets and a plan.

Very early the next day, with our having gotten the Dreschers packed, to the station and all aboard, our train departed the Frankfurt Hauptbahnhof.

We were counting on the near certainty that heavily-wrapped Winter would help hide our actions, and that the Christmas-weekend crowds would be self-absorbed and distracted from others' activities. Our departure so early in the morning, at just after 05:30, meant that the numbers within those crowds should be reduced, and those who were there, sleepy and inattentive: common effects of cold and a surfeit of Christmas 'cheer'.

To be confidently inconspicuous, Papa and I wore our uniforms: the same ones that we had publicized while standing guard on Kristallnacht. Although I was wearing a heavy coat over my jack-booted uniform, I made sure that it stayed unfastened, so that it could fall open, for propitious display at any exigent moment. Very often you can be more certain you'll be ignored if you're a flagrant, or even an obnoxious, part of people's expectations, than if you're quiet!

The train would take us from Frankfurt, south along the Rhine to Offenburg, then southeast through the Black Forest to Singen, a small town very near the Swiss border, just 8 km to the northwest of the westernmost arm of Lake Constance. With this town's being so far from any non-Teutonic frontier—sitting between the German-speaking part of Switzerland to the west and, to the east, the Austrian frontier that had disappeared the previous March—we expected minimal risk of being stopped and checked. To be certain, we would leave the train there. To have continued by rail from Singen directly across the Swiss border into Schaffhausen would have been far too dicey!

Only some 130 km into the 350-km trip, at the station in Karlsruhe, two men got on the train and walked slowly through our carriage, scanning everyone seated there. They had the typical look of Gestapo agents—not particularly bright! —too heavy on the skulking, too obvious in their visual investigation of the passengers, but intimidating, nevertheless. They took the best unoccupied seats they could get, to afford a view over all the other passengers.

To keep my composure, I decided that I would have to exert control of the situation. First, I got out my Hitler-Youth copy of *Mein Kampf*, handed it to Daniel while mouthing, "hold this."

Then I stood up, took off my overcoat and stretched, extending my arms and shoulders as wide as possible, and puffing out my chest slowly and deliberately, so that everyone around us, including those agents, could get a good look at my HY uniform, its blatant swastikas, and the ribbons and awards I had won.

In a voice just loud enough to be heard by our visitors, I said, "Keep my place in the *Kampf*, Fritz! I still have to read before the Führer's speech tomorrow!" Then I stretched again.

"But my legs are getting stiff from studying so long!"

Daniel caught on quickly, despite the name-change—I had explained the rationale for the uniform the previous night—and replied, "Certainly!" quite loudly.

I walked slowly down, then back up the aisle, making sure that my footsteps were stern, to draw attention to those heavy, SS-style jackboots, that I had worn again just for this effect. As I came back up the aisle, I noticed Papa standing to stretch. He moved into the aisle for a second, too, making sure that his party-membership pin was visible to anyone who might look up.

We both sat down and assumed our original activities. I watched those agents, subtly, over the top edge of *Mein Kampf,* letting Hitler dither as I kept watch.

Every so often, one of them would take out a pencil-stump, check his watch, then jot something down on a dingy little pad. However, our performances had apparently had their desired effect. It wasn't long till I noticed that one of the Gestapo agents had nodded off, and that the other, the note-taker, was staring blankly out the window.

After 75 km, at the Offenburg station (the end of that stretch of our journey paralleling the Rhine and the French border), they grabbed their black fedoras, rose and left among the other exiting passengers. We all relaxed just a little when they didn't reappear, nor others materialize among the thinning passenger load.

The route through the Black Forest wound circuitous, looping tightly through woods and wintry mountains until we at last passed through Donaueschingen.

Farther, nearing our railway-goal, the train slowed as its tracks ran within the snow-draped shadow of the ancient volcanic core that is the Hohentwiel, and made a wide curve, swinging around eastward into the terminus at Singen.

It was an immense relief that Bartomeu was there waiting, after having driven through the snow from Zurich to meet us at the station. With his help, we struggled as surreptitiously as possible with the luggage, and to ease Hannah from the train onto the landing. We migrated uneasily, en masse toward the station exit.

I kept praying silently, "Please, keep moving! Please, go! Faster, faster, please!" as we stepped, slipped and slid, carting the bags, and Papa and Frau Drescher worked so carefully to walk, at times carry, Hannah through the station, to the automobile awaiting us in the darkly snowy afternoon.

As the most ostentatiously "Nazi," I stood alongside, pointedly on display.

At last, packed tightly into Bartomeu's rented, German-marked, but quite drab (as requested) car, we set out on those seven kilometers farther, that would take us from Singen west into the middle of Gottmadingen.

Within that village, we turned south.

Although our fleeting drive from the center of that village was less than a kilometer to the border, it was as heart-pounding a journey as I'd ever made: and it wasn't from the 8 cm of snow on the road!

A car looked to be following us! Fast, and faster, it came ever closer; we sweated and prayed!

No, it turned onto another way!

But the one behind it sped up! Closer, ever closer—was it after us? Through the window frost, dancing with my every heartbeat, I watched, on thinnest, teetering edge. Gestapo?

Arrest, torture, death!

At last, it slowed, slowed into the distance, then swung off, onto a branching farmhouse drive.

We came quickly, suddenly, to a multistory house on our right, guarding the Swiss border, and slowed in nerve-shredding caution. But the minimal barrier had been left open on this slight, farming road, and there was no one attending!

We had timed the crossing to occur at dusk, suppertime in the early evening of Christmas Eve, and that was exactly when we passed, speeding down the road past the snow-laden, fallow fields of Blindenhusen. The frigid weather—it was 6° below freezing!—and the day's new centimeters of snow seemed to have ensured that everyone had been ready and determined to wrap themselves within a warm home that Saturday evening, there to commence Christmas celebrations. And they had indeed done so!

The drive from there through wintry, north Switzerland was tortuous, with an occasional slide and reactive half-Catalan, half-Swiss-German cuss from Bartomeu, but lively with the excitement of escape.

As the distance from the border increased, a gradual muting, then quiet fell over the passengers as thoroughly worked muscles and overwrought nerves melted into a stunning exhaustion. There was no reason to worry about the driver: Bartomeu had lived in Zurich long enough now that he proved very experienced in the snow, and had prepared the car for it.

The valley's level, curving road, skirting red-tile roofed, fachwerk farmhouses with their green, red, or blue shutters pulled tight against the biting wind, was separated from dormant, snow-laden fields by a guardian line of gnarled, ancient trees. It proved an easy, albeit icy, track.

Bartomeu drove the five kilometers directly into the pacific village of Ramsen, where he had made arrangements to switch to his own car, and for us to stay at a small hotel.

The silent night sang like liberating angels; slumber fell blessed, quickly.

In the middle of the night I was awakened by intermittent beeping.

I arose stealthily, pulled the curtains aside and gazed out over the snowy vista from our gable-centered, uppermost-storey window.

A car was parked with its lights on, shining onto the whitewashed base of a house sitting beside the nearest of the distant-stretching fields. A heavy-coated woman rushed from the vehicle as a tall youth carrying a very small calf walked into vehicle lights, revealing the still-dangling remnants of an umbilical cord. A man leading two cows followed, one struggling more than the other through the icy drifts, toward the ancient house's ground-level barn-door, that the woman rushed to shake and pull open, despite the obstreperous, piling snow.

My mind flashed, "winter calving must have come a few weeks early, unexpected—probably the weaker one's first calf!" but this too mundane, farmer's observation faded, replaced by the soothing melody of a choir, caroling *Quem pastores laudavere* [*He, whom shepherds praise*].

Gazing out at fields and farmhouses, across heavy, Swiss winter, I besought that Shepherd's and Our Lady's help for that family, those animals, and that I might, like these diligent stewards, truly be one of those men, my great-aunt's asserted "good ones—so many in our own family!"

I stepped over, tucked the covers more tightly about Daniel's neck, then turned away, slipped back into the arms of my own featherbed, and blessed the comforter.

We remained there into the morning, as we waited for Hannah's medicine to clear the congestion the escape's anxiety had driven into her lungs; then we set off again. The next 70 kilometers into Zurich were so snowy that we could go only very slowly in several sections of the road, despite the easy inclines of this Swiss landscape, still north of the foothills of the Alps.

By early evening, though, we were within the city, on the hills stretching above Grossmünster. After the racking anguish of those myriad frightful, fret-filled centimeters of snow, I stepped quickly from the car to cool my nerves in the icy, cedar-fresh air of this life-lifting Christmas Day.

Zurich was peaceful, so resolutely removed from our home-world of terror.

I looked out, far beyond the street to the long-remembered, but now snow-cloaked lake, the distant, beckoning hills, the farther, pristine Alpen peaks, and felt the warm wash of Heaven-blessing, soul-affirming relief. Bartomeu, Papa and I were no Magi, but we had, at least, delivered these precious children of Abraham beyond the savage grasp of our too-current, Teutonic Herod.

Our gifts delivered, this task was done. We had succeeded!

Sursum corda! [*Lift up your hearts!*]

The high mountains of my heart resounded with pulsing drums and trumpets, lofty with Bach's echoing Christmas-choir: "Jauchzet, frohlocket! Auf, preiſet die Tage!" [*Rejoice, exult! Arise and praise the season!*]

Bartomeu's house glowed warm, huge, and gorgeous!

Rapt in the season, he had erected an immense, Germanic Christmas tree, but beside it stood an intricately realistic, almost life-size, Mediterranean-style crèche, as well. Surrounding it all was a sea of cinnamon- and citrus-scented candles, and American-style menagerie of holly, ivy and mistletoe, Santa Claus and reindeer!

And in the corner, specially lit, stood a golden menorah, ready for his guests on this, the eighth, final, liberating day of Hanukkah, AM 5699.

His grand house made our poor farmhouse look like a hovel, but Bartomeu had set on making its size an asset now, using it to provide sanctuary for the Dreschers. Indeed, he was hiring Frau Drescher as his own housekeeper, and had also contacted local doctors to care for Hannah. With the monies secreted and maintained from the boarding-house sale, he had arranged an exclusive, private school for Daniel, affording the quality that Germany had set itself on denying him. Privately that evening, Papa offered several times to help with funding their refuge, their care, but Bartomeu wouldn't hear of it.

"It is my great privilege, Herr Meyer, to fight the Fascists with the few means I have at hand! We will guard your funds for the fight you, and Edi, still must wage."

With heavy knocks percussing the clock-towers' peel of the 9 a.m. hour, two somberly dressed gentlemen appeared at Bartomeu's front door on Monday morning, the very day after Christmas. Bartomeu had arranged for officials from the Swiss immigration ministry to come right there, to his house!

They set quickly to registering the Dreschers as refugees, without fuss. While they were busy, poring excitedly over their cherished paperwork, Bartomeu whispered to me, "Nothing gets Swiss bureaucrats off their asses and moving faster than a well-placed phone call from a bank!"

"Now, gentlemen!" Frau Drescher interrupted their paper-play to ask quite frankly, "What is the process for changing one's citizenship?

"I do not wish to remain a refugee! Despite my family's thousand-year life there, we must leave today's *death's head* Germany far behind!"

Daniel seconded his mother's desires: "I'm ready both to change my citizen-ship and to join the Swiss Army!"

The bureaucrats laughed at that, the shorter of them asserting, "We'll be sure to come back to take you up on that offer! But in a couple of years, when you're of age! Switzerland is so small in comparison to our neighbors! We can certainly use all the capable, strong young men we can muster!"

After this year's sudden seizure of Austria and the subsequent gang-rape of Czechoslovakia, even the Swiss were wary of German belligerence and the shad-ow of war. This union of the oldest of cantonal democracies must certainly have seen clearly now that tyranny breeds war, that war fosters tyranny.

Papa and I rose early the next morning, December 27th, and, with the forged border passes that Bartomeu had obtained for us, took our leave of the Dreschers.

It was so difficult to say good-bye! Daniel didn't help: he looked so sad that I could almost feel the waves of loneliness emanating from him. I knew he would be safe there, but it was very trying for me to have to bid farewell to someone who had become so much a little brother, of whom I had become so protective!

On the train-station platform I hugged Bartomeu very tightly, and perhaps for too long, but insecurity drove me to hold him, and to smell that cologne—his and my uncles'—just once more.

I had no idea what might face me so soon in Leipzig. It was going to be my first extended stay away from my family: from both my families, now.

Auf nach Leipzig — Chapter 12 — On to Leipzig

I sat bundled alone on the early express, distanced from the few other travelers.

Rushing across Germany in this Leipzig-bound train, my mind spun, not just from everything surrounding this trip itself, but from all that had happened just since the start of November.

It was the 7th day of January, 1939. That sole, previous long-distance, life-changing train-ride, across France into Catalonia, was now more than ten years in the past.

My life in those years seemed to have plunged through those mounting waves of spiritual decadence inflicted by Hitler's conservative revolution faster even than this speeding train could push its way through the freezing morning's Thuringian-forest fog.

After 14 hours from this early-morning's farmhouse: in Saxony at last!

The taxi-ride from Leipzig's railway station had gone much faster than I had expected, giving me far too little time to appreciate that area of the city we traversed: between the station and the noted *Music Quarter*, travelling a quick route from the northeast, around the University, into that famed neighborhood just south of the old city, the area surrounding the present, second *Gewandhaus*. However, despite the afternoon overcast of that late-January day, what I saw was certainly impressive: 𝔓𝔯𝔢𝔦𝔰𝔢 𝔡𝔢𝔦𝔫 𝔊𝔩ü𝔠𝔨𝔢, 𝔤𝔢𝔰𝔢𝔤𝔫𝔢𝔱𝔢𝔰 𝔖𝔞𝔠𝔥𝔰𝔢𝔫! [*Praise your luck, blessed Saxony!*]

Standing before those steps leading to the door of the big, stone house on Beethoven-Strasse ("How appropriate!" I laughed to myself), I glanced around while absentmindedly smoothing and straightening my uniform.

I ascended, stopped, took a deep breath, stood tall and rang the bell.

Almost instantly I heard footsteps, muted, deep-chested barking and matching assertions of *shush!*

Frau Gellert flung the door open, and a boxer muzzle bounced up into my face!

"Molly! Settle down!" she exclaimed, trying to grab the big puppy, to quell her jumping.

I knelt quickly; Molly came right to me and almost pushed me over as she wiggled her fawn butt against my side while turning so tightly, swiveling her torso, trying to lick my face.

"Well! I know now who *her* favorite is!" Frau Gellert laughed.

I stood up, expecting her to extend a hand for me to shake.

Instead, she grabbed my upper arm enthusiastically and pulled me forward into a ferocious hug, then pushed me, holding me at arm's length.

"Eduard! My dear! Tall and more handsome than ever! Come in, come in!"

I reached down and toyed with Molly's ear with my free hand, to excite her again; she ran back into the building ahead of us.

"My Dear! You must be exhausted after such a journey! We must talk and then go to dinner! Oh, my! Now that I see you in good light, you've grown even more gorgeous since I last saw you! Were you such a golden blond then, too? How did I not see that!"

She ran her hand from the hair above my ear, down across my cheek.

"You are a most delectable specimen! We shall have to fight the girls off! And strong, too!"

She grabbed my upper arm again. Well, I *had* still been helping around the farm!

She snapped back to task, "Oh, but your baggage! And the taxi! Go, go, get your things! Quickly!" she shooed me back toward the door.

I leaned over, cupping Molly's face, "Don't worry! I'll be right back, Puppy!" trying to reassure her, so she wouldn't bolt again.

Opening the door carefully, I made certain that I wasn't being tailed by the tailless pup, before edging through the door and fully outside.

The driver helped me tote my luggage to the landing. Frau Gellert managed to step outside unchaperoned, to supervise, flooding the street with suggestions, directions, comments.

Having dispatched the driver with his tip, she opened the entry-door tentatively, shooing Molly back out of the away so that I could heave the baggage-loads in, just over the threshold and beyond the door quickly, without letting out too much heat: the clouds and breeze made the near-freezing temperature feel much colder!

Just as she had said, her house was large, larger actually than Bartomeu's, but both sparser and more cluttered. Perhaps, despite the high, nineteenth-century ceilings, it was because of all the musical scores piled on top of and beside the three concert grands in her salon! Two of them were side by side; the other was reversed, tucked bend-to-bend into the one on the left. Nearby were identical, modern-looking sofas, placed together closely, spaced only by tables at their junctures. A rather grand staircase led to the first floor.

Obviously, the Party had been good to her! That was most likely because they didn't want her to escape the dictatorship and go over to the Allies, like Marlene Dietrich and so many others had!

"Come, Edi!" — She was already calling me by my 'family' name!

She grabbed my hand and pulled me, "I'll show you your room. It's rather large! It was the dining room here at one time, I think…"

She led me past the sofas, straight down the hall stretching from the entryway and parlor, continuing to talk an uninterrupted stream as she walked along and pointed things out.

"My suite is upstairs; the new dining room is off the front room—did you notice the big door past the far piano? There may be other protégés to move in with us; I hope you don't mind. I get rather lonely here at times, and it's always nice to have someone around! Anyway, if we find some excellent musical talent, we'll both decide whether we'll take them on; is that alright with you, dear?"

I wasn't certain that she had paused her monologue; with a jolt of recognition, I answered, "Certainly, Frau Gellert, whatever you think best!"

"OK, enough with the 'Frau' stuff, Edi! If you are to live here, you must call me *aunt*: *Tante Geli* for 'Angelika', or simply *Tante*! I have no children of my own—I've had to evict all three of my husbands: scoundrels! damned scoundrels every one of them! One of them ran off with an opera singer, an *opera singer*, can you believe it! What he saw in that huge mouthed, emaciated stick of a woman, I cannot imagine! her Italian was horrendous! *atroce*! *pessimo*!—we must talk much more, very soon, Edi! I am so pleased you're here at last! Having young people around is such a delight for me!"

"Thank you, Tante Gelchen!" I said with a smile.

She laughed. *Dear Little Aunt Geli*: I think she liked that!

"Fantastic! It's so nice to see you have a sense of humor! So many artists nowadays don't understand the benefit of a good laugh! Or of harmony and melody! That Schoenberg fellow! Horrible, simply horrible! Does he think audiences want to be hammered by his twelve-turd, atonal noise?! No! Of course, not! He should stop trying to force-feed the audience *dreck* and give them something that they can feel, hum, sing along with while they darn socks, chop cabbage or work in the garden!

"And Edi, take off that hideous Hitler Youth outfit and put it far, far in the back of your armoire! I don't want to see you in it again, ever! Simple armbands will do fine! You see, we have no uniforms in the *KdF*, and never shall we! We are artists, not cadets!"

She finished with a most flamenco flourish of her hands.

I laughed again, "Thank you very much, Tante! I was growing so very tired of khaki!"

She clapped her hands and laughed again.

"You and I will get along famously! How could we not? You were chosen by Molly before you walked through the door!"

Molly had been standing, leaning against me the whole time we had been talking. She kept looking up, turning her head, wagging her butt, "Pet me, love me, talk to me, too!"

"Perhaps she knows what happened," I ventured.

"I lost my boxer at the start of last December.

"Eva was 12. She always slept with me. But now she sleeps beneath the apple tree at the corner of the farmhouse."

I had to catch myself. The pet-death pain hit hard.

"Oh, my dear, dear, Edi!"

Gelchen hugged me. That made it harder for me to control the feeling of loss. She pulled back and stared deeply.

"No wonder Molly was so eager to greet you! They know! They know!" she said emphatically, "But, you understand that very well! They always know, and they will always find a tender heart!"

This had to stop, or I would lose it. So, I turned and stepped into the room she had just said was mine.

Exactly as she had described, it was quite large. Almost the entire side of the house, it had ample space for another full bed, and more. The windows were tall and faced the northwest: chilly for now, but nice in fall, and wonderful in spring and summer!

"Will it do, dear?"

"Definitely, Frau … Tante Geli!"

"Fantastic! Now, get all your baggage in here, and get settled. As soon as you have done all you can, and changed clothes, we shall go out to have a celebratory dinner! Let's see! Where? Ah, Auerbach's of course—I am desperate for some wine and you must have a beer—we shall have a little feast! Then you must rest.

"Tomorrow we shall play among the pianos, so you can practice, and learn their tones and temperament!"

I smiled. Obviously *protégé* to her was still also *student*, at least to some degree. Then she dropped it on me.

"I hope you have brought something nice, and less *Hitlerjugend*-ish to wear!

"You see, we're going to have a special guest tomorrow night for a little soirée.

"Propaganda Minister Goebbels and his wife are in town for an official engagement, and will be stopping by. He is very interested in seeing if everything I have told him about you is correct!"

She must have noticed the look of shock on my face.

She touched my arm, "Don't worry, dear! Despite his Ph.D., he's as lacking in taste as the rest of the government—they wouldn't know Mozart from a mop if I didn't tell them!

"But you mustn't repeat me on that!" she whispered, smiling conspiratorially before returning to her monologue.

"At dinner, we will talk more about what you'll play, and what I'll say to him, just so that you will know what to add to the conversation, and everything will be fantastic! We must talk, too, about what music—composers and nationalities—you can and cannot play. It's depressing, horrible! But that's the way of things right now… At least with Franco's victory you can play your Barcelona-music again. It's always such a nuisance to try to remember what instructions this or that silly directive has brought from Berlin!

"But, Edi, I assure you that by this Wednesday you shall have the entire Propaganda Ministry with you, and you will be able to move between the *Gewandhaus*, the Music Conservatory and the University as you wish."

I didn't understand.

"Tante Geli, the *Music Conservatory*?"

"Yes, dear! Oh, didn't I tell you?

"You will be able to take classes at both the Music Conservatory and the University! In fact, some at the Conservatory—it's just down the street!—have already asked about your availability to give a few master classes. They knew already, of course, that *I* was far too busy, but that you had been an instructor at the *Hoch'sche*!

"From Clara Schumann's *Hoch'sche* to Mendelssohn's *Conservatory*, in the very city in which dear Clara was born! What a marvelous path for any pianist! Of course, I told them we would see, but if you were free, that would be a marvelous idea!

"That was OK, wasn't it, my dear?"

"She's got me working already!" I thought, then smiled.

"Certainly, Tante, anything you feel will help you, and the *KdF*!"

Diplomacy would have to be my second face and become my cardinal, defining characteristic if I were to be certain to please her and survive this ordeal by music, and conversational flood!

Dinner was exquisite fun. Gelchen had an irrepressible, amazingly vibrant, bubbly personality, even stopping graciously to sign autographs when she was recognized during our walk to dinner.

Leipzig was indeed a town, musical like no other!

Dr. Goebbels and his missus showed up, as expected, the very next night. I had not realized he was such a slight, oily, devious-looking man. But I forced myself to swallow my perceptions, to remember to address him as *Herr Doktor* (because of his Ph.D. in literature), and to play specifically to our audience.

Tante Geli entertained them with a couple of pieces, after which I played.

Goebbels then started talking. And talking. Ultimately, Tante Gelchen had to interrupt him—*she* had to interrupt *him*!—to keep the private concert going! We played a Mozart duet that we had worked up that day. Earlier in the year she had sent me the music, in the thick envelope along with her address and all the other information I would need. I'd had no inkling that I would need it so soon!

Frau Goebbels was pleasant enough, but seemed a bit distracted, distant, and didn't say a lot, except to express her husband-echoing and Hitler-referent compliments. Gretchen whispered only later about their on-going marital difficulties!

At the end of the extended test-recital, the propaganda lecture/rant, and all, Goebbels betrayed an air of excitement: from what he said, he seemed to have found more than expected. As they were just at the front door, ready to depart, he stopped to announce that he planned to write a full report of "a glorious evening of the most radiant of Aryan talent" to the Führer. I knew he meant me, in particular, with that tag. But, what could *I* do about it? It was propaganda directly from the minister!

Gelchen had been right, again. We got complete *carte blanche* from the Ministry.

From winter into spring and throughout its summer, 1939 was an exciting flash of performances, study and teaching, including concerts during the first weeks of July that Tante and I gave on two harmonious Norwegian-fjord cruises we worked on, aboard the *KdF* ship, the *Wilhelm Gustloff*.

But then September came with the dire dissonance of sudden war: our troops were invading Poland!

Although it was a horrific, numbing shock, we felt truly relieved after the first few weeks, when the entire misadventure had transpired with so light an amount of bloodshed, as the newsreels and newspapers told us.

But the quick declaration of war by Britain and France had sent a shudder of *déjà vu* through the older members of the population, and among the younger ones with whom they had shared their too painful experiences.

There was doubt: doubt that you could hear in people's voices even though they didn't dare say it outright. Hitler had pulled off some amazing stunts: re-militarization of the Rhineland, and seizure of Austria. Next (oiled with Judas-like British, French and Italian connivance) came the three-step dismemberment of Czechoslovakia: annexation of the Sudetenland, quick seizure of Moravia and Bohemia, subversion of Slovakia.

But almost everyone shared a soul-churning, gnawing fear that the present events Hitler had set into motion in Poland would lead ultimately not to success, but to the catastrophe of another defeat, and to a humiliation far worse than that of Versailles.

However, by that Christmas, when Britain and France had again played fee-bly along and done nothing, and the Western front had mellowed into the *Sitz-krieg*, we began to relax. Maybe it would stop there, and we could go on with our lives without the cataclysm of another Great War!

Tante Geli and I gave several concerts for soldiers—many of them wounded—and continued our scheduled concerts for industrial workers and the general public. I certainly got to see more of Germany than I had ever thought about vis-iting!

Like too many Germans, I granted myself the spineless indulgence of ignoring the ever-present swastikas.

But I found myself loving Germany more, the more I saw: from the mountains of Bavaria to the seashore and heath around Hamburg and Lübeck, from Frei-burg, Stuttgart, Cologne, Hannover and Bremen to Königsberg, Danzig, Marien-burg, Posen and Breslau!

Even my simple train-ride home and back gave me a thrill, for I knew that I was travelling among the very cities associated with the lives and journeys not only of Goethe and Schiller, but of Bach and Handel, as well: Frankfurt, Fulda, Eisenach, Gotha, Erfurt, Weimar, Halle, Leipzig.

Berlin was monumental, imposing; Dresden was beyond beautiful—I had sat in overwhelmed, awestruck silence at the wondrous, Baroque nave and vault of the *Frauenkirche*—but the Taunus, the Rhineland, and Frankfurt were home.

Leipzig, however, was becoming very dear, too.

Whenever I heard one of my students playing his best *Bach*-organ in the Thomaskirche, or I walked beneath the trees in front of the Schumann house on Inselstrasse and heard my Clara's voice humming a melody from Robert's "Pa-pillons" it grew ever dearer.

I was living the beauty of German culture while, all around, the oppressive stench of Nazi dreck surged, striving so viciously to drown it.

I could do nothing but walk on.

————[1940]————

In April of that next year, 1940, we invaded and occupied Denmark and Norway.

It went so quickly, what could one say? We needed iron ore from Sweden, and with Britain and her mighty Royal Navy at war with us, it made sense to secure the Norwegian shipping routes: if war ever makes sense!

That May 10th I was in the great hall of the Conservatory, on the stage beneath the wide, toothy grin of the old organ, straining to reposition the piano while also pushing chairs out of its way, struggling to arrange it all for a next-morning recital.

One of the upper classmen ran in, breathless. He stooped, leaning over to support his panting torso on the back of the very chair I was just then trying to move.

"Manfred, what is it? And let go of the chair!" I said.

He released it and plopped onto its neighbor; he had tiny beads of sweat glinting on his forehead.

"We've just …"

He had to take a breath.

I stopped rearranging momentarily to pay attention, "We've just *what*?"

"We've just invaded the Low Countries — and France!"

It hit me like a punch to the gut; I had to sit down, to catch my breath, too.

"Are you sure? Look! That's not funny if it's supposed to be a joke!"

"No, Edi! No joke. We're marching into France … again … at this moment!"

I could hear Gramma scream.

I felt, saw, smelled the horrors of Passchendaele: of gas attacks, of young, beautiful men with shattered faces, of devoted fathers in their thirties coughing their lungs out one minute, then turning blue in suffocation the next, of widows working themselves to an early grave striving to keep a fatherless family together, fed, dry, and warm.

All the anguish, terror and death that Gramma had talked of, the privations we Germans had faced: little food, no coal, church bells seized and melted down for weapons, desperation twisting the faces of young mothers as their children cried from hunger, their stomachs bloated from malnutrition! This was not what I wanted for the Germany I had just been discovering! This could not be inflicted again on the Germany that I had just now truly, fully begun to love!

The next few days exceeded anguish. We waited each moment to hear what we feared most, of the big Anglo-French push — France still had the largest army west of Russia! — that would freeze the front and return us to the murderous years leading to the dreadful catastrophes of 1914-1918, and beyond.

But it never came.

After we had swept through the Netherlands and Belgium, the French government had collapsed in upon itself. Only the last-stand, Spartan-like bravery of the French Army in Dunkirk had prevented the maelstrom from sweeping it away, and the British Expeditionary Force along with it. Within only six weeks, German forces had defeated France and made us masters of central and western Europe. And all the while, ever since Poland, the Communists had been … our allies?

Was Stalin blind, stupid, or both?

In the Hitler Youth, I had been forced to read *Mein Kampf* beyond nausea. Even scanning it just once should have told him what to expect. But, if he wanted to be a complete idiot, to sit there and not bother us, that was fine with me!

Worst of all this was that Hitler was now a damned, untouchable hero. He had done what neither German king nor Kaiser—nor Bismarck, Ludendorff and Hindenburg—had been able to do: to place France utterly, completely under German control. He had crushed ole Napoleon in a single act of Teutonic revenge. Screw Pétain! I knew he had sold out his whole country, even if he pretended his remnant of France around Vichy was independent!

All Germany erupted in celebration: except for Gramma, except for her family. Never could I applaud.

Indeed, I felt only sorrow, not because I was less *German*, but perhaps more *European* in the same instance. I had seen so much more of Germany only recently, yet this made me appreciate not only it, but the wealth of excitement and beauty to be found beside it, in other parts of Europe. Perhaps it was a true Rhinelander's gift: that multinational river valley was so different a "Germany" from that of Brandenburg, or even of Bavaria—and certainly distinct from that of Silesia or East Prussia!—that at times it seemed a separate nation.

It must be no mistake that the most Classically international of German writers, Johann Wolfgang von Goethe, was born in Frankfurt, within a shout of the Rhine, of *my* Rhine!

Papa had started teaching me French right after we got back from Barcelona, and I had practiced with both the English and French sets of gramophone records that we had ordered. Here in Leipzig, I had decided to pursue advancing studies in both languages.

English courses were not particularly popular right at the moment, so I had the professor largely to myself. With my existing skills in English, we branched off, to include Old English (officially, and on record because, with its alternate name, *Anglo-Saxon*, it was more obviously regime-pleasing "Germanic") to study *Beowulf*, the homilies of Wulfstan, and the writings of the great West Saxon, Alfred. We still carried out the coursework and all translations of Anglo-Saxon poetic license in English, to broaden my expertise in this language.

But speaking French had made me sensitive to the people of France, just as speaking American had taken me closer to them. I understood the French better than most Germans did simply because I had gained greater insight into their culture. Gramma and Papa had long asserted, "Language is culture, and culture, language."

So, I ached for the French: mes français, mes chers français! [*My French, my dear French!*]

I was glad, though, that if it were going to happen—and this was certainly well beyond my ken or control—at least the invasion had been quick and didn't kill anywhere near the vast number of French and German soldiers slaughtered in the previous war.

The greater pain, though, was that I could not see the French now helping us with the liberation we needed, the extrication from this gangster-tyranny.

Fretfully, neither could I do anything myself, except try to survive until we, as a nation, might find our renewed strength, to rekindle the spirit of that liberal revolution, of Frankfurt, 1848.

————————

Cousin Albert had gone from his stabilizing life on the farm right into semi-nary. It seemed he was indeed going to honor his grandmother Waltraut's great, dying wish, for him to enter the priesthood.

In the midst of his studies, though, he had decided to take some time off from the seminary in Fulda to see a little more of the secular world before hiding him-self beneath the cloth, locked within the binding collar. His father's old friend and Nazi mentor, Father Hagen, was now working on the staff of the bishopric of Meissen, stationed here in Leipzig, so he invited Albert to work with him. And Albert, needing the parochial experience, agreed, despite his continuing distaste for that seemingly bad-luck embosomed priest.

It was good to have him, my cousin, around again; his presence brought an air of home to my Leipzig life.

He even took some vocal and cello master-classes at the Conservatory!

Often, when he'd drop by, I'd accompany him in duets. Tante Geli especially loved to hear him play Beethoven's and Brahms' works for cello and piano. I would be the first to assert that his rendition of those was particularly masterful. On the cello, he was also no *Dreikühige*!

"Any time you want, you can be part of our company!" she always told him while applauding his performance.

He would say, "Well, maybe some time!" and laugh it off.

Albert was still determined to finish his seminary studies, even if he did give every indication of being on an extended Saxon sabbatical!

————————

In the late afternoon of Monday, the 16th of December, 1940, two young people were to appear at our door.

With the extending draft, we had seen so consistently disappointing a stream of those aspiring to be chosen Tante Geli's protégé that I almost didn't break out of my class- and tutoring-routine, to come home to help her evaluate them. The war had ravaged the conservatories, reducing, near devastating, the rolls of mu-sic students: not a single applicant had been up to her standards this far; so why did she need me?

But I heard someone whisper, urging me to be there, for this audition.

Was it my dear Clara?

Just as I walked in, Tante Geli asked me to raise the lid of the nearer Steinway to its high, performance angle. I got it set, then sat on one of the couches near it to work on repairing an accident I'd had with a musical score.

Tante went to the door herself when they arrived.

I stayed in the parlor, seated on the sofa, trying to organize score-pages after I had dropped the book in my rush to get back to the house. The binding's stitches had popped loose, shuffling the sheets across the slickly polished floor of one of the central halls at the Conservatory. I was having to be very careful to make sure that I had all the pages, and could butterfly the signatures back into their original, bound order.

Our visitors walked in; I fussed with the pages until I got them in a state in which I could put them safely aside, then stood up.

Gelchen introduced them to me.

The young lady had dark brown hair and green-chased blue eyes, which shone as she introduced herself as Ulrike Maria von Eisenberg. The young man introduced himself as her brother, Thomas Dieter von Eisenberg. He had richly black hair; and his long, jet eyelashes made his large blue eyes, well, shockingly alluring. She was slightly shorter than he; he also looked shorter than me, but certainly not by more than two centimeters. There was a mischievous sparkle that I sensed from him; she was a bit more stiff, almost officially professional in her bearing. Perhaps it was just nerves showing in different ways from each of them.

I yearned to luxuriate in attention to them but, still painfully distracted, worried by the score (it was from the Conservatory library, and it was a case of fix it myself or pay Versailles-level reparations!), I returned to the unavoidable distraction caused by the volume of my task.

Just as I sat down to resume the re-assembly, the bell at the front door rang again.

Tante Geli was talking to the pair with her usual, unstaunchable animation, so I put the score aside again, stepped quietly around the conversation—I heard her chirp, "Thank you, dear!" with barely a break in her delivery as I walked past—and went to answer the door.

It was Albert.

Motioning for him to move backwards, I stepped outside with him and explained what was going on, in case he didn't want to sit through the auditions. He said he didn't mind: it could be fun! He had left his cello here and, if nothing else, he could use the quick-exit excuse of needing just to pick it up, then rush away.

We went back in.

Still standing at the front-door side of the parlor, Tante introduced Albert to the pair, while I went back over to the sofa and my scattered score. As I had done at these interviews in the past, I sat where I could look into the face of the person playing the audition, a view that was particularly direct if they chose the nearest piano.

That one was the dark red, black-veined African mahogany Steinway that Geli had brought home from New York in 1924, on returning from one of her several American tours. She had filled most of those top-floor rooms of her house with photos, books, furniture, all the souvenirs of her world-touring days, but at least the three pianos, including that reddish one, and the antique, Hamburg-built Steinway (it was the one Tante had played as a child), had been left down here in the large sitting room!

In contrast to the New-York-born Steinway, its neighbor, a Nazi-made, regime-supplied, Berlin piano, despite being a concert grand, reminded me so much of my childhood up-right, back at the farm, in timbre and sound profile, especially in the (at points, too uneven, or even ponderous) lower notes.

Sometimes I would play the same piece, switching from one piano to the other, just to hear the differences their variant voices and key-actions affected in a melodic line or changed in the density of harmonies.

Tante caught on to my process very fast, too, and soon started doing so herself, or she would sit and listen intently while I did the "piano tango" as she jokingly called it. After a period of doing this, I had pegged my own preference, aligned with the enduring love for my own 'ole Steiner', and so settled quickly back into the consistent and irreplaceable, technical and aural brilliance of the Steinway.

Geli took a seat on the sofa directly across from me, but to my right, at the far end, away from the piano itself. She had explained that it was a better position in the room for her ears. "And I have to sit with them!" she'd laugh.

The young man, Thomas, was going to play first. He announced that first on his program would be Bach's Partita in B flat major, BWV 825.

I stopped paper-shuffling to rest my head back against the sofa; I closed my eyes.

I could not fault his playing. Contrapuntal technique, phrasing, sense of melodic line, all were right on the money! I opened my eyes a slit to watch him play the flashy final movement, the *Gigue*. He was good, really good, almost as good as me, in some respects, maybe a little better?

I felt a twinge of jealousy—something brand new to me! But as I watched the unexpected, intriguingly sensuous musical motions of his playing, his ease, his tactile mastery, the sight through those eye-slits forced me to ask myself, "Was it envy of him, or of the piano?"

Pulling myself upright, I leaned forward when he told Geli his second piece: Beethoven's sonata No. 24 in F sharp major, *à Thérèse* [*For Theresa*].

I watched his face intently as he prepared.

He looked up.

I couldn't breathe, couldn't blink, couldn't look away.

The depth, the yearning!

Those first nine chords! He was playing them as he stared directly into my eyes, as Clara sang new words to the melody: "Wie darf ich sagen, wie tief ich lieb', ich liebe dich…" [*How dare I tell you, how deeply I love, I love you…*]

He smiled slightly when the music led on, beyond that ninth chord.

I was melting!

He looked down, to the keyboard and his hands. I kept gazing, waiting, wanting desperately for him to look back up, to look at *me*!

Every time he did, something between us arced; thoughts, emotions, lives.

My palms tingled; my breath caught; my heart banged in counterpoint to the music! I had felt this only once before, at the interrupted concert, so had no practice in such overwhelming exhilaration. I didn't know what to think, didn't know how to act! All I knew was that, somehow, for whatever reason, he was becoming the key to my world, the dominant resolution, centering my every thought!

The final movement of that sonata, the *allegro vivace*, provided musical material that allowed him to demonstrate his sense of humor. He would look up and smile, raise one eyebrow slightly; I smiled back, feeling rather silly at how closely I was approaching an overt admission, an irremediable declaration! To say that he played it well would be a ridiculously feeble understatement.

When Thomas finished, he stood up, cocked that left eyebrow, smiled at me again, turned and moved away from the piano.

Tante said, "Thank you very much Thomas! Outstanding technique, excellent interpretation, of *both* works!"

Thomas thanked her, then stepped to the side and sat on the other piano's bench, facing his sister as she took her place at the keyboard and announced her selection.

Since Albert had first walked in, I had also noticed how he had been studying the young lady. He had started watching her as soon as they were introduced. As far as I could tell, from the lofty aerie of my own *Shangri-La*, he hadn't been able to take his eyes off her!

 Ulrike also played a Bach partita as her first selection, BWV 826, in C minor. I turned my attention, albeit a bit distractedly, to her performance: I still had my duty to render Gelchen a valid appraisal!

It was another stellar rendering of Bach, of the final, *Capriccio* movement, in particular.

She announced that her second piece, rather than mirroring Thomas's second, Beethoven offering, would be Brahms, his expressively romantic Rhapsody in B minor, Op. 79 No. 1.

Thomas was sitting on the edge of the neighboring piano's bench, facing his sister. She seemed to gain confidence from his attentive presence.

Her spirited rendering of the Brahms was yet another flawless, deeply musical performance: she was certainly as good as her brother!

As she raised her hands from the keyboard, Albert stood, exclaimed, "Brava!" and started clapping. She smiled at him, coyly, obviously embarrassed by such exuberant attention, and unique acclaim.

Tante Gelchen rose from her sofa and walked toward the siblings. She rubbed her palms together, holding her hands wide open, moving them in slow circles against each other; her fingers passed over each other lightly in each cycle. Then she stopped, the points of both hands touching her chin. In these twelve months, I had learned that this was a sign that she had been well pleased and was contemplating a positive course of action. I was so very glad!

"Excellent! Excellent, both of you! … Now, if you'd excuse us, I'd like to talk to Eduard privately."

She grabbed my hand, almost jerked me up from the sofa and led as we walked together down the hall. We reached a point presumably far enough to be out of earshot, but she whispered anyway.

"I think these two are good enough to be our protégés. What do you think?"

"*Our* protégés?" I mused but, as quickly as possible, whispered my answer, "Tante, if they could move in tonight, I'd be helping them with their baggage right now!"

She laughed. "So that's a 'yes', isn't it?

"Very well! You and I are of the same mind in so many things! From the first moment I heard you play, it was as if you were more than a student, more than a protégé—very nearly my own other hands, heart and mind. We play so much alike and think so much alike, you and I! This is why you were the first I let into my house!

"Good! We are once again agreed!"

But she began to tap her chin with her right index finger.

"But I'd like to hear something more, before we tell them. I doubt it will change my mind, but I want to see some resilience, some adaptability, less emotional stiffness, particularly from the girl."

My stomach flipped and churned, knotted in an atonal duet with my brain. I begged Heaven desperately that anything, *anything*, that might happen wouldn't change her mind!

I followed her back into the main room.

She stepped to the side of the concert Steinway, near the keyboard and stood, once more a judge, with one hand resting atop the red and black mirroring polish of the piano's mahogany frame.

"Does either of you have experience in recital with a singer or instrumentalist?" she asked.

Ulrike raised her hand slightly—as if in the class of an irascible teacher—and replied, softly, "Well, yes, I have, Frau Gellert. I have worked regularly with string players, and with vocalists."

"Good!" said Geli. She clapped her palm on the piano frame.

"Albert, warm up your cello! First movement! Opus 99!"

"Certainly, Frau Gellert!" he said. Springing from his chair, he leapt leopard-like to grab his instrument.

"Now, Ulrike. Do you know the Brahms Cello Sonatas?" Geli asked, apparently not realizing that she probably should have checked with the girl first.

"Yes, Frau Gellert, but not by memory."

"No problem. Edi, where's that piano score?" she snapped without turning to look at me.

I dug quickly into the pile beside one sofa; it lay fourth from the bottom.

I handed it to Ulrike, who placed it on the piano's music rack, then motioned for Thomas to hold it open and turn pages for her.

Albert had moved chair and cello into position beside the piano so that the two players could watch each other during the performance. He had memorized his part, so had no score in the way: other than to blink, he never took his eyes off Ulrike!

It was nine minutes of enchantment!

There was a definite connection, surmounting the merely musical, between the two of them, something that Albert and I hadn't found whenever we had played it. Albert could not possibly have watched her more intently: he read every nuance in her face, in each movement of her hands!

"Wonderful!" Gelchen exclaimed in the silence of the fading final chord, "You two play like you were meant to be together!"

Uli dropped her head, a blush spreading, sweeping aside the cream of her complexion. Albert was trying, unsuccessfully, to subdue the pleasure in his smile.

Geli turned. "And Thomas, have you done any ensemble work?"

"I've accompanied instrumentalists on the harpsichord. And I've done some vocal accompaniment on piano."

"Albert has been working on the *Dichterliebe* song-cycle. Do you know them, Thomas?" I asked, hoping anxiously that he did.

"Yes. I've worked with all the Schubert and Schumann songs," he replied confidently.

"OK, Albert, which of them will you do?" asked Gelchen.

"The first and the fifth of the *Dichterliebe*."

"Is that alright, Thomas?" he asked.

I had to fight back the excitement as I pulled the Schumann score from elsewhere in this same, predominately Albert-music stack.

I knew exactly why Albert had chosen those two: someone in this room had knocked him on his emotional ass!

At least I knew without doubt now that I wasn't the only one in trouble!

Thomas looked over at Albert and replied, "That's fine with me." Then he glanced at me; I could have sworn he had that mischievous glint in his eyes again.

He knew, dammit, he knew!

Thomas returned to the Steinway.

 I faced him as he played. Albert stood with face angled toward Geli and Ulrike, a tenor voice for those lyrics, saved from condemnation by insidious Nazis who attributed them now not to our dear poet, Heinrich Heine, but to some obscure, Nazi-sanitized, pseudo-Aryanized *Anonymous*:

Im wunderschönen Monat Mai,	In the most beautiful month of May,
Als alle Knospen sprangen,	When all the buds were bursting open,
Da ist in meinem Herzen	There, in my heart,
Die Liebe aufgegangen.	Love sprouted forth.
Im wunderschönen Monat Mai,	In the most beautiful month of May,
Als alle Vögel sangen,	When all the birds were singing,
Da hab' ich ihr gestanden	There have I confessed to her
Mein Sehnen und Verlangen.	My yearning and longing.

Thomas flipped the pages quickly, to Albert's second selection.

Ich will meine Seele tauchen	I will plunge my soul
In den Kelch der Lilie hinein,	Into the chalice of the lily,
Die Lilie soll klingend hauchen	The lily shall breathe, sounding
Ein Lied von der Liebsten mein.	A song about my dearest.
Das Lied soll schauern und beben	The song shall quiver and shake
Wie der Kuß von ihrem Mund',	Like the kiss of her mouth,
Den sie mir einst gegeben	That she once gave me
In wunderbar süßer Stund'!	In a wonderfully sweet moment!

When Albert had finished his songs, Tante Geli jumped up, grabbed his arm and locked his gaze intently into her own.

"Wunderschön! [*Absolutely wonderful!*]

"Albert, I know you could have a music career, if you would only decide on it!"

She moved over to put her hand on Thomas's shoulder.

"Ulrike and Thomas, the two of you play exquisitely!

"And we," she nodded toward me in inclusion, "would like you two to be our protégés, to perform with us in the *KdF* Classical Music program. You may also live here with us, as offered in my letter."

Thomas and Ulrike looked to each other, apparently seeking mutual permission. Thomas nodded in agreement, whereupon Ulrike said, "We would like that very much, Frau Gellert! You have been an inspiration to us throughout all our studies!"

Tante glowed from the compliment, which I knew she valued because of the high estimation she had already expressed of the persons paying it.

"Excellent! And I will let Herr Goebbels know of our momentous decisions!" she said.

I held my fist to my mouth and cleared my throat, rather obviously begging attention.

"Yes, Edi?"

"But Tante, since you hired the live-in housekeeper, there is only one free bedroom, the smaller one just along here. The only other open space is in my room."

I didn't want to remind her that we could always clear some of her mounds of tour-memorabilia junk out of one of the rooms on the upper floor! No need to set her off onto another tangent! And that option was one I was definitely not interested in, anyway!

"Oh, dear, yes! That's right!" she exclaimed.

"Would you mind having an extra bed moved into there, Edi?"

"Not at all!"

"Well, Thomas. Would you mind having a roommate?" she asked.

"If it means being to work with you and, of course, if Eduard doesn't mind, then I don't mind either!"

"Fantastic!" Gelchen exclaimed.

"Edi, take Thomas and show him where it will be!

"Ulrike, come with me and I'll show you your room!

"Albert! Stay there until you agree to join us!"

Albert looked rather dumbstruck; I knew he was love-struck! Was he starting to consider her proposal?

At that, we moved toward the hallway. Geli and Ulrike stopped to tour the room that would be hers. I opened the door to what had been solely my room, and a boxer jolted, butt wiggling in unrestrainable excitement, into the hall.

Molly came to greet me, sniffing my shoes and shins, then went immediately to Thomas. He knelt down, held her and talked to her. Shaking, groaning, trying desperately to lick his face, she again reacted as if she had been suddenly reunited with a long-lost friend.

When Thomas and I stepped into the room, Molly jumped immediately into the middle of my bed and lay down, watching. I pointed out where his bed would be, that there was already an extra armoire, where we could put an additional table for him, possibly a dresser, and so on.

I may have sounded rushed. His glances emphasized his movement, grace, the color of his eyes. I returned us to the front room quickly.

Once we had all gathered again around the pianos, Tante Gelchen said, "Edi, would you like the encore?"

I wasn't sure what she meant, certainly wasn't expecting that phrase, and must have looked at her with a most quizzical expression.

She laughed, then explained slowly, as if describing to a child where to find middle-C on the keyboard.

"They have played; you have all heard me perform. But would you like to play something for our new house-members?"

"Oh. Right!"

I moved, tentatively, to the Steinway and sat, only to stare for a moment at the now-mute keyboard. What to play, what to play?

I looked up; Thomas had moved to the bend in the frame. He was looking directly at me. Those eyes, those deep, drown-me dammit, blue eyes!

Clara voiced softly, "Barcelona, Edi! The charming, tender rhythms!" and without over-thinking it, I began playing *Andaluza*, the same 'number 5' from that long-ago trip to Spain.

Tante Geli moved to stand closely beside Thomas; she reached behind him and placed her hand on his lower back, closed her eyes and swept softly with the swaying-palm rhythms.

Thomas's eyes opened wider, softer.

I closed mine!

Images of warming light and errant shadows in the incense-perfumed cathedral nave, the caress of sea breezes flowing through the palm trees centering the boulevard before the *Palau*—no, that wasn't Andalucía—but this *was* Granados, and it was my Barcelona! I looked up; he was still watching, intensely. Then it hit me! He had those same, full, Cupid's bow lips as Bartomeu's secretary, Joaquin!

I *had* to shut my eyes!

As I finished, my eyes opened to the applause arising from the group, except for Gelchen, who was still dreaming. She opened her eyes slowly, looked at me and said, "Such a controlled, masterful gradation of touch! Such a gift for melody! Oh, such a gift, my dear!"

"Thank you, Tante!" I replied.

"Play something else," Thomas said, "please."

"Anything!" I thought.

Preserving the mood, I followed with *Valencia*, from the same set of *Spanish Dances*.

I was launched afar again, to Catalonia: a child again, bouncing along enchanted, ancient stone streets and plazas, on avenues of angels and princesses; swinging around rough-barked palm trees; overwhelmed by home-hearth aromas of fresh-baked bread, roasting beef, of the delicate, sensuous delight of *crème catalan*-filled pastries and orange- and lemon-scented chocolates!

I didn't dare look at him more than twice during the almost five minutes of this *danza*; I knew what was happening to me. He was overwhelming me, sweeping me away! I didn't stop at the end of this selection—did I forget to pause?—but went directly into the following dance, the *Sardana*, "Asturiana", with its beautifully lyrical melody that sounded to me so much like intertwined waves of midnight, Catalan murmurs of love, *moltíssim t'estimo: I love you so very much*!

I finished. Not a sound from any of them.

Thomas whispered, "Magical!"

Tante Geli agreed softly, "Exactly, Thomas," then added, "The simplest of melodies takes the greatest art! Edi, my dear, exotic fantasies—simply magical!"

Her voice trailed off, as if launched into a new, ever-distancing dream.

With a jolt, Geli's ebullient, mother-bird awoke; she fluttered from one of us to the next, from me to Thomas to Ulrike and Albert, effusive in her praise, telling us what excellent musicians we were as she caressed our hair, smoothed our clothes, patted our arms, clasped our hands.

She cycled back to Thomas, lay her hand on his shoulder and said, "Thomas, *I* know all about you two from your letters and application but, you and Ulrike, do tell Edi and Albert something about yourselves! In the meanwhile, I will get the housekeeper to bring us some refreshments!"

We moved from the pianos over to the couches. Albert made sure he was seated within direct gaze of Ulrike. I had no such work. Whenever I looked up, I caught Thomas: his furtive glance, or a longer stare.

All seated, Thomas at last said, "Well," and started to talk as Tante marched from the room, "we're from Cologne." Then he paused.

"Our parents were killed at the train station during the first air raid, on May 12. Since then, we've been living mainly at the family estate outside Bergisch Gladbach. We have had to find our own way in life these past few months, searching for lodgings in Cologne while we attended the music conservatory, the *Staatliche Hochschule*, there. Because of the growing destruction the bombing raids are inflicting, it has been more and more difficult to continue our studies in Cologne.

"Sometimes it seems it's the only city the RAF can find!" he added with an air of bitterness.

"We gave a concert in Düsseldorf this past September, at which Propaganda Minister Goebbels heard us play Mozart's *Concerto for Two Pianos* in E-flat major.

"He made a point of meeting us afterwards, and suggested strongly—almost ordered!—that we get in touch with Frau Gellert.

"Herr Goebbels was so impressed with our performance that, after he asked my age (Uli and I are 17 now, 18 this next January 3rd) he promised me a draft exemption on the condition that Frau Gellert accept us into her *KdF* program. I believe he has communicated that to her. He explained that he had obtained an exemption for another of Frau Gellert's stars, and asserted that it would be no problem to do it for me, too. I take it that by this he meant you, Edi?"

"Yes, that's right, I guess!"

I laughed, still unaccustomed to hearing the label, *star*. "It must be so, since I'm the only one here with her right now!"

Tante Gellert walked back into the room, trailing our stout housekeeper, Frau Nussbaum, who held a large tray with a tightly centered bottle of wine and five glasses, enclosed within a circling assortment of small pastries. Frau Nussbaum leaned over, installing the tray on the table nearest me; I smiled up at her and whispered, "Thank you!" She grinned back a likewise "You're welcome." Tante announced good-naturedly, "Thank you, Elsa! That will be all for tonight!"

Elsa said, "Yes, madam," made the slightest hint of a curtsy, turned and left.

The five of us lounged on and around the sofas and talked until quite late that evening. Tante Gellert started going over expanded plans she had for concerts she wanted us to be involved in, lamenting the war's reduced options, of musicians (the *KdF* had been severely depleted by draft and munitions-work), and of venues, particularly that there would be no more leisurely Baltic or North Sea cruises aboard the *Wilhelm Gustloff* or the *Robert Ley*.

Ulrike and Thomas stepped gingerly through Tante's long-flowing stream of dreams, to ask me about the University. I started to lay out the information I had, but Tante Gellert jumped back into the conversation to add extensively how they would also be allowed to attend the neighboring Conservatory, for specific classes or seminars, mentioning that I was already doing some teaching there.

She also promised the two that she would get a harpsichord for us to have here at the house, as they had inquired. Those letters to Gelchen had apparently reported their continuing study of quite a bit of Baroque and pre-Classical-period music in Cologne, both keyboard and woodwind.

"I will speak to Goebbels," she said, "about whether we might make some gramophone recordings for the *KdF*, and for distribution to the troops. I believe he will agree: he has praised the consistently great affect we have on morale! Germans love great music—but that's only natural after all!—so much of it is *ours*!

"Now, Ulrike and Thomas! You will be moving in on what day? It will be soon, won't it?"

"Yes, ma'am," he answered, "We can return on Monday, the 30th of December."

"So, Edi! We have some furniture—and a harpsichord!—to procure!

"We must get busy at once! You will be going back to your parents' farm for Christmas?"

"Yes, Tante. I leave on the 21st and return on the 28th. They're both Saturdays."

She turned back to our new friends, "Then Edi and I shall have all accomplished this very week, and ready for the two of you when you arrive on the Monday after he returns!"

After the rather lengthy, lingering exit and their requisite, repeated thanks, I walked to the street with them, simply because I just could not surrender myself easily to yet another good-bye! They hurried off to their hotel, thence to catch the morning's first train toward Cologne.

Later, I lay in bed staring into the darkened ceiling, replaying every sight, everything that was said, every detail that had transpired that night. I would definitely make sure Tante contacted Goebbels for Thomas's draft exemption—immediately!

I had never been so reluctant to go home, nor so anxious to leave it, as I was that Christmas season of 1940!

Erstes Konzert – Chapter 13 – First Concert

Tante Geli got not one, but two harpsichords!

She told us that Goebbels had been so intrigued with her proposal to extend our concert repertoire more fully into the German Baroque that he had committed extra funds for the needed instruments!

The second bed was also delivered, bringing in tow its dressing table and another bedside cabinet. Thomas's bed went flat against the far, northwest wall; the headboard of mine remained against the near wall, with the bed itself sticking out into the room. That arrangement made mine look more senior which, after all, I was!

True to their schedule, Thomas and Ulrike reappeared with trunk, other luggage, boxes of music and duplicate sets of wooden transverse flutes and recorders on that next-to-last day of 1940. The following two months were a whirlwind of activity for them, as they arranged their classes, pulling both Albert and me into the vortex as we helped them learn their way around Leipzig and its institutions.

I was in paradise, being able to see Thomas almost every hour of the day!

Every moment away from him was innervated by the reminder of just how soon I would be near him again. I spent several evenings watching as he sat on the edge of his bed, with now 19-month-old Molly sitting on the floor between his legs, looking up at him adoringly. He stroked her and talked to her, "Pretty Molly! You're a big, beautiful bear, aren't you Molly Bear? Moll-ly, Moll-ly!" Except for her stump of a tail, which set itself to re-stirring the milky universe, she would just melt into his hands, her big brown eyes staring up at him. Damned lucky dog!

As I was no longer the sole protégé, traffic through the house became not quite constant, but unpredictably disruptive; I could no longer practice there freely. So, the three of us signed up for practice hours at the Conservatory. Thomas and I learned not to choose rooms too close to each other: the temptation to stop and try to listen even to those few *fortissimo* sounds that might filter out from each other's sessions was just too great!

And now, Albert began to appear at the front door, sometimes puffing in breathless haste, every moment he could get away from his parochial and diocesan-staff duties. I hadn't seen him this much since the years he was living with us on the farm!

But it wasn't me he was dropping by, so eager to see. There was someone else here to whom he was drawn, dragging him towards her with what I knew were longed-for tendrils of desire that his deepest needs spun, that grabbed him and held him so strongly. I could see it in his eyes, his actions, and hear it in his sighs.

Did he admit such things at confession? I thought not!

Well before Thomas and Ulrike appeared, I had volunteered to take over duties at the Thomaskirche whenever the organist there needed to miss a service: he was now too often alone at his post, after his assistants and pupils had been drafted into Wehrmacht, Luftwaffe or war-work. Although I still treasured the antique stateliness of the Latin mass, I had also come to love the musicality of the Lutheran service, particularly Bach's settings of the old hymn tunes, with the chances they afforded the organist to spread his wings and how, in the hymns and chorales, the congregation would soar with him.

I would often take Thomas with me to the Thomaskirche when I played there. He would help me set the organ stops and, on occasion, turn the pages of those very few scores I hadn't had time to memorize: a new hymn, prelude or fantasia, toccata or fugue. But he never wanted to play the organ himself; he asserted he just couldn't play keyboard and dance at the same time. I had to accept that: it took a certain degree of physical exertion, and *daffiness*, to play one!

But I loved being with him, having him attentively near, showing off for him. It was after one of my "Thomas in the Thomaskirche" jokes too many there that he finally told me, in no uncertain terms, to call him *Thomi*. Rats! It had been the glint of fire in his eyes that had made me keep bugging him with that joke!

With two harpsichords at our disposal, Thomi and I started toying with the soloists' parts of Bach's concertos for two, three and four harpsichords, testing ourselves and the instruments. Soon Uli (she also wanted to go by her less formal name) had joined us, working into the rota with us to cover all the parts.

When Tante Geli heard the Bach-commotion arising from the parlor, she came downstairs to watch and listen to our Baroque version of *musical chairs*, or *musical benches*, echoing my own *piano tango*.

As we explained what we had been doing, an excited look invaded her face.

"That's it!" she exclaimed, "That's what we can do that will be sure to get us on the radio!

"Edi, let's see about renting a couple of additional harpsichords! We will move the pianos toward the far wall, although that will make it tight to get to the keyboard of my old piano—why it's in here, I don't know now, it just seemed a good idea at the time, and you know this room *is* quite large, so I thought, well, let's just put the third grand in here, but now, even with all of us here, it's so rarely ever played it doesn't really make sense to keep it, but just where would I put it if it were taken elsewhere?"

She stood with her hand propping her face, scanning the room, drawn off onto a different vector. I ahem'ed into my hand and she snapped back around to us.

"Anyway, there will be room, I'm sure of it! Edi, find out the cost and see. We will arrange them together so that we can get used to playing them ensemble!"

And we will ask a couple of the more advanced students from the Conservatory to play the orchestral reduction on the pianos.

"Oh, no! The pianos! The harpsichords! The harpsichords are tuned to the same scale as the pianos, right, Edi? I will call Goebbels and suggest the program! We can do it from around the corner, right here at the *Gewandhaus*. I will check with Herr Abendroth to see when we might squeeze an extra performance into their schedule.

"With the Ministry's backing, I'm sure he'll agree—he pounces on every extra-income opportunity he can find for his fiddlers!"

She seemed to have reached a felicitous pause, so I jumped in.

"Yes, Tante, the harpsichords are in tune with the pianos. I will see to the rentals tomorrow morning. We already have the solo-scores, and small orchestral scores. We should be able to find playable piano-reductions of the orchestra parts fairly easily. After all, we *are* in Leipzig!"

Thomi stepped up and handed me the C.F. Peters catalog, open to the page, pointing to the section. My finger led my gaze down the listings.

He piped in, "I'll run with Edi to the music store to check the rentals and see which scores they have in stock."

Tante was very excited!

"Uli, you and I will roll the pianos into whatever pile we need to make it so that we can get everything in here. We may have to summon Albert, oh, but I'm sure he will be along soon! We may create quite a blockage!"

"Aux barricades!" [*To the barricades!*] I said loudly, raising the fist of revolution.

Thomi grinned; he understood exactly what I meant, and toward whom the covert idea of revolt should be aimed.

Uli laughed, turned herself about on the harpsichord bench, and started playing "*Les barricades mystérieuses*" by François Couperin.

We froze in place: she definitely had the touch!

When she was done, we applauded.

Not to be outdone (or outshone!), I moved quickly to the other harpsichord and dashed off Domenico Scarlatti's Kk. 381 Sonata in E major!

Then, in a continuing show of musical rivalry, with the end of my piece, Thomi scooted his sister off the bench and launched into the third movement, the *presto*, of Bach's *Italian Concerto*.

When he had finished, we applauded and laughed, but then challenged Tante raucously to choose which among us was the winner!

"But my children, you played pieces incomparable because they are different styles, from different nations! French, Spanish and German? You are all winners! You are all *my* winners!"

She came over and gave us, each and all, a confirming hug before returning to stand at the corner of the red-glowing Steinway.

I had already moved over to sit on that piano's bench to watch Thomi's hands on the harpsichord. I didn't know why, but I suddenly had to play something special! There were emotions building up within me. I had to assert them!

I spun to face the expectant keyboard, then looked down, noticing anew those

Rachmaninoff hands and knew, in our vehemently anti-Slavic climate, that they—that *he*, in particular—hadn't heard what I had: that music sent to me by my uncles. I closed my eyes and felt the ardent, *Ivanovka*-wind: caressing the birch trees, tousling their tender leaves on an early-summer, radiant morning. I knew what to do.

My hands fell strong: rocketing into *fortissimo, maestoso*, surging arpeggiated, deep, bass-anchored waves, driving, sweeping through the master's B-flat major prelude. The lyrical, baritone line sang beneath the joyous shimmer of the soprano-notes: the glint of the sun from the sweet, *Tambov* tea-glasses, the echoes of Natalia's loving laughter.

I so wanted to be good, to someone, for someone! I ached to impress Thomi, to invite him somehow to return my longing!

With the fading of those final, booming chords, my vision returned; I looked up.

In the silence of the room, Geli seemed transported, transformed, exalted.

I had never played our secret—"our" Rachmaninoff—for anyone besides the two of us. And she had never rebuked me for those recitals of the regime-forbidden music of that Russian composer, now for so long in America. How much more abuse would this, perhaps our greatest living composer, have to suffer from self-serving political operatives, or from tone-deaf, emotionally dead modernists?

She repeated her longing, almost bereft, oft-asserted appraisal, "You remind me so much of dear Serge! And on this very piano that he himself played!" then leaned over, hugged my head and kissed my hair.

I put my right arm around her hips and hugged my dear Gelchen as she still clasped my head to her. Then I looked up and smiled, before breaking into a laugh.

"So, you will take us to dinner tonight?" I asked, hoping so!

It was the housekeeper's day off, and scavenging our way through the war-wizened kitchen was not my idea of a great meal!

She laughed, too, and with a shoulder squeeze, agreed.

"Oh, alright! If we are all ready to go, we four …"

The doorbell interrupted. Tante went to answer it, then reappeared leading Albert by the arm.

"Five!" I proclaimed.

"Yes, we *five*, can go to a nice restaurant," a jubilant Tante was finally able to finish, "You see! I *knew* he would be by to help!"

"Wait. Help? What?" Albert sputtered in confusion, casting a look toward Uli, expectantly.

"Never mind. We'll explain everything, including your work-order, as we walk!" I said.

"OK, let's go!" Gelchen called out.

We grabbed our coats, a stack of ration cards, and laughed and joked as our little group spilled down the stairs and out onto the sidewalk, toward Wächterstrasse, on our usual walking-route around, toward the Augustusplatz, directly into the Music: the Old City of Leipzig!

The night of the concert came far too quickly.

As it happened, there had been only one opening in the Orchestra's schedule at the Gewandhaus, on the evening of Sunday, March 3, only four weeks later.

"That's perfect!" Tante Geli had proclaimed, "All of Germany will be at home, rested or resting; it will be a perfect prelude to the audience's work-week! I know this is what Goebbels will want to think, so I will say it in a way to make it seem that he had thought of it first.

"You see, Uli, this is how you have to work with men! Even though we women do the actual thinking, we still have to make sure that the men can act as if they had thought of it first! Oh! And Uli, we must pick out what we will wear! Ah, it's so much easier for you boys! Just put you in a nice suit and the girls flock to you!"

Everything else had also come together with amazingly few wartime glitches. We had been able to have only one long rehearsal with orchestra and all four harpsichords. By the end of it, though, we had achieved a level of confidence that would certainly suffice. Then, on the night of the broadcast, even the radio crew had their equipment set up and working without great delay or technical catastrophe, something that Tante Gelchen said was practically unheard of!

I had called Mama and Papa and told them about the concert as soon as we knew the schedule. The performance was to be broadcast live here, in Berlin, and in other, larger cities around the nation. On a later, specific schedule, the performance would be re-broadcast, using something (the technicians had explained, secretively) called *Magnetophon*-recording, all across Germany and into the occupation-thick parts of conquered Europe.

The present conductor of the Gewandhaus Orchestra, Hermann Abendroth, was soundly capable—"but no *Bruno* [Walter]!" Tante Gelchen whispered in confidence. At least he did agree with Geli's effusive praise of our talent, and he was very helpful in making sure everything was in order, including stripping the orchestra down to Baroque dimensions. Of course, conducting a national event, one that the Minister of Propaganda himself would introduce then eulogize, wasn't going to hurt his public reputation, or his standing with the regime, either!

Goebbels was complementary in his opening statement, and unexpectedly brief.

He mentioned Tante Geli a few times, then added me, Uli and Thomi, hailing all four of us as "outstanding, supreme examples of ever-growing, German Musical Greatness."

The program was all Bach, all harpsichord concertos, and was scheduled to run just over an hour, including a very limited intermission. In some cities of the world it would have been difficult to fill an auditorium for such a program, and a fairly short one at that. But this was Leipzig, after all, and Bach stood atop everyone's list of favorites!

Gelchen opened as soloist, in the solo-concerto in E major, BWV 1053.

Such a consummate show-woman, she emphasized her movements to make sure the audience could see, as well as hear, her work! Even her dream-like head movements demonstrated that she was not only performing, but listening along with her fans: she let them know that she was sharing in *their* experience!

The audience knew very well that she was one of "their own" and they demonstrated their devotion enthusiastically. Only musicians, actors and poets touch people at this, the very root of their humanity, and garner such deepest affection. The performances of such transcendent artists become indelible parts of the profoundest emotional life of their listeners!

That night's second piece was a musical surprise for most. It was BWV 1057, the Concerto in F major, which most people knew only in its alternate form: as the fourth Brandenburg Concerto. As '1057', however, it features a solo harpsichord, and two recorders—*flutes à bec*—which are played very much as an instrumental duet. It is a refreshing variation on the Brandenburg!

This performance found me on harpsichord and, standing nearby, Thomi and Uli playing the recorder parts, instruments they had studied at the Cologne academy. Unfortunately for me, despite its "harpsichord concerto" name and Bach's interesting approach to casting the music, it is really more of a double recorder-concerto than a stellar one for harpsichord! But still, I enjoyed being on stage, and having the thrill of watching them be the 'stars' in this, their first public performance for Tante Gelchen!

At its end, the three of us rose to stand in self-conscious syzygy, to bow from the front side of the harpsichord. The applause was quite good, augmented suddenly by the assuring reappearance of Geli at this, the end of the 40-minute long first-half of the concert.

We were relieved! It's so hard to judge the reaction of a classical-music audience! You get no indication (unless you get boos, or rotten produce, of course!) until everything's over and too late to amend!

After only ten minutes of intermission, Tante Geli and I started the second half of the program as duet-soloists. We performed the C Major Concerto for two harpsichords [BWV 1061]. The instruments were placed to the left of the conductor so that we were side by side, with my keyboard pulled back a piano-bench width and a half, so that I was visible to more of the audience. Because of her smaller stature, and greater musical prominence, Geli sat at the keyboard closer to the audience.

The following finale was the "show" piece: Bach's A minor Concerto for Four Harpsichords.

Geli and I stayed in position from the previous item. Uli and Thomi came on stage to acknowledging applause, bowed and sat at the harpsichords reflected across from us: Uli opposite Geli, Thomi facing me.

At only around ten minutes, this was the shortest piece of the evening, and the most showy. With our arms moving in rising-lowering rhythms, it must have looked rather like one of those American movie musicals with all the dancers stepping together, or with the stacks of synchronized piano players. Thomi called this concerto "the 40-finger monster." It required massive restraint, mental and emotional self-control to keep our keyboard parts from pushing it faster, ever faster!

With that *monster,* and the close of the program, we received a standing ovation!

Goebbels was ecstatic! We had to stand in place after our bows as he effused unctuously, "heavenly German music performed by the best, the purest of Aryan youth and experience, a display of supreme, serene artistry, a shining light beckoning to a world sickened by the plagues of bolshevism and overweening Jewish decadence, proving through the unbounded gifts of its people that, as our Führer has proclaimed, the Third Reich will live a thousand years!"

Having heard it so often, I didn't think much about it. And Dr Goebbels did tend to blither on!

The audience returned its boisterous agreement, not considering that this ready applause betrayed its co-conspiratorial approval of his self-damning harangue.

The local political and cultural apparatus held a reception after the performance, for Dr. Goebbels and all the regional party big-wigs. Tante Gelchen was compelled to attend but, with our thanks, excused us as having studies to return to.

It was only a two-block walk from the *Gewandhaus* back to Gelchen's house on Beethoven-Strasse. We walked slowly; Uli and Thomi barely said a word. I was getting nervous, hoping it wasn't something that I had done, insecure that, somehow, I might have misstepped.

Molly raised her head from a drowsy curl-up on one of the sofas, jumped to greet us as we walked into the parlor.

Thomi pushed past us, darkly ignoring Molly's effervescent 'hello,' strode single-mindedly to the piano, and dropped onto its mahogany bench with deliberate heaviness.

Uli and I remained standing nearby, unsure what was happening.

He fisted his hands in obvious, seething anger—at the piano or something else?—like he was torn whether to punch or to play!

In a flash, Chopin's Reich-denigrated "Revolutionary" Etude, blasted forth, in an unapologetically disobedient, Nazi-defying sweep of power, of rage subsumed in musical treason, notes sparking and sparkling like anti-aircraft fire arcing across the night sky!

He stood, roared a soul-angry "Aaaungh!" raised his hands and brought them fury-fisted down hard to pound the piano, but stopped just a hair's breadth before he struck it!

Never looking up, he walked angrily to our room; the door closed firmly, almost a-slam.

Uli turned to me, looked off toward that still-echoing door, then looked back to me.

"I think he just needs someone to talk to. The past year has been very difficult for us, especially for him," she said, touching my arm lightly before turning away, into her own bedroom.

I stood alone.

The pianos rested mute, their heavy wooden frames perfuming the room with agèd scents of forests unknown, bereft now of the society of birds.

Silence.

I stepped softly down the hall, stopped briefly for a breath of strength then, with a light turn of the handle and a gentle push, opened the door to our room.

Still sullen, Thomi was sitting on the edge of his bed.

I closed the door silently, turned to him.

"You know we're just pawns, fucking tools of the dictatorship!" he spat.

"We're collaborators! doing nothing but making it easier for the lies and murders to continue! Germans are not ignorant bumpkins! Why did they let it happen; why do they let it keep happening? Why don't they rise up against it? Where are the barricades? Where is the revolution?"

He stood, confronting me as I walked closer.

"We're pipers, leading the mice, the children, to the serpent's mouth! Why are we doing this? Why? Why can't we stop it? It is so wrong!"

I knew he was right; and the knowledge shamed me.

"We both know it's wrong, Thomi! But we're too few!"

"If we were to strike against the viper, it would just turn and devour us, too—joyfully, with no glimmer of regret! That would do no good!

"We would do nothing but cause the most temporary, fleeting irritation, something that the regime could and would turn easily, to use against us, our families, friends and everyone else who might be courageous, or merely nearby. You can't kill a snake with indigestion, no matter how righteous the heartburn!"

For the first time in our lives—suddenly, almost ferociously—he hugged me, pressing his face tightly against my shoulder. A nervous shudder rocked him, a jolt springing as his anxious, angry tension escaped in a plaintive, "But what are we to do, Edi?"

Immobile only a moment, he pushed himself backwards, turning aside in a sudden re-seethe.

"Why the hell do we have to have this crap lying around! Why do we have to be so fucking afraid!?"

He reached over and grabbed my 'safety' copy of *Mein Kampf* from the dust it, and the small table that held it, had been gathering.

"Why do we have to keep this shit on display?" he yelled, throwing it onto my bed.

It hit, then bounced up from the bed. Its pages sprang open and out flew a singed scrap.

He grabbed it forcefully in mid-air as it tumbled toward him. His palm opened; he stared at its captive.

He looked up, asking in a shockingly hard, accusatory tone.

"Where did this come from?"

But as his question faded, so did his anger.

His stare dropped to the scrap.

Looking up at me again, plaintively he asked, "Edi ... *where did this come from?*"

He moved slowly to stand directly in front of me, so closely, as he held it out toward me.

"It flew to me as Papa and I were standing, heartbroken, within the burning ruins of the main synagogue in Frankfurt, on Kristallnacht," I replied.

"I know that it's in Hebrew. I had meant to try to read it, even to return it, but

I forgot it was in that book. It's been nestled there, between the same pages, since November, 1938."

Thomi looked into my eyes, searching, seeking, almost yearning: for exactly what, I didn't know.

Then his eyes returned to the slip of parchment.

To my surprise, he said, "It's not quite complete.

"The verses above, the ends of some lower phrases have been burned away."

He ran a finger along its charred edge, leaving a slight, ashen streak across his fingertip.

He sighed.

"Va yomer Adonai eth-Qayin."

He stopped to swallow, and breathed roughly: his voice unsteady as he read further.

"Éy Hebel akhika?"

It got more and more difficult for him as he continued: reading or reciting, I couldn't distinguish.

"Va yomer, ... lo yada'thi ... ha shomer akhi anoki?"

Another fraught pause, he continued.

"Va yomer, meh 'asitha? Qol daméi akhika tsa'qim éla min-hadamah!"

He swallowed slowly, painfully. His voice lowered, thickened; his gaze rose, staring out, across a room unbounded as he recited.

"V-'athah arur athah min-hadamah asher patsthah eth-piah laqakhath eth-daméi akhika miyadeka!"

He stood silent.

I could hear his struggle, wrestling against emotions. He moved closer, holding the slip of parchment to my chest. I brought my hands up and placed them on the outer points of his shoulders, supporting him in a steadying, open embrace.

He kept his face lowered as he translated, barely breaking a tormented whisper.

"And the Lord said to Cain,

"Where is Abel, your brother?

"And he said ... I don't know. ... Am I my brother's keeper?"

He paused; my heart flailed, frantic to stay afloat in the flood of lamentation flowing from his voice.

"And He said, What have you done? Your brother's voice cries out to Me from the Earth.

"And now you are cursed by the Earth, who has opened Her mouth to receive your brother's blood from your hand."

He leaned forward, resting his forehead beneath my chin, at the top of my chest just above where his hands still cradled the parchment to my chest, pulsing with my every heartbeat.

"Why do they hate us?" he asked, an almost silent plea.

"The pain, Edi! the helplessness! the loneliness!—so terrible! so unbearable!

"Except for my duty to go on, to help, to protect my sister ... sometimes I wish

I had not been rescued!"

"What do you mean, Thomi?"

I heard him swallow.

"We were visiting Frankfurt once. I fell into the river and a man ran down, jumped into the river, caught me and pulled me out just as I was about to be swept away, to drown."

My breath caught in my chest. I cradled his head in my hands and tilted it upward. He raised his face, his eyes half-closed in sorrow. I caged my erupting emotions with all the strength I could muster before allowing myself to ask,

"Trout?"

His eyes shot open.

"Edi?!"

"I almost lost you!" escaped me and, without thought, doubt or care, in a *presto tempestuoso* maelstrom, I kissed him!

I was consumed, exalted irretrievably within an up-surging, mind-blasting swirl of overwhelming, life-shattering heat! He wrapped his arms around me tightly and returned the kiss, almost frantically!

The heavens flashed open and everything that had ever happened in my life came rushing in, the sounds, smells, tastes—all those melodies, all those memories!—burst through my mind in an explosion of exaltation, of clarity, a seething, doubt-sweeping whirlwind of fevered, ultimate, radiant understanding!

At last my life—my longings, my passions, my existence—made joyous sense!

He had handed me his life.

And I had become his keeper.

———————————

When I awoke the next morning, my nose was tucked into his nape-hair.

Music wove through our bedroom; in the parlor, one of Uli's soprano students sang.

We lay on a single pillow. My right arm stretched forward, beneath the hollow of Thomi's neck, wrapped around his chest to hold his left arm; my left draped over him holding his right. His hands held both my arms, intertwined in place. Our legs were lying against each other's from hip to toe. We could not have been wrapped more tightly.

His breathing told me that he was still asleep. I didn't want to move.

For the first time in my life, I felt complete: complete understanding. At last, I knew that love-beyond-description that bonds two people.

The sun was rising; the jealous wind pushed frantic against the window frames. I had no idea what time it was, and didn't care. I dozed off, awoke to kiss the nape of his neck, then fell asleep again.

Tugging at my Taunus-dreams, from the front of the house floated a practiced, near-angelic soprano voice, one finishing her vocal warm-up exercises.

The house grew quiet; Uli must have been discussing lesson plans.

Clara's voice whispered, "But Edi! Listen!"

 Through the shimmering lightness of the morning air, melody filled the house, that of Robert Schumann's setting of the poem *Widmung* [*Dedi-*

DMD-13e

cation].

I held my David tightly, tightly, as closely as I could.

Du meine Seele, du mein Herz,	You my soul, you my heart,
Du meine Wonne, du mein Schmerz,	You my wonder, you my ache,
Du meine Welt, in der ich lebe,	You my world, in which I live,
Mein Himmel du, darein ich schwebe,	My heaven, you, in which I float,
O du mein Grab, in das hinab	Oh, you my grave, down into which
Ich ewig meinen Kummer gab.	I always banished my cares.
Du bist die Ruh, du bist der Frieden,	You are rest, you are peace,
Du bist vom Himmel mir beschieden.	You are destined to me by Heaven.
Daß du mich liebst, macht mich mir wert,	That you love me, makes me worthy of myself,
Dein Blick hat mich vor mir verklärt,	Your glance has transfigured me,
Du hebst mich liebend über mich,	Lovingly, you raise me on-high above myself,
Mein guter Geist, mein beßres Ich!	My blessed spirit, my better self!

Friedrich Rückert

When she sang the final "My blessed spirit, my better self," I raised my head from the pillow and kissed the soft outer-edge of his left ear. He sighed and pressed back against me. I lay my head down, my blond nose safe again within his jet hair: and we dozed.

Molly lay asleep atop the covers, wrapt in chasing-rabbit dreams, curled within the hollow of my knees.

The next night we lay in my bed, after we had messed his own deceptively, holding each other and talking.

Yes, I did remember from that long-ago park that his name was *David Schraeder*, and that Uli's was *Esther*, or at least that's what they used to be, when their parents had visited Frankfurt, checking on their store there. But I wanted to know what had happened, when and why he and Esther had assumed new identities!

The explanation was intricately unusual, its execution and perpetuation dangerous, the rationale familiar and painfully justified.

When the evil intentions of the Nazis had become unbearably obvious, David's parents had tried to emigrate but, because of the large number of Jews going through the process, they could not get visas for entry into another country. The West was already entangled within its own medieval, hypocritical anti-Semitic rhetoric, and had placed stringent limitations on Jewish migration.

Their only means of escape was blocked because, being documented, wealthy owners of a set of stores, the physical movements of the elder Schraeders were already being watched closely. They never had a chance to escape clandestinely over a border in the way we had been able to slip the poor, and therefore near-anonymous Dreschers to sanctuary in Switzerland.

The Schraeders also considered themselves to be upright, law-abiding Germans.

Like so many German Jews, they just could not conceive that a nation, particularly one that put so much pride in its culture, in its self-concept as a leader of European Civilization, could degrade itself to the point that it was capable of allowing those Nazi thugs to carry out their threats! We had all learned too late: never underestimate the conniving lies, vicious rackets and murderous acts that such conservative fiends are capable of!

The unusual twist in their situation was that, although David and Esther were definitely Jewish, like their parents, they did not present the deliberately exaggerated physical image of "Jews," so hatefully caricatured everywhere in Nazi propaganda. The children had been gifted with their mother's blue eyes, inherited from her family, the Tischmanns.

Thomi's practiced pianist fingers stroked my face as he explained, "If you love my eyes, you must thank my grandparents, Marcus and Malka. They both had deep, blue eyes.

"*Zeyde* [*Grandpa*] Tischmann was a cantor at the Choral Synagogue in Smolensk until 1898.

"When a synagogue in Berlin invited him to emigrate, he decided to escape the interminable troubles Jews have always faced in Russia, suffered in particular by those of us residing outside the Pale. *Mameleh* [*Mom*] and her sisters were then born in Berlin."

Although Esther's eyes had gained golden specks, changing them so slightly greenish as she had aged, neither of the twins drew attention as looking *Nazi-typically* Jewish. They had also been raised with other German children, of assorted religion and confession, and spoke and acted just like so many other, urban, urbane Germans. With this in mind, and all other escape-routes having been closed, their parents had decided in desperation to hide their children—in plain sight.

"Our parents had a close personal friend and business partner in Cologne who wasn't Jewish, was a member of the minor gentry, and was married but had no children. He and his wife, Wolfram and Sigrun von Eisenberg, agreed to shield us. They adopted us, and brought us into their house as their own children, the unfortunate orphans of Sigrun's late, widowed, Graz-resident sister. Our foster parents bribed a bureaucrat to certify new birth records, and explained to any who might ask, that those outside their family had never met us simply because Sigrun's sister had sent both of us off to a Swiss boarding school."

With a deep, anxiety-lofting sigh he continued, "It all had been a complicated, tenuous exercise. However, the arrangement was completed successfully five years ago, in 1935, when we were 13. Like so many German families did, the von Eisenbergs had registered me in the Hitler Youth when required, but then had created convenient health-excuses to keep me away from its meetings. The set-up had worked well ever since, until recently.

"We last saw our parents the final week of April, just last year, when they had been invited by the von Eisenbergs to spend a hidden Passover with us at the mansion in Cologne."

More distressed, he added, "Esther and I haven't heard from Mamesheh and Tatesheh since—we fear, we're terrified of the worst!"

"This entire arrangement became far more complicated two and a half weeks after that last visit, when the von Eisenbergs were killed. The train car they were in was sitting within the station in Cologne. The blast of a direct hit blew it apart, during one of the first Allied air raids on Cologne, late in the evening of May 17, 1940!

"As the von Eisenberg's legal children, we inherited the certified 'Aryan-owned' business, along with all the property and titles of the von Eisenberg's.

"Although sale of the von Eisenberg's holding of our parents' original, Tiergarten-area store in Berlin and the branch in Frankfurt went through easily, we were compelled to spend quite a bit of the legacy during disposal of the one in Cologne. With the persistent threat of Allied bombing, there were few offers, even to buy just the real estate within the city! At last, the mayor's office and the gauleiter stepped in and arranged a merger, at a hefty discount (and payola, the Nazi crooks!), with another large store.

"And so, we have been orphaned," said David somberly, "not once, but twice!"

I wrapped him in my arms and held him. I understood deeply the crush of loss falling upon ever-mounting loss!

"I love you, Edi," he whispered in my ear before he kissed me.

"I've loved you since I first saw you, wet, wrapped in that big towel, fished freshly from the river! You were so beautiful, and so cold!"

He sighed into my neck, "Yeah, but I'm not cold now!"

I promised myself I would be his warm shelter, imperfect as I was, and so limited, so constrained being now my abilities.

I would strive to be a better, inseparable *Jonathan* to this David!

Auf Tournee – Chapter 14 – Touring

"I promise! I will never call you *David*, and especially never *Trout!*"

"And never say anything in Yiddish, either!" he added.

I promised again; I understood.

Either of those would be an immediate give-away if his sister were to hear, telling her instantly that someone beyond the two of them was privy to, perhaps had uncovered, their secrets. The distress and anxiety this might bring her, he was ever unwilling to chance. Fiercely dedicated to her, he sought to spare her all worry, all pain.

That diligence was also why he made an unfailing habit of messing up his bed at night before stepping over into mine, and then making sure both our beds were immaculately restored in the morning, hotel perfect, before we stepped out of the room. The housekeeper loved him for that. So did I.

His and my relationship became ever tighter as we spent so much time together.

When no one was around, we would indulge in the now-forbidden, foreign books he had discovered, hidden, apparently purposely misfiled from the book-burners, deep within the University stacks. I would call him *Tommaso*; he would laugh and call me *Angelo*, whispering, "l'amor mi prende e la beltà mi lega..." [*love seizes me, and beauty holds me fast...* {Michelangelo}]

More somber, we delved into those situations and circumstances before we had met, first in Frankfurt, then in Leipzig, of our childhoods in such different sections and neighborhoods of Germany, of our common experiences at the academies, of our families. He spoke dejectedly, painfully of his mother and father. Although they had not been strictly observant Jews, they had always kept the Sabbath together, if possible. I told him that if he wanted to celebrate it—as much as he could remember, since we had no texts—that I would certainly be his *Shabbes goy*, or even an ersatz *oyrech*, with what little we could make of the *simcha*.

So, every Friday evening that we were at home in Leipzig, although having to wait well after sundown to avail ourselves of the privacy of night, he would celebrate his heritage, and I would help however I could. I was deeply pleased by the peace that came over him whenever we did this: it gave him the comfort of union, of restored, unbounded acceptance, and cemented the fact that we truly belonged together.

On Saturday night, with the timing again offset because of having to secrete ourselves and our activities, I would attend while he closed our Sabbath by reciting the *Mourner's Kaddish*, driven by knowledge that his adoptive parents were dead, and the gnawing, inescapable suspicion that his own parents were no longer alive. I heard him say the Kaddish so often that I had soon memorized it, too.

The first time we did this, after our final "Omeyn", he broke down; I held him tightly, silently as he mourned. With the passage of weeks into months, he became less overtly distressed. But he never lost a wrenching, aching sorrow, and I never stopped holding him.

To help myself maintain the inner strength I felt I needed to carry on, both for myself and for Thomi, I had retrieved Father Vogler's gift, and started praying the Latin rosary, Sunday mornings after the *Kaddish* evenings. Thomi would sit beside me quietly.

And as I finished, Thomi—no, my *David*—would say, "Amen."

We were committed, together.

———————————

As the war in the East dragged on (and was turning so obviously against Germany that even the Propaganda Ministry was unable to disguise the awful, foreboding truth—an intelligent person would see stock film-footage in newsreels only so many times before apprehending fully what's going on), the house filled with talk often about the abysmal drop in enrollments at both the University and the Conservatory. Young men were failing to show up at the start of semesters; some would evaporate right in the middle of classes!

Tante Geli told us that she had heard that Goebbels was still trying fitfully, in an attempt to preserve his vision of German culture, to make sure that at least the most musically-gifted young men were not sent directly into the army. However, his sporadic efforts didn't result in enough matriculations to guarantee the continued existence of all the several German conservatories.

Throughout this time, though, Uli stayed very busy with her own studies, her pupils and projects, blossoming from the attention she received from her very appreciative conservatory-students, and its expansion of her self-confidence. She was becoming very much a real "knock out" as the most beautiful American movie stars had been called.

It seemed Albert was at the house more and more: he had definitely noticed!

———————————

With Tante Geli's persistence, Albert had at last requested, and gotten leave from the suffragan bishop, his father's friend Hagen, to travel and perform with us for several of our out-of-town concerts. Even after his ordination in 1942, Albert returned to his assignment in Leipzig, and traveled with us frequently.

With each trip, though, he seemed to be more and more taken with, almost overwhelmed by Uli. Although he and I still talked, he no longer confided his passions to me. I could only sense that they were singularly-directed, intense and growing. I dared not ask about his private world, hoping by this to avoid inciting his prying into mine. He did have the chance, though; he ate at least one meal with us every day or two!

His meal-taking here was not a major problem, though. Tante Geli's tight connections amongst the insiders at the Propaganda Ministry provided her with extra ration cards herself, and additional ones for each of us, too.

Although rationing had been introduced in late 1939, immediately after the invasion of Poland, it wasn't until after the attacks on Russia had unmistakably failed and the Wehrmacht was being forced to pull back, mid-1943, that our household started feeling the full effects of Germany's mounting military failures.

Individual rations were reduced tremendously. And it took more of our extra allotments to make up for the difference, given that there were any victuals in the shops to purchase! It was then that the average German went from looking no longer merely thin, but gaunt. Albert was now slimmer, too. Odd it was for me, though, that Bishop Hagen was still as vermillion-faced fat, if not even porkier than he had been before the war!

As musicians, we were engaged now either in playing to smaller audiences, outside the larger cities and their increasingly frequent bombing raids, or in entertaining recuperating soldiers.

I felt guilty. In those audiences I saw men, mostly my age or younger, whose bodies and lives had been forever mangled by this war, at the very time I was being coddled by the same criminal regime that they had gone—innocently, idealistically, naïvely—to extend and preserve.

Heartbreak, guilt, anger were assuaged only by the look of appreciation on their faces, comforted by the music or simply its demonstration that they had not been forgotten. If it lay at all within my power, I would make sure the music said that to them. I just could not understand why German "master-race" leaders were so easily set on maiming, on slaughtering these, our beautiful German babies!

Those leaders were unquestionably insane. You cannot be a "master race" if you do not master yourself first. But having mastered yourself, you can only realize, in humility, that there is no such thing as mastery of others and, more deeply, that there is truly no such thing as *race*.

By the fall of 1943, we were travelling in the north and west of Germany no longer by train, but primarily by bus. The need to avoid these major city-centers, to maneuver around damaged roads and blown bridges meant that we were often delayed, circuitously detoured in getting to our concert-venues.

We were practically the last vestige of the *Strength Through Joy* program.

Goebbels seemed to be hanging onto us partly for propaganda purposes, and otherwise simply to maintain his bureaucratic position, retaining control over all still-active cultural resources.

Filling both goals, he had lately informed Tante Gelchen that he expected us to be involved in providing the score for the big project whose production he had started earlier that year, a movie called *Kolberg*.

Those 120 km of tortuous, as-yet unbombed, but ill-maintained rural, mountain roads across the Eifel and through the Hunsrück on the last Saturday of October meant that, although we had left Bonn in the early morning, we reached the site of our next concert, in Oberwesel on the banks of the Rhine, only just after lunchtime.

The ancient bus trundled up into the open lot on the north side of the village's *Liebfrauenkirche,* complaining ever louder as it convulsed, arcing around to a stop.

We stumbled out into the afternoon's weak sunshine, stretching and groaning away the road-weariness.

A gust of wind eddied the aroma of the dense forests of the Taunus on the far, eastern bank of the Rhine: we stood only 20 km to the southwest of the farm in Singhofen! I looked away toward it, and let my longing for home absorb me.

Here, only one Rhine-bend south of the Lorelei, I, unlike Heine, knew exactly why I was so sad: it was no fairytale from ancient times. Gramma, Mama and Papa, my home, my own *German night-thoughts,* stood near, yet now so many ages afar.

But I shook it off.

Oberwesel, caressing the wavy flank of the swollen River, was too lovely not to seduce me away from such melancholia. I glanced at Thomi, my secret "Trout" awash in the Rhenish breeze, and could not help but see in him the well-proved verse, *"many waters cannot quench love, nor can the floods drown it."*

If we might just continue treading water until rescue must surely come…

Thomi, Uli, Albert and I left our few fellow passengers and meandered around the parsonage toward the gallery at the north entrance to the church. The slight, 11° breeze would have been quite chilly, but the sun had finally pierced the overcast, so our light coats were all we needed in the crisp, Rhine Valley air as we approached that north-facing side of the Liebfrauenkirche.

With the clearing light, Albert stopped and posed the three of us, to snap a photo before the sea-bound river, and its age-cut cliffs.

The sides of the very tall, black-roofed octagonal spire stood bright in the inciting October sunshine; the quadrangular stone tower on which the spire sat warmed its flush tones. The weathered-rose, almost-red, lofty stone heights of the nave-exterior were in shadow, letting the rays that shone through the fully sunlit southern side reflect through, to penetrate the lance-like windows of the tall, northern wall.

We walked into the open arcade that roofed the entryway; an ancient door led into the half-nave-height north aisle.

The door stood ajar, propped open for quiet passage. We could hear the rustle and murmur of a crowd inside the church. The four of us stood out there, reveling in the medieval arches and their stonework tracery, supporting a covered, cloister-like walkway: an entrance-pier, just outside the nave, this moored *church-ship.*

Thomi and I had strolled off toward the western end while Uli and Albert stayed near the door.

They edged ever closer to each other.

Her face turned fully to his, Albert was staring into her eyes, ignoring us and the world around them.

Suddenly, Albert pulled her close and, at last, kissed her. Deeply.

At the very moment their lips touched, the voices of the choir inside broke gloriously into the chorus of a Bach cantata.

Der Himmel lacht! Die Erde jubilieret	Heaven laughs! Earth rejoices
Und was sie trägt in ihrem Schoß.	Along with what she bears in her womb.
Der Schöpfer lebt! Der Höchste triumphieret	The Creator lives! The most-high triumphs
Und ist von Todesbanden los.	And is freed from the bonds of death.
Der sich das Grab zur Ruh erlesen,	He who has chosen the grave as rest,
Der Heiligste kann nicht verwesen.	the Holiest one, he cannot waste away.

BWV 31

Still locked, eyes closed, tightly entangled, within that same kiss, they stood immobile.

Not to be outdone, after making sure that no one could see, Thomi pulled me aside into a quick, silent kiss, too, then grinned so mischievously as he moved away.

The choir finished the chorus.

Uli and Albert broke apart only after hearing the choir director raise his voice, expounding the corrections he wanted within a particular section, followed by the well-known shuffling noises of musicians and sheet music.

The conductor had started giving them more, and more extensive instructions as we opened the door wider quietly and stepped as discretely as possible into the north aisle.

This church was one of those almost breathtakingly marvelous jewels of the German Late Gothic. Red sandstone columns of the long, rectangular nave exalt-ed the golden stars of its lofty ceiling; stained-glass windows soared, piercing the Heaven-seeking height of the walls extending above the aisle-arches.

The clearing sky let the sun play vagrant, bright and shadow, as its rays shot through the southern windows and bathed the interior floor and pews in a kalei-doscope of fluctuating hues and shades, scattered and re-colored by the after-noon's light-wrestling, south-rushing clouds.

From the far western end of the aisle, we turned and walked up the nave to-ward the singers and attendant, small, instrumental ensemble. About halfway, I stopped, and turned.

A Late-Baroque-period organ loomed majestically on one of the low arches that created the narthex. It looked a miniature version of those glorious organs of Holland and north Germany, built by Schnitger and his contemporaries 250-or-so years before. I could have stood there in trance unbound, gazing at it. To me nothing—perhaps except for a piano—promised such a wealth of music as did the glinting pipes of a classically built organ.

Thomi tugged my sleeve, recalling my attention.

As we neared the choir, one of the singers pointed toward us, prompting the conductor to turn. He stepped over to us quickly and introduced himself as Herr Stresemann, director of this, the combined choir drawn from Oberwesel, Sankt Goar, from all the Rhine valley immediately south of the Lorelei. His ensemble was going to perform the following weekend. We explained that we were the ones advertized as performing there in the church the afternoon of the very next day!

As we chatted with the director, a thin, elder priest stepped through the same door we had used, and walked briskly, his cassock rippling behind him, through the shade of the north aisle and directly toward us. He waved "hello" to the musicians, who returned his greeting with mixed-chorus hello's and *good-afternoon-father*'s. Albert had loosened his jacket so that his clerical collar showed, and when he turned to face the approaching priest, the meager pastor smiled and walked purposely in Albert's direction. As the priest approached, he extended his hand in greeting and said, "Ah, Father Neumann may I presume?"

"Yes! Father Egger?"

"Indeed! But please, do call me Klaus! We received all the information about the concert from the Ministry along with a note from Frau Gellert. We are very pleased to have you, you all," he turned as he motioned to the remaining three of us, "visit us here!" But after that sweep toward us, he stretched himself to his full height and looked around, beyond us, as if scanning a field for lost sheep.

"Where are the others? Is there not supposed to be an orchestra, too?"

"Yes, father, there is," I replied.

"A very few of them are outside, near our bus with the instruments. However, the remainder of them are on a second bus, and we have lost contact with it!"

"Oh, my! That doesn't mean the concert must be cancelled, does it?"

"That's uncertain right now," I ventured. "Would you have a telephone I might use to check on things?"

"Certainly! If you would come this way!"

Father Egger rushed us into the vicarage. I placed calls to Bonn, to Cologne, and finally discovered what had happened. The other, even older bus had broken down not 2 km from the site of our last concert, near Bonn. With a blown engine and wartime privations, it wasn't going to be able to deliver its load of musicians to Oberwesel in time!

I realized that we had no choice but to improvise a program. So, we set to work immediately, to overcome the fact that the musicians present were either too few or instrumentless.

Using the church's own harpsichord and organ, Thomi and Uli's recorders and Albert's cello, the four of us were successful in bringing together a Baroque-only concert that next afternoon.

Despite the hardships, or perhaps because of them, the reduced concert was very well received, and Tante Geli told us after we had returned to Leipzig that Goebbels himself had been exceedingly pleased by the local gauleiter's report of the incident. Goebbels was full of admiration and appreciation for our resourcefulness in the face of all the war-time problems.

There was even a rather detailed article not long afterwards in the Nazi-official *Völkische Beobachter* newspaper, praising us for showing "resourcefulness in the face of great adversity, true dedication to the happiness and welfare of the German people, and strongest determination to fulfill their pledge to the Führer that is, indeed, a great example to us all!"

We didn't know about any such *pledge*, and certainly none to that *Alberich*!

We were just doing what felt right and natural. Musicians simply must make music, and it takes more than a busted bus to keep us from it!

Sunday night, the 14th of November, 1943, was cold and raw in Leipzig.

The dark afternoon had been barely able to hold itself above freezing, and the personal discomfort of the persistent drizzle had descended into communal misery.

We sat together on the gathered couches in the parlor, in the glow of that toastily rich-veined Steinway.

Albert had said mass four times that day and was starting to sound hoarse when he walked through the door around six. On hearing his greeting rasp, Tante Geli sprang into action immediately, with all the home (or hotel) remedies that her years of touring had taught her, and whose ingredients our increasingly limited rations still permitted into the house.

Franco's Falangists had started rebuilding Spain's orange and lemon industries (with Catalonia at gunpoint, I wagered) and small shipments of those fruits found their way here into Central Europe, although in quantity only on the black market. Our housekeeper had been able to procure three, still mainly green-skinned lemons. Tante Geli had Elsa juice half of the ripest one and add that to some honey and half a glass of her prized, long hidden-away reserves of Tennessee sipping whiskey for Albert.

He nursed the nectar; his voice loosened; his public, priestly reserve relaxed.

While we sat, lounging about with blankets for extra warmth, I looked over at Geli and called out, "Tante! Tell us about how you came to get the special Steinway!

"You've mentioned several times to me that it came from an admirer, but you have never revealed the full details!"

Well, Geli had decided that she merited medication, too, so she was sipping on her own, larger glass of *cure-all*. She had offered some to each of us, but Thomi and I knew not to take the chance that liquor might cause a slip of the tongue. It seemed Uli understood that, too, so we three just sipped carefully at our mist-lofting cups of broth.

"Edi! You ask me in a condition when I may not be able to guard my secrets!" she laughed.

I knew that those lingering sips of liquor she had so far indulged in were going to get us more personal information than she would normally allow herself to divulge! All we had to do was to get her started, and she would entertain us for the next few hours!

"Oh! He was absolutely the most beautiful man—beyond anything I had ever dared dream! Blue-eyed-blitzing, deepest chestnut hair, baritone voice so luxurious, so scintillating: a Stradivarius would weep in exquisite jealousy!

"Aleksey, a Russian count, not long escaped from those dreadful revolutions: you know the communists stole everyone's property—not just from the nobles!—well, he had been smart, and escaped with everything he could ship out right after the first, Tsar-toppling revolution, so he was gone before the onset of the Bolshevik terror! Ah! The eyes of a saint, the body of a Greek god, skin like cream, the hands of an artist, the legs and marble-hard butt of Michelangelo's *David*, the c—" she caught herself. Her face turned slightly red and she giggled, "Well! We won't talk about *that* piano stool!" She took another sip, coughed slightly, cleared her throat shaking her head and remarked, "Needs more vodka!"

"But, Tante, I didn't think it had any in it!"

"You're right, Edi! That's exactly why I said so! … But, oh! the Count was amazing! It was New York, 1924, just heading into '25 … almost before I had registered at The Plaza, he started showing up at every one of my concerts, bringing flowers, candies, champagne … always *dressed to the 9's* as they say in English, so elegant in black tails … at last, how could I refuse his invitation to dinner? … his limousine was exquisite … the moment I sat in it he wrapped me in the most exquisite sable stole—it was almost as big as a tablecloth! I wore it everywhere we went! to restaurants, to the theatre … oh we did so enjoy that year's new musical, *Lady Be Good!* George was such a gentleman, and such an amazing talent!"

"George?" I interrupted.

"Gershwin, of course, dear! Oh, *Fascinating Rhythm,* such a fantastic piece of syncopation! We met him after the premier—he said he adored my playing, of course I could not deny my enjoyment of his music—such delight, such fun! He invited us to a soirée at his apartment … his brother Ira and his sweet-heart, Leonore, were there, and others—I certainly had not expected such a crowd, nor so large a flat! But after all, it was New York!

"After he begged me, I gave in and played some Mozart and Beethoven, then I asked George if he would play something for us. He sat at the keyboard; Ravel and I stood aside as George played his solo-piano version of *Rhapsody in Blue!* Oh, it was amazing! If Aleksey could just have stopped for a second his talking to Serge—yes, your *Rachmaninoff,* Edi! Those exiled Russians could be so clannish and morose: Serge was *always* looking for fellow White Russians to smoke and mope with! … Russian governments seem always to have excelled at doing the most stupid, oppressive things just to run off their most talented! Serge! Stravinsky! even Serge's friend, that *flying-boat* man, ummm, Sikorsky!—I'm sure Aleksey would have enjoyed it as much as I did! … George promised he would send me a copy of the score. And he did, written in his own hand! I'm sure it's upstairs in one of those boxes! There were some other friends of George and Ira's around, including Russians, Americans and a few Germans, all of whom had helped George by putting money into the musical. In fact, two of them—startlingly handsome—looked very much like you two, Edi and Thomi! Although I do believe you have them beat! Too bad for the ladies, though! I heard from someone there that they were 'an item', if you understand. Still, they were the most charming, polite and entertaining men: so funny, brash and both so full of tall tales of Texas, cows, and those tumbling things out there! George often called the blond one 'Spats', teasing him mercilessly about his always wearing cowboy boots, even with his tails!"

I could not believe what she was saying! She had met my uncles? It simply *had* to be them! And Edo and Reinhold were just like, well, me and David? It shocked me that I hadn't realized that, but then, I had been so very young the last time we were all together! And Gramma! She knew! She had called both of them "my sons"! I suddenly realized just how wonderful, loving and special, my Gramma was! And Papa and Mama: they must have known, too!

I wanted to yell the joy I felt, but didn't dare reveal the slightest hint of reaction to what I had just learned! To have done so could have caused so much trouble for me, my Thomi, and for our Uli, as well!

"George wanted to keep talking shop with me and Maurice—you know, music, and the show. And Ira, and everyone else it seemed, wanted us to stay, for us to play more. But Aleksey wanted to leave, so we said our sad adieus and went back to his place.

Geli paused for a long, fortifying sip of her elixir.

"By that time, I was really feeling the champagne! We walked into Aleksey's suite; he closed the door and slinked up to me moaning softly, so sexily in Russian. Oh! Being made love to in Russian! Every word, every sweet, sumptuous sound brought his luscious mouth closer and closer!

"О! Моя любовь, свѣтлая! Свѣтъ міра! Любимая любовь! [*Oh! My love, {so} radiant! Light of {my} world! Belovèd love!*]"

She paused, seeming lost in lyric memories, unconsciously fanning her rising flush with one hand, taking sips from the glass held by the other, working to catch her memory-abated breath.

"When he put those beautiful arms around me, and held me, well, his lips burned through my soul and I was just *gone*! He had us both gloriously naked before I realized he wasn't still kissing me! And when he asked me to wear just that stole and my high heels, what was I to say?" She stopped and looked at us.

We were staring at her, utterly rapt.

"Am I shocking you, dears?"

"Well! You're all adults now: you need to know about these things!

"So, I did as he asked, trailing the edge of the stole over his body, tickling him, wrapping it around his … bench … teasing him. I had thought that *I* was the musician, but someone could have written concerto after concerto about *his* rhythm, all his *allegro tempestuoso*'s, *adagio amabile*'s and *presto* groan-*issimo*'s! The next morning, I awoke to find him propped up on his arm beside me, staring at me, too handsome to be anything but a phantasm! a dream! I felt something just beneath my chin, and when I reached for it—stop laughing, Edi!—found a diamond and ruby necklace!

"After that, I wore the stole as I came on stage for every performance and, as our own little joke, left it draped over the bench beside me as I played. We were together so often those next two years—even on my tours in northern Europe, he came along! When I would return to Germany, he would go back to New York, then I would arrange another schedule of performances over there. Whenever we were away from each other, he would let me know the times he would be near a phone for us to talk!

"He called me *моя любовь, my love*, always; and taught me to say *мой любовникъ, my love, my lover*, back to him. He went out and purchased that piano right there especially for me, and if you look inside, along one edge, down near the soundboard, he wrote *для моей настоящей любви: for my true love!*

"Everything was going absolutely wonderfully, or so I thought, until the day that his milk-cow, butter-fat countess wife and their eight children showed up on a ship from Rome!

"Of course, he pleaded with me!—he wanted to get a divorce, but it was impossible because of the perpetual, incorrigible backwardness of the Russian Orthodox Church! Couldn't things stay the way they were? He really loved only me!

I was the love of his life: the only woman for him! …

"I snapped back, 'Of course, Aleksey, the only woman! … and those children just popped out of *where*?'

"Well, that ended the affair right there!

"Of course, I kept all the things he'd given me! And I made certain to take *that* piano! If he had been treating me like a courtesan all that time, I was damned sure that I was going to be well paid!

"Then, despite the anger, the pain-splattered rage, I simply *had* to cry on someone's shoulder. George ran over immediately! Such a wonderful man! He seemed terribly lonely back then; I was so happy and relieved when he finally met Kay!

"Not long after that emotional cataclysm, I rebounded into the arms—the utterly boring arms, I came to find out—of the man who would be my first husband; and two years later, the equally spindly arms of my second husband, and then of my third husband.

"That third one, I may have told you, was the one who ran off with the emaciated soprano! A scrawny, off-pitch, nasal-whining, swan-legged, crow-voiced stick! And he could have had these!"

She cupped her hands in front of her Teutonic breasts.

"At least being so often in New York with George and Serge gave me the opportunity to hear new music, and to experience exciting and innovative ways of interpreting classical European music! One of the utterly romantic pieces that showed up over there around then, one that I adored, was Max Bruch's *Concerto for Two Pianos and Orchestra*. Indeed, I was so fond of it that I arranged to get a copy of it, and to have it made into a three-piano reduction! It's upstairs, too, probably with that score of *An American in Paris* that George sent me."

She pulled herself, unsteadily, to the edge of her seat, "I know! Let's go upstairs and see if we can find some of that music!"

I stepped over to help brace her wobble, but she took off up the staircase before I could reach her! Thomi joined me, laughing as we sprinted after her. We were finally going to get to look through some of her secret collection!

When the two of us caught up with her, she had already unlocked and was within one of those side, treasure rooms, scanning the labels on the sides of the boxes that had been cataloged and stored there, in orderly, stacked rows. She tapped one box stuck into the topmost tier but one.

"Edi, you're taller and stouter than I am, come grab this one!"

Thomi helped me get the one above it out of the way and I managed with difficulty to extract, then set the one she had requested onto the floor. Tante untied the twine securing it, pulled off the cover and started looking through its contents. She would ooh, laugh, "now, where did that come from?" hand us pieces of paper, photos or little objects with finger-pointing commands, "Look at that!" "Can you believe that!" But that wasn't the box!

Considerable hefting and two case-pilferings later, at last she found a packet that contained a manuscript. On the front, it said "Bruch" and from it Tante pulled the three-piano reduction of his double-concerto and spread out the first of the hand-written sheets.

While we were lost in our musical adventures, perusing the score, Albert and Uli appeared at the door.

"Good night, Geli!" Albert called, "I have to run; I must be up early tomorrow!"

"Oh, OK, dear! Be careful! And be sure to keep warm! Wrap your throat securely against the cold!

"Ciao, darling!" she called out, unable to divorce her attention from the music for too long.

Uli chimed in, "Tante, I'll be in my room. I've got several things to review and plan before the morning's lessons. Good night!"

Geli again didn't arise but looked up to the doorway and said, "Certainly, dear! Good night!"

The two of them disappeared from the hall, down the stairs.

After shifting through the rest of the box's contents, Geli sighed, "Well, there's nothing else interesting in this one! Shall we see how the Bruch sounds?"

Instantly down the staircase, we three laid the contents of the packet out on one of the sofas. A quick survey showed that all three parts of all four movements of the concerto were there.

"Who gets which?" Thomi asked.

Tante answered him promptly, "You play first piano.

"Edi, you take second. I'll play the orchestra-reduction. I want to hear how the two of you handle those solo parts. If I can convince Goebbels that Max Bruch wasn't Jewish, which he wasn't—just because he wrote a piece on Hebrew melodies doesn't mean he's automatically Jewish! And dammit! Why should that even matter?—we may have another broadcast extravaganza!"

 So, with Thomi in place on the New York, *Aleksey* Steinway, me on the Berlin-piano, and Gelchen across from us on her original, childhood Hamburg-Steinway, we set ourselves here in Leipzig into this new score.

Sight-reading our parts was not the easiest thing, particularly as we'd never heard the music before! We did a remarkable job, though, despite having to push ourselves through some difficult passages. However, by the time we got to the end of the third movement, Geli was definitely starting to fade. Her 'medication' had brought on her almost uncontrollable yawn.

So, we called it a night, and headed, still humming, to bed.

When Thomi and I were finally alone, I had to tell him my secret, the revelation hidden within Geli's rambling. He was astounded.

"You mean, Geli actually met your uncles back then? And she doesn't realize it? That's amazing!"

"Yes, it is, isn't it? But it does explain why one of the packages of piano music I received from my uncles was—except for Rachmaninoff's Op. 23—all by Gershwin. *And*, every one of those pieces had been autographed by him, many with notes to Edo and Reinhold personally! Atop the manuscript of one song, the one whose original title said, *The Girl I Love*, Gershwin had crossed out the word *Girl* and above it written *Man*!

"But Geli's memory must have been a bit pickled tonight."

"How so?"

"Although Rachmaninoff has been in the U.S. since 1918, I know that Ravel wasn't in New York until 1928! She must have met him there, then, perhaps around the debut of Gershwin's *An American in Paris*, instead of the musical she mentioned."

"But, even so, it's amazing, Edi! Your uncles met and helped Gershwin, and you met and actually performed with Hindemith! Now, you're working with a lady who, along with your family, has known Gershwin, Ravel, Rachmaninoff, and (didn't she tell us a funny story the other day about his preoccupation with bowel movements?) Stravinsky, too! You and your family have been in the middle of modern music history without even trying!"

I pulled him tighter, melting into the correction: "Our family!"

But he was right. Without realizing it, we had truly been in the midst of it! There wasn't a better word for it: amazing!

We talked more after we had lain down, those soft, gentle words one mouths breathily while floating within that glowing aura of unbounded companionship, to fall asleep, cocooned within our own eider-down, sable stole.

Deep in the thin air of the night I thought I heard the quick snap of Uli's bedroom door being shut, footsteps, then the clink and soft creak of the front door, pulled open warily before being closed even more carefully.

Molly's claw clicks ran down the hall to our door; she pawed at it and whimpered. I got up and let her in, looking down the hall into the front of the house to see what had happened. I saw nothing.

Guessing that I had dreamed the noises, I lay down again, slipping my arm beneath Thomi's neck as I slid into place, to spoon tightly behind him. Molly jumped onto the bed, circle-tromped out the snakes—one, two, three times—then curled up tightly beside us and fell quickly into soft boxer-snores, asleep.

Harmonie und Verrat
— Chapter 15 —
Harmony and Betrayal

Sun-rays sparkled in the frost: a wintry morning that made you love hot coffee and lust after a warm bed.

Thomi had already gotten us up, made the beds and left for his advanced counterpoint class at the Conservatory. It was still a couple of hours until my French tutorial, and our reservations in the practice rooms: I was in no great hurry to rush out into the cold. So, I stood at our private windows, watching the strands of vapor jump from the surface of the water in my cup into the warming sunbeam that had invaded the room.

A knock at the open door, "Yes?" and I glanced up to see Uli blinking through the sunlight reflected from the polished wood of the floor.

"Edi? Can I talk to you?"

"Certainly, Uli! Come in!"

She stepped into the room, turned and pushed the door closed softly. As she crossed the room toward me, she seemed radiant, her visage very, well, *womanly*. No longer a girl growing out of her teens, almost 21, she had gone beyond beautiful to sultry.

She came over to my bed and sat on the edge facing the windows; she patted the cover to her left, silently bidding me sit.

"When Tante was talking about New York last night, the musicians and Broadway musicals, the tall buildings, grand hotels and everything … I so much wanted to go there, to be there!

"I've always wanted to see one thing in New York, in particular. That statue! The 'Mother of Exiles': *I lift my lamp beside the golden door*…I do so want to see her!"

"The Statue of Liberty?"

"Yes. … Once, when I was young, we vacationed in Paris, and there I saw the smaller version, the statue that stands there, beside the river. But I want to see the real one! You want to go see her, to New York, don't you Edi? You mentioned that you had uncles who used to live there. Wouldn't you like to go see where they lived? I would!"

"Definitely, Uli. After the war we can go visit, perhaps even tour there!"

"That would be so nice. Promise me, promise, Edi! We'll go and see the Statue! Promise we'll all go!"

"I promise, Uli! Just as soon as this mess we're in has settled down, we'll all be together, there, looking up into Liberty's face, at her torch. Perhaps by then she will have come back to live here again, too!"

"Thank you, Edi!"

She paused, seeming uncertain, but after a couple of parted-lip, tongue-to-teeth-touch sighs, continued.

"Thomi said, and I know, you keep your promises!"

She smiled, clasped my left hand tightly as she lowered her gaze. She paused before looking back up into my eyes, becoming more earnest.

"Edi. … You are such a good friend to my brother! He has told me that he trusts you with everything, that he loves you more than a brother. I am so glad that he has finally found a true friend! He was so very lonely when it was just the two of us, before we came to live here. He says he can talk to you about any-thing …"

A furtive look-away pause seemed to search the room nervously…

"Yes, he can, Uli!" I replied, although unsure, getting a bit nervous. Just where might she be headed with this?

"Unfortunately, I have no one to talk to, no one I can share things with, things I cannot tell my brother. Certainly, I can't share personal things with Tante Geli!

"But I need to talk; I *must* talk to someone!

"I have to express my feelings, about what happened—to remember them, to know that all that happened was real! I'm almost bursting with the need to tell *someone!*"

"Uli, you can tell me anything and it will stay between us. I promise."

"Thank you, Edi!" She leaned over and kissed me on the cheek, then leaned back, preparing herself.

I waited, not sure what to expect.

"Last night … while you and Thomi and Frau Gellert were having such a good time, going through the boxes upstairs, and Albert and I said good-night to you all … well …

"He didn't leave. He came down with me into my room.

"We sat together on the bed, like we're doing now, talking. We heard the three of you come downstairs—so happy!—talking, laughing, setting up the pi-anos, shuffling scores. Albert and I talked on until, when the beautiful, heart-wrenching harmonies of the first movement started, Albert leaned over and … kissed me.

"I couldn't help myself! My hands rose and held his beautiful head; I pulled him to me! Oh, Edi! It was paradise! To have so handsome, wonderful, caring a man touch me, kiss me, want me, need me!

"His hand moved to my leg; my thigh tingled all the way to my spine as his hand moved closer and closer! He pulled me against him; he was so strong, gen-tle, and warm! Oh, the wonderful smell, that intoxicating aroma of a man's desire!

"Edi, I couldn't stop! I couldn't! I didn't want to!

"Our clothes flew away … we lay beside each other … his broad shoulders, the soft, tender hairs of his chest, his narrow waist, his hard body pressing against my thigh … his lips on mine, down my neck, on my breasts, my stomach and then … oh! his tongue! … the bed shook, I couldn't stop! he wouldn't stop! he groaned and groaned … the bed shook and shook!

"He raised himself, pushed his tongue deeply into my mouth, lying on me, covering me, protecting me … he pushed into me quickly! oh, the pain, so sharp and sudden! … I screamed into his mouth … he held me tightly, kissing fiercely as he started moving and the pain was shoved away by immeasurable wave up-on wave of bliss … the bed shook again! Oh, such heaven, such shattering ecstasy, Edi!

"Albert stared into my eyes as he moved … he said things to me that I had never heard—never expected to hear—from a man … *love, treasure, jewel, baby, sweetheart, lover!*

"Suddenly his head reared back, gasped, then shoved hard, so hard! I felt him, his heartbeat throbbing and pounding and I … I couldn't help it, I shook all over again, more than ever! Oh! I wanted it to last and last, to keep him there, to be one like never before with this man that I loved, that I adore!

"He leaned forward and kissed and kissed and kissed me as he stroked, moved and moaned. At last he lay still, still with me, still on me. He looked at me, so tenderly, and said softly, 'You … are the light of my life. … I love you.' Then he kissed me again, and didn't stop.

"Those wonderfully romantic melodies of that third movement filled the room.

"We lay there, touching, kissing, whispering, still as one, until we fell asleep."

She stopped to get her breath; she was flushed.

"Sometime after 2 this morning we woke up. He panicked when he realized the time, but then he looked at me, and his dreamy eyes softened. Again, he kissed and kissed and kissed … and we, well, it was even more glorious that time!

"He dressed, then slipped out the front door. I hadn't noticed that Molly had been asleep in her little corner spot that whole time—she must have slipped in while Tante was talking last night—so I let her out before closing my door and going back to bed, to try to fall asleep."

She paused, still flushed.

"Oh, Edi! I wish you and Thomi could find someone to love, to love so deeply! to give someone beautiful the experience I had! I had no idea that we could feel like that! So heavenly! So fulfilling, united, connected! It's almost impossible to explain! It's like all of Beethoven, Schumann, Chopin, Mahler, Rachmaninoff, all combined, harmonies, flowing, overwhelming, blasting out, all at once!"

I put my hand on hers; she grasped mine, "Uli, I'm sure it will happen to us one day, soon, don't worry!

"The important thing is that you accept Albert's love, and return it with all the happiness and love that you can. I know he must be touching the clouds with joy this morning, too!"

"Thank you, Edi! I knew you'd understand!"

A tap on the door was followed by a man's voice, "Edi? Are you awake?"

I recognized the voice: "Come in, Albert!"

He stuck his head around the half-opened door; he looked surprised at seeing Uli, then grinned. I had never seen Albert's smile grow that wide! It was as if his joy wanted to punch through his teeth from the inside! I motioned for him to come in and shut the door.

Uli stood and walked toward him. He rushed to her, grabbed her almost desperately, staring into her eyes, caressing her hair.

I moved around them quickly, stepped into the hall, slipped the door closed behind me.

A swish and a groan fell feebly from the staircase, above me.

Bed-headed Tante Geli, disarrayed in an equally disheveled dressing gown, was feeling her way down the banister with one hand. Her forehead and vagrant locks of hair were nested in her other hand, pressed over her eyes.

"Unh. I could never handle my lemon juice!"

"And good morning to you!" I whispered when she reached the final step.

"Shut up! No need to shout!"

Well, if she was going to be mean about it…

I walked right over to the *Aleksey*-piano, sat down and started playing a Gershwin song, the score that I knew now had its own, inside-joke, that autographed, *The ~~Girl~~ Man I Love*.

She teetered feebly those few feet further, over to the piano and plopped down onto the bench beside me, leaning into me. Her head lay on my shoulder, her left arm stretched around my waist.

I knew she had drifted off to the arms of her one true love, the Russian who had gifted this very piano. And I was sensing the tight grasp of my own love, too, the grandson of a Russian Jew. Our emotions were traitors to the Nazi-Reich and its insane war, and we relished it!

With the end of that piece, she stirred slightly and sighed, "That was so-o-o-o nice," then muttered, "Too loud, but nice."

I decided to see just how hung-over she really was, so I set immediately into *Oh, Lady Be Good!*

She raised her eyes and muttered, "You smart-ass! I *am* good!"

OK, it was on; let's see if she could handle another. So, I went right into *I Got Rhythm*.

She whispered, "You play those so much like George did!" then launched herself unsteadily to her feet, angled toward me.

"You know, it's good that you're so talented … and so damned pretty," she said, playing with the hair above my right ear.

"Of ik würt di slaage!" [Plattdeutsch: *Or I'd slug ya!*] she whispered, then kissed my head.

I stood up with her. Somewhere beneath all that hang-over hair she was still smiling. I moved beside her, put my arm around her waist to hold her firmly and said, "OK, sweetheart! Let's go see if the housekeeper has any *safe* remedies in her pantry!" and walked her down the hall toward the kitchen. I made sure to keep chatting, to be as distracting as possible, as we lumbered past my bedroom door.

After getting Tante Geli under repair, upstairs and back into her bed, I headed out toward the university. I cut my French tutoring short and looped back to the Conservatory. I found Thomi at the practice rooms, waiting. Damn! He took my breath away, he was so startlingly handsome! We were early, but one practice room was already free.

"Let's get this one *now*," I said emphatically, with what must have been a revealing smirk, "I want to start practicing a duet *right now*."

He grinned; we signed for it and went in together. I made sure the door was closed securely.

Luckily, the solid, wooden doors and their acoustic seals made the rooms practically soundproof—only the loudest instruments or musical passages could normally be heard from them—because I had barely barred the door when I turned, grabbed him and set us running toward Uli's 'find someone' paradise!

Looking forward to another routine morning, I swung the front door and held it open for Tante Geli. She was taking Molly walking, out into the weakly rising sunshine, before the promised rain. The 24th, this last Wednesday of November, 1943, we were all getting ready again for a normal day, or as normal as a day can be when your nation is losing yet another world war.

Back in the privacy of our room, Thomi and I were standing in our coats at the foot of the bed, arms around each other tightly, foreheads touching, talking between quick kisses about the schedules we too soon had to hurry to, what rations we would use for lunch, and where.

We were both perplexed. Albert hadn't been by since Sunday, three days ago. It was unusual that he should break his routine so abruptly, startling that he should not drop by at all. I tried to think of some rational reason for it. It had been only a week and a half since Uli had confided in me; and every time since, whenever he had come by, it was obvious that his emotions were only mounting. My only suggestion was that, perhaps, it could just be diocesan business: after all, it was only four days till the first Sunday in Advent.

We heard the front door open, harder than usual, but I thought it had probably just taken a good Molly-bounce.

Steps, pounding steps came running down the hall; the door swung open and, before we could react, a man dressed all in Gestapo-black burst into the room, caught sight of us and yelled "Seize them!"

Trench-coated men rushed in from behind him, grabbed us and wrenched us painfully apart.

He gloated, "Well! Jewish queer trash and a trash-loving faggot! Sorry to break up your little love-nest here, boys!

"But in the name of the Reich and the German people, you're both under arrest!"

Utter terror screamed across Thomi's face.

The two thugs that had grabbed us yanked our hands behind us and shoved us out toward the hall.

When they got us into the hall, we could see that others had already taken Uli and were muscling her out the front door, past Geli, standing just outside, her mouth open in unspeakable shock.

Thomi couldn't stand it. At the top of his captivity-anguished lungs he yelled, "Es—sther!".

It echoed down the hall; she turned her head and looked back, aghast.

When they got us to the street, the man who had broken in on us directed, "the girl into the first car, that one into the van. And the faggot-traitor into the other car!"

As they jerked my dearest away from me toward the van, my guts seized.

As loud as I could push it out, I yelled, "Thomi!"

He turned to me, and with a mournful, defeated look, mouthed, "David!" and before he could finish the last word of "I love you," they had thrown him into the van and slammed the door.

Geli's scream, "No! … My babies! NO!" ricocheted through the neighborhood as she collapsed, sinking to her knees.

Molly jumped, struggling against her leash; she jerked out of Gelchen's enfeebled hand and ran over to me. One of the men beside me grabbed the lead.

"Take the dog back to her! And get her inside and quiet!" the officer ordered before looking at me, laughing.

"Save your tears, queer! You'll need them where you're going!"

He spat on the sidewalk beside my shoes in unmasked, hateful pleasure, then shoved me down, head-first into the car.

––––––––––

The process at Gestapo headquarters flashed by, with excruciating, obdurate German efficiency.

I sat in the ill-lit cell, alone. I could barely remember anything that had transpired: mug-shots, fingerprints, terror-driven interrogation, a yelling, abusive asshole of a magistrate, guards with their sadism barely concealed, scarcely subdued.

No jury, no trial, only punishment: under the *Führer-principle*, you had no peers. Superiors ruled: no right of appeal.

"Ein Reich! Ein Volk! Ein Führer! — Ein Verderben!" [*One nation! One people! One leader! — One doom!*]

Geli, dear Geli! the image of her tore a deep, bleeding gash across my soul. Her cry of anguish shattered my mind, cast me right back onto that cold pew at Edo's funeral. I felt weak, helpless, abandoned, just like I did then, a ripped-apart six-year-old. But this time, I had no family with me. I gasped. What will happen to them?

And what of David and Esther? No need to hide their true names, now, at least in my mind!

Oh, David, my David!

I sobbed, aching, the deepest, bone-breaking yearning. A strangled wail, ever so silent—I dare not call a guard's attention to myself, thrust now into the pit of despair—forsaken, deserted, afraid. Only a sniffle allowed: my nose had burst, bleeding when the interrogator backhanded me because I wouldn't give information about David or Esther.

I was still David's keeper.

I would not have *his* blood crying from the earth! I dared not think more about that. Imagining his pain only cascaded into, and roiled multiply with my own. I prayed for Esther, my delicate, loving friend and begged Heaven repeatedly, pleading for a second Purim!

I shivered, cold, desolate. I envied Daniel in the lion's den, for he at least had his predators right there with him! I, however, was surrounded by a nation whose lions played invisible, just as vicious, just as deadly, yet far more heartless and stealthy, immeasurably less human, too inhumane.

"Oh, Daniel!" I thought, soothed by involuntary, but welcome visions of the Dreschers' refuge in Zurich. At least you're all safe! Why could I not have saved my own David, our Esther?

"Failure, failure, failure! Hold him, love him, unguarding, selfish, inattentive failure!" my whimpers scolded. How could I have let this happen?

Germans don't fail!

We had had that notion thrown at us so much that we had fallen into its trap: we believed it.

We Germans did not fail—except ourselves.

Paragraph 175.

I was to be sent for "re-education"—harsh re-education, too—as a registered, Regime-certified faggot, but far worse to this government, a Jew-hider, a Jew-protector, a Jew-lover.

Where now was *my* Germany, my beloved Germany?

Der Viehzug — Chapter 16 — The Cattle Train

Shoved head-first, again, into a plain black car: its musty, horse-hair stinking upholstery and blacked-out, rattling side-windows swayed and bounced over railway tracks, hurrying me out across the freight yard.

I was not allowed to see Germany. She was not permitted to see me, any longer to know me, any more to care about me.

Saturday morning, November 27, 1943.

I had started drilling the calendar into my head, accounting the passage of time as if doing so gave me some degree of fleeting power over the uncontrollable. The dehumanization, the helplessness, the hopelessness: I was learning from direst experience that emotional violence was, by far, the Nazis' greatest weapon against the free individual.

Extracted to stand cold on the siding, I could not see all the way to the engine, although I knew it was far ahead, waiting at the coaling station. An uncountable line of cattle cars, it was the only train nearest the auto-accessible road; the guards had brought me to its very last carriage.

"Aus dem letzten Wagen hob man soeben das kleine Tobiäschen.

"Es war tot."

[*From the last train-car, just then, they lifted tiny little Tobias. He was dead.*]

I recited Gerhart Hauptmann's Kaiser-era lines to myself, feeling here those too intimate pains of bouncing, rubber ball-like, beneath the heavy-handed railroad-machinery of Nazi injustice, denuded of any basic humanity, unwatched by even the most inattentive, dismissive of railroad-crossing guards.

Yellow-star Jews from a Polish-marked, occupation-area train that had pulled earlier not too far from this one were fleeing from it into the cars to which the guards were also leading me. Every-day railroad workers and select SS-enforcers were rushing, driving the unlucky stragglers, struggling across tracks with bundles of their few possessions, the final, meager remnants of lives just now ripped from their hands.

So, this, here, was the dawning truth of that pair of Nazi "*re-*'s": *re-settlement* and *re-education*!

––––––––––––

Cast into that final, ill-patched, decrepit wagon, I was greeted by the disbelieving, fearful stares of what must have been around thirty people, guarding

186

their bulky hoards, standing near or sitting on them, closely shepherding their monstrously misshapen sheep: bulging, overstuffed bedspreads.

All the passengers bore the yellow *Magen*, some displaying within its center the added, Nazis' feeble attempt at castigation, "Jude" [*Jew*].

Only one family aboard had small children. Amongst the group, a couple of teenagers rested, but there were no other youngsters. As the final carriage, it had not been stuffed like the others had been, with guards still shoving people and parcels atop each other through already overcrowded carriage doorways.

I found an empty space along one side-wall, pulled my coat tighter, and stood alone.

The wagon smelled slightly a barn: small remnants of dried dreck were still visible in the deeper cracks of the floorboards, tendrils of cow hair still pluckable from within the larger splinters of the walls. I made sure I found a more solid, less-haired area before leaning my coat against it. The cold morning air told me I would need this fortunately-rescued jacket.

A guard, one who walked in a stiff-legged falter, had come into my cell early that morning to wake me, to tell me to prepare for relocation. Saturday morning meant the police compound was quieter than it had been the previous days; it had given him the opportunity to bring along my coat, to return it.

Handing it to me, he apologized, almost tearfully, "You and dear Frau Gellert played for us at the Wehrmacht hospital in Aachen, after I had been wounded, my leg shattered in France. Your concert meant so much to all of us—it helped so many of us forget our pain, to reclaim joyful times, if only for a few minutes!

"If I only could, I … I … but forgive me! I must follow orders!"

I was so very grateful for his gifts: the coat and the remembrance! Simply returning the jacket could have exposed him to untold trouble!

The morning was coasting along near freezing; clouds assaulting the late-rising sun declared that the weather was not going to get much warmer. The cracks in the wagon, its thin, corrugated-steel roof, and the four small, high windows holding neither glass nor shutter, but only spare wire mesh, would guarantee a constant flow, the occasional flood, of frigid wind.

With heavy, boot-on-gravel steps, an SS guard rushed by to slide-slam the door shut. The hinge screamed as it turned; the latch was seated: trapped within a jail cell, again.

Pulling my wrap tighter, I leaned into the rickety wall, looking at times through the cracks in the sides and the floor of the carriage, and occasionally into the faces of my travelling companions.

Their expressions betrayed suspicion: what was an obvious German, "Aryan" doing here? Was this blond another guard? Gestapo? Was he a spy? What did his presence mean? Of course, fearful people will find ever more things to be afraid of. I could not blame them; I had known pangs of near-paralyzing suspicion while rushing the Dreschers out of danger.

After a few minutes, the father with the young children sat the older two on the family's bundles, alongside their mother, who was cradling an infant. He stood near them, produced a small, thick book and started reading to himself from it, rocking subtly. I noticed soon that its text must have been in Hebrew letters, from the direction in which he flipped the pages.

Then it hit me—it was Saturday: *Shabbes*!

After a few minutes he stopped, removed his glasses and rubbed his eyes. A man amongst the rest of the group spoke up, asking something in what sounded Polish. However, I heard him address the standing reader as *Rebbe*.

The rabbi responded to the question in Yiddish, "Ikh vays nit, Ephron. Oyf 'm onzog vom himl, geduldik muzn mir vartn!" [*I don't know, Ephron. We must wait patiently for heaven's message!*] With that, I started to understand who it was that I was riding with. Finding out even that little bit allowed me some measure of relaxed companionship, of harmonious, soothing understanding.

Strident whistles, the banging of cars jarring each other into compliant motion, a final, heavy jolt, and the journey began.

———————————

The sun's occasional winning struggle against the clouds, plus the shelter of being in the last cattle car—and therefore mostly blocked from the wind that the train drew in its wake—started to warm the carriage reluctantly.

After what could not have been more than half an hour of the slow, trundling-carriage journey, the rabbi's daughter started whispering to her mother, to which her mother answered, "Nor varte un mir vet zen!" [*Just wait and we'll see!*] But, the little girl was persistent, to the point that I understood that she was telling her mother that she 'had to go'! (My Yiddish lessons with Daniel had not gone this far into the colloquially intimate.)

After a few minutes of this, her mother looked up at me with a pleading expression. Perhaps she thought that I, obviously German, had some additional capacities that they, as exiles, outcasts, had not been vouchsafed.

I looked around the wagon from where I had sat down. It was such a run-down old carriage! How many loads of cattle stolen from Poland, Ukraine and Russia had it spirited back to the pilfering Fatherland? I stood and moved around it as best I could to reach each of its corners, checking, analyzing the woodwork the same way we had to inspect the barn at home every spring, to discern the repairs required by that winter's insidious damage.

As I did this, my fellow inmates parted and moved away, the way flocks of birds give way to hawk or eagle. As they did, stepping at times on their bundles, I could hear metal rubbing against constrained metal: some had brought the kitchen utensils needed to start a new life. The faint hint of mothballs rose from other bales. They must have grabbed their most precious, long stored-away heirlooms, their family-treasures, brought along in hopes of passing them on to their children, their grandchildren and *their* children.

I ached for the Dreschers' ancient mezuzah, just one touch, one rub: to be able to say a passing, threshold prayer for "the days of your children" just once again!

My attention re-centered, I finally spied what I needed, near enough to one of those corners; as the carriage moved, it was at the trailing end. I knelt and started pulling at the one floor-board that looked more decayed, worn and friable than the rest. I was able to dislodge some larger splinters. The board next to it was worn also, but too strong. I pulled off one shoe and started banging that board with the heel, stopping to flex the wood up and down, then hitting it again.

When I looked up, my audience appeared worried—I was destroying official property! I hit the board harder; frankly, I didn't give a damn now if I were damaging government goods or not! I *was* now government goods!

Finally, I had worked sufficient board fragments loose to create an opening I thought large enough for the task without hazarding a fall. I stood, reshod myself and called the rabbi over. In Yiddish as good as I could manage, I explained its purpose, indirectly.

"Have your little girl come over here with her mother, and the other ladies stand around both of them, as a wall, a shield."

His face flashed with surprise and immediate understanding, "And the men can do the same, after that!" he replied, revealing his immediate grasp of the process I had in mind.

He went to his wife and explained. She smiled with relief. As she walked by, she touched my arm and said, "Filn dank! a toyzend brokhes oyf ir! toyzendmol bentshen!" [*Thank you very much! A thousand blessings on you! May [one] bless a thousand times!*]

It hit me like that interrogating, nose-bleed guard's slap! She used phrases so close to those that David's mother had spoken that first-hand-hold, river-afternoon in the park!

I choked back that reaction, and replied "Zol es tsu gezunt!" [*You're welcome!*]

She smiled; whether in acceptance, or at my Frankfurt-dialect Yiddish, I was not sure. But I smiled, too.

As the rebbetzin led her daughter over to the corner, her husband explained the procedure to the others in the carriage. The other women stood quickly and moved into an arc looking outward, surrounding the impromptu latrine, and the men, as if synchronized, stood or moved in their seats, turning to face away from that corner. With this, a pattern was established that held throughout the trip, for both women and men. Whenever someone busy at *di mitl* [*the device*], as they started calling it, would make noise, those standing in the semicircle would immediately start singing to assuage any embarrassment the noise-maker might feel. It proved again what I already knew: these were definitely not the subhuman, diseased scum that that asshole Hitler preached!

As morning dragged into afternoon, inexorable hunger crept in. But more gnawing than that was thirst. I was feeling the deprivation more deeply now than in the Gestapo cell, for here was no chance of calling out to anyone for help: we had no human turnkey, no guard even to beg for water.

Germany was our jailer: no one else in the world knew that we were there, locked within that cattle car. And no one cared.

At last, sunset came and it became clear to me, again, just why my companions had stood aside, not helping while I banged those floor-boards open.

With the completion of the rebbe's close-of-Sabbath prayers, they had come alive, shifting and resettling their bundles, and building lively animation into their conversations. One of them had retrieved a little hammer from his precious store of belongings. He came over to me and, in Yiddish flavored with a Polish accent, told me to give him my shoe; he pointed at the one I had used to bash the boards.

He took it carefully, turned it round and round, checking it over, then sat down. With it between his knees he hammered carefully at the heel, making sure it was still seated firmly on the sole, then handed it back to me. "Thank you!" I said in Yiddish. He grinned and said, "You're welcome!" repeating the Yiddish phrase exactly the way I had said it earlier to the rebbetzin.

Once they had assured themselves that I was neither spy nor other, fearful ogre, they worked to bring out some of the bread that they had grabbed and put away when compelled to leave their homes in such obvious, precipitous distress. The cobbler handed me a palm-sized chunk; I was so grateful! I broke off small pieces of rye and held them in my mouth until they were moist, then chewed them slowly, saying an *Ave Maria!* with each bite, both to pace myself and beseeching Her, my only, final Refuge, for continued strength and compassion.

I had sat most of that afternoon, dozing fitfully with my head resting on my knees. But at nightfall, the rebbe invited me to share the edge of their bundle as a pillow. I had to curl my legs, with knees pulled toward chest, to stay warm. At least my coat wrapped my torso and arms!

Lying at the outside of the rebbe's little family group, my jacketed back turned toward them helped shield the children from the pernicious breeze.

The next morning, my tongue felt thick, swollen. The wisps of coal smoke from the engine had on occasion even reached this final wagon, and its irritation had made my nasal passages swell. I must have slept part of the fitful night breathing through my mouth.

Thirst was near unbearable; I had no idea how the children were able to cope. The rebbe's infant was still nursing, and it could not be long before the rebbetzin would be too dehydrated to produce nourishment for it.

I dozed—it was my only escape from the worry, the tedium, the aching misery. I awoke from a dream that I was sleeping in my own wide, soft bed at the farm, with Taunus raindrops tapping the windowpanes.

Rain! I raised my head to listen. Yes, it was raining! I stood up and leapt to the nearest of those four rectangular openings cut high into the sides of the cattle car, then stepped carefully around my new friends to check the other three.

One of the windows had a good, little stream flowing down past it, cascading from the roof. The train had been going so abysmally slowly that there was almost no wind from its motion, and the stream stayed together as it flowed in a slight arc past the opening.

Damn! There was that wire-mesh screen over it!

The cobbler wasn't quite sure if he should, but the rebbe convinced him to lend me his little hammer. I used it to prize the screen out of its mounting on two sides. Evron was obviously relieved when his precious tool was returned to him safely!

With that mesh curled out of the way, to avoid the wet, I removed my coat, rolled my sleeve above the elbow, then stuck my right arm out, reaching my hand up into the stream, while I held myself up to the level of the windows with my left arm. I managed to catch a handful of the run-off and brought it in to wash my hand, then held it out again, gathering half-handfuls to drink.

Oh, the nectar of the gods could never have tasted so sweet!

The problem with this invention was that, with the angle formed by my extended arm, there was more water dribbling down that arm and into the carriage than I could catch in the hollowed palm of that hand. The rebbetzin, though, must have noticed; she came over with a child's cup. I rinsed my arm, then re-extended it out the window so that my hand caught more of the rain. The water ran down my arm and flowed off my elbow into the cup.

Soon, others came over with cups; someone even had a vase! Someone also produced an old, rather battered cook-pot for me to stand on, to make the process easier.

Because of the chill—it couldn't have been over 5°!—I couldn't keep my hand out the window for long. So, a rota was formed, with the men holding their larger hands out the window, and the women, or men whose arms were recovering their warmth, holding the catchment vessels. After an extended shift of this work, all had had enough water to drink to refresh themselves and to survive. Everyone worked to make sure that the children and teenagers got all they wanted; we were even able to fill the vase and cook-pot, then let everyone's hands warm. While one of the men was drinking, he laughed, pointed, then called me *der Fintstr-Moishe* [*Window-Moses*].

After we had worked together and restored our vitality, I was invited to sit with the rebbe, rebbetzin and their children. He had introduced himself earlier as Aaron Schulmann. His wife was Rebekah; his eldest son, Isaac, 9; daughter, Sophia, 6; and infant, Benjamin, just 8 months old. The rebbe and rebbetzin spoke some German; whenever they couldn't remember a word or phrase they needed, we'd work as a team, taking words from Yiddish back through the sound changes that this language had gone through in evolving from its Germanic, Hebraic and Slavic roots.

When I told them my full name, the rebbetzin's eyebrows rose in surprise. She asked if I happened to be a musician. And when I confirmed it, she asked if I hadn't been on the radio.

I sighed, "Yes, ma'am."

She explained that she remembered my name because she had taught piano in their little village. It was one within the pre-1918, Prussian-ruled province of Posen, in that part that the infamous Treaty of Versailles had handed over to Poland.

The rebbetzin was extremely complimentary. They had been able to listen to broadcasts that Geli and I had done back in 1939, before the invasion. After the fall of Poland, however, the SS had seized their radio, in a preemptive drive to counter any threat of espionage or organized resistance, so they had heard nothing more recent.

Needless to say, she was shocked to find me there amongst them, another one bound for resettlement.

I corrected that, explaining that I was being sent for "re-education" because of my crime.

Rebbe Schulmann asked, "And what crime could that be, from someone who smote the window and brought water to Hebrews in this new desert?"

"For protecting Jews, people wanted by the Gestapo merely because they were Jewish," I replied, expressing that one real reason for which I knew that I was there, condemned to this journey. I had understood from the magistrate's mutterings that, with only a Paragraph-175 conviction, I should have been sent to a prison-camp within Germany. I had heard him mention Dachau.

From the words the rebbe used, and the reaction of those around us, I could only assume that he had repeated what I had just said, in Polish.

"And this? To give refuge, hospitality! This is now a crime?"

"In Germany today, anything Hitler doesn't care for is a crime," I averred.

Everyone in the cattle-wagon fell silent.

The eternal metronome of clicking and clacking wheels lurching from one rail to the next, the ghostly creaking torque of a rusty carriage-frame, of metallic grinding of the trucks as the train's inertia alternately propelled or dispelled this ultimate car, it all echoed without relief through the rough-hewn walls. The train had been sidelined several times as we were passed by faster-moving ones carrying tanks and other military supplies toward the east. This dreadful trek was slow, painfully slow.

That Sunday afternoon, I sat again with the rabbi's family. We rested against the forward-lurching wall, bundles before and on either side of us as we sat shoulder to shoulder for warmth. Isaac, who already looked so much like his father, stayed beside the rebbe. The rebbetzin cradled the infant; I held their daughter.

Sophia was so chilled that I took my coat off and spread it across her legs. She snuggled into it, tucking her legs and pulling its collar up to her neck to cover her entirely, as she rested on my lap. To help pass time for the children, their parents had been reading to them, although the adults had grown ragged-voiced around noon. After an hour or so of silence, Sophia asked me to read to her. She handed me the text her mother had been using. It was a Yiddish translation of the Hebrew Scriptures. I asked what she wanted me to read.

"Rooss!" she exclaimed.

I smiled. Daniel had explained the differences between the various ways Jewish communities pronounced Hebrew, the contrast between the *Ashkenazi* and the *Sephardi* ways. So, my sight now accustomed to those slender beams shining in from the cracks and small windows, I turned the pages of the *Tanakh*, past the *Torah* and the *Nevi'im* until at last, amongst the *K'tuvim*, I found the book of *Ruth*.

Sophia lay her head against the front of my left shoulder, to listen as I read aloud.

"Und es iz gevezen in di teg ven di shuftim hoben regirt, azoy iz gevezen a hungersnoit in dem land, und a man iz avekgegangen oys Beys Lekhem Yehuda, kedey tsu voynen in dem folk von Moab, er und zayn vayb und zayne tsvay zihn..." [*And there was in the days when the Judges ruled, a famine in the land, and a man set out from Bethlehem of Judah, to live among the people of Moab, he and his wife and his two sons...*]

To me, the Yiddish sounded rather *verdeutscht*, as if it had been tailored for the use of those more familiar with German. (Daniel had taught me that the past participle of "to be" was *geveyn*, not *gevezen*!)

I flipped quickly over to the title page. Yep. It was a 1904 translation by a German-speaking Jew, Mordecai Bergmann—published in London, of all places! The condition of its language was neither an inconceivable, nor indeed an unusual situation though, given that the rebbe's community had been firmly within what had been the officially German-speaking borders of the Prussian kingdom from the second partition of Poland, in 1793, until only twenty-four or so years ago.

My curiosity settled, I returned to task.

I started off reading slowly: so many years had passed since Daniel's lessons at the boarding house in Frankfurt! Sophia would giggle and shake her brown curls whenever I read a word wrong. Then she would correct me, and I'd start that phrase again.

I had not realized how emotionally difficult it would prove for me to continue reading, specifically when I got to the sixteenth and seventeenth verses of that first chapter.

"Ober Rus hot gezogt, bet mikh nit dikh tsu ferlozen, oder dir nokhtsugeyn, vorin avo ahin du vest geyn vel ikh oykh geyn, und avo du vest nekhtigen vel ikh oykh iber-nekhtigen, dayn folk zal zayn mayn folk, und dayn got zal zayn mayn got.

"Avo du vest shtarben vel ikh oykh shtarben und dort wil ikh begroben veren, Got zol azoy tsu mir tun, und nokh mehr, nayert der toyt alayn zol manen ayne ofshay-dung tsvishen mir und tsvishen dir."

[*But Ruth said, don't ask me to abandon you, or not to follow you, for wherever you go, I will also go, and wherever you lodge, I will also lodge, your people shall be my people, and your god, my god.*

Wherever you shall die, will I also die, and there will I be buried, God do so to me, and more, too, if anything but death cause separation between you and me.]

I had to stop, to stare into the distance, to breathe. My eyes bore a huge hole, shooting through the trailing, western wall of the carriage, back into Germany, searching, frantic for my life, my *Life: my better Self.* Where was he? Where, where, sweet Mary, *Panagia! Pantánassa!* Where was my David?

I had to wonder, too, if I would have been able to say to David what Ruth had said to Naomi. Yet, could there have been anything in the world powerful enough to have kept me from it?

But now—would I ever have the blessed chance to find out?

I swallowed my emotions and forced myself to return to reading for this dear, little Sophia. After all, my personal calamities were not something to lay on the head of so innocent, so precious a young life.

It became obvious toward the book's end, just why Sophia liked the story. It was one reveling in the triumph of Life over the challenges that Life itself can throw into one's existence. It was full of the hope that comes from love and dedi-cation to others, to each other.

I could not help but think of home, of the farm, when I read her the fourteenth and fifteenth verses of that final chapter.

"Und di vayber hoben gezogt tsu Naomi, gebensht iz Got vos hot nit gelozt tsu dir oyfheren haynt a goyel, az zayn nomen meg ongerufen veren in Israel.

"Und az er zol tsu dir zayn a derkvikung fon dayn nepesh, und az er zol dikh dernehren in dayne elter, vorin dayne shnur vos libt dikh, und vos iz beser tsu dir vi ziben zihn, hot ihm geboyren."

[*And the women said to Naomi, blessed is God who has not abandoned you today without a kinsman, that his name may be famous in Israel.*

And he will be a restorer of your life, and a nourisher in your old age, because your daughter-in-law, who loves you, and which is better to you than seven sons, bore him.]

It reminded me so much of my Gramma's high opinion of my mother, her own daughter-in-law. And as that daughter-in-law's only son, I had to repeat my question from that ride into Bad Ems, to Edo's funeral mass, "Shall I be among the 'so many' good ones, too?"

Sophia had fallen asleep before we had reached the list of males bearing sons in the final verses, so I just read them to myself as I held her. Her head lay on my shoulder, her curls tickling my neck.

Is there anything more precious than the life and happiness of a child? I felt blessed by her acceptance, her allowing me to be part of that innocent joy.

My long-sleeved shirt allowed that, as I became more accustomed and resistant to the cold, I could let Sophia continue to wear my coat, even if its edges sometimes bounced from the splintered floor of the cattle car. She was happy when she was warm, and her joy was a light to the world, to our so tightly constrained, captive cosmos.

Other than within veiled threats, no Gestapo officer had disclosed fully where I was being sent. This was both worrisome and frustrating, so I worked, trying to derive it by watching out the windows for signs every time the train became even slower than its infuriatingly lazy pace had been, as it approached yet another town or rail-side village. We had passed through Dresden without stopping. Then the names had progressed, Bautzen, Löbau, Görlitz, Liegnitz, Breslau, Oppeln.

Unease mounted, the farther east we went.

With Kattowitz this Monday morning we were no longer within Germany's, the German Republic's, borders. We had left Silesia and crossed well into what, from 1921 until autumn, 1939, had been Poland, and before that, Imperial Russia.

I had never heard of the town whose sign we had just seen when the train, again, started to slow: "Oświęcim — Auschwitz."

We came to an unexpectedly hard-jolting, painfully screeching stop.

All hell broke loose.

The door was unlocked, flung open; the cold morning air rushed in with a new, sickly sweet stench, mixing with that of a crowd of long-trapped, unwashed human beings. SS guards with guns, truncheons, dogs, and men in striped, ill-fitting pajama-uniforms bearing numbers above yellow stars were yelling at the people, forcing them to jump out of the cattle cars. The passengers tried desperately to pull their possessions from the carriages before any guard—especially one holding a snarling dog—might walk up to them. I could hear those striped-pajama men yelling into the open doors of the cars in Yiddish, Polish, German, Dutch, French, what sounded like Czech, and scraps of a few other languages.

"Leave your belongings, your bundles. You will be able to retrieve them later!"

Some of the passengers didn't hear, didn't understand, or couldn't abide the thought of leaving their few possessions behind, so they lugged them from the train on their shoulders, struggling beneath the weight.

There must have been over a thousand people who had jumped, tumbled or been dragged from the train.

With all the SS and the pajama-men working their way amongst them, it looked like a small town had just been dumped beside the track with all its laundry! But this town, the people and the boxcars (most, unlike ours, with no windows at all!) reeked of days of close captivity: of sweat, of dreck, of those who had died on the way. Yet that stench was as nothing compared to the whiffs of burnt-sugar-fat sickening sweetness that drifted in and mixed with those odors around us whenever the north wind itself had to stop and turn its head away, to catch its breath.

One of the SS-officers yelled, "Women and children line up over there; men and older boys over here!"

As the cry was echoed by other SS-men, the crowd shuffled, parting slowly. I heard one of the striped men say to the rebbetzin in a stern whisper, "Hand the baby and children to their grandmother, quickly!" She was confused, afraid: I knew there was no grandmother of theirs nearby. She just stared at him blankly while pulling Benjamin more firmly to her breast.

He turned and walked away, with "I tell them! But do they listen?" shakes of his head.

A small group of SS-officers was working its way down the men's line.

Whenever its leader spotted an old man, a young boy, heard someone cough, or spotted evidence of any notice-demanding health problem he would motion him across, over to the line of women and children.

When he came to me, he looked surprised, almost startled. He asked me who I was. After I told him, he got a smirk on his face, "Another pretty boy for re-education, huh?"

"Jawohl, Herr Obersturmbannführer!" [*lieutenant colonel*] I answered at attention with my well-practiced, but long-unused Hitler Youth voice. He seemed surprised that I had recognized his rank, obviously not a common occurrence amongst those train-loads of innocents, the arrivals he was dealing with!

As he stared at me, apparently pondering what to do with me, an attending Oberscharführer [*staff sergeant*] came over and passed one of the folders he carried to the Obersturmbannführer; the Gestapo must have forwarded the paperwork. The officer stepped back, read a page quickly, then suddenly boiled into agitation and shoved the folder forcefully back into the hands of the Oberscharführer.

"To the main camp!" he yelled.

A tall Oberführer [*senior colonel*], the only officer in the group who outranked the colonel and who, with cap pulled tightly down over his eyes, had been standing back, watching and listening, spoke up immediately.

"But, Obersturmbannführer, if I may remind you, he's obviously a *Reichsdeutscher*! [*an ethnic German*] He must go to the re-education section!"

"With respect, Herr Oberführer, I am camp-commandant now! He has been living with the Jews, making love to Jews: he will stay with the Jews! That is final!"

"I see," the taller officer said flatly and took a step back, farther away from the line. Even in his tactical retreat, he didn't appear to have been shaken at all by this sharp rebuke from someone he outranked. The slight gray at his temples showed that he was older, more seasoned. I could not see his eyes beneath that low-set visor, but his steady voice betrayed no disturbance in his mien. Indeed, to my ear, the Oberführer's voice had maintained an almost reassuring tone, rather like that woody, soulful, tenor range of an English horn; the commandant, on the other hand, had all the warmth and grace that squawks from beginning clarinet players!

I was petrified that this analogy might make me laugh; but the thought was interrupted.

"See to it that my order is carried out!" the commandant barked to an attending Obersturmführer [*first-lieutenant*].

"Jawohl, Herr Obersturmbannführer!" the Obersturmführer snapped in reply.

The commandant moved on. The moment he had progressed farther down the line, his attention returned quickly to what seemed an almost joyful task of pulling men out of line, to what end, I did not yet grasp fully.

The Oberführer, still standing aloof nearby, called both the Oberscharführer with the folder and the Obersturmführer who had accepted the commander's order over to him. He took the folder and looked through its contents apace, but with greater attention than the commandant had paid.

He stopped at one particular sheet that lay deeper within the small stack and read it more slowly. He flipped through the rest of the contents before returning to that one page. With a quick jerk, he freed it and looked up at the folder-toting Oberscharführer. The Oberführer's distance, and the noise of another train arriving behind ours meant that I could just hear him say, "I will hold this form for the moment. There is no need to record the fact."

He told the Oberscharführer to ask me my occupation. Before the question was repeated, I answered, "Musician—concert pianist, sir."

On hearing that, the Oberscharführer made a step closer and asked, "Are you any good?"

Defiantly, I answered, "Herr Propagandaminister Goebbels and the German people thought so!" but was internally ashamed even to mention that troll.

At that point, the Oberführer pulled a golden pen from his pocket, stared at me a few seconds, his eyes glinting secretively from beneath that low, black visor of his cap. He wrote something across one of the forms at the very front of the folder then re-read it while waiting for the ink to dry. He closed the folder with a militarily crisp snap of the pages, before recalling the Oberscharführer and handing the folder back to him. This was accompanied by a distinct, precise order to get the entire contents of the folder and all related documents onto his desk the first thing that afternoon. He replaced his pen, folded the sheet of paper he had extracted and slipped it carefully into a pocket of his tunic.

He spoke sternly to the Obersturmführer, "Carry out your order from the Obersturmbannführer as issued. But see that the prisoner goes to *Kanada*, and *nowhere else*. And, by all means, keep Mengele away from him! All I've said to you right now is a direct order!

"And if the commandant questions these instructions at any time, tell him you are doing so under direct order from *me*. Then come to me immediately, *with him*."

At that last phrase, he had tilted his head, motioning toward me.

He turned back to the sergeant, "Oberscharführer, you will draw up the forms that state that Obersturmführer Hofmann here has been reassigned, that he reports directly to me now, as a staff-officer."

The NCO *heiled* his salute, and both officers were dismissed. With that, the Oberführer walked away briskly, returning to the Obersturmbannführer, to witness him, plying his happy trade, progressing farther down the seemingly endless line.

———————

After we had stood there several minutes, a muffled order passed down the rank that we in the men's line were to set aside anything extra we might be carrying with us, and prepare to move toward the camp for registration and delousing. But before the shuffling of packs had died down completely, before the final order to move out, I spotted Sophia running from the women's line, across the railroad tracks' gravel bed toward us.

I knelt as she came near, holding my coat out toward me.

"Thank you!" she said and grabbed my neck in a farewell hug.

A welcome, but chillingly fresh breeze blew in, sliding towards us from beneath the carriages, while pulling its own cloud-train in from the overcast, graying north.

"No, Sophia, you must keep it!" I said softly to her.

"You will need it more than I!"

She smiled, her eyes wide with innocent joy. I took it from her hands, swung it around and draped it over her shoulders like a cape; I fastened the top button to secure it.

She embraced me, whispering, "Bay mir bistu sheyn!" [*I think you're handsome!*]

I kissed the curls above her ear and whispered back, "Un bay mir bistu di sheynste!" [*And I think you're the most beautiful!*]

She laughed.

Then stepping over, she hugged and kissed her father, who had knelt beside us.

He held her, spoke softly to her, "Take care of your mother and brothers, sweet Tzofi! Remember always that your papa loves you!"

He smoothed her hair, caressed her hands and looked into her innocent treasure-face as long as he dared, before surrendering to the painful recognition of his utter inability to avoid having to say good-bye.

"I love you, Papa!" she said.

"Thank you! I'll see you soon!" she said to me cheerfully, before turning and walking carefully—being certain to keep the coat up out of the gravel—back to her mother and brothers.

The two of us stood up.

Rebbe and Rebbetzin gazed at each other, unmistakable, unfathomable dread written across their faces. The rebbetzin turned Benjamin toward his father, so he could look into the eyes of his youngest.

Sophia leaned against her mother; Isaac reached over and took his sister by the hand as they stood together closely, facing their father as if posing for a holiday snapshot.

———————

I turned for a glimpse of them as we were led away.

Kanada — Chapter 17 — Kanada

Walk. Speed up. Faster. Faster! Run!
Run!

Leipzig's frequent journey, often several times each day between house and university had made my legs resilient. Most of the other men had not been so well prepared.

Thoroughly winded, by the time the rebbe and I struggled at last through the camp gate, we had left a goodly part of the men's group behind us. Few of those, including many from our own train-car, did we ever see again.

Stripped, heads-shaved, beards-shorn, rough-showered—boiling water, freezing water, you could hear the gasps and moans as the fascist at the taps played his childish torture-game—and that damned, painfully inflicted, dark-blue deep-inked tattoo. I had never hated numbers before; I would quickly learn to despise these, and that pink triangle.

"Pajama"-ed and badged, I had been pushed into one line heading out the door when that officer who had been reassigned by the Oberführer, appeared suddenly.

He walked quickly through the clamor to the SS-bureaucrat Scharführer [*sergeant*] who was divvying us up according to a list he held, counting us, checking his list, counting again. The Obersturmführer pointed to me and said something to this Scharführer; the shuffling clamor in the room blocked distinction of their verbal exchange. The Scharführer *heil*'ed, looked down his list, and yelled out a number.

It meant nothing to me.

Then I noticed the Obersturmführer motioning for me to come to them.

I looked down at my left arm. The tender, white inside of my forearm shone red with specs of blood and irritation surrounding the dark blue digits. The colors set me apart as an enemy: an Ally.

That Axis bastard had yelled my number!

I hurried over as fast as I could in the loose, roughly carved wooden shoes I had just been assigned. I could already feel the blisters that they were going to raise, burst, abrade.

The Scharführer pointed with his pencil to the small group of men that I was to join, pulling more men from our cattle-car over into our rank. He re-counted us, then made more jots on his list.

The man standing at the front of our group wore a different type of star. Its upward-pointing yellow triangle lay behind, but the top, downward-pointing triangle was green instead of yellow. I found out fairly quickly that he was our *kapo*.

A petty thief from Riga, he was someone we would discover we were lucky to have. "I'm a thief, not a murderer!" was something he would say under his breath whenever he was compelled to beat one of his crewmembers in front of a guard, just to retain his position as company thug. We learned, as well, to make his blows look more painful than they were: we would soon hear that too many kapos gladly beat their own men to death, even when no camp officer was around. But our kapo's innate, singular bent toward thievery and subterfuge was a skill that we all came to value, vitally.

In the deepening evening gloom, we had to run to the barracks, sabot-splinters scraping into the deep flesh of still-tender, naked feet.

The barracks were dark—no windows, just open skylights running along the peak of the roof—and smelled like a combination of our barn on a hot summer's day; that critical, no-hope ward at the hospital where Waltraut had died; and the worst, sick-to-death, make-you-want-to-vomit farts you could ever imagine. The kapo yelled for us to find a bunk and get in it, four or more to each one; it was past dinner and there would be no food or drink till morning.

Only half-occupied, the barracks had bunks available about mid-way through the building. An inmate on the next bunk told us that the SS had caught previous crews in a minor infraction and had reassigned them all to *Sonderbehandlung* [special treatment]. As he said "reassigned," he moved his pointing index-finger upwards in tight spirals, then made cloud or snow-flake motions with his fingers. I wasn't sure what he meant. He recognized my confusion, mimicked a pistol shot to his head with his hand and added, "You don't have to worry about them—they will never come back to claim their beds!"

The mattress felt barely more than a couple of thin blankets thick; the blanket itself could be considered no more than a sheet. One of the first into the barracks, I had grabbed a mid-level bunk. Everyone shied away from me—the pink triangle was having its maleficent effect—until the rebbe, the cobbler and another man from our train-car approached me. I was so pleased to see friends again, especially under these forsaken conditions!

There was room for the four of us to lie on our sides. The rebbe tried to get me to take a space in the middle—he remembered that I had lain exposed in the cattle car, to shelter his children—but I had to lie on the outside, on my right side.

Despite being exposed to the cold, it was the only way I could fall asleep now, after having slept on my right side continuously these past, almost two years with David.

The blistering abrasions from the clogs fought to prolong their discomfort, to keep me from rest. I removed those wooden torturers, stuffed my cap into one and cradled them both within my arms. A few quiet moments, and sleep slammed me into oblivion.

I dreamt I was at home, cradling Eva. Someone behind me moved; a push and I was in Leipzig, petting and talking to Molly. Then it was David I caressed: I could smell his hair, feel the tender skin of his arms. He rolled over toward me and smiled. But his blue eyes sank with explosions of crows flying out amid circling vultures; his skin melted away, leaving only vacant bones; I awoke with a start. I was gripping the clogs desperately.

Morning came at last; we were led through the new rigors of reveille. "Always have your cap and shoes on at roll call! Or else!"

We were forced to stand in place as the unrelieved minutes stretched. Some wavered, but none fell.

With the conclusion of that test, we were allowed our "breakfast": fake coffee—or tea, one couldn't tell!—but no food. The prisoners who had been there a while produced edible remnants from the day before. But because we had missed the chance at that, we new inmates stood and waited, our stomachs rumbling from the effects of something unsavory that had been tossed, or had fallen, into the brew.

The unusual thing I noticed at this first roll call was that, although everyone in the ranks had his striped, prisoner cap on, many of them wore civilian clothes, either fully, or over parts of their prisoner-pajamas. We found out all about this presently.

Beneath horribly tinny loudspeakers and their unending musical scratch, we were marched into nearby barracks. The one we entered was stuffed with pile after pile of goods that could only have been taken from those railcars hauling the transportees to the camp. Sadly, I recognized that these were the contents of those "you'll be able to retrieve them later" bundles, now obviously irretrievable. More, massive piles leaned against the back, outside of these barracks, having been trucked over from the railway siding by other inmate-gangs.

"Open the pack, sort and throw its contents into the correct pile! Quickly!"

Men's, women's, children's clothes and shoes; bedding; baskets; books, photos; flatware, dishes, cooking pans; and sometimes … food. We learned fast that the food was not usable by the SS, nor did they want it—it could be neither sold nor sent back to Germany—so we ate it, or hid it away (like our kapo taught), as we found it. This had been why those other prisoners had not minded the meager, sump-water breakfast! And anything that could replace the horrid turnip-water that masqueraded as our paltry daily ration of soup was a treasure!

Mounds of goods were also delivered from other regions of the camp, not bundled, but loose. These were almost always clothes. But among all the garments came sacks or loose loads of eye-glasses, dentures, canes—even gold teeth, and artificial arms and legs!

The first thing I did was find a jacket that would fit me, and not too tightly.

Getting the pink triangle out of sight was something I knew would help me survive: I had already been the target of sneers and verbal abuse.

Even amongst the most oppressed surges that pernicious urge to pass on the pain, to degrade others.

Abuse is father of the abuser.

Two days later, while going through those random stacks of loose clothes and personal belongings, I spotted something that almost stopped my heart.

My own coat!

I clasped it to me, breathed through its fabric; yes, it was mine! From its collar floated a couple of long, baby-fine, curling brown hairs, caressing the breeze.

Tears welled! Her sweet, child's laughter at my Yiddish mistakes! Her acceptance! Her innocent compassion!

With a furtive eye-wipe and a quick glance around to see where the other prisoners were working, I shoved it, crammed it deeply within the already-separated pile of men's jackets. The rebbe must not see it, even if there were only the slightest chance he might remember it: our last, *sweet Tzofi* blessed sight of it!

Not long after that, in the limited time we might relax at night, the rebbe spoke of his family. I knew what he was trying to say, although he couched it in vague, Scripture-avoiding phrases.

His wife had a "bachelor" brother, who had worked diligently during the worst Depression-years, buying food, clothes and gifts for his family with any surplus he might scrape from his meager earnings. When the threat of German troubles had started rising, around 1936, this brother-in-law had joined the Polish Army, and in 1939 had just been made an officer. He had then rushed off to the east to fight the treachery of the invading Soviets. No one had not heard from him since then, and they assumed he had been killed.

"No matter what anyone might say," he continued ruefully, "Anshel was a good man. He loved his family, always kept Shabbes, and died for his country! If that is not *a trayer Yid*, [*a real Jew* {or *person*}] then no one is!"

To this, our constant friends, Evron the cobbler, and Fishl the tailor, replied, "Omeyn."

At the end of April, 1944, our *Kanadakommando* started getting the occasional new, replacement inmate, paroled from those first trains of Jews and other prisoners arriving from Athens.

Among those was Nikos Ioanninopoulos, a political rabble-rouser. A stout man of stouter opinions and readiest expression, he had nevertheless learned quickly to keep his mouth under control. He had what looked like a permanently black left eye to show for the lesson.

Nikos didn't speak German, but his French was good enough that he and I could get into some seriously heated conversations. There were no other Greeks within our *Kanadakommando* detail, and no one else spoke French well enough to keep up with him, so I was pretty much his only, well, friend, if you could use that word. "Conversational target" might be a better tag.

He was such a lecturer that he would maintain his disputation untiringly while working. He called me "Megakhéria" [*big hands*] because my wide hands and nimble fingers permitted me to sort the goods we worked through faster than anyone else in the *kommando*. I called him "Moyzlekh" [Yiddish: *little mouse*] just because that was the last thing he was!

At 35—thirteen years my senior, near the age of a world-wiser, elder brother—and a classically well-educated, self-assured man, he was never fazed by the occasional glimpse of a pink triangle.

In one of his lectures he had detailed, "the old priests have done nothing but hold us back, trapping us within the most backward medieval superstition, slavery, and Byzantine mumbo-jumbo!

"The Greeks keep forgetting Harmodios and Aristogeiton!

"It is intelligence, devotion to each other and fearless action against tyranny that will free us and lead us forward!"

The simple fact was that he hated the Nazis with an unquenchable, burning passion, and with them, all Germans. He blamed every one of us for what we had done to Europe, to Greece, to his family and, interestingly, for what the Nazis had done to the word "socialist"! (Beyond that, I learned quickly never to get him started on Stalin or Franco!)

He would almost scream, "*National Socialism*! Bah! Socialism does not invade other nations! Socialism does not kill innocent people!

"Fascism, communism and blind capitalist greed kill people: steal their food, their lands, their freedom! None of these is socialism!"

Even while he was not close to raving, I sensed that there was a cauldron seething beneath his bearing, just waiting for an errant whiff of extra fuel to invite an explosion. But every conversation we had, he always finished by repeating one phrase to himself, a single phrase in Greek. I asked him about it: he explained it and I learned it. He would say it, as a blessing before eating, and I would repeat its verb, "Zíto!" That pleased him beyond my expectations. My meager attempts to demonstrate that at least I, of all Germans, did not support this tidal wave of Pseudo-Hyper-Teutonic dreck sometimes even made him smile.

My efforts at Greek seemed to convince him that he might crack open his high wall of personal isolation.

He spoke of having been born in a village just west of Argos, of sitting atop the mound at Mycenae, looking out, beyond its great stone walls over the sun-bleached hills, streams and vast carpets of olive groves stretching across and down the valley toward the distant, siren Aegean shore: τὸ κοίλον Ἄργος, Homer's storied *Vale of Argos*.

"... τοὶ δὲ νεέσθων Ἄργος ἐς ἱππόβοτον καὶ Ἀχαΐδα καλλιγύναικα," he recited, then translated this, the Iliad's "... let them return to Argos, pasture-land of horses, and to Achæa, land of beautiful women!"

He was very proud that his grandfathers had worked with the German-American Heinrich Schliemann in the 1870's, when he had excavated the ruins of Mycenae and, Nikos asserted, had proved thereby—twice!—that Troy was indeed Western-Civilization, Greek fact, and far from any of what he held to be old, ridicule-inviting, superstitious sacred fiction.

Only in time did he share with me more intimate, sacred jewels from his life.

His father's family was originally from Epirus, having moved from there into the Peloponnese in 1830. From Feres, in Magnesia, (he detailed, exposing the upside-down inside of his left hand and pointing to the index-finger knuckle at the edge of his palm) had come his Vlach grandmother. She had thrilled him as a boy with tales of her, the Kyriazis, family's fight for Greek Independence. With those intense personal epics, she had instilled within him her vast, unflagging and indelible devotion to Greece.

Nikos's wife, Diotima, had been born in Argos, her family originally from Ar-
cadian Tripolis. The two of them had met, fallen in love there in the Argolid, then
had made their home near *The Pantánassa*, in the Monastiraki of Athens, in a
house from whose citrus-flowering terrace he would witness the sunset, spreading its pink and orange-pastel hues aglance across the north portico of the Erech-
theion and the northwest-watching, Doric column-tops of the Parthenon.

His hopes, his children, had been born there…

With a plaintive, almost whispered "τὴν Ἑλλάδα χωρίς, δὲν ὑπάρχ' ἡ ζωή"
[*without Greece, there is no Life*], further revelations evaporated. This was as far
into his private life as he could then allow. When he approached that close to the
door securing this private *tholos*, the treasure-house of the life he had lost, his
emotions reached up and throttled him, choked him into head-bowing silence.

I dared not press him. It was enough that he had honored me, one of the despised Germans, with this degree of confidence. But the way he spoke of Greece,
his detailed, intricately marvelous descriptions of history and people, his deep,
spiritual connection to the land, mountains and sea, had opened magical, basil-
scented, grape- and olive-bough vistas; I was falling in love with Her, too.

At least once a month during the spring and early-summer, the Obersturmführer delivered me from the *Kanadakommando* to the residence of the Oberführer,
the one who had retrieved my records on that very first day, while we were yet
standing beside the train. I played piano, entertaining groups of his guests.

My arrival was always early, while his quarters were empty; I was hidden
away, instantly behind a screen. This was unquestionably both to keep me from
seeing who was present—even the Oberführer kept his invisible distance—and
so that none of them would have to face in me a living image of their activities,
their crimes.

Nikos thought it amusing that I was a 'local celebrity' but lectured me mercilessly, too, about being naught but a performing monkey on a chain, giving aid
and comfort to the enemy, even using some of his newly-learned German vulgar-
ities to punctuate the imagery. His criticism stung, but those concerts were the
sole moments of connection to my life, the now-distant, joy-filled life, that had
been ripped away, torn asunder, crushed.

Falling quickly into a pattern, Nikos and I worked side by side simply because
I was fast and he was strong. A co-worker, Josef Piontek, a young Silesian bearing a political prisoner's red triangle, found us hilarious when we'd argue; the
rest of the time he seemed to have adopted us in place of the family he had lately
lost. Sixteen years old, and with one foot partly malformed, it surprised me that
he had survived the selection process. But he was very fast, a quick learner, a
good worker and an attentive listener. Whenever I called him "Josel" [*little Joseph*],
he'd grin: that's what his own family had called him all his life.

By the end of July, 1944, we were being forced to work faster and faster, a
grinding problem that arose from three, unfortunately confluent events.

The most serious of those was that a spur had been built during the Spring to extend the rail-line from the edge of the town directly here into the Birkenau area of the Auschwitz-Birkenau camp. The transports now unloaded faster, and increasing numbers of victims were arriving. So, too, ever more goods were being stolen and sent to *Kanada* for processing and shipment back into an increasingly materially destitute and desperate Germany.

Adding pressure to this was the change in the Hungarian situation.

We knew from other, more recently arrived prisoners that the government of Hungary had stood steadfast in refusing almost all Nazi demands to arrest and export their Jewish population. However, word passed into the camp that on March 19, the Wehrmacht had seized Hungary and deposed that protective government. As rapidly as possible, the Army and SS had begun arresting Hungarian Jews and shipping them en masse to Auschwitz, working feverishly in the face of the Soviet army's increasingly rapid, rabid-vengeance march, in from the east.

The third event was that we had lately lost our protective kapo: "*der Litvaker gonif*" [*the Lithuanian thief*] as Fishl had often called him with an air of chuckling appreciation. The *Litvaker* had been caught hoarding and trading sausages taken from the bundles of those Hungarian victims. He had forbidden us to eat them, explaining, "That paprika will stain your mouths, and then they'll have a ready excuse to accuse you of stealing—or of anything!"

He had used his stash to bribe one particular group of homesick SS-guards, all originally from around Eisenstadt, a mixed, German, Hungarian and Slavic region in southeast Austria. He paid them off so that he could relax in private with his friend from the women's camp, one who came regularly into the *Kanadakommando* to help; he had also given her some of his purloined *Kolbász* to use as graft back in the women's barracks. We teased him that she was just using him for his sausage. He'd just laugh, say, "Yeah, she likes my sausage … and loves my sausage!" and grab his crotch.

Our area commander was gone along with him: he had also been "reassigned."

The commander's replacement, Rottenführer [*specialist*] Bohm, was a totally by-the-books with-a-side-of-sadism bastard! He brought in the kapo from his old command. Both of them forced us—searched and beat us—to turn in all the foodstuffs we found amongst the bundles; he took them for his own, private black-market use, back in an ever more-starving Germany. We grew hungrier and hungrier, far hungrier than before, as we were constrained to single, secret, desperate bites of what we discovered, and to those scraps of standard-issue sawdust-bread, and turnip-dreck wash-water.

By August, slow-stifling starvation meant that all of us were having trouble keeping our rates of sifting and shuffling high enough, so extra guards had been brought in, to whip us into moving faster.

As the war turned ever worse in the East (such news filtered into the camp with the new prisoners from the East), more and more of the native-German SS stationed at the camp were being moved out, into fighting units. To fill the growing gap in coverage, replacements called *Hiwi* (the *Hilfswilliger*: "those willing to help") were recruited from the most sadistic, violently Anti-Semitic of the Baltic and the East, and were being brought in to take their places. Most were curt, severe, almost gleeful in their new-found positions of authority within the Nazi State. One, though, seemed less brutal, but with it, was shifty-eyed, obviously calculating.

One quietly routine afternoon I noticed that *Hiwi* call Josef by himself over to the farther side of the barracks, down a row of high boxes and containers. Since he was the only guard present at the moment, I was able to move stealthily around the piles to find out what was going on; I found a tall crack in the inventory stacks that let me see.

In the flitting shadows at the far end of the row, the *Hiwi* turned Josel around and put a big chunk of fresh, guards-ration bread on the box he faced.

Famished, Josel grabbed it and stuffed it into his open mouth. Quickly, the *Hiwi* pushed his gun-belt to one side, opened the fly of his uniform pants, pulled himself out, lowered Josef's pants and shoved his erection into Josel.

He screamed into the bread.

The *Hiwi* kept pumping into him, hard and fast, his wedding band glinting with each hard sway, within an errant, directed streak of light. Josel bit into the bread, his hunger more vicious than the pain.

I was paralyzed with rage, white-lipped, gut-spasming rage!

But, so famished and weak, I could do nothing: the fury could go nowhere! Unrelievable, stomach-twisting frustration twisted me aside, to retch turnip-water froth.

Nikos had stepped up, behind me; he had seen, too. He walked away: another two guards had stepped inside at the far door.

I turned and looked back. The *Hiwi* had finished; he wiped himself on Josel's pants, restuffed and quickly closed his own. Then he snatched Josef's cap, to jam it down into the pocket beside his loaded pistol. To the far end of the stacks and out, he rushed away.

Josef stayed in that hidden position, the tears running down his face as he continued to gnaw at that precious lump of bread.

The afternoon passed in *stay-busy, what-can-I-possibly-say* silence.

That night, Josef lay at the isolated edge of his bunk, curled tightly on his side, trembling, distant. I sat nearby, rubbed his arm, tried to say something to comfort him.

Twice he murmured, "My cap ... my cap!"

He knew what its theft presaged: in the morning, at roll call, definite trouble— possibly, probably fatal.

Eventually, his shaking waned and, at last, exhaustion pushed him into sleep.

I moved to my own bunk; everyone else looked and sounded asleep. Nikos was leaning up against the wall at the head of his own bunk; he often slept that way, as if perpetually on guard.

Lying there, looking over at Josel, I ached for him. Was there anyone left in the world to care about this child?

Stealthily, I rose, took my own cap and placed it securely within his grasp, careful not to wake him. Then I lay down, preparing myself for the morning, for the terror, then the ultimate peace it must eventually bring.

Dawn and roll call on August 15th came far earlier than expected.

It always does when you're starving, when you awaken, to lie in the dark, swallowing air just to fill your stomach, to push its gnawing, rancorous walls apart, to break the shooting pangs.

I rushed outside, took my place in line. Josef, as usual, stood just to my right.

Rottenführer Bohm *Mussolini*-ed down the line, strutting along in front of our ranks, searching each and every person for any infraction possibly inviting his fury.

He paused and yelled a number, "Front and center!"

Nikos stepped by me and as he did, turned quickly to say, in a French whisper, "Ne m'oublie pas!" [*Don't forget me!*] He then walked calmly to face Bohm.

"Where is your cap, scum?"

I reached up and touched mine; I hadn't realized that I had it with me! A glance over, Josef was touching his, too: a quizzical look, trying to grasp what was going on.

Nikos waited a second, apparently baiting Bohm, letting his anger rise, then said simply, "Lost!" rather flippantly.

This just fanned Bohm's rage. Shorter, he puffed himself up to get right in Nikos's face and, spit-flying yelled, "You lazy, shit, Jew-boy, communist scum! Where the hell is your cap?"

Nikos exploded and slugged him one, two, right in the gut. Bohm fell backwards onto his saggy ass.

Two guards grabbed Nikos by the arms and pulled him back. At the top of his lungs, he yelled, "Ζήτω ἐλεύθερη Ἑλλάδα!" [*Zíto eléftheri Ellátha: Long live free Greece!*] lunging, pulling fiercely against the restraints, directly toward Bohm.

Bohm jumped up in a fury. He rushed Nikos, kicked him in the crotch, grabbed his truncheon, turned slightly and slammed it against the side of the Greek's head.

Struggling in a frenzy to get himself free of the guards' heavy grasp, through the pain, Nikos again screamed, "Ζήτω! ... ἐλεύθερη Ἑλλάδα!"

Another, thudding truncheon-blow to the head and Nikos fell to his knees.

"Ζήτω!" he managed to say in our direction, before being cracked twice again and falling forward. He lay on the ground, his legs and arms spasming, his eyelids fluttering in a concussion-induced seizure.

Bohm took out his pistol and shot Nikos in the head.

Still wheezing his seething wrath, tightly wound, a snorting bull, just waiting to charge, Bohm stared his flaring anger into the bleeding, now silent corpse, then snapped his gaze up to me. He raised the pistol slowly and pointed it at my face.

"What the hell did he say to you?"

I looked past the gun, directly at him.

Clearly, so that the rest of the crew might hear, I replied, "Not to forget him. ... Sir."

In unblinking red-faced furor, he stared, ripping me apart with his eyes.

"You'll be wishing he was the only thing you could forget!" his voice ground.

Deliberately, he lowered his pistol, arcing its aim down, down along my body.

He stepped through the front row and shoved himself close against me, snarling right into my face, "I may not be able to touch you, you pussy, Jew-fucking faggot!"

An evil, predatory smile spread across his crimson, rage-flushed face, then he added, in an ominous whisper, "… but I don't have to!"

Without stepping back, he yelled my inmate number, "will report immediately to Crematorium 5! *Sonderkommando!*"

Das Kindlein — Chapter 18 — The Infant

"Guards! Seize him! Rip off those *Kanada*-clothes and see that he's dressed for the crematorium! Then escort him posthaste to his new, *proper* place of employment!

"With all the additional trash coming in, he's going to be damned busy — while he survives!"

Stomping away, pushing through the prisoners' petrified ranks, Commander Bohm swiveled a hard kick, slamming Nikos's prostrate, still bleeding body.

"Make sure the bunks are packed as tightly as they can be; we've got train-loads of Yids coming from Theresienstadt and Hungary to stuff into there!

"And have these lazy bastards take this sack of shit to the crematory pit!"

He turned, shot me a self-satisfied glare, then stomped away.

I was shoved back into the barracks, stripped down to my original, pink-triangle-badged, ragged-striped pajamas.

Dragged, bouncing along the ground, my now-sockless wooden shoes hammered the ground in a hollow, clonk-clonk-clonk, accompanying the loudspeakers' mocking, thin-echoing spew of *Siegfried's Rhine Journey*.

The two guards wrenched me across the loose gravel of the yard, past the barracks, beyond Crematorium 4, its burning trenches, then over the dirt road that separated those from its neighboring oven-building and the smoldering ash pits hidden at its northwest corner.

Crematorium 5's chimney belched its eye-stinging, lung-wrenching smoke.

Wagner would have been proud: Fafner was awake and hungry.

Tenor notes of Siegfried's horn lofted as they pushed me headfirst into the kommandoführer's office. The kapo, bearing a yellow star augmented by the band of a unit-boss, leaned in beside him. They both smirked. I knew what they were thinking when they saw the pink triangle and heard my escort's word, *Sonderbehandlung* [*special treatment*]: "just one more faggot to kill."

I stood as tall and unbending as I could. Defiant in my mind, in body, I was not so sure.

Gratuitously harsh, threatening crematory work-instructions ruptured mechanically from the purulent mouth of the SS-kommandoführer: an arrogant, self-inflated cog within this noxious apparatus.

That *Sonderkapo*, a shorter, but unusually still powerfully built young Jew, led me out of the office, past the incinerator—its lair brutally hot, with men already shoveling coke into its fire-eating gullet, stoking the ovens' overbearing heat—and thence beyond, into what he tagged "the changing room."

Rags, wraps, detached personal belongings lay piled in scattered mounds, thrown toward the wall; they didn't look soiled, but the room stank of death.

Scurrying errant among enforcer-guards, prisoners tugged at those remnants hurriedly to clear them out (and over to *Kanada*, I realized), as quickly as they could. Soon, very soon, there would be more clothes, with the surge from more disemboweled bundles to divide: evidence to steal, to disperse, to hide.

"This same room over in Crematorium 4 is now the barracks for us Sonderkommandos, while they're working to get the ovens in the unit over there going again.

"Don't forget! You will not return to your previous barracks!" the kapo said sternly. He spoke German tinged with a Plattdeutsch, or perhaps Dutch, accent.

I answered, "Yes, sir. I won't forget!" using as much matching, northerly Rhineland, Cologne-area dialect as I could remember and pack into so short a phrase.

He looked at me in surprise and laughed, then replied, in plain *Kölsch* [*Cologne dialect*], "Good ear for a queer! I thought it was your other holes that were supposed to be so talented!"

I said nothing.

Just past the changing room, he led me to the remainder of the crew, tens of pajama-clad, smudge-faced, wan-eyed men, standing about, waiting in the ante-room. On the right were two smaller rooms that had been Sonderkommando quarters, now filled with yet more pilfered property awaiting its shift, over into *Kanada*. The door to the left, the victims' entrance, was closed. The next group of Jews was already standing outside, waiting.

Bearing a foreign-volunteer SS-battalion's insignia, one huge, heavy-browed guard was stomping about, scanning every room minutely on his threatening rounds. He menaced into the next room, away from us.

"Beware of him!" the kapo whispered, "if the goon thinks one of us too slow or not pulling his weight, he will beat all of us!" He reached up, rubbed his shoulder, as if the mere statement recalled too vividly some recent encounter.

In the ante-room he pointed to me, announcing to the rest of the *kommando*, "*Kölle* [*Cologne(-boy)*], here, has been assigned to work with you. Get him a gas mask, show him how to load the trolleys, then how to stuff the ovens."

That said, he turned and hurried away.

The rooms had already been loaded and the sequence started; we had to wait.

Meanwhile, the other kommandos explained the tasks, in sanitized, self-effacing euphemism: all three "shower-rooms" would be filled with "material to be processed." The doors would be locked, the room allowed to warm above 26°, "the medication" dropped in. After around twenty minutes, when "the party" inside had quieted, the ventilation fans would be turned on. After a few minutes more, we would go in, wearing gas masks, and start shifting "the contents" from the showers into the "changing room," there to await "final handling."

One younger crew-member spoke up, almost a-panic, shedding the sheltering analogs, "Make sure the arms and legs are straight down their sides as you pack them into the stacking room! If they're lying too loosely and rigor mortis sets in when their limbs are bent, they won't fit easily through the oven doors, and we'll have to waste time dislocating or breaking 'em! Then *that* guard will lead the others…" His anxious, teen-aged victim's voice shook as it faded.

The minutes dragged; I forced my mind blank.

The signal came.

Gas masks on, we grouped for work.

The doors swung open: my mental vacuum screamed!

Mind-choking horror!

Young! Old!

Women! Men!

Teenagers! Children!

Babies!

All lay heaped in the naked agony of death!

The stinking floor was slick with the reeking, convulsed drainage of human misery: shit, piss, phlegm, vomit, blood, semen, menses! The bodies were slick with sweat and the splatters of everything human bodies racked in desperate, convulsing death-throes could exude!

Then, having to touch them! bare-handed, to touch them! to heave them like nameless, spiritless, slimy logs!

If you didn't grab a corpse tightly enough or in the right place, it would slip limply out of your hands, slide around into others, getting naked arms, legs, heads, hair mangled, wrapped, snarled in a tortuous mass.

Worse yet was when the corpses would tumble, face-banging, off an overloaded cart on the way to the changing room!

Any slow-down threatened us with our own torturous demise!

The crew considered it great fun to force the faggot to handle the females, especially if the throes of death-cramps had caused one to menstruate—her blood, her feminine life—a flow unceasing.

Don't breathe!

Don't see!

Don't think!

Don't feel!

I shocked myself when, too soon, my self-consoling, anguished stream of *Ave Maria*'s was interrupted by the thought, "This setup is pretty damned inefficient!"

My soul shrieked, for with this impulse I knew that I had experienced the first symptom that this horrific, unspeakable process could become unthinkingly remote, impersonally automatic!

The rash of murders still to be managed and the backlog accruing from each time-consuming cremation had required that the next congregation be compelled to strip outside.

The door from the showers' ante-room into the still corpse-littered changing room had been shut so that these naked newcomers could get no better idea beforehand of what was awaiting them. While their journey commenced, we were ordered to shift the cadavers, ever more cadavers, from that charnel to the ovens.

When, later, that same ante-room door was again open, the ventilation fans hummed loudly, rattling above the murder chambers at that farther, complicit end of the building.

———————————

The kapo ran in, yelling, "Crematorium 4 is on fire!" then raced out to find the kommandoführer.

They both rushed back into the room, the frenzied kapo still declaiming, "with this flood of inmates on top of all the Hungarians to handle, they decided to try re-firing 4's ovens, and got 'em too hot! The fire-bricks have started exploding and the chimney is threatening to collapse!"

Instantly, the kommandoführer snapped at me and four other Sonderkommandos to stay, to continue clearing out the corpses. Then he ordered that most violent guard to stand over us remnant few, and had the kapo, too, stay to hurry us along. He then left, rushing the rest of the crew and guards out the door toward unit 4.

SS, guards, kommandos: they would all catch abject hell if one of the crematoria burned down!

We worked as fast as we six could, shifting the last few of the waiting bodies from the changing room to the ovens under the continually hateful glare and continuous, abusive threats of that guard.

By the time we had struggled those corpses away to the ovens, the poisonous fumes of Zyklon B had been well exhausted from those, as yet untouched, still-stuffed murder-rooms. Air-inviting doors propped wide open, we left all the exhaust fans on, too, to make sure we could work there safely as we returned, without the stifling, smothering masks.

The first load gathered, I wheeled my cartful away, into the changing room. By the time I'd unloaded it and returned, the others had spotted something they would laughingly force me to confront.

A young lady, so slender, so gaunt—from the growing stubble of her shaved head and lack of an accompanying *property-of-the-Reich* tattoo, obviously one of those transportees being cleared out of another camp—was leaning, knees half-bent, against the tangled, still-steaming pile of corpses.

Between her legs, hanging from her distended vagina was a cord that extended, looping as a dark blue and gray streaked, ashen white rope to its goal, a connected fetus, lying face-up on the floor in a pool of the outflow-dreck from his neighbors, mixed with the water and blood that had splashed down with him from his mother's womb.

Time slowed with each approaching step, almost froze as I looked into her meager, but still-so-beautiful face. My chest broke into tiny, breath-grabbing spasms, quixotic: unsure whether to retch or to scream.

My heart saw hair still flowing in enticingly rich curls, springing from this vision of dark brown stubble-shave, the baldness with which her executioners had tried to shame her. The green and gold sparkles within her blue eyes were fixed, gazing off beyond the confines of the concrete ceiling toward a distant, inattentive heaven. I closed them softly, carefully.

I picked up the child—born a-dying in his mother's own extreme agony—holding him as carefully as I would any newborn, cradling his head, his fragile neck in my hand, his tender back braced along my forearm. His slight, still wet, blond baby-curls and large, blue eyes summoned inexpressible waves of migraine-pounding, pounding, pounding! explosive sorrow!

I closed those eyes, too.

Across his forehead and in his flaxen eyebrows still shone that white, powdery-wax, the protection of the freshly newborn; the fluid-stopping plugs yet filled his nostrils. So beautifully, delicately formed, he was obviously full-term, so ready to come screaming, gurgling, cuddling into the world.

But not this world.

I rested him tightly against this new mother's now even more-sunken stomach.

With my left arm wedged beneath her back, her sweet face shouldered softly into my neck, I managed to lift her and the child together.

Bending to shift, to settle the two of them gently, still united onto the empty cart, I struggled, set the child softly, face a-sky onto his mother's too famished chest, near her still-expectant, maternal breasts.

Travail had made me weak, but the will triumphed.

Mother and child, and them alone, I pushed slowly from there, a silent recitation racking my lips.

The trolley moaned a matching dirge, forlorn with each eternal trudge, trudge, from the murder site, beyond the changing room, to the ovens themselves. Our SS-guard screamed: I was a slacker, Jew-loving, pussy, shit! But he was as nothing.

I slogged on.

Naked-bulb shadows of the others fell around us, tailing the curse-howling guard, watching: attentive, unsure, afraid.

From the cart I slipped her onto an oven's slide-in tray, and there arranged the two again in mother-and-child pose: her arms across her torso, her delicate, care-abraded fingers touching, soothing her silent child.

I stood, unsteady, continuing my soft recitation of deeply shared verses, that had grown so familiar.

The guard screeched unceasing, stamped over, grabbed my shoulder from behind, spun me around and shrieked into my face, "What the hell are you doing? What the fuck are you saying?"

I replied with the recitation's next verse, loudly enough for everyone in the room to hear over the ovens' unheeding roar, "Y'hei shlama raba min shmaya v'khayim aleynu v'al kol Isra'el. V'imru …" [*May there be abundant peace from Heaven and life upon us and upon all Israel. Now say…*]

A braver few of the crew ventured an answering, "Omeyn."

The guard grabbed me by the collar with both hands and jerked me forward almost off my feet. In pyroclastic rage he spat in my face, and spewed, "Fucking

Jew-loving fucking faggot! Fucking Jew!" then spat again.

Putrid gobs trickled from my forehead, eyebrow, dripped down my cheek as he glared at me, his crushing arms locked in immobile, trembling-manic furor.

I nailed my gaze to his and bellowed back at him, completing in unbridled defiance the *Mourner's Kaddish*: "**Oseh shalom bim'romav hu ya'aseh shalom aleinu v'al kol Isra'el.**" [*He who makes peace in His heights, may He make peace, upon us and upon all Israel.*]

At the start of that verse, behind the guard, the kapo had grabbed the broken-off spade of an iron ash-scraper noiselessly from the floor. Now, with two silent paces nearer, he hefted the rod and tensed, poised to swing with both arms.

I shouted "**V'IMRU …**" and closed my eyes, fearing the kapo's aim.

He yelled, "**OMEYN!**"

A wisp of whirling air, a dull-metal clang: the thud of spreading flesh on crackling bones punctuated his word!

Sudden release of my collar: my eyes shot open!

Staring above, unblinking, beyond, the guard shuddered, slumped forward towards me slightly, then lurched away, a spastic, stridor-voiced bellows, collapsing sideways onto the floor.

The others ran over, screaming, "What have you done? They'll kill us all for sure! right now!"

The kapo yelled, "Shut up! They're going to kill us anyway! Now, help me!"

He tossed his iron bat and bent down, feeling for the guard's heartbeat.

With a muttered "Shit!" he grabbed the guard's head and gave it a sharp, spine-shredding snap.

In a flash, he had rifled the guard's pockets. Grabbing holster, gun and ammo, he shifted everything to the others with the stern order, "Stash it all with the rest!"

They ran from the room.

The kapo stood, stepped over to my shocked, frozen form and reached up, using his soot-heavy pajama-sleeve to sop the still-sliming spit from my face.

"Thank you, Kölle!" he said, "You helped us more than you know."

"Thank you," I managed to reply, "… you saved my life!"

He stopped wiping, and stared.

"But you, *you*, an utterly condemned, despised *feygele-goy*! You defied the SS to its very face, honored us and our faith, and the life and memory of these victims! … You stood—unafraid, unashamed—ready to be killed for the Kaddish!"

Resting his left hand on my shoulder, with a squeeze he said firmly, "You're a *mensch*, Kölle!"

I cast my eyes down, ashamed, to the oozing, accusing dreck on the concrete slab. How could I be a "mensch" when I had now become an intimate participant in this murderous madness?

"It was…"

I struggled to look up at him.

"It *is* my duty … my sacred duty."

He looked at me, disbelieving, seeming to search his way among the words.

"A mitzve!" he whispered barely heard, before mouthing, unsure, "Halevai?

A lamed vovn-...?"

Vaulting his voice mid-word, our brother-workers ran breathless back into the room. His phrase derailed, he dropped his hand from my shoulder and sped to direct the others.

"Quickly! Help me get the momzer up onto the slider!" he yelled.

"What about his boots? His clothes? Can we use them?" one of them asked.

"No! They would only cause more questions!

"Remember! We don't know where he went! He just stepped out and never came back! They know he's fucking crazy and might do anything! Besides, he's not a German! They already believe the very worst about him!"

Surrounding the guard's corpse, each grabbed limb or head and hefted him boot-first onto the nearest slider. The kapo yelled, "Fast! Go get more fuel! The steel studs of his boots have to melt!" One leapt off toward the storeroom, then ran back with a shirt-load of lumps of coke.

They stuffed them on and around him, jamming several between his legs, shoved vindictively into his crotch, loading his thick thighs and overfed gut.

The slider squealed as they forced the weighty pile into the oven-fire; the kapo swung the consuming iron closed with a heavy, final clang.

He turned, clapped dirt from his hands and proclaimed with a vengeful laugh, "Azoy hoben zay dem Haman oyfgehongen oyf der t'liyeh vos er hot ongebrayt far Mordekay dem Yiden!" [Yiddish: *So they hanged Haman on the gallows that he had prepared for Mordecai the Jew!*]

––––––––––––––

Still standing on edge, I had to steady myself with a quick reach behind, to grasp the slider-rail at my back.

Returning to mother and child, I pulled myself slowly about.

Holding her nearer, dearest hand until the flames forbade, I edged them slowly, slowly toward their own heat-glistening, searing coals, reciting *lento, pianissimo*—more for myself than for anyone, anywhere—disjoint phrases swirling through a mind thrashing to rise for air, gasping against an unrelentingly subversive, plunging maelstrom of mounting bereavement, "*Ave Maria, ... gratia plena! ... ... Benedicta tu ... in mulieribus ...*" [*Hail Mary, ... full of grace! ... ... Blessed art thou ... among women ...*]

Thus I consigned the young woman and her son to the flames.

Und sie erlischt — Chapter 19 — And It Flickers Out

"Please, stop! Stop!" I prayed.

But they would not stop!

These legion, blessèd dead — *V'imru: omeyn!* — could not hear!

The bodies just kept coming: in their hundreds, hundreds, upon thousands. And no one was listening! No one, anywhere! No one!

The weariness, the mindless, dulling weariness!

We few slogged on.

The Sonderkommandos who had been pulled away to fight the incinerator fire in Crematorium 4 continued to work over there, repairing, rebuilding.

Our remnant worked as long as we were able that afternoon, but when, at last, even the kapo was exhausted, he called a halt. I heard him explain to an SS-officer that our guard had run out of the building during the noise, without saying what he was doing and that he hadn't seen him since. Because that guard spoke little German beyond vulgarity, and rarely ever said anything except to curse the prisoners, such reticence wasn't unbelievable: even those fellow-guards had feared his brutal insanity.

The kapo got those of us forced to stay there in Crematorium 5 a little extra bread and tea. I wolfed it down, forgetting that I was no longer in the *Kanada-kommando*, and that I would now have nothing to eat with that watery, morning brew that was the only "breakfast" provided.

The devastating emotional turmoil, inflamed by the physical effects of sudden, rushing nourishment from the few crusts of bread overwhelmed my mind. Dazed, I meandered unawares, unthinking, back toward my previous barracks: that's where my mind saw rest, and soothing friendship …

I heard loudspeakers somewhere spitting out Wagner; in some sick Auschwitz-joke, it was his opera, the fatal love-story, *Tristan und Isolde*.

I trudged on.

 "Rette dich, Tristan!" [*Save yourself, Tristan!*] sang Kurwenal, the baritone, to his friend.

But, like Tristan, I could not save myself.

Stumbling mentally and physically, I had reached the front of my old barracks.

There stood a group of prisoners—I recognized Evron and Fishl amongst my former crewmates—surrounding someone on the ground. I walked over.

The observers glanced up at me and parted. I must have reeked unbearably with the day's labor, and its substance.

I looked down at a horribly gaunt figure, a shadow-man captive to a pink and yellow star. His resting torso held off the ground, propped by Rebbe Schulmann, he looked up slowly from that recumbent position. His face so thin, his sunken blue eyes stared at me. Slowly, he smiled; my shock shattered into ten thousand screaming splinters.

"Edi!" he whispered as he reached a ravaged, skeleton's hand out toward me.

"David!" I yelled and knelt down so fast and hard that my pajama-pants ripped open at the knees.

His fragile form I had to pull into my arms.

I held him, cradling his horribly feverish head. The men around us turned to face outwards, just as my *shtetl* had done on that distant train-ride, guarding privacy, dignity: turning away trouble. Only the rebbe stayed beside us as David spoke, gasping roughly against the smothering air.

"I've been searching, searching for you ever since they shipped us here! I was certain I'd see you again, that we'd live, be together again!" he said weakly.

"They tried to kill me in Treblinka—but I fought them! I fought! I wouldn't let them!

"I survived!—and did everything I could to make sure that Esther was OK!

"She worked in the stockpiles, with the stolen goods being shipped back to Germany."

He had to pause to rest, his breath rough, his breathing thick, painfully labored.

"She would smuggle food to us. My precious sister! Have you seen her? The SS was bringing survivors from Theresienstadt here; the guards brought me here last week … She must be here! They must have brought her here to *Kanada*!"

He struggled to raise himself, to search for her, but was too feeble.

"Wherever she is now, I'm sure we … will see her soon!" I tried to assure him.

He smiled weakly.

"Yes, we will," he replied, struggling to wet his parched lips. He looked directly into my eyes.

"Edi! I love you!" he said softly.

"I love you, too, Baby!" I replied in a fervent, constricted voice.

He fixed his eyes on mine, raised a gnarled, ancient-young hand to touch my face, but spoke no more.

I could only watch from the crushing depths of helplessness, witness his struggling, phlegm- and blood-strangled breaths fade shallower, shallower, shallower. In my arms, his blinking ceased; his fever-ravaged breath faded away.

"David!" I yelled after him, in a strangled whisper. "My David!"

The rebbe started to rock gently, to pray.

I froze in place, holding David, staring into his face, running my hand over the stubble on his head, where his lustrous black hair had once dazzled, its aroma filling my so tightly-held night-inhalations, lulling me to warm, velvet sleep.

My chest spasmed, seized, burning raw with inexpressible sobs.

Holding one long, last, desperate look, their blue burned into my being.

I closed David's eyes.

A sunburnt, desert August breeze scoured the barren ground.

"I must take him," I said at last.

The rebbe shook his head slowly in agreement before reaching over, starting to unfasten the pajamas. David could not be laid to rest with them on; the guards would have their clubs ready.

"Please, hide these, save them," I begged.

Again, the rebbe nodded.

With his help, and strength borrowed from Evron the cobbler, I stood up.

David's lifeless corpse lay limp, draped across my arms.

"I almost lost you," resurged to mind, "I almost … lost … you!"

I took a step, unsteady, then another, walking slowly, consumed by an unfailing call. I must carry him. I must.

Within a few paces, I felt a small hand grab at the ragged bottom hem of my pajama shirt. I knew it was Sophia, dear, little, *di sheynste* Sophia.

With the shortest pause, the loudspeakers had reached the last scene of the opera: the slow notes of Isolde's extreme aria.

The orchestral rhapsody rising, upwelling all around us. The voice, the soprano voice came not from the speakers, but from Sophia at my side:

Mild und leise	How placidly and
wie er lächelt,	gently he smiles,
wie das Auge	how tenderly
hold er öffnet —	he opens his eye —

The farther I trudged with my David, the more I felt the growing presence of others: an ethereal upwelling, a vast, artesian forest of attendant souls.

Seht ihr's, Freunde?	Do you see it, friends?
Seht ihr's nicht?	Don't you see it?

They walked with me, those thousand dead that I had witnessed with my very hands that day, the heaping myriads, thousands upon thousands killed in the camps of Auschwitz, Monowitz, Treblinka …

Immer lichter	How he shines,
wie er leuchtet,	brighter and brighter;
stern-umstrahlet	bathed in starlight
hoch sich hebt?	he lifts himself high?

… Blechhammer, Jawiszowice, Jaworzno, Lagisze, Myslowice, Trzebina …

Seht ihr's nicht?	Don't you see it?

… Sobibor, Belzec, Bergen-Belsen, Theresienstadt, Chelmo, Majdanek, Sajmište, Maly Trostinets, Buchenwald, Jasenovac, Dachau, Sachsenhausen …

Wie das Herz ihm	How his heart
mutig schwillt,	swells boldly;
voll und hehr	how fully and sublimely
im Busen ihm quillt?	it wells in his breast?

… the unknown murder-fields, the uncountable death-trenches, stretching deep, unheralded across the burning East …

Wie den Lippen,	How blissful,
wonnig mild,	mildly,
süßer Atem	sweet breath
sanft entweht —	softly wafts from his lips—

… filled unspeakably with the voiceless victims of SS, Wehrmacht and too-eager Axis soldier: their pistol, rifle and machine-gun fire sounding across sanguinary fields, the disfigured Earth forced, forlorn, to open her mouth to receive that blood from their hands…

Freunde! Seht!	Friends! Look!
Fühlt und seht ihr's nicht?	Don't you feel it and see it?

… The tens of thousands dead at Babi Yar, Rumbula, Ponary, the countless, unsung, unvoiced victims of century upon unceasing century of European and Asian pogroms …

Höre ich nur diese Weise,	Do I alone hear this melody,
die so wundervoll und leise,	which wonderfully and softly,
Wonne klagend,	lamenting delight,
alles sagend,	telling all,
mild versöhnend	mildly reconciling
aus ihm tönend,	resounding from him,
in mich dringet,	invades me,
auf sich schwinget,	echoing on itself,
hold erhallend	sweetly resonating
um mich klinget?	rings around me?

…the lovers, the singers, the dancers, the joyful—Jews, Roma, Sinti, Socinians, liberals, churchmen, homosexuals, socialists—all those caught acting righteously, on conscience, conviction, courage and true, unashamed nature …

Heller schallend,	Sounding more clearly,
mich umwallend —	undulating around me –
Sind es Wellen	Are these waves
sanfter Lüfte?	of gentle air?
Sind es Wogen	Are these billows
wonniger Düfte?	of delightful fragrances?

…swirling, new-born clouds of sweet-breath, laughing children, the million infants who knew no better, had no say, but went, ever-trusting, ever-loving to their deaths…

Wie sie schwellen,	How they swell,
mich umrauschen,	how they surge around me,
soll ich atmen,	shall I breathe,
soll ich lauschen?	shall I hearken?

… all rising to stand with me, countless witnesses to the fact that I must attend: never to let love, the love that many waters cannot quench nor the floods drown, go unloved: unrequited, forsaken, unmourned!

Soll ich schlürfen,	Shall I sip,
untertauchen?	submerge?
Süß in Düften	Sweetly in fragrances
mich verhauchen?	breathe my last?

Roiling clouds of acrid, ash-laden smoke inundated the soaring harmonies as I knelt, to lay David gently on the weeping clay of the crematory pit, augmenting a growing pile of now-nameless, once-loved, ever-belovèd *others*.

I had almost lost him, only to lose him and, utterly powerless, to witness the loss, to tumble powerless, lamenting to the feet of world-breaking Fate.

In dem wogenden Schwall,	In the swelling torrent,
in dem tönenden Schall,	in the resounding echo,
in des Welt-Atems	in the World-Breath's
wehendem All —	wafting All —
ertrinken,	to drown,
versinken —	to sink —

Sophia released my stain-rancid shirt, and sank, dropping down beside David, nestling within his left arm. Curled warm within my own coat, she sighed, put her thumb to her lips, dissolved to a skeleton, and vanished into the Earth.

David's gaunt, disease-ravaged, haggard body remained.

Now at rest, on swelling waves of heavenly wings, he suffered no more.

unbewußt —	unconscious —
höchste Lust!	supreme joy!

Wagner

I arose, unsteady, held my hands over my stinging eyes, staggered, then turned slowly to retrace my steps.

My vision foamed a bleak, dismal, deepening fog.

I paused, blinked: in murky eyes, I had no tears. This gloomy, accursèd world turned dark, darker, black.

The last lamp of my life, the light, was gone: *und sie erlischt.*

Utterly defeated, I had failed.

Bereft now of sight, I could not abide; I tacked to another course.

I knew where they were: I had to reach them!

With heavy, weary-weaving steps, I traced the invisible vectors of my mind's broad sea-chart, striving for the strength to find them, to reach them, to touch them at last!

Now very near, the siren, buzzing charge of the wires called me, beckoned me!

"Hilf' mir! Hilf' mir! **Helft mir!**" [*Help me! Help me! (Both of you) Help me!*]

From that hissing darkness, I reached out, groping: searching to grasp that rocky-surf static roar, the release, the relief.

Frevel — Chapter 20 — Outrage

"What the hell does the prisoner think he's doing?"

Hands seized my wrists and pulled them roughly to the side, jerking me a-round. I knew the Oberführer's voice.

"Let me go," I protested weakly.

"Just let me go."

"No!" he said with scolding authority, "You idiot! If I hadn't been here, the guards would have shot you!"

"Obersturmführer, take him to my office!"

Someone else standing nearby seized me by the upper arm, and began to pull me toward him quickly, forcefully.

"Wait!" the Oberführer yelled, before continuing more calmly, "Both of you report to my quarters instead. There is no need to parade him in front of the staff!

"And clean that stench off him before you bring him in!"

With a quickly snapped "Jawohl, Herr Oberführer!" he hurried us away.

I could tell from the abating odors that we were walking farther from the cremation pits, away from Crematorium 4's damage-reeking, heavy coke-smoke, beyond the thick, sweet-soul sickness spewing from the ovens of Crematorium 5.

From changes in the unseen textures under foot I knew that he had pulled me through the guard post, beyond the barbed wire fence onto the road that ran between the barracks of the original camp and the extension on the north side, that area yet under construction that everyone called *Mexiko* because its inmates, left naked, had been forced to scrounge for things to wear. Having found multi-colored blankets and scraps to drape over themselves, they had looked too much like those Central American peons posed by Europeans for photos in geographical magazines.

My wooden shoe clipped the top of a rock protruding from the rough surface of the unpaved road. I stumbled; the lieutenant caught me before I fell.

His voice boiled in aggravation: "Watch where you're going!"

"I can't," I said blankly.

"What the hell do you mean, *you can't*?"

"I can't see. Anything."

He stopped us, turned me toward his voice.

I felt the wind from his hand across my nose and cheeks as he waved it in front of me.

"My life is but a breath; my eyes will never see happiness again!"

The voice of Job fell heavy on my mind.

The officer exhaled, full of frustration, "Oh, shit!

"Your wandering off may have cost me my commission! And now this!" Through his still-tight grasp, it felt like he was shaking his head.

"Fuck! Now what! I lose sight of you just one day in all these fucking months, and look what the hell happens!

"OK, just walk carefully. I'll warn you if we approach something," he said, sounding irritatedly resigned to his fate, attentive now to keep anything else from going wrong with me, and more importantly for himself, it seemed.

We walked on.

"So, this is the lieutenant who was my shadow when I first arrived," I thought. After that first day and its redirected assignment, he alone had been the one to fetch me for those concerts at the Oberführer's. I had noticed him only on a few occasions otherwise. But then, it was always him, and no other.

He led me soon into a building that I could not recognize by location or stench: it smelled clean!

"Take off your shoes; leave them right there."

I kicked them off; he led me across a cool, tile floor into an adjoining room.

"Stand here. Use this," he handed me a slick-feeling bar. I raised it to my nose. Real soap!

He turned a shower on, testing the temperature carefully, then urged me forward into the spray.

"Wash yourself and your clothes! Quickly!"

He walked away.

The water was hot, perfect! It was not scalding like they used in tormenting new arrivals and certainly not the icy cold, dirty fluid that had been our only wash-water for so long. I spread the lather all over the pajamas, stuck the bar inside them to scrub myself. Dried, dead layers of emaciated skin panicked, and peeled off into my hand. I had almost forgotten that feeling, the purification of soap and water.

"At least, whatever else happens today, I will die clean!" I thought gratefully.

"Hurry up!" he yelled from the door.

But I was slow because I could now only feel my way, even cleaning my own body. I thought I had scrubbed all of me, but wasn't certain. However, everything felt so much better now that any stray, unwashed areas no longer mattered. A quick rinse, I felt for the shower controls. I turned one, but aaugh! frigid water! Another knob, a twist of both, and the water was off.

"Where do I go?"

He stepped in, took my hand and led me, alive, out of this real shower room.

"There's a bench right in front of you, and towels. Sit and dry yourself quickly! We're already in deep shit with the Oberführer! Don't pile it on worse by making us late!" Even in his eagerness, his voice was losing its hateful edge.

Was it pity? Had he realized that he simply couldn't hurry me—or that rushing merely called the hour of his own accountability closer to hand?

The towels were thick; the thin material of the inmate-pajamas dried quickly.

As I listened to ambient noises, getting my bearings, I realized that he must have brought me to the showers used by the SS-guards themselves. At this time of day, they were all out in the camp on duty, so it was fairly safe for a prisoner to be within this facility.

"Here," he said, placing lumps of knitted fabric in my hand.

"Put these on. We don't have time to get you any leather shoes."

Socks! The ones I had been wearing, rescued in *Kanadakommando* from among the possessions pilfered from the murdered, had been stripped from me early that morning before I was hauled to the crematorium. The sores that I thought long healed had been scraped into new, raw life in just those few hours. I was so grateful! In the midst of depraved desolation, the smallest donation, the slightest kindness becomes a universe of pleasure. Friends know this and use it to the comfort and encouragement of others; tyrants grab this and twist it to their selfish advantage.

"It was painful to watch you walk," he said.

And I knew then which he was, beneath that SS uniform: what he actually saw himself as and, perhaps, still wanted to be. He must be like most Germans had been forced to become: trapped between his goals, his desires, his root-goodness and the Fascist fact that the only way to move any of those goals forward now was to let yourself fall into the vicious behaviors the dictatorship demanded.

I recalled the Oberführer's quarters as we approached. I knew the layout of its main floor from all those times I had been taken there to entertain his guests. He had always been distant, having the lieutenant shepherd me at all times. I expected nothing more from so high-ranking an SS-officer. Indeed, I presumed much less.

As head of the financial arm of the SS camps, and because (as I'd overheard during more than one of those private concerts) the Auschwitz camp-complex was one of the biggest of Himmler's moneymakers, the Oberführer had been assigned there, billeted within the largest of the original houses from which the Poles of the area had been evicted, when Auschwitz-Birkenau's construction was commenced in October of 1941.

His piano-resident parlor, with home office at one side, was on the first floor; the ground floor was kitchen, housekeeper and quarters given over to his staff, including this Obersturmführer. The Oberführer's private suite was at the top of the house, the entire second floor.

Having led through the front door, the lieutenant told me to take off the wooden shoes, then helped me mount the stairs; at the top of the stairs we turned to the left and walked through that door into the first-floor parlor.

I pictured it from memory. The large desk was centered before a wall of three large windows to our right, overlooking the meadows to the southeast, bordered by the camp, the original town and the old, pre-Hungarian-Judaic-rush railroad siding. Beyond the desk was a local-brand baby-grand. The Oberführer didn't play, but he kept it here on-hand for entertaining his guests; it was the one I had played.

"Serviceable," I recalled, "but not my *Steiner!*"

The air was so pleasant here, away from the twinned stench of decay and death. The aged-wood aromas of this antique house summoned so much the aura of the farmhouse. I stood, savoring pianist-memories within the redolent breezes, but was torn *sforzato* by the realization that this was only temporary: I would obviously be sent back. To *Kanadakommando*? To the crematorium? What hell-hole would they find for me now?

The heavy fall of jackboots mounted the stairs and stepped into the room. The thick door shut with a brass-solid clack. The footfalls stopped. We were already facing the Oberführer's desk: the chair creaked as he sat.

"Obersturmführer, would you kindly fill me in on the day's details, and tell me what the hell happened?"

"Herr Oberführer!"

Nerves rankled his voice.

"I made my daily trip to the *Kanadakommando* late this afternoon to check on the prisoner's condition and whereabouts. I had been delayed today because of our meetings with the camp commander concerning the great increase in numbers of new arrivals!

"When, at last, I reached *Kanada*, he was nowhere to be seen! I checked with his kapo and, rather hesitantly, he said to ask the section leader. When I found Rottenführer Bohm, he laughed and said the prisoner had been reassigned."

"Reassigned? By whom? By whose authority?"

"Rottenführer Bohm himself, sir!"

I heard the Oberführer drum his fingers on the desk.

"Go on," he said gruffly.

"When I found out where the prisoner had been sent, I rushed, but he was not there either, nor was his crew. He also wasn't among those crewmembers when I was able to locate them."

"And that's when you had the Hauptscharführer [*master sergeant*] run to fetch me?"

"Yes, sir! I continued to search for him, and was finally able to direct you to him just before he…"

"Just before he grabbed the electrified fence."

Reluctance rusted his reply, "Yes, sir."

The Oberführer produced a long, guttural sigh, then silence. He stood up and took two steps farther from us; I could only guess he had moved to look out the windows.

I heard him turn sharply back toward us.

"Thank you, Obersturmführer. You did nothing wrong."

He tapped his desk slowly with a fingernail, then continued.

"In fact, your haste in summoning me saved this prisoner's life, and avoided a difficult situation. … I am much obliged, Hofmann, and will see that you are commended for your quick action in protecting the property of the Reich!"

"Thank you, Herr Oberführer!"

Relief dripped from the Obersturmführer's voice.

"And now," the Oberführer addressed me by number, "Please tell me every-thing that happened that produced this situation."

I had felt myself wavering. I could see nothing to gauge my posture, and now was about to fall.

"But first, both of you sit down!"

The Obersturmführer grabbed my arm to steady me with one hand, and used the other to scoot a chair across the floor into position for me to sit. I was his commendation now; he seemed set on taking care of me. Guided into the chair, my thin-pajama butt slid across its slick, highly polished wood. I heard him take a chair beside me, after the Oberführer himself had sat.

I cleared my throat, took a deep breath and proceeded to lay out in detail all the things that I wanted him to know.

Our starved exhaustion after Bohm had started stealing food; Josef's food-rape by the *Hiwi*; the stolen cap; Bohm's murder of Nikos; Bohm's threat to me; the reassignment, working in the crematorium; the death of a friend, whom I had carried, according to the rules, to the cremation pit: I detailed each of them.

He didn't have to know about the details of the crematorium, nor about Da-vid's true meaning to me. The pink triangle condemned me in their sight: like Nikos, jealously would I guard my own treasures, those few that kept me human, and sane.

I finished my exposition by telling of my blindness, its sudden onset at the cremation pit, within the smoke.

The Oberführer slammed his fist on his desk.

"These goings-on, such conduct cannot be tolerated!"

I heard him stand, almost jump from his chair. The Obersturmführer vaulted, too, the chair sliding back from the sudden, wisping push of his slick-booted calves. My muscles seized in benighted panic.

"Obersturmführer! You will take Untersturmführer Gleiss and Hauptschar-führer Mannheim with you!

"Go, find out who the *Hiwi* guard was that was on duty yesterday.

"Backed by those officers, you will arrest him *and* Rottenführer Bohm and bring them both here! Order Oberscharführer Huber to fetch Bohm's records and bring them back, along with him! And when you discover who the *Hiwi* was, have Huber retrieve his records, too—as quickly as possible!—and bring them along! Take a couple of extra SS-men with you, to help control each of the prison-ers.

"Do this now! Quickly!

"Oh. And you will locate this lad." His voice turned toward me, "You said his name was what?"

"Josef. Josef Piontek, sir," I answered. "He's in the *Kanadakommando* barracks."

"You will locate him and bring him here, too. I want this all taken care of as rapidly as possible! Is that understood?"

"Yes, sir, Herr Oberführer!"

With "Dismissed!" the Obersturmführer rushed from the room, his jackboots clomping down the stairs, hitting every other one as I counted them. He wanted that commendation!

The Oberführer took his place behind his desk. He was quiet, but I could hear from the gradual slowing, the diminishing of his enraged breathing that he was watching, looking in my direction.

"So. Your sight faded after you lay your friend in the pit? You have become completely blind?"

"Yes, sir. As I turned away from the pit and the heavy smoke rising from it, sudden grayness, then black, covered my vision."

I heard him remove, then place his cap on the desk.

"I had noticed your lost, muted reactions, at the fence … Yes. I've heard of such sudden blindness before," he said before becoming quiet again.

Moments passed; then my stomach growled.

"You're hungry?" he asked quickly.

"Yes, sir. Extremely."

"Stay seated" he said, then arose, walked out the door and down the stairs. In the stillness, I could hear the ticking of a small clock across the room. It threw me back to the metronome Herr Fuhrmann had made me use when I was so young, practicing those Czerny exercises, and from there, to images of the old farmhouse, of Mama, Gramma, Eva and those early-developing, *rocket-man* hands.

Two sets of footsteps, one heavy, the other dainty, made their way back up the stairs and into the room.

"Just there, Frau Berg," the Oberführer said, "We'll move the stand close by him."

I heard furniture, then dishes being moved and arranged. A woman's slight, tender hands took mine and pulled them forward, to the small table that had been shifted over next to me.

"Here is some bread, with butter and some strawberry preserves. I hope you like it!" she said as she held my hand to let my fingers identify the location of the crust.

"And here is some hot tea!"

She pulled my right hand, saying "Be very careful!" as she placed my fingers cautiously out around the cup so that I could feel the heat and the handle. She understood my condition very well; the Oberführer must have explained it to her.

"Thank you, Frau Berg!" I said.

"You're welcome, dear!" she said, before stepping away softly.

"Yes, thank you, Frau Berg," the Oberführer repeated, in a voice so mellow that it sounded like home.

She closed the door as she left.

I felt the bread. It was warm, the smell of it with the butter and strawberry preserves was nothing short of heavenly! The Oberführer can only have watched as I chewed so slowly, luxuriating in private, infantile memories of raucous, family-crowded, steaming meals around the big table. Within that butter-savor, I could still hear the 'A' of that Frankfurt oboist, tuning the orchestra of that distant, long-ago interrupted gift. And the strawberries—my mind, sensations, emotions, and helplessness—were rushing me toward my childhood.

"This lad you mentioned, he is a good worker, and trustworthy?" he asked calmly. Something in the almost familiar tone of his voice made me relax. For some reason, I felt I could trust this officer. But caution overruled: only time could tell.

"Yes, sir, both. He is slightly crippled in one foot. Nikos, the one whom Bohm killed, and I watched out for him, tried to make sure his problem didn't attract attention, and that he had plenty to eat."

"He's Jewish?"

"No, sir, I don't believe so. Like Nikos he was brought in as a political prisoner: his badge, his triangle, is red. He talked about how his father had been active in the *DDP*, the old left/liberal *German Democratic Party*, and had written several articles in its *Volkswacht* newspaper before it was shut down in '33. When the Gestapo discovered that his father was secretly still politically active, they arrested him and his entire family. As far as I know, Josef is an ethnic German just like I am."

"I see."

I could hear his breathing move to one side as he looked away, then turned back toward me, seeming from the sound of it almost anxious. But he let me chew in peace, several minutes, before continuing.

"You may find it unusual, but almost every time I have talked to Himmler since you first played for him, he has asked about you. You made a very favorable, quite memorable impression on him."

"Thank you, sir," I answered, even though I certainly didn't give a damn what that fuck Himmler thought!

"I have read in your file that you worked in the *KdF*, for Goebbels."

"Yes, sir. It was all arranged by Angelika Gellert, the pianist."

"Ah, yes, Frau Gellert. She was a very humorous, marvelously talented woman! Not particularly lucky when it came to men, but she was so charming, delightful and caring."

"You knew Frau Gellert, sir?"

"Yes. ... We met a few times. That was quite a few years ago, though."

He was sounding more human, and less SS, to me. He had met Gelchen and liked her!

I chewed the bread slowly—it was so otherworldly soft! Fresh, homemade, with sweet-creamy, real butter! I hadn't had anything like it beyond these past nine months! And the tea was real, not watered-down dregs left over from wash-up in the SS kitchen! I decided that, if this were going to be my last meal, I would relish it! So, I made it last. The Oberführer sat quietly, apparently watching me as I nibbled.

At last I finished and, despite the utter uncertainty of my situation, felt myself gradually meandering in the breeze, along that moonlight-mottled, tree-shaded path toward sleep. I had been up since before that summer daybreak; it must now have been almost evening.

Sudden shouting and jack-booted scuffling echoed from the road fronting the house.

The Oberführer told me to stand. He guided me over to the sofa—farther into the parlor-area of the room and out of the way—where he seated me. Then he went back to slide my bread-table far to one side, out of the way, and to scoot the two chairs back, clearing the area in front of his desk.

Two sudden raps pierced the door, tailed by the perfunctory, "Enter!"

Obersturmführer Hofmann reported in. Successful in finding all three men, he placed Bohm's and the *Hiwi*'s records on the desk, as requested.

I was impressed, but then remembered that this was the efficiency, the damnable Teutonic efficiency, that Auschwitz—indeed, the entire murder machine— ran on!

The Oberführer ordered him to bring 'the lad' in first. Hofmann stepped from the room to the top of the stairs and called for Josef by number.

I heard Josef walk in; the unevenness of his pace betrayed his anxiety. His gasp in my direction spoke volumes.

The Oberführer called him again by number, then "You are Josef Piontek?"

"Yes, sir!"

"You were working in the *Kanadakommando* yesterday?"

"Yes, sir."

"And did one of the *Hiwi* guards abuse you sexually while you were working there during that time?"

He gasped again, then answered, in a voice so utterly terrified, "Yes, sir."

We all knew the terminal penalty imposed for being caught in such acts.

"Josef, take a seat in that chair, right there," the Oberführer ordered.

I heard him move to his left and sit. The chair scraped against the polished wooden floor. He must have sat down too fast, nervously.

"Bring in the *Hiwi* ..." the Oberführer flipped open the guard's records and read out his name.

Three sets of boots entered the room and shifted about, into a position that partially blocked the Oberführer's voice.

He called the *Hiwi* by his full name, "Were you on duty yesterday in the *Kanadakommando*?"

"Yes, sir," he answered in a heavy accent.

"And did you take sexual advantage of the prisoner sitting to your left?"

The *Hiwi* stood without reply; I guessed he just didn't understand the question.

The Oberführer yelled, "Did you fuck that boy yesterday?"

With that, he must have pointed at Josef.

Sounding like his head was turned toward Josef, the *Hiwi* started spewing out loudly what could only have been a native flood of cursing.

"Guilty as charged," the Oberführer said flatly.

"You two, take him downstairs, strip off his uniform, and that wristwatch, wedding ring, and any other jewelry he may have on him. Hold them as repayment for his meals, clothes and housing, then march him to processing. Naked.

"Sonderkommando duty!" he added forcefully, before yelling, "Now get him the hell out of here!"

A rush of commotion; down the stairs; yelling in the yard; a solid, flat punch to naked skin, and it was quiet.

The Obersturmführer stepped into the room and reported, "Your orders are being carried out, sir."

"Excellent, Hofmann!" he replied calmly.

"Now bring in Bohm!

"Josef, move your chair fully out of the way, farther to the right," he instructed, patiently. The chair was picked up and put down with another slide, even farther to my left.

Three pairs of boots again walked heavily into the room. Another, I thought probably the Obersturmführer's, then stepped alongside as they took their places before the Oberführer's desk.

"Rottenführer Bohm, what happened in your command at roll call this morning?"

"We had a disturbance, sir. I had to discipline a prisoner for failing to appear at roll call properly dressed."

"And did that discipline require killing him?"

"It was self-defense, sir! He attacked me!"

"Rottenführer Bohm, since when has saying the word 'lost' been a weapon?"

"He punched me, sir! Twice!"

"And the SS didn't teach you how to defend yourself without resorting to beating a restrained prisoner to death?"

Bohm asserted in a tense, low growl, "I was following orders, sir, as I saw fit, acting as commander of my section."

He had turned his head around to look at me: I heard the pig-snort when he recognized me.

"I'm over here, Rottenführer," the Oberführer said flatly. Then he launched into a "don't pull this bullshit with me, soldier!" lecture.

"The fact is, Bohm, that you destroyed Reich property, wantonly and for your own personal vengeance and, I must also assume, pleasure!"

"I am allowed to discipline my command, sir, as I see fit, sir!"

The Oberführer continued as if Bohm had said nothing.

"With the demands of the war, one of my directives has been these past several months that no prisoner assigned to work who is producing well and conscientiously be harmed by direct action of any officer, guard or other person having control over him.

"Other commanders have had no problem with following my directive, but you, Bohm, *you* violated that order!

"I've gone over your record, Bohm. This is not the first case of insubordination, nor does it appear to have been the last, just today!"

The Oberführer's voice was growing louder and angrier.

"Rottenführer Bohm! Did I or did I not give you a direct order that the prisoner seated over there was never to be placed in danger? Did I not tell you that this was the desire of Reichsführer-SS Himmler himself?

"I shouldn't have to say that, now should I, Bohm? I outrank you by how many levels of command? It's twelve by my count. I am your superior officer; do you not think it your duty, your sacred, sworn duty, to obey? Or does Rottenführer Bohm now think he is somehow exempt from his oath?

"By sending that prisoner into the Sonderkommando of Crematorium 5 this morning, you placed him in direct danger!"

The Oberführer spoke directly, ominously, loudly, "Bohm, you disobeyed my direct order, an order reflecting the will of Reichsführer-SS Himmler. You have disgraced the SS. You have added strength to our enemies by destroying productive property of the Reich during time of total war.

"You, Michael Bohm, are a traitor. And you will be dealt with as all traitors must be.

"Obersturmführer, take this traitor and have him held for execution."

Heavy commotion, scuffling and cursing broke out at the desk.

Bohm turned my direction and yelled, "I'll get you, you slimy-ass, worthless faggot! I'll kill you! ..."

I could hear his fierce struggle to get himself loose, to do just that.

The Oberführer interrupted Bohm's tirade with overpowering, distinctly calm, resigned authority, "Never mind the transfer, Obersturmführer, just get him downstairs and outside."

I heard a desk drawer slide open, something heavy slip across its wooden interior before being picked up, then a quick metallic click and snap.

"I'll not wait for that vapid bureaucrat, Höss, nor even that ass Baer, to take action: I'll just handle this myself ... now," he said resolutely. Louder, he then ordered, "Mannheim! Draw up the paperwork: Rottenführer Bohm, executed for gross insubordination, theft and treason!"

An avalanche of pounding jackboots flowed in a tumult down the stairs, carrying something scraping and bouncing along, hitting each descending step twice in an off-rhythm, ker-thump, ker-thump. Bohm uttered not a word.

One, then another gunshot.

Through the open doors I heard, "Strip him and leave his uniform here. Gleiss, take three men and throw this carcass into the nearest slime pit. Obersturmführer, come back upstairs with me."

The Oberführer walked back into the room, tailed by the other officer. He took his seat, slipped the gun back into the drawer and pushed it shut.

"Well done, Obersturmführer! Now I need your help with two more things this evening."

"Anything, Herr Oberführer!"

"First, take Josef here to the *Kanadakommando* and have him pick out some sets of clothes, three for himself and three for the pianist, including a couple of pairs of real shoes for each of them. Get those stinking rags off him and get him cleaned up—wash him down like you did the other. On your way back, gather a crew to clean out this big storage room here, and put two soldiers' cots in there.

"It looks like I can't trust anyone to keep this prisoner alive, so he's going to stay here, billeted in that storage room. Josef here is going to stay, too, to take care of him, since the pianist has gone blind.

"Tomorrow morning, you will bring Dr Schreiber from the infirmary here to check the prisoner's eyes. Then, you will bring the camp electronics crew. We're going to wire a feed from this piano to broadcast into the camps. I'm so gawd-damned tired of those fucking records I could crap! And I know that that un-relieved noise is impeding productivity!

"I realize it's starting to get dark, Hofmann, but those first two things have to be done this evening. Oh, on your way, stop downstairs and ask Frau Berg to get Josef something to chew on while you're heading out. I know he must be fam-ished."

"Yes, sir!" the Obersturmführer answered, with undisguised enthusiasm.

"You can count on me, sir!" he added.

"Yes. After today, I know I can, Hofmann!"

My clothing requirements noted, he and Josef walked out.

The door closed.

[August – September, 1944]

Erkenntnis – Chapter 21 – Perception

The Oberführer moved around the room, shutting windows and pulling down shades before the approaching evening's chill.

He walked over and grabbed my hand.

"Come back over here and sit. I'll have Frau Berg bring up some real food. We must get you and your fingers back into shape!"

Before rising, I said meekly, "Thank you, sir."

Despite his official pronouncements—and even after having been waist-deep in corpses in the gas chamber—I couldn't shake the fact that he had just executed a man.

"You killed the man who murdered my friend and was set on killing me!"

"No thanks needed. He disobeyed orders and was a continuing danger to everyone … but especially to you."

I was startled by his statement. Suddenly I realized that almost everything he had done that evening had been centered on my safety!

"Stand up," he said.

In front of me, he took my hands in his, and said surprisingly warmly, "I'm just sorry it has taken so long for me to be able to get you to safety!"

He paused, then added, shakily, "I just wish Edo and I could take you back to the zoo!"

I was dumbfounded!

"What?" My mind spun with the words!

Then he said, in English, congested with emotion, "Edi! Look at what *we* found!"

Eva! What? Reinhold? Reinhold?? Reinhold!

Suddenly a six-year-old again, I grabbed him and burst into tears.

Then I pushed him away.

Over his own sobs I started pounding him, "You bastard! You fucking bastard! You asshole! stupid mother-fucking son-of-a-bitch fucking stupid fucking bastard shit!"

I hit him, punctuating each pitifully weakening slug with every curse word I had ever heard, or thought I'd heard, and went back for more! He just stood there, holding me by my shoulders, taking my feeble, starveling punches until I had no more strength and just fell against him, holding him as tightly as I could.

The mask of Oberführer had fallen away; I answered his sorrow in kind.

Moments of silence: I was the first to speak, to plead.

"Reinhold! ... Reinhold, how could you have done this? To yourself? To Edo?" He choked.

"I don't know how it all happened, Edi!" he answered haltingly, "Things just fell apart so horribly after Edo died..." Another sob wrenched him.

"I tried to make sure you and your family would be taken care of ... but then I couldn't care for myself!

"When I came out of the coma, the headaches, the visions, the anger, the terrors throttled me!

"After I left the sanitarium and returned to the apartment, the loneliness, the emptiness, the tomb-like quiet slammed me to the ground! I crawled the floor, weeping, crying out, my brain aching, pounding while I searched, searched desperately for any evidence that Edo had ever existed!

"I had nothing! After twelve years of fantastic, blessèd friendship, partnership, union! Nothing!

"My vibrant past! My intimate present!

"Every moment of my future, now damned! vacant! empty!

"Nothing!

"The housekeeper had already been in; everything there was spitefully clean.

"Scouring the apartment on hands and knees I searched and searched! I was able to find six blond hairs—just six!—and that was all I had of my Edo! I lay them securely behind the glass of a small picture frame with one of his last notes to me, an ancient *minnelied*. I've kept it with me these past seventeen years!"

He stopped talking. I could feel the quaking shivers as his chest, his breathing spasmed. His tears dripped from his cheek into the inmate-shorn bristles of the back of my head.

"For the first month or so after returning home, between memories and the sudden onrush of wretchedness, I struggled to return to normal. I was able to remember and to act on the things that Edo had desired, financially, for you and your family. Acting on Edo's wishes, I even asked Bartomeu to arrange your introduction to Frank Marshall in Barcelona—to see if you might study at the academy there!

"But things started changing, everything started going awry! I realized that I had not lost just Edo, but without him, I had lost all of you! I had no friend, no companion, and now, without Edo I had lost my family, too!

"I was completely alone, orphaned again!"

He stopped, swallowed, murmured, "When the brain breaks, the heart dies in its utter solitude.

" ... ...

"Allein ... Ganz und gar allein ... ... [*Alone ... Totally alone ... ...*]

"Todeinsamkeit ... so morgen wie heut' ... in ew'ger Zeit ... so dicht gereut ... [*The loneliness of death ... so tomorrow, like today ... forever ... so heavy with remorse ...*]

" ... ...

"As the months passed, my emotions ran riot more and more, chasing revenge! Revenge! But on whom? I didn't know, but didn't dare ask myself!

"I could make it through a couple of days, then burst volcanic, explosive at anything that happened to hint of Edo.

"I would awake screaming in the night, watching that truck plow toward us! I had ripped and shredded the sweat-soaked sheets where I had reached over, trying to grab Edo to pull him out of the way! I lay there, afraid to sleep, terrified that that truck would roar out of the darkness, to kill us again!"

He paused, breathed; his voice grew more steady as he recovered his strength, slowly, seeking to explain it all. He talked beside, slightly over, the top of my head. The stubble of his day-old beard, of that cleft chin, rubbed into the meager, unshielding hairs of my head.

"I felt such a failure! I blamed myself for his death, searching, praying for something—anything!—I could have done differently to change things, to avert our path, to keep us from that place, that road!

"I dared not face any of your family, to beg to be allowed back, an orphan held again within your Gramma's so-loving embrace! I had lost her son, her elder son! Seeing any of you would have refreshed my anguish, my utter desolation!

"That's why I avoided your father, communicated solely through my attorney.

"For a while, I grasped at anything—tried alcohol, medications; they made it all much worse and, often, simply made me very sick. With drugs addling me, I couldn't handle money anymore. My solicitor stepped in, took control and saved me from losing everything. My mood swung so easily, so drastically! For days, I would hide myself away—weeping, wondering if life were worth all the agony. Then suddenly, I would burst joyful, enthusiastic, aflood with ideas. But the big plans would soon show themselves to be idle fiction, and I would plunge again, deep into the subtractive, smothering pool of anguish and intractable self-loathing.

"I could become so angry! Uncontrollable rage would erupt onto anyone who crossed me: no matter how trivial their action. I lost my ability to connect with others. My memory was failing: Edo was the last one I could still remember who was human for me!

"But I was never able to say goodbye to him: I would raise my voice, pleading for a sound, trying to talk to him, to speak and hear his voice just once again!

"Within months, I started hearing voices in the water streaming from the shower, voices that would whisper words that made me rage with face-punching, bone-breaking anger, or cower in terror in the corner of the tub. I had no hope: days came in which I was afraid even to go near that shower! I would avoid it, shun the voices, and just stand at a basin, sponging myself instead, never daring the slightest glance into the mirror, terrified of who or what might be glaring back!

"I even tried marriage, to see if there were some heaven-sent curse for my life with Edo.

"That was worse than anything! Not only did it not help me in the least, it made her life a living hell, too! She was a saint; but that life was false—an antique, sadistic, superstitious fake, never mine!

"Memories of the years before the accident faded slowly, piecemeal, till I could sometimes not force the recall of names, or the years things had happened:

234

acquaintances, anniversaries, but especially the joys of my earlier life.

"Slowly, my symptoms began to stabilize, but they would recur, in rounds, in pounding bouts. I struggled, searching for a cure—or just the merest relief! I saw a doctor whom I could trust. He found nothing wrong with me physically, but said that he had seen other head-struck, accident-victims, ones who had awoken from injury or extended coma, have the same kinds of trouble develop after such an incident, a blow to the head in which there was no outer scar, but inner turmoil, confusion, innermost devastation. He tried to help, but it was of little, too little avail.

"No one understands concussion: a brain afire, accursed within its unique, unseeable calamity! No one!

"Searching for sanity, I struggled to block, to repress, to seal away utterly all my memories!

"Viciously, the repression took hold. With the facility established, I could block any sentiment, all compassion: condemned to replace friendship with distance, understanding with disdain, humanity with monstrous hatred.

"I drifted, unloved and unloving. I rebuked my feelings—my desire for anyone!

"I even had to deny my dearest love for Edo, or face forever those continual terrors of the night alone!

"Then in one day's explosive fit of rage, I fell in with some brownshirts beating up communists. The *shirts* were very impressed: whenever that fury would hit, there was no stopping me!

"They urged me in and, before I knew it, I was a Berlin section-leader. I reorganized their finances successfully, and when Himmler caught wind of this, pulled me over into the SS. I've done so much, so well in his eyes that I have risen to this rank, now with unfiltered access to the Reichsführer himself.

"After Heydrich's assassination, Himmler promoted me to be one of his direct reports, auditing and augmenting the finances of all the SS-controlled camps and their sub-camps. He appreciated my unimpressed, unshakably dismissive demeanor when dealing with the executives of the large corporations to which he wanted to sell slave labor. I knew, angrily, that those executives were just like those American bankers we had dealt with in 1920's New York—they'd sell their children's souls for the mere promise of a glimpse of gold—and my anger played them for it. Because of the cash I have brought in, the last time I saw Himmler he had even mentioned a promotion to Brigadeführer [*brigadier general*].

"It has not hurt my position that I fought with the troops when we raged across Belgium and France: it proved my warrior credibility, even if our German forces accomplished that quick conquest more by using drugs—tablets to keep us unexpectedly awake and viciously uncaring—than with true, soldierly courage."

A slight tremor had seized his left arm; he paused.

"It was so easy for me to go along with all this because, with the Nazis and within the SS, there was always someone there to tell me how to act, what to think, what to remember. I had stopped thinking: not to think was soothing. It was too easy for me never to question!

"If doubts ever started creeping back, the headaches, anxiety, nausea and night-terrors would rush back in! Being a vapid tool of Führer and SS provided easy escape from my injury. With that, I could rebuff the shower-voices: they had to be quiet and obey orders just like I did!

"With the blocking of memories, the loss of human connection, I had also stopped feeling. I repressed all compassion. *Desires are weak; hatred is strong*—at least that's what was drilled into me by the SS! And I came to depend on it!

"Because I've worked at such a high level in the SS, I have been isolated from the suffering in which I have trafficked, the agony of death that I have helped inflict, that I have myself inflicted.

"This complete and utter repression of emotion, of desire, of love, allowed me to treat all humans as outside of myself: the SS had told me that I was an *Übermensch*, responsible only to my superiors and to no other earthly, or heavenly, power. It was the opiate to my misery. Propaganda anesthetized my still-raging pain: this made me numb to the suffering of others.

"But then I saw you there, our own baby standing obediently with the Jews!— all those Isaacs, bound for slaughter on the unholy altar of National Socialism!

"The shock, the shrieking terror of that moment awoke in me the sudden, insufferable realization that these trainloads were not going meekly to their deaths because they were what, so viciously, so successfully, the Nazis have inculcated, *Untermenschen*, vermin deserving extermination.

"The Jews are dying not because they are weak, but because they are strong!

"Their faith keeps them from thinking the worst; they believe, purely, unblemished, unsullied, in a better human nature, in a better Germany, one far better than we ourselves have believed in and have borne! They die because they believe—in us! *We* have been weak; it is *we* who have failed!"

In audible pain, he paused.

I felt, and knew only too well, the shame.

"You looked so much like Edo! So much like he did when we met in San Antonio, when we were so happy in New York City, in Berlin, on the farm, but especially in Texas! Your beautiful face—so much like Edo's, your hair, eyes, even the way you talked ... Cowboy!"

A shiver rattled me: no one had called me that since Edo died!

"I locked myself down that very day! Memories of that happier, joyful, loving life crashed back into my mind with more force than that fatal truck could ever have wielded! The horrible spell of unrestrained hatred had been broken, but suddenly I had to confront my own *Frevel*: my sin, my crime, my self-treason!

"The pain and suffering I have caused rushed in and threatened to crush me! But before I could allow that to rip me apart, I had to make sure that you, before anyone else, were safe!

"That's why I ordered the Obersturmführer to tail you, to be your unheralded guardian. I had to fight so fucking hard to stop myself from yanking you out of that line, wrapping you in my arms like I had held you that fever-break morning in Berlin, and carrying you right back to your sweet mother in Singhofen!

"I wanted to hug you, to hear and see our spoiled, strawberry-demanding Edi again! But I couldn't! I couldn't!

"To have done so would have meant certain death for both of us!

"To have an SS colonel step out of line and rescue a paragraph-175-convict, and a Jew-hider, too! The Nazis would have cried, 'Perversion and treason!'

"The only thing I was able to do right then and there was to grab your folder and extract the most incriminating, most dangerous documents. I started that very day striving to protect you, searching for any way possible to keep you alive, scheming ultimately to use the camp-system itself to get you safely out of here!

"The first thing I had to pull out of your folder was that draft-deferment signed by Hitler. If it had gotten back to Berlin that the Führer were in anyway associable with so well-known a KdF-performer, an adjudged paragraph-175 convict, it would have meant a bullet in the head for you, right then!

"I burned it the very first thing that afternoon, right here in this fireplace! Then I knelt, and dug and stirred and dug more at the blackened pieces, forcing them into the ashes, to ashes, to ashes … to make sure that they disintegrated — mixed indistinguishably with those of the wood fire.

"Edo said so often to me that you were the closest to a son that he would ever have. He sought, and I gladly gave, my promise to protect you.

"My disgrace slapped me awake: I had failed those 17 years to act on that promise fully, actively. When I saw you there, I was gut-punched, painfully re-awakened: it was time for me to change, to live up to my word. I had to act!

"The vision of you cracked my heart open again, restoring long-strangled emotions, forcing me to sense, appreciate, even to honor again the needs of others. This was the shock that unscrambled, made visible and returned legibility to the original text of my life, restored from that violent palimpsest my injury had made of my mind! It has been so very painful to recognize again so suddenly what I had seen in you: that all these prisoners, these Jews, are not the Nazi's *them* but our, Edo's so often asserted *us*!

"I saw you give your coat to that little Jewish girl. In the simplest act, you gave her joy, hope and compassion in a world the Nazis, and my own injured, insane anger, have striven so feverishly to fill with sorrow, fear and loathing, and to destroy.

"At that moment, I knew that — somehow, and soon — I had to work to resolve myself from that fetid world!

"This is why I moved so quickly today. That is why I killed that bastard. He was too much like the old *me*: the corruption of Germany from which I am now trying, struggling to arise! And he had nearly robbed me of you — our little boy! — and denied me the ability to fulfill my own oath to Edo, *mein besseres Ich* [*my better self*]!

"I had brought you here all those times, to play for visiting officers, executives and government officials to curry their favor — and, in my own way, to show you off, to exult in my own private pride in you — but I was forced to distance myself from you so that you could never recognize me. I hid you behind the screen, too, so that any who might have seen you previously, while performing with our dear Geli, couldn't glimpse, and possibly identify you!

"At last, I was able to get Himmler to visit long enough to hear you — you know that he has come back twice more! With his approval, I was going to issue orders making sure that you were protected better than before. Finally, just this week, I thought of the idea of having you live here and play this piano over the camp loudspeakers.

"Then that dumb-ass Bohm had to act up before I could get everything arranged! Well, it's all in order now! You will not return to the camp: today, I finally succeeded in arranging a way to keep you safe!"

I felt weak. With mention of the camp, he had reminded me of all the tragedies, the screaming, grinding misery of this fateful, fatal day.

"But *I* have failed," I mourned into his tunic.

He pushed me away from his chest, "What do you mean, *you've* failed?"

It was my turn to struggle against jagged emotions.

"That friend ... I carried to the cremation pit ... was David, *my David* ... he was ... *my Reinhold*! Frau Gellert said once that he and I looked like ... like you and Edo!

"He died, and I ... could do ... nothing!"

He hugged me and held me tightly as I released all those months of deathly sorrow, of anguish and guilt, loneliness and pain, of the compounding, excruciating, eviscerating loss.

The day's date whispered; the thought dug deeply into my mind.

August 15. It was the Feast of the Assumption of the Virgin, of *Pantánassa*: Vessel of the Shekhinah, She of the divine *Sophia*.

The metronome-clock on the mantel contrived the sweep of time.

Two-decade-deep tidal-waves of release had at last ebbed, dragging mounds of debris and devastation with them, washed away, into a resolving, solicitous sea.

Having led me to a chair before his desk, Reinhold was again seated behind it.

Boot- and shoe-steps ascended the staircase, then a quick, military rap rattled the door.

It was the Obersturmführer and Josef; they walked in, to stand alongside Reinhold's desk.

"Yes. That's much better!" Reinhold told them. "No more stench!"

"Josef, sit there."

I heard him take the chair to my right.

Suddenly, more footsteps came up the stairs and stood waiting in the doorway.

While leading them in, the Obersturmführer gave them their instructions. Soon, noises echoed from a small side-room, things being cleared out, cots cracked open, put down, pushed around.

Hofmann said, "Very good! You remembered pillows and blankets!"

Soon, the Obersturmführer ushered the crew out, closed the door and returned to ask Reinhold if there would be anything else.

"Yes, Hofmann! I would like you to stay, to hear what I have to say to these two.

"There will be no prisoner-numbers used here! Josef, if you don't know already, this is Eduard, but he says we can call him 'Edi'. You will act essentially as his valet, responsible for making sure he has everything he requires, and that he can get around with no problem, given his disability. The two of you will sleep

"This floor of the house will be always locked while I am not here, but you will be free to move about on this level, so long as my own use does not demand your seclusion. There is a restroom and bath next to your room. Keep it clean! You will be served your meals here by Frau Berg, who will also see to your laundry.

"My suite is on the floor above, and the housekeeper and members of my staff are on the ground floor, below, so you must remember that your movements can be heard at all hours.

"And both of you must be sure not to talk while Edi is playing piano over the loudspeaker system, which could be as much as a few hours in the morning, and additional hours in the afternoon!"

"A new work-detail," I thought. It would be taxing, but paradise compared to the crematorium, or even *Kanada*!

"Neither of you is allowed away from this floor of the house without a guard escorting you! Do you understand? Josef?"

"Yes, sir," he answered.

"Edi?"

"Yes, sir," I said, trying to make sure it sounded like I was responding to the present Oberführer, and not the hidden Reinhold.

"And Obersturmführer, since you no longer have to shadow this prisoner, you will be assuming greater responsibilities tomorrow morning, as my aide-de-camp.

"On your way out, please stop downstairs and ask Frau Berg to bring up three light dinners as soon as she can have them ready. Be at my office at 8 o'clock tomorrow morning. Dismissed!"

The Obersturmführer snapped to attention. I even heard a pert little, Prussian heel-tap as he said, "Yes, sir! Thank you, sir!"

He walked to the door, opened it, and repeated, "Thank you, sir!" before closing it behind him. I could have sworn he bounced down the stairs like a kid!

"Now, Josef, what is that extra bundle you brought back with you?"

"Well, sir, the rabbi asked me to bring something to Edi."

"And what is that?"

"The prisoner's uniform that Edi's friend was wearing when he..."

"I see," Reinhold interrupted.

"Is that something you want, Edi?"

"Just the badge, sir," I replied, swallowing a renewed surge of memory.

"Very well. I'll see to it that it's put aside."

"And," I said reluctantly, "I want my own, this badge." I pulled it away from my chest, as if he didn't know what a badge was. "And if I could get one from the Jewish women's camp, I'd like it as well."

"Why from there?" Reinhold asked.

"Just in remembrance of someone."

"Certainly!" Reinhold replied. "No one will miss mere scraps of cloth! Josef, you'll have scissors tomorrow morning to cut the stitching, to remove them from the pajamas."

A light knock and the door opened. Frau Berg announced the meal.

Josef pulled the small table between us, handed me a fork and tried to tell me where on my plate the bread, cheese, tomato and sliced boiled egg were laid out.

"Think: he's looking at a clock.face," I told him.

"Oh! OK … right!" and he described the exact hour of each morsel.

Frau Berg had gone downstairs, but soon returned, announcing more hot cups of tea. This time, she showed Josef how to teach me where it was—with directing hands instead of words, for surety.

"That's all for the evening, Frau Berg," Reinhold explained warmly, "You may retrieve the dishes tomorrow morning."

She left, again, graciously.

Avoiding our own personal topics during the meal, Reinhold mentioned the music he wanted me to play. We also got Josef to talk some of his boyhood in Gleiwitz, but soon exhaustion, and the influx of extra calories, cast its pall over both of us.

Reinhold walked behind us as he had Josef lead me, pointing out the locations of doors, furniture, the bathroom, and finally the cots. That room had its own light; Josef assumed responsibility for making sure to turn it out before retiring.

Too tired to change from my prisoner rags, I lay my head back onto the pillow, and it was only then, on my back, staring off into an impenetrable ceiling of blackness that it hit me: I was blind, and more helpless than ever!

I fell asleep with tears still coursing into my ears, spilling out, into a quietly receptive pillow.

———————————

The next morning, Josef woke me. Frau Berg had just come in and left our breakfasts on the small table in the big room. Josef had already washed up.

"There's hot water, and plenty of it!" he crowed.

"But let's eat before you shower!"

A fried egg, jam, butter, a large roll and hot, real coffee! It was like we'd died and gone to the Ritz! We made short order of the meal, only to sit in postprandial torpor. Then I had Josef lead me quickly back to the bathroom. The sudden change to higher calorie food was having not the most pleasant of effects!

Just before I went in, he described quickly where everything was (now being clock-wise), from sink and toilet, spigots and soap to the location of my new, clean clothes so that, starting that morning, I would be able to undress, shower and re-dress with nothing more than introductory, verbal assistance. I was de-termined that this blindness would not devastate my independence!

Recovered and clean-togged, I felt my way tentatively from the bathroom into the front room. Josef jumped up to help.

"To the piano," I directed, wanting to make sure the chairs and breakfast table were either exactly where they had been left, or moved completely out of my way.

I felt around on the piano to learn what state it had been left in. Its lid was down, front and back, its keyboard-cover flipped down and closed. Well, at least it hadn't been left exposed to every breeze!

After getting it once again into its familiar concert configuration, I started practice runs to check its tuning. Some rough notes, slower answering keys: I'd have to talk to Reinhold about that. But I was not going to let that childhood, "grand-piano attitude" arise and get in the way of staying alive! So, I started playing, flipping mental Czerny-pages, working to rebuild my finger strength, to pull my coordination back up to par.

Hofmann reappeared with Dr Schreiber. An examination from the piano bench, and his diagnosis was that the blindness was temporary: that rest, nutrition and diminished nervous distress (including a light-deflecting, eye-covering compress) were the only things needed for ultimate restoration. Relieved, I returned to my Czerny-preparations.

The door swung open. I heard Reinhold say, "Good! You've started work!"

"The electronics crew is here, and will be running the lines needed to get the microphone to the piano."

After telling Reinhold the piano-repair requirements, I worked with the electricians. With everything set up, we went through preliminary sound checks.

Mentally, I began walking methodically through the regime-delimited repertoire—Beethoven, Mozart, Bach, Schumann, Schubert and Brahms, plus Grieg, Granados and Albeniz—in preparation.

That first afternoon I played for three hours. After just this first performance, Reinhold started getting appreciative responses: it seemed he wasn't the only one who was dead-tired of the old records!

Late that evening, after I had lain down, I heard the squeaks and rattles of Josef dropping himself carefully onto his cot. He tossed a bit, then whispered softly across the nearly empty room, "Edi! Are you awake?"

"Yes, Josel. What is it?"

"Well. It's been bothering me: I'm so confused!"

Tensely, almost timorously he asked, "What happened yesterday? Do you know how the officer knew what was done to me?"

"Josel, the colonel knew because I told him. It was actually your incident the afternoon before that started off everything that happened yesterday."

"Really?"

"Yes. Both Nikos and I saw what the *Hiwi* was doing to you. I'm so sorry, but we couldn't stop him! By the time we could have done anything, two other guards had already shown up. And if they had found out what was going on, things would have been very much worse. You know that everything that had happened would have been made your fault—and yours alone.

"And, I saw the *Hiwi* steal your uniform-cap.

"That night, when you were moaning, 'my cap ... my cap,' I knew exactly what you meant: you knew the rules, and were terrified that, beyond everything that had already happened, you would be beaten, or worse, the next morning for not having it with you.

"I simply could not let you suffer more! So, after you fell asleep, I put my own cap under your arm, for you. Then I lay down. I was so ready for that next morning to bring me relief from my own anguish that I fell asleep almost immediately.

"However, when we were awoken yesterday morning, I was still so exhausted that I just grabbed for my cap out of habit. Because one was there, I put it on and leapt up, without thinking. It was only when Nikos was pulled out of line that I realized what he had done. I saw in your face at that same moment that you also didn't understand, that in the rush you had forgotten about your own, stolen cap just as I had my gifted one!

"Nikos had left my cap with you, and had placed his own where I always held mine."

I could barely get the words out: to continue, to speak the fatal truth.

"I tried to save your life; Nikos stepped in, and gave his life for both of us!"

Josef lay there, silent, for several minutes.

"Thank you, Edi!"

"You're welcome, Josel."

After another long pause, he continued, "He told you not to forget him, didn't he?"

"Those were the last words he spoke directly to me."

"You were very brave when Bohm pointed his pistol at you!"

"Bravery or just bone-braking weariness, Josel, it's hard to tell the difference!"

In my darkness now, that morning seemed years ago, but too vivid, too painful not to review, to remember, and to try somehow to make sense of Nikos's actions.

"One of the things that Nikos was very proud to repeat was his single line of English, one that he asked me to help him with. It was what Churchill had said in 1941, while Greece was, once again, fighting to repel her invaders: '*Hence we will not say that Greeks fight like heroes, but that heroes fight like Greeks!*'

"At that moment, facing that gun, I *did* want to be Greek, too, to answer Nikos's extreme courage with bravery of my own."

From studious silence, he ventured, "I won't forget him either, Edi, I promise!"

"That's good, Josel. But there's more that you should know."

I stopped, and sighed: it was disturbing to relate the terrible facts. But someone else, at least one other German had to know!

"Nikos explained to me that the reason he hated Germans was because of the looting and outright theft that started in 1941, with our occupation. The Wehrmacht has taken so much food from Greece, along with the fuel needed to distribute what little the Army has left behind, that at least 400,000 Greeks have now starved to death. His mother, his wife and their only two children were among those who perished.

"But because our German army and bureaucrats have also stolen all the industrially useful metals and other material they could lay their hands on, Greek carpenters had no nails with which to build coffins. His family was laid to rest in only their shrouds.

"Now, the SS has also rushed there to extract Jews, hauling them to their death here, from those parts of Greece Mussolini had occupied, where Italian officials had refused to let the SS touch them, so long as they could.

"Goethe must, right now, be hiding his face in the deepest, abject shame!

"Nikos's rage at all of us Germans had been his strength, his reason to survive, to return to Greece, to avenge his loss!

"But yesterday he gave his life out of deepest friendship, to protect, to save two Germans. Promise me you'll help me remember him, and learn the one phrase, the blessing he would say before he took the first bite at any meal, the very last words to pass his lips."

"I promise, Edi. Teach it to me!"

"OK. It's only three words; say each of them after me:

"Ζήτω …" — "Zíto"

"ἐλεύθερη …" — "eléftheri"

"Ἑλλάδα." — "Elládha."

"Ζήτω ἐλεύθερη Ἑλλάδα."

"Zíto eléftheri Elládha. … Edi, you'll have to remind me! I've never spoken anything but German. What does it mean?"

"Long live free Greece! The first word means 'long live'; the second is 'free'; and the third is 'Greece'."

"Zíto … eléftheri … Ellátha. Is that right?" he asked before repeating it forcefully, adding a verbal exclamation point.

"Very good, Josel!"

He seemed to be thinking it over, letting it sink in. At last he said, "Zíto, Edi!"

"Ζήτω, Ἰωσήφ!" [Live long, Josef!] I answered, following it in my mind with the deepest, grieving wish, "Νίκο! Ζήτω! Καὶ ἡ ἀγαπημένη Ἑλλάδα μας!" [Live long, Niko! And our beloved Greece!]

Sitting alone in the evenings, after Josef had retired, Reinhold read me timely reports coming from the front, catching me up to and keeping me apprised of our current situation. Just this year, the Western Allies had captured Rome and moved north, had taken both Normandy and Brittany, and from there had rushed to surround an entire German army near the French village of Falaise. I also learned quickly how desperately dismal Germany's situation had become in the East.

Right after rescuing me from the crematorium, Reinhold had revealed that the Red Army, having taken all of Poland east of the Vistula, had already overrun the ruins of Treblinka. Now, camped just beyond the border of East Prussia, it had advanced to just north of Tarnow within the first two weeks of August. The front line was only 130 km away! But a week went by, then two weeks, and they made no further movement toward the west. Yet who knew when another, sudden push might be launched towards us?

I could hear the mounting concern, the rising tension, in Reinhold's voice.

Within a few days of our extraction, Josef and I had fallen into a routine, much like we had within the camp, albeit without the stench, the sadistic guards, the ever-present hand of death.

Josef would wake me. Then, breakfast and shower and a shave out of the way (I did manage it myself, with some painful, nicking self-corrections), I would sit at the piano and prep for the "broadcasts", as we called them. Between performances, Josef and I would talk, or I'd teach him things I thought he would need whenever we should get out. Or he'd sleep. After all, he was still a teenager, and one who had been severely nutrition- and sleep-deprived for almost a year!

At lunchtime, Reinhold often accompanied Frau Berg as she brought in our meals, and he would eat with us quickly, before having to rush back to his duties.

We never engaged in anything but small talk during the day, or when Reinhold sat regularly with us at dinner. In the evenings, though, Josef often went off to sleep early, allowing Reinhold and me to sit and talk quietly. Our conversation complete, Reinhold would leave to go to bed, always certain to lock the door, both to keep us in, and to shut Auschwitz safely out.

Three weeks into the new routine, I awoke to find that I could distinguish at least some level of shadows. The promise of the return of my sight would have exhilarated me, except for the worry I discerned in Reinhold's voice.

The Western Front was collapsing.

Paris had fallen; modern tanks were rolling vengefully over the still too fresh, antique trenches of Verdun, the Somme. The Americans and Free French had landed in the Riviera and were moving rapidly up the Rhône.

But Reinhold was under extreme pressure here, ever mounting as the Eastern Front continued to surge toward us.

By September first, the Red Army had taken the eastern half of Romania.

Around the fifteenth, they had overrun the northern half of Bulgaria, Moldavia and Wallachia, and were charging beyond the Carpathian Alps, through the forested hills, past the seven Saxon-Lutheran towns of Transylvania, rushing ever northwards.

Within a week the Russians were in northwest Romania, at the southern, pre-war border of Hungary, only 400 km away. It could not be long until this area was surrounded!

At dinner one night that week, after Josef had turned in, Reinhold sat near, speaking at a very low volume, to let me know the bad news, with no chance that Josef might overhear.

Orders had come from SS headquarters in Berlin to plan the logistics of closing the Auschwitz complex, both the main camps and all those sub-camps housing the thousands of slave-workers used within the IG Farben, Krupp, Siemens, and other, factories. All prisoners still alive at that time were to be moved by any means necessary and available from the Auschwitz camps westwards, to existing concentration camps within the original borders of Weimar-era Germany.

He lamented, "We're losing this war, and all Berlin can think about is killing more of these unfortunate human beings! I do not understand how a nation can be led so stupidly, so insanely, so ... well ... sinfully!

"I was blind to it all, more blind, by far, than you have been!

"My own sin remains that I have been part of this process of wholesale murder, only one part of it, but still there, within it.

"But now, I have at last been able to start making some meaningful changes. I've issued orders to see that Jewish doctors be taken from the death lines to work with the sick, and that at least some Jews be moved into lower positions of authority over their companions to lower the death rate, all in the pretense of increasing war-production. But no number of such minor commutations now will release me from my ultimate responsibility.

"My physical injury in the wreck denied me the ability to see past my own rage, to regain the ability to love," he replied. "At last my emotions were ripped free from its tyrant-grasp by the shock of seeing you there, a prisoner: captive, condemned. Our own baby! Our little boy!"

I heard him swallow hard, sniff, clear his throat.

"Dictatorship is a disease lying dormant within every democracy.

"If the democratic system suffers injury, if its people lose their ability to think clearly and for themselves, roiling in fear and anger, they will too easily turn to tyranny for relief.

"Within such trauma, those blithely benefiting from freedom become too easily distracted, arguing and fighting over insipid, inconsequential issues, insanely taking true liberty for granted. They fall asleep, assuming that the blanket of freedom will be always there to cover them.

"But the tyrant pulls that cover away ever so slowly, slowly until, too late!

"The sleepers awake to find that it has been ripped away, utterly destroyed and that they must then face the frigid, heartless night of dictatorship, each of them, helpless, alone.

"People afflicted by economic woes or terrorized by their and others' timidity will accept, unconcerned, any conservative devil who will promise them a return to ill-remembered, false-nostalgic money, jobs, or security, who will pledge to make them "great again," even if that weakness were just his own, pernicious lie.

"Having seduced them, he will turn citizens into ravenous swine, to whom he will cast his enemies and, ultimately, his own people.

"And those swine will devour them gladly unawares: forswearing any possible thought of their own responsibility!

"Tyrants, and the mob, feast on obedience perverted into subservience.

"We Germans have never produced a Moses. We have just wandered, staggering blindly from one pharaoh and his plagues to the next."

He stopped, his ragged sigh sustaining the onus of Atlas.

"Weiche man von der Freiheitsbahn ab, folgt die Strafe danach, wenn auch noch so spät!" [*If one stray from freedom's path, punishment will follow, even if it is so very late!*]

As if all his deeds, his ravaging losses, were arising, pummeling him yet again, he paused. His few, deep breaths resounded contrition.

"Whatever the rest of the world may do, Germany must neither forgive herself, nor allow her children to forget! When she learns this, accepts it, and resolutely, bravely shoulders her own responsibility, she will truly have become, at last, the most adult, and most honorable of nations!

"The Germans did not become suddenly evil in 1933.

"Too many good people believed simply that their own goodness forbade evil; and this childish faith left them naked, unprepared for the full onslaught of evil that was to come.

"The problem is that, once tyranny has taken hold, it becomes almost impossible for the enlightened to free himself of the enforced discipline, of the monetary rewards, for him to re-establish an everyday, moral independence: to supplant the certainty of slavery with the self-reliant responsibilities of righteousness.

"We must remember to be ever vigilant against tyranny masquerading as redemption. For, redemption comes not from others, but awaits the dedication, the wisdom, the strength that must burgeon within each of us.

"I doubt now that the world will ever excuse us, ever forgive Germany. And that may be best: I'm afraid that the world might forget.

"Humans forget things far too easily, too willingly, and the more terrible those things are, the faster they forget!

"I cannot ask for forgiveness.

"Just remember of me that, when I did finally awaken to my fault, I did what I could to start setting at least a few things aright, to try to practice what Edo and our Berlin-friends always called *tikkun olam—repairing the world.*"

He seemed to stir himself, to sit with regained purpose.

"Edi, I must get you and Josef out of here and returned safely home! I will start working on arrangements tomorrow morning. I am determined to have us out of here by the middle of next week at the latest! Don't be surprised if we have to move very fast!"

That week, Reinhold sent out orders that all crematoria in the Auschwitz system be brought down starting the afternoon of September 26, to cool and be readied for full inspection the next day.

Privately, he told me that he had been ordered by Himmler to see how much effort and expense would be required to destroy the entire complex, to wipe away all evidence of mass murder. It was to be a repeat, albeit much larger and far more complicated, of that futile disguising of guilt that Himmler and the SS had attempted at Treblinka.

Reinhold let me have that next day off, too, and ordered Hauptscharführer Mannheim to take Josef back to the *Kanadakommando* to get us more sets of clothes.

When Josef returned with the goods, he was ebullient.

"Edi! You won't believe it! It's so quiet! All the inmates were at ease, still in their barracks! I saw the rebbe: he said to say 'hello' and 'thank you'!"

"For what?"

"For all the music—he said they especially appreciated your rendition of *Vltava.* And for today, too—he said it was called *Yonkipper*—the guys think you had something to do with the stand-down!"

"Reinhold, you sneaky bastard!" I smiled to myself, seeing him in even more expansive light. He had given the prisoners Yom Kippur: he *was* working to keep his promise, working the flagrantly abusive Nazi system against itself in small ways, unnoticeable by the thugs, by the soulless bureaucracy, but highly meaningful to the inmates. I wouldn't take the acclaim.

"No, Josel, it wasn't me. But I'm glad it turned out that way! Did you see any of the others?"

"Fishl, the tailor is still there. But Rebbe Schulmann said that they barely have enough of our original crew left now to make a *minyan*, whatever that means! The cobbler died of dysentery two weeks ago. He drowned in his own filth while SS-guards from the East stood around, watched and laughed. The rebbe told how he had taken Evron's body to the same pit to which you took your friend.

"He said it's much more shallow now."

I paused in painful memorial, at such saddening news. Evron had been a good, a constant friend. *V'imru: Omeyn.*

"Josel, I never asked you. Were any within your family Jewish?"

"Yeah, my mother's mother was—but not really a practicing one, except in all the food that *Bubbe* made for us! She was always cooking, always trying to feed us!"

So. He was a quarter-Jew, degraded as a *Mischling* [*mongrel*] according to the Nuremberg Laws, but cherished as a Jew by rabbinical precept. Although disguised as a political act, that's why the Nazis had sent his whole, Silesian German family to Auschwitz, and not just his father!

I heard Heine! The cry of 1848 rose, but it must now be sounded, not from here in the Silesian East, but from the West!

Im düstern Auge, keine Tränen ...	In a gloomy eye, no tears ...
Wir weben hinein den dreifachen Fluch —	We're weaving into {it} the three-fold curse —
Wir weben, wir weben!	We're weaving, we're weaving!
	{Old Germany's burial shroud}

Yet another blow: another blessing, another blessèd one, had been ripped away!

This news of losing yet another precious friend, Evron the cobbler, summoned memories of that horrific cattle-car ride, the stench of aged cow shit and fresh human terror. He had been so afraid that I would harm the precious hammer he had brought along from his shoe shop. But then he had been the first to jump up, to ply his trade to help me, a stranger among that displaced, but still-welcoming *shtetl*.

Rebbe Schulmann had spoken to the car-load calmly that day: "Un ayn fremdling zolstu nit paynigen, un du zolst ihm nit onterdiken, den ihr zayt fremdlinge in dem land mitzraim." [*And thou shalt not vex a stranger, and thou shalt not oppress him, for ye were strangers in the land of Mitsraim.*]

The rebbetzin had said a soft *Omeyn* to this. And, without looking up from fiddling with one of her buttons, Sophia had added a loud, 'Ó-méyn', punching each syllable with her sweet, child-soprano voice. It was the only time during that entire journey that I heard my companions laugh.

I knew that the verse, and its reception, had been directly about me.

 As for the music, I had snuck that piano-reduction of Smetana's *Vltava* into the middle of one of my broadcasts specifically because of its main melody.

The Germans would hear that tune simply as one that Mozart had used in a set of variations. Any English or Americans within the camps would hear a childhood tune, "Baa, baa, black sheep," "Twinkle, twinkle, little star" or perhaps (like Edo and Reinhold had taught me to sing), as "the alphabet song".

But the Czechs would recognize it as a piece by one of their own composers, using one of their folksongs; and the Jews would hear the melody as that of their own *Hatikvah*.

It was the single piece I could play that carried so many messages: of home, of hope. And that was vital, sustaining, empowering.

A child's voice whispered to me, floating soft, as if from afar:

עוד לא אבדה תקותנו...   *"Od lo 'avdah tiqvatenu..."*   *Our hope is not yet lost…*

When an unexpected Reinhold strode in to join us for lunch, he sent Josef downstairs for more food, to wait there while Frau Berg got it all ready.

While we were alone, I chuckled and expressed my earlier thought.

"Reinhold, you sly bastard!"

He laughed and said, with an audible smirk, "Now what?"

"You know! Scheduling a down-day on Yom Kippur!"

He chuckled again, then said seriously, "I had the opportunity—the reason and the authority—to schedule it. I asked Dr Schreiber about it, and that was when I picked the day. I'm afraid others will find ways to get around my orders: Mengele remains beyond control. But I did what I could.

"Edi, I find myself able to remember more and more things from back, before the wreck! I struggle with it: the injury and my self-inflicted fugue still plague me.

"But now I am able, better and better, to recall memories of happiness, of our beautiful Berlin life, of trips to the farm and those loving receptions from your grandmother and parents.

"Your uncle and I had so many good friends in Berlin, and we had always been so pleased to be able to help them! For some of them, we would run their stores on the few days they couldn't because of observances, especially around Yom Kippur, Hanukkah and Passover. One of those families made sure we always had our choice of the most expensive clothes they could find in Germany. You may remember that Edo was very demanding about his pants, in particular. His trousers had to fall just right for all his El Paso-made cowboy boots!

"I remember those Schraeders, in particular, and how they could find such outstanding merchandise for us.

"I urged and urged them to expand to Frankfurt, so they'd have a store closer to the farm! We would stop by their Berlin store, along the street toward the Tiergarten to check for any new goods they might have gotten, and to play with the twins they had had in 1922, a beautiful little boy and girl named…"

He paused, as if searching his memory. Then, he must have noticed my face, quivering, my bitten lip. He took my hand.

Painfully, I managed to say, "Esther. And David."

"Right! … But? … that beautiful little girl … you mean that they? … that precious little boy we held … who played and played with the chimes of my pocket-watch … that was? …"

"My David!" was all I could say before hanging my head, overwhelmed by yet another flashback of my own *better self*—haggard, pale, lying forever silent at the edge of that smoldering, stinking pit of corpses.

"Oh!" he said, his voice growing tight, broken within one strangled word.

He dropped my hand, rushed out the door, up the stairs to his private quarters. His door slammed, and an anguished roar bellowed through the house.

Papa had been right.

"You will never fully understand how much they mean to you, until you lose one that you love."

Ausbruch — Chapter 22 — Escape

"Come with me!" Reinhold said, the Friday afternoon two days later, as he led me upstairs to his personal quarters for the first time.

Sitting at a large, dark wooden table, I watched—my slacking vision now allowed some shadows, forms, and vagrant hues—as he returned to sit beside me, to place a small stack of folders in front of us.

"Because of my rank, and through the right SS connections, I managed to retrieve the original sets of records from the Gestapo archives. They were delivered late yesterday."

He announced whose folder he held as he pulled each from the stack, spreading all of them before us, "Yours, David's, Esther's, Albert's, Frau Gellert's and, from the Frankfurt office, your father's."

"Albert's? ... My father's?"

"Yes. When charges of suspicious activities got to them, the Gestapo investigated everyone who frequented Frau Gellert's house. Albert and Frau Gellert, and the housekeeper, were cleared, and you would have been, too, except for how the agents found you and David.

"Then, because of this, they scrutinized your father. They found nothing in his case and that's as far as it went, except for putting the farm's phone line under observation. Luckily, with its being locked away, your parents had never become accustomed to using it!

"I know that you have not heard, and realize that you don't need more bad news, but I wanted you to know ... Frau Gellert was killed in the massive air raids on Leipzig, December 4th of last year, only ten days after your arrest. The report states that during the week previous to that, she had become a matter of public concern, walking the streets at all hours of the day and night, calling for all of you by name, especially you, and muttering, "my baby, my babies!" almost constantly.

"In the early hours, she had been seen wandering through the Augustusplatz, directly in front of the university, just before the bombs hit. Workers found her body two days later, before the ruins of the *Augusteum*, directly at the foot of the facade, where parts of it had collapsed. If she had just stayed at home, she would probably still be alive. The bombs spared the area around her house, the area south and west of the Conservatory, but she had wandered directly into the path of destruction. The *Augusteum* and most of the University there no longer stand undamaged."

The news shot yet more holes through my soul. My dear Tante Gelchen! And my beloved University! I felt hollow. When you have plummeted onto the jagged rocks at the very bottom of the abyss of mourning, there is no farther to fall. But with each new lamentation, those rocks grow taller, sharper, rip ever deeper.

Reinhold continued, "Albert's report details who the Gestapo's informant was, how the entire proceedings were kicked into gear."

I asked him, so he read me Albert's entire transcript: I had to know who had turned us in!

With that one read, Reinhold expanded those details with more, personal information.

"Do you remember having loaded a small box with a ring and some jewelry from that golden pile in the *Kanadakommando*?" he asked.

"Yes, I was told to pick just a few items. The kapo had told me to do it.

"I remember the ring in particular. It had a delicately worked chain of twenty-one interlocking circles running along its outer edge. It reminded me of David's description of his parents' rings, rings like those he had wanted us to have, too."

"Well, that box went to the informant as a gift, provided by the SS, from the Gestapo commander of the Saxony region. Such exchanges are not uncommon, but remain unknown to the public, as marks of evil courtesy, or bribery, between those two sections of Himmler's organization.

"A hand-written note in the record mentions how much the Gestapo owed to that snitch: because of him, they were able to seize the fortune David and Esther had inherited from both sets of parents. It seems that the fink had even turned in his own superior, a Bishop Vogler, originally from Frankfurt, now reported dead in the Mauthausen camp, arrested for hiding Jews and Gypsies within his cathedral. When you return home, be sure to stay clear of Cologne: the informant was recently elevated within that see."

My dear friend, Father Vogler, gone, too! The losses kept compounding!

I was able to force my voice, "I will.

"Now, what about Papa's dossier?"

"After you were Paragraph-175'd and all, an investigation was made into your father's and your family's activities. They found nothing: your father's membership in the Nazi party helped deter a lot of trouble." Then he added with a chuckle, "I bet your grandmother had a fit when he told her he had joined!"

"Yeah," I said, "but she suffered through it when she heard him tell about all the trouble the party had been inflicting on non-joiners. She learned to keep her free-thinking to herself. We had all learned quickly that the Nazis won't put up with any talk of government and social responsibility, or of personal liberty!"

"According to the records, your Paragraph-175 conviction was never made public—the whole affair appears to have embarrassed the Gestapo, because they had cleared you, and David, before each of you had received your draft-deferments—so your family doesn't know anything about it. Your father traveled to Leipzig looking for you after the arrest, inquiring about Army orders, the draft and such, but apparently was told only that you had been taken into protective custody. The Saxony Gestapo is also notoriously tight-lipped about their activities. It will be up to you to let your family hear what you want.

"Although, as demonstrated by their always-loving acceptance of Edo and me, you have nothing to hide."

"Thank you, Reinhold. That's comforting to know."

"Do you want me to read you anything from the twin's dossiers?"

"No. I don't think so. Not right now, thank you, Herr Oberführer."

"Yes, well.

"I've forgotten that I hadn't told you a couple of things, and that you wouldn't have been able to see them.

"Last week, when I got back from Berlin, I hadn't just been to Berlin. I had run an errand for Himmler.

"He has been skimming funds from those the industrialists have paid for the slaves the SS has been supplying the work-camps. His 'fee' has, of course, been going into a Swiss bank account. Himmler had me fly into Geneva, and then back from Zurich. He wanted some of those funds in gold coin that he could keep with him. So that's what I did: act as a black-market bag-boy for the Reichsführer-SS. By the time I had made the delivery to him in Berlin he had also read my report on output increases that had set in after I had curtailed the worst abuses against the camp inmates.

"He was so pleased with my speedy and accurate delivery, and with my report, that he skipped a level over his original threat, and promoted me to SS Gruppenführer [*major general*]. And he added oak leaves to my Knight's Cross of the Iron Cross."

He paused and took an ominous breath.

"Something else I haven't told you is that I have applied for transfer out of the camp system and back into the Waffen-SS, for duty on the Eastern Front."

I panicked, almost jumped.

"But, Reinhold! What will happen to Josef and me?"

"Don't worry, Edi!" He placed his hand on my arm to calm me. "My transfer is part of the plan to get you out of here. It's complicated, but we can pull this off! Trust me!

"The Allies have just liberated all of France except for Alsace-Lorraine. Getting you back to the hills of the Rhineland is the safest thing I can do for you, to get you far away from the Red Army.

"We'll have to see where Josef wants to go, but I must get you out of here and back to Singhofen!"

He laid it all out for me. He was right; it was complicated. But then, every detail had to be covered to make it safely feasible!

Toward the end of our conversation he added, "Oh, and by the way, Bartomeu says 'Hello': he and the Dreschers send their love. Hannah is doing much better under the care of the Zurich doctors, in the region's clear mountain air, and Daniel did enlist in the army. They're all Swiss citizens now, even Bartomeu.

"He was not completely happy about it, but said that he was constrained to do it. He will probably never be able to return to Barcelona. You see, his family had been in the vanguard, fighting against Franco, who had subsequently revoked Bartomeu's passport, trying to force him to return to Spain. Bartomeu hasn't been able even to set foot out of Switzerland since 1940 because of its being surrounded by the Axis. He and his family were installed on the Spanish dictator's enemies-list, and that was then forwarded to the Gestapo. From there it went to OVRA and the Milice.

"That was quite a scheme you cooked up with your dad, to get the Dreschers out of Germany! I'm glad you went into the *KdF*, and not the Security Service— you're far too cunning! I'd probably be reporting to you!" he laughed.

"Bartomeu wanted me to let you know that, because of the early Swiss fears of a German invasion, he had transferred all the holdings in your family's accounts to the bank's branch in New York City just before the fall of France. Everything is safe. He has been greatly apprehensive for your family's safety, so he has avoided trying to get in touch with your folks since that summer of 1940, except to let Aunt Franziska drop hints in her letters, particularly after the war had curtailed Mama Meyer's visits to Zurich.

"He asked me to assure you that he will come to Singhofen as soon as the situation allows, and detail everything that has happened."

I was immensely pleased. I had some friends, dear friends of my childhood, who were yet alive.

My parents' faith in Bartomeu had not been misplaced!

———————————

That following evening, a Saturday, Reinhold had a banquet prepared, and all his staff to dinner. I played for them, once again invisible behind the screen, while Josef also stayed obediently out of sight.

The pinnacle of the evening was when Reinhold promoted Obersturmführer [*second lieutenant*] Hofmann to Hauptsturmführer [*captain*], and awarded him the Iron Cross First Class (with grant of 2nd Class).

From that same, hidden position, I had often heard Reinhold's staff officers in less formal settings with him before, regularly. I knew their vocal patterns, recognized their jokes and japes. But now, all that was much reduced.

It seemed that Reinhold's promotion, his approaching transfer, plus those oak leaves, had instilled a greater level of respect, of restraining distance. Yet, an air of foreboding permeated that reserve.

As time approached for them to leave, Reinhold asked Hofmann to stay behind. When the three of us were at last alone and together, Reinhold addressed him.

"Hofmann, I'm sure you appreciate the distinctions I've secured for you, just as I value the extremely able work and unbounded dedication you have demonstrated under my command."

"Yes, sir! Without question, sir!"

"Good. As I'm sure you remember, I am being transferred to the Waffen-SS, and leave this next Wednesday, the fourth, after one more camp inspection. Would you like to accompany me, and help defend the Reich from its true enemies, the communists, or would you rather stay here and babysit prisoners?"

"If you'll allow, sir, I'd much prefer to go with you."

"Good, Hofmann! I was hoping you'd say that. I've had transfer papers drawn up, needing only your signature.

"But I require something else, too. And for this I need you to swear your personal loyalty and willingness to carry out all orders I may give you. Can you do that?"

"Without hesitation, Herr Gruppenführer!"

"Good. Your steadfastness and abilities have been exemplary, Hofmann!

"Now, as a personal favor to me, I need your help in getting three inmates out of the camp and sent safely on their way home. We will do it in such a way that no doubt can arise about anyone's activities, or endanger your or my standing in rank or capacity within the SS. You must be able to keep secret all that I tell you and all that we do.

"Can you do that? Will you do that? I must remind you that if anything goes wrong, we will all be implicated—and shot—so success is the only option!"

"I will follow your orders, sir!"

"Excellent, Hofmann!

"First, I want to introduce you fully and correctly to this"—I could see the light from his hand raised toward me—"young man. This is Eduard Meyer, and he happens to be a member of a family that is very, very dear to me. I have obtained his dossier from the Gestapo, and determined and verified that the claims made against him are completely unsupportable.

"However, I cannot, even with my rank, interfere with Gestapo business to force them to rescind their report. So, *we* will see that this injustice against a true, ethnic German is undone, and send him home.

"Do you have any questions, Hofmann?"

"No, sir!"

"Thank you, Hauptsturmführer! We will need to send the young lad who has been helping him along, too, to see that Eduard arrives safely. And, to facilitate this mission, we will also be taking Dr Schreiber, who will look after Edi's eyes, as needed.

"I will also tell you now, Hauptsturmführer [*captain*], that when this has been accomplished, and you and I are established in the Waffen-SS, that I will promote you to Sturmbannführer [*major*], and you will be my executive-officer. I realize that you have been too long held back in your current rank, and I wish to remedy that by recognizing your talents and your loyalty.

"Now, is there anything about this that you cannot or will not do?"

"No, sir! I will carry out the general's orders to the greatest exactitude!"

Reinhold definitely had Hofmann's number! That guy was rank-, honor- and action-starved! He was even being offered promotion yet another level up!

"Now, Hofmann, you realize too that you can tell no one anything I have said, including concerning your upcoming promotion. I expect you to abstain from all alcohol for the next week, to keep your head clear and your mouth shut. Is that understood?"

"Completely, sir!"

I could feel the excited pride radiating from his voice! His exuberance was undiminished.

"Good! Be here at 08:00 tomorrow morning and we will go over the details!"

With dismissal and salutes, Hofmann was out the door and gone.

The next morning, Reinhold had me try on the field-gray uniform of an Ober-sturmführer to match the appointment papers he had created for me.

"You do remember your *Hitler Youth* training, don't you, Edi?" Reinhold asked.

"Certainly, sir!" I snapped in crisp salute.

He laughed, "Yep, looks like you do!"

So, I was to be protected behind the mask of a war-blinded, not Wehrmacht, but Waffen-SS first lieutenant.

I was just glad that I couldn't see myself then, in what my life had come to view as the most repulsive set of clown costumes.

Well before roll-call Wednesday morning, Hofmann had a lorry parked before the house, its driver waiting. On the pretense of giving a distant concert, and of having my vision checked further, we were leaving Auschwitz.

Josef led me down the stairs; Dr Schreiber helped me up into the truck's fabric-vaulted rear while Josef hefted our travel-bundles.

I was again in prisoner clothes; my uniform had been folded and packed away. It felt odd, but I was already wearing the jackboots beneath my pajama trousers. Something lay on the floor of the truck, opposite where we sat. I had toed into it with my boot when I turned around to sit. It wasn't hard, but returned a soft, almost squishy report.

As planned, within the glare of the truck's lights, Hauptsturmführer Hofmann kept the driver, a raw SS-Schütze [*private*], busy with road-routing instructions while the three of us took our places in the back of the truck. It was vital to Reinhold's scheme that the truck driver not see who might get into the back.

Reinhold sat beside Hofmann, who drove the staff-car in the lead, toward Kattowitz, only around 40 km to the northwest. Once there, the west-bound road pointed us toward Gleiwitz. Josef kept standing to look out the back of the truck, growing more excited as we got ever closer to his hometown.

Within the heavy woods some 10 km west of Ruda, we slowed to a stop beside the road.

Hofmann walked back to the truck driver and explained that the general needed to stop for a piss. He offered him a smoke; the driver got out of the cab. We could hear them step off, a good ways ahead. Then Hofmann started whistling *Lili Marleen*. That was the signal!

Josef helped me down from the truck and, grabbing our packs, led me away quickly.

Then he ran back to the truck, and he and the doctor extracted each of those oblong objects. They pulled them away, into the edge of the woods; I could just see that Reinhold had come close to where they were dragging them. When they had gotten all three of them into position, Josef and the doctor rushed over to where I was, making sure we were well hidden.

Reinhold yelled, "Stop! Prisoners, stop! Hauptsturmführer! They're escaping!" then fired his pistol five times in quick, syncopated succession.

I could hear Hofmann and the private running back down the road, around the truck. Reinhold announced that he'd shot all three, that their bodies should be lying just within the woods "over there." The driver and Hofmann located each of "our" bodies, dragged them back to the truck and tossed them inside. Once they'd recovered them, the private asked, very nervously, what he was supposed to do.

Reinhold answered, "Just wait, Schütze! Hauptsturmführer Hofmann will fill out the paperwork. Then you will drive back to the camp and report what happened here to your officer. We will provide instructions as to what to do and how to dispose of the corpses!"

"Paperwork?" the private asked.

Reinhold laughed, "This is Germany, son! There's always paperwork!"

Hofmann got up into the truck, checked the numbers on the arms and uniforms of the dead, and filled out the forms. After the still-rattled private was laden with bodies and bureaucracy, he was dispatched back to the concentration camp. At last, Hofmann came over to get us.

Josef and Dr Schreiber had shifted quickly into their civilian clothes, so they helped me change quickly into the Obersturmführer uniform. The rest of our bundles landed in the trunk of the open-roof staff-car. The doctor sat in front; Josef and I sat in back on either side of Reinhold for the remaining 20 km into Gleiwitz. I kept the bandage over my eyes wrapped tightly beneath my cap's visor, against the ride's wind and unremitting sunshine.

For security, we hadn't revealed the entire arrangements to Josef, so he had questions, especially about those bodies.

Reinhold explained, "Those unfortunates had been recently brought-in, unregistered prisoners in Dr. Schreiber's care, but who had succumbed yesterday evening to the ravages of their incurable disease. During the night, the doctor had tattooed the ID number of each of you three into the arm of one of the dead.

"There's no need to worry about the minimal blood-flow from their gunshot wounds: the long drive back to camp will avail. Plus, after having murdered millions, the SS will not notice: there is no one in the SS who will suggest an inquest for three more lonely corpses.

"This way, when the private gets those bodies back to the camp, it will be you who are recorded as having died. There will be no record of successful escape attempts, and no one called to task—a procedure that would have presented the supreme danger."

"So, as far as the SS is concerned, we're dead now?" Josef asked. "And there's no reason for them to come looking for us?"

"That's right," Reinhold answered with a laugh.

"The three of you are no longer living inmates of Auschwitz. That doesn't mean you're safe, but it does mean that you are far closer to having a real future than you were, only hours ago!"

In Gleiwitz, Hofmann drove us directly to the ponderously tall, gray-red mass of All Saint's Church. Reinhold got out and went in.

He returned presently and ordered, "Everyone inside! Quickly!"

Just within the shadowy narthex, Reinhold introduced me to Father Dominik Schaletzski, and a nun, Sister Maria Franz. But before Reinhold could say another word, the sister exclaimed "Holy Mother of God! Josef Piontek!"

I felt a breeze as, wimpled and in full sail, she rushed past me to envelope him.

"Hello, sister," I heard him say, with the echoing unease of a teenager being sucked reluctantly into the inescapable, hugging gravity of an aunt or grandmother he hadn't seen in ages.

Sister started explaining joyously, "But Josef—dear little Josel!—was a student in my first class, when I started teaching here in our elementary school!"

The sister's embracing amazement expressed, Reinhold asked quietly, "Father, did she arrive?"

"Yes. Yes, she did! The evening before yesterday, as a matter of fact!

"She's expecting him. Just a second and I'll fetch her from the rectory!"

Billowed by her second wind, the good sister burst into extolling how it were surely a saintly miracle to have Josel restored, particularly on that day, the feast-day of her own *Sankt Franz*: Francis of Assisi! Of course, she then had to regale us with a tale of little Josef's antics while he was so very young. I could sense the teenage-embarrassment glowing from him.

At last, two sets of footsteps echoed in approach.

A girl's voice called out, "Edi?"

"Edi! We've been so worried!" she said as she rushed to grab me, wrap me in a tight hug, before putting her head securely on my chest. It was my little sister, Gretchen!

I hugged her, breathed her hair. She felt taller; she smelled like home.

"Gretchen! What are you doing here?" Reinhold had not mentioned her part in this escape!

"Edi! What's wrong with your eyes?"

"Problems—they're getting better. But don't answer a question with a question! Why are you here?"

"An SS-officer drove up to the house, with a message, train tickets and security passes for me—just me—to come here to Gleiwitz, specifically here to All Saint's, that someone had found you! Edi! We had no idea where you had gone! No one would tell us anything!"

"Yes, Gretchen. I was the one who sent them," Reinhold volunteered.

She turned her head, "Thank you! But, you are…?"

I answered, "Gretchen, you're too young to remember him the last time he was with us in Singhofen. This is your uncle Reinhold."

"Reinhold?" she paused as if she were trying to piece the information together, to quell her disbelief.

"You mean the *Edo* Reinhold? Edi? The one in the *Tiergarten* photo by your bed?"

She released me.

"Oh, Reinhold! Gramma, Papa and Mama will be so pleased!"

I heard her hug him, too.

"Are you coming back with us?"

"No, Gretchen, I have duties here." He turned. "Father, would it be possible for us to move into a more private area?"

"Oh, pardon me! Yes! Please! Come this way!"

Gretchen walked on my left, Josel on my right, directing me as we made our way up an aisle, and ultimately into what must have been part of the vestry. It had the unmistakable aura of old books, incense and prayer.

Reinhold started addressing each of us, deliberately and with some emphatic speed, as soon as the door clicked into its frame.

"Dr Schreiber, you have passes, clearance and a new identity card that should let you head west whenever you need. I do suggest that you not return to Litz-mannstadt [Łódź]—there will be too many there who might recognize you. And the front, the Red Army, is much too near it!

"Josef, the good father here has volunteered to keep you in hiding within the parish if you want, or you may travel west with Edi and Gretchen. If you stay, though, it is vital that you keep out of sight, never recognized!

"Gretchen. You will take Edi, with Josef if he wants, back to Singhofen. The Allies will either be stopped at the Rhine, or they will rush around the Taunus toward larger industrial and population centers. Either way, it's better to be there than to be trapped by the Russians!

His orders complete, he risked a repeat.

"Are there any questions?"

Gretchen asked, "What do I do about Edi's eyes? Does he have ointment or drops, or does his dressing need to be changed?"

"There is nothing necessary," the doctor offered, "just keep the wrapping over them so that there is no shock to his system from piercing lights. At the rate he's progressing, and given that he has no more physical or emotional trauma, his vision should certainly return fully within a very few weeks."

Josef finally spoke up.

"Sister, do you know if any of my family is still here?"

"No, my child, there is not a one left here! … Will any others be coming from the camp?" she asked with unremarkable, regime-manipulated naïveté.

"No. None," was his heartbreaking answer. He was an orphan; that fact seemed to have registered only just now in his 16-year-old mind.

"I'll stay here, anyway," he managed to say, "if it's alright with the Father and Sister Maria. I'm afraid if I were seen by the wrong people during the trip west, they would demand to know why I'm not in uniform!"

"Certainly, my child! We'll keep you here!" the sister answered quickly. "Af-ter the SS scoured the town and took away all the Jews not yet in sanctuary, they have not come back to look for more. We have places to keep you safe here, with us!"

"And, Doctor," the priest added, "if you would consider, we have people in the area—people of all confessions, including so many hidden—who could bene-fit much from your expertise, and vital discretion."

"Thank you, Father. If I could, I *would* like to stay here to help, to recover some direction in life. So much has changed so drastically—I, too, have lost my family—that I must take time to steady my mind. And, with the new identity card the general has provided so generously, I will again be able to practice medicine!"

"Excellent!" said Reinhold. "Father, and Sister, thank you very much for your help! I know it was frightening for you to accept my initial inquiries—I value your trust."

I heard him shift his position, as if reaching for something.

"And here is 8000 Reichsmark to help with any needs that might arise."

"Thank you so much, general!" the priest responded. "That will help us greatly!"

Reinhold stood up.

"And now we four must get to the hotel! There is much more to talk to the Meyers about. If you'll excuse us, Father, Sister."

With that, he stepped toward the door through which we had entered.

Josef grabbed me, hugged me hard.

"Zíto, Edi! Remember me! I'll never forget you, and Nikos!"

"Ζήτω, Josel! I'll never forget you, either! And remember, if you need us, we'll be in Singhofen. All you have to do is ask anyone in the village and they'll tell you how to get to the farm!"

He held and held my hand, my arm. It reminded me of how I had not wanted to let go of Bartomeu at the Frankfurt train station, all those years ago, in that other world when I was, what, twelve?

Gretchen pulled me away, leading toward the door, down the nave and outside. I felt the sun on the exposed parts of my face, then heard a nearby clock tower strike the morning's eleven o'clock.

Once Hofmann had loaded Gretchen's bag, we took our seats in the staff car. There, I was shaken by the sudden realization: Josef, the doctor and I were destitute!

Beyond the rescue, we now had nothing!

I was seized by apprehension, with fear of our surroundings. I hoped no one had been watching, that none of the regime's ubiquitous, suck-up snoops and snitches had noticed that we had dropped off two men, and were now leaving with only one female. Even in the company of an SS-general, when you're under the constant, conservative eye of the dictator and his homeland-security machine, fear never abates.

———————

Reinhold had arranged our Gleiwitz-accommodations through the SS.

After lunch, while Gretchen and I lay down in our rooms and rested, Reinhold and Hofmann went out to take care of SS matters. One of the Auschwitz satellite-camps was located nearby: I guessed that this was where they had gone, an inspection creating Reinhold's routine justification for the trip, and its expense-report.

They returned late that afternoon. I did not ask where they had gone, what they had done. I didn't want to know: I wanted only to be as far removed from the death-camps as possible.

We hurried down to dinner. The three of us must have made rather a startling impression in our SS uniforms: the general and his two officer-aides, along with what might have been the general's daughter. The dining room fell stark silent

258

for a moment as we entered.

Our own conversation warmed quickly. Reinhold and I caught up on every-thing that had happened around the farm, with Gramma, with Mama and Papa, and with Gretchen herself. I hadn't seen her in over a year; Reinhold hadn't seen her since she was less than eighteen months old. Hofmann sat politely quiet, sharing only a few details of his home in Stettin, and his youth, spent playing on its Baltic beaches.

However, those pleasant visions of the north coast vanished for me the mo-ment that Gretchen revealed that the Old City of Frankfurt had been devastated back in March, the night of the 22nd. She reported that the *Dom*, the *Hoch'sche* and our boarding house—the sites of so much of my early life and accomplish-ments—had been bombed, completely burned out, and that Frau Guenther, the grandmotherly manager that the anti-Nazi Lutheran minister had found for us, to replace Frau Drescher, had been killed that night, along with nine of our boarders, including a family of four that had struggled their way south from Düsseldorf, seeking refuge from the fire-raids for their small children.

Sadly, in modern war it isn't only rain that falls on the just and unjust alike.

Because of the sheltering eye-band, I couldn't fend those rapid-replay visions of the Altstadt—*my* Altstadt—from filling my mind. It was heart-breaking to see, feel and taste those memories so vividly, and realize that to glimpse it now would be to awaken within the midst of an even greater nightmare!

Gretchen brought at least one, more welcome snippet of news. Despite ever more frequent, concerted Allied air-attacks, the trains along the central route she had ridden were running almost unaffected. The destruction from Allied bomb-ers came more often to housing, school and church than to transportation, indus-try or, indeed, military.

Reinhold explained that Germany was fighting a petroleum shortage, but coal production had, so far, not been affected seriously, so trains were still running. Even bomb-damage at the stations was still cleared and service restored quickly.

Gretchen and I were to leave at just past 23:00 that night. The route, a long, winding, local-train trek out of Silesia, across Saxony, Thuringia and Hesse, would carry us at last into Hesse-Nassau, the Prussian Rhineland. It was along this same route that I had travelled so often between farm and Leipzig. But I al-ready treasured the fact that this time, with every hour survived on the train, I should be that much farther away from the hell-hole of Auschwitz, and just so much nearer home.

Dinner and conversation done, we arose and headed to our rooms. Gretchen and I would rest a little before having to catch the train. But as we left the dining room, Reinhold asked us both to come to his room, at the same time directing Hofmann to fetch a special package from the staff car, to bring it to us there.

In his room, Reinhold explained, "I asked you here because there was some-thing else that I discovered in Edi's, and in Frau Gellert's *KdF*- files.

"Edi, Goebbels had arranged for the two of you each to receive a reward, the Iron Cross Second Class, for the work you had done in the *KdF*, particularly for all the concerts you gave for wounded soldiers and airmen, and for that handful of sailors not lost at sea.

"I see no reason why yours has to be withheld any longer. I hold it right here."

At Reinhold's urge, I stood while he directed Gretchen in attaching both the ribbon and the cross itself to my tunic.

"If for no other reason," he continued, "displaying this award on your uniform should smooth your way, and help in getting the two of you home safely.

"Edi, I know that all you and Frau Gellert did, you did for the love of music and your dedication to bring joy and solace to the people. I hope, whatever may happen, that you will keep this award, at least to remember the thankful applause and accolades that the soldiers gave you, as an expression of that purer love for people and nation in which they strove. It is not just the man behind the gun who fights, but all those who stand devotedly alongside!"

"Thank you, Reinhold," I said. Then I did my best Hitler Youth snap to attention and military salute, "Thank you, sir!"

He laughed. It was so nice to hear. Ever since he had learned the fate of his own, our little David, he had grown quieter, so often somber. He understood everything now, fully: he had lost one that he loved, through his very own actions.

The award attached securely, he said, "And now, dear Gretchen, Hofmann, if you'll allow, I need to speak with Edi alone."

They stepped out of the room. He had me sit in one chair, then seated himself nearby, facing me.

"Edi, take off the bandage. I want to look into your eyes."

I removed it, shaded my vision from the painful glare of the light bulbs, blinked, then again. I could now see his outline, some details of his face, his eyes. Now I could discern, beyond the wearing of age and abuse of experience, the still-handsome features of our Reinhold.

He raised a thick envelope in his hand, brought my right hand closer and inserted the envelope before closing my fingers around it tightly.

"Here is all the information about my affairs. Bank accounts, property, my will, everything that is left from my true life—with your uncle—and that beyond, all certified. I want you to hold onto it.

"Edi, we are losing the war. With France, Belgium and Italy in Allied hands, and the Russians driving quickly into Hungary, it will not be long before it's over.

"I have directed the SS bureaucracy that, if anything happens to me, they are to send my effects to you in Singhofen. If I survive, I will come to the farm; if I don't, there will be a package delivered to you there, one containing the trinkets of my current career.

"Within this envelope is the claim, entirely as Edo wanted it, that you have on the rest of the inheritance, all that was left after my diseased misfortune from the accident, and all that I have been able to regain since. Bartomeu has copies; I can't guarantee that my solicitor in Berlin will outlast the air raids, but he has copies, too. But you have the originals. I know they will be safe with you at the farm, far away from the worst of the devastation that Germany has yet to endure.

"Be certain not to miss your rail-connections—you and Gretchen must travel beyond the cities as quickly as possible, ahead of the cataclysm. The faster you can get away, west of Erfurt, into the farms and forests north of Frankfurt, the better."

"Thank you, Reinhold! You have saved my life! You rescued me!"

"No, Edi, it is I who must thank you. You not only saved my life, you brought that life, my real life, back to me! You showed me just how much of a miserable, damnable failure I—and the Germany I have helped create—have been. You gave me a chance to do something—far too little, far too late—but still *something* to begin to rectify it!

"This is so little to be able to say, so damned little..."

His voice trailed away, as if sensing again that repentance were futile.

Then he continued, "We each had our comas.

"Yours opened the gates of a world of joy and human expression, of intimate understanding.

"Mine slammed the gate, with me barely half-way through, and held me prisoner to its infirmity. Only when I saw you there, standing condemned beside the train, was I able finally to force that oppressive iron off me, to dispel the animosity and the drugs I had used trying to dull it, to open that portal. You restored to me the most precious thing that I had subverted, and very nearly lost: my deepest memory of just how much I had loved your uncle, and how deeply he had loved me!

"I had charged through life with physical bravado, but you restored the emotional, moral courage, the strength to break down those walls of inhuman hatred I had built up, that I had used to shield myself from my actions, my responsibilities, and their dreadful consequences.

"I had to re-learn to be human.

"Love is commitment. Love is work. Love is bravery. If there is one, most important realization that you have awoken in me, that haunts me now, rebukes me for my vile, spiteful life, my damnably accursèd, vicious actions these past fifteen years, it is the utter knowledge of my own wrathful weakness.

"Hatred is the laziest form of cowardice!

"But you have demonstrated courage beyond your years."

He stood; I rose quickly and grabbed him. We stayed there, holding each other. Five, ten minutes? I wouldn't count, daren't keep track.

He kissed the top of my head, the slowly re-sprouting hair, where twenty years before he had kissed my infant curls.

"It is far better to love, braving any chance of being wronged, than to hate, and with it, to be eternally wrong.

"Edi, continue to love, to love courageously.

"Don't be like me: living, just waiting to die, wrapped in the shroud of my own regrets."

Rough, ragged, congested, his voice asserted gently, "You have a long, productive, wonderful life ahead of you. If we don't see each other again, soon, please remember me just as you have been doing all along, as one of those uncles who chased the chickens out of the barley with you, counted the barn cats while you laughed and wiggled through the hay after them, who sent you your special piano.

"You will always be our only nephew, our little boy. And we will always love you."

That child again, I grabbed him tighter and sobbed.

I murmured, "Don't go. Don't go! Losing Edo once was agony enough, but now, Reinhold, to lose you—twice!"

"Don't say that, Edi! You know I have to go! You must let me go!

"Germany, what little is yet left of the *real* Germany, needs me now. She will need you, everyone will need you, and need you badly, later. You're a witness. And all you have witnessed must never be forgotten!"

He started pulling away; I had to release my grip.

From that deep vacuum of the hollow, six-year-old's shell to which, again, I had been reduced, I heard my voice ask him the time; it was already almost ten o'clock.

We sat, silent, the few minutes before Hofmann knocked, then stumbled in from his room, bleary-throated from so short a nap.

"Sir, we will need to leave within the next few minutes."

"Thank you, Hofmann! Please get the car ready!

"Oh, and Hofmann!"

"Yes, sir?"

"We will be getting a driver soon—being a mechanic *won't* be part of your normal assignments as my aide!"

Reinhold laughed, and in a relieved tone, Hofmann replied, "That's good to know. Thank you, sir!"

After he had shut the door, Reinhold pressed a wad of folded paper into my palm.

"Here is $\mathscr{RM}$ 5000 in 10-, 20- and 100-Reichsmark bills. Let Gretchen hold onto some of it. This should cover any expenses, or emergencies, you might have on the way."

"Thank you, Reinhold!"

"Don't thank me!" He chuckled softly.

"It's come from your inheritance!"

Gretchen sounded fresh, ready to set out when she stepped into Reinhold's room.

"You, my dear, are a knock-out!" he told her.

"Thank you, Reinhold!" she answered, audibly quite pleased.

"Here," I said, handing her the money.

"Split this in two, hold onto both, but give me five twenties from my half."

I put the bills into a pocket of my tunic, along with my fabricated, but not counterfeit, SS identity card. The wrap went back into place: my eyes were still very sensitive and starting to hurt.

"May I fold the envelope, Reinhold?" I asked.

"Actually, I have a portfolio you can use. I made certain to place all of those folders we went through back at Auschwitz in there, as well as other information you may need in the future, too. It locks."

He pushed a small key into my left hand, making sure that it was tightly within my grip. My right hand he guided to the thin case; the cold brass had just one rough area on its polished surface.

"Here, Gretchen, is the second key," Reinhold said. "Each of you, be sure not to lose yours! No one else must see the items this case contains!"

Having unlocked it, I flipped the leather tongue out of the way and inserted the financial-records envelope before snapping the flap back down quickly and feeling my way to lock it.

Hofmann reappeared to announce that the car was ready, waiting in front of the hotel. Reinhold and Gretchen helped me downstairs and out into the vehicle. A short ride and we were at the Gleiwitz train station.

Standing aside, I heard Hofmann jump out, rush to place Gretchen's small suitcase beside the car, then run to open her door. Apparently, he seconded Reinhold's appraisal of her!

With our gear gathered, Reinhold told Hofmann to stay with the car. The three of us walked into the station, with me in the middle.

The rush-about noise of passengers and baggage told me we were far from alone, seeming to part as we strolled ahead. I heard someone approach, rushing past all others, in shoes beating a brisk, breathless tempo into the station's landing.

"Herr Gruppenführer, sir! I am Lothar Hirsch, assistant station-master. Is there any way I may be of service to you?"

"Herr Hirsch! Good of you to offer your assistance!" Reinhold said in a very "general of the SS" voice.

"This wounded young officer and his sister need transportation back to their home near Frankfurt am Main for his recuperation before returning to action, to defend the Fatherland. Their tickets have been purchased, and they need to get underway. Could you please make sure that everything is in order?"

"Yes! Certainly, Herr Gruppenführer! If I could but look quickly over the ticket-details…"

While enjoying the station-master's old-fashioned, bureaucratically formal address, from beneath the bandage's edge I could just see Gretchen reach down into her bag and pull out a long envelope.

"Thank you, gnädiges Fräulein! [*dear miss*] Ah, let's see. … Yes, umm … yes. Yes, Herr Gruppenführer, a route not optimal for speed, however these arrangements are exactly what they will need for the train they will catch here. It is on time and should be arriving within the next several minutes. I see that they will need to change trains in Görlitz and in Erfurt. If you would but allow me only a few minutes, I will write up information on those stations so that our young hero and his sister will face no delay or inconvenience there!

"If you'll excuse me…"

He stepped back quickly, spun and his *allegro assai* footsteps were gone.

I felt Reinhold bend over toward me before whispering right into my ear, "He's a bit of a suck-up, even for a bureaucrat!"

We both chuckled.

Innocent of our fun at his unctuous expense, the assistant station manager returned in high spirits, to detail a sheet full of instructions for navigating those next two, train-change stations. He explained that he had even written the names of their station-masters (and their assistants) across those typewritten forms, just in case.

Reinhold made sure to let him know that we were all very grateful, even asking him to jot down his own name and details so that the SS could thank his manager, the station-master, for his such diligent help.

"Ass-kissing from these nazified, Kaiser-era officials must always be recognized and rewarded," he said after the little guy had almost kowtowed in bureaucratic thankfulness, before rushing back to his office, "otherwise, they'll stop doing it, and the whole Reich will collapse!"

———————————

The wind shifted, and I caught a familiar, piercing odor. There were cattle-cars sitting on a siding not too far away. And they didn't contain cows.

"Reinhold," I said, "there's a shipment for Auschwitz somewhere nearby."

He replied, "Yes, Edi. Straight ahead and to the right, I can see part of it on the farthest track."

At that point a whistle blew, and freight cars rattled away from that direction.

"They're rolling out. Please, Dear Mother of God, be with them! Because I can't!" he said dolefully, resigned now to his new position, and to his newly re-established recognition of our personal responsibility.

He bent closer to my ear to say, "Edi, I hadn't told you, but Himmler agreed to my orders to get prisoners more food and bedding. On Josef's last trip through the *Kanadakommando* I also had him slip information about schedules, and even some area maps, to the rabbi that was in your section.

"When the Russians get closer, prisoners not needed for the camps' destruction will be marched back toward Germany, after the ovens are shut down and destroyed. There is a chance that some may be able to escape at that time. I don't know if any of that will help since I will no longer be there but, thanks to you, I have at least now tried!

"That bastard Eichmann is still dragging Jews out of Hungary and the Czech lands, despite direct orders to the contrary! There are official reports stating this, detailing the conditions and population of the camps over the years, between the papers in your satchel. Use them if anyone ever tries to weasel out of his complicity!"

I whispered back to him, "Thank you, Reinhold!"

"Don't thank me, Edi. It's my responsibility. This, my responsibility to the people, the entire people, to humanity, should always have overridden any diseased oath to the puppet-master."

Loudly spewing coal-noxious steam, our train approached. Wartime's diminished maintenance shrieked in ear-abrading, high-pitched squeals as it ground to a stop. We waited for those who were exiting here in Gleiwitz to make their way from the train and away, then Reinhold and Gretchen walked me over to the door of the carriage.

I heard Reinhold bidding farewell to Gretchen. Then I turned toward where the bandage-slit revealed the toes of his boots, and saluted. Gretchen told me later that he had returned my salute, and had held his until after I had lowered my arm.

Had I ever, in these months, ever told my uncle that I loved him? I hoped so. But I knew from that salute that I had far more than love from him: I had respect.

Up the stairs and into the car, Gretchen directed us over to an empty bench, facing forward, toward the engine: travelling looking backwards had always made her sick. The carriage was fairly full, so we held tightly to her bag and my attaché case. After only a few minutes of chatting, the whistle blew, the conductor yelled the 'all aboard' and the train chugged slowly out of the station, weaving its way into the Silesian night.

———————

In a fallback to how we had to live in the barracks, always in fear that someone might steal cap or shoes, cup or bowl, I had stuck the attaché case behind my lower back. I soon fell asleep on it, shielding it.

I awoke to Gretchen's screams!

We had fallen asleep in an empty church and soldiers had rushed in on us! Speaking some ba-ba-language, they were laughing and calling her names; they had dropped their guns and were pawing at my sister!

I grabbed one of the abandoned assault-rifles and started spraying them with bullets. Gretchen dropped down behind a shielding pew while I stood in the middle of the nave, firing continuously, blasting every soldier that popped up.

Then Hagen, Hagen was everywhere! I followed his fat, mocking face, firing round after round, bursting fonts, statues, stations, and frescoes as I swung the arc of fire around the inside of the building, until the crashing bullets neared a statue of the Virgin. It was rocking—it was going to fall!

I threw the gun down and ran over to it! I held the image's legs securely to my chest until its pitching stopped. I released my grip, arising slowly, making sure it was standing still: solid and safe.

I gazed at Her sandals, then lifted my glance, taking in each detail: the gold embroidery entwined within the dark blue and glinting white of Her robes, the celestial blue of Her eyes, the golden star-burst floating, circling above Her head, that gentle, assuring smile.

The church wall roared down, collapsing where I had been firing, crushing the rifle. I looked back to Her face. Her cheeks were warmer, her eyes glistening!

"*Ave, Regina cælorum!*" I whispered to Her, and turned to walk back, over the rubble of the now-collapsed wall, to where my sister had hidden.

 I heard a soprano's voice intone the final melodies of Handel's *Salve Regina*: "O clemens! O pia! O dulcis! O dulcis Virgo Maria!"

I turned back to look at Her.

She was now holding a curly-blond-haired baby. Rows of candles surrounding her had come to light, wrapping her in warmest, suffusing aura, reflecting in the Baby's own, shining, blue eyes.

———————

I jerked, started, sat up, suddenly awake.

The carriage had swung heavily with the rattle from crossing switch-points leading off to another siding.

"Edi! Are you OK?"

Gretchen worried, "You were making odd little, jerking movements with your legs and hands!"

A moment to think, to return: "Yes … Yeah, I'm OK," I finally managed, as my mind cleared enough to realize again where we were, and what we were doing.

"How far are we now? What time is it?"

"We've just passed some place called Penzig and I think we're only about half an hour or so from Görlitz; the sun is just now trying to come up."

"We'll have to wait there, won't we?"

"Yes, about an hour and a half for the train to Erfurt. The notes we got from that station-master in Gleiwitz say that there's a place to get a little something to eat there."

"Good! I'm getting very hungry. But … before we get there, you're going to have to walk me to the toilet."

"OK. It's just to the rear of us, about four rows. I'll open the door and tell you where things are."

I carried the attaché case in unbreakable grasp: it would take each step with me.

———————

Well fed (Reinhold had been right about the uniform and medal's effects), refreshed and on a less-crowded train to Erfurt, Gretchen and I talked, catching me up more on what she had been doing. At just eighteen, she had a lot to tell her big brother about: she had started noticing guys, and enjoying the attention they paid her. The trouble she was facing was that, although she liked their notice, she hadn't found any of them particularly appealing.

"They're all so immature," she complained, "or they're not that smart, or not ambitious. I want a guy who knows who he is, where he's been and where he's going!"

"You'll find one soon enough, Gretchen!"

From the open, bottom slit of the eye bandage, I had noticed repetitive movements in the shadows of her hands.

"What *are* you doing?"

"Oh, the only yarn I can get tends to come unwound too easily, so I re-spin the strands more tightly as I pull the yarn from one ball to another. Gramma and I do it so much better by hand than any machine-made you can get right now."

"So, when did you start knitting? I don't remember you doing any of it the last time I was home!"

"I've been knitting and sewing on and off for about three years now. I just didn't do it when you were home because we were always rushing around! We had so many other things to do!"

"So, what are you working on now?"

"I was going to make a new shawl to replace the one I made Gramma two years ago."

"She wears out her shawls that fast? Or was it just not very good?"

She jabbed me with her elbow.

"Don't be mean! Yes, it was good! I just wanted to make her another one!"

"Why don't you knit some socks for Reinhold, or Hauptsturmführer Hofmann?

They're going to need warm clothes in the East in the wintertime! And, it sounded like Hofmann was trying to be extra nice to you!"

"Yeah, he was very nice. But …"

"But what?"

"Well … he smokes, and you know how you and I are about that—it makes me sick just like it does you!"

"Yeah, clean country air does make you wonder why anyone would suck on a chimney! But if he's cute, maybe you could change him!"

"No chance! Mama's already warned me about trying to change men! She told me, 'You can't straighten out a tree after it's grown with the wind!' and I think that's right!"

"Well, after the war, maybe you can go stay with Marianne and Fritz in Wiesbaden, or Liesel and Gerhard in Darmstadt! You could try to chop down a tree there that's already grown the way you like. There have to be more men for you to knock down in a city than in our village!"

"We'll see, but I'd like someone homey *and* exotic, familiar, but with spice: enough to be interesting, but not so much that you get a stomach ache!"

At eighteen, she sounded a growing enthusiasm, set to run out and grab life on her own terms. I was now 23; life had rushed in, shown me all its possible delights, but then crushed me with every demented torment it could possibly inflict.

What bargain had I made whose price had required so great a premium?

I was tired. Tired of pain, tired of trains, tired of life: I just wanted to go home.

We arrived in Nassau just past four in the morning: Friday, October 6, 1944.

Here was no fawning assistant station-manager, although the elderly night-guard did offer to let us into his little office to sleep and wait for the warmth beyond the dawn. But I wanted to be home, even if it meant having to walk all the way, through the darkness.

The night-watchman warned that security officers had been going around, cutting telephone lines to keep them from falling into the hands of the approaching Allies. The Wehrmacht's so rapid, cataclysmic loss of France had made the local Nazis very nervous—back in Gleiwitz, Reinhold had said that the Allies were in Luxembourg, less than 120 km west of Singhofen!

So, we knew that we had to find our own way to the farm.

Even if we could have phoned the house, we didn't know if the car would have been able to make the trip! Gretchen said that fuel-supplies for farm equipment had been sufficient only to start the harvest. Beyond that, Papa had been compelled to hitch up the horses, to help our neighbors, all working together to make sure the barley, rye and potato crops, and the winter's vital supply of hay, were brought in. Some farmers had even resorted to swinging antique hand-scythes again!

The weather was clear. With the temperature hovering around 9° in the pre-dawn, I was afraid it might be too cool for Gretchen. But she got out a thickly knitted wrap, from among her own spinning, and declared, "If you think you can handle it, let's go!"

From the Nassau train station into Singhofen was about 6 km, with the farm another 2 km farther. The biggest problem was that the first four and half kilometers of the trip required climbing directly up 240 m of those hills rising from the river valley to the level of the plateau on which the village was nestled.

The watchman was gracious enough to share some bread and apples with us and gave us a little jar of homemade *Ebbelwoi* to warm us on the way. He was full of tales about the Great War, apparently feeling a significant camaraderie with someone he accepted as another soldier. But after only one episode, we had to interrupt him, excuse ourselves and set off.

Once we had crossed the Lahn, I stopped to remove the head-wrapping. My sight was recovering, albeit still slowly. I could now see well enough to walk by the light of the moon, half-way between full and last quarter, as it hung in the darkling sky.

Unbandaged but bundled, we started the slow climb up into the forested hills to the south of the river. I hadn't worn a military cap consistently since those days in the Hitler Youth, but it was a welcome piece of kit this morning, averting the night-chill from my camp-inflicted, still sparsely-furred scalp.

More than an hour later, we had finally surmounted the slow incline from the river valley onto the hill tops. We paused for only the quickest rest. Just three and a half kilometers to go, yearning for home compelled.

Eeriness—walking through a silent, sedate Singhofen after so much had happened—contrasted with a tense excitement. My sight was now so new to me that I kept my head turning, trying to watch every shape and color grow and change as the lightening eastern sky presaged the dawn.

It was just past sunrise when we reached the eastern rise opposite the farmhouse, above the dip in the road at the base of the hill on which the house sat.

We stood and gazed.

Hauntingly other-worldly, it was difficult for me to believe that I had survived.

We had not moved when I saw a dog dart out of the front door of the house. It ran as fast as it could, its paws flinging a trail of tiny dust-clouds, as it rushed towards us, across the east side of the farmhouse, down the hill and then up the rise to where we waited. I knelt as it neared.

Molly! Oh, Molly! My Molly Bear! I held her and sobbed.

The only living being left of my home—of our life, our wonderful Leipzig life!—was in my arms, wagging, squirming, trying to lick, to jump! She wiggled, whimpered, yelped in frustration: she simply could not be happy fast enough!

At that moment, Doctor Marianus burst into his baritone with Mahler's lushest choir, singing as I rose to face the farm, and we set off, slowly, toward the house:

♪ DMD-22b

Blicket auf zum Retterblick,	Look up to the redeeming glance,
Alle reuig Zarten,	All penitent creatures,
Euch zu seligem Geschick	Seeking to transport you
Dankend umzuarten.	Gratefully to a blessèd state.
Werde jeder beßre Sinn	Let every better sense
Dir zum Dienst erbötig;	Serve you unrestrained;

| Jungfrau, Mutter, Königin, | Virgin, Mother, Queen, |
| Göttin, bleibe gnädig! | Goddess, be ever gracious! |

Goethe

Suddenly at the farmhouse door, I was encircled, standing within the enclosing, nurturing arms of my little sister, my mother, my grandmother: this company of strong women.

A growing, rose-fingered glow, dawn shot her dew-drafting shafts of golden, glancing rays, piercing the shadowing trees, coursing across the cool hills, fields and forests of a tacit, sleeping Taunus.

And I felt my home-sun rising warm, once again.

Zusammenbruch – Chapter 23 – Collapse

"Where's Papa?" I asked them at last.

"He and others in the area were summoned to Frankfurt to see about helping, before winter comes, all those people who are still homeless, burned out by the fire-bombing last March. Did Gretchen tell you?"

"That the Altstadt's gone? Yes, I had heard. I can't believe it's gotten this bad.

"It seems the Allies want to bomb Germany into dust and ashes, so she can be swept off the face of the earth."

I sighed, looked weak-eyed out across that distant-feeling, autumnal morning, heard the distant, painful echo of David's voice: "And now you are cursed by the Earth," and half-murmured to myself, "Although, with what I've seen, what I've been forced to deal with, I'm not so sure that that might not be best."

"Surely it can't be that bad!" Mama replied.

Gramma jumped in, "With that damned bunch of crooks, anything—the absolute worst—is possible!"

She pulled back from her hug, looked my uniform up and down and said, "But Edi! You didn't join the …"

"No, Gramma!" I interrupted her.

"Let's go inside. The sunshine hurts!"

It was such a relief to get my too-sensitive eyes into those sheltering, ancient, wood-perfumed shadows within the farmhouse!

I stepped over to my *Steiner*, lifted the woven dust cover, and stood, rubbing in small, caressing circles the mirror-polished wood of the Steinway's reassuringly strong, ebon frame.

"Thank you for covering the piano!" I told Mama.

"Don't thank me! That was your grandmother and little sister's doing! Mother Meyer has been teaching Gretchen to sew, knit and crochet!"

"Thank you both," I said as I hugged each in turn.

Gramma raised one eyebrow. She might have turned 70 this year, but she was still sharper than most 30-year-olds!

"OK, Edi, what about this damned uniform you've got on. Oh, and an Iron Cross, too?" she exclaimed, touching it.

"The Iron Cross *is* mine, Gramma. Second class—it was awarded by the Propaganda Ministry for Frau Gellert's and my *KdF*-work, entertaining wounded troops. But the uniform is temporary, part of the plan Reinhold thought up to get me and two others safely out of the death camp at Auschwitz."

A visible shock shot through them both.

Stunned, Gramma sat.

Mama stepped near, placing a tentative, protective hand on my shoulder.

"Baby! You were in a … *death* camp?" Mama teared, in post-reactive fear.

With incisively narrowed eyes, Gramma completed the line of questioning.

"And you saw Reinhold?"

I was beginning to think that nothing would faze this old bird: she was tough, savvy, and direct.

"*Yes* to both questions! Reinhold sends his love." I nodded specifically toward Gramma.

"During the last part of this miserable odyssey, I lost my sight, so there were people and things that I only heard, smelled, sensed, but could not see, except very poorly as my vision started to return. How did he look, Gretchen?"

"Tall, well-built, very handsome, black hair with a touch of gray—amazing blue eyes! He looked really smart in his SS-Gruppenführer uniform."

Gramma slammed the tip of her cane on the floor and stood, almost leapt from her chair.

"What? Reinhold a general in the SS? Is that true, Edi?"

"Yes, Gramma, it's true. It's a very long story!"

I urged her to sit back down, to calm herself.

"I'll reveal it all, but I'd like to wait, to relive it only once!"

"Mama, when is Papa due back?"

"Probably tomorrow morning, or the day after. It's not been easy getting messages around here since the Gestapo cut the phone lines, stopped mail service, even blocked some of the roads. Maybe we should go back to messenger pigeons!"

"But then we'd have to shoot 'em and eat 'em like the soldiers did in the first Great War!" tapped Gramma out with her cane, spicing her response with a bitter, "I told you so!" laugh.

"Is there any food, Mama?" I asked tentatively.

"You can have some eggs, sauerkraut and potatoes," she said, "or some dried apples and cheese. But anything beyond the merest staples that we've grown, produced, or preserved ourselves is not likely to be on hand."

"That will do fine: just no turnips—never ever again turnips!" I replied.

"Is my bed, my bedroom, still available?"

"Certainly, baby!" Mama said, stepping over to rub my back reassuringly.

"Good. I've worn these boots for three days, and when they come off, I am going to collapse! You'll probably want to burn the socks!"

Papa returned from the city that next morning, just before noon. The tires on the car were worn, in places bald, and he had to park facing downhill since the battery was long since dead: the car could be started now only by pushing. Tires, batteries, fuel: almost everything needed for modern life was in short supply. Only the black market was operating efficiently.

"Still too many homeless in Frankfurt, Wiesbaden and Mainz. The entire Rhine-Main valley has been almost wiped out by Allied bombing attacks. I don't know how we'll get through this," Papa told me. "It's a thousand times worse than anything that happened in the first war."

He sounded so dreadfully weary.

Of course, he had greeted me with a surprised, long, tearful but strong hug and a "Welcome home, son!" when he walked into the house. But he seemed so downcast, I wondered if I might better have gone ahead and revealed my details—ones I knew would cause them all so much distress, anger and pain—to Mama and Gramma yesterday. Papa sounded now near collapse.

I thought I should wait at least until after Mama had gathered him his lunch, and he had had time to recover from the drive home. So, I took the cover off the piano—with Gretchen to help me fold her and Gramma's handiwork nicely, of course—and sat down at the keyboard to see how *Ole Steiner* had fared this year.

I played a few scales and it sounded … wonderful! Completely in tune, the keys were still balanced and beautiful. I was amazed and so, so very pleased!

The first thing I played was Beethoven's *Les Adieux* sonata.

Oh, I could have melted in the full, warm, glistening tones of this— again! at last!—my very own *Steiner*!

When I had finished and finally looked up, Mama was standing, clasping a dish towel to her breast, glowing.

"It's a miracle to have you home, Edi!" She came over and kissed me on the cheek. "Your sister has been playing, too! But not on this one—she wouldn't hazard the chance of hurting your piano! But she *is* very good, and now I'm sure you can help her play even better!"

Papa looked up from the few remains of his lunch and asked her, "You haven't shown him, have you?"

Mama glanced at him, shook her head, stepped over to him.

"No, dear. I was waiting until you came home," she said, clasping his hand.

"Shown me what?"

Kissing, then releasing Mama's hand, he stood and walked to the farther edge of the kitchen.

"OK, Edi. Come with me!" he said, calling me over to the door at the top of those wide, heavily reinforced stairs leading down into the basement.

That staircase was family history: Gramma had told me that Grampa's father and grandfather had been forced to expand and strengthen it when the late winter and spring of 1860 had been so cold that they had been forced to bring the cows with calves into the house! "Like the Swiss have to do!" she had said in awe.

"There have had to be a few changes downstairs," Papa said.

He descended the staircase ahead of me, and turned the ceiling light on. At least the Gestapo hadn't cut the power lines! They can only have needed electricity for themselves, for their own radios!

At the far side of the room, ahead of us, the top of that wall of the basement had been sliced into, to add a row of small, curtained ventilation windows facing out onto the field behind the house.

And sitting in the middle of the room, under a dust cover similar to the one upstairs, was a third piano, another grand piano! Even its bench was covered! I walked over to it slowly, wondering what this could mean.

"Lift the cover," Papa urged.

I grabbed the cover's low-hanging corner, and raised it carefully, exposing more and more, dark red- and black-veined, highly polished mahogany. It was Gelchen's *Aleksey*-piano, the Steinway she had brought back with her from New York after that torrid, love affair with the Russian count!

I stood and stared, hearing Gelchen's rapt, reminiscing phrase, "свѣтлая— моя любовь" [*radiant is my love*], deathly afraid that if I broke the vision with sigh or syllable it might vanish—or I might wake up, still captive in Auschwitz!

Suddenly, it dawned on me: I hadn't asked about Molly!

"Papa, why do we have this? And why is Molly Bear here?"

"They, and other materials, were shipped in from Leipzig.

"During that week after you had been taken away, as soon as Albert had returned from the retreat his bishop had ordered him away on, he went to see Frau Gellert.

"He said that she appeared more random-headed than usual, totally incoherent about what had happened, sitting, moaning, "My babies! My babies!"

"He thought she meant that you had been taken away for the army or something. That was all he could discover, and that's all we ever heard.

"But she was clear—and adamant—about one thing. She had re-drawn her will, and in it had left everything to you: the three pianos, the harpsichords, the house and all its other contents, *and* the dog. While Albert was there that day, after some effort, he convinced her to allow him to collect everything of yours from your bedroom, to ship it here.

"However, after her death—you have heard, right?—the Leipzig gauleiter intervened and disallowed the majority of the bequest.

"He and the Party took everything except the things Albert had been able to ship quickly with the money we sent him, or had brought immediately: this piano, Frau Gellert's souvenir boxes, and Molly.

"We cut those thin windows through the wall to ventilate the basement better against the damp so that we could bring this piano down here: there simply wasn't room upstairs. Some of Frau Gellert's boxes are in the spare room, or in what used to be Albert's room; the rest now fill the house the Fuhrmanns lived in.

"When she first arrived, Molly wandered the house, searching. She would sit at the door to your bedroom and whine until we let her in there. Then she would dart around your room sniffing, searching, almost desperately seeking her quarry. After she hadn't found what she was seeking, she'd come back to us at the door, sit and look up, with an air of unfulfilled expectation pulling the wrinkles onto her face."

"I see," I said quietly. I knew she had been searching for me, and for David.

Even now, so often with the look of loss, she had left my side only rarely: she was pressing tightly beside me, just then. With her touch, I heard the echo of Geli's voice: "They know! They know!"

I raised the keyboard cover and pressed keys, savoring those rich tones of the few notes my ravaged spirit could manage. It was also perfectly in tune and in excellent condition! This was another instrument that I would cherish deeply: all four of us, my entire, lost Leipzig life, had played it!

That afternoon, I gathered all the family together at last to tell them what had happened, although it was necessarily abridged. About Auschwitz, I could reveal only dry facts: I could not bring myself yet to speak of David's death, nor of the specific events, the personal horrors of the gas chamber. My eyes would not let me see.

But, of course, Mama and Papa were shocked, Mama near devastated. They had heard of concentration camps but, with that rampant homeland-security apparatus, only whispered, illicit rumors of death camps had ever reached them.

Gramma became angrier than ever, and vented her expletive-extended rage.

But in the eyes of everyone, she was now completely vindicated.

Always had she been right, and her strength, her righteous, liberal indignation ever squarely on target!

The saga of Reinhold's injury—his trauma, brain injury, coma and his struggle through the anguish, self-set fugue, and personality changes that had resulted, and then his awakening, recognition and acceptance of personal responsibility—I told in the greatest detail.

Gramma had loved him as a son, Papa and Mama, as a brother.

They deserved to know why he had been so intrinsically supportive, instituting those extensive bank accounts, only to avoid us, seemingly to reject us, for all those years.

But I did tell them one thing, something that shocked them to silence.

His devotion had never left us.

Aside from the financial arrangements, it had, in fact, been Reinhold who had asked Bartomeu to contact Sr Marshall in Barcelona.

Reinhold, acting on Edo's aspirations, had been the one who had started my career as concert pianist, my life as a musician!

"So, everything about the Barcelona trip was set up by Reinhold for our, and your, benefit?" Papa wondered.

"Yes," I said, "From the trains to meeting Bartomeu, from the hotel, the bank, the accounts, to meeting Sr Marshall, even those packets of pocket money had been his doing.

"At every step, known or unknown, he has been with us. So long as he was mentally and emotionally able, he struggled against his injury, his illness to be— as he told me, reminiscing specifically about you, Gramma, just what he had heard you teaching us, and Uncle Edo, to be—an unsummoned angel."

Her grief mounting, renewed, Gramma shook her tearing head sadly.

I never mentioned the dossiers that Reinhold had given me. They would have been too hard on them, particularly on Papa. From Gretchen, I retrieved the second key, and made certain that the attaché case stayed locked, always hidden away.

But I would not, could never destroy its contents: they held the plot of a chapter of my life that I simply had to keep!

The morning's clear and crisp, 6° dawn was supposed to climb beyond 20° by mid-afternoon. The surfeit of warm, autumn sunshine had called everyone out of the house but me, yet guarding my still-faulty eyes.

Gretchen had walked down into the village to help a friend; the rest of the family had gone out into the fields to finish preparations for hard winter. It was October 12, and chilling-autumn rains threatened their sweep-through the very next day. The foreboding list of final, harvest chores was being ripped through as rapidly as possible.

Papa had asked Gramma to go to the fields with them. She had been through so many winters, and had outlasted so many shortages in her seventy years that her knowledge and wisdom were nigh irreplaceable, particularly since wartime privations had, once again, forced most of German agriculture back to the tools, processes, and draft animals of the 19th century!

A knock at the door drew me away from continued, finger-strengthening exercises on the *Steiner*. Before I could get up to answer it, the door opened, letting the daylight pierce the room's imposed, eye-shielding gloom. Albert stuck his head in and called out, "Anyone at home?"

"Yes, Albert!"

"Edi? Edi! Where have you been? When did you get back? What's happened to Uli and Thomi?" His flow of pressing questions led the leggy sweep of his cassock through the door and over to the piano.

Utterly taken aback, I was stunned. Those names! So, he didn't know!

I answered plainly, directly.

"Albert. I've been dying with the Jews at Auschwitz."

He must not have expected so direct an answer: the color drained from his face.

He tugged a chair over from the kitchen table, sat quickly, leaned toward me and in a low, conspiratorial voice asked, "So, you mean it's true? The alarming rumors we've been hearing are true?"

My irritation was unmaskable. I knew what was in those dossiers!

"What are those rumors, Albert? I've been away. The most startling thing I've heard has been the groaning, screaming and praying of Jews trying to claw their way out of the gas chambers!"

I didn't think he could get any paler; but he did.

"Yes," he swallowed, "those saying that the resettlement trains are actually taking them away to be killed," he said quietly, almost fearfully.

I continued, rather matter-of-fact-ly, "I calculated that at Auschwitz alone several thousands, if not tens of thousands, were being killed each day. The one day I was forced to work in just one of the crematoria we burned the bodies of almost a thousand Jews, whose murder I witnessed. That part of Auschwitz had five crematoria that the SS tried to keep running twenty-four hours a day—not always successfully—but they strove to keep them all working."

He sat, silent, almost without breathing.

I stood and walked away from the piano, nearing the wall at the far side of the room. I had no idea how I was going to tell him!

After several tense minutes, he stood up and walked over to me.

"Well, at least you were released! And you're home now."

"I wasn't released: no one living was ever released.

"I was helped to escape, me and two others. An SS-officer took pity on me because I could play so well.

"When he was promoted to general and was about to be sent to the Eastern front, Reinhold arranged for the three of us to leave Auschwitz with him. It was only his help that allowed me to escape death: all inmates who have tried to escape Auschwitz on their own have been caught, killed and disposed of immediately."

"Reinhold?"

"General Reinhold, that was his name."

Shit! I didn't want to have to remind him of Edo and Reinhold, then have to go through the whole damned explanation again!

"Why, Edi? Why were you sent away?"

"The Gestapo raided Geli's house. They had determined that there were two Jews living there in hiding, and they came to arrest them."

"What? What two Jews?"

"Albert! Thomi and Uli!"

I was growing angry rapidly, but had to restrain myself. I had to remind myself of what he didn't know!

"Except those weren't their real, their birth names. They were born David and Esther Schraeder!"

"Esther? ... And David? But they didn't look or act Jewish!"

The anger flashed.

"What the hell does that mean, Albert? There's no such thing! There's no such fucking thing as a "Jewish *race*"! God damn the word! They're not a race! They're not **them**! They're **US**! They're born, they live, celebrate and suffer—they love, and damn it, they die—just like we do!"

He stood at arm's length, looking through, no longer at, me.

He cleared his throat, paused, swallowed painfully, cleared it again.

"I was very fond of her. You know that; you saw."

"Yes, and I loved *him*. That's why they took me! They came to arrest Esther and David, and walked into the bedroom while I was holding him, kissing him!"

He looked at me suddenly, shocked.

"Yes, Albert. You were right, back in the Frankfurt train station before we left for Barcelona. I'm a faggot! A queer! A homo!

"And I was the only one he ever loved!

"I know that because he survived the horrors of the death camps just long enough to find me, to see me again before he died.

"But then I had to carry his lifeless body, to place him in the cremation pit!

"And what's worse, Albert—Albert! I had to walk away!"

A hand jumped up, protective, over my eyes. The pain shot through me again; I staggered, but had to go further. I had to look at him. I had to tell him.

"Yes! I know you were fond of her! And I know more: much, so much more!"

"You *loved* her! You loved her with every fiber of your being! And she loved you, just as much, perhaps more! I know because she told me! She told me everything!"

His mouth dropped, agape, apprehensive.

"Yes! *Everything*!

"You were able to make her feel more human, more complete, more loved than she had ever felt—ever!

"You and I each had that gift with these two Jews, to make them feel loved and beloved in a world that sought nothing but to make them suffer, and after a hell of suffering, to kill them!

"The man who turned us in was … your bishop, Hagen!

"Hell! He even turned in his own superior, my friend, Father Vogler, because he discovered that Vogler was hiding Jews and Gypsies on the cathedral grounds! Vogler was murdered at Mauthausen!

"Hagen either got angry at Gelchen, or someone piqued his suspicions, but it was *he* who called the Gestapo, to have them target Geli! They discovered the arrangements Esther and David's parents had made to hide them as another, non-Jewish couple's children. And then they came to get them!"

My rage roared suddenly, like an overcharged incinerator!

With both hands I grabbed his cassock near the collar and shook him!

Terrified, he reached up and grabbed my wrists, holding them, trying to restrain my grip.

"*I* had to put Esther's emaciated, murdered body—the one *you* caressed, *you* kissed, *you* made love to—onto the platform, to slide her into the flames!

"But you know what else, Albert?

"Albert! She was not alone!

"In the agony of dying in the gas chamber, surrounded by hundreds of other suffocating, writhing, panicking, Hebrews, Esther gave birth! To the most beautiful, blue-eyed, blond-haired baby boy!"

I was sobbing and yelling at the same time, "Albert! It was your son! Your beautiful, *beautiful*, little Jewish, German son!

"They killed them!" I shouted, shook him, and shoved him hard against the wall.

"**They killed them!**"

Suddenly, my anger collapsed; my grip failed.

The awful truth had to pass my lips! In a spasm of anguish, I froze, struggled, forced the horrid confession.

"**We** …

"*We* killed them!"

I turned aside.

His heavy-flagging hand caught the rosary hanging at his waist, tangled in it, ripped it apart.

The crucifix, torn loose, hit the floor among fleeing beads, tumbling, bouncing in front of me, and hit the base of the wall with a muted clink.

I covered my eyes as I sobbed, staggered, held onto the piano's curve to steady myself.

Standing there, I repeated the verse softly that the kapo had pronounced with vengeance in the crematorium that dreadful, dreadful afternoon.

"So they hanged Haman on the gallows that he had prepared for Mordecai the Jew!"

Turning away, I trudged up the stairs to my room, one aching, harrowing step after the other.

When, at last, I came back downstairs, the ground floor was quiet, luminous in now fully restored, vibrant shades, exquisite in minutely detailed, delicate tints, bright hues and deep shadows.

I could see clearly.

Albert was gone.

Eindringlinge – Chapter 24 – Invaders

My heart feared what my mind fully expected.

Delivered from SS headquarters in Berlin, that box, the one that Reinhold had warned me of, sat ominously on the kitchen table.

Although it had arrived on the third of February, 1945, the letter accompanying it said that he had been killed in action the second week of January.

Having rushed into Hungary, Reinhold had been killed leading his men in a counterattack against a Red Army offensive near Lake Balaton, fighting to retain the oil fields there, the Reich's last natural-oil supply.

Our nerves ached still raw, recovering at the farm from the renewed terror of the USAAF bombing raid that had hit Bad Nassau the previous day, wreaking its fearful, fatal havoc fewer than nine kilometers from the farm. This new anguish was worsened by our own experience, just of last December 28: although only two of the ten-or-so bombs dropped in the area had landed on buildings in Singhofen, the abiding unease and visions of the (luckily, only few, lightly) injured and of the damage were, still, hard to shake.

Papa, Mama, Gramma and Gretchen sat around the table with me.

The knowledge of Nassau's recent dead deepened the foreboding, funereal air as I opened the box and started extracting, scrutinizing each of its carefully wrapped contents. It was a somber experience for all of us, particularly for the four of us who remembered Reinhold as the irreplaceable man, called 'son', 'brother' and 'uncle' purely from deepest affection, who had lived all those years with our special Edo. He had been the other half of that team, and—I understood now only too fully—the one who had made Edo whole, so alive, full of drive, and irrepressibly joyous.

Gramma suffered the anguished loss once more of a son: Reinhold had indeed been so. In all his years with Edo, he had returned Gramma's affection, addressing her always as *Mama Meyer* or, in that orphan's fullest-heart, gratefully gifting way, simply as *Mama*.

I took the internal parcels apart, pulling the packing paper open carefully, arranging each item with its label or any accompanying information. Much of the content had to do with honors gained during Reinhold's SS career.

The most impressive of those was his Knight's Cross of the Iron Cross.

The medal, its wear-worn neck-ribbon and matching ribbon bar had been removed from his final uniform, cleaned and returned to their presentation case, along with all the commendation forms signed by Himmler, and bearing Hitler's depressing, downhill scrawl.

When Reinhold had been promoted this last time, he had told me about receiving the Knights' Cross augmentation of oak leaves along with his promotion.

An inserted, newer commendation form stated that now, posthumously, this honor was also to be extended with swords. Obviously, Himmler had been as impressed with Reinhold's military drive as he had been with his organizational abilities, and his capacity for shaking down the industrialists.

It seemed that Reinhold showed no more fear of the communists of the Red Army than he did of that self-serving, laissez-faire, corporate mob—often had he declared them the same, two-headed ravenous beast bent on sucking Germany dry.

Beneath the other military honors and swastika-decorated trinkets, yet atop the bottom-most layers was a note from the promoted, now Sturmbannführer [*major*] Hofmann. It detailed Reinhold's actions, expressed his admiration and sorrow, and explained his motives for trying to send along everything that he had learned was dear to his commander. He regretted his inability to send Reinhold's service pistol along in tribute, but no arms could be spared from those too-few still left on the front. Along with that note was a personal thank-you to Gretchen—they had each appreciated her gifts very much—he apologized for not having sent his thanks earlier. The field-colored mittens and socks had been very welcome, especially during the cold winter nights in the field, out on the windy Hungarian plain.

She blushed slightly and said, "Well, we had all that extra wool that Gramma and I had dyed in the old way, using wild flowers and herbs…"

Alongside that, there was another short note added by a Hauptsturmführer [*captain*] Weiss.

Waffen-SS Sturmbannführer Hofmann had been killed before he could complete the shipment; this Hauptsturmführer had finished it, and sent along in that note his condolences for both fallen officers.

In the bottommost layers were photographs, still in their frames, and other of Reinhold's personal mementos. One was his and Edo's copy of the *Tiergarten* photo that I still kept beside my bed.

In another frame, slightly smaller, was a simple card, foxing from the edges, that bore a verse from a well-known, anonymous medieval-German love poem, an eight-century-old *minnelied*.

> Dû bist mîn, ich bin dîn,　　Thou art mine, I am thine,
> des solt dû gewis sîn.　　of that, thou canst be sure.
> Dû bist beslozzen　　Thou art lockt away
> in mînem herzen.　　within mine heart.
> Verlorn ist daz slûzzelin;　　All-lost is the little key;
> dû muost immer drinne sîn!　　therein must thou forever be!

The signature of its sender, "Edo", stood out in age-faded bluish ink angled into the bottom right corner. A few, short blond curls flowed across, pressed into the surface of the thick paper, stretching across the text.

Composure, Edi! Composure!

But my right eye leaked: it was too weak. Such dire emotional pressure it simply could not withstand.

Painfully unable to say anything, silent beyond any attempt to explain it, I handed the frame to Gramma.

She read the text, moved the frame about under the light, studied the words and peered at the contents behind the glass. Tapping at the hairs with the labor-thick nail of her farm-work gnarled, aging index finger, she asked, "Edo's?"

I could only nod in agreement.

"Bless him! Bless him!" she said softly, raising a cloth to dab her cheeks.

"All that happened, we must remember and lament; but in our hearts he was, and will always be, our dear boy."

I watched her with full eyes and fuller heart. Although bruised from the pain of repeated loss, Gramma's love proved undying: unconditional, all-empowering, everlasting.

Thereafter, accompanying Reinhold's copy of the 'zoo' picture of the three of us and her ancient, ever-present photograph of Grampa, Gramma would keep that poem, and its frame's precious treasure of those so few of her elder son's hairs—the only physical evidence of her child!—beside her bed all her remaining years.

They became the golden triptych of the altar of her life.

Two weeks later a letter came for the family from the director of St George's Philosophical-Theological College. The letterhead bore a Frankfurt address, but we knew it couldn't be from that area: that part of the city had been bombed out by the Americans in the big, March 18 raid the previous year.

The director had written to allay our concerns, to let us know that Albert had been with them at one of their temporary locations, near Marienstatt in the Westerwald, since the middle of the previous October.

Albert had confined himself, he reported, entering into a period of silence and fasting for six weeks, after which he had emerged, pledged himself to the Jesuit Order, and rededicated himself to the Church and to the Holy Mother, and had commenced a renewed, exhaustive study of Hebrew and Yiddish.

A penitential, Albert had walked the previous December the entire 152 km from the college's location outside Müschenbach to the bomb-damaged ruins of the Liebfrauenkirche [*Church of Our Lady*] in Trier.

On his way back in mid-January, he had ministered both to German soldiers and to their American prisoners of war, as our troops rushed in retreat from a great battle that had just transpired to the west, beyond the Eifel, in the thick-forested Ardennes of Luxemburg and Belgium.

The director concluded with the assurance that Albert would be staying there with them for the time being, if we needed to contact him.

Along with that letter a second one, from Albert, came sealed, directly to me.

I took it up to my room, to read in private.

My Dear Cousin,

As you became, on that distant trip to Spain, my true and faithful, secret-guarding friend-confessor, I express to you, alone, these private sins, my bleakest, true contrition, and ever-growing blessings.

I acknowledge my innumerable grievous errors, and apologize as profoundly as humanly possible for all the hateful, mean and unloving things I have said to you, or enacted toward you, throughout our lives. You know the circumstances from which they arose; I beg your forgiveness for my loathsome, unconsidered and inconsiderate behavior toward you. Mea culpa, mea culpa, mea maxima culpa!

I wish, too, to express, in this so feebly limited way, my deepest appreciation and admiration for what you did for our dearest friends: our very own little family! And I pray that the blessèd Virgin will keep you always within Her prayers and protection, for the selfless care and devotion you showed our beloved in that horrific situation.

While a pilgrim at the Liebfrauenkirche in Trier, I slept in the crossing of the war-ravaged church, its roof open to the sky, and often fell asleep watching the wondrous transit of the stars. In a dream, I saw the Queen of Heaven, Her arms outstretched, protecting Esther, who was holding our son in her arms.

My dearest had been blessed, hearing your Kaddish, but you could not hear her answering 'Omeyn'. She said that she knows you will keep your promise to her; that she will see you again, after you deliver the gift: you alone may know what she meant by that.

I will never love another as I did, and ever do love her. I am now content in abstention to lead my life as I have been called. She was the most perfect, most beautiful, most loving of women! That first night, she professed her undying love for me; I pledged mine to her.

Whatever happens, wherever you may go, you will always have my prayers, my blessing, my eternal thanks. The Blessed Virgin, the sweetest of sorrowful, painfully bereft parents, is bestowing Her peace upon me. I beseech Her daily in my perpetual contrition, that She and Her Son may continue to bestow Their loving grace upon you.

Your devoted cousin,
Albert

Mother knocked on the door softly, then pushed it ajar, to look inside.

"Are you alright, dear? Is everything OK?"

I glanced up from the beautiful script, the marvelously steady, clear-hand *Kurrentschrift*, of his letter.

"Yes. Everything is fine, mother! Thank you."

She smiled, and closed the door softly.

I went to my bureau, reached into the topmost drawer and took out the rosary Albert had retrieved from my bedroom in Geli's house. It was the one given to me by Father Vogler, bishop and martyr.

I held its image of the Madonna gently to my lips, then slipped the beads silently back into the drawer, secure atop the folds of Albert's letter.

———————————

The morning of March 22, Gretchen burst through the front door, froze in place and yelled, "The Americans have reached Berg! They've stopped just outside there, on their way to Singhofen!"

Mama almost screeched Papa into the front room, "Hans! Hans! We must find a way to tell them our intentions, to make sure they won't attack the farm! They mustn't bomb again!"

Papa turned to my sister, "Gretchen, what happened to that Wehrmacht unit that was stationed on the road into Nassau?"

"They were planning to leave two days ago, Papa. One of the men told me that they were preparing to pull out toward Limburg."

I smirked: nothing better than a pretty girl to get information from a soldier!

"We have to take the swastika flag down right now!" Papa proclaimed, almost in a run out the front door to fetch the stepladder, to give him the reach needed to grab the pole and take it down.

He came back in with the bloody-red banner crumpled unceremoniously into a wad. Carried directly to the fireplace and shoved into the fire, its cotton flamed up quickly. Hurriedly, Mama took the propaganda posters and pictures down from their allotted space near the door; Papa grabbed them from her and stuffed them in, around the burning flag. Gramma raised her hands in defiance and exclaimed, "Hoorah! Burn all the trash! Down with the kakocracy!"

Mama asked quickly, "Hänsel, shouldn't we put out a white sheet, or something? Anything to keep them from firing artillery or whatever they have, onto the house?"

I interrupted.

"Papa, Gretchen! Beyond the Wehrmacht, are you certain there are no SS or Hitler Youth units lurking in the area?"

"I haven't heard of any in the local Party reports or scuttlebutt," Papa said, then asked, "Gretchen, have you seen, or have any of your village-friends mentioned any such thing?"

"No, Papa. None at all."

Mama reasserted, forcefully, "But we have to put *something* out to let the Americans know that we're friendly!"

As we stood, almost frozen in uncertainty, I heard Edo's voice yell, "Get busy, Cowboy!"

I laughed out loud.

Mama looked at me, quizzically.

"We won't put out a surrender flag!" I said firmly, still smiling. Even Papa was looking at me as if I were going a bit crazy.

"Where's the stuff that Edo and Reinhold brought us, from their travels?"

"Most of that I hid in a hole I cut into the outside wall of your bedroom, behind your armoire," Papa said, still not sure why I was asking.

"Let's get it!" I commanded, turned and raced up the stairs, followed by Papa, Gretchen and Mama.

As we rushed in, Molly looked up from the middle of my bed, wagging her nubby 'hello' in delighted surprise.

We pulled the armoire away from the wall. I couldn't see anything amiss.

"Where is it, Papa?"

"I had to hide it extremely well. I got word that the Gestapo was coming through Singhofen, oh, over two years ago. That's why all of Edo's souvenirs had to be hidden!"

He hit the wall with the ball of his hand, listening for reverberations.

At last he found the cavity he had been sounding for, and we pried the covering boards from the wall. Out fell one box; we pulled two more from deeper in the recess.

After scooting Molly off the bed, we set the boxes out on it and started searching through them. The box that had sat lowest in the cache had some water damage, although that looked old. Nevertheless, the object I had sought was in it, at the bottom, of course! The slight soaking had caused it to start falling apart.

"Damn! That one won't work—it won't hold together!" I told them.

I opened the second, larger box and shifted its contents. I found a replacement and pulled it away from the other items. We unfolded it on the bed. It looked pristine: its substance hale, all like new.

"*That's* the one!" I said with a knowing smile.

"Are you sure?" Mama asked, not quite convinced of the scheme.

"Definitely!" I said, then hugged her, trying to allay her ill-ease.

Papa held it up to the light, surveyed it and said, "I think this will work!" Then he rushed down the stairs, to carry it outside.

The arrival of the Americans at the farm towards the end of March was so important an occasion that I came to hear of so often and again from all those involved in the event, especially from the American—augmented by my own participation within the very details—that I could hear it, see it, watch it play out, told by a hidden narrator: as if I were leaning back, sliding down into a seat lit only by the flickering shadows of a movie…

*** *** ***   *** *** ***   *** *** ***

Colonel Paul Ziegler was chewing his *Wrigley's Spearmint* with a slow vengeance, studying a map. He had his knees resting against—and the toes of his cowboy boots wedged under—the back of the front seat of his jeep. He had stopped his unit at the eastern edge of a little village named Berg.

"Now the instructions were supposed to detail how to get from Sankt Goarshausen toward … Bleidenstadt and Hahn … before we head down into Wiesbaden. Where the hell did they get us off track?" he muttered to himself.

He was so engrossed in his puzzle that he didn't notice when a jeep carrying one of his command's majors, James O'Henry, bounced in from the opposite direction and skidded to a stop right beside his.

The major called out, "Sorry to interrupt, Colonel, but I have to ask you.

"Respectfully, of course, suh", he added, in a comically-exaggerated, Senator Claghorn-style, Southern accent before lapsing into his Vermont dialect and spitting out, "but just how the hell did **your** people get here before the rest of us?"

"Jack, don't mess with me. I'm not real happy right now and don't have time for your jokes!"

The major laughed, did a "you're not gonna believe this" shake of his head.

"No, Colonel, it's no joke. Come with me—it's just up the road about a mile! If you don't take a look for yourself, you'll never believe what I've spotted!"

Exasperated, Paul huffed, stared back at the map, ground his gum a few more times and sighed, "OK, major. I can't get this damned GI map to work right. I should have brought one from home! Let's go see what you've got."

Paul straightened up, stretched one arm high and bent slightly to stretch out his back, folded the map tightly and stuffed it into his hip pocket, then jumped from the jeep. He turned and told his driver, "Ron, wait here till I see what this

284

damned goat-roper thinks he's found."

He pulled his jacket a little tighter.

"Crisp, beautiful morning just like in the Hill Country!" he thought.

Then he vaulted onto the back seat of the other jeep, much like he'd done so many times (he grinned to himself) getting up on his palomino mare back home—but she was prettier and smelled a damned site better than any old jeep!—and they started off, with Sergeant Grayson whipping the wheel to miss the potholes in the war-pitted road.

When they'd gone almost a mile, the major tapped Grayson on the shoulder and said, "This is close enough."

Sarge pulled the jeep to a stop half-off the road. Jack handed the colonel his own binoculars, pointed off from their position, up a private road that swept down, then curved up and around toward a southeast-facing farmhouse sleeping in the morning sun.

"Take a look, there."

The colonel put the binoculars to his eyes and before he could think about it, muttered, "Cotton Himmel!" [*Damn!* (German: *Gott im Himmel!*)]

He blinked and rubbed his eyes to make sure he wasn't imagining what he had seen, brought the binoculars up for a second, longer look then pointed off toward the building and barked, "Sarge, take us up there!"

The major choked, then almost yelled, "What the hell, Colonel? The three of us going up against who knows how many there could be waiting to jump us from that farmhouse or that barn?"

"Sarge, go! That's an order! Major, trust me on this—no Nazi bastards would ever have any idea of putting *that* on a building anywhere in Germany!"

He had raised the binoculars to scan the buildings again, and almost toppled backwards into the seat when Sarge popped the clutch and the jeep lurched onto the road to the farm. Paul put the binoculars down, spat out the gum he'd almost just swallowed, regained his stance, and stood like Patton, holding the back of the seat, staring intently at the farmhouse while they bounced along toward it.

Quietly, the major got his side-arm ready for a quick draw. But it was Sarge who was scared—white-knuckled steering-wheel-strangling, throw-up-if-you've-got-it scared—he thought the colonel was shit-faced crazy for doing this!

But then the jeep got close enough so that he could see what the officers had spied.

Reflecting in the morning sunshine, from the single pole angling out from the lintel above the front door was hanging...

a Texas flag!

"What Germans in their right mind would be flying a Texas flag in Nazi-insane, *follow-orders-until-you-die-or-we-will-slaughter-you-ourselves* Germany?" he wondered.

As they got nearer the farmhouse, they could see a small cluster of people coming out of it, gathering to stand passively, all facing the oncoming soldiers. They had frightened, half-smiles on their faces.

"Civilians—in traditional, Hesse-Nassau peasant clothes," thought the colonel. "If I had a nickel for every time I've seen the same thing back home..."

Occasionally, as the jeep approached, the older man would ask something of the young man standing next to him, to which the younger one replied.

The Colonel, now close enough, heard the last thing said, distinctly: "Oberst." [*colonel*]

"Wir ergeben uns! We surrender, sir!" said the older man rather haltingly, his hands raised a little over halfway, unsteadily. The others raised their hands in reaction to his statement.

The colonel barked roughly, trying to put some Teutonic heavy-handedness in it, "Gibt's Wehrmacht oder SS hier 'rum?" [*Are there any soldiers or SS around here?*]

The father answered in German, "No, Herr Oberst. Here it is only us. We are all anti-Nazi, anti-fascists."

Just hearing this statement—a so-often-repeated claim made by Germans trying to avert suspicion or to cover up their nefarious activities—made Paul nervous. Unbidden, his forearm rubbed against his own side-arm, making sure it was there if he needed it. He looked them over quickly, continued to speak German to them.

"Truly?" he started, then paused and thought.

"Hands down!" he ordered, thinking further on how to test those claims.

Suddenly, he had an idea, one that went back to his early home- and school-lessons in the language, to the first-year German literature classes he had taught as a grad student at the University of Texas, and to the many, orderly rows of ancient, Fraktur-format books in his own grandparents' Familienzimmer [*family room*].

"All of you who can, finish this verse: Deutschland hat ew—". [*Germany has an eter—*]

He paused at that syllable, without finishing the last word. His left eyebrow rose expectantly as he used his studied, officer's glower on the group.

The Meyers looked puzzled, shuffled nervously, glanced at each other, searching for a hint, a clue, any encouragement.

The colonel repeated the phrase slowly, more forcefully, "Deutschland hat ew—".

At that point, the young man's face brightened, and he answered, almost shouting, "ewigen Bestand!" [*an eternal existence*]

That said, he paused, looking into the colonel's face for some kind of response.

Seeing no sign of denial or refute, he started again, from the first of the phrase, this time to be joined quickly at various points by his sister, grandmother and parents as they, too, recognized the verse, so that they all ultimately recited with him as he repeated, "Deutſchland hat ewigen Beſtand." [*Germany has an eternal existence.*]

With no interruption from the colonel, the young man led the group in reciting the subsequent lines of that stanza, "Es iſt ein kerngeſundes Land — Mit ſeinen Eichen, ſeinen Linden — Werd' ich es immer wiederfinden." [*It is a nation good at its core — With its oaks, its linden trees — I will always find it {so,} again.*]

The young man then reached backwards in that poem for two lines, lines he recited with unmasked melancholy:

Zwölf Jahre ſind ſchon hingegangen;

Es wächſt mein Sehnen und Verlangen.

[*Twelve years have already flown; — My longing and despair are growing.*]

When they had all absorbed the heady harmonies of the verses, Paul paused to consider, "It has been twelve years of Hitler, hasn't it?", then acknowledged their effort with a small nod and an accepting, "OK. Na, gut." [*OK. Good.*]

The sternness in his face faded. He stood looking out over the little group.

The Meyers shaded their eyes, squinting at him through the growing glare of

Paul kept replaying his realization: the fact that he knew damned well that any Germans who, after those twelve years of the Nazi's lying, abusive propaganda, could still remember anything of the poetry of the regime-obliterated Heinrich Heine—and by heart at that!—could very well be telling the truth about being anti-Nazi.

With Paul chasing his thoughts, things grew increasingly quiet.

None of the Americans responded with any other questions or orders. The colonel just stood, pensive, a bit lost.

But the young man, trying desperately to gauge exactly what his family was facing with these, their new captors, felt the onrush of panic—he wanted desperately for this all to go well!

Then he remembered the one phrase in English that his uncle had spoken with such hearty gusto, while recounting his adventures in the United States.

Piercing the still morning, he called out nervously, almost shouting,

"Remember the Alamo!"

A jolt rocked the Americans, the shock growing slowly beyond the initial, disquieting exclamation.

The colonel started to chuckle, then he broke into a gut-bending laugh. From him it spread to the other two soldiers, from nervous giggles to outright guffawing. And they kept laughing, and laughing: almost falling-over-themselves laughing.

The young man was petrified, his family more and more nervous—was this bad?

Had he done something wrong? It had been so long since he had been taught that phrase! Were they in trouble? What was going on with these crazy Americans?

When the colonel had pulled himself together sufficiently to notice their growing looks of consternation, he wiped away the water his laughing had squeezed from his eyes, and said, "Herzlich dank, Junge! Das war wunderköstlich!" [Thank you very much, young fellow! That was damned funny!] Then he chuckled more.

After the family heard the colonel say this, though, they began to relax again.

When he could at last breathe, Paul decided it was time to get serious, to try for more information. That outburst, the poem's recitation by heart, the family's so familiar bearing, all convinced him that the father had told the truth.

He dismounted, the tall heels of his non-regulation cowboy boots ("Hell! If Patton can carry those damned, non-regulation revolvers...") clanging as they hit the naked steel step of the GI jeep.

The major again reached nervously back toward his pistol: his training just kept kicking in. But the Colonel walked—no, he swaggered his slim, six-foot-four Gary-Cooper frame—over to them. He stopped close to them and, as if he were about to chat with the schoolmarm, pushed his officer's cap up slightly, exposing a few shocks of short, blond hair. He asked the father:

"Wie heißen Sie, mein Herr?" [What's your name, sir?]

The father responded, "Wir sind die Meyer, Herr Oberst. Mann und Frau, Großmutter, Sohn und jüngste Tochter." [We're the Meyers, Colonel, Sir. Husband and wife, grandmother, son and youngest daughter.]

"Ziegler heiß' ich, Oberst Paul Ziegler der Armee der Vereinigten Staaten." [Ziegler's my name, Colonel Paul Ziegler of the United States Army.]

From his own standing position in the jeep, the major looked over at Paul quizzically—where the hell did that 'ow' in his first name come from, and what about that 'ts' at the front of his last name? The major had never heard the colonel speak German until this morning. And that pervasive Texas accent of these past several months had never even raised an inkling that the colonel could or would speak anything but his particular, southwestern brand of English!

Paul pointed backwards toward his men in the jeep, continuing in German, "That is Major Jack O'Henry, and this is Sergeant Grayson."

As each of the men heard his name, Jack nodded, and Sarge raised his right hand from the steering wheel in a small wave in acknowledgement. Neither of them, though, had anything beyond the merest grasp of what might have been said with their names, other than recognizing their introduction.

"Herr Meyer, I must ask you some questions about the lie of the land in this region," the colonel continued. "Please come over here."

He motioned Herr Meyer, and the major, over to the front of the jeep.

As Herr Meyer approached, Paul extracted his misbehaving, under-performing map and spread it out over the hood. Colonel and Major then started asking him a series of questions, piecing together as much information as possible about military and civilian matters in the area between the farm and Nassau, extending their questions to include the rivers, from the Lahn toward the Main.

The young man had stepped over with them and was jumping in as needed, to help his father understand the GIs' English, and translating German into English for the major, when the colonel hadn't thought to. He couldn't look at the map for very long. Although he could see very well now, the unfiltered morning sun still pained his eyes, and much of the time he was forced to shield them with his hand, or even to stand with his eyes closed to avoid the overwhelming dazzle of the crisp morning's late March sunshine.

The four men at the jeep busied themselves, poring over the map, more questions and answers, drawing lines and loose polygons, while scribbling notes among those. After several minutes, the pace of questions and answers cooled. The Americans were pleased with the knowledge they had gained from the civilians, and the Meyers had become more at ease with the occupiers, even if not yet quite sure of the occupation.

The grandmother, Frau Meyer and her daughter left, but soon reappeared from the farmhouse with fresh pastry, and pitchers of milk and of apple jack, carrying them over to where the men were still gathered around the jeep.

They offered refreshments first to Sarge and the major. Each took a small sample, although neither was quite sure what he was getting: they were still apprehensive—would this be the chance these krauts had been waiting for, to poison them?

But as the two of them were hesitating, the Colonel glanced over and exclaimed, "Haddekuche!"

Like a famished kid reaching out to snag candy, the colonel flung his arm past anyone who might be in the way—he didn't care!—toward the mother's tray, to grab a piece as fast as he could! He took a big bite of it and a swig of apple cider, chewed almost ferociously, then swallowed, groaning in guttural rapture.

Once he had stopped to catch his breath, he was off again, but this time talking, explaining effusively, and again in his birth-dialect-spiced Hochdeutsch, about how his own grandmother would make fresh haddekuche, and serve them with steaming cinnamon-apple juice, as a reward when he and his little brother came home from school.

The Meyers listened respectfully rapt to this obviously foreign, yet so Taunus, so Hessian a tale.

As their own anxiety from the encounter had been assuaged, the young man and his sister started concentrating intently on the colonel's words, trying to discern exactly which German dialect might be hiding behind his speech.

They recognized that it was standard German, *Hochdeutsch*, but there was something both very familiar and quaintly old-fashioned about it, with an occasional Anglicism thrown in. The pair would whisper to each other whenever either of them thought they had found another clue. Then it got to be too much, and the young man had to ask.

"Please, Colonel! We've noticed that you speak a form of standard German, but we can't determine which dialect might be residing within it. Might we ask you to tell us how, where and why you, an American, learned to speak German?"

The colonel nodded and through a mouth still half-full of haddekuche muttered, "Gewiß!" [*Certainly!*] trying—still as if half-starving—to consume the last bits of his third piece of pastry before continuing. He choked a little, had to pause again, glancing at the ground to concentrate, to get his breath and bearing. Then he looked up.

Why the hell hadn't he noticed her before?

He took a long, long moment to sip some milk this time, to calm his throat, stealing engrossing glances at this marvelous Mädel, all the time feeling his heart pounding, moving with each pulse up his throat toward what had started as only a dry Kuchen-lump.

So much like the girls back home in Fredericksburg—radiant, golden blonde and blue-eyed—she was simply the most beautiful young woman he thought he had ever seen! But this Mädchen, he realized, had something more, something that just made him sweat his britches every time she glanced at him. Romantic image, he smirked to himself: sweaty britches!

Paul snapped himself out of his reverie. GI business first, he reminded himself reluctantly, and forced himself to concentrate, to try to calm the growth in those sweaty britches: not to be pulled toward that vision, this girl he so desperately wanted to look at. Again. And again. Then he spoke—still clearing the cookie, "Zuerst ... aber ... das Militärische. [*First ... however ... military matters.*]

"Herr Meyer. I must request that you allow me to use your farmstead as my headquarters for a couple of days."

"We would be greatly honored, if we could be of help, Colonel!"

"Danke sehr, Herr Meyer." [*Thank you very much...*]

Paul excused himself, turned, stepped back towards the major and motioned for him to walk with him. When they were far enough away from the others, the Colonel's directions started coming, rapid-fire.

"Jack, go back to the men and have my gear brought here. And bring a couple of tanks up here, too, just in case some snipers or damned SS try to show back up. Otherwise, move the troops and tanks beside that main road down there—we may have to move out real fast. You noticed that we can see into Singhofen from the hilltop here at the farmhouse, right? The barn sits even higher—we need to check out the vantage point. Get Communications up here, but first see if battalion headquarters can tell us how far things have gotten in the push into this region. Find out particularly what areas have been taken and secured—things are moving fast around here, now. I'll clear everything with Command. There's no need for our hosts to know much more about our situation, but this is a good place for a short breather, to regroup. Get ready to secure the village—shouldn't be much trouble, once they see we hold the high ground—then get all the vehicles down on this section of the road, backed off out of traffic so that they can pull out in any direction we may need to push. I'll wait here."

Jack suppressed a smirk when he heard "short breather" and Paul's plan to stay there; he had noticed Paul's heavily smitten-teenager reaction to that farmer's daughter!

He considered reminding Paul about that regulation the Army had issued last September 12th against fraternizing with German civilians, but, as a high-ranking officer, Paul was pretty much exempt, and able to communicate with anyone he judged necessary or beneficial. And, the Meyers' reactions, particularly their ready demonstration of an eagerness to help, made them seem nothing like enemy.

Jack found himself wondering … if the French could be treated as allies despite their involvement with Vichy, the Italians so quickly forgiven their poison-gas, Fascist history, and both nations welcomed so easily back into the Allied camp, why couldn't decent Germans be accepted as friends, possibly allies against fascism, too? "Besides," he thought, "If I could get away from having to shake hands with myself, and attract some attention from a pretty frahline sometime, I wouldn't say 'no' either!"

Paul had staunched the flow of his instructions to pause, to give himself time to work mentally through a growing laundry-list of possibilities, digging through it to see if he had been able to uncover and detail everything that might be necessary immediately.

Then he snapped, "And have Ron get my jeep up here. It's been a nice diversion, standing around chatting, but we have to get ready to keep things moving. We don't want to take any shit from the General."

"Yeah," Jack thought, "Patton's high-pitched, nasal, cussing shriek is the last thing I want to hear!"

He saluted Paul with a perfunctory "Yes, sir!" ran back to get Sarge and jumped into the jeep. Sarge ground the starter, popped that noisy clutch, made a wide-sweeping arc to get the old girl turned around and headed back quickly toward the main road.

After tucking his hat under his left arm, smoothing his hair and subconsciously fiddling nervously with his collar, forgetting that he wasn't wearing the formal-dress tie that he now felt he really needed, to make himself completely presentable to these parents—ones he definitely wanted to impress—Paul sauntered back toward the farmhouse.

When he had reached the little group, he turned to them and asked, "Is there anyone among you that can help me understand the routes, roads and lay-out of this region better?"

That young woman moved forward slightly and volunteered, "I can, Colonel."

"Cotton Himmel!" he thought, turning nervously white-faced and flustered, "Germany be damned—I'm going to have to conquer myself, first!"

"Thank you, miss! And you are?"

Herr Meyer stepped forward.

"Excuse me, Colonel! I have been impolite; I haven't introduced you to the family formally!" He pointed out individuals as he presented the members of his small family.

"This is my wife, Maria Anna Meyer; and here, my mother, Gertrude Magdalena Meyer."

"Es freut mich, gnädige Frauen!" [*I am pleased {to meet you}, dear ladies!*] responded the Colonel, with a quite formal, slight (but old-fashioned) bow.

They each returned his greeting with an ever-so-slight curtsy, and Frau Meyer acknowledged with a soft, "Herr Oberst." [*Colonel*]

Herr Meyer reached beyond the young man to add, "And this is our youngest daughter, Margareta Anna, whom we call Gretchen."

"Es freut mich, gnädiges Fräulein," Paul greeted her, with rather nervous, stiff German courtesy, just like his very own Oma [*grandmother*] had taught him, back in the Hill Country.

"And this here, the real English-speaker, is our son, Eduard Gottlieb Meyer. A casualty, he was only recently allowed to return home from the East. He was blinded, but not permanently, Gott sei dank." [*Thank God.*]

"Ah, Gottlieb — Amadeus!" answered the Colonel, laughing and shaking Edi's hand, switching unconsciously back into more relaxed, American mode.

Edi responded, "Ganz richtig, Herr Oberst." [*Exactly correct, Colonel!*] Edi then spoke again, before the Colonel had a chance to ask any more questions, particularly ones that might dig more deeply into Edi's situation, as his father had already started wandering into too deep detail.

"Colonel, you promised to tell us the facts of your German accent."

Gretchen, sensing her brother's attempts to deflect questions from himself, stepped up to add, sweetly, "Doch, Herr Oberst! So haben Sie uns versprochen!" [*Indeed, Colonel! You promised us!*]

When he looked into her eyes as she spoke, his mind started swimming. Every part of his body started sweating again, just as they had, back when he was 13, trying to get up the courage to phone Susanna Bergmann to ask her to that first winter dance in middle school.

His voice, reenacting the memory, cracked slightly, "Bestimmt!" [*Certainly!*] but he forced it under control (and to regain its maturity) before continuing.

"Well. Its origin stretches into the past…"

He paused again to gather, to organize his thoughts.

He was nervous. Not the short-term, "they're shooting at us and I have to lead my men up the hill to stop them" nervous, but a visceral, gut-to-finger tingling, "if I can just impress these people, I will make my life so much better," best-job-in-the-world, rest-of-your-life nervous. So, he dug deep, probably deeper than necessary, given this oddest of circumstances. But he already knew his emotions had launched themselves from the cliff, and he wanted, somehow, to invite, excite, entice this beauty to follow him aloft, into the mounting thermals of his soaring flight. There was no war for him now, just her!

He wanted desperately for her to know him, his family, their lives, and to care: so, he dug deep.

"In 1815 … my great-grandfather, Rudolf Ziegler, was born … in Bad Nassau."

Paul's arm sprang up, but Gretchen pressed it gently into a different direction.

With a polite, self-effacing grin, he dutifully accepted her correction and reset his indication, not realizing what he had just demonstrated to her so fully, in that moment: his acceptance, his esteeming her as a knowledgeable, valuable and valued person, and his willingness to listen to her.

"His wife, Minne-Katrina Schultz was born that same year in Schaumburg. Their son, my grandfather Johannes, was born in 1846 in Frankfurt.

"Great-grandmother's extended family contained a member of the Frankfurt Parliament, and both of my great-grandparents were deeply involved with the liberal struggle at that time for German unity and freedom.

"After the revolution was crushed, Rudolf and Minne felt compelled to leave Germany, because of their revolutionary activity. At that time, they had heard a lot of good things about the German colony in Texas, so when they were forced to emigrate, they decided to go there.

"After arriving in Galveston, they, along with many Rhinelanders and other Germans, headed west, out onto the central plateau, and established farms, ranches and businesses there. In this region, west of San Antonio and Austin, these immigrants established the only successful agrarian colony that Germany has ever produced. Because of this, the countryside stretching from the area south and southwest of San Antonio north, almost all the way to the Red River, came to be called 'the German Hill Country'.

"The two, currently most famous German-Americans from this German settlement-band are General Eisenhower and Admiral Nimitz."

A quick breath, a glance-about to get his bearings, and he returned to his family history.

"There, living in the Hill Country, my grandfather met a young lady, Brünnhilde Weißmüller. She had also been born near here, in Limburg, before her own family was compelled by the reaction of those same conservative imperial and reactionary religious forces to emigrate. They were married in Texas. My father, Heinrich, was born over there in 1883, where he also later married my mother, Ingrid Biermann, whose family had immigrated from Koblenz.

"It was my exiled grandmother Brünnhilde who would curse the Kaiser and thunder, 'Righteousness will never return to the German people until the gold returns in freedom to the flag!' "

The grandmother exclaimed, "Exactly! A wise woman! A wonderfully wise woman!"

Paul smiled and continued, "I was born speaking both English and German, and at school or at home, we learned to do everything in both languages. Because of that intense double-education, a large number of children from the Hill Country have attended university.

"With a higher level of education, and our family histories, the people of that area of Texas have often been more progressive, more enlightened in their views. It was the main area in Texas that supported Sam Houston's call to preserve the Union, to vote against the treason of secession—𝔗𝔯𝔢𝔲𝔢 𝔡𝔢𝔯 𝔘𝔫𝔦𝔬𝔫! [*True to the Union*]—at the start of the U.S. civil war.

"So, although my family took their middle-Rhine, Goethe-dialect into Texas with them, there were so many settlers from other German regions there, including some Sorbian speakers welcomed from the area south of Berlin, that we minimized our family dialects, and spoke proper Hochdeutsch as a sign of mutual respect."

"Only our great-grandparents and grandparents would speak to us in their original dialect, and then, only when our parents weren't around. Our parents always drilled us in Hochdeutsch."

Frau Meyer then spoke up, "Ausgezeichnet!" [*Excellent!*] through her own family's snickers. The colonel chuckled with the rest of them, then returned to his exposition.

"So. When I speak, you are hearing standard, 19-century-based American Hochdeutsch, with middle-Rhine, and Texas-German influences.

"Did you understand all of that OK?"

He waited for any questions. His audience appeared to have been overwhelmed with all the information, unable, as yet, to fish any questions from that flood of data. So, he posed his own.

"Well, Edi! Now, how and why did you learn English? And who taught you that phrase about the Alamo?"

Edi replied in English, "Colonel, the flag might have hinted that we already know a lot about that area and the Germans over there!"

"Is that so?"

"My father's elder brother, Eduard Friedrich Meyer," he said, emphasizing the differentiating middle name, "emigrated to Texas before the Great War, into the Hill Country. He worked all over that area.

"In San Antonio, he met his business partner, Reinhold Keller. They were very successful there, took their business to New York City and then expanded it to Berlin once the Mark had begun to be stabilized. They used to visit us here a lot, and it was they who taught me to speak English, to speak just like the two of them, and 'all y'all'!"

Paul had to laugh at that sudden turn into deep Southern-dialect.

"And," Edi explained further, "He always warned me never to ask Americans if they're from Texas!"

"Now, why would he say that?" the colonel asked, concerned about any bad, foreign reputation his home-state might have acquired.

"My uncle said that if those you meet are from Texas, they'll tell you. And if they aren't, you don't want to embarrass them!"

Paul chuckled at the joke, but looked down, kicked at the ground, a bit embarrassed, himself: he had just done exactly that!

"Yes, Colonel," Hans Meyer stepped forward to say, "If my late brother and his partner had not been able to help us during the hyperinflation years, from their success in Texas and the U.S., we would most likely have lost the farm! So, our appreciation of their opportunities there is heart-felt."

Edi added, "And, Colonel, Uncle Edo always wore his cowboy boots, even in Germany—just like you!" They all laughed when the colonel raised one leg across the other knee, patted the pants leg covering the tall side of his boot and smiled.

Silence settled over the group, as if they were letting the rush of information sink in, take root. But then the grandmother, leaning forward from her cane, spoke up.

"Es ist interessant, nicht wahr, Herr Oberst, daß Sie hierher durch Feuer, Blut und Tod gebracht worden sind, aber trotz allem finden Sie hier eine starke Hingabe an Frieden, Freiheit und Familienliebe?" [Interesting, isn't it, Colonel, that you have been brought here by fire, blood and death, but despite all that, you find here a strong devotion to peace, freedom and love of family?]

"Freilich, gnä' Frau! Sehr interessant!" [Indeed, ma'am! Very interesting!]

The peaceful, persistent breeze travelling the countryside inspired quiet, almost homesick yearnings in the colonel. He looked out over the Taunus and thought, "Hill-people that leave them, always move to other hills. Perhaps it's the view into the distance that has made us restless, perhaps even visionaries, always wanting to learn about that next peak, and who and what lie beyond it."

With his thoughts directing his attention, Paul glanced accidentally at Gretchen. His heart raced, but he made sure to look away before she could notice. He smiled to himself, "Family love ... Oh, Oma, if you only knew the depth of what I'm feeling for this one, particular member of your family!"

Herr Meyer broke the silence: "Colonel, would you like to see the layout of the house, so that you can choose where to make your office?"

Paul drew himself up to attention, "Thank you, Herr Meyer, that would be most helpful! But I do not want to be too much trouble to you," he turned slightly to the rest of the family, "all," making sure to include the others—especially the young lady!—then returned to Herr Meyer.

With this, Colonel Ziegler stepped along after Herr Meyer.

They, in turn, were tailed by Gretchen and Frau Meyer, with Edi and Gramma in the final rank, into the farmhouse to see how its antique rooms could be adapted for the new use of the U.S. Army.

With this not only began, but was welcomed, the occupation of the Meyer farm not by an enemy, but by a long-lost neighbor's son.

*** *** ***   *** *** ***   *** *** ***

We walked the colonel through all the rooms on the ground floor, up to the first floor; then Papa led him into the attic. I knew that Papa would want to make sure that there was nothing about the house hidden or unknown to the colonel: better to cover all bases now than have to fix, explain or excuse things later!

Except for that side-trip into the attic, Gretchen had tagged along, silently. I could tell something was going through her mind; I would dig into that later!

When Papa had led the colonel back into the big room, we all gathered around again. The day was tilting perilously toward lunch time. We were grateful, and eased, to be able to speak German to this foreign officer; he appeared to enjoy it, as if doing so opened a door to a very pleasing arena of his own life.

"If you would consider it, Colonel, we would be honored if you would join us for our simple noon meal."

"I appreciate that very much, Herr Meyer! And I would be very pleased to accept your kind invitation!"

Mama placed her hand on my arm, "Edi, can you play something for us?" then hinted, "Perhaps something more *American* for the colonel?"

I moved to the bench, thought for a second, with almost a laugh, "Ah, *his* music would be perfect, wouldn't it, Uncle Edo!"

Before moving my hands into place on the keyboard, I flipped through the music mentally, watching clefs, notes and measures flow by. With our liberation, and now fully allowed, it had been so long ago—that morning with Gelchen!— since I had enjoyed Gershwin.

I had already noticed that the colonel had been sneaking more sly, smiling glances at my little sister (and her at him), so I launched right into *That Certain Feeling*. I followed this closely with the slower, more lyrical *So Am I*.

They all applauded, of course. Then Mama said, "Edi, play mine!" I smiled and set right into Gershwin's full version of *Swanee* for her.

After this, they all laughed and clapped. Ours was probably the only house in Europe—certainly in Germany!—that had the so-happy, inspirited music of George Gershwin echoing through it!

Once the fun had settled, Papa shifted our mood into a more serious direction.

"Colonel, I must explain our situation in greater detail—I will hide nothing from you. I must admit something to you before it comes otherwise to your notice."

The colonel looked puzzled, a little nervous: worried that he had misjudged my family?

"You see, Colonel, I *was* a member of the Nazi Party. I was forced to join in order to protect my family. At that time, I was, and have continued to be, anti-Nazi."

Colonel Ziegler shifted, obviously growing uncomfortable at this turn.

"I used the information I obtained as a party member to help preserve us, and others, during these horrible years. I realize that you will hear many people make similar claims, but I have proof of my and my entire family's dedication to fighting the Nazi nightmare we have struggled under these past many years.

"Colonel, in the eyes of the regime we are criminals, all criminals.

"Yes, including my agèd mother."

We had both noticed Paul's quick glance at Gramma when Papa had asserted *all criminals.*

"If you, Colonel Ziegler, and the rest of you," he motioned toward us, "will accompany me…"

Paul looked increasingly uncomfortable, but when Gramma stood, walked over to him with her cane and held out her hand to lead him, he took it. Not to be outdone, Gretchen stepped up, slid her fingers into and clasped his right hand. This sealed the deal.

We all moved toward that door leading into the basement, turned and made our way down its over-wide flight of stairs.

First to reach the lower level, Papa flipped on the light, and began speaking as soon as we had gathered.

"Colonel, this is another room you may make use of, if you need. As you can see, it is well ventilated, partly because we have this very expensive piano stored down here."

He lifted the cover to show the colonel. I took a second look; I was certain I had closed that keyboard cover! Had Gretchen been on it while I had been out of the house?

The colonel looked around apprehensively.

What he saw was a variously columned, full-house basement, with shelves everywhere covered with home-made preserves, or laden with heavy jars of sauerkraut that I was certain—because of those thoroughly explained, extensive German roots—he simply had to be intimately familiar with!

He looked beyond those, into every corner of the room, at every post. I knew he was scanning for the least, suspicious movement.

Papa stepped over to the shelves on the west wall of the basement, then called me to help.

I looked back at the four left standing in the middle of the room, watching us.

Paul was awash with worry, but he was also almost deliriously distracted.

Gretchen had moved against him tightly, his right hand still in her left, her right hand wrapped at his elbow, her left breast pressed securely against his upper arm.

From one of the shelves Papa took down a Luther-Bible that had been nestled tightly beside a square cookie-tin and flipped its pages quickly to one particular selection: verse 19 of Psalm 118. Having run his index finger along the text, he motioned for me to join him as he started reading, loudly, directly toward the wall behind the shelf.

Tut mir auf, die Tore der Gerechtigkeit, daß ich dahin eingehe und dem Herrn danke.	Open to me the gates of righteousness; I will enter into them, I will give thanks unto the Lord.
Das ist das Tor des Herrn; die Gerechten werden dahin eingehen.	This is the gate of the Lord; the righteous shall enter into it.
Ich danke dir, daß du mich demütigst und hilfst mir.	I will give thanks unto Thee, for Thou hast answered me, and art become my salvation.
Der Stein, den die Bauleute verworfen haben, ist zum Eckstein geworden.	The stone which the builders rejected is become the chief corner-stone.
[Lutherbibel, Ausg. 1912]	[KJV, 1611]

I heard rustling; a click from the bottom of other side of the wall was followed by others, mid-ways, then toward the top of the wall and the shelves. To my shock, an entire, shelf-holding wall-section creaked open slowly, tentatively, until … out stepped … Herr Fuhrmann!

Papa exclaimed, "The Americans are here, Shmuel! You're free! You're all free!"

Herr Fuhrmann's shocked expression was rapidly overwhelmed by joy. He and Papa greeted each other, hugged and patted each other's back in an emotion-charged celebration.

Herr Fuhrmann turned and called out, "Golda! Leah! Es iz itst sikher, oys tsu kumen! Es iz farbay! Mir zaynen fray!" [Yiddish: *It's safe to come out now! It's over! We're free!*]

From around the corner of the hidden room's door peeked a very cautious Frau Fuhrmann, and their daughter. Leah had to be about six years old now! How many of those years had she spent, hiding away, imprisoned like this?

Mama and Gramma rushed over to greet them. I couldn't move. I just stood in amazement: they had told me nothing!

I *had* thought there was something strange about the basement, though. I had spent little time down there since coming home, but it had seemed somehow different when I had last gone down there back in 1943, on one of those very few, short visits home I had made from Leipzig, but thought it just an illusion, likely from having finished the last of my teenage-growth while I was away in Saxony! Even now, within a near-empty house, I had noticed no extra rushes of movement, nor soft murmurs of distant conversation.

Herr Fuhrmann took my hand.

"I hope you don't mind, Edi, but I played your pianos, and kept them repaired and in tune, waiting and ready, praying for your return!"

I could only grab him and hold him: he had never lost faith that I would come back!

At last calling the Fuhrmanns together, Papa led them over to meet Paul.

"Colonel, these poor people, this family before you is the reason I can assert to you that we are all anti-Nazi."

"This is entirely true, Colonel," Herr Fuhrmann volunteered.

Papa explained, "When the party members in this district were informed of an upcoming visit by security officers to round up the area's Jews, I let slip to the local party-leaders my own intent to go ahead and drive the Fuhrmanns to Frankfurt for secure delivery to the resettlement authorities and, so, went by the Fuhrmanns' house and picked them up in my car. But a few kilometers away, I stopped, hid them within the car, then journeyed the long way around, back here to the farm. In complete secrecy, Herr Fuhrmann helped me rebuild the basement, digging out and creating that hidden room in which they could take refuge, and there they have hidden for these three and a half years!

"Because the farm is at some distance from the village, well-separated from any other homes and on a rise, we could see anyone who might approach, to make sure the Fuhrmanns were out of sight, safely concealed from the danger of arrest.

"Their presence here was known only to my mother, my wife, our daughter and me. We didn't even tell our son because he was away, ultimately another victim of the regime, and couldn't reveal it to him until just now, after all danger of re-arrest and interrogation be past. We, the Meyers, could not, and would not stand by and see our dear neighbors hauled away, never to be seen again!

"It was only when our son returned that we learned that the very worst of the rumors we had heard was, indeed, true."

Paul looked confused, overwhelmed.

I put my hand on Papa's arm, signaling him to pause.

"Mama, Gretchen, why don't you take Frau Fuhrmann and Leah upstairs to find something to eat," I interjected.

"It's past noon and I'm sure they must be hungry!"

"Yes, yes, indeed! Golda, Leah, come upstairs! We'll fix a good lunch!" Mama said as she reached her hands out to them. "The kitchen is still *kashrus*, just for you, Golda, like you taught!"

The last of the ascending procession, Mama turned back to me and, nodding her head, mouthed, "Well done!"

The four of them topped the stairs and soon cup-clicks and dish-clattering descended from the kitchen. When they were well away from the revelations to follow, I said, "Now, Papa. Please continue."

"Colonel, the rumors, whispered throughout the community—very, very carefully—were that the regime was not resettling Jews in the conquered eastern territories as it claimed, but was killing them, along with anyone else it alleged problematic, or simply found distasteful to their ignorance. We didn't know until Edi was restored to us that those rumors were indeed true: the Nazis have been slaughtering multitudes of Jews, and others—including Christians and other, conscientious Germans!—since just after the war began. Some they murdered years before, just after their seizure of power!"

"So those reports that the Soviets started putting out last summer haven't been just propaganda? They've been right all along?" Paul wondered aloud.

"Yes, Colonel," I answered.

"Colonel Ziegler, I was sent to the death camp because I had helped harbor just two Jews, a boy and girl, in Leipzig. For this, they marked me as expendable refuse."

I pulled up my sleeve to show him, them all, for the first time, that horrid tattoo.

Gramma gasped, "Oh, baby!" and reached to touch it. I had been careful not to show her before. Any tattoo were the mark of the devil to a Christian: a transgression against that divinely bestowed beauty of the bodily temple. That it was an everlasting memory of our own, indelible national monsters now made it vastly more so.

"I am a witness, Colonel: no longer a victim, but an active witness of the atrocities!

"At least a million Jews have been killed in southwestern Poland, within the Auschwitz camp-complex alone. At the height of operations, there were six large murder-camps operating just within the pre-war borders of Poland. There were more in Germany, Bohemia, the Netherlands, some still operating right now! An SS-officer admitted to me this past September that the total number of ghettoes, prison compounds, concentration camps and death camps set up by our Nazi government throughout enslaved Europe has exceeded 40,000."

Gramma tsked and shook her head in disgust.

"For a nation of fewer than 70 million, that's one interment facility for every 1600 of its own people: a torture camp for every village! Does that by itself not indict the German nation and the very government they themselves ... we ourselves ... allowed to take control?

"Those branded undesirable, who were not killed outright in the gas chambers, have been worked to death, beaten to death, starved to death, or allowed to perish from ordinary, treatable diseases of filth, overcrowding, malnutrition. But what will never be visible—and I fear could be forgotten because there can be no single place of remembrance!—is that even more Jews, Poles, Serbs, Greeks, Russians, were killed in Eastern Europe, shot by SS Einsatzgruppen [*action groups*], by ordinary, Axis soldiers, and by ever-eager, local collaborators, than were killed in the camps!"

"Edi, how do you know all this?" Papa asked.

"Reinhold had access to all the paperwork travelling between the camps, the Einsatzgruppen, the Wehrmacht and Berlin. He said that Army and SS-officers, even Himmler and Goering, talked about it all openly, but that there was a set of code words they had to use in sending reports to Hitler, so that it would look like he had no idea it was going on. But he knows, he has definitely, always known! He has been working toward it since at least 1923, although Reinhold asserted that it had taken real evil geniuses, like Heydrich and Eichmann, to set up the automatic machinery of mass murder."

I stopped when I noticed Paul dropping heavily to sit on the covered piano bench. He leaned forward, his elbows at his knees, and lay his face in his hands. His face covered, he just sat, breathing thickly into his palms.

He said nothing; we stood silent, watching him.

At last, still hiding his face, he spoke with sorrow, weighted even more heavily by regret.

"So, *this* is the German heritage I have now, that my children, my grandchildren will have to confront—as if that damned fool Kaiser hadn't been bad enough!"

Gramma stepped over to him, rubbed his shoulders, then bent down closer to him.

"Yes, my dear, it is," she said.

"The righteous will never forget nor, righteously, let it ever be forgotten!"

Die der Brünnhilde Rache
— Chapter 25 —
Brünnhilde's Revenge

Colonel Paul Ziegler and his GI crew slipped into the house quickly and, even more rapidly, evacuated.

The minor tank skirmishes required in fully taking Singhofen (like so many small towns) notwithstanding, the drive of the Allied forces across Germany was gaining speed, as ever-increasing numbers of Wehrmacht units determined it was far better to be a captive of the West, than a corpse in the East.

I was certain that we'd see Paul again. When you catch someone kissing your sister—and more importantly, her kissing him back!—you will arrive easily at such predictions, very fast.

Not long after the Colonel had left, Gretchen started receiving a trickle of letters from him. The U.S. Army had stepped in and taken over the postal system very quickly, primarily for censorship, to guard against the threat of coordinated sabotage or enemy-reorganization. So, Paul wrote only in English: writing in German would have been too suspect, with the war's still being prosecuted so enthusiastically.

My sister came to me for help with translation.

At 27, Paul was about eight years older than she; you could read the maturity in his measured tones, his education in both vocabulary and style.

After one too many of Gretchen's recitations of his charms, I had to tell her to stop: I really didn't need to hear the megillah again! Yes, he was handsome, intelligent, statuesque, spoke such lovely German, with its Hessian, old-fashioned politeness, and … It was just more than I needed!

In the letters, their relationship revealed itself deeper, more serious than anyone might have guessed. He wrote beyond the trivial, about his feelings and concerns: he was already treating her as a respected companion within his own emotional life.

This came across most clearly when Paul wrote his growing anxiety, ever since his brother, Georg, a bomber pilot in the Army Air Corps, had been shot down during a flight of his B-17—bearing nose-art proclaiming "Brünnhilde's Revenge" after their German-revolutionary, exiled grandmother—over Cologne back at the start of March.

It pained me, in particular, that neither Paul nor his family had received word whether Georg was still alive, so very much like my own family had suffered with my secretive seizure and separation those eleven months.

Gretchen wanted very much to answer his letter with words of encouragement, of loving understanding. I saw in this that she was maturing, too, simply by learning about Paul, his struggles, concerns and goals. Their relationship might have started as infatuation at first sight, but it was growing steadily into a deep, adult, stand-together-against-the-world love. I could recognize it as such because I had already experienced it myself. I prayed she would not lose it, that her world would not reach out in insane rage, to crush it and them.

She begged me to help her improve her English, so we started lessons.

While we were talking, working through the chapters of the phonogram set that I had used such a long time ago, she let it slip that they had been 'friendly' one time during those few days that the GI's had been here, but then swore she hadn't let it go too far. (How the hell did she know about "going too far"? Hey! That's my little sister, GI!) She gushed, rather impulsively, about how smart, how sweet, how funny, how, well, *everything* he was! I let her talk on, even if I had to set my mind into automatic, not-really-listening, Czerny-mode.

––––––––––––––

My dreams since returning home had become more distinct, more wild and far-ranging, more anxiety-riven. I found myself slipping into a distant, phantom, terror-world so quickly, whenever I would fall asleep, whether abed, or just sitting still during the day.

I fell into a panic, rushing—by train, by bus, running, even flying like a bird—over so many places, distinct and indistinct—an inarticulate conglomeration of every location we had ever traveled—searching, desperately searching for Thomi, for Uli, for Gelchen.

Suddenly, a train rumbled and squealed to a steam-belching halt beneath my feet. I ran from the carriage, out of the station, across the city: past the *Paulinum* and through the Augustusplatz, around the museum, through the Conservatory courtyards and suddenly onto our street. I saw Thomi opening the door, stepping into Geli's house, our house!

I rushed through the entryway; they were standing in the grand salon in front of the *Aleksey*-piano, smiling, gazing at me serenely. I stood paralyzed before them, heart pounding—breath, breath, out of breath!

Geli said, "Dear, you cannot come with us!"

Esther agreed, "Edi, you cannot follow us!"

David moved towards me, reached up, caressed my neck, whispered, "Baby, you must stay, for now!" and when his lips came so close, so very close, nearly touching mine, he—they all!—vanished into a swirling mist.

I stood there, in a suddenly, dreadfully empty, echoing, deserted room, in a distant land, living darkly: abandoned, dejected, rejected.

A looping stream, a plethora of repeating, helpless-pursuit-dreams peppered my naps, my sleep, every moment of rest: wrapped my existence in a featureless fog of indecipherable, ever unreachable, unresolving sadness.

My thoughts, my intellect, my outlook had changed.

I was now highly sensitive to the passage of time: everything was fleeting, transitory, too temporary.

Each thing, each moment would be lost!

I found myself staring, studying people, their movements, their words, their actions and reactions, exerting myself to grip each gesture, catch every nuance, to remember every tiny thing. Grasp and hold! Grasp and hold: no one shall ever steal my memories!

Great loss compels dread anew of every approaching, attending loss.

It was overcast and, at around 2°, cold for the last day of April; but at least there had been no frost that morning.

Cocooned before the fire, in one of the high-backed chairs randomly peopling the big room, I nestled into my old, Leipzig study-text of *Beowulf*, stepping through the poetic lines, translating into archaic English the verses of this ancient, Anglo-Saxon report of yet another community-consuming, Teutonic monster.

...	Þu wāst, gif hit is,	...	Thou wost, if it is,
swā we sōðlice	secgan hȳrdon,	so we soothly	saying heard,
þæt mid Scyldingum	sceaða ic nāt hwylc	that midst Scyldings	a scathing, I wot not which
dēogol dǣdhata,	deorcum nihtum	hidden fiend,	during dark nights
ēaweð þurh egsan	uncūðne nīð,	showeth through terror	un-couth envy,
hȳnðu and hrāfyl.		hatred and slaughter.	

That fiend had been another demon also removed ultimately only by the most determined heroic action! I read on.

"Se wæs betera þone ic!" [*He was better than I!*]

Thus exclaimed King Hrōðgār of the death of his elder brother, Heregār. It was too close to my own family: the still-sorrow-recalling voice of my own father.

While poring over the ancient text, I had also turned the radio on, hoping the propaganda static-level would be minimal, the music maximized. The U.S. Army's Signal Corps had run wires across the beams in the attic as an extended antenna. Those, plus the elevation of the house's high roof had meant a much improved quality and distance of reception once our own radio had been connected to it.

Pleasingly, music was indeed playing but the selection that morning was again Wagner. Yet another re-broadcast of his *Ring Cycle* had arrived that morning at the final opera of the four, *Götterdämmerung* [*Twilight of the Gods*].

The quality of the singers and orchestra, of the signal, and of the broadcast (it, like our Leipzig concert, must have been recorded by *Magnetophon*) was quite high. It could only have been pre-war, or at least from those few, short years before the continuous air raids had started, making grand performances in the large cities too dangerous, the burial sites of so many mangled and muted musicians.

I drifted, dozing into, around and through my agèd Anglo-Saxon, and Wagner's idiosyncratically antiquated German text during those three-plus hours swallowed by the opera's first two acts. Teasing the tedium, I ate an apple, sliced before the onset of the third act; the snack primed me for sleep.

 The *sforzato* chords at the start of Siegfried's funeral march roused me from my torpor. I stretched, stoked the fire, wriggled around to get comfortable, then pulled the blanket up, tucking it tightly over my shoulders.

Such beautiful melodies for the horns and the brass: it was such a pity that Wagner was so ready a tool for the fascists!

 Heavy lidded, lofted afar, during that final scene's "Starke Scheite schichtet mir dort" [*Build for me there a mighty funeral-pyre*], I fell ever further into ancient Germanic dream as spear-lofting, shield-flashing, Teutonic-voiced drama flowed: "Fliegt heim, ihr Raben …" [*Fly home you ravens…*]

Rooks' raucous rabble!   Sudden, rearing schimmel I spy,
shimmering stallion,   white steed racing
hoof-fleet across flood-swept,   storm-forge, barring
dikes of deserted, northern coast,   disheveled, white mane
flying backward, whipped   in rain-drenched wind
and wild spray cast from terror-billows,   tossed in furious tempest.

He rears, hoof-shrieking, a-sky,   shifting a shining-corseleted,
wing-capped woman—   his mighty rider wielding the rune-bright reins,
brandishing her brass-gilt spear.   Rising to blast rain-frenzied
thunder clouds asunder they fly,   Grane's fleeting hooves flailing
'gainst wild, world-whipping winds.   Woman and steed
bend to sky-vessel, Valhalla-bound,   on blast-carrying course,
rushing on racing, breaking crests,   ever higher, ever farther
from grass-carpet cushion-field,   receding North-folk countryside.

Closer on, to Colonia they soar,   contending as one,
Grane—his mistress aback—   borne blatant in bomber-nosed art
Flashing its warning frank   and fearless: 1848.

Wafting shaft from the west,   shells shattering all 'round,
one failing engine forlorn,   faltering plane's nose sinks;
another flames out; flinging one, two, away: nine swan-chutes unfurl,
lacking one, left, alone—   shall it loft at last rejoining,
spring out, float nigh, then plant?   Plane holds its path, pounding
cylinder-hooves bearing it onward: toward the bridge, the bridge,
blackest iron-braced bridge ...   runs bane-Hagen in red-faced fear,
terrified, torn from the temple—   at river's clipping rand he trips;
Pained engines shove shining plane   and baleful bombs to shatter Earth.

Cathedral-besting, ever-swelling: the savage blast of Brünnhilde's Revenge
exploding rips him, wafts him,   the wooden box he bears, wayward,
his ruing yell "Back from the Ring!"   beyond the besting river shore.

Fracts the box: a-bursting, the booty,   unfast from fatal capture,
sails high in celebration—   slow, joyous gyres, arcing, seven-fold,
seven-fold, then thrice: again   circling, fleeing seven-fold,
high over waves, floating, tumbling   hanging in sensuous, heart-rich
caress of open air, rolling.   Rings, rejoicing, soar,
consort slowly down, setting,   settling toward surface waves.

Rhinemaidens' ravaged arms   shoot up from River's flow!
Grasp their long-purloined prize   in sister-proud, secure-sheltering hands!

Slowly the now youth-born arms   bend, turn, bidding:
their slight palms give   that treasure's eternal glint to glaring sky,
heaven-flaring brazen-red.   Fires fell the fortress:
deceit-fed, death-robed,   immolating demigods destroyed!

Midst waning lays,   the maidens lower now spotless arms,
drawing down the hoard,   deep again to ancient, rightful Home,
Palms soft-kiss sated River's   now soothing flood.

Golden streaks shoot   a-flash from the moist-auric hoard
to bedraggled bunting, hanging   forlorn from wreck of bridge, burg,
nation—Death-defiled,   debauched, bloody bands of
red, white, black fall: instantly renew, rising
in shining, rebirth-resilient   black, red, gold!

The sky screams, explodes in white   and golden stars: shimmer
driving away death-dread fright,   flooding with flashing rays
the radiant blue night,   cyaneous robes of mighty Maiden Mild,
staunch before Rhine   brandishing colors new, bold
sword defensive, now brightest reborn,   with resolute gold,
aurific democracy audacious: a new-blessèd dawn.

Chest-heaving gasps!

I spasmed erect, jumped to breathe, awake, awake, fully awake!

Startled, confused, uncertain, I found myself still at home, within the Taunus-farmhouse and no longer standing afar, beside the cliff-bound Rhine, watching there with unashamed cathexis that good, that belovèd flag, ancient Frankfurt's liberal-revolution, *Germania*'s tricolor waving: enrobing a new-rising phoenix-nation.

I slumped back into the chair's warm, blanketed embrace, knowing now, somehow, and at last, in the mind's easy breeze of anguish-earned contentment, of comforting, caressing realization:

Our agony was coming to an end.

Hagen was dead.

Brünnhilde had wrought her revenge.

The following day, those aching love-dreams, those visions still surging in flood, withdrew only to expose a minefield, a listing mental vessel, full of emotions, but famished, awaiting, expectant.

After a morning of lying in bed, dozing in guarded moments, I returned that afternoon to the high-backed chair by the fireplace, nursed hot soup and tried to distance my loss. I turned the radio on, for company, for noise.

Interruptions every twenty minutes or so stated that an important announcement was going to be made at 22:00 that night. The entire day's music languished lugubrious.

I would get irritated, turn the radio off, get bored with the quiet after a few minutes, then switch it back on.

Gretchen came in and sat a while, before becoming irritated.

"Make up your mind, Edi! On or off!"

After another stint of enduring my mood- and radio-switching, she jumped up in a snit and left.

Later, with dinner done, I went up to my room to read, or at least to try to catch something to leaf through. But I flustered aimlessly about, found nothing, then decided to descend to the basement.

With the security of the Jews now established by the Allies within the region, we had removed Frau Gellert's boxes from the Fuhrmanns' house and into the former sanctuary-room and basement, to allow the Fuhrmanns reentry into their home. At the earlier resettlement-expulsion, Papa had purchased their house to keep it safe; we returned the house, along with its Nazi-denied true value, as a second-chance, life-affirming gift.

However, when the Fuhrmanns got there, saw the anguished, burned-out ruin of the synagogue and realized that there was no Jewish community left for them in Singhofen, they had re-packed their meager remnants, returned the house-deed to us, and set off for Nastätten to search, to see if any of Frau Fuhrmann's family had survived or would return. It was yet another difficult good-bye, to say farewell to the teacher whose skill and devotion had set me soundly on my professional path.

So, I went downstairs and rifled, reading the labels on the outsides of the boxes, sticking my nose into some of them. They still exuded Leipzig life: aromas that both made sense of my mood, and were comforting, too.

It hit me: I was just going stir crazy! Cabin fever was dragging me down. I had spent most of my life travelling from place to place: on trains, on buses, or simply out walking through Frankfurt or Leipzig every single day! Although I had been tightly confined at Auschwitz, the terror of daily life there forbade boredom ever to take root.

Now, I had nowhere to go, no one to teach, no one to cuddle with. Well, except Molly. I wished something would just hurry up and change. I could feel my mind, my life closing in on me; I needed to be out and active, with and in front of people! It just seemed this dismal war would never end!

After I had realized what was bringing me down, I searched out all the boxes that bore some sort of 'Music' label on them and dug through them. I found a few new, unfamiliar or forgotten pieces, including an early edition of all of Chopin's works. Many of them I hadn't seen, or I barely remembered, since Geli and I had been forbidden by Goebbels to perform "decadent" music, whether German, Slavic or any other.

I clasped in my arms all that I'd found and trudged with it up the stairs.

By that time, the much-heralded broadcast was scheduled to begin, so I put the books on the corner of ole *Steiner*'s bench and sat with the rest of the family, already gathered around, watching the radio.

Grossadmiral Dönitz spoke. In somber tones, he announced that Hitler had "fallen" the previous day, and that now *he* was the new boss, the next *Führer*.

So, after twelve years of fear, devastation and murder, that despicable man had gone to perdition. I didn't know whether to celebrate, cry or—or anything! So, I just sat, benumbed.

But Gramma clapped her hands: "Well! That's the first shoe! When's the next one going to fall?"

"What do you mean, Mother Meyer?" Mama asked.

Papa and I answered at the same time, "The surrender."

Then Papa continued, "That's the only logical next step. And with that insane cretin now out of the way, some logic must, surely, return to the government!"

Another surrender.

The thick, threatening cloud of uncertainty that cloaked what lay in wait on the other side of that chasm made me shiver with dread.

This time there could be no simple armistice, no repeat of Versailles.

That earlier situation had required a German government with whom the victors would treat. But there could be no German government when the Allies were through this time.

Just as they had refused to speak to the Kaiser then, they would not deal with the Nazis now and, without the Nazis, the current government was gone: the Nazis had simply eliminated or murdered all alternatives.

Germany would be a blank slate. Whether this would be better, or worse, only Heaven knew, and the blessing of time would reveal.

I arose to walk slowly across the soothingly familiar, long-suffering timbers of our sheltering, nurturing farmhouse and out the front door.

With no protection against the chill, I stood, watching the pregnant clouds blow in, wrapping the woodlands, farms and hills of the longer-suffering Taunus in swirls of mist, glowing in the few visible house-lights of the distant, half-empty, Jew- and democrat-bereft village.

What did I feel for a nation that had so eagerly, so easily, so unthinkingly put in place a government that had driven away my good friends, killed my dearest, and done its best to press the very life from me?

I knew I still loved it, or at least part of it: that Germany of the '48'ers, that Germany of the more-recent, ill-starred Republic, that abiding Germany of Lessing, of Goethe, of Thomas Mann, that *kerngesundes Land* [*good-at-its-core nation*] unceasingly yearned for by our liberal, conservative-exiled Heinrich Heine.

That nation simply must lie still hidden somewhere, having waited, sleeping fitfully for so long—so painfully, so damnably long.

And now fallow, facing a new, unknown season, Germany must awaken again, to bloom.

Spring had come at last; but was it too late?

Frankfurter Hochzeit
— Chapter 26 —
A Frankfurt Wedding

The surrender on the following Monday, May 8, ended the cataclysm of war, but ushered in a year and a half of misery: of disappointment, disillusion—of bureaucratic dysergia—and famine.

None of the Allies wanted to feed the Germans after they had defeated us.

Even the Germans who had opposed Hitler—but worse, the German victims of the Nazis—were treated as criminals by the victorious, occupying armies and their naïve governments, now caught up in the Allies' own, Four-Power shotgun-marriage crisis.

All the problems within Germany were abetted by the colossal mistake the Allies, the U.S. in particular, made concerning the food supply.

American bureaucrats had failed to take into account all of the Germans displaced by the Soviet seizure of East Prussia, the eastern regions of Pomerania and Brandenburg, and all of Silesia, including Gleiwitz and its young Josef, as far as I knew. These Reichsdeutsche [*ethnic Germans*] had fled, flooding westward, needing to be housed, but more pressing, to be fed. However, the American command had severely underestimated the number of these people, not by thousands, but by tens of millions, thereby inflicting widespread famine.

Of course, by causing this mass shortage of food, the one thing the Americans had done was to make sure that the black market in cigarettes and chocolate—and bed-based bartering—flourished. The U.S. Army's response was to impose regulations that penalized soldiers for any unofficial contact with the German people, rules which, of course, were doomed from their very conception.

The U.S. government, military and occupation authorities had failed utterly to learn anything from that nation's thirteen-year "noble experiment," that abysmal failure, Prohibition. What was it with those conservative Americans and their persistent, ever-failingly insane, Pollyanna-fascist drive to legislate morality?

When you create artificial shortages in staples, or any other sought-after goods or services, anomie, then self-organizing crime will step in to fill that demand. So, official American puritanical, vengeful stupidity resulted in the undeserved deaths of already defeated, de-Nazified Germans, particularly of the innocents: children and infants.

The conditions were not so severe in the countryside, but that included a mere pittance of the population.

The situation the year after the surrender was made even worse when those same bumbling occupation-bureaucrats caused a shortage of fertilizer. This meant that, on top of the Soviets' theft of the agricultural wealth of East Prussia and Pomerania, the proportion of food we could produce ourselves dropped even farther because of inability to maintain crop yields.

It was fortunate for us few that Mama and Gramma had canned so much food, so frugally, just before and during the earlier years of the war, while farm work could be carried on more normally. They had been preparing to continue providing food in secret for the Fuhrmanns. But they had since departed; this reduced the load on our stocks.

Finally, in late 1946, the incompetents were shipped out of the U.S. Sector Command. Humanitarian activities were greatly increased, and some sense of humanity returned gradually to the American sector, and from there, throughout western Germany.

Colonel Ziegler kept us apprised of the problems. He had been on Patton's staff in Bavaria until the general was relieved of command of the Third Army on October 7, 1945. The colonel had then been reassigned to American-sector headquarters in Frankfurt.

With those draconian rules against fraternization in place, Paul committed himself to finding "official" reasons to travel into the French occupation-sector, into which Singhofen, and the farm, had fallen.

The French government had pressured the three active Allies into letting them have a zone of occupation. And, mainly to get their prime minister, General de Gaulle, to shut up, the Americans (always sentimentally attached to France, but especially so after having received the unreserved help, and witnessed the selfless, heroic suffering of the French—of the people of Normandy, in particular) had caved in and given it to them.

This new border, that the American command had drawn within its original occupation zone, had split old Prussian Hesse-Nassau and put our western slice of the region into the French occupation zone. So where formerly we and Frankfurt were within the same province, we now had an internal, internationalized border running across the hills between the farm and the City!

Colonel Ziegler had become terribly distressed when he learned the extent to which the U.S. had bombed his ancestral, little Bad Nassau (not once, but twice!), destroying eighty percent of the city, including two hospitals—one full of wounded soldiers—and killing 300 people from a population of only a few thousand. The bombing had also devastated the mineral spring there, destroying the city's distinctive and ancient designation as a spa, a bath-city: no longer officially "Bad Nassau," it became permanently simply "Nassau."

All this spurred him to become active in trying to do what he could to help keep Nassau alive and in doing so, to visit its (and our) region.

The colonel had located a French officer assigned to Nassau, one whom he had met some years before, and had lately renewed his friendship. That French captain was well-versed in *les affaires douces et enchanteresses du cœur* [*the sweet and enchanting affairs of the heart*], as he called them, and quickly found a multitude of issues and excuses for Paul to come over here into the French zone, at least once a month.

Although billeted on those trips in Nassau to work with reconstruction, the colonel spent the free hours he could arrange at the farm. On occasion, that French officer would come by as well, for a short visit—I got to re-learn some of the French I had studied so long ago with the gramophone records and at the university in Leipzig. But he was neither thrilled with German farm-cuisine, nor captivated by country life—certainly not with helping someone he considered a country-bumpkin speak French—so his stops were abbreviated, albeit cordial. (I thought he really came by only to see if another buxom, farmer's daughter might show up, so he kept his disappointment to a minimum, with the shortest of rare visits.)

The early morning of the 22ⁿᵈ of November, 1945, we were surprised when Paul's jeep came to an unannounced, but now-normal, clutch-grinding stop in front of the house. (He would laugh, "I go through jeeps faster than Sam Houston went through horses at San Jacinto!") His 'horse' had now acquired thin, cold-weather plastic and fabric covers; and the riders needed them, too, even in their warmer, GI-ubiquitous, riveted-denim civvies! It was barely above freezing that morning, with no sun, too!

Accompanying Paul were two lower-ranking officers, according to his introductions. Having brought extra food along, they had already decided that they would treat Paul's German friends to a real American Thanksgiving!

Mama released her kitchen to the three GI's, albeit nervously. She stood not more than a few steps away from their banging around within her personal fiefdom—at least until she fatigued of guarding, and just gave up and sat down.

"You'll pay for anything you damage!" she threatened, making sure Paul knew he would hear of any cracks, pits or catastrophes!

Paul approached Papa and started talking with him about the small greenhouse. (Papa had installed it, leaning against the farmhouse, as a disguising and insulating weather-cover over that basement-extension: the Fuhrmanns' refuge.) Paul abandoned his subordinates to finish getting the food ready while he and Papa stepped outside. It wasn't long, though, before Papa stuck his head back in the door and asked Mama to get her coat and come outside, too.

At last the cooks had everything that they had brought along baked or bashed (and some, a little burnt), and loaded into serving bowls; then they called us to the table. Papa, Mama and Paul came back in. Mama's face was a little red; the wind must have picked up.

We were stunned by the amount of food!

Did Americans always eat this much?

They assured us it wasn't typical of every day, but just of this one day. Oh, and Christmas day, and the Fourth of July, and Labor Day, and birthdays, and anniversaries, and church picnics, and …

It was really quite good, except for this stuff called "cranberry sauce." Ugh. Too bitter!

309

We younger, still underfed four, devoured everything we could possibly contain. But Gramma ate slowly, deliberately taking her time, savoring her meal. She remembered too fiercely those so many German years now of war, of deprivation and misery, of disaster.

Molly was in heaven: scraps of turkey, mashed potatoes and gravy, and lots and lots of exuberant attention! The GI's didn't speak very much German, and what they did, certainly not very well! ("You can't use *das* and *es* with just every noun!") We had a great time laughing at their mistakes and trying to correct them, listening to their fevered attempts "zu bekommen es recht" [{*broken German*}: *to get it right = "es gut zu machen"*)].

Those younger two GI's kept going back for more of this, a ladle-full of that; but Paul didn't. He looked nervous, taking small bites, then pushing his food around with knife, then fork, like there was something else more important that he was trying to arrange, something very serious.

Paul pulled rank again and ordered the other two officers to "KP duty," telling them to "make everything shine!" But we all pitched in and helped. Those GI-cooks had dirtied almost every pan in the place during their rush to get things ready that morning, so dish-duty was more than one day's work for two guys, anyway! The only two who didn't move into the kitchen to help were Paul and Gretchen. They had disappeared. I had seen them put on their coats quietly and slip away, outside.

However, about fifteen minutes of all the banging, clanging and laughing in the kitchen was all Mama could stand. She exclaimed, "Aaaaaaugh! Men!" and drove all of us, except for Gramma, out of her province, swearing that she'd do it herself! It wasn't very long after that that our two missing persons came floating back in through the front door.

Gretchen called for everyone's attention; she announced that Paul had asked her to marry him. Of course, she had said, "Yes!"

This set off a round of congratulations and toasts. One of the GI's had snuck a bottle of whiskey up from Frankfurt, and Papa fetched a bottle of his stoutest Ebbelwoi from the basement. The stream of well-wishes was punctuated by the clinking of glasses, quickly followed by more toasts, handshakes, kisses and hugs.

This celebration soon succumbed, though, to sedated, postprandial, 'round the fireplace, naps. One of the GI's grabbed a pillow, one of Gretchen's hand-knitted coverlets and sacked out on the floor, beside my *Steiner*.

After that evening's gut-stuffing replay of the noontime feast, and the late departure of the three back to Frankfurt, I heard more of the details of that morning.

Paul had actually asked Papa and Mama to come outside so that he could seek their permission to ask Gretchen to marry him. At that, Papa had been floored; Mama was still beaming. They declared that they hadn't felt this honored since Hindemith had asked them if I could accompany him at his concert!

"Paul's action, his concern mean so much!" Papa explained.

"It tells me that someone still respects us, as parents and, yes, as Germans! This American colonel, he expressed himself, all this, in such lovely, classical, Goethe-sounding German!"

Mama nodded in agreement.

To this Gramma extolled, "And he is such a good Taunus lad: a fine, polite,

310

handsome, Hessian boy!"

The rationale behind Gramma's place-labels for him had been proved during one of Paul's frequent, earlier visits. We had cleared off the kitchen table and laid out one of his big, Army charts of the entire area. As he stepped again through his tale of that past century and a half, verbally retracing his family's local history, we circled each of the German towns and villages he mentioned. Not a one was more than 85 km from that very table!

Indeed, from his working lately to help the U.S. Army restore Singhofen's Nazi-wrecked Jewish cemetery, Papa had documented the name of one Jewish forebear that Paul knew of. One of his paternal great-great-grandfathers had been a close relative of Israel Baer Kursheedt who, ultimately the first Torah scholar in North America, had been born right here in Singhofen in 1766!

During the previous July, after the war had been lost in May, Bartomeu had sent a private courier from the Zurich bank to the farm with a note for Papa. In it, he informed Papa that the bank would continue holding all disbursements until the attitude of the occupation-forces could be fathomed.

Bartomeu had become extremely concerned that Papa's sudden spending, or even receipt, of any monies (whatever the currency) during this time could inflame problems with the overly-cautious occupation authorities. Because the transfers were still set up to go through the Frankfurt bank, this could alarm the Americans, in particular. The state of the economy, and the Americans' imperialist rules against fraternization, made their military command extremely suspicious whenever a German flashed cash, particularly when that cash included dollars. The Allies had already started trying to lock down the old Nazi currency, preparing to remove it from circulation, to replace it soon with something of their own design.

Finally, in mid-December, 1945, Bartomeu had been able to take the train himself from Basel to Strasbourg, and from there to Nassau. With the French Zone fully active, his route along the Rhine avoided crossing into the American sector. And with his Swiss passport, the French had no qualms about giving him unimpeded transit of either their own territory or their occupation zone within western Germany.

Bartomeu had not warned us that he was coming; he had set out assuming, correctly, that we would not be travelling so soon after the war. His professional reason for the visit (and, with it, avoiding the chance that the occupation forces might intercept a letter or telegram) was to bring Papa up to date with all the account figures. Long-delayed, these constituted those from the bank's activities during the war, the result of Bartomeu's preemptively transferring our physical assets to New York, unknown to us (until Reinhold's revelation to me), after he had broken off all communication in fear for the family's safety.

His goal in both these last two actions had been to hide our accounts from the Nazis. The dossier on Papa that Reinhold had retrieved from the Gestapo mentioned nothing about them, so the blackout had been successful: the dossier's very existence demonstrated that the deception had been a vital, unfortunate necessity.

Bartomeu revealed that, with the money the bank had earned on the account during the war (the permanent account holdings had essentially doubled), there was plenty for us all to leave Germany and resettle anywhere else in the world. Yet none of us would even consider such an idea. The Nazis had not driven us out: if at all possible, we would not now abandon our home just after they had been defeated and their heinous curse lifted, at last.

Before he left Singhofen, he acted on his personal reason for the trip: he and I had the chance for a long talk. I was finally able to be fully open, to tell someone everything that had happened, unbuffered, uncensored. He was shocked, appalled, supportive, comforting.

Bartomeu revealed more: what he already knew about what had gone on.

"Reinhold may not have told you, but he was in Zurich on SS business the very month after he had recognized you on the railroad siding. Suddenly and after years of silence back in touch with me, he was distraught, panicked, struggling to keep his sudden realization, his mental breakthrough, his drastic change of deep personality, all secret, completely constrained in order to avert another mental breakdown.

"Finding you there, seeing you in that condition, that predicament, had blown apart the comfortable world of denial that he had constructed to control the trauma of his mental injury: his acceptance of the Nazis, his betrayal of what he and Edo had accomplished together, their very life together.

"In all those years long ago, he had rarely mentioned your family to me, and then, only in quickest context of setting up the accounts. But after that encounter, your safety was his continual, overriding concern!

"It was only that following August, just before he had succeeded in spiriting you out of the camp, on his final assignment through Zurich, that he seemed to have attained a degree of purposeful peace, of clarity and surety, so near to that which I, myself, had witnessed so long ago, during his years with Edo. He asserted that he had committed himself to getting you out of there and back home, no matter how high the cost to himself.

"You were truly your uncles' special baby, their *golden boy*, their entire lives!"

Paul and Gretchen's engagement dragged on ("eternally!" as she lamented) for eleven months, forced on them by the U.S. Army's restriction, barring GI marriages with German women. I didn't see how this prohibition could possibly stand, given Paul's estimate that over four million German soldiers—husbands, fiancés, boyfriends and friends—had died in the war. This had left emotionally destitute too many German women, "some of the best women in the world!" Paul had asserted, to Gramma's knowing, and loving, smile.

Then, with cooler heads prevailing, by the end of September 1946, the restrictions on everyday fraternization between soldier and civilian had been lifted, and the restoration of more personal freedoms both to GI and "kraut" had begun.

As a colonel within the occupation command, Paul had early knowledge that the marriage ban was to be lifted completely during that coming December, 1946, but he couldn't wait. He sought, rushed and received quickly, the official waiver required to marry Gretchen two months before that date, before the wind could have a chance to teethe the wolf-days of winter.

312

They scheduled the wedding for Friday afternoon, October 11, to take place within the still ruined, but under reconstruction, St Bartholomew's in Frankfurt.

This posed a new set of problems for me: Gretchen and Paul had asked me to supply the music.

The biggest obstacle was the organ. Having evaporated in flames during the British firestorm that obliterated the Altstadt on the 22nd of March, 1944, the stolid, antique-Victorian instrument was no more.

Neither could I find much help among the musicians of the City. I had become involved that year with local attempts to resuscitate the area's musical life, but this was not without a mountain of difficulties.

The classically 19th-century, Hoch Conservatory building, like the late-medieval *Dom*, had been gutted during the firebombing. Jewish members of the faculty that I had known were now dead, had already flown or were now fleeing post-war Europe. And the other few teachers I could locate were simply too overwhelmed by post-war misery and those on-going shortages.

The city- and the cathedral-staff had begun working diligently to restore at least minimal religious services to the *Dom* as soon as practical. The grand organ bombed and burned away, a work-around had been obtained in the form of a smaller, two-manual-plus-pedal semi-portable organ. This *portatif* sat on the floor of the nave, wrapped within a tarp-framework. The roof was being rebuilt, and the windows stood still open, unglazed, so the portatif was uncovered, repositioned and played only while accompanying those resurrected hymns or masses.

Yet this return of services to the *Dom* shone a powerful sign of hope for the ultimate rebuilding of the City. The Cathedral, the site for 500 years of the elections and coronations of Holy Roman emperors, and one symbol of the 1848 liberal revolution, was the immortal phoenix around which the City would arise, reborn.

But any organist performing there now just had to hope to Heaven that all the seasonal, and day-into-night changes of temperature and humidity in a building open to every mood of wind and weather wouldn't have driven that poor portatif horribly out of tune, or caused even one of its wooden mechanisms to swell and seize. Organists' prayer-service actually started well before they had even walked into the building!

The Old City being still in ruins and the electrical system still undependable, Paul had to find an electrical generator to keep on hand to power any temporary lights or equipment needed. A tech sergeant was very happy to requisition one, bring it by and maintain it that day in exchange for the colonel's deliberate amnesia concerning the NCO's (still forbidden) German wife and new baby.

With the organ capable of taking its wind-pressure either from a small electrified turbine or from its hand-pump bellows, this power supply reassured me that it would be playable.

For the service then, and for me, in particular, lurked the problem of the music itself. I definitely was not going to perform that damned wedding march from Wagner's opera *Lohengrin*, the notorious "Here Comes the Bride" ("big, fat and wide" as Paul sang it). It wasn't allowed anyway. The colonel and his family were Episcopalians and this denomination forbade that operatic monstrosity in their services. I liked them already!

An young oboist, once my student at the *Hoch'sche*, was available. But, having to work around the organ's limitations, in war-worn Frankfurt, I could find only a single arrangement for oboe and organ that would work as a slow processional. I simply didn't have time to extract one from an orchestral suite myself, nor to charge through Gelchen's boxes in an unbounded rummage-quest for something else.

This singular work was the *Arioso*, the opening *Sinfonia* from Bach's cantata No. 156, "𝕴𝖈𝖍 𝖘𝖙𝖊𝖍 𝖒𝖎𝖙 𝖊𝖎𝖓𝖊𝖒 𝕱𝖚𝖘 𝖎𝖒 𝕲𝖗𝖆𝖇𝖊" [*I stand with one foot in the grave*].

When I told Gretchen, she was a little taken aback, but Paul almost bent double, laughing. She wasn't sold on it; he wouldn't have anything else.

"It's too perfect!" he laughed.

October 11, 1946, dawned at last: cloudless, bright, and promising warmth after a week of clouds, rain and cold.

That morning we drove from the farm to the *walls-standing-broken-and-forlorn-amid-cinder-and-brick-piles* that had once been our vibrant, imperial, *Altstadt*. From there, my family went to the few rooms that we had been able to rent. Some streetcar lines were running again; I rode, then walked directly to the *Dom*.

Now, every time I approached the cathedral, or stood within it, waves of intimate sorrow from seeing a city, a history, a people lost crushed me with ever greater vehemence. This was the site of my youth, the *Dom*'s tower an axle of constancy around which had revolved everything that seemed so permanent in my earliest years.

The ruins of the *Dom* itself reminded me, too mournfully, of the mindless injury inflicted on the main synagogue, the one Papa and I had visited that sorrowful, terror-riven night almost exactly eight years before. It was then that Germany had sealed her fate. A nation cannot flourish on hatred of others, for that hatred will always turn about, to rip hater himself asunder.

The perpetual division of mankind into "them" and "us", the *Saints* and the *Sinners*, the beloved and the despised, had wrought ruin once again upon a never-learning world. One faction always asserts "We are the best, the wise, the strong, the ruling race", but there is no super-race. There are, in fact, no races: there are only humans.

I exerted myself, exalted my spirit from such sorrowful musings.

"Sursum corda," [*Lift up our hearts*] I whispered, thinking gratefully of the blessings my life had accrued from the Dom's martyred Father Vogler, only to sense a distant, mass-echoing, "Habemus ad Dominum." [*We lift them up unto the Lord.*]

Walking about the building, I scanned its fabric, checking the state of preparations. Amid reconstruction, the building itself was bare, bereft of the golden altars, saintly images, and shining, commemorative decorations that had so brightened it those years before. But the portable organ had been moved into place, its room-brightening pipes cleaned and aligned.

Earlier that month, I had been able to locate Heinz Neustadt, a tuner of the *Dom*'s previous organ, when I had played it for those early masses. He was already at work that morning, assuring the portatif's fitness for service.

While he and I chatted, a couple of U.S. soldiers came in and lay a ladder up against the pier to the right of the choir and altar. One climbed as the other held the ladder steady.

At the exact height he wanted, the ascender searched carefully, then worked until he was able to get a hook-holder wedged securely onto the red sandstone pier. The groundling then handed up to him what must have been at least a two-meter-long rod-bundle. From that hook soon hung a cord stretched into a triangle as it held that rod by its extremes. He untied two knots before allowing the fabric wrapped around its inner dowel to fall. On the right unfurled the U.S. flag, its 48 pristine white stars shining 6 by 8 against a navy-blue field, the 13 red and white stripes flowing down, around it. To its left hung a Texas flag: the single, large white star on its wide, blue field, its individual red and white stripes moving with the light breeze coming through the unglazed, gothic windows of the *Dom.*

I stood and stared.

The two soldiers stepped back to plumb their work, clapped their hands to scare away some too-interested pigeons that had flown in onto the nave scaffolding. They then moved to the opposite pier, on my left, and went through the same motions of setting up the ladder, and looping the rope holding a second rod through the mouth of the hook placed there.

When the GI atop the ladder let the fabric down, the flag held on the right was that of the city of Frankfurt, so much like that of Texas, except instead of the blue field with the star, it had a white field with a gold-bordered, red shield bearing the old, white, imperial eagle.

And to its left—it made me catch my breath—was the black-red-gold of the Republic, the flag of the Frankfurt Parliament! Paul had found one!

That flag of the liberal revolution hung now almost directly above the spot where, thirteen years before, I had sought Father Vogler's help with my conspiracy to protect Hannah, to shield a helpless unfortunate against the mindless machinations of Nazi tyranny. To me, it was as if the '48-ers were somehow acknowledging, commemorating an act they approved of, that at least some of them would gladly have undertaken themselves, if they had but been vouchsafed the chance.

Paul had made certain that his grandmother, her spirit, his ancient family, would be here!

Herr Neustadt stayed on hand after completing his tune-up of the *portatif.* He loved listening to organs as much as tinkering with them.

Sarge pulled a line in from the generator outside, to tap into its electrical system to drive the portatif's blower. I tried to play it, but something was amiss: no power was reaching the organ!

In quick solution, Heinz stepped in, push-pulling the levers working the original bellows. The little organ began to sing out, to fill the open space of the *Dom* with its music.

But, dammit! What now?

Although the portatif had two, matching bellows that filled alternately when hand-pumped, one of them had begun suddenly to wheeze from an air-siphoning leak! We had no time to take it apart to find the rip and fix it! As long as the wind-chest was forced to depend on those bellows, instead of its electric-power fan, only one of the two manuals could be used, and I had to limit the air-demand from the number of voices required on that manual as well as by the pedal-board. We were going to have to wing it.

Talk about having one foot in the grave!

Passing through the occasional U.S. Army MP's stationed at the doors to keep any who hadn't been invited out of the building during the rite, the guests started arriving, filtering into the rows of temporary seating.

Paul had set up the ceremony, as close as it could be under the circumstances, to be in the American style he was accustomed to. I wasn't sure what a wedding should look like under these conditions: my two older sisters had had simple, civil ceremonies. The only religious wedding I had been to was the Fuhrmanns' and I was fairly certain there wouldn't be any wine-glass crushing or cries of "Mazel tov" during this *simcha*!

The congregation included at least one general that I could see, standing beside Catherine, the lovely English wife of Paul's brother, George. She was the daughter of the vicar of St Nicholas's in Wells-next-the-Sea, the town nearest the grass-runway, Norfolk airfield that George and his bomber, the "Brünnhilde's Revenge," had been stationed at during the war, until it and he were shot down over Cologne.

In our side of the seats were Mama, Papa, Gramma, as well as my older two sisters, their husbands, and their young, growing, and surprisingly well-behaved broods from Wiesbaden and Darmstadt. Several family-friends, including the Brandts and their extended family, had come into the city from the Taunus.

The priest and Colonel Ziegler walked into the south transept.

Behind Paul came his still-bandaged brother, (for a proud month, and now blue- rather than green-uniformed) U.S. *Air Force* Colonel Georg Ziegler, followed by an officer that I recognized as one of those Thanksgiving-day-celebration cooks. They all walked slowly toward a temporary altar, with seats and prayer bench, that had been set up in the crossing.

Paul was so handsome in his full-dress uniform, with his ribbons and decorations! He, his brother and friend stood to the nave-facing chaplain's left, on the same side as the U.S. and Texas flags.

Matching them, almost immediately, Gretchen's best friends from Singhofen, Anna Zimmermann, Helga Riemann and Bettina Arnim-Scholz, carrying small bouquets, moved toward the altar from the north transept to stand on the opposite, the German side. Paul had said that this wasn't the usual custom—they should have walked in long, slow procession before Gretchen—but (given the need to clear out for the reconstruction workers) they had opted for quicker simplicity.

I motioned to Heinz to start working the levers that pumped the bellows; the oboist stood at his music stand, watching for my cues.

We started together and—I was amazed!

Because of problems with scheduling during on-going reconstruction, we had

316

not been able to practice here within the still-skeletonous *Dom*, so the sounds were new, and rapturous. Even with its reduced voice, the organ provided a warm harmonic bed for the magical, poignant tones of the oboe, echoing from the red sandstone columns, re-calling from the empty, airy spaces of the aisles, the transepts and the choir! With the skyward-reaching regions of the roof, and the windows still unglazed, open to the sky, it was much like being within a sun-streaked glade, deep in a forest.

So lovely, my little sister walked slowly from the west entrance, up the center of the nave, between the halves of the congregation, split to her either side.

Gramma had used satin purchased several years ago to create a shimmeringly light blue dress, layered in antique white lace. Gretchen carried a simple bouquet, decorated with two sets of ribbons that fluttered down from it; one set was red, white and blue, the other, black, red and gold.

Her blond hair cascaded in large, open curls from beneath a simple veil matching her dress's intricate lace.

I glanced up from the keyboard; she winked at me as she walked past—she couldn't stop smiling!

As she came to where the congregation sat, the Americans all rose to their feet as soon as she stepped nearly abreast of them. The Germans quickly copied the maneuver.

When she got to the altar, she stopped and turned to face Paul. The oboist and I finished; the priest awaited the silence, ushered within the oboe's plaintive, fading resonance.

Then, he began loudly, in English, "Dearly beloved ..."

I was awestruck! Perhaps it was the limits of my experience, but I had never heard a congregation called that, or by any comparable German or Latin phrase in any of the services I had ever attended, been organist for, or witnessed! These Episcopalians sounded different: less cowed, more intimate. I'd have to watch how things went with Gretchen and Paul. I hoped this might be a sign that she would be truly happy!

Still at the console, I worked to set the organ's voices to those I wanted for the final piece, hoping that it could continue to wheeze through my selection on its one good lung.

Sarge interrupted, pssst-ing from the back side of the nearest pier. I looked over; he gave me the thumbs-up signal.

I flipped the blower switch to its 'on' position, heard the whispering air pressure rise in the organ's wind chest, and happily added the portatif's louder, brighter voices I wanted for the ending piece of the ceremony.

Lacking hymnals, there had been no congregational singing, so my two pieces were the only music.

Soon, though, I heard the phrase Paul had told me was my cue, "You may now kiss the bride!" I looked around the edge of the organ case and watched my sister being pulled into the arms of her husband—an exact repeat of what David and I had experienced in our room that first evening, standing together, in Gelchen's house in Leipzig.

I burst the little organ open with the joyous melodies of the third movement of Bach's Organ Concerto No. 1 in G major. The organ was now loud enough that it startled pigeons that had returned to the *Dom*, roosting among the scaffolds. The birds flew down into the nave, circled above the group standing at the altar, then shot out through the windows, into the afternoon sky.

Sitting back from that finale, I heard my sister call, "Edi!"

I peeked around the console. I thought that Paul had said that the previous piece would accompany the recessional but, to my surprise, he and Gretchen were still standing in place, holding each other and smiling.

"Edi! Laß uns mal tanzen!" [*Let's dance!*] she called.

I laughed; I knew exactly what she meant: Bach's *Fugue à la Gigue*.

In the midst of playing, from the corner of my eye I could see some among the congregation swaying, almost bouncing, to the rhythm. "Just like they did in Leipzig!" I chuckled to myself.

Everyone applauded and laughed; it was so rewarding to see that they were starting off with such joy, that I had been permitted the distinction of helping incite.

Still standing at the altar, Paul explained, in German then in English, that in many American weddings at that point, the bride and groom would run from the church-building to escape in their car, while their friends and family threw rice at them for good luck. However, he said firmly, given the continuing food shortage, this was not something he would allow!

"I have been informed by my well-wishing associates," he motioned toward his brother and fellow officers, "that there will be a reception, with food and drink, somewhere nearby. They hope that all of you will grace us with your presence there." He paused, looked down at Gretchen. She smiled and nodded; he continued.

"But before that, my wife and I would be deeply honored if you would accompany us on a short walk. We would like to do something to honor the heritage of the families that we now share."

The congregation stood; he and Gretchen retraced her earlier path between the halves of the congregation, down the nave and toward the west tower. She held his hand in her left, and still carried the bouquet at her waist, in her right hand.

This was a development that they had not even hinted at!

When they paused and motioned for me to come with them, I walked over and got into position behind them, with Mama and Papa, my hand held securely within the firm grip of my Gramma.

The newly-weds led us out of the *Dom*, guided our steps carefully through the rubble that lay heaped to its west, out into the wasteland cleared from the rubble of what had once been houses and shops between the medieval streets of *Alter Markt* and *Saalgasse*, and past the ruin-piles of the Römerberg.

By crossing the plaza, the extension of *Bethmannstrasse* toward *Wedel Gasse*, they led the procession directly toward their goal: the Paulskirche.

Its bombed-out walls still stood, but stark, roofless: a disconsolate skeleton, propped up by mere scaffolding.

Paul and Gretchen stopped at the southwest corner of its south tower.

He turned to us, tucked his cap beneath his arm and spoke in German, with Gretchen repeating each sentence in her now well-practiced English.

"In this *Paulskirche* only two years shy of a century ago, members of our family strove to bring democracy to the German people. The crushing of that revolution by vicious conservative, imperial forces is perhaps the single most direct reason why we are here, and in this condition, today.

"We would like to pay honor to them and to the effort exerted by them then, in the prayerful and determined hope that, at last, they may be listened to *now*."

There were some quiet *amen*'s, and one 'hear, hear!'

They both turned toward the ruin. While Paul bowed his head, watching her, Gretchen stepped toward the corner of the tower, and placed her double-ribbon wedding-bouquet at the wall, beneath one of those plaques memorializing the long-ago, liberal, Frankfurt, assembly. She then stepped backwards, rejoining Paul, still facing the building.

After a few silent moments, Gretchen looked up at Paul. They kissed.

Turning about, they nodded toward Gramma. They lowered their gaze as she took half a step forward before reciting, in a raised, serious voice, a truly personalized version of Christmas-cantata lyrics that she had chosen from among those she had cherished for so long:

Höchster, schau in Gnaden an	*Highest, behold with Grace*
Diese Glut gebückter Seelen!	*This fervor of reverent Souls!*
Laß den Dank, den wir dir bringen,	*Let the Thanks, that we bring Thee,*
Angenehme vor dir klingen,	*Sound before Thee pleasantly.*
Laß uns stets in Segen gehn,	*Let us walk steadfastly in Blessing,*
Aber nie wieder geschehn,	*But may it happen **never again**,*
Daß uns der Tyrann möge quälen.	*That **the Tyrant** might torment us.*

[BWV 63: "Christen, ätzet diesen Tag"
Johann Michael Heinecius (?)]

Again, some quiet *amen*'s spirited amongst us.

Paul replaced his cap, looked at Gretchen and smiled. He then turned toward the small crowd, pushed his cap at-ease, farther back on his head, and with a huge grin called out loudly, "Läßt mal ess'n! – Let's go eat, y'all!"

♪ DMD-26b#c

Des Musikers Leben
— Chapter 27 —
A Musician's Life

Augh! The house was dead!

With my little sister married and gone, only Molly pestered me for attention!

I had become so bored that I had even worked through Mr. Czerny's dreaded *School of Velocity* backwards. I didn't play the exercises in reverse order: I played the actual notes in reverse order! And when I got to the front, I returned to it from there, switching staves, playing the left-hand notes with my right hand, up an octave (or more) and Czerny's right-hand notes with my left, transposed down an octave. Excellent practice, challenging, but just how out-of-your-mind blasé do you have to be to do something that crazy?

I couldn't find decent housing in Frankfurt, to permit me to stay there and help with rebuilding the Conservatory, and travelling back-and-forth like I did when I was a teenager had now become too difficult and time-consuming, both because of fuel shortages and the continuing interference at the internal border installed between the French and American occupation forces.

Everyone in Germany was feeling unsettled, unsure, uneasy: how long would the occupation last, how would the nation be reorganized, if it were to be allowed to re-form at all? I felt trapped within a Germany whose blind, at times fumbling, search for itself only complicated my own attempts at self-reconstitution.

I received the letter the afternoon of Friday, November 8. I read it, then re-read it; the very next day, I told my parents about it, and revealed my plans.

"Stockholm? Are you certain, Edi? It's 1500 km away—that's even farther than Barcelona!" my mother responded.

She questioned my decision, reviewing my reasons patiently, but ultimately supported me in it, despite her unmistakable, deep desire to keep me there, at home. She was simply too strong to let her own needs interfere with the lives of her children.

The Swedish Royal College of Music had invited me to join their faculty as a visiting professor of keyboard performance, and counterpoint. I thought myself an odd choice, for them to seek someone from so far afield, but the letter did mention some of their faculty's attendance at certain long-ago *KdF* concerts, citing my performance there of Bach's and the Schumanns' works, in particular.

Stockholm it would be!

January 22, 1947, I rushed to make that Wednesday morning's train.

Excitement whitewashed my nerves. A new people, new language, new institution: this would definitely further my education and experience, certain to be of use when (I never thought 'if') I return home.

At last—after two, exhausting days of crowded trains and queasy ferries!—I stepped out into the frigid air of the Stockholm station and rushed into its enclosed, waiting area. I didn't know why the greater cold hadn't crossed my mind! Obviously, Stockholm would be more frigid than Frankfurt: it was almost exactly a thousand kilometers closer to the North Pole!

One step outside the station brought my first real look at this new land.

Shock, homesick memories and abyssal regret awaited any German who might now chance upon this large city, serene, pristine, with neither wreck nor scar of war anywhere to be seen!

So I stood, attending the flood of melody, of soothing refreshment, of a soul longing to be restored.

The arctic breeze seized and shook me! Such free-embracing, world-opening, sparkling cold I had not felt in so many years! The shimmering blue sky, the golden sun: the wind-stroking Swedish flags. They beckoned a refuge to one, now standing solitary, adrift: *Du gamla, du fria ... Du tysta, du glädjerike sköna.* [*You ancient, you free ... You quiet, you joy-rich beauty.*]

I stood entranced, in the overwhelm of new, iced sensation.

Then the cold tickled its way into my wrap: a warm apartment awaited.

I hailed a taxi and set off!

The College staff had been very helpful, finding me temporary housing fairly near campus—less than a kilometer distant: on Sibyllegatan, near Karlavägen—until I might find something for myself.

With the hyper-sensitive Allied occupation still imposed on Germany, Bartomeu could only disburse small amounts of cash from the accounts to my family there. However, he was able to transfer to me in Sweden any amount that I needed, either from those accounts, or from the ones I had lately inherited directly from Reinhold. Those funds gave my search for longer-term accommodations in Stockholm both extended freedom and vastly more possibility.

Aided by new-found college and community friends, I was soon able to track down and obtain a lease on a two-level, top-floor apartment in a building within sight of the RCM, along the strikingly wide, almost forested length of the great boulevard, Valhallavägen.

Shortly after moving in, I had my *Steiner* delivered to me there. With the extra open-space, I was able to put the piano on the top floor, with one story's insulation to guard against its sound's carrying, disturbingly into adjoining apartments.

This wide distance between the piano and my neighbors was vital: many nights found me utterly unable to rest.

I would fall deeply a-dream, precipitously asleep, so quickly that on some mornings I would find large ink spots in the sheet, soaked down into the mattress, where I had plummeted unconscious while holding a fountain pen, marking my own music scores or my students' papers.

But soon in the night, I would too often wake with a start, my heart racing, the bed wet with sweat, from the specter of being chased by demon brownshirts, by *Hiwis*, while trying desperately to rescue a multitude of suffering, fleeting spirits.

Other nights, the beloved would come.

David and Esther! the Rebbe and Rebbetzin! Edo and Reinhold flashed into view! Before my sorrow-swollen eyes, they led visions, thousands upon thousands of faces, of smiling lives and undeserved deaths of women, men, teenagers, children, grandparents, infants and elders, of scholars, lovers and fighters!

Marooned on mountain top—glacial precipice, Áhkká—I could not, dare not turn away! I had to look each in the eye!—each face: the unyielding, undying glow of divine memory! And I could not quiet the *Deutsches Requiem* psalm, enrobing each of them, chanting sparrows and enchanting swallows, soaring, diving, sweeping: ever northward-streams rising from the sylvan length of Valhallavägen, encircling me from soft push to shaking pulse of free, high-soaring waves! 𝔚𝔦𝔢 𝔩𝔦𝔢𝔟𝔩𝔦𝔠𝔥 𝔰𝔦𝔫𝔡 𝔡𝔢𝔦𝔫𝔢 𝔚𝔬𝔥𝔫𝔲𝔫𝔤𝔢𝔫, 𝔥𝔢𝔯𝔯 𝔷𝔢𝔟𝔞𝔬𝔱𝔥! [*How lovely are thy dwelling places, O Lord of Hosts!*]

The ache! the ache! the never-ending, heart-, back-, soul-breaking ache!

The clock! the clock! turn it back!

Oh, damn it! Germany! Help me, damn you! Turn the clock back, all those years, back! Return what you have destroyed, all that you have stolen from me!—that I helped destroy!

Blind as Höðr, we let Loki raise our arms, aim the loathsome dart!

Loosed, again and again—unstoppably again!

The beloved! The beautiful! The fair ones fell, fell, kept falling, falling!

Stop!

Mid-scream I awoke, a-blur, jumped from the bed, paced the floor, my heartbeat pounding in the soles of my feet as, sweat-slick, they touched the death-cold, wooden floor. Across the room, down the stairs, into the kitchen—why was I here?—I stared out the window, scanned the distant darkness!

The city slept. I searched.

The Seeress sang, "Níu man eg heima, níu íviði, mjötvið mæran fyr mold neðan. ... Baldr hugrakkr, fallegr Baldr: Baldr mun koma!" [Old Norse: *Nine homes I remember, nine fading abodes of the great World-Tree beneath the ground. ... Baldr the brave, the beautiful Baldr: Baldr will come!*]

Cold, numb, I returned to bed, grasping at sleep, lying on my David-hugging right side, holding tightly a too-yielding pillow: ersatz companion, thin, poor pain-deceiving comfort.

But there, with rising streams of blue-nascent, gold-morning light the blessed Madonna, sweetest *Mamesheh*, enfolded me, soothed my worldly woes, bade that wide-stretching cosmos recede, and those precious tabernacles settle, rest, retire.

322

Life beyond the house assuaged those hidden travails.

My tenure as a teacher at the Kungliga Musikhögskolan [*Royal College of Music*] was challenging, highly interesting, and as rewarding as my time at any school, particularly after my introduction to the Royal Family.

Not long after my arrival in 1947, I had been invited to perform for Crown Princess Louise, originally of Battenberg, who was charmed to find a fellow Hessian who could also speak English with her. She spoke so glowingly, so powerfully of her adopted homeland, of the wonder of its people that she became, to my mind, rather a Nordic Nikos. I just prayed that none of my beautiful Swedes would ever have to pay so high a price for this nation, as he had for his.

The Crown Prince, Gustav Adolf, was also favorably inclined toward me and my endeavors, increasingly so after I had expressed my condolences over the death of his eldest son, Prince Gustaf Adolf, Duke of Västerbotten (who, at only 39, had been victim of a plane crash in Copenhagen), and extended this commiseration by relating the similarly distressing, sudden demise of my uncle. It was a so common, too-human pain.

Often sought out thereafter for personal recitals or receptions at the Palace, I tried to include at least one of my pupils, always making a priority of introducing my students to this prominent, public realm.

I was well aware that they were my charge, for whom I had been brought there: not to be a German prodigy on display, but to nurture Swedish talent and place it before the nation. I was determined to do for them in this place what Hindemith, dearest Geli—and Reinhold, too—had done for me in mine.

However, the professorial rewards of those productive years at the KMH were not without personal trial. The fleeing-chase dreams and angst-fueled night-terrors dipped in frequency, but worsened in intensity.

With deep relationships so very difficult, and my aging Baby Bear, Molly, left comfortably with my parents at the farm, I surrendered myself when not in class to that one delight to which I was able to dedicate myself, completely and without reservation. That was to perform. If I didn't have a concert scheduled, at the College or within the city during the week, or one booked somewhere else on the weekend, I'd arrange a private one at the apartment, in the evening late after lectures and lessons, or on Saturday.

Food and refreshments were only a pretense: I held these soirées purely for the chance to chat, more so, to perform! I had become able to open myself to others fully, emotionally, only while on stage.

————[1950]————

These years passed quickly in Stockholm, with teaching, concerts, the recurring opportunity to play at Drottningholm Palace.

Such a beautiful city! Its northern Venice-like character, nestled among Nordic inlets, lakes and streams soothed and inspired. Late hours spent nestled on the organ, within the baroque splendor of the Katerina Kyrka became the frequent balm to my persistent aches, to my inner self, so painfully riven, bereft.

Then, one mid-Spring evening in 1950, I held another of my friends-and-faculty dinner-concerts. Two of the guests were the Järnssons, Fredrik and Emilia, both Ph.D.'s from the University. Emilia held her degrees in biology and comparative anatomy; her husband, in physics.

Each of them was extremely fond of obscure, interesting or provocative facts about their subjects or, indeed, details of any developments they might have heard of from their fellow-professors. I could count on them to spur lively, even provocative conversation.

Apparently inspired by our dessert that evening, Emilia revealed that the white of an egg is essentially the same thing as the fluid that flows when a pregnant woman's water breaks.

She added excitedly, "And humans also still produce the attached container for yolk! But little is ever placed within it: it atrophies early during pregnancy! So, we mammals still develop within the structure of an egg!"

Her captive, soirée 'class' commented politely how interesting that was, despite any queasiness it might otherwise have evoked during our meringue-based dessert-course discourse!

My local solicitor and sometime dinner companion, Jörgen, stayed over that night. In the morning I rose early and, despite feeling lung-congested, feverish, and a bit woozy, stepped quietly into the kitchen to start breakfast. Our usual breakfast tended more toward brunch, and was rather more substantial, northern-European farmer-fare—ham, eggs, sausage, oatmeal, coffee—than strictly continental.

Hoping the meal and an escorting, slow, dark cup of coffee might restore my state, I started getting the required ingredients out and ready.

I placed the chosen eggs on the counter, thinking they were well secured.

But one of them rushed the edge, hurled itself off into space, and arced onto the tile floor. It broke open, the yolk almost intact, the white running to escape the sharp-edged shell.

I knelt to sop it up.

The dessert-lecture-primed vision—golden yellow of the yolk, the large, blue sparkles within the floor-tiles—and suddenly I was back in the *Sonderkommando*, extracting Esther and Albert's baby from his womb-water, flowing out into corpse-effluent, ejecta-dreck.

But I couldn't grasp him! He kept slipping and slipping and slipping out of my hands! The SS-guard was going to beat me! When I thought I had finally taken hold, he fell apart, disintegrating into a nauseating soup of vernix caseosa and lanugo, of baby-skin, blond hair and blue eyes.

I fell back onto my butt, against the cabinet, the room now hidden in a growing, darkening mist.

"Jörgen! Hjälp mig!" [*Jörgen! Help me!*] I yelled, as I slumped over.

The morning fell dark.

Two days later I regained full consciousness between the callous sheets of an antiseptic-reeking hospital bed.

Bacterial pneumonia: the doctors and nursing staff had been working with American and British suppliers to secure more penicillin, enough to get me fully out of danger. The first courses of treatment had pulled me back from death; the doctors were yet watching for signs of life.

I tried to raise myself: I was stiff, achy, hungry, thickly congested.

I angled myself up slightly, turned my head to see who might be in the room. In a diaphanous corner stood Edo and Reinhold, arms around each other's waist. They smiled.

I was exhausted. I flopped back down on the pillow and exclaimed, "Und ich möcht' doch **Erdbeeren**!" [*And I still want some* **strawberries**!]

I laughed, coughed, then coughed out my laughter. No one else there understood.

It was time to go home.

The following week, well on the way to what should have been a restful recovery, I paced the apartment. I couldn't relax, wouldn't allow myself to put up with the postal delay: to write a letter, then have to sit, raging with impatience for several more days, hoping, fiddling, waiting: desperate for a reply. It was already April and I had to let the director at the Royal College of Music know very soon whether I would remain on staff, starting a new year in the fall!

A Stockholm telephone operator put me through to Germany, and I finally got an operator in Frankfurt who understood what I needed.

The new director of the *Hoch'sche*, Walther Davisson, wasn't available; I left a wordy message with his secretary.

When I hung up, I could barely remember the conversation. It had been emotional and vitally draining; I hoped I hadn't sounded too desperate! Of course, the secretary didn't remember me, but surely Herr Davisson must! We were together at the *Hoch'sche*, and then again, at the Conservatory in Leipzig!

Within interminable minutes, he returned my call. I told him to hang up and I would phone him, to pay for the call, to save the *Hoch'sche* the expense. He agreed laughing; we hung up. And then I played operator-footsies again, working to make a clear connection from Sweden, across the Baltic, then down through Denmark and the western occupation zones within Germany, to Frankfurt. But we did reconnect!

"Yes, Edi! I remember you very well! I still cherish having been witness to your accompanying Hindemith in that amazing concert the two of you gave in Frankfurt back in what, 1930! Several of the faculty have been asking if anyone knew where you were!"

I was so relieved! I continued the conversation quickly, before he might mention or ask about Thomi and Uli from our shared, Leipzig Conservatory days.

"Yes! Yes, here I am, Herr Davisson! I have been working in the Swedish Royal College of Music. Herr Davisson, I wanted to ask if there is any chance you might be able to use me on the faculty there in Frankfurt this coming year…"

"Certainly, Edi! We are in the process of planning our move next year into the new building, the one that is going up where the old one was standing, you will remember, at the Eschenheimer Tor! We are also completing plans for how the Conservatory and the Music College will fit together in their offerings—no need for them to compete! Several faculty members have been asserting that we need you here desperately, to teach, to guide and inspire! With the pace of reconstruction picking up now all throughout western Germany, churches will be needing organists and choirmasters, and theaters, opera houses and orchestras will be requiring new, highly trained musicians! Now, Edi, tell me, what is your salary expectation?"

"Herr Davisson, that doesn't matter to me just now! Simply tell me that I am on the faculty starting as soon as possible, and trust me, we can work that out later. The most important thing to me is that I return to Frankfurt and to the *Hoch'sche* as soon as possible!"

I had to squelch my unbidden, but intensely emotional reaction to that phrase. I continued, momentarily, "I must tell the director of the RCM presently whether I will remain here this coming year or not."

An aside, "Fräulein Brauer!" I heard him call out, "do you have the new schedule and faculty roster at hand?" I thought I heard a questioning response, but it was faint. "For both this summer and the fall," he replied.

Just a few moments and I heard him say quietly, "Thank you, Fräulein!" A minute of paper shuffling and his voice returned, "Edi, we need you here the first of August. Let's see, that's a Tuesday. Can you arrange that?"

"Without a doubt, Herr Davisson! With no inkling of a doubt! Thank you so much!"

"Thank you, Edi! You will be a cornerstone of the new *Hoch'sche* and our revitalized Hochschule! I will post your offering letter of appointment this afternoon. If you will sign it and return it as convenient, I will push it through the bureaucracy and everything will be official!"

"If you will send that letter by airmail, Herr Davisson, I will reimburse the cost! And I will return it the same way the very hour it touches my hands! Thank you, Herr Davisson, thank you so very much!"

He laughed. "You are most welcome! I will be awaiting your acceptance, and I will be most proud to be the first to welcome you back to our dear Conservatory!"

"It will be more rewarding for me than I can express, Herr Davisson, to be an active and productive member of staff there again!

"But, if I may ask, has anyone found the portrait of Clara Schumann that hung in the larger recital hall?"

"Yes, Edi, it has been found. It is unblemished, awaiting its return to a place of honor in the new building!"

The mere thought of that image choked me—my Clara, my dearest Clara!

I thought I might have worn out the *thank-you*'s; I didn't remember how often I'd said it by the time we hung up.

I stepped away from my desk and sat down at the *Steiner*'s keyboard, played a *forte* E-flat major chord with an octave in the bass: I smelled the sweet breeze rising from the Rhine to flood the forest, the Hunsrück, the Eifel, the Taunus. The tones echoed, echoed, faded softly down that long, blond soundboard. I pressed the keys until the strings slept, voiceless.

The sweeping melody of Schumann's *Rhenish Symphony* burst the banks of my mind and swept over every thought, every concern, every doubt.

I was returning to my Hesse, my Frankfurt, my *Hoch'sche*: I was going home!

Settled again in my city on the Main—and, once the Conservatory was within its new building, rebuilt on its previous site—routine kicked in.

The music college, however, didn't yet have its own building, so we had to scrounge to find public places, or we held classes and individual instruction in private homes, even in mine.

I was actively content, but I dared not say that I was completely happy.

This shadow was simply because the city of my aspirant youth, of my dreams and expectations, was gone. Utterly obliterated.

From Stockholm, I had longed, yearned, truly ached, to return to Germany, to *my* Germany.

It was only with my return that I saw—experienced viscerally—that it was no more.

Even more disconcerting was the realization that *my Germany* had probably never been. At least physically.

My Germany had been one of Music, the music of sounds, of words, the music of sights and smells: of Goethe, of Beethoven, of thickly packed fachwerk houses and quaint, village-costume-clad *"noch ein Bier!"* welcoming, *oom-pah* celebrations and boisterous almond-ginger fêtes.

Language, history and tradition, it had been a phantasm: the *Greater Germany* of the mind. That widely shared, Teutonic fantasy had glued this amorphous amalgamation together, variously and varyingly, across so many centuries, mixing peoples, spanning that multitude of borders: free-cities, counties, duchies, prince-bishoprics, kingdoms, empires and, too late, democracies.

My *Germany* was a sense of being, of *Volkeinheit* [*Folk-unity*], of *Volksgemeinschaft* [*Folk-community*] that had existed long before Hitler had perverted those phonemes. It had long exerted the agglomerating pull that drew us into a fractured but consoling, dialect-spanning cultural unit. But, because it was self-defined, incompletely formed, malleable and too easily manipulable, it had also fired and fueled the blindness that had seared our souls into hardness, into that insufferable, inhuman superiority-callousness that ultimately spells doom to all who fall its prey.

Germany united by militarism had been a threefold failure: Bismarck, Kaiser, Hitler.

But with this now fallow field, a Germany laid utter waste, the opportunity had arisen for us to forge a new nation, mindful of, but wisely no longer imprisoned by, the past.

It was well time that Germany not be known for Prussian compulsion, goose-step and guns, for training and inciting the armies of other nations. It was now time for true leadership: building on the foundations laid by Lessing, Goethe, Kant, Schiller, Heine and Mann, echoing even more widely through Bach, Händel, Beethoven, Schubert, Schumann, Brahms, Mahler and beyond.

Edo and Reinhold, then the Zieglers, had revealed that to be German within America had been to be well-educated, dedicated to family, business and to the welcoming, progressive community those founded and funded.

It was then these same Americans who, in Germany's time of greatest weakness, and Berlin's hour of greatest distress, had bombed its German children.

But those bombs had been candies and chocolates.

Germany had come through its 40 years of wandering in that dismal valley of the shadow of death: of defeat, of financial ruin, of cultural suicide, of war and death. It must now find its way onto the plain of enlightenment. We had to rekindle that fabled *Kerngesundheit*, that healthy core, and if it could not be restarted, to rip out those roots, to replant it and nourish it anew. Only when the highest praise other nations might aspire to should be, "Wir genießen deutsche Freiheit!" [*We enjoy German Freedom!*] would we know that this had been fulfilled!

But for now, it seemed, physical, not spiritual, reconstruction was all that mattered. The resulting phrase most seen or heard seemed always to be "neulich wiederaufgebaut." [*recently restored*] Allied bombing had devastated 60% of urban Germany. At this moment, physical rebuilding was all we had.

Yet this clean-up and construction in Frankfurt was now happening (as in those other parts of Germany I had just crossed) far too quickly, and the city was being stuffed with the ugliest of aluminum-stick and glass-sheet, faux-Bauhaus, characterless boxes. It was not "form follows function", but "form lies dead and bleeding after its assault by false frugality, and a misdirected conceit of usage."

I would never become accustomed to it. I would just learn not to see it, but to envision, to cultivate the Germany of my mind and memories.

Paul Hindemith paid a return visit to Frankfurt from America in 1952, and he and I took the opportunity to reprise our concert of 1930. The music was definitely easier for me at 31 than it had been when I was 9!

An unexpected feature of his visit was his agent, brought along surreptitiously, specifically because Hindemith thought it was time I should meet and talk to him.

Needing an agent was something that had never crossed my mind!

After Hindemith and I had recapped our ancient performance, his talent agent, Bernard Rosenfeld, came backstage. Paul had been teaching at Yale during most of his exile in the States, and had become an American citizen in 1946. He always spoke to Bernie, a New Yorker, in English, and that's how he introduced us.

After we had conversed a while, I noticed Mr. Rosenfeld cock his head, staring at me. He said, "Whoa, kid! I gotta astya—just what part of da Sout' are ya's from?"

I laughed and told him, "My uncles who taught me English lived in Texas."

"Yeah, I t'ought so!"

"And they lived in New York City, too!"

"Yeah? Dat's rich, kid! But I doan heah how it improved ya's tawkin'!"

Well, the conversation was joking and lively from there, with "Bernie" telling me everything I should be doing, how to build up my career and all the details. He would call me "Tex" and be my agent for the next decade, until he retired, when he handed the business, and me with it, over to his son, Mort.

I worked with the Conservatory and Hochschule essentially full time for the next five years, with Bernie finding me "gigs" (as he called them) for whenever I didn't have to be on site. These took me to most of the music centers of Western Europe.

By the end of those five years, I was sufficiently well-known and had a large

328

enough following from record sales—particularly after LP's had become prevalent—that I went on part-time status. I never left the *Hoch'sche* or the Hochschule
officially: I just moved gradually over into my own world.

By 1957 I had attained fame enough to be a fulltime "concert artist."

I still taught and performed in Frankfurt each fall semester, but the rest of the
time I was on the road, or in a recording studio, almost constantly.

With my earnings, plus money coming from the inheritance accounts, I
bought a newly constructed apartment building along Hasengasse: simply for its
location, not looks. It was within what had been the Old City—near the old Le-
derhalle, along where the post-war Hasengasse had been extended to include the
ancient Trierische Gasse. It was only around 400 meters in a line from where our
Drescher boarding house had stood (near the now-extirpated Konstablerwache)
and stood within easy sight of the tower of the Dom.

Having that vista helped settle somewhat my unceasing nostalgia for the obliterated beauty, that historical, real-life quaintness of the medieval-Imperial, half-
timbered, quarter-Jewish city.

The best thing about the building itself was that it provided a personal refuge.
I reserved the top storey for myself, and had its floor reinforced and sound-
proofed before taking possession. As soon as possible, after expanding and
strengthening the freight elevator to grand-piano dimensions, I had the venerable
Steiner brought over from my previous lodgings, and contracted to have the *Aleksey*-piano moved in from the farm.

Mama and Papa had brought that piano up from the basement to the big
room as soon as I had shipped my Steinway to Stockholm, so it had been well
cared for. I had made sure of that during my frequent return trips to the farm, to
my Gramma, to my childhood Singhofen, and the apple-tree graves of Eva and
Molly.

My eldest sister, Marianne, her husband, Fritz, and their younger children
were now set and ready to move back to the farm from Wiesbaden to be with
Mama and Papa and help them with the crops and chores, and with Gramma—
now 83, physically slower, but mentally as sharp and as out-spoken as ever!—so
they needed it out of the way. But they did still have the old *Dreikühige*!

Among the materials also shipped to me were those boxes of Geli's.

While going through them, cataloging their contents, I discovered a concert-
publicity photograph displaying a wonderfully vibrant image of her always-
radiant personality. I had it framed: it went onto the *Aleksey*-piano, in a place of
honor.

Within one of her stored-away books of Schumann *Lieder*, the one from which
Thomi had played and Albert had sung that first night of the twins, I found a
hand-written note of hers. On it she had inscribed each of our names—mine,
Thomi and Uli's, Albert's—along with our birthdates and a date-column she had
labeled "came into my life."

At the bottom, she had scrawled another date, inked painfully within a paper-
wrinkling arpeggio of tears: 24.11.1943.

Slamming my emotions, keeping my own losses carefully from staining it further, I slipped that sheet behind Geli's photo, snug within that frame, never to be lost, as we three had been on that date: the day she had lost her babies.

Gretchen and Paul's first child, Paul Jr., had arrived in Frankfurt during 1948, while I was in Sweden. Just like almost every grandmother in the Western World, Mama had chuckled in her letter announcing the birth, "He looks so much like his dad it's pitiful!" Their first daughter, Trudi (apparently not so pitiful: looking less like her father), was born in 1951.

With the retirement of Paul's rancher-father in 1952, the new parents decided to return to Texas to take over the "little Ziegler-family spread" as Paul always called those eight thousand scattered hectares his grandparents and parents had acquired, stretching west, outside of Fredericksburg. So, their subsequent children, the twins Astrid and Elektra (1953), Margaret "Gretel" (1957), and their youngest, a younger son, were born over there.

Paul had driven the family down to Houston to see me perform in concert in 1956, during my first tour—and first adventure in America. At this time, that large, Gulf-coast city was a low, spread-out town: humid and without much architectural character. Galveston was the little, neighboring, sea-coast town with real history and style, from its long-ago stint as an immigrant port-of-entry, and cotton port-of-exit. Yet it was the out-going, unreserved good nature of the people that gave both cities their can-do character. That was my first taste of what had drawn Edo to this region.

Being the largely absent uncle, I received letter upon overstuffed letter of extended epistles and photographs. Of course, these centered on baby pictures, christenings, birthdays, first bikes, and festival, holiday and vacation snapshots.

Although Paul's family had long-departed from their more Germanic religious roots, they still celebrated—and photographed!—every aspect of Advent and Christmas as if they still lived in the Rhineland. Paul's grandparents had been drawn to the Episcopalians because, he had explained in detail, they had found all the other local, American protestant groups of the time "little different from the rawest Calvinists—way too much of endless preaching, of unending, finger-waggling *thou shalt*'s, and utterly bereft of any European sense of the ancient, enlightening spiritual awe inherent within time-honored dignity, ritual and sacred continuity."

Without a local church in Fredericksburg, Paul and Gretchen's community—later including then-Senator and Lady Bird Johnson—had convened in members' homes or driven into Austin. So, while Paul, Jr., and Trudi had been christened by the Army chaplain in the *Dom* in Frankfurt, the younger ones had been christened in Texas. I had been "godfather in absentia" for Paul, Jr., present and standing for Trudi's christening in Frankfurt, but had missed those of Astrid, Elektra and Gretel.

Just as soon as Gretchen knew she had become pregnant with another child, she had told me his name: she was somehow certain she was carrying a boy.

Although my little sister had been the only one in the family to whom I had revealed everything, all the details of Leipzig and Auschwitz, her decision still came as a most pleasant surprise.

I rescheduled all my concert appearances to be certain I could be in Austin at the very start of 1960, when time came to church the baby that, if indeed a boy, would bear the name *David Eduard Ziegler*.

If she and Paul were going to give him those two names, I was damned sure I was going to be present there in person, with this David, at St. David's!

Although I'd seen all of them in Germany several times before, a concert in Dallas in March 1965 was the next time after David's baptism that I saw my little sister's family in Texas. Paul's brother, Georg and his wife and their two children had tagged along, too. Only Paul, Jr., could not be there. He had joined the Army after ROTC in high school and was going through basic training at Fort Polk in Louisiana, before officer training, and duty in Vietnam. He had always been determined to follow his father's military example.

I was organist for this concert's performance of Mahler's Eighth Symphony.

The organ was old, acoustically fluffy—as almost all organs in the U.S. tended to be at the time—but could be loud: it was certainly serviceable enough for this Romantic-era symphony. With the German poetry of the symphony's second part, I knew the Ziegler kids would at least enjoy trying to follow along. Although schooled in English, they had grown up largely speaking German with their mother, and often with their father and his folks, so that, whenever amongst their growing throng, I was bombarded by a passel of German-chattering Texas kids. It seemed they just *had* to see if they could manage the language with a native speaker other than their own parents!

At the reception after the concert, I noticed that little David had the arms of his jacket tied around his waist. I asked Gretchen about it.

In whispered German, she revealed, "When you hit that first chord and the orchestra and choir answered, he wet himself a little! Then, when the first section ended, and the final notes of the *Gloria Patria* faded, he turned to me and said, 'Wow!'—his eyes were as big as saucers! I cleaned him up as well as I could during intermission—the jacket's there to hide the spot. I couldn't get it fully dry!"

I laughed. He was following family precedence! But I had to hide my deeper, intense family-association with that symphony. Gretchen had been far too young back then to remember now that horribly truncated performance at the *Alte Oper* in 1927, but my memories rang, still deep, intimate. Today, at least, I was *there*, an uncle determined to avoid such devastating interruptions.

"You've started his piano lessons, like you did with the girls, right?" I asked.

"Over a year ago," she said. "None of them has seemed to be especially interested.

"But he…

"His teacher says he's exceptionally gifted: that she's never had a pupil progress as rapidly as he has. She has to slow him down, to make him concentrate on his lessons: he tries to play—and usually does!—every piano piece he hears on the radio!"

I knelt down and asked him, "Wie war das Konzert, David?" [*How was the concert, David?*]

Our beautiful five-year-old's copies of his mother's blue eyes grew huge as he said slowly, emphatically, "Unvergleichlich! Ausgezeichnet! Perfekt!" [*Incompar-*

able! Superb! Perfect!]

Within twelve months, Gretchen was driving David into Austin twice a week to study privately with members of the music faculty at the University of Texas, his tuition paid by funds still drawn on those Barcelona/Zurich accounts.

Just as I had my own, I could see the sails being lifted, the boom swung about, the tack set in preparation for David's own journey of discovery.

But I understood intimately something that they could know now only secondhand: the money paying for David's lessons was coming from Edo's death, and Reinhold's undying devotion.

It was, once again, the guiding, nurturing hand of the unsummoned angel.

[1978]

Texas-Hochzeit
— Chapter 28 —
A Texas Wedding

"Every time, so much new! New cars, new buildings, new houses and roads!

"How do they do it? Everything new, new, new! How do they keep up with such changes?" Mama had exclaimed after the latest visit with her distant-ranch, American children.

By 1964, she and Papa had travelled to America twice to see Gretchen and her family, each time taking ship from Hamburg, then riding the train from New York into Texas. Their adventure in 1970, though, was on one of Pan Am's brand-new 747's (That irked me: I had wanted to be first to ride one!), and then on the seemingly ever-expanding American Interstate Highway system.

With each exploit, their astonishment at the size of the U.S.A., particularly of Texas, grew. ("Just one state almost a quarter larger than the old Empire! And so full of German descendants!" Papa marveled, "What the hell were the Kaiser and Hitler thinking?") They seemed to be continually amazed.

Along with that, during the late 1950's stretching into the early '70's, Gretchen and Paul had tried consistently to get back to Singhofen once a year, for at least two weeks each summer. During those visits my elder sister, Liesel, would bring her children there, too, to join Marianne's brood already living there, for a great, jumbled camp-out at the farm. There would be cousins everywhere!

Of course, Mama and Papa were ecstatic when everyone showed up, but utterly exhausted by the time their grandchildren had, at last, been split between those that stayed and those to leave, and Liesel and Gretchen had packed up their tribes and headed off into their separate directions.

Paul and Gretchen always spent the final few days of their vacations with me in Frankfurt. Paul used my apartment as the base-camp for those "teach the kids their heritage" trips they would make, around Frankfurt and the Taunus, but sometimes farther afield, north along the Rhine to Bonn, Cologne and Düsseldorf or Hannover, south through Stuttgart to Zürich, eastwards into Bavaria: to Munich and Dachau, and even farther, to Salzburg and Vienna; one of their flights took them into West Berlin.

They even went to Regensburg (to get some small idea of how Frankfurt had

332

once looked) and visited its nearby *Walhalla*, that ersatz Parthenon, sitting high on its isolated hill above the Danube.

David and his sisters always slept in my music room, where David would spread his sleeping bag out right under *ole Steiner*. He said he slept better hearing it breathe its excellence for him during the night.

As he got older, he and I would play duets, or sometimes "dueling Beethoven" in competition to see who couldn't follow whom in sonata passages we'd start at random. His parents often had to tell him to get off the piano and go to sleep, but he always woke us by 06:30 every morning. That was the practicing schedule he had adopted, and he was determined to keep to it!

David had started bringing staff-paper with him on these visits. He would pull music from my collection and make his own, handwritten copies of the things he wanted to study or play back home.

Not long after, I had noticed him, writing into his staves. I watched him intently as he made his "copies." He would mark the first note of a measure clearly, but then add only lines, sprinkled with dots, accents and x's, for the contour of the following notes of that measure. I asked him why he wasn't putting the notes in for those other, following beats.

"That's all I need! Once I get the shape of the lines, the music of each page flashes and sticks in my mind, and I don't need the individual notes anymore — or even these scores for long!"

"So, I'm not the only crazy one who sees mental music-landscapes!" I thought with a chuckle.

I stepped over to the piano and played a chord, "What flavor is that, David?"

"E-flat major ... Haddekuche ... by the Rhine!" he said, without stopping to lift his head from his score-scribbling.

Yep!

In late May of 1978, my sister Liesel and her family detoured their way from a farm-visit, back to their home in Darmstadt, to bring Mama and Papa into Frankfurt.

From Rhein-Main, my parents flew with me into Dallas, for transfer to the smaller jet carrying us into Austin.

Now 21 and 18 respectively, Gretel and David had driven from Fredericksburg to Mueller Airport to greet us.

Standing on the wide sidewalk before the terminal, after pointing out the University Tower in the distance, David announced, "Mom and Dad send their apologies for not being here to pick y'all up. But they're crazy, rushing around, so busy getting everything ready for Astrid's wedding!"

The afternoon was warm and waxing. We soon got all the luggage stuffed into the old van, and Gretel drove us away. The eighty winding miles onto those rolling hills of the Edwards Plateau beckoned us outwards, into Uncle Edo's storied cowboy country.

The air became drier, our skin cooler, the sky even clearer as we travelled west and up, gaining the twelve-hundred feet in elevation from Austin. Soon, we were passing stands of leafing mesquite, what had once set my uncles laughing after I had called them "mosquito" trees. The spring had been a good, wet one. The creeks were running, the fields were green, and from the road to the farthest hills, the countryside was overlain in a random tapestry of painter's palate wild flowers.

Mid-morning, the day after our arrival, Mama walked out onto the wide front porch of the Ziegler house.

I followed, walking my coffee out beside her, and hugged her into my left side. We held together, looking out over grass-furred rises and hollows marked by errant groves of pecan and live oak, listening to the distant calls of birds we didn't recognize, and the scratches of high-plains insects we couldn't name.

"Hügelig, wie zu Hause," [*Hilly, like back home*] I said.

"Yes, but so open, so peaceful and—with no village in the distance—almost lonely," she mused quietly. Looking up at me, she smiled, then gave me a cheek-pressing, tighter hug.

"Well, back to getting ready," she sighed before stepping back into the house.

I could not believe that my young mother, that girl Papa had always flirted with, always eager to grab and kiss, was already 81, and Papa now 82. My dear Gramma had departed 18 years before. The on-rushing threat of recurrent, personal desolation was already tugging at me.

Eventually, we must all greet our orphanage.

I stood, gazing across vacant Spring meadows into the bosque, the field-edging copses, hearing a distant, now solo-singing bird.

Alone in this scant, scattered forest, I felt the connections, the ties of my life spin like the wisps of white fluff, flowing from those open, spreading arms of tall, stream-shading cottonwoods. Albert's Uli-enraptured tenor floated with the ghosting-fiber melody, intertwining once again with Thomi's playing, his furtive, enticing glance, "Im wunderschönen Monat Mai…" [*In the most beautiful month of May…*]

The wind caressed my hand, crossed my fingers, teasing my touch, just as my David had, there in Leipzig, within deepest, wielding and yielding night.

The afternoon of the wedding was again sunny, with the occasional, parallel slivers of *armadillo clouds* spinning in from the southwest. The noon-day sun was coaxing shiver-waves of heat to rise shimmering from the green and browning grass that kowtowed in repeating ripples to the breeze.

Through the screen door, Gretchen called for me from inside the house. I turned to go in, to hear our assigned seating in the big SUV.

Now dressed, I clomped around a bit unsteadily: in keeping with family tradition, I was wearing my newest, Edo-style—"Keep that champion attitude, cowboy!"—boots to the wedding.

Travelling eastwards into Fredericksburg by the main highway, Paul turned to go down South Bowie. (I was warned that "round these parts" it was pronounced "boo-ee" or best you just didn't say it!)

He turned the ponderous car-truck and parked it at an angle on West Creek Street, pointing it into the shadow beneath two big deciduous trees. They stood tall beside a sparser-shading fir, all cooling the northeastern side of the church lot.

Astrid was already in the small chapel near the street, changing into her wedding dress.

That diminutive building was an old, local farmhouse, purchased by the parish and converted in 1954 into the first St Barnabas's. You could tell it had been built by a German immigrant because of its fachwerk construction: exposed and darkly painted timber framing filled with intimately cut blocks of the pale, local limestone. This chapel reminded me so much of Frankfurt's Old City, before the war: especially of our boarding house!

The thought of that lost home, and of the Dreschers, summoned a promise from myself that I would travel to Zurich to see Daniel after I had returned to Europe. At his mother's funeral—a few years after Hannah had died—he had asserted that I was his one remaining relative of his own generation. Before his sister succumbed to her frailty, his wife, Olga and he had named one of their daughters "Hannah" in her honor. I must not neglect, never neglect.

This daydream of Daniel, and the memories of his mother and of our Hannah, conspired to inflame depression, the loneliness that had become too close a stalking companion. Of advancing age? No, I had known its stealthful, ever-lurking presence each of those fifty-one years since Edo's funeral.

I throttled my weakness. Seeing my sister's joy, I smiled, and the demon was cast off, driven far away.

Gretchen stepped into the chapel to see if she could help her daughter; Paul led the rest of us farther, into the sanctuary-building itself.

Mixed flower-pot upon planted pot of bluebonnets and Indian paintbrush covered every available space in the room. It looked like the pews had been transported, arranged in their rows across one of those prismatic Hill-Country-spring fields.

Paul greeted the vicar, who immediately turned to us, too, and made us welcome, with hand-shakes and pre-wedding small-talk before we made our way to the bride's side of the nave, to take our seats in a pew toward the front. Papa moved in, then Mama, then me. We left space for Gretchen and Paul at the center aisle. Gretchen would soon take her place beside me. Paul was in the first part of the wedding, "giving away" his daughter, traditionally, after which he would sit at the aisle, with us.

Suddenly, it sounded like we were being invaded!

David, and the University musician friends of his that he had rounded up, running late (his mother would have added, "As usual!"), had burst through the front door and were rushing inside to loft-positions around the organ console. And, conspicuously—except for David, who had on a dark suit with his persistent, black cowboy boots—all were wearing burnt-orange and white, including some who were in their Longhorn Band uniforms!

Astrid and her fiancé, Henry Gruenblatt (whose ancestors had immigrated to a farmstead close to Luckenbach in the 1850's but had both German and Slavic, *Sorbian*, roots), had known of each other most of their lives there around Fredericksburg. After a meeting arranged by Astrid's twin, Elektra, and her long-time roommate, Henry's cousin Marcie, they had dated throughout their years at the University.

Henry had been a trombone player in the University Band so, of course, David had had an easy time convincing some current band members, and several other friends from the Music Department, to travel all the way there to take part!

David's promise of a keg of *Lone Star* after the ceremony hadn't been unproductive, either!

Henry and Astrid were both about to graduate from UT Medical School in Galveston, and they wanted to "tie the knot" before hospital-residency might take them (only temporarily, they swore!) out of the State.

I watched with amusement those 'kids' pushing their seats and music stands around. Pairs of violins, horns, and trumpets, a viola, two cellos, a bass, an oboe, trombone, tuba and a snare drum—a snare drum?—had to be fitted into close position. But then, another sonorous, empty-barrel din arose as two kettle drums were wheeled in! Astrid had asked David to handle the music, but I wasn't sure she had expected it to be so thoroughly manhandled!

While that ensemble's din waned, Paul stood in the aisle chatting with us, down along the pew. Suddenly, he looked up and hurried off, toward the door. One of the guests of honor had arrived and he wanted to be certain to greet her and conduct her to the pew just behind us.

This was the home church of that guest, Claudia Alta Taylor Johnson, and had been her and President Johnson's refuge since the early 1950's. The Ziegler children had grown up with Lady Bird and Lyndon; indeed, she had taken time from her pre-inauguration duties as wife of the Vice President-elect to come into Austin, to stand, along with me, as one of David's godparents when he was christened in 1961.

I had not seen her in person since she and the President had asked me to play a recital at the White House in 1966. Recognizable from the vast, open-coiffed curl above her right eye, she was the soul of grace: always so charming, in her open-hearted, Hill-Country, Southern ways, greeting us each warmly, unfailingly always by first name.

David ran over to hug and schmooze with this, his favorite godparent (as he joked with me). He kissed her cheek, then hurried back to directing his cohort.

With our special guest seated, the near-orchestral ensemble started playing arrangements that David told me later he had written himself, and then been forced to revise after a couple of bandmates had pulled out.

"They couldn't get out of finals!" he had explained, "but I still wanted to do Handel because he's so cheerful!" He laughed, and in a co-conspiratorial, breathy whisper added emphatically, "And *gay!*—*Hallelujah!*"

David started the ceremony by conducting Variation 2, *Alla Hornpipe*, from Handel's Suite in F Major, *Water Music*. At the end of this, the priest, groom and groomsmen took their places at the altar rail. Immediately, the smooth melodies of number three from Handel's *Music for the Royal Fireworks*, "*La paix*" [*Peace*] followed.

This had introduced the slow, bridal procession. Paul Jr. and his wife Lenora's elder little daughter, Amalia, was flower-girl, and their young son Nathan "Nat" (or "Gnat" as his uncle, David, teased him, mispronouncing it, "*Guh-nat*") walked along as ring bearer, followed by Elektra, with Marcie, and other of Astrid's friends completing the long line of bride's maids.

Piercing the silence just after the music had ended, Nat sneezed, hard.

In the sneeze's arm-jerk shockwave, the ring-tied pillow he held flew into the air. With a quick swipe of his nose along his sleeve, he dove after it as it flew away. Then he popped back up, holding it aloft like a well-caught football, smiling.

Standing before the altar, Henry started laughing, guffawing a deep, guttural release of his groom-awaiting-execution tension. David held the music while the laughter spread, then ebbed into a communal, relaxing joy.

The *forte* brass of the *Fireworks' La réjouissance*, "Rejoicing", announced the arrival of the bride. Astrid entered, flowing in bluebonnet-embroidered, lace-draped, whitest silks and satins. Stepping slowly toward the altar, she processed with that ever self-confident, proud Ziegler bearing that all their children and grandchildren had inherited. Almost giggling, she winked at Nat.

Everyone at last in place, once again I heard that Elizabethan phrase of magical resonance, "Dearly beloved..."

A warm press of hands, one on each shoulder told me that Edo and Reinhold were there with us, for me, for their youngest niece, my sister, the third of their unforgettable "beautiful princesses," and for all this congregation of our own *dearly beloved*.

Ending the solemnization, the 'per regulation' kiss signaled David to burst into the same exquisitely joyful Bach organ-concerto movement that I had played at the identical point within Gretchen and Paul's wedding, in the *Dom* in 1946. And, just as then, the bride and groom didn't move, but stayed in place, hand in hand, facing the congregation, listening.

With the fading, final echoes, Astrid called out from beside her new husband, to her little brother, "David! Laß uns mal tanzen!" [*David! Let's dance!*]

I heard him laugh, take a second to reset the voices; and he indeed played Bach's *Fugue à la Gigue*, completing this commemorative double-parallel between the two weddings.

Gretchen took Paul's hand in one of hers; the other grabbed mine, and she started rocking back and forth with the dancing rhythm, just as the she and Paul had done on their wedding day in the Dom, thirty-two years before.

I glanced back; almost everyone in the congregation had joined in the rhythmic sway of celebration.

In afterward's milling about, I made my way to speak with our Lady Bird.

I simply could not miss the chance, for talking with her, hearing her voice, witnessing her soft manners and gentle mannerisms was like taking a cool, refreshing drink on a dusty, hot, Hill-Country afternoon. She spoke and we, her wildflowers, were refreshed.

Then, with the rising ruckus of laughter, the calls and hoots 'n hollers of "ya'll come on, now!" the family exited the church, moving to pack ourselves into the "now, who's ridin' with y'all? You sure ya'll got room? Nathan! Honey, y'ain't gonna fit in the back of that van! OK, well, you can ride with 'em; David, make sure he sit down! Ya'll gonna be too tight in there? Ya know, we got more cars!

Oh, well! OK!" vehicles for the short ride to the reception.

With Paul Jr.'s youngest, 18-month-old Maria, hefted onto my left arm, I wedged my vacant shoulder through the front door into the crowding banquet room, stopped and almost melted.

The smoky, sweet-tangy aroma of barbecue held me captive. I closed my eyes and breathed, until my tongue and stomach (and Maria's exploring finger in my ear) jolted me back into action. There was a long table spread out with so much food! Except for the mounds of barbecue at the far-left end and the ranks of pecan pies at the other—"Remember! Say *pih-káhn*! Every other way ya hear it is jus' plain Yankee!"—it looked like the Rhineland had exploded and its food come to earth right here! Sausages, more sausages, sauerkraut, cole slaw, potatoes in every form possible, breads (light and dark), Roggenmischbrot, Zwiebelbrot, haddekuche, kirschtorte, cheesecake and, of Frankfurter Kranz, I counted at least three! Four different kinds of light and dark beer, plus already-tapped and eagerly flowing kegs of *Lone Star* that David had had delivered from San Antonio for his bandmates, separated the long table from a smaller, round one on which the tall wedding cake perched.

We ate. And ate. The band Paul had hired played a couple of polkas, some *conjunto* and *tejano*, some beer-hall sing-alongs, some cowboy-Western. They tried their hand at some more rock-ish numbers, but (with that prevalent accordion) went back quickly to the German-folk, and Western, country favorites of the crowd.

I was truly pleased that, for once, no one even breathed a word of having me play anything! I was so full: luxuriously, Thanksgiving-style, just-roll-me-over-by-the-fire-and-let-me-sleep-dammit stuffed!

But I had to awaken, at least partially; the American marriage-ritual continued.

The bride and groom cut the wedding-cake, shoved pieces into each other's faces, missing mouths and laughing as they spread it around.

Too soon, the pair rushed off for their honeymoon trip. But, despite being bereft thereafter of its two, central characters, the party went on, with *ritardando* then *accelerando* repeats, as our stomachs conducted us back onto, and then away from the wide-arrayed buffet.

At last, our family grumbled its weighty overindulgence into the vehicles, now somehow much shrunken, and slogged away, back to the ranch, and rest.

David knocked softly on my door before dawn that next morning, calling a quiet "Uncle Edi! Get up or you'll miss it!"

Readily awake, I echoed a soft, "I'll be right there!" before slipping into some comfortable, early-morning jeans and a new, Longhorn t-shirt.

The carpet was cool, almost moist-feeling from the country air that had flowed down over it from the open windows during the night. I felt my way along it, following David's rug-silent path through the still-dark house, certain not to let the screen door slam as I stepped, with barefoot caution, out onto the unlit, east-facing, kitchen porch.

David's legs dangled, swinging slightly from his seat at the edge. He handed me the cup of coffee he had brought out for me, and moved a bowl of the cold, fresh strawberries he had chosen between us. The eastern sky was not yet start-ing to lighten; the countless stars of a Hill-Country night still held sway against the merest, reticent glow of a sleeping sun.

"Listen!" he mouthed before swallowing a strawberry and wiping his mouth with the back of his hand.

A mockingbird perched in the trees at the north side of the yard had just start-ed to run zestfully through its repertoire. Among the songs, calls and noises that it had heard and learned to mimic, it emitted a thumping, almost growling sound.

"That's the old tractor that we use to brush-hog this field," he whispered.

With a sudden lift, his pointing finger flew quickly to a tree at the opposite side of the yard. There, a second mockingbird had just landed, flashing the shin-ing white stripes of his fighter-wings in the still, thin air.

"His competition's here!" he breathed.

The birds dueled in a wing-flashing vocal duet for the next twenty-plus min-utes as we sat and listened. Only one silent trip in and out of the kitchen for more coffee interrupted the concert, our view of the now-nascent sunrise.

Just as solar limning outlined a distant stand of trees, David motioned a rein-forced silence, then pointed off toward the first notes of an alto-flute's song streaming from the tall trees. It was answered from the roof of the house.

"It's here!" he said, barely mouthing the words, "the doving hour!"

So, this was what he had meant!

"Mockingbirds sing the passing stars; doves serenade their rising sun!"

After the first few melodies had floated by us, he took up the soprano record-er that had been lying beside him and recreated the lament of a mourning dove. After he had done it twice, one flew into the nearest tree and answered him. He and the dove sang their call-and-answer duet for much of the next few minutes, then David put the recorder down.

"This one always sings in F!" he whispered.

With the growing flood of light, disparate bird-nations threw their throats to the fray. But at last, we heard his mother, clattering silverware and cups in the kitchen.

"Thank you, David! That was amazing!" I said.

"You're welcome! I thought it would be something you had never experi-enced before—*the Texas doving hour!*"

Another jangle of pans, and a persistent, siren sizzle wafting from the kitchen brought bacon's irresistible *Lorelei* song.

David twisted toward the door, called out, "Mom! You're gonna need to make more coffee!"

We jumped up and stepped off into the kitchen in file, abandoning the fantas-tic for the familial, familiar and mundane, for breakfast.

Paul and Gretchen simply were not going to be rushed! After all the frenzy of wedding preparations, then the wedding itself and its reception, they were set on relaxing with their leisurely cups of coffee, while waiting for our parents to stir.

My sister and brother-in-law were flying to Germany with Mama and Papa later that afternoon, and had committed themselves to a morning of calm organi-

340

zation.

It helped, certainly, that they were flying with neither children nor grandchildren this time! Last year they had brought Paul Jr.'s wife and three small children with them, along with David and Gretel; by the time my sister had arrived in Frankfurt, she was edging on nervous wreck, and Paul was swearing that they would never try *that* again!

While their parents loaded the SUV for the trip to the airport, David and Gretel were moving quickly to gather all that we would need that afternoon and the next and pack it into the van. Gretel would ride in the family car with her parents and grandparents to the airport, before picking up her boyfriend, Jake, in Austin and driving that vehicle back, to leave here at the ranch. Then we four would pile into David's van and travel the twelve miles north of the ranch, to visit Enchanted Rock. Uncle Edo and Reinhold had mentioned it often in my childhood, but in all my years of wandering, I'd never had the chance to see it!

After lunch, the kids bade their annual good-byes to their grandparents, while I consoled Mama and Papa with "I'll see all of you after I return, the weekend of next week!"

Later that afternoon, Gretel and Jake drove in, returning from Austin.

We grabbed the cold-beer ice-chest, jumped into the old van, and left, heading out through the Hill Country.

Rolling into the parking lot at Enchanted Rock at close to four that afternoon, we found a place to camp and unloaded our kit. It was still early in the season for vacationers, and as end of day approached, we were the only ones still there.

We got a little fire going, heated up some of the sausages and barbecue left over from Astrid and Henry's wedding reception, added potato salad, sauerkraut and beer, toasted some hunks of the Weizenmischbrot over the fire, and lounged about in the shade.

As dusk lowered, we walked over to the access trail and began our climb, up the side of the Rock. David was toting a portable cassette player: he had told me earlier about one musical selection that he wanted me to hear, but from the summit.

The moon had already risen, sitting a few degrees above the eastern horizon; not yet quite full, in the clear air, it was amazingly huge, stark white, hanging still in a sky that was descending into ever deeper shades of blue around it.

At the summit, we stood and looked out, far over the west Texas landscape.

I scanned an arc, turning, trying to take in the panorama, although the view was too vast to be absorbed all at once. David was pointing out parts of the countryside, like Sandy Creek, and one boundary of the ranch, just visible in the southwestern distance. Gretel and Jake were standing off to the side, holding each other and whispering, stealing little kisses between their private confidences.

When the sun had nearly set, David motioned for me to come over to the rounded top and sit beside him, on his right, facing out toward the west. He put the cassette player beneath his right knee so that its sound could be heard between us.

"This is a grad student's work, something I conducted. It's the second movement of his second symphony. He calls it 'Playing With the Boxers in Sandy Creek'. The boxers running toward and playing with the cows are the louder portions, the 'B' of the piece's simple, AABBAC structure," he explained. "And where that playing in Sandy Creek was is right down there, on the north side of the rock," he motioned, before reaching down to press the 'play' tab.

He rested the bend of his elbow atop my shoulder as we listened to the English horn and the oboe singing longingly to and with each other, like those doves had done this morning, serenading a now dusking West Texas sky. The tender melody summoned all those memories of my uncles, their tales of this rock and their happiness right here, so many years ago.

As David had explained, within those final, louder measures I heard the composer, voicing baritone the tune of his young niece, Amanda's sing-song calling to those boxer pups, "Maggie Bug, Maggie Bug, Cassie, Maggie Bug!"

I yearned for Eva, our Molly, for my David, who loved her so much.

Sirius awoke far in the southwest sky; Luna lolled with Spica in the east.

The darkling wind swept the day into pastel shades and gray-cooling shadows, welcoming a fresh, vast universe of stars.

———————

My back was so stiff the next morning! I had spent the night within a too-thin sleeping bag on the floor of the back of the van—the 'kids' had slept in a couple of small tents outside—but despite the fact that I thought I had slept well, the morning greeted me with an abiding ache.

This had to be fixed. I was due to be at rehearsal in Dallas two days later, for performances that next week, before returning to Frankfurt. I simply couldn't be in spinal agony while having to perform! The drive to Dallas was going to take over four hours, and despite the fact that we could drink beer on the way, I was definitely going to need something a bit more directly analgesic! With luck, Gretel had packed some extra medication!

Aside from skeletal ague, I was also feeling a bit feverish, sunburned from all the unaccustomed southern exposure: we were 1400 miles due south of Frankfurt—like being almost in the middle of the Sahara!

I was able to stay awake as we drove through the rugged wonders of the Hill Country, northwards through Llano: across the wide-rolling landscape, the river and its *Highland Lakes*, then eastwards into Burnet. About 40 miles before reaching the interstate and the long road north, toward Dallas, we stopped for gas.

David started speaking Spanish with a family, sitting despondent there at the station, idled by two unaffordable flat tires, their children growing hungry. Without a pause, he handed them all the money he had on him. I paid for the gas, then we made sure that this family had water and something to eat.

To their grateful complaints of inability to repay he answered simply, "Ayuden a otros cuando ustedes serán en condicione de hacerlo. ¡Para mí, suficiente será eso al reembolso!" [*Help others whenever you shall be in a condition to do so. For me, that will be repayment enough!*]

Sitting again in the van, he explained, "*Tejanos* on the road are never on vacation.

"They're always going from one job to the next: always struggling, always working so hard, never paid enough.

"It feels good to help at least some, though," he added as we drove away.

342

Once we had passed through Georgetown, and had settled onto the monotonous concrete-desert of the interstate, my back relaxed; I drifted off, nodding along, most of the way.

 My indolent slumber floated with the melody of David's rich baritone, at an octave below the radio's lilt, of Dolly's *Coat of Many Colors*. So soothing, it lulled me into deeper sleep.

Only later was the spell broken by David's happy singing along with the live 8-track of our *Divine Miss M*; he was driver-dancing, tapping his thumbs against the steering wheel to the rhythm.

"Friends…" I mused in a touch of melancholia—dispelled, though, in watching his ingenuous joy from the melody, his utter, unreserved delight in this, his beloved Bette. He said we had just passed through Waco, still a hundred miles south of Dallas.

"You didn't miss anything there!" David laughed.

"That's for damned sure!" Jake seconded, adding a boisterous, and decidedly Longhorn, "The only place there's less to see is College Station, or Norman, Oklahoma!"

David chuckled and started to explain it to me. But I interrupted him.

"I know, David! Ik nikt keinen Aggie zein!" [*I not no Aggie to-be!*] I detailed painfully in heavily broken German.

When Gretel heard that, she laughed a swig of beer up her nose, and started coughing it out between paroxysms.

Amid the uproar, David yelled, "Hey! Don't waste it! We won't have beer money till we get to Dallas!" and joined in the laughter.

———————

We arrived at the hotel, checked in, cleaned up and went to dinner.

"Well, it's Saturday evening," I said as we crossed our knives and forks on the plates and sat back from the table.

"What do we do now?"

"Rest a spell," David said. "Because we're going to head out around ten tonight and go dancing!"

It was news to me! I had always been a 'home body' not a partier, although I had certainly attended more than my share of overdone receptions, both pre- and post-concert, and at record releases.

David picked out my costume for the night, one of his tighter t-shirts, jeans and those cowboy boots I had ordered from the *Champion Attitude* Stiefelmacher [*(tall) boot maker*] in El Paso, for my niece's wedding. I had stopped wearing Uncle Edo's pair long ago, but had ordered replacements immediately. I had found that the tall heels helped ease those "sitting far too long at the keyboard" back pains.

An American-trained chiropractor in Frankfurt had averred that they would help restore and maintain the curvature of my lower spine. I remembered how Uncle Edo had shown me to walk in them, in a loose, swaggering lope with your hips and lower back unlocked and swinging counterpoint to your shoulders. He had warned, rightly, "If you lock your hips, you'll injure yourself!"

The t-shirt was tight enough. I had never been 'magazine' muscular; but I was trim, so he had picked a burnt orange one with the white UT longhorn on it that pulled in and showed off my flat stomach. Not bad for 57, but with blond hair hiding the still-reluctant gray, and no wrinkles from having ever-avoided the sun, most thought me still in my thirties!

Gretel sketched their usual night out at the dance clubs: a straight one for her and Jake, then a gay one for David, another straight one and, lastly, they'd head to their favorite gay, western dance-club on Cedar Springs.

I knew the music could be too loud for me, so I hid some small cotton balls in my pocket. I used them in the first three clubs, then took them out while we were heading, at last, toward our "last round up."

No cover charge there: a few pool tables toward the front, a short passage and the club opened into a large room with walk-ways and edge-railings to keep you from misstepping and falling onto the narrow platforms that acted as steps onto the sunken, wooden dance floor at the center of the room.

Just as we had moved in through the crowd and settled near the edge of the dance floor, the opening notes of "Cotton-eyed Joe" came on.

David grabbed Gretel's hand and they rushed onto the floor.

The tune following that was what David called "country swing" and he and his sister almost took over the floor, dancing to it. Those already there around them moved back to give them room! David told me later that his sister and he won dance contests there regularly. In fact, they had won so often that they had voluntarily 'retired' by entering only about a third of the ones they would have been able to attend, and win.

Their foot-work was very good—now I knew why he wore his boots to play the organ and realized that the tall heels and sharp toes would actually be better for playing the pedals than those almost-ballet style shoes some of us had been taught to wear in Europe!

By the time they came over to where Jake and I were standing, David was sweating. Jake and Gretel started baby-kissing, then latched together for a little heavier *tongue-wrasslin'*. We all needed a beer, so I offered to go fetch us some cold ones.

I had already noticed a tall, muscled, sandy-blond standing at one of the bars. Now that he had turned more or less to face our direction, I could see just how well-built he was—big arms, wide chest and sturdy thighs stretching his pale and worn jeans—he was tanned, and with his sun-sculpted face, looked a little older than the rest of the men trying to get to the bartender. Late 40's? Perhaps a bit older?

But what had really caught my eye was that his tight t-shirt displayed a lone star just behind the state flag over an outline-map; and around it all in an arc were the words

Tief im Herzen Texas
[Deep in the Heart of Texas]

under which, filled with a black-red-gold gradient swath, appeared the single-word assertion "Texanerdeutsch!"

OK, my interest was beyond piqued.

344

I walked up to him, pointed to his t-shirt and said, "Also, Sie sind eigentlich Texanerdeutscher?" [*So, you're really a Texas German?*]

He looked surprised, then got this aw-shucks grin.

"Ja!" he said haltingly, "aber jetzt ist mein Deutsch nicht so gut. [*Yes! but my German is not so good now.*]

"Sie sind Deutscher?" [*You're a German?*] he asked.

To spare him any more discomfort, I switched into English. "Yes, from Frankfurt."

A huge look of relief spread across his face. His smile raced in the wake of that ease, and from that point he opened up—he was definitely a Texan: he needed no further prompting! He told me all about where he was from, his ranch about 16 miles southeast of Llano, 15 miles or so east of Enchanted Rock, and started explaining how his German family had come to Texas. But there I had to interrupt him, and order the beers. I got him one, too, then motioned for him to follow as I took the rest back to our little group. It had already grown by one, as David had located a friend, Jess, he had met on a previous trip to Dallas and had become immersed in talking to.

I handed out the beers, stepped backwards and found myself flat up against "Lukas Johannes Oldenburg, but the Marines just called me LJ—amongst other things!" He had tagged along closely, and when I stepped back against him, he put his arm around my waist and pulled me tightly against him. I sighed, bent my non-beer arm around my back and his blue jeans, and held him closer.

While he was holding me against him, I raised my left arm to scratch a nose-itch. He pulled his arms away, stepped backwards, then spun me to face him. He grasped my left arm, pulled it toward him and ran the tips of the fingers of his right hand back and forth over the fading numbers. Painfully inquisitive, he looked up into my eyes.

"Auschwitz," I said.

With sudden fierceness, he grabbed me and pulled me tightly against him, locking me closely to him by my waist with one arm, and rubbing deeply across my shoulders, neck and upper back with the other. It felt like he was trying to absorb me, the pain, or was he imparting, sharing something deeply troubling within him? Did he understand this—his, our—inheritance?

I relaxed against him, my arms around his broad back, my face against the side of his neck, he smelled tanned, Hill-Country, soothing. We spent the rest of that night talking, laughing, commiserating, understanding, over all the different beers he'd order. Okinawa, Auschwitz, Korea, Germany, Viet Nam.

We were good listeners, laughers, survivors, witnesses.

LJ turned out to be one of the best friends I would ever make: steadfast, always true. A U.S. Marine—never 'ex', never 'former'—he understood very well what it was to put your life on the line for your friends, for others. We would visit each other often after that, on his ranch, at my apartment.

He became my Hill Country treasure, my listening-partner in the *doving hour*.

Auf die Bühne — Chapter 29 — Onto the Stage

"Edi! I need your help! It's David! I'm at a complete loss!"

Gretchen had phoned me, her voice overwrought with a mother's worry.

David's graduation in Austin last year, attaining his master's degree in Music at the age of only 20, had failed to provide him with any sense of direction to his life.

After having received letters of acceptance for advanced studies from his choice of two of the most prestigious New York music schools, he had spent part of a year there, but then had returned home discouraged and disenchanted. His mother described how he would sit now at the Steinway (the concert grand, 16th birthday present that I had bought him), and play one piece after another without a break. One day it would be Beethoven, the next Chopin, then Bach, then Rachmaninoff; he was playing through composers' entire piano-work opus-lists without stopping! She was terrified that he was becoming neurotic. So, I called, making sure it would be at the hour Gretchen and I had arranged for David to be at home alone.

"OK, cowboy. What's up?" I asked. "Who put the burr under your saddle?"

That, at least, made him laugh a little.

"Dunno. Just down," he muttered, "I just ... well ..."

He paused.

"You just *what*, David?"

"I just failed in New York!" burst out, among sobs.

"What do you mean, 'you failed'?"

I waited, waited, then heard him blow his nose.

"They threw all this 'tonality is dead, atonality, dissonance, post-modern music is the only thing that matters' at me! And I hated it! Twelve-tone, atonal, what the hell is the use? Modern music—CRAP! Who the hell walks out of a performance of 'modern music' humming the tunes? Who drives to work the next morning having that noise go through their minds, thinking 'Oh! That caterwaul will help me get through my day!'? NOBODY!

"It has no flavor! It has no aroma! It has no aura! ... **It has no music**!

"I couldn't play the noisome junk they required!

"Every composition student there was striving to see how strident, crashing, *painful* they could make their works, and then the professors expected *us* to 'render' those scores! They even tried to force me to write it! I couldn't do it!

"I refused even to sit down at a 'prepared' piano! *Prepared?*—my ass! It was damaged! So painfully abused! Why does anyone think that stuffing nails, tissue paper, paper clips, plastic sheets, or any such garbage in, on or between the strings of a precious piano is music? It's noise and it's CRAP! It's just high-fallutin', snooty-nosed bull-shit!

"Noise is noise! Even the mourning doves know that!"

I couldn't contain it: I had to laugh. It was too much like listening to myself!

"Those damned dudes, those goat-ropers treated me like an idiot, a country bumpkin because I didn't like it, didn't worship it—and had a real, physical problem playing it—that was the first time I have ever had stage fright!"

"David!"

I had to interrupt his tirade.

I had to nip this anxiety, his disabling dismay now. I could not let it grow to be a major problem, like the anxiety that had debilitated my dear Horowitz during so much of his adult life. David needed reassurance: let him see the utter folly of his foes, then reinforce, pound home the power of his own prodigy.

"David! You're exactly right! It is noise, and it is awful!"

I gave him a second to absorb this. It was something that I had faced, I had seen (and heard, painfully) and I knew how excrementally frustrating it could be!

"The problem is that present music-composition students are still subjected to Wagner's curse! They are tricked, cajoled, or outright bullied into believing that they must follow the baleful path preached by Richard Wagner, that to be a 'true artist' they must compose in a style different, as different as possible, from all composers before and around them! And to be different, they must selectively throw away ever more parts of what they are brainwashed into castigating as 'old fashioned': the music from 1600 to the present, of the *Common-practice Period*!

"This means, unfortunately, that they must turn more and more from harmony to dissonance, from music to noise, and pretend—as hoity-toity pseudo-*artistes*—that only *they* know what music is, and that all who disagree, even their painfully assailed audiences, are hopeless, backward, ignorant rubes!

"However, you have already witnessed the three principal outcomes of this!

"The first is that orchestras must still—always!—perform harmonically pleasing selections or they will have no audience! All these new, sterile works have to be 'cushioned' selectively, individually between the insulating emotional wealth of Mozart, Tchaikovsky, Bach, Beethoven or Brahms, or the audience will bolt!

"Modernist noise is an audience-killer: a market shrinking, money-loser for all musicians!

"Second is that the closer to us in time these composers are, and the more closely involved they are with this 'noise-is-music-*because-I-say-so*!' movement, the less well- and widely-known they become. Just think of how many people have heard of (and regularly, faithfully enjoy) Beethoven over Schoenberg, or worse, John Cage!

"The third effect has been that, since the First World War and the cultural discord it bred, what was once *classical* music has grown ever more distant from the popular ear: it has been derailed by dissonance. Mainline musicologists proclaim—wrongly!—that the common practice period was moribund with Mahler, and had already died before Rachmaninoff. But it wasn't, and it didn't!

"Because of modern, so-called classical music's headlong rush to follow the descent of the plastic arts into their anti-human, anti-humanist modes—their disheartened isolation and out-right painful, sociopathic angst—listeners are staying away from orchestra-performances in droves! By the 1920's, popular music was fleeing the symphony halls, taking refuge in dance halls, saloons, musical theater. Subsequently, it was taken up by movie soundtracks, by crooners and the big bands. Now, the banner of living music is carried by rock and roll, country music, disco, even heavy metal: all sorts of music listened to by everyday people, every day!

"In the 19th century, classical music, the music of Beethoven, Schumann, Brahms, Verdi, Puccini and Strauss was the music of the people! But because over-schooled, tone-deaf professors failed utterly to consult the audience—and the till—this mantle migrated to those, by academe denigrated as *amateur*, execrated as *popular*, but who continue to sing of and celebrate the magic of life!

The scepter has passed to Ella Fitzgerald, Louis Armstrong, Glen Miller, Paul Robeson, Carmen Miranda, Ethel Merman, Frank Sinatra, Elvis, Barbra Streisand, Aretha Franklin, the Beatles, Johnnie Cash, Elton John, Cher, the Rolling Stones, Diana Ross, the Supremes, Bette Midler, Barry Manilow, Dolly Parton, Tina Turner, Willie Nelson, The Jackson 5, ELO, Three Dog Night, Cyndi Lauper, Gino Vannelli, The Carpenters, Eric Carmen, Christopher Cross, Earth Wind & Fire, ABBA, Journey, the Bee Gees, and a vast multitude of others!"

"Damn! How do you *know* so many of those?"

"It's the 1980's, David! Germany isn't a desert island!"

"But, hush! I'm not through!

"Humans have sailed—living, loving and dancing—from Beethoven to *Boogie Wonderland*, while the harmonically estranged purveyors of all the deranged scholastic, *alleged*-music have missed the boat!

"One may even see in this a sign of musical racism!

"The more popular the pure, tonal, living music of black communities, or the adventurously tone-stretching music of black-rooted jazz, has come to the fore, the farther these Wagnerites, these Schoenbergians have pushed into their angrily contrasting, and contrastingly sterile, forms of noise-as-music prejudice!

"Just remember: music must come from within, from life!

"If it isn't *soul music*, it isn't *music*!

"The fact is that those (usually *nouveau*) wealthy, snob-wanna-be's who commission "modern" works from today's note-scribblers—I cannot elevate them to the status of *composer*—will shell out the cash, glory in the fact that their names and patronage are cited publicly in the printed program, then swell with pride while the unfortunate audience is subjected first to the unlistenable composition, then compelled thereafter to voice something vaguely fawning at the always unavoidable, dreary post-concert reception. But the fact is that such a commission-piece will essentially *never* be performed again!

"Why will it go directly to collecting dust?

348

"Because non-harmonic, atonal music—noise!—will never be hummed by the mother changing her child's diaper, by a father tucking a tot into bed. It will never be played at christening, marriage or funeral!

"The fact is that all sensate living-beings avoid noise and are drawn to melody and harmony—the human songs of the womb and childhood—like your early *Looney Tunes* cartoons! Don't let those noise-besotted idiots 'kill the wabbit'!"

He laughed so hard he had to pull the receiver away from his mouth and cough out his paroxysms: I had at least drawn him out of his funk!

"Uncle, you do realize that you just declared that the majority of composition professors today are insensate, dead! And *wabbit kiwwers*!"

"Yes, David … well, in this matter, too many of them just stumble-bumble along, continuing to spout the noise-bound blather they were taught, that if you do not smear excremental dissonance over your compositions, you can never achieve your own style, and that consequently, the more dissonant, the more fleetingly "stylish" your works must be!

"Just remember that true style comes from how well you know and use your tools, to express the humanity—the love, the sorrow, the joy, the joke—within your message. The expressive use of considered, practiced, subtle instances of dissonance, such as by Vaughan Williams or Hindemith, shows mastery; the 'shovel it on' approach of Schoenberg, *Les Six*, Cage and their other bastard children, is just hack!

"Aleatoric crap: anyone can piss random notes!"

At this, *I* had to pull the receiver from my ear, he was laughing so hard!

"Now, David. If you don't have still have it, retrieve a copy of your Professor Kennan's counterpoint book, his orchestration book, along with a good, German edition of Fux's *Gradus ad Parnassum*, too! We'll work through them all, together.

"But at this moment, step away from the piano! Get out of the house: just go somewhere!

"Go to the Rock; listen to it; listen to the world around it: listen to yourself as you arise, re-enchanted! You will find your center once more: your bliss. Remember to be ever dedicated: to yourself, to your passion, to your *own* music, your own *soul* music!

"Keep in mind, too, what your dad has always told you: 'Get off your ass and get busy—Texans don't mope, they move!' And David, I'd add that if you don't know into which direction to move, just stand up and dance! It will come to you!"

He laughed again, freely now, sounding so much like a baritone version of his mother, and his great-grandmother!

"Alright," he sighed though an audible smile. "I'll find the books and call you as soon as I have them all together."

I made sure he knew that he was never alone, that he could always count on me, and then said our good-byes and hung up.

Clara's voice wisped to mind, "You know what we're going to have to do, don't you, Edi?"

"Yes!" I answered before taking a long sip from a tall glass of Ebbelwoi. "Yes, my dear Clärchen, I do!"

As David worked diligently through all the exercises I had assigned him, his mother and father both testified that his native ease, confidence and propensity for showing off had rebounded. They had returned both at home on the piano as well as in the church services in Fredericksburg and Austin for which he played organ, or piano for area chorus and choir practices.

In celebration of our completion of the studies, and his irrepressible recovery, I had him and Gretchen fly into Hamburg to meet for a short vacation-excursion, from there across the fens, flats and beaches of northern West Germany.

But before we set out, I had them come to the final concert of a series I was performing with a Hamburg symphony. A new Viennese friend, just hired by an orchestra in Frankfurt, Maestro Seidler would be guest-conducting those three performances that I was giving with the orchestra there on the North Sea.

I had my agent, Mort, come there, too, with the new and current contracts he needed me to review. Bored as usual with concert-life, he spent most of his time camped out in my dressing room, playing solitaire, or poker with any unsuspecting stagehand he could entice into a game. To keep us both apprised of on-stage activities, I checked with the symphony hall-theater's technical staff, to make sure that the audio-feed from the stage into that dressing room was working, and working well.

After some shorter pieces, the main item on the opening, first half of that night's program was my Clara's Piano Concerto in A minor, her Opus 7. Just one part of my continuing attempt to revive public appreciation of Clara Schumann's compositions, the performance, accompanied by her ever-present, mental encouragement and delight, was made that much more pleasant for me because my *Steiner* was there, too. This was a requirement that I had learned from Horowitz about touring: pack light and always bring your own Steinway!

At intermission, Gretchen and David walked with me from where they had been standing, attending in the wings, through the maze of backstage curtains and towering props: the hall's management was preparing to stage *Aïda* there the following weeks. They shadowed me into my dressing room.

Mort was stretching in a consuming yawn. Not having found a "pigeon" for a game of poker, he was trying desperately to remember a card game other than solitaire to allay his ennui.

Gretchen settled quickly back to her knitting. David lounged, flipping distractedly through some of the several magazines the concert hall's staff had provided. "For Reichspräsident von Hindenburg!" he complained. I stepped into the attached bathroom.

After brushing my teeth—a habit I had gotten into because the mint in the toothpaste always helped wake and restore me—I filled the tumbler at the sink to rinse my mouth. Soap residue lurking slickly on it, it slipped through my fingers. As it fell, I grabbed with my right hand; the glass hit the unyielding side of the porcelain basin and shattered.

I grabbed a towel, wrapped my hand and cried out, "Mort!"

Hearing the crash of the glass and my yell, he appeared instantly, seconded by David. I kept my hand bandaged, not wanting anyone to see any injury. Mort held it securely, keeping the pressure on.

"Not very deep, but not pleasant, either," I grimaced. "I can dress it, but there's no way I'll able to play the second half of the program, especially since it's all Beethoven."

Mort looked terrified.

I winced, pointedly at him, and said, "Of course, this means that we may have to give the audience at least part of their money back! ... Unless ... David, you could play in my place."

I knew that Mort would think immediately of the contract, our lost revenue, and our potentially damaged reputation from a truncated performance. He jumped on it.

"That's a great idea! You can do it, kid! You're great! They'll love you!"

It was just what David needed to hear.

"Well ... OK. ... But I don't know the 5th piano concerto well enough to handle it tonight! The *Fantasia* I can do—it's simple," he replied.

"Instead of the Beethoven concerto," I offered, "you can play that Schumann sonata you played for me and Seidler at lunch. After all, at just over thirty minutes, it will be the perfect substitution for the Beethoven!"

"So, will you do this for me, David?" I asked.

"Of course I will, Uncle!"

With a sudden flash of doubt, he added, "But I don't have a tux!"

"Just a second!" I said. "Gretchen, have you seen my other tails?" I turned to David, "Close enough to your build, it shouldn't be a bad fit!"

She pulled the extra tux from the tall cabinet. It was still in its wrapping from a cleaner. David took it and moved quickly toward the bathroom before he froze.

"But I don't have dress shoes!"

"Just buff 'em up: those black cowboy boots will do!" I said with a grin.

He laughed, "Well, OK! If you say so!"

"Family tradition!" I chuckled to myself.

I sent Mort to fetch the conductor; we three talked out in the hall. Seidler was extremely solicitous, almost panicked when he first heard of the glass incident. But when I explained the minor nature of the injury, and the substitution plan, he calmed quickly, then became rather excited at the prospect.

"That's a marvelous piece and he plays it exceptionally! I will let the audience know, and we shall have his debut here in Hamburg!"

"With Gelchen," I mused. I had not forgotten our dear Tante Geli's birthplace!

Mort and I stepped back inside the room. David was standing in the coat-tails.

His mother adjusted the bowtie as he squirmed, tugging at this or that part of the upper half of the ensemble, at whatever didn't seem to be in quite the right place. But the pants didn't fit, damn it! But, they should have!

"Well, you'll just have to button up your jeans and wear them!" I told him.

"Good!" he laughed. "I hate dress pants and their flimsy-ass material, anyway!"

"I'll be so much more comfortable in these!" he said, thumb-holding a loop of the beltless waistband out toward me.

Yeah, I wished I had thought of that! They were definitely a lot more comfortable, and easier and cheaper to launder!

I slipped a properly folded handkerchief matching his tux-shirt into his tail-jacket pocket: I was afraid he might need it, and wanted to be sure to remind him it was there!

At the end of a slightly extended intermission, Maestro Seidler walked to the center of the stage to an automatic round of applause and called out, "Ladies and gentlemen!"

Amidst a soft sea of muffled coughs, the audience settled.

"There has been an accident during the intermission that has made it impossible for tonight's soloist, Eduard Meyer, to perform the second half of the program."

With gratitude, I heard murmurs of disappointment within the resulting, minor tumult.

"However!" he interrupted them.

"However! ... In this unforeseen situation, Maestro Meyer's nephew, David Ziegler, a prodigy from Texas, in America ..."

I had to laugh: Herr Seidler was notoriously clumsy with geography!

"... has graciously offered to perform for you in this emergency, in the place of his uncle.

"Rather than the fifth Beethoven piano concerto with the orchestra, he will perform, solo, Schumann's *Great Piano Sonata* No. 3 in F minor, often called the 'Concerto without Orchestra'. After the four movements of this sonata, he will return, joined by instruments and chorus, as scheduled, to perform Beethoven's *Choral Fantasy*.

"I know that you will welcome him in his first-ever, public concert appearance here before you, our marvelous Hamburg audience!

"Herr David Eduard Ziegler!"

The speakers in the dressing room echoed David's familiar, easy lope across the stage. The audience responded with polite applause: his hybrid, piano-riding-cowboy costume might have taken those more straight-laced among the audience by surprise. I knew most would be welcoming: David was tall, svelte, wide-shouldered, with curling, sunshine-blond hair, an amazingly handsome twenty-year-old.

LJ had been right when he had remarked to me after seeing a picture of Uncle Edo, "*Hot* runs in your family!"

Then, unexpectedly, I heard David speaking German.

"Thank you. Thank you very much!" The applause faded quickly.

"With your kind indulgence, I would like to play two pieces on this, my uncle's beautiful, Hamburg-born Steinway, to warm up my fingers before starting the sonata. You will understand that my performance for you has come unexpectedly to all ten, no, *eleven* of us!"

He sounded so relaxed! The audience laughed at his fingers-plus-himself joke, and burst into applause. I wasn't sure if it was for the joke itself, or for his seemingly unanticipated, spotless Hochdeutsch!

A few steps across the stage: he must have arrived at the piano. There he announced, "Schumann, *Kreisleriana* ... Op. 16, Number 1."

His performance was crisp, exact, flowing, flawless! The audience loved it!

Relayed through the speakers, it sounded like he had stood up and turned to face the audience. Then he addressed them again.

"My uncle has always told me to be dedicated — to music, family and heritage.

"This next piece bears my dedication to him and to those, those no longer among you, that he has, that we all, have lost."

He returned to the piano.

In pride-bound melancholy, I turned and stood at the window, looking expectantly out at the clouds fleeing over the moon, lighting Hamburg's North Sea night.

In keeping with his statement, David played Franz Liszt's piano adaptation of Robert Schumann's song, *Widmung* [*Dedication*]. When he came to the notes singing the phrase "𝔐ein guter 𝔊eist, mein beßres 𝔍ch!" [*My blessed spirit, my better self!*], I raised my hand and kissed the soft side of my left index finger, the same way I had kissed the tender edge of my own David's left earlobe that first of our mornings together, in Leipzig, those thirty-nine years before.

The audience showed even greater appreciation for this selection. Although musically simpler than the first piece, it was a song so well known, so intricately entwined within the lives of so many Germans, they responded gratefully.

After this round of applause, the longest of any so far, I heard David sit on the bench again. He scooted it a little, probably back some: this Schumann sonata demands elbow room! I just hoped he wasn't getting hyped up, and doing the usual, wipe of his hands down the thigh of his jeans! And I hoped he had remembered not to sit on the tails!

 I was nervous, more nervous than I had ever been before my own performances! I counted down, through the first three movements: *Allegro brilliante … Scherzo, molto commodo … Andantino, Quasi variazioni …*

The music flew by my mental eye as he played.

He missed not a note!

His phrasing was fantastic, the melodies soared, melted, melded then resurged perfectly! I could hear my dear Clara humming along — or was that me?

Then came the final movement, the *Prestissimo possibile*! [*as very-fast as possible*]

Oh, he was so good with those bell-like tones of the melody! Our Steinway loved that boy, and he was echoing that adoration for the world to hear!

The last movement's final notes resonated across the soundboard, beyond the stage, throughout the hall, then … silence. Not a breath!

Silence.

Suddenly the audience erupted in applause and cheers. This accolade continued unabating, for what the concert-master, sticking his head inside my dressing room door, reported as a standing, three-curtain-call ovation.

Without looking up, speaking into his solitaire hand, Mort remarked matter-of-factly, "You know, I may just have to sign that boy."

As on the previous evenings, I heard the orchestra move in to take its place, and the chorus file onto, then spill across the risers behind it.

Applause trickled, then rose quickly. I could see in my mind, from those earlier performances, Maestro Seidler walking with deliberate steps out onto the stage, followed by the vocal soloists, then David, taking my place. Once they had arrived at their stations, the conductor would direct the entire stage to rise, and having turned to face the audience, bow. Then he would have the soloists bow acknowledging the applause. Finally, he would turn around, and with a single motion, signal orchestra and soloists all to sit.

The *Fantasy* opened with almost four minutes of solo piano, the section Beethoven had written specifically for himself as a show-piece. David had been with me to each of the rehearsals and, in fun, we had even played through it in my apartment earlier in the year (after I'd received the program for these performances), using a two-piano arrangement that we would play, swapping the piano part alternately as we laughed our way through it. So, he knew this work very well, and he had seen and heard how Maestro Seidler wanted it rendered. He was playing it with almost every nuance I had brought to the performance last night: he had a damned good ear!

About half-way through this twenty-minute piece, I told Mort that I was going to the stage to join my sister.

In the bathroom, I slipped the bandage off hurriedly, argued my tux back from disarray, and in a rush pulled the bandage back on, then stepped quickly, quietly, out beside Gretchen. She had been standing there in the wings, watching her son the entire time he had been performing.

I put my arm around her. Watching this younger David perform, I couldn't help but think of the other David, *my* David, and of how far from those too-few, blessed days with him I had now traveled.

I noticed my sister looking at my arm during the choir's first singing of the chorus-text,

Großes, das ins Herz gedrungen,	*Greatness, that has penetrated the heart,*
blüht dann neu und schön empor.	*flourishes, then rises new and beautiful.*
Hat ein Geist sich aufgeschwungen,	*When a spirit has arisen,*
hallt ihm stets ein Geisterchor.	*it is greeted always by a heavenly choir.*
Nehmt denn hin, ihr schönen Seelen,	*Then accept, you beautiful souls,*
froh die Gaben schöner Kunst.	*joyously, the gifts of beautiful Art.*
Wenn sich Lieb und Kraft vermählen,	*When love and craft are wedded,*
lohnt den Menschen Göttergunst.	*divine grace is bestowed upon humankind.*

Kuffner (or Treitschke)

The bandage was on that hand of her attention; otherwise, I didn't really think much about her inspections.

She, however, continued to glance at it, look away, then back at it.

Suddenly, she grabbed my left hand, slipped the bandage off it, pulled my right arm from around her waist and put my right hand into the wrap. She looked up at me and laughed, kissed my cheek then hugged me.

"Thank you! You dear, wonderful fraud!" she whispered.

"You're welcome," I said smiling: such happiness and relief!

I stepped around her and put my left, now properly un-bandaged arm, around her waist and whispered to her, *"Der* ist aber keine Dreikühige!" [*But* he's no Dreikühige!]

The two of us laughed at the old family joke, then sang along with the chorus's final repetitions of "𝔚enn ſich 𝔏ieb unð 𝔎raft vermählen, lohnt ðen 𝔐enſchen 𝔊öttergunſt." [*When love and craft are wedded, divine grace is bestowed upon humankind.*]

The applause was long and loud for orchestra, soloists and conductor.

Then Seidler came over and pulled me out onto the stage: the audience stood in acclamation. I motioned for David to come out there, too, and the *Bravo!* calls started, from audience, orchestra and chorus.

David and I took a second curtain call. Then I sent him out into the boisterous accolade by himself. Seidler was motioning him over to the piano; David looked back at me, quizzically.

I yelled, "Revolutionary!" He didn't quite get it, so I yelled it again. That time he understood. He returned to the bench; the house took its seat and got very quiet.

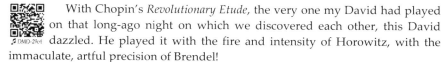

With Chopin's *Revolutionary Etude*, the very one my David had played on that long-ago night on which we discovered each other, this David dazzled. He played it with the fire and intensity of Horowitz, with the immaculate, artful precision of Brendel!

The audience went wild—at least for Germans!—again.

To my utter surprise, after his bows, he sat right back down and played Franz Liszt's virtuosic, solo-piano version of Schubert's song-setting of *Die Forelle!* [*The Trout*] It grabbed me, shook me: I was stunned! Had he somehow sensed my reminiscence of his namesake?

He stood, bowed several times, returned to the wing, just inside the proscenium arch, where I stood, getting a hold on myself, still packing away the rush of memories: the surge of those alpen-abyssal emotions.

Again, the audience would not let him go: "What do I do now?"

"Do you remember Granados' *Allegro de Concierto*?" I asked him.

"Well, yeah. You think that one? But it's over eight minutes…"

"Yes! It's marvelous, and they won't be expecting it!"

"Should I announce it?"

"No! Just sit, then amaze them! With that one, you're done for tonight! Now, go! Shine!"

He returned to stand at the piano, bowed, sat down and gave them the *Allegro*. He had such lyrical, Barcelona-summoning, *Rambla de Sant Josep*-scented turns of phrase in the melodies: our dear, *ole Steiner* sang so wonderfully for him!

Again, at the finish, the house sat silent as if stunned, then burst into riotous applause. He stood and bowed, then bowed again, and again, before making his way to the wings.

He hugged me, "Thank you, uncle!" He was near tears.

His mother was already having to wipe away her own as she grabbed him and hugged him. She grasped my bandaged hand and, over David's shoulder mouthed "Thank you!" to me within a tear-framed, mother's smile.

Later that evening, at the reception arranged hurriedly by the symphony board, David was swamped by local reporters and the ubiquitous music critics.

He charmed them all, particularly with tales of his mother's leaving her wedding bouquet at the Paulskirche in Frankfurt the day she and his Hessian-American dad had been married. He asserted his desire to take at least one of the bouquets the audience had launched at him that evening and place it there, too, in commemoration of his father's family, and honoring his German heritage.

From there, he wound out the tale of his relatives and their involvement in the Frankfurt Parliament and the liberal revolution. Of course, the West German press ate this up! It demonstrated a direct connection between the new democracy of the Federal Republic and the older one in North America. And with the new decade's on-going Cold War tensions, such a bond could only make the West Germans feel more secure—and more proud of their own post-war, democratic accomplishments!

The next morning, the music critics proclaimed that a new star had burst forth within an older constellation! That 'within' was me, but I didn't mind at all. At least an "older constellation" is still stellar! But he was my nephew, so pride was natural and, after all, it was I, with Clara's blessing, who had arranged the whole thing!

And it had all occurred on my—Edo and Reinhold's—magnificent Steinway!

Tough as a week-old bagel, Mort worked every offer that came along hard, starting that very night. Soon David had a recording contract with my same label, and had already been booked into several performances. Mort was even starting to plan possible tours. He had mentioned having the two of us appear in concert together, particularly playing selections written for two pianos, like the Mozart concertos Geli and I had played. If it would help David's career become established, I would certainly do it!

––––––––––––––

Aged 84, Papa died later that year. His funeral mass was sung at St. Martin's in Bad Ems, just as his father's, his brother's and his mother's had been.

My friend, LJ, flew in from Texas to be with me. As he drove the two of us, in 1980, from the farm over that same, ancient road through Nassau into Bad Ems, I could hear Great-aunt Franziska's assertion, and had to ask myself the question I had posed in 1927, "Shall I be among the 'so many' good ones, too?"

Kristallmacht — Chapter 30 — Crystal Might

David's eye still showed blotches of black and blue, touches of fading green.

"Three young guys jumped out of their car and rushed my friends on the sidewalk, yelling, 'Faggots!' One had a bat he held high, threatening them.

"Automatically, I ran over and, before realizing it, I had swung around and slammed the tall heel of my right boot through that bat-wielder's ribs. He dropped the bat, but managed to reach out, to land a glancing punch to my eye. I swung—with my whole upper body!—punched him flat in the face and yelled, 'Don't fuck with a Texan, asshole!'

"He teetered back about four feet, wheeled over a parked car and collapsed, holding his side, groaning. The other two punks high-tailed it, jumped in the car and sped off, abandoning their buddy, the fucking cowards!

"My friends calmed me down. While waiting for the cops, we stood over the guy on the ground. I had blood running down my face; and whenever he moved, I'd jab his tender gut with the sharp toe of my cowboy boot.

"He looked terrified—none of the 'phobes ever expects that gays can or will fight back!

"The car was traced to a residence in Marin County. Typical spoiled, rich brats, so terrified of their own sexuality! Egged on by their parents' hateful, conservative bullshit, they have to take their personal anguish out on others!"

"Yes," I nodded, "it's too typical."

This was America—the "land of the free"—where the brave were forced to fight the superstitious, the bullies, the posers, the cowards.

"I had never hit anyone before," he added sadly.

"It was a white-lipped automatic, unstoppable eruption of rage, this defense of my friends."

I felt again that unseen wisp of air, heard once more the bone-shattering crunch, fought the sudden, roiling, silent recall: "V'imru: Omeyn."

Quiet fell over the small table, our round refuge beneath the wide window in the corner of my kitchen.

At the moment, David was still nursing jet-lag. I was warming myself with a mug of coffee, the reward for a quick trip to the corner-shop to get a bag of fresh croissants—buttery, some chocolate—perfect to start off an overcast, 8° morning in Frankfurt, its grayness blanketing the Altstadt view through the wide, unshuttered, top-floor kitchen windows.

This year, 1989, had not been easy.

In her 92nd year, Mama had passed away in July, after nine years of mourning Papa: 62 years after we had lost Edo. I had always marked time since that cardinal date, my own sixth year.

Could I really have survived that long, have gotten this old?

Age sneaks up on you, like unwelcome winter snaking around a windowsill: and the loneliness of loss can be just as cold.

———

I had decided to take all of November and December off. Aside from the aching requirement of emotional restoration after my orphanage that year, I needed to play deaf to those bone-biting cries warning of the imminent rebirth of wolf-howling winter.

The vacant rest could also help dispel the disappointment of the now-normal, unfortunate few bookings during those months, at least for those infrequent performances that didn't involve the now perpetually predictable seasonal concerts or, particularly in America, Advent's growing infestation with torrents of off-tune *Messiah*'s and unending, kiddie-matinee *Nutcracker*'s.

Americans didn't seem to appreciate—or hid desperately any possible recognition—that both composers of those, their adored Christmas standards, were ostentatiously, unapologetically and, in their day notoriously, homosexual.

Pulling at the flake-shedding layers, David picked the croissant apart piecemeal, intently, with a hint of the morose: unusual for someone whose ebullience usually shone, even through a jet-lagged fog.

"I lost another friend."

I looked up from the torrid swirls in my coffee.

"Joel, the personal trainer in San Francisco," he explained, stopping between lament-laden phrases to chew.

"He lasted barely three months after his symptoms started. He was twenty-nine. His partner, Mike's business was still booming, too, right till his last—he had made sure that Joel always had a new, scarlet sports car to drive into the City to work! Joel was always cheerful, always ready to help: he was, well, a facilitator.

"Joel was Jewish; Mike, Armenian. With another friend, Steve, that's two Jews and an Armenian—the first of my own friends—that I've lost! I never thought I would come so close to the personal pain of those two holocausts. It's as if the twentieth century had walked up and punched me in the heart!

"You will never truly understand how much they mean to you, until you lose one that you love. Isn't that what Opa Meyer taught?"

I nodded.

He sat quietly, sipped his coffee, cast his moist gaze out the window, toward the diaphanous-fog-stirring tower of the *Dom*.

"I spoke with his mother, Naomi, at the memorial service. She was resigned to it, his death. She had had several months to prepare herself for the inevitable. But still, he was her only son, and … well … I can only imagine a mother's grief.

"Yes," I agreed quietly. "I believe … that no *man* can understand that grief.

"To do so does come easier to us, us gays, because we span that gap. We link the emotional chasm between male and female psychologies because, mentally, internally, we so easily understand both extremes.

"We are the genetic, the bio-chemical, the very human bridge.

"Just look at the emotional depth that Michelangelo summoned within the Madonna of his *Pietà*, and the gender-bending phrases of his sonnets, or Leonardo's soft, so spiritual faces within his paintings. Listen to the tender depths of Schubert's *Ave Maria*, to the sweeping resonance of the vast soul of Beethoven in the *Kyrie* of his *Mass in C*—or in those first nine chords of his twenty-fourth sonata."

"*à Thérèse*," David said, "…wie darf ich sagen…" twisting his mouth as he repeated my lyrics, repressing emotion, still watching the cloud-shifting tower. I observed him intently: I sensed, but wasn't sure what was going through his mind.

Finally, he spoke, in subdued sorrow: in tones I had heard before.

"Why do they hate us?"

I didn't rush an answer. Some replies must await the better angels, the truer messengers of our understanding. Still, I had to reply with reassuring strength to this cry of this new *Abel*, another victim of the rampant, slavering *Cains* of hyper-conservative American religiosity.

"Because they're afraid.

"Your great-uncle, Reinhold, in his final days averred adamantly that all hatred, all animus is cowardice, gutless fear! He knew it intimately.

"Hatred is the laziest form of cowardice!"

"But fear of what, Edi?"

"Everything. Everything new, everything different, everything that could possibly question the ossified tenets and superstitions on which they've built their wee, timorous lives."

"So, when the American press and news media started labeling AIDS 'the Gay Plague' they were acting from fear?"

"Exactly. Indirectly, but exactly.

"They were exploiting fear to sell magazines and newspapers.

"The American media was dipping yet again into its bottomless well of sensationalist, yellow journalism simply to drive sales and circulation by drawing alarmist attention to their headlines.

"Those news-rags know that the very best way to be noticed, and (far more importantly) purchased, is to play on the public's fears: to inflict, incite, then wring cash from the terror they themselves have contrived."

"And the ministers, priests and preachers who are drawing such crowds now with their rabid cries of 'all our problems are the fault of the gays and gay-coddling liberals'?"

"Religion has become for many ministers in the U.S. solely a business, a way to make money. Just like the news business, those evangelists get their cash from how well they can excite a crowd, incite emotional overreaction, and thereby sell tent-show tickets and pull donations from their hatred-inflaming performances. Although there are, undoubtedly, priests and ministers who have pledged themselves to their communities and work in vows of compassion, even of poverty, there are far too many who just want all the huge houses, fast cars, and bimbo babes—or hidden guys!—that they can fleece their flocks for.

"Unfortunately, America seems to have established an insidious tradition of breeding preachers who are only too willing—under the pretense of 'freedom of religion'—to forgo the Gospel for the most self-serving, attention-grabbing of paid politics, like that horrible, pre-war Anti-Semite, 'Father' Coughlin!"

"Yeah, even into his old age, Grandpa Ziegler would mention him in the same angry breath as Charles Lindbergh, as blood-sucking 'America First' Isolationist-Fascists who had throttled the country, and almost killed his son, Uncle Georg."

This mention of true-voiced family brought my Gramma and her Frankfurt-revolutionary zeal to mind: I had to try to continue the tradition.

I knew so many Americans who labeled themselves "conservative" only because that was the word their parents had used; or they'd been taught by others who thought that the only other, possible political label was "lib'ral"—a word that their preachers and politicians had smeared with the taint of irreligious, ineffective, free-spending femininity.

Most of these good people were better called *frugal moderates*, instead.

Yet David deserved a deeper, the deepest of explanations.

————————

"More, ever more social and political problems will arise from, and for, the ultra-conservatives, the literalists of every tenet and creed as their mental, moral and political distress deepens.

"Because the emotional effect—the cash-bearing yield—of the terror they incite fades inevitably with time, it must be heightened in ever-worsening cycles: their old alarms must be sounded in more sinister or new threats; new enemies must be invented, inveighed, and attacked. Such conservatism is inescapably circumscribed: predictably, fatally constrained by its chicken-heartedness, and by the golden profits those fears must lay.

"Every tyrant is conservative: every conservative-lackey, a would-be tyrant.

"Just as, before the war, backward, religious alarmists joined the Nazis joyfully in targeting the Jews, they heartily condemn homosexuals now.

"That's where their publicity, their marketing, their dirty money is: the very source of their vapid sense of power.

"Fighting against freedom, they turn again and again to enforced, legislated observance of their shady dogmas, their antique superstitions. What they do not realize is that the moment any religion does not lead by persuasion, by conviction, by life-empowering, free example, but must turn to government, police and violence to prosecute closed observance of their literalist law-codes, that religion has already failed!

"Any religion that must turn to government for enforcement is already dead.

"And whenever the members of a religion attack others because of their alleged *sins*, their solely creed-defined *crimes*, those attackers are doing so to hide their own, internal failures. The greater their tumult, the far vaster are those wracking, hidden transgressions!"

"But what about the homo-hateful parts of the Bible the fundamentalists cite, over and over again?"

"The fact that these individuals quote, and proclaim condemnation from individual, cherry-picked commandments, while they blithely ignore Patriarchal violation of those very statutes (for just one instance, Abraham married and had at least one child with his sister, Sarah), while they, themselves, regularly, without forethought, or penance thereafter, break the vast majority of the multitude of damnation-dealing or death-demanding rules just within the text of Leviticus alone means they are themselves suffering from what might be called, given their doctrine, textual-idolatry-schizophrenia.

"For example, the link such people make between the storied destruction of Sodom and Gomorrah and punishment for homosexuality is disproved by quotations from Ezekiel and Amos that say specifically that the reason for those cities' destruction was their populations' arrogance, gluttony and lack of concern for the poor, something that any cash-crazy preacher is obviously going to ignore.

"The talk in other verses of "sexual perversion" actually refers to any of the myriad of sexual obsessions that plagued (and continue to derail) father-god religions. Their fetish in attacking any male activity that would not result in the birth of more children is expressed in the dictum that a male never "spill his seed", whether by masturbation, *coitus interruptus* (the actual *sin* of Onan), homosexuality, the uncleanness of "nocturnal emission" or any other means.

This is simply because their worldview was predicated on the belief that the male creates complete babies in his sperm, and passes those to the passively waiting female. This was most infamously reflected in how certain the English king, Henry VIII, was that his wives were killing the male children he was planting in their bellies, so he sought judicial and religious justification for divorcing or killing those wives.

"Because sex determination wasn't understood until genetics became clear during the 1920's, all writings and pronouncements on that topic previous to that discovery are simply wrong: whether they be secular or sacred.

"Fundamentalists must have literality: they must enforce unquestioning obedience to their own, specific, verbatim-seeking, law-imposing interpretations.

"Yet, to maintain this conceit, they must, at the very same time, forcibly ignore all the literality-exploding conflicts within their idolatry of those texts.

"While trumpeting their text's infallibility, they ignore the fact that, within its pronouncements there are the barest of citations that do not get even the simplest of contentions correct! For example, it states plainly that rabbits chew their cud, that grasshoppers walk on four legs—and that there's a male in every species of animal—yet none of those is true!"

"Wait!" David said, "you mean…"

He considered; I waited, watching him frame his question.

"You mean there are species with no males?"

"Of course. Among both plants and animals: from the microscopic, on up."

His mind whirled across his mien, into almost a frown, then an ideating sigh.

"But that implies that those old stories of the male's being the first, original sex, of woman's being just an 'oh, yeah, I forgot!' afterthought, and a spare-part, spare-rib knock-off aren't true?"

"Not only is that proposition not true," I said, "It can't be.

"Literally, it *cannot* be true."

He looked puzzled, almost worried.

"David, did you ever notice the line that looks like a sewn-up, post-operative suture, that dark scar running from beneath the scrotum, up the underside, or front of an erect penis?"

Blush flooded his face. Uncles don't talk of such things, even if they're gay, too!

"Well, that's where our fetal, external labia fused."

Sudden puzzlement: he looked askance.

"What?"

"We all, male and female of all species, start life with the form of the female.

"Much like those angst-soothing, disguising analogies that were used to hide the truth from those victims being herded into the gas chambers, Western anatomists still use the male-pandering, sanitized term 'indeterminate form' for the fetus in its early stage.

"It's the fog those very embarrassed, male Victorian biologists hid within and behind, still abjectly ignorant of the genetic basis of sex selection (because, like I said, genetics itself was not understood at all until its revelation began in the 1920's), but desperately alarmed at the implications this discovery had for the validity of their political and economic—religious—divine-male, male-superiority tenets.

"In mammals, including humans, very, very soon after conception the male's female-specific X chromosome shuts off his male-engendering Y chromosome, and doesn't revive and release it until around the 10th week of development.

"Before that, during this entire early period, the still-active X chromosome directs our bodies to grow into those of almost complete, tiny females: with clitoris, dual sets of labia, gonads in ovary-position, fetal vagina and uterus..."

His mouth had dropped almost to the table.

"Wait! How do you know this?"

"German and Austrian schools and media teach and talk of facts of biology that Americans are terrified even to approach. From those proscribed, words-and-phrases-never-to-be-used guidelines I was bombarded with, before several of the interviews with the U.S. press, I doubt they will even hazard the word 'clitoris' in public!"

He nodded. "Yeah, that's true. Just hearing the word would obviously make U.S., WASP teenagers run out, listen to rock music, use drugs, and have wild, pre-marital sex! They might even become friends with *Nee-grohs!*"

I just smirked. Within American society, beyond the groveling media, I'd witnessed that extreme level of repression, of moronic prudishness, too. But American backwardness in its citizens' perpetual push to define freedom of religion as "*my* freedom of *my* religion, not *you* or *yours!*" demonstrated by their drive to destroy any influence of Science—all a part of their desperate attempts to stave off conservativism's looming defeat in their Kulturkampf—was a different, conversation-fertile tack, so I returned to topic.

"At or shortly after that 10th week, the X chromosome awakens the Y chromosome.

"The Y chromosome resets the endocrine system, which then begins to shift from its original, female-mode to flood the XY-fetus's female-formed body with hormones: with testosterone, in particular. This surge turns off those X-chromosome genes that would have directed the body's simple maturation into a female, and turns on those Y-chromosome genes that are then responsible for that drastically severe, destructive-creative re-plumbing of the original, female-form fetus into the form of a male.

"The huge variety evident amongst different guys, their 'junk', as you've called it"—David chuckled—"comes from the great variability in each individual's level of those Y-chromosome-driven hormones, and his genetic sensitivity to them.

"Nowadays, it is also influenced heavily, or interfered with, by the poison of organic, estrogen-mimicking chemicals spreading so insidiously throughout the environment.

"The great similarity of all females' reproductive equipment is simply because their bodies never undergo this full-body remodeling: the female form is already the result of eons of genetic refinement.

"The clitoris is extended to form the core and head of the penis; the vagina and uterus merge and consolidate primarily to create the male's prostate.

"During this extensive re-plumbing, those pleasure-sensitive nerves already formed within the clitoris remain within its extension into the penis: those of the vagina stay connected to his prostate.

"However, because of the huge number of cells involved in recasting the male's body, there are always some cells that miss the full effect of the chemical messages. So, every male goes through life with at least some of these 'sleeper cells' from his fetal uterus and vagina yet living on or within his prostate.

"When age decreases the active level of suppressant testosterone, these cells may reawaken, their genes still set on completing that fetal womb. But without the surrounding, matching tissues to emit the necessary, controlling, development-directing electro-chemical signals, they can grow and replicate, enlarging the prostate and, at times, turning wildly into cancer.

"This could truly be called *Eve's ultimate revenge*.

"The discoveries made this century in genetics and embryology have made it irrefutably, literally clear. Every male is simply a female: one adapted for sex."

The kitchen resounded with his quick, "Don't I know that!" laugh.

"Despite what any long-dead writers of any culture may have scribbled in haughty presumption, the female is the original, source-form of life. Even among animals, there are species maintained solely as and by females, who carry on merely by cloning themselves, asexually. Males simply cannot do that: the destructive nature of our re-plumbing makes it impossible.

"Beyond that sexual fact, in gender studies, homosexuality has been discovered and documented, occurring naturally and beneficially within essentially all animal species so far investigated.

"Although some will, of course, still voice the convenient lie, that ancient conceit that humans are separate, and not animals—and therefore both elevated to special position and subject to unique conditions and regulations that only those prevaricators themselves are privy to!—is just so much effete, infantile, mythic snobbery.

"I've even heard some assert, too, that humans aren't really mammals and that to call us such is an insult. Mammals are distinguished by the production of milk for their young, and that means we are defined by cardinal characteristics of our mothers, not of our fathers, although they, too, bear the prominent, life-long evidence of this trait: we all have nipples because humans are mammals and that early expression of our ruling X-chromosome demands that we all have nipples."

"The findings of science prevail: homosexuality is natural, thus any point of view or philosophy, any creed that has not adapted to the revelations of that knowledge, that still claims otherwise is logically, by its very own definition …"

"Unnatural," he interjected flatly.

"Exactly."

Even with that shy blush not yet flushed fully from his cheeks, David seemed to be settling into this.

"Ancient, and continuing, ignorance of basic biological facts, and reliance on the misleading idea that the male produces the 'seed' while the female is just a vacant, male-owned furrow, awaiting his pleasure in the planting, is the root of those patriarchal textual errors. It is also at the root of what you and I have both witnessed: their idolaters' ever-growing frantic, violent denial of science, their 'talk love, practice hate' schizo-morality.

"This was the basis of the Nazis' amoral pushing of their definition of community, while freely murdering members of that community, just as it is the basis of today's 'love the sinner, hate the sin' propaganda: the spouters of such dare not chance the loss of their ability to define 'sin' in others, and to act on that conceit in any way in which their self-doubt demand its prerogative.

"As we see in the accelerating decline in church attendance throughout the Western World, any creed that fights science and the natural wonder and liberation it brings will become more and more irrelevant, and pushed aside, as it digs itself ever more into the quagmire of denial, and angry, dissipating self-deception.

"The ancients, everywhere, put forth their best (or, at times, the most politically, financially or sociopathically opportune) guesses of things that they did not then understand, nor (with their limited technology) could ever have understood.

"There are those now who realize rightly that all sacred texts exist for example and guidance, for faith, enlightenment, encouragement.

"Only those who seek desperately for some external force to wash away their personal responsibility, who search masochistically for others to rule every detail of their lives, hold such texts as infallible, unchanging, absolute: a fossilized, obsessive-compulsive definition they can idolize as an authoritarian figure, controlling all aspects of their tremulous existence.

"Those first are the people of faith; the second, the slaves of fiction.

"The worst condition, in my opinion, is that the preachers of such literality, who puff themselves up like Goering-on-parade, are ignorant of one thing. They are, in fact, not *Christians*. This is because they actively turn aside, they purposely violate specific teachings of Jesus.

"There has been a multi-millennium long, deliberate ignoring, misunder-standing and misuse of the two most important commandments of Jesus."

Obviously more intrigued, David leaned forward, waiting for me to continue.

So, I decided to delve into this issue more deeply.

"Just a second," I said as I put my mug down, rose and stepped into the front room. There, I grabbed a book from the shelf quickly, and brought it back to our small corner of the kitchen.

"After I met the late Father Bartlett, of the Episcopal church here in Frankfurt, at a military-memorial concert, he and I spent many hours over coffee and *Kranz*, scaling a virtual Everest of cultural, social and theological points and concerns.

"This had started when he admitted to being quite intrigued by my mention-ing to him just how much that one, time-polished, Anglican liturgical phrase, *Dearly beloved*, had come to mean to me, after your family's weddings I had at-tended.

"He could not fault my position on our topic directly, and had difficulty tak-ing issue with it, even indirectly.

"But we were of one mind about one ancient presentation, in particular."

I handed David the book and said, "Turn to the 22nd chapter of Matthew, then read verses 37 through 40 aloud."

Flipping through, searching and smoothing those tissue-thin pages, passage found, he started reading.

"Master, which is the great commandment in the law?

"Jesus said unto him, Thou shalt love the Lord thy God with all thy heart, and with all thy soul, and with all thy mind. This is the first and great commandment. And the second is like unto it, Thou shalt love thy neighbour as thyself. On these two commandments hang all the law and the prophets."

"Re-read that last sentence."

"On these two commandments hang all the law and the prophets."

"That is the verse, reinforced by its parallels throughout the Gospels, that con-demns the haters, particularly those who spew other Bible verses in their at-tempts to cast their own condemnation upon others.

"The condition within that verse, that is ignored utterly by them, is specifical-ly that those phrases *the law* and *the prophets* are each ancient Rabbinical terms. Of course, this fact is blithely ignored by many ministers, unschooled—by conven-tion, laziness, or theological bigotry—in Hebrew, in Jewish theology and in reli-gious history, in the history of all religions.

"Now, what is 'law' in Hebrew?"

"Isn't it *torah*?"

"Right. And as a proper name, *the Torah*, it is applied to the core of the Heb-rew scriptures, the first five books. Now, what about 'prophets'?"

"No idea."

"It's *nevi'im*. It is used as a name of the second section within the threefold, rabbinical division of those scriptures. The third group, with Psalms, Proverbs, Esther, Ruth, Jonah and other books, is called *khetuvim*: the "writings". The initials of the three sections, $t - n - kh$, with an 'a' vowel stuck between them for pronunciation, is what forms the primary Jewish name for the entire Hebrew canon. That is, the *Tanakh*: it is the word used for what Christians cite, at times disparagingly, as the 'Old' Testament.

"But 'the Law and the Prophets' is itself an age-old, standard phrase denoting those first two sections of the Tanakh: often treated, as here, as a single unit, in contrast to the *K'tuvim*, the *Writings*."

David interjected, "So what Jesus says in that quotation is that, for his followers, these two commandments supersede *everything* in those two sections of the Old … the Tanakh?"

"Exactly. The verb of that quotation, in the Greek, states that everything in those two sections, *The Law and The Prophets*, depends on, literally *hangs (down) from*, those two commandments given by Jesus.

"Thus, anything within those two, older sections of scripture that does not now measure up to either of those two, his own commandments, are thereby disallowed—effectively done way with for his own followers—by this, in our Western estimation, greatest of Jewish teachers, Jesus.

"These two commandments are the filter through which all other Christian texts, all Christian teaching, indeed, all Christian actions must pass. Whatsoever does not survive this test, does not measure up to these teachings of Jesus and is, therefore, *not Christian*.

"That means, in turn, that any who would put anything in the Old Testament —or in the New Testament outside the Gospels!—before, over or in the stead of these two commandments are not *Christian*. Any who would do so put the writers of those texts before Jesus, but don't have the moral fortitude to realize, to acknowledge that they are, in fact, pushing Jesus aside.

"The call of faith of true Christians, these two commandments are the treasure of the faith. They set Christianity on a burgeoning path of personal responsibility, of human and humanist value, of divine love and care, that is ethically paramount, most valued, most valuable.

"The failure of self-labeled Christians to apply these two commandments, to follow the teachings of Christ—to treat the Jews, indeed, to esteem all as their precious neighbors—stains the pre-war churches, the entire West, and its leaders.

"Now, it confronts, even condemns all those who celebrate the arising of AIDS amongst humanity—gay or not—seeing within it the spiteful justification of their own personal, petty, unnatural hatred.

"What it truly means is that Jesus himself taught brotherhood and acceptance, toleration and forbearance, unity and community: a universal, divine love for all, all-transcending. This great task, this grand vision, is the unique way in which Christians, all Christianity, can move ahead, discard the ancient, contemning inaccuracies and lead, with Love Divine, to a community of compassion, of tolerance, of an ever-extending understanding.

"Just remember, David, that, as proclaimed within the simple, direct words of that most beautiful phrase of the Church of England, you are, we all are, always, the *Dearly beloved…*"

David nodded slowly, a look of contentment softening his countenance. His shoulders rose; he sat taller.

Had this exposition truly helped him? I hoped so! At least, with an intelligent audience, it had let me release a very deep level of long-restrained frustration!

David gazed from his chair, out the window to the tower of the Dom, watching the fog hug and swirl around the looming steeple.

He turned back and, with intermittent licks, pushed the tip of his finger deliberately across the plate, picking up the last crumbs of those breakfast rolls. After he had prized all he could from the chocolate-butter smear that had oozed across the clearing white porcelain, he looked up.

"Edi, do you still go to mass?"

"Sometimes I walk over to St Leonhard's, in the quietest times, day or night, to sit with the solitary compassion of Fr. Vogler's rosary. There, I look around, at that building, one of the very few spared the fire-bombing of 1944, dreaming there of what Frankfurt used to be, and should have remained.

"But, no. I haven't in a long time, particularly not since services were demoted from Latin into the colloquial." I sighed, suddenly longing for those ancient, elevated rhythms.

"Your cousin Albert sought and received special dispensation from his superior, the Patriarch of Jerusalem, to continue to say the Latin Mass there.

"On his final visit here, Albert was the very last from whom I have received the sacrament.

"Sursum corda. [*Lift up your Hearts*] I still hear this, his call, with my solemn response, Habemus ad Dominum." [*We lift them up unto the Lord.*]

Quiet, subdued, we sank back into our mahogany brew. At last David spoke.

"Is it true that Albert was killed trying to save an Israeli, a Jew?"

"During the Six-day War, in 1967.

"The report we received was that he was running down one of those summerdusty, narrow streets in Old Jerusalem, trying to get water to an Israeli soldier he had seen being shot, when he himself was gunned down. There was relatively so little blood-shed involved in this latest seizure of the Old City—who knows why someone would shoot a priest...

"Albert had carried those files that Reinhold had given me—the death-camp records, to Tel Aviv to make sure what they held about Eichmann got to his prosecutors there. Albert was absolutely determined to help me make sure that I carried out Reinhold's wishes: to be certain that that bastard Eichmann not escape his deeds, his responsibility, his crime."

I peered beyond the window, out into the cathedral mist.

"After Albert had learned of the identity and the death of Esther, and of their son, he had rebuilt his life around their living memory, and ever-palliative dedication to the Madonna.

"He was killed the morning of June 7, the day before my 46th birthday.

"Because of the war, he wasn't buried until four days later, on the 11th, the feast-day of St. Barnabas, the Peacemaker."

He glanced up, eyebrows raised. I nodded in recognition: Fredericksburg, his home parish.

"You said that he truly loved her," he said solemnly. "He did, didn't he?"

"More than anyone.

"Albert barely remembered his mother; he had been abused by his father and his fellow-hoodlums. His grandmother was the only one in his childhood home who had loved him, but even she had made it conditional on his attending mass with her.

"Uli—Esther—was the only woman who gave him what he had sought for so long, so deeply, almost desperately. She loved him utterly: without demands, without preconceptions, totally, unconditionally, purely.

"After their immediate, at-first-sight love, and two years of unremitting, unfailing growth in *hohe Minne* [*exalted, chaste love*], crowned at last by a mere seven days of intense, all-consuming passion, he was struggling with leaving the priesthood, to be with her, to stay with her, at the very moment our lives were ripped apart … so suddenly … so horrifically."

David looked up; I had to turn away.

The words of Albert's dossier scorched my mind! If Albert had only not gone to talk about Uli, his deep emotions, his plans, to his bishop, Hagen!

If only … if only … !

We settled into a transcendent silence, dusted by the solitary, whispered-*adagio* tock-tock-tock of the kitchen clock. The rhythm lulled me into a quieter, more meditational state of mind. I continued, subdued, introspective.

"After the war, I found myself feeling distanced from society by the resurgent push of conservative German constriction, the revival of ever more Third-Reich-style and Nazi-period laws that were being ensconced anew, or reinstated hatefully, senselessly, merely as pre-existing, 'pre-Nazi or pre-Weimar' laws: that male-homosexuality criminalizing Paragraph 175, in particular.

"The percentage of gay men murdered while in Nazi custody was higher than that of any other group, even than that of the Jews and Roma: essentially 100%. Yet we have been treated as if we never existed by this 'free' government, locked down by the loving hand, the closed, conditional fist, of conservative German, political religion.

"Inspired by your family, I have spent festival days, particularly Christmas Eve, with the local Episcopalian congregation. After everything I have seen, experienced, survived, it is very difficult to abide continued bullying from anyone—any society, any creed—who holds us less than human because of nature: our innate, divine-instilled, divinely instituted nature!

"Your great-grandmother knew about your great-uncle, Edo, and his lover, Reinhold. She treasured them both, praying the rosary for them as one.

"Your grandparents also knew, and when they realized my gift—and along with your parents, yours—it changed them and their love for us not one bit. They defied superstition-concocted, theology-enshrined, biology-denying hatred. It was far more important to them that we grow to cherish commitment, integrity, and love for one another, than to participate in the animus-addled, literalist-idolatry of some rabbit-cud-professing fundamentalists!"

He laughed even harder. "You really know how to dig it deep, don't you!"

"I've had plenty of practice: as a mythoclast and beyond!

"When you are loved, you share that love in common; but when you are hated,

you bear that hatred by yourself. Love shines on each and all: the shadow of hatred sticks to each of us, alone. You must be strong, prepare yourself, steel your
soul: let its abiding glow dispel the shading gloom."

"Do you hate the haters?"

"No. Your great-grandmother taught specifically against feeble hatred.

"It is more that one should rebuke and pity them: for haters walk in darkness,
stumbling in fear, inexorably toward the pit of their own despair.

"I know you remember Reinhold's profession of Gramma's life and teaching:
Hatred is the laziest form of cowardice."

David nodded, sighed, then looked down at the table and its persistent selection of books.

He picked up another text lying nearby, and turned it over and over. It lay
there often, being read or waiting. He flipped it open and peeked inside.

"Is this Hebrew?"

"Nope. Yiddish."

"Isn't Yiddish just German written in Hebrew letters?"

"Only if Dutch is German written in Roman letters!"

"What do you mean?"

"Yiddish is a separate, unique language, derived and unified about 800 years
ago from common, early-medieval German dialects, after which it developed into
a lingua franca used between widely scattered Jewish communities. Those were
the dialects spoken in the German towns and villages, like Singhofen, in which
the Jews were accepted as part of the community.

"Only some centuries later did those same German dialects influence the Saxon Chancellery's creation during the Renaissance of that widely understandable,
mixed written-dialect used subsequently by Luther in creating today's standard
German."

"So, the Jews standardized German before the Germans did?"

"You could say that! As that early language was used further, especially within prayer books for women, it took on more and more Hebrew loan-words. After
Western hatred, greed and jealousy had forced so many Jews to migrate into
Eastern Europe, Slavic elements extended its vocabulary and its range of expres-
siveness, making it truly a fully separate language. But Yiddish retained its German nature because the Slavic-speaking peoples in eastern Europe forced the
Jews to remain separate: the German root of Yiddish stands as a memorial to how
the Jews were received and treated in a friendly manner in early-medieval
Germany, before the horrific insanity of the Plague years.

"The myth that Yiddish is just a derelict, debased German dialect, and not a
'real' language, is a noxious, 19th Century, anti-Semitic fable that the Nazis
played up and that, unfortunately, is still in circulation, even amongst some Jews!

"But at night, before falling asleep, I often read or talk to myself in Yiddish,
just to hear it, its personal, deeply pleasing mellifluence.

"It is the voice of the six million, the mother-tongue voice of my boarding-
house friends, of dear little Sophia, of my own David!

"I cannot bear to see it perish, as I was forced to watch him die!

"So long as Yiddish survives, their voice is not stilled; their spirit, never conquered; their lives, ever treasured!"

David scanned the book then lay it carefully, almost tenderly, onto the table.

Just then, he looked up and flashed a mischievous grin, so much like his great uncle!

"Let's play something!"

He jumped up and dashed into my parlor, the big, piano room. Before I could push myself back from the table and join him, he had sat himself at the *Aleksey*-Steinway and was playing "I Got Rhythm."

He looked so happy! But then, Gershwin will do that!

"What do you want us to play?" I asked after he looked up from listening to the strings' fading vibrations.

"That two-piano version of *Rhapsody in Blue*!" he replied with a laugh.

I located copies of the score, handed him his and, as he leafed through it—but before he could steal the stage again!—I played Granados's *Asturiana*, from his *Danzas Españolas*. I looked up; David sat watching, deeply attentive.

"Wow!" he whispered when I had finished it. "I know now why you've always played that as your signature encore! It's wonderful, magical!"

"That's what my David said," I explained. "It was his favorite, too. I taught him how to hear words in parts of the melody, the Catalan phrase, *moltíssim t'estimo—I love you so very much*!

"And I promised him that, whenever, wherever I might play that piece, I would always be singing those words in my mind to him."

As we started the *Rhapsody*, I also pledged to myself right then that I would check with Mort about our bookings. Perhaps, one day soon, David could accompany me, on a journey retracing my joys, back through my enchanting Barcelona. I needed its warmth, its wonder; and I knew he would love that beautiful city, too!

That evening, our digits had ditched the pianos, our attention turned to television, until our popcorn-messy celebration of Hedy Lamarr's birthday (watching her in *Samson and Delilah*!) was interrupted precipitously.

Sudden sounds and images flickered into Frankfurt from West Berlin, gripping, charging emotions! To those of us who had fought through the previous fifty-plus years of turmoil, defeat, shame and, at times harrowing, rebirth, they were nothing short of breath-taking!

Gates within *The Wall* had fallen open and East Germans were rushing, surging into the celebrating West!

Those murderous portals were being held open politely, almost joyfully, by erstwhile trigger-happy East German guards! The flood had broken through, and a sudden, new tide of freedom was now working to sweep away decades of doubt, self-belittling regrets, and death.

My emotions walked an undulating knife's edge. I was close to tears of joy, but fear slammed them back.

Terror gripped me: something might still happen!

In reactive, suppressive, repressed-conservative rage, some angry arm of tyranny might still lash out from the Politburo to smash this long prayed-for, physical reuniting of this, our so viciously twinned people!

This night, merely by its date, now almost deadened me with dread!

I didn't know if David had perceived my predicament, but he looked over at me, watching, then said, "Come on! We've got a couple of places to visit!"

We threw our coats on, pulled them tightly against our necks to shun the wind, and stepped out into the moist-cold, overcast night of November 9, 1989.

The neighborhood stores already closed; we stopped by the corner café.

Detlev, our Munich-transplant waiter, let us take a couple of small bouquets from tables they had already closed and cordoned off.

Passing vagrant glimpses of the *Dom*, beneath the spying light of its tower's bright clock faces, we crossed Berlinerstrasse, and braved the chill along Battonnstrasse to a grove of trees protected by a high, white-washed wall.

We stopped to peer through one of its black, iron-grill gates.

The destruction of the old Jewish Cemetery was still visible within, from that horrific, hellish night, even after those fifty-years, to that very day. I twisted one of the bouquets' stems into a point, and forced it securely into the gate's decorative metal fixtures.

Braced against the breeze, my left arm securing the loop of his right, David and I stood before the gate.

As if my own David could hear me there, I had to call out one part of a verse that I had read to little Sophia, snuggled within my jacket, while that cattle-car rolled us along toward Nazi-prescribed, German-perfected, hell.

"Got zol azoy tsu mir tun, un nokh mehr, nayert der toyt alayn zol manen ayne ofshaydung tsvishen mir un tsvishen dir." [*God do so to me, and more, too, if anything but death cause separation between you and me.*]

David reached out with his left hand and caressed one of the bouquet's rose petals between his fingers, "For Joel and Mike, Steve, and all the victims!" To which I replied simply, "Omeyn."

Each deep in bereavement, within our individual, painful memories, we stood together: against the wind, against the world.

Somewhere across the city, a church bell's rapid peal cut a brassy, knife-edged swath through the increasing swirl of lowering clouds. The rising noise—bells, horns, anything that could shatter the atmosphere—revealed that the old, Imperial city of Frankfurt was waking up to this, yet another cardinal day in our German history.

We pushed against the chill, down toward the river, but then quickly around, through the cathedral square, past the rebuilt beauty of its *Emperor's Portal*: the door I had so often hurried through during my youth, rushing from playing organ for morning mass to catch a streetcar, off to the *Hoch'sche*.

David hurried us past the Römerplatz, shoulder-slicing the waves of the breeze that flowed around us along Bethmannstrasse, to reach the spot at which, forty-three years previously, his mother and father had led their intimate congregation of marriage-witnesses from the *Dom*, across the rubble of a newly liberated, utterly devastated *Altstadt*.

At the side of the rebuilt Paulskirche, before that same plaque memorializing the Frankfurt Parliament, the Revolution of 1848, we stood side by side, arm in arm again.

David sighed.

"It is well and good to remember: my ancestors at the Parliament, their work abrogated on this very day, in the execution of Robert Blum by the reactionary tyranny of the Austrian emperor; the abdication of the insane Kaiser; the proclamation in Weimar of the Republic; the Beer-Hall Putsch; Kristallnacht; and now, at last, the fall of that accursèd Wall. It's been one hell of a hundred forty-one years!—so many things to have happened, each on November 9!

"May Great-great-grandmother Brünnhilde finally rest fully in peace, knowing that the gold did return, righteously, to the flag and that it has been maintained, the cherished emblem of that liberal democracy of which she dreamed, toward which our family strove!

"Now, at last, may Germany maintain that democracy, in lasting, bravely benevolent unity!"

All I could say to that was, again, "Omeyn."

Monday morning of that next week, David asked about the *Hoch'sche*, the *KdF*, and my Iron Cross, so we looked leisurely through boxes of mementos, trinkets, and baubles from my distant life.

Among those were odds and ends, autographed scores and programs, documents, clippings and awards—from those early Conservatory days, the *KdF* tours, our Leipzig life and, ultimately, from the camp.

Three of the most flimsy, he extracted from their package, took in his hands and, as gently as in the slow movement of a Mozart sonata, played his fingers across the tender fabric of their sad, stain-spotted surface.

"When you no longer need them, may I have them, the entire packet?" he asked softly.

"Of course, you may!"

I almost gave them to him right then.

But my own, sentimental, choking pangs held me back.

That wrinkled wrapper contained the final and most intimate of my most endearing memories.

As with all my family and friends, his visit was too brief, his flight too soon.

My life continued to flow from one good-bye to the next.

"Uncle, you can't live alone! Not at your age! You must have some company!"

He expressed his worries, "You must at least get a dog!"

David insisted, persisted till I assured him that I would find one—it would have to be a boxer!—for safety, for companionship, for the high-spirited bounce and ever-happy butt-waggle! That promise was the only way I could convince him to get on the plane to fly home!

I took those fragile requests of his and returned them to their time-shielding packet. Their delivery to him was another promise I pledged that I would not fail to keep.

Krankheit — Chapter 31 — Illness

"Dallas" shown from among the post that littered an August afternoon.

The airmail, business envelope was unexpected. Its content, an invitation to perform on the new Fisk organ in the Meyerson Symphony Hall, was a most welcome surprise!

Ever since its installation had been completed the previous year, 1992, David had raved about the instrument: its sonorities, its effect within the hall, its visual grandeur.

"Black shadows, red-tawny casework, and the golden reflections in the exposed pipes—visual echoes shining across the light wooden fixtures of the stage! It sits well into the room, not boxed away, hidden in the wall behind a screen like too many school- and concert-hall organs! It is a real instrument, standing close, amid the music of the others! Its amazing voices sing with, among the orchestra!"

As soon as the intractable time zones would allow, I telephoned the music director, proposed a program, and confirmed the concert dates.

October it would be!

———————————

My niece and her husband, Gretel and Jake, now Dallas residents, stood waiting where the jetway opened suddenly to spill the cramped plane-load out into the terminal. They were pleasant, welcoming, yet nevertheless clouded by an unmistakable melancholy.

David had come to Dallas to see his specialist: they had left him there to fetch me. With customs already completed in New York, I was able to leave with them quickly, rushing back to the doctor's office.

I tried desperately to hide the visceral shock that gut-punched me when I saw my nephew.

He was almost as thin as I had been at Auschwitz. At just 33, his eyes were sunken: he looked weary, struggling through a too-frail emaciation.

Our David looked too shockingly like *my* David!

Despite this, he told us emphatically that he wanted to stay in the city that weekend, to delay the grinding discomfort of that long drive back home, into the Hill Country.

Weak, he could now play piano for no longer than a few minutes at a time.

His life had gone from a racing *allegro* with fierce, sky-scorching, *prestissimo tempestuoso* lightning-flashes to an interrupt-riven *adagio*. It was descending rapidly toward a mournful, Mahler-esque *sehr langsam*: a soul-wrenching *lento*.

———————

The cool gray stone surrounding the ogive-sweep of the aluminum-framed glass curve of The Meyerson was welcoming on so hot an afternoon for October.

The new organ was aurally amazing, the acoustics phenomenal, the orchestra unexcelled. The rehearsal, and the following nights' concerts of Karg-Elert, Bach, Mendelssohn, Jongen and Saint-Saëns went without problem, echoing to the ultimate applause of an audience we spoiled happily with splashy, organ-rumbling encores.

David sat amidst our family: a prodigious master-musician reduced to a mere observer, sentenced simply to listen.

———————

That Saturday night, after the second and final concert of this booking, David wanted to go out, dancing if he could. His sister would not say, "No."

LJ met us at the country-western dance-bar, the same one he and I had met at, those fifteen years before. He had gotten us all new copies of his original, 𝔗𝔦𝔢𝔣 𝔦𝔪 𝔥𝔢𝔯𝔷𝔢𝔫 𝔗𝔢𝔵𝔞𝔰 [*Deep in the Heart of Texas*] t-shirt.

Mine fit perfectly; David's, however, fell loosely over his shrunken frame.

David wanted to dance, desperately, as if his psyche demanded proof that he could still move, that he was still alive. LJ led him out onto the dance floor. Radney Foster's "Just Call Me Lonesome" was finishing; the plaintive, slow melody of Dwight Yoakam's "The Heart That You Own" followed it directly.

His sister turned away, burying her face in her husband's chest to hide her tears.

I watched these two men, swaying in easy circles, wide, but getting smaller: a still thriving 67-year-old having to secure, to prop up a frail 33-year-old. David's strength waned quickly. Soon, his struggling steps could barely keep his boots' slight movements matched to the rhythm of the music.

Gretel had Jake wipe away any stains from her makeup before LJ brought David back over to where we had stood, watching. But that didn't disguise the watery glance, the welling congestion of her swelling sorrow. He was her best friend, and she was being forced to watch him fail. But she would not turn away.

I understood, innately, intensely.

The two walked back to us slowly: David content, smiling all the way.

I embraced both men, then made sure to express my deep appreciation to LJ for what he had just done for David, for all of us. The big Marine just sighed and said quietly, "'Twern't nothin'! Just somethin' friends do."

David wasn't supposed to drink because of his medication, but he couldn't pass up at least one longneck that night.

His voice was phlegm-graveled, his breathing strained.

"You do remember your promise, about the packet, don't you? From that November?"

"Certainly, David! You know I remember, and keep, my promises!"

He smiled, reassured, then raised his beer and took a long swig.

It was while he was holding the beer-bottle high that I noticed the dark, circular spots on his spindly arm. He had put makeup over them. With the disguise, they were almost unremarkable, those purple splotches.

I rushed my emotions brusquely aside to reassure him.

"I'll bring it to you as soon as I can!"

He smiled again.

I watched, scanned, recorded everything.

I wanted desperately to save that momentary picture of his contentment, of that fleeting happiness still shining out, vibrant from the depths of those already-fading blue eyes.

Nimmer stirbt der Tod
– Chapter 32 –
Death Never Dies

The call came on Saturday, January 8, 1994.

David had celebrated—if that word could be used in the circumstances—his birthday just six days before.

The day following his, the third of January, was my own David's birthday. My sister had said that this close coincidence of birthday and due-date was one reason she had been adamant about his name: only my little sister had known everything about him and our life together.

This birthday would have been David and Esther Schraeder's seventy-second, although each was now forever twenty-two.

That week had already been too much eaten away by resurgent memories and caliginous melancholy, by all the 'what-ifs' and 'if-onlys' that beset a long life, burdened by decades of unbounded bereavement, of guilt from wondering how, and why, I had been the one to survive.

David had died at home, in his childhood bed, within the surroundings of those early, soothing years of innocence. He passed just minutes before the heavy phone call had come: his pneumonia intractable, his death inescapable.

Like Edo, he was "so young, just 34!"

I argued with myself.

Which of the two situations made me feel more helpless: watching people I loved be ground to dust by immoral, mindless tyranny, or by the hatred of equally immoral, mindlessly tyrannical religiosity?

Death, inflicted actively or through spiteful neglect, seemed still to be the only way such oppressives—such sociopaths, such *veneropaths*—could ever deal with others.

"Death never dies, does it, Clara?"

"True, Edi. But then love never dies, either. Its song is eternal! Melody, Edi, melody!"

The words floated, perfuming the memory-sodden breezes of my mind.

I stood, walked to the piano, sat before it.

There, spread atop our steadfast *Steiner* and its partner, *Aleksey*, were so many pictures, the images of my life: Gelchen, my nephew, my nieces, my older sisters and their families, my parents and one of Gramma and, beside it, her own photo of my late *Opa*, and my now almost ancient *Tiergarten* photo.

In the center was that one photo, the only extant image of us—of that moment's Uli, Thomi and me—that Albert had snapped outside the Liebfrauen-kirche in Oberwesel, 1943. I stared at the figures in those images, listening to them talk and laugh, staring at my beloved, my David, holding him again, smelling his hair, kissing his ear.

My fingers moved, pulling sounds from piano keys unbidden.

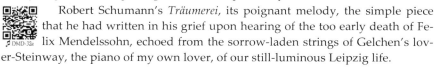 Robert Schumann's *Träumerei*, its poignant melody, the simple piece that he had written in his grief upon hearing of the too early death of Felix Mendelssohn, echoed from the sorrow-laden strings of Gelchen's lover-Steinway, the piano of my own lover, of our still-luminous Leipzig life.

Tears flowed, counterpoint, singing this song eternal, beyond words.

So unlike David's personality, the mood of those at his funeral was somber, depressed by the weight of a vast treasure lost: irretrievably, far too soon.

In Fredericksburg, St Barnabas's was wrapped within the bright shine of a star so luminous within its lustrous blue, daylight sky that it threatened springtime in the midst of heaviest winter.

But my constellation had lost its star.

David had chosen everything for the service: site, readings and music. And, with the bishop's support, he had specified that the *Book of Common Prayer* of 1928, with its beautifully classical language, be used for the service.

Stemming from his joyfully recounted summers in Britain, his annual, organ and choral concert-pilgrimages to St Mary Redcliffe in Bristol—"the most beautiful church in Christendom!" he so often asserted—his choice of hymns celebrated the English Church: *Jerusalem, For All The Saints, How Shall I Sing That Majesty*, followed by the lilting, almost waltz-like, Welsh setting he so cherished of *Love Divine All Loves Excelling*.

Father Barton eulogized.

"*Love Divine, All Loves Excelling*... Just how appropriate that is to David's life, few know, for he strove always to excel: beyond music, in love, charity and devotion. He helped the Church, and the greater community publicly, but privately, anonymously, even more so—in ways of love in which he chose to remain unknown—seeking always to return prayer for prayer, blessing for curse. He would be the first to say of anyone, 'This is my friend', expressing in all things that divinely ordained love of neighbor, striving always for a more perfect, Christian loving-kindness." His voice quivered as he struggled, "And I am most proud to be able to say ... that this, ... our David ... godfather of my own children ... was my neighbor ... my friend."

The final hymn, *I Vow To Thee, My Country*, David had explained within his instructions: it was included specifically in honor of his father, his father's brother, and his own brother. With its first phrase, Paul Jr's soldierly grief broke its restraints and burst forth. This was, after all, his little brother—his very own little brother! — that he had lost.

The single text he had chosen was those verses he had read from the book of Matthew while he and I were sitting at my kitchen table, that wet-cold, fog-wrapped morning, only five years before.

He had taken the words to heart. I knew he had chosen them for me, for the two of us, for those we had loved, for the entire world.

Members of the faculty, alumni and student classmates from the University of Texas were there, as were staff-members from his favorite, publicly-financed (and thus, always grateful for his attention) classical-music radio station in Austin.

St Mary Redcliffe, and his aunt's St Nicholas's, in Wells-next-the-Sea, were also beneficiaries of his affection, his devotion, his deep love for those golden summers of adolescent wandering across the British countryside: from Wales to The Wash, from Dover to Dunvegan.

He had always had a ready *shilling for the poor-box*. Supporting the University, that radio station, and his involvement with this, his English Church had been the firm foundation of his greatest pleasures, his greatest joys.

Beyond the hymns, closing the service, David had chosen songs that he cherished, with messages he treasured, starting with his beloved Bette Midler's *The Gift of Love*.

A reflecting, quiet minute then, for his brother and sisters came, as he had requested, Willie Nelson's *Blue Eyes Crying In The Rain*, its words almost too painful, expressing my losses double, now treble.

Beyond another moment followed the selection he specified as last, memorably, Billy Dean's *If There Hadn't Been You*, dedicated to his family, and to his Fredericksburg, his own fan-congregation, entire.

With a few, dismissing, too-final, parting words, the rite was over.

Elektra and Marcie had sat at my sides, truly with me: their own, devoted, deepest-companion hands comforting my perpetually snatched-empty ones. They, this company of strong women, helped me stand, and together, we moved resolutely forward.

Setting out bravely, through a sea of community condolence, the family left, returning to the ranch to stage the final act of David's request.

Tilting the simple, glass container as we walked, we each took turns, scattering David's ashes across his home's favorite field.

There, lofted high within the thick arms of the trees at its crest, as a boy, David had first caught distant sight of that massive, pink-granite tumble of Enchanted Rock.

Those wide-spreading, tall-grass-carpeted acres were bordered by great arcs of live oak, mesquite and pecan.

Among those swaying branches would soon, with the distant, leafing Spring, resound David's beloved mockingbird chorus, heralding the star- and Milky-Way-lit, deepening-rose dawn, and the cooing, soft-mourning calls of the *doving hour*.

Ankunft: Das Geschenk
— Chapter 33 —
Arrival: The Gift

A sudden jolt: I awoke with a start!

The cabin's lights had flashed the morning. In the squinting brightness, I perceived a slight downward tilt, sensed the subtle onset of gliding descent.

Extra coverlets pulled away slough-eyed crabby in static-affection clumps. The flush of cool air revived me more, but resurgent sorrow tainted the arising recollection of exactly where I was, and why.

A panic-shaft shot through my stomach.

I grabbed for the packet!—where was it?

With a sigh I settled, recalling more of the previous night's arrangements. It was safe, within my jacket, stowed in one of the near-to-hand, hanging-bag closets.

I lay back, and sighed.

A cart loaded with breakfast and beyond, pulled Andreas and Sonja into view, offering a selection for our morning refreshment. Their simple dance as they dipped and swerved to serve us meant that, between Sonja's snug cleavage and Andreas's tight uniform, everyone in first class had something to watch, while rousing themselves from the night's exhausting, long-haul passage.

Our descent was rapid.

Having landed, now waiting at the gate, I sat still, waiting quietly while the plane disgorged, avoiding the nerve-jangled rush that seems always to overtake airline passengers on landing. Their desperation to get out of their aluminum-cylinder prison seemed to impart panic second only to their anxiety to rush on board.

Andreas returned from his exit-station, to tell me that the way was finally clear.

Assured that I had all my impediments, he grabbed his own kit, helped me down and out of the fuselage, then walked beside me along the jetway and out into the lounge. From there, we circuited the maze toward customs.

As we walked, he became quite talkative, seeming suddenly, gratefully unburdened by the reserved formalities required of his job, enforced by strict, traditional German-hierarchical management.

"I'm supposed to be met by my friend! His family is from the Hill Country, somewhere south of Llano, do you know where that is? His name is Nathan and his family came to the U.S. from around Frankfurt a long time ago."

I smiled. I wasn't going to ask his friend's last name.

"Well, Andreas," I said, "when you are talking to Nathan, ask him if he has ever heard that Llano County is geologically the oldest part of Texas, the part that all the rest stuck itself onto, and that this makes the area in and around Llano County the real, physical heart of Texas!"

He stopped and stared; I paused with him. I could almost hear the mental wheels whirring. He smiled, then broke into a co-conspiratorial laugh.

"No! That's great! He'll love that! Thanks!"

We walked on, chatting: even insulated within the terminal, the morning was already warm, and looked to become even hotter.

"Oh! Here's customs!" he said, pointing energetically toward its entry point.

"You need to go through there. Sorry, but that's where all the rest of the flight is having to wait. I can slip through the flight-crew line over there.

"Ciao, Maestro! It was great having you on our flight!" he said before exerting an unexpected, non-corporate hug.

He walked off briskly, making his easy escape while I moved toward the ever-lengthening line awaiting the interrogation that a minutely invasive, and ever more timorous U.S. political system had imposed on the rest of us.

I laughed to myself, knowing now that one of the Zieglers wouldn't be in the crowd outside to greet me. But then, the Vogler rosary shifted, a slight jingle in my pocket. My right arm shot up, touched my coat.

My fingers searched, sensed the lump of the packet, reassuringly, but mournfully still clutched at my chest.

There was another Ziegler who wouldn't be there, who couldn't be there.

Jake drove the SUV. Gretel had insisted that I sit in front, in the other captain's chair. She had taken the backseat with their youngest, another Margaret, called *Gretchen*, like her grandmother. Their other kids climbed back and forth throughout the back, sparring over who got to sit where, to fiddle with door, window or seat controls, or to play with whichever of the toys they'd brought along.

Lulled by the sway of the car, I dozed to and fro. Jetlag and the extended stand-about in customs were taking their unwelcome toll on my contrarily aging frame. The CD in the car's audio system struggled against the road- and wind-noise and the kids' playful *Germglish* to reproduce Mahler's 8th Symphony. It was one of my favorite recordings of it: Georg Solti conducting the Chicago Symphony with the Vienna State Chorus.

The *forte*'s of the first section drew me back to the *Alte Oper* in Frankfurt and then to Dallas, when I, and later, our David, had heard it those first times.

Monday morning traffic was extremely light; we reached the convention center with no noticeable delay. Jake had remarked that this was typical for Labor Day, especially when the forecast threatened temperatures over a hundred degrees.

I wasn't aware of American vacation patterns. All I knew was that it definitely was already torrid for a European: not a cloud in the sky here, before ten o'clock on this, the morning of the 4th of September.

Jake was able to find a shaded parking space, although distant from the front of the building. It wasn't until I set foot on the pavement and felt the oven-like blast surging from the overheated cars around us that I realized just how desiccatingly far the path stretched across this concrete Sahara to the front door.

Our third *Margaret*, six-year-old Gretchen took my right hand and urged me on, as we lagged behind. The other youngsters had run to the entryway as fast as they could and ducked into the cool. Jake and Gretel were not far behind them. But the two of us, oldest and youngest, made our way, avoiding any unnecessary exertion that could incite even more heat-inflicted misery.

Gretel pushed the door open. We stepped inside; she walked quickly ahead.

Passing through a wide, double doorway, the floor held a wide field of colorful cloths stretching away to the far side of the hall.

Arranged with walk-ways between their groups, rectangular swatches held names, dates; some bore pictures, others none; a few had toys or other mementos attached; others were simple, rudimentary, looking almost abandoned, although at least still remembered.

Slightly more than half-way across the room stood several members of my family, of the Zieglers—my sister, her husband, Paul, their five remaining children, many of their grandchildren: Gretel's sisters, brother, and their families. Off to the side, Nathan and now out-of-airline-uniform Andreas walked along, standing tightly shoulder to shoulder, reading panels, pointing things out to each other, whispering, their hips touching, pressed together reassuringly from time to time, one's arm slipping to the small of the other's back to comfort.

Little Gretchen led me along the pathway toward her mother, the panels exploding into vast fields of Hill Country blooms—blue, gold, red-orange-yellow and white—blossoming amongst the green as we passed.

My sister Gretchen grabbed my hand, kissed my cheeks as I stepped amongst her family. I slipped my left arm around her waist.

"Es freut mich so sehr, Brüderchen, daß du hier bist!" [*I'm so pleased you're here, dear Brother!*]

I held forth the hand still being clasped so firmly by our younger Gretchen and replied, "Bin gut g'führt g'worn!" [*I was led well!*] and chuckled.

"I have always been blessed by the company of strong women!" I added, smiling before hugging my baby sister more tightly.

The time had come.

From the depths of its secured seclusion, I drew out that wrinkled, precious packet, the gift—David's gift—slowly, feeling guardedly for those catches and pulls that pockets can so often surprise us with. The paper was now more fragile, so frail after those repeated perusals and proddings of security and customs.

Yet even with greatest diligence, as I reached to pass it to Astrid's daughter, Helga, the parchment rent and its contents fluttered away like leaves, joyous in their final flight, onto the ready fabric beneath, then lay flat to welcome the gifting.

Each piece had launched itself into its separate, airborne liberty, insistent on finding final repose.

They were put in place quickly; Elektra and Marcie stitched them into position, completing their exquisite, extensive embroidery. The seamstresses stood up, stepped back. Marcie grasped Elektra's hand; Elektra extended hers, hugging her mother, and with her touch, conducted their strength.

Gretchen dabbed a handkerchief beneath her graying eyes.

Lying before us, forming the background of the quilt panel was the vast, intricate embroidery that Marcie and Elektra had done from David's youthful, lovingly precise, pencil and watercolor sketch of the great southern extent, the glowing, long prospect of Canterbury Cathedral.

Within an arc formed of a musical staff bearing those poignant, first nine chords of the "*à Thérèse*" sonata, stood the declaration

DAVID EDUARD ZIEGLER
2 JANUARY 1960 – 8 JANUARY 1994

Framed by the façade of Barcelona's cathedral, the large, central photograph of our beautiful David proclaimed his unfading joy, his ever-playful zest. Attached nearby was one of his earliest, favorite childhood toys: a small grandpiano. The surface bove its tiny keyboard still bore the word that young David had painted onto it, (as he explained) "to make it a *real* piano": *Steinway*.

Near those was the copy he had requested of that picture of Uli, Thomi and me, the one that Albert had taken at Oberwesel's Liebfrauenkirche, on the bank of the Rhine. It brought us in, making us part of his personal composition, as the lessons of our lives now joined with his: he had once sworn to me that he would never forget them, that he would let no one forget.

Just below lay the gift, those three fragile parts of my promise to him.

The star worn by my David—yellow triangle beneath pointing upwards, pink triangle above, point-down—was on the left.

My own pink triangle-badge rested on the right.

Between them, centered witness for all to see, was the golden star for Esther, the *Magen David*, now circled by the Hebrew text

מים רבים לא יוכלו לכבות את-האהבה
ונהרות לא ישטפוה:

Running in an arcing, riverine path from David's star, past Esther's to my own badge flowed its English translation from the *Song of Songs*,

Many waters cannot quench love,
nor can the floods drown it.

Spreading beneath it all, in the beautiful old, pre-Nazi script—that of Lessing, Goethe, Schiller, Heine, and Mann—was the pronouncement, that Reinhold, at last awakening, like Germany, from the depths of a living hell, had asserted to me in Auschwitz—one of those things most cherished by our David, and by which he had lived:

Der Haß ist die faulste Form der Feigheit.
Hatred is the laziest form of cowardice.

Gretchen held my left hand in her right, rubbing the ancient number on my arm lightly with the soft pads of her left hand's now-knotted, age-worn fingers.

She looked up into my eyes.

"David talked to me often about your promise, your gift, and how he would treasure it. You went through so very much with it, now to bring it from so far, to fulfill your promise!

"You are a good man, Edi," she said, "among all those so many good ones in our own family!"

Der Kreis wird nie gebrochen werden: Versprechen gehalten
— EPILOG —
The Circle Won't Be Broken: A Promise Kept

Those quilt panels grow, flutter, stretch their floral enticement afar, into the distance as walls and ceiling of the hall dissipate into the pregnant air.

Music surges, filling the sky—a celestial orchestra sounds sumptuous, broad-flowing Mahlerian harmonies.

Amid the golden harpists' bright-toned shimmer, *Mater Gloriosa* summons those coursing around, above, below me:

Komm! hebe dich zu höhern Sphären!	*Come! Lift yourself to higher spheres!*
Wenn er dich ahnet, folgt er nach.	*When he senses you, he will follow.*

Surrounded by clouds, sweeping in—hiding, disclosing, filling again the gossamer, gleaming hall—*Doctor Marianus* summons all, throughout the watching heavens!

♪ DMD-34

Blicket auf zum Retterblick,	*Look up to the redeeming glance,*
Alle reuig Zarten,	*All penitent creatures,*
Euch zu seligem Geschick	*Seeking to bring you, thankful,*
Dankend umzuarten.	*To a blessèd state.*
Werde jeder beßre Sinn	*Let every better sense*
Dir zum Dienst erbötig;	*Serve you unrestrained;*
Jungfrau, Mutter, Königin,	*Virgin, Mother, Queen,*
Göttin, bleibe gnädig!	*Goddess, be ever gracious!*

A hand on my shoulder, I spin around.

My David!

Baldr! fallegr Baldr! his eyes bluer than the jealous firmament!—kisses me, pulls back, smiling, takes my hands!—they're young again!—raises them to his lips, and says into them, "V'imru..."

A massive, electric shock rockets through me, a spasm, earth-shaking surge through deepest core as six million souls cry out, "Omeyn!" with an undeniable myriads' resounding "Ամէն!" [Armenian: *Amen!*] and yet another half-million's cosmos-quaking, "Ζήτω!"

Albert smiles, clasps my shoulder. Our beautiful Esther hands him the child, who reaches out, laughs and grabs my hand with firm, chubby fingers.

Esther hugs me so tightly, kisses both cheeks and, for the first time, calls me "Brother!"

A radiant mist spins 'round her, spiraling outwards, wrapping the five of us in diaphanous, swirling wind.

Tante Gelchen arises within, encloses all in her embrace.

She takes the child's hand, kisses it, holds it to her cheek and claims us hers aloud, her beloved *Leipzig*, once more: "My babies!"

Nearby, Nikos smiles, nods, his wife, mother and children gathered 'round.

Jakob and Deborah, the beaming Schraeders, stand with Frau Drescher, now-hale Hannah, beside Rabbi Schulmann, Isaac, and the Rebbetzin.

My nephew David there, at the Rebbetzin's elbow, teases her Benjamin, a now-laughing tot, with David's friends: Joel and Mike, Steve; Sammie, Manuel; and those two, dear Rainbow-Bend brothers with their sweet borzoi.

Mama and Papa hold young, gooey-eyed hands beside Grampa, laughing with Edo and Reinhold radiant, their shoulder-to-shoulder arms entwined, again so movie-star handsome: a protective arch over Gramma, who beams, holding them both tightly, so tightly once more.

A tug on my sleeve: I look down.

Sophia!

I pick her up, lift her high and spin us around for all the universe to see, hear her laugh, watch her brown curls bounce in free-swelling breeze!

Tight against my chest, I hold her secure on my left, kiss her forehead amongst the fluttering ringlets. My right arm grabs David's waist, pulls him close. I drink from his brilliance, kiss him, love him: *aleynu shalom!*

Esther caresses my arm. Standing before us, her voice soothes the surging air.

"Always—I knew!—I knew that you would keep your promise, my brother!

"Unknowing, innocent, walking unawares, you have been, ever-steadfast, our unsummoned angel!"

Sophia turns her head over my shoulder and summons you—**yes, *you!*—** standing there behind us, listening, watching, weeping all these years!

Her tender fingers wave you toward her.

Come near! Nearer!

As you approach, she points farther forwards, up, past us, beyond.

Your eyes follow the forward sweep of Sophia's small hand, past her pointing finger. Love for Sophia compels: you must follow her sign!

It is the patina-bronze foot of a statue.

The planted sandal peeks from beneath linen delicately draped.

Your gaze moves higher; voluminous folds of frozen cloth are pushed forward by a knee poised in progress, in mid-, forward-striding step.

Alles Vergängliche	All that is transient
Ist nur ein Gleichnis;	Is but reflection;

Drapery-folded bronze draws you upwards, ever upwards.

Spreading swaths of fabric wrap the metallic, motherly frame in wide-falling folds; her soft, strong hand holds the tablet at her waist.

Das Unzulängliche,	The inadequate
Hier wird's Ereignis;	Here becomes perfection;

Her unbending neck, her fearless glance, her heroic coronet of rays: enlightenment piercing the tyranny of hatred, neglect, oppression.

Mother of Exiles, her resolute, demanding right arm strikes high-lofted the glistening, sun-surfaced torch. It radiates shimmering gold amid red shafts, shooting new sunrise up, into the lustrous black body of day-begetting night.

Das Unbeschreibliche,	The indescribable,
Hier ist's getan;	Here is accomplished;

Bursts of fire-worked brilliance, of white, of red streaks flare from the torch, strike out across Heaven, shooting circling patterns of five-point, six-point, five-point swirling stars! Cycling white and gold, they weave their singular, enmeshing, shifting twelve-star, thirteen-star, circling-orbits across the endless, embracing vault of the Eternal's cerulean sky.

Sophia laughs with Esther, clasps our Gelchen: the triple, nine-home World-Tree enfolding.

All, now placid, sing irenic once more…

Alles Vergängliche	All that is transient
Ist nur ein Gleichnis;	Is but reflection;
…	…
Das Ewig-Weibliche	The Eternal-Female
Zieht uns hinan.	Leads us ever onwards.

J. W. von Goethe

11080410R00221